THE
SILENT
HOUR

ALSO BY MICHAEL KORYTA

THE SILENT HOUR

Michael Koryta

MINOTAUR BOOKS
New York

This is a work of fiction. All of the characters, organizations, and events portrayed in this novel are either products of the author's imagination or are used fictitiously.

A THOMAS DUNNE BOOK FOR MINOTAUR BOOKS.
An imprint of St. Martin's Publishing Group.

THE SILENT HOUR. Copyright © 2009 by Michael Koryta. All rights reserved.
Printed in the United States of America.
For information, address St. Martin's Press,
175 Fifth Avenue, New York, N.Y. 10010.

www.thomasdunnebooks.com
www.minotaurbooks.com

LIBRARY OF CONGRESS CATALOGING-IN-PUBLICATION DATA

Koryta, Michael.
    The silent hour / Michael Koryta.—1st ed.
        p.   cm.
    "A Thomas Dunne book for Minotaur Books"—T.p. verso.
    ISBN-13: 978-0-312-36157-0
    ISBN-10: 0-312-36157-2
    I. Title.
    PS3611.O749555   2009
    813'.6—dc22

                                            2009010485

First Edition: August 2009

10   9   8   7   6   5   4   3   2   1

To Don Johnson and Trace Investigations—
with deepest gratitude

ACKNOWLEDGMENTS

This book and its predecessors wouldn't have existed without the faith, hard work, and keen eye of Peter Wolverton, who has been both an editor and a friend, and I'm deeply indebted. Thank you, Pete, and thanks to everyone else at St. Martin's, Minotaur Books, and Thomas Dunne—Andy Martin, Thomas Dunne, Matthew Shear, Katie Gilligan, Elizabeth Byrne, Hector DeJean, and all the rest.

Much gratitude is also due to:

David Hale Smith, agent extraordinaire.

George Lichman of the Rocky River Police Department, a friend and helpful resource.

Laura Lane not only offered a critical eye to the early pages but guided me to the genesis of the story several years ago. She had no idea of this, of course, but deserves credit nevertheless.

A pair of deeply valued early readers: Bob Hammel and Christine Caya.

Michael Connelly, for countless kindnesses.

Dennis Lehane, with a standard but important additional note of thanks to his Writers in Paradise conference at Eckerd College, www.writersin paradise.com.

Tom Bunger, who answered a lot of truly strange legal questions involving the missing, the dead, and their homes. If you're missing or dead and you have a home, I'd suggest you call Tom.

The many booksellers and friends who have been gracious hosts over the years, including but certainly not limited to Jim Haung, Robin and Jamie Agnew, Richard Katz, Jon and Ruth Jordan, Steve Stilwell, Barbara Peters, Otto Penzler, John and Toni Cross, Mike Bursaw, and so many others.

A motley band of assorted generous folks: Dr. J. D. Headdy, Ridley Pearson, George Pelecanos, Laura Lippman, Gena Asher, Lawrence Rose, Brad Petrigala, Tony Mitchell, George Juergens, Louise Thurtell, Robert Pepin, Roger Levesque, and my family.

PART ONE

WHISPER RIDGE

1

He'd sharpened his knife just an hour before the killing. The police, prosecutor, and media would all later make great use of this fact. Premeditation, they said. Proof of intent, they said. Cold-blooded murder, they said.

All Parker Harrison had to say was that he often sharpened his knife in the evening.

It wasn't much of a defense.

Harrison, an unemployed groundskeeper at the time of his arrest for murder, took a guilty plea that gave him a term of life in prison but allowed the possibility of parole, the sort of sentence that seems absurd to normal people but apparently makes sense to lawyers.

The guilty plea prevented a trial, and that meant Harrison's tenure as the media's villain of the moment was short-lived. Some editors and TV anchors around the state no doubt grumbled when they saw he was going to disappear quietly behind bars, taking a good bloody story with him. On the day of his arrest, he'd offered something special. Something none of them had seen before.

The victim was a man named John Maxwell, who was the new boyfriend of Harrison's former lover, Molly Nelson. The killing occurred in Nelson's rental house in the hills south of Xenia, Ohio, a town made infamous for a devastating tornado that occurred the same year Harrison went to high school, destroying homes, schools, and churches while killing thirty-four people and leaving nearly ten thousand—including the Harrison family—homeless. It wasn't the first storm of breathtaking malevolence to pass through the little town: The Shawnee had named the area "place of the devil winds" more than a century earlier. The winds certainly touched Harrison's life, and a few decades later the locals would claim the devil clearly had, too. A Xenia native who was half Shawnee, Harrison had been separated from Nelson for more than a year before he returned to town and they reunited for one night together. It was passionate and borderline violent, beginning in a shouting match and culminating in intercourse on the floor. Evidence technicians later agreed that the abrasions found on Harrison's knees were rug burns from that night and had no relevance to the killing that took place two days later.

After the night of sex and shouting, Nelson told Harrison she was done with him, that it was time to move on. Time to move *away.* Get out of town, she said; find something else to occupy your attention.

Apparently she didn't convince him. Harrison returned to her house two nights later, hoping, he would say, for more conversation. The police would insist he returned with murder on his mind and a recently sharpened knife in his truck. Harrison's story, of an argument that the new boyfriend turned into a physical contest, was never proved or disproved because there was no trial. What went undisputed was the result of the night: Harrison punched Nelson once in the jaw as she went for the phone, interrupting her as she hit the last of those three digits needed to summon help, and then turned on Maxwell and killed him with the knife. Harrison disconnected the phone, but a police car had already been dispatched, and a single sheriff's deputy entered the house through an open side door to find Nelson unconscious and Harrison sitting on the kitchen floor beside Maxwell's body, his cupped hands cradling a pool of blood. He was attempting, he said, to put the blood back into the corpse. To return it to Maxwell, to restore him to life. He was, he said, probably in shock.

That detail, of the attempt to return the blood, added a new twist on a classic small-town horror story, and the crime received significant media coverage. Front-page articles in the papers, precious minutes on the TV news. The murder was well documented, but I don't remember it. I was an infant when Harrison was arrested, and his name meant nothing to me until almost three decades later, when the letters started.

2

He wrote me for the first time in the winter, about two weeks after my partner, Joe Pritchard, left for Florida. I remember that because my first instinct was to laugh out loud, and I was disappointed that there was nobody around to share my amusement. It was a crazy letter from a crazy killer who was already back on the streets. That life sentence only held him for fifteen years. He'd been out for thirteen when he made contact with me, sent a letter explaining that he had a matter of "grave importance" to discuss, but wanted to tell me his personal history before we met. It was an issue of honesty, he wrote. He had recently learned the importance of total honesty, of accountability, and therefore he would not hide from his history. He proceeded to describe, in a formal, matter-of-fact fashion, the crime he'd committed and the time he'd served, then left a phone number and asked that I call him when I was ready to meet.

The letter went into the trash without ceremony, and no call was made. More than a month passed before the second one arrived. This time, Harrison was more insistent and even stranger. He wrote that he'd followed my career in the newspapers and believed that I had been chosen for his task. He knew this must sound strange, but I needed to believe him, needed to meet with him just one time. There was talk of me being not a detective but a *storyteller*. Harrison had a story, and he needed to know the ending. No one could tell the ending but me. Was I intrigued?

I was not.

This time I considered burning the letter, or tearing it to shreds, but then decided that was too much of a gesture. Instead, I tucked it back into its envelope and tossed it into the garbage. Four companions soon found their way to a similar demise in the months that followed. Harrison was growing more persistent, writing so often that I at least took the time to look into his background to see what sort of psychopath I was dealing with. I considered contacting his parole officer but never did. His correspondence, while annoying, also seemed harmless.

He gave up on the letter campaign and decided to arrive in person on an unusually warm afternoon in the first week of May. I was in the office and engaged in critical business—browsing the ESPN Web site and pondering what lunch should be—when there was a single soft knock on the door. Walk-in business isn't just infrequent at our agency; it's nonexistent. There's no sign on the building, and that's by design. Joe had a theory about walk-in clients being the sort you wanted to avoid in this business, so we kept a low profile.

I pushed back from the desk, crossed the room, and opened the door to face a man who couldn't have stood an inch above five-six. He had a thick build, the natural sort rather than a weight-room product, and his hair was cut very close to his skull. There was one scar on his face, a dark imprint high on his cheekbone, offsetting a pair of coal-colored eyes that were fastened on my own.

"Mr. Perry." It wasn't a question; he knew who I was.

"Yes?"

"I'm Parker Harrison."

He saw the look that passed over my face in response.

"I'm sorry if the letters bothered you," he said. "I didn't want to be a bother. But I also thought . . . you were a police officer, and I thought maybe the name would mean something to you. So I said, well, better to be up-front about things, right? Then, when you never called, I decided maybe that was a mistake. I was hoping you'd welcome me."

"Welcome you."

"Yes."

We stood there in silence for a moment, and then he made a nod at the interior of the room and said, "Are you going to let me in, or do we have to talk on our feet?"

"On our feet," I said. "It's not going to take long to finish the conversation, Harrison. I don't investigate thirty-year-old murders committed in front of a witness and then *confessed* to. Besides, you're already out. You did some time and now you're done. So what's the goal? I don't understand it, and I don't want any part of it."

For a moment he just stared at me, looking perplexed. Then his face split into a smile, one with some warmth to it.

"Of course you think that's what I want. Why wouldn't you? I'm sorry about that, Lincoln. May I call you Lincoln? I apologize for your confusion, but the last thing on my mind is my own case. I mean, there *isn't* a case. As you said, I confessed. That wasn't a joke, something I did for kicks because I wanted to spend my life in prison. I killed that man, Lincoln, killed him and never denied it."

He must have seen some reaction in my eyes, some hint of the chill that had gone through my stomach, because he stopped talking and frowned.

"I say that like it's nothing," he said, "but that's not how I feel about it. Not at all. I regret it terribly, would give anything to see him have his life back. So if you hear me talk of it like it's nothing, please understand that's just a product of familiarity. When you spend every day living with the price of destruction—of someone else's life and your own—it becomes awfully familiar."

He spoke very well, gracefully even. I said, "All right, it seems I misunderstood, but why tell me about your case in that first letter if it's not your current concern?"

"I told you," he said. "I wanted to be honest."

I raised my eyebrows. "You know, Harrison, there are some things we all keep to ourselves. If I'd killed somebody with a knife, I'd probably put that one on the list."

"Are you going to let me in?" he said.

I hesitated for a moment, then sighed and swung the door open and walked back to my chair behind the desk. He sat across from me, on one of the stadium chairs. He gave it a curious look, as most people do.

"From the old stadium?"

I nodded.

"When I was a child I saw Jim Brown play there," he said.

"Lots of people did."

He frowned at that, bothered by my unfriendliness, and said, "I have six thousand dollars. A little more than that, but roughly six thousand. I meant to lead off with that, do this properly, with the retainer and all."

"I'm not really looking for work right now, Harrison. Pretty backed up, actually."

He looked at my desk then, perhaps noting the absence of paperwork, and I reached out and turned the computer monitor to hide the ESPN screen. Like I said, pretty backed up.

"I read about you in the papers," he said.

"Terrific. I wasn't real happy about being in them."

"I felt the same way when I made the front page."

I cocked my head and stared at him. "Is that supposed to be amusing?"

"No, it's supposed to be serious."

Neither of us said anything for a minute. I was studying him, that scar on his cheek and the steel in his eyes. He had a soft voice. Too soft for the eyes and the scar.

"When I read about you," he said, "I knew you were the right person for this. I *knew it*. You've shown compassion for people who have done wrong. You've done wrong yourself."

He seemed to want a response to that, but I didn't offer one. After a pause, he spoke again.

"I knew that you wouldn't treat me as worthless, as diseased, simply because one day I made a terrible mistake and somebody died."

A terrible mistake and somebody died. That was one way to phrase it. I pushed back from the desk and hooked one ankle over my knee, keeping my silence.

"You're looking at me with distaste," he said.

"I'm sorry."

"It bothers you very much. Being in this room with me, knowing that someone died at my hand."

"Being in the room doesn't bother me. Knowing that you killed someone does. Are you surprised by that?"

"You've never killed anyone, I take it?"

My hesitation provided his answer, and I disliked the look of satisfaction that passed over his face. Yes, I'd killed, but it was a hell of a lot different than what Harrison had done. Wasn't it? Of course it was. He'd murdered someone in a rage. I'd killed in self-defense—and never reported the death.

"Mr. Harrison, I'd like you to go on your way. I'm just not interested in continuing this conversation, or in doing any work for you. I'm sorry if that upsets you. There are plenty of PIs in this town, though. Go on and talk to another one of them, and do yourself a favor this time and keep the murder story quiet."

"You won't work for me."

"That's correct."

"Because I told you that I killed someone."

I was getting a dull headache behind my temples and wanted him out of my office. Instead of speaking, I just lifted my hand and pointed at the door. He looked at me for a long time and then got to his feet. He turned to the door, then looked back at me.

"Do you believe that prison can change someone?" he said.

"I'm sure that it does."

"I mean change them in the way that it is supposed to. Could it rehabilitate them?"

I didn't answer.

"You either don't believe that or you aren't sure," he said. "Yet you were a police officer. You sent people to prison. Shouldn't you have believed in that idea, then?"

"I believe that we don't have any better ideas in place at the current time. Does that satisfy you?"

"The question is, does it satisfy *you*, Lincoln."

"If all you wanted was a discussion about the system, you could have had it with your parole officer."

"I didn't want a discussion about the system. I wanted you to treat me like a functioning member of society. You've chosen not to do that."

I rubbed a hand over my eyes, thinking that I should have left for lunch ten minutes earlier.

"Prison didn't rehabilitate me," he said, "but another place did. Some other people did."

He was still standing there, hadn't moved for the door, and now I gave up. It apparently would be easier to hear him out than throw him out.

"The job," I said. "What is it? What do you want from me?"

He gestured down at the chair from which he'd just risen, and I sighed and nodded, and then he sat again.

"I got out thirteen years ago," he said. "Spent the first year working for the most amazing woman I ever met. She was someone who operated on a level above most of the world. Kind, compassionate, beautiful. She and her husband built a house in the woods that was as special a place as I've ever seen on this earth, just a gorgeous, haunting place. If you go to it, and I hope you will, you'll understand what I mean. There's an energy there, Lincoln, a spirit I know you'll be able to feel. They came up with the idea for the home themselves, and it was incredible. Built underground on one side, so that when you came up the drive all you saw was this single arched door in the earth."

He lifted his hands and made an arch with them, revealing tattoos on the insides of both wrists.

"The door was this massive piece of oak surrounded by hand-laid stone, and it was all you could see. Just this door to nowhere. Then you could walk up over the door, stand on a hill, and even though the house was directly beneath you, you couldn't tell. There were trees and plants growing all over the place, and no sign that a home was under your feet. At the top of the hill they built a well house out of stone, styled in a way that made you think it was two hundred years old. There was no well, of course, because the house was beneath. If you kept walking past that, you'd come to this sheer drop."

Again he lifted his hands, making a slashing motion this time. "That was the back wall. Two stories of glass, all these windows looking out on the creek and the pond and the woods. It was only from the back that you could see the house. From the front, it was just the door in the hillside. Alexandra wanted it to feel that way. She wanted it to be a place where you could escape from the world."

I had a strong sense that he was no longer seeing me, that I could stand up and do jumping jacks and he wouldn't blink. He was back at this place, this house in the earth, and from watching his face I knew that he recalled every detail perfectly, that it was the setting of a vivid movie he played regularly in his head.

"I helped them grow vegetables, and I kept the grass cut and the trees trimmed and the creek flowing and the pond clean," he said. "In the fall I cleared the leaves; in the winter I cleared the snow. No power tools, not even a mower. I did it all by hand, and at first I thought they were crazy for requiring that, but I needed the job. Then I came to understand how important it was. How the sound of an engine would have destroyed what was there."

"Who were they?" I asked, and the interruption seemed as harsh to him as a slap in the face. He blinked at me a few times, then nodded.

"The owners were Alexandra and Joshua Cantrell, and while I was not close to Joshua, I became closer to Alexandra in a year than I would have thought possible. She was a very spiritual person, deeply in touch with the earth, and when she learned I had Shawnee ancestry, she wanted to hear all of the stories I'd heard, was just fascinated with the culture. I learned from her, and she learned from me, and for that one single year everything in my life seemed to have some harmony."

He paused, lifted his head, tilted it slightly, and looked me in the eye.

"They left that place, that beautiful home they'd built, without any warning, just drove away and left it all behind. I never saw them or heard from them again. That was twelve years ago."

It was quiet, and I let it stay that way. One of the reasons I didn't speak, truth be told, was that I could feel a sort of electric tingle, and I wanted to hold on to it for a moment. It came not from his story, which was intriguing but could also be total bullshit, but from the way he told it. The light in his

eyes, the energy that came from him when he spoke, had an almost raptur-
ous quality. There was a depth of caring in what he said that I hadn't seen
often before. The depth of caring you could probably develop if you spent
more than a decade in a cell and then were released to the place he'd just
described.

"I'm sure there's a simple explanation," I said. "One you could probably
find with a little computer research. Maybe they overextended when they
built that house, and the bank foreclosed. Maybe they moved to be closer to
family. Maybe they decided to go overseas."

"You think I haven't done computer research?" he said. "You think that's
a new idea to me? I've researched, Lincoln."

"You didn't find anything?"

"Nothing. I turned up some addresses for people with the same name,
wrote some letters, never got a response unless the letter bounced back to
me."

"Not all of them did? Then you probably got through to them and they
didn't care to respond. No offense, Harrison, but correspondence with a
murderer isn't high on most people's list of priorities. I can see why they'd
ignore your letters. I tried to do the same."

He spoke with infinite patience. "Alexandra would never have ignored
my letters. She was a better person than that."

"People change."

"I have six thousand dollars," he began again.

I waved him off. "I know, Harrison. You've told me."

He looked at me sadly, then spoke with his eyes on the floor.

"I need to know what happened. If it takes every dime I have, I won't feel
that it was wasted. What I told you in my letters came from the heart. I see you
as a storyteller. You take something that's hidden from the world, and you
bring it forward, give us answers to our questions, give us an ending. It's what
you do, and you seem to be very good at it. I'm asking you, please, to do that
for me. Give me those answers, give me the ending."

I didn't say anything. He shifted in his chair, looking uneasy for the
first time, and I had an idea of how badly he wanted me to take this job.

"You just want to know where they went?" I said. "Is that it?"

He nodded. "I'd like to speak with her."

"I won't facilitate contact for you. I believe there is a very good chance that one of your letters got through, and they did not wish to hear from you. If that's the case, I'm not going to pass along any messages or give you their new address. I'll simply tell you what I can about why they left."

"The address is important to me, though, because I want to send a letter. I have some things I need to say."

I shook my head. "I'm not doing that. The most I will do is tell them where you are and say that you'd like to be in touch. If they want to hear from you, they can instigate it."

He paused with another objection on his lips, then let it die, and nodded instead.

"Fine. If you find her, she will be in touch. I'm sure of that."

"You said you weren't close with her husband," I said. "Perhaps you should consider the possibility that he didn't think highly of you, and that he's one of the reasons you haven't heard from her."

"He's not the reason."

"We'll see."

It went quiet again, both of us realizing that the back-and-forth was through, that I had actually agreed to do this. I'm not sure who was more surprised. Harrison shifted in his chair and began to speak of the six thousand again, to ask me what retainer fee I would require.

"None, Harrison. Not yet. I expect this won't be hard. What seems altogether mysterious probably won't be once I dig into it. Now, you gave me their names, but is there any chance you remember the address of that house?"

"It's 3730, Highway 606. Just outside of Hinckley."

Hinckley was less than an hour south of Cleveland. I took a notepad out of the desk drawer, then had him repeat the address.

"There's a stone post at the end of the drive that says Whisper Ridge," he said. "That's the name Alexandra gave to the place, and it was a good choice. Appropriate. It's the quietest place I've ever been. Alexandra said one of the contractors told her it was built in an acoustic shadow. Do you know what that is?"

I shook my head.

"I'd never heard the phrase, either, but apparently in the right terrain you can have a situation where the wind currents keep sounds from traveling the way they should. I have no idea if that's true of Whisper Ridge, but I can tell you that it's an unnaturally quiet place."

"The house will give me the start," I said, not interested in hearing another spiel about the property. "I'll be able to tell when they sold it and whether there was a foreclosure involved. Sudden departure like that, one could be likely."

He shook his head. "That's not going to be your start."

"No?"

"Well, the house will," he said. "The house absolutely should be. I'd like you to see the place before you do anything else, but there won't be any details in a sale that will help you."

"You say that with confidence."

"That's because they never sold it."

"You're sure."

"Yes."

"Then who lives there?"

"No one."

I cocked my head and studied him. "Positive about that?"

"I'm positive. I've had correspondence with the sheriff out there. The house is still owned by the Cantrells, the taxes are current, and according to him, it's empty."

"It's been twelve years," I said.

"Yes."

"The house has just been sitting empty for that long?"

"That's my understanding."

"A house that is worth—"

"Several million, for the house and the property. I know you expect this to be easy, but I have a different sense than that. I think it will be anything but easy."

3

I left the office a few minutes after Harrison did. I stood on the corner waiting to cross Rocky River and walk over to Gene's Place for some lunch, trying to enjoy the warm breeze and the sun and not dwell on the fact that I'd just
agreed to work for a murderer. Not even an accused murderer, which was the
sort of thing defense investigators did regularly, but an admitted murderer, a
guy who'd sat across the desk from me and talked about the man he'd killed
with a knife.

I'd had him on his feet, headed toward the door, and now I was working
for him. So what had changed? Why, after ordering him to leave, had I agreed
to his request? I could pretend part of it was the story, the intriguing question
he'd presented, but I knew that wasn't enough.

You're looking at me with distaste, he'd said, and he'd been right. I was
disgusted by him when he walked into the office, disgusted by him when he
wrote the first letter back in the winter. He was a killer. He'd ended a life,
shed innocent blood. I was entitled to my disgust, wasn't I? Then he'd looked
at me and asked if I believed in his potential for rehabilitation, asked if I
believed in the work I'd done with the police, and somehow in those questions he'd guaranteed himself my help. I didn't want to refuse him on the

grounds that he was a lost cause. Didn't want to walk out of the office feeling like a smaller man than when I'd walked in.

The light changed, and I crossed the street and cut through the parking lot to the restaurant, thinking that Harrison was a clever son of a bitch. It had been a nice play, that final question about rehabilitation, and in the end it got him what he wanted. Part of me felt honorable for my decision; another part felt manipulated. Played.

Maybe I'd made a mistake. This wasn't the sort of client I wanted on the books. Granted, we hadn't signed anything, and I could always back out . . .

"Joe will be furious," I said aloud, and then I managed a laugh. No, my partner was not going to be impressed with this story. I could hear him already, his voice rising in volume and exasperation as he explained to me the hundreds of obvious reasons why I shouldn't have taken this case. That alone could justify taking it. I had a hell of a time getting under Joe's skin now that he was in Florida. This one just might do it, though. This one just might have enough annoyance to bridge the miles.

It should be simple, too. I added that to the pro side of the list as I walked into Gene's Place and down the brick steps beside the old popcorn machine that had greeted people just inside the doors for years. Honestly, it should take me no more than a day or two to determine where this Cantrell couple had gone. I'd give them a call or drop them a note and explain where Harrison was and what he wanted. If they agreed to contact him, fine, and if they didn't, I would still have held up my end of the bargain—and, hopefully, would have satisfied Harrison into silence.

I ate a turkey club and drank black coffee and listened as people around me discussed what a beautiful day it was, how nice the sun felt. It had been a cold, angry April, with a late-season snowstorm that canceled the early baseball games and then settled into a few weeks of gray sky and chill rain. That looked to be behind us now, finally. Today's weather seemed to be an official announcement, winter waving a GOING OUT OF BUSINESS sign at the city. CLOSED FOR THE SEASON sign, rather. It'd be back soon enough, as everyone in Cleveland knew.

Still, today it was gone, and staying indoors seemed like a crime, unappreciative. I had no real need to make the drive to see the Cantrell house—this thing could probably be wrapped up without leaving the office—but the day called for an outing of some sort, and this was the only one that had offered itself. I finished my lunch and left, walked back to Lorain and past the office and a few blocks down until I got to my building. I own a small twenty-four-hour gym and live in the apartment above it. The original plan when I got kicked off the police force was to make a living on the gym. Then Joe retired and coaxed me into the PI business, which was fairly easy to do based upon the meager profits the gym had been turning. A few short years later, Joe was gone indefinitely, and I was running the agency by myself. Man plans, God laughs.

I stopped in the gym long enough to say hello to Grace, my gym manager, and then I got into my truck and headed south for Hinckley. The Cantrell house was supposed to be just off 606, which was a winding two-lane highway that cut through small towns and farm country. I came onto it too far south and had to backtrack. Ten minutes and one more turnaround later, I located 3730, a beat-up metal box on a weathered wood pole, the painted numerals chipped and peeling. The pole sat at an unnatural angle that suggested previous contact with a car. I wasn't surprised. Winter storms came in fast and hard out here, and the rural communities always had more roads than they had snowplows.

The mailbox was on the opposite side of the highway from the driveway, which was identified, as Harrison had promised, by a stone post calling it Whisper Ridge. I turned off the highway and drove past the sign onto the rutted gravel lane. Well, it *had* been a gravel lane, at least. Most of the stone had either washed away or been beaten into the dirt, and grass was beginning to reclaim the drive. I made it about fifty teeth-rattling feet before I saw the gate.

Parker Harrison hadn't mentioned the set of steel bars at least eight feet tall blocking the rest of the driveway, outfitted with an electronic lock. On either side of the gate was a metal fence with barbed wire at the top.

I turned the engine off, climbed out of my truck, and studied the obstacle ahead. There was no need to risk setting off an alarm or angering a neighbor with an attempt at trespassing, but now that I was all the way out here I wanted to actually see the damn house. There had to be a way down to it; it just wasn't going to be as easy as I'd hoped.

My first choice was to walk the fence line to the left, and that was a mistake. After battling through the undergrowth for about thirty feet, I ran into water. The fence went all the way to the edge of a creek that was maybe fifteen feet wide and at least a few feet deep. Wetter than I wanted to be, that was for sure. I backtracked and walked in the opposite direction only to find that on this side the fence ran into thickets of thorns and tangled brush. On second thought, the creek might not be that bad. It was closer to the drive, and Harrison had talked about the house looking out onto a pond and fountain, right? Well, the creek must feed the pond.

I clung to that belief as I set to work ruining a good pair of shoes. Originally I'd had hopes of jumping from stone to stone, but it turned out ol' Lincoln wasn't as nimble-footed as he remembered. I splashed my way around the fence, grumbling and cursing, and then battled through more of the brambles until I came back to the driveway, this time inside the gate.

From there it was an easy walk. It was a long driveway, at least a half mile, and it curved through a border of pine trees so that my truck was quickly hidden from sight. At one point a dirt offshoot led to the right, but I figured that probably led to some sort of outbuilding, so I stayed with the gravel, tramping along down the middle of the drive, stepping around the occasional hole or downed branch until it came to an end in a stone semicircle.

At first I couldn't see anything but trees and ivy. It was very overgrown, and even though the sun was out, all the shade left it dark and gloomy back here. Then I saw the hill rising steeply in front of me, and the door in the middle of it.

Harrison's description was dead-on. The door was a massive piece of oak encased in an arch of rough stone, and everything was so weathered and unused that it just blended right into the hillside.

There was one wide, flat stone inlaid beside the arched door frame, with words carved into it. I walked closer, pushed ivy aside, and read the words.

> *Whisper Ridge*
> *Home to Dreams*
> *October 2, 1992–April 12, 1996*

An epitaph for a house? I ran my fingertips over the carved stone, then across the heavy wood of the door, and let out a breath that I hadn't realized I was holding.

"Unreal," I said, and it was. I'd never seen anything else like it. There was nothing here but a hill covered in ivy and groundcover and this single, solitary door with the words carved beside it. On a second read, I decided I was wrong—the epitaph wasn't for the house, which, still standing, lived on. It was for the dreams.

I stepped away and looked around at the empty trees and the drive I'd just walked up. All right, the house was here, and he'd been honest about the door. Let's see about the rest of it.

I walked up the side of the hill, which flattened out on top. A stone path was barely visible in the tall weeds, and I followed that until I came to the well house. It, like the door casing, seemed to be built out of hand-laid creek stone, and Harrison was right—it looked like it was two hundred years old. As I walked past I felt a strange, powerful need *not* to peer down into the well, as if something might come snarling out. I forced a laugh and shook my head and then went up to the edge and looked over, ignoring the prickle that climbed my spine.

The bottom was covered with plywood that was rotted and broken, weeds and mud caking the jagged edges of the boards. I leaned back and surveyed the hilltop. It looked like hell now, all the thickets and tall weeds threatening to take over, but I could imagine how beautiful it had been when Parker Harrison tended the grounds and kept the woods at bay. It was a solitary place, that was for damn sure. I couldn't hear a sound except wind and birds. Even though the highway was less than a mile away, I couldn't hear any traffic. That seemed impossible to me, so I listened harder and still couldn't hear a car. Finally I gave up and walked away from the well.

At the far end of the hill there was a little ridge of stone, and once I got up to it I realized it was the top edge of the back of the house. I walked along it until I came to the end, and there I found a little path that led back down the side of the hill and emptied out behind the house.

It was just as Harrison had said—two stories of almost sheer glass looking out on the water. There was no fountain now, and the pond was covered with a skim of algae and leaves and hidden behind a cluster of dried, broken reeds, but I hardly cared about the water. The house held all my attention. It should have been gorgeous, but instead it was buried under a heavy layer of grime and disrepair. The windows were broken in several places and covered with dirt, but even so you could see what it must have been, what it could *still* be if only someone had taken care of it.

I walked up to the lower-level window and used my shirtsleeve to rub away some of the filth, then pressed my face to the glass, shielding my eyes with my hands like someone window-shopping at a store that had closed for the night.

A swimming pool was just inside, long and deep. A lap pool. Empty, of course, with stains and corrosion lining the cracked tank. Around the pool was a floor of Italian tile, many of the pieces broken, and behind that the thick plaster walls were bare. I could see two ornate columns rising behind the door that led into the next room, and a curving stone wall with a fireplace.

I stood there for a long time. Didn't move until my breath began to fog the glass and I could no longer see. Then I stepped away and looked from the house to the silent pond and back again, suddenly feeling very ill at ease.

This was not normal. The housing market in Medina County wasn't booming, but some people were willing to trade a long commute for a little country living, and the price tag on a place like this would have been mighty. So why not sell it? Why did you let a home like this sit empty and exposed to the elements for twelve years?

I walked away from the back of the house and up the other side of the hill. I found an angle that allowed me to look in at the second story, in at more beautiful but empty rooms. All the way around the hill was another entrance, a sunporch with almost all the glass broken out. I stepped over the jagged shards and walked to this door and repeated my face-to-the-window act. This time I saw a hallway bordered by a short partition that had recessed floodlights and doors opening to hidden rooms beyond. Back through the broken glass and into the woods, and now I was walking away from the house faster than I'd walked toward it, returning to my truck with a strange tightness in the middle of my back and sweat-dampened hair clinging to my forehead.

I splashed back through the creek without a single muttered curse or a thought about my shoes and climbed up to the driveway.

People did not leave homes like this. I'd never seen anything like it, and maybe that was why it was affecting me in this way, why I felt almost relieved when I was back in the driver's seat and had the engine going. It was just something . . . different, that was all. Felt a little off because, well, it *was* a little off. Abnormal. Still, I could figure out what had happened, and I could tell Harrison, and I could be done with it. I owed him that much, because his request certainly seemed genuine, convicted murderer or not. This much of the truth he had told me: The door was there in the earth, and the house beyond it was empty.

4

My shoes forced a return home. I was tempted to head straight for the Medina County Recorder's Office, find out who held the deed on the property and whether there was a mortgage, and then continue on to the auditor's office to see whether the taxes were truly paid up and who the hell was paying them. My shoes and the lower third of my pants were soaked and coated with a slimy creek mud, though, and I didn't want to go tramping into the county offices looking like I'd just emerged from a swamp.

I was back in the city, only a few blocks from my building, when Amy called.

"Guess who visited today?" I said in place of a hello.

"Who?"

"Parker Harrison."

Amy Ambrose, friend-turned-girlfriend—a process not without its bumps—was well aware of the letters I'd received from Harrison.

"The psycho?"

"The rehabilitated murderer, Amy."

"Fava beans," she said. "Tell me he talked about fava beans."

"Sadly, no."

"Well, what the hell did he want? How was it? Is he crazy? I bet he's charming. Those guys always are. Or did he get angry? I could see him getting—"

"Amy."

"Sorry. Got carried away."

"Indeed." I turned left across traffic and bounced into the alley beside my building.

"So?" she prompted.

"He is unique," I said. "More toward the charming side, definitely."

"Please don't tell me he *charmed* you into working on his case. From what I read, the guy couldn't be any guiltier."

"That isn't in dispute." I parked and shut off the engine. "He candidly admitted his guilt."

"What did he want with you, then?"

"Help with the most minor of investigations. I mean, it's odd that he went through all the dramatics of the letters, because this is something that shouldn't take much time—"

"Oh, no. You agreed to do it, didn't you?"

"Why do you say that?"

"Because you're trying to explain it in that rational, matter-of-fact tone you always use to justify something stupid."

I smiled and didn't answer.

"Speak," she said. "Tell me I'm wrong."

More silence.

"Lincoln!"

I explained it to her then, told her about Harrison's story as quickly as possible and went on to describe the house. I knew the house would pacify her. Amy's natural curiosity well exceeds my own.

"How much do you think the place is worth?" she asked when I was done, her voice softer.

"I'm not good with real estate, but I'd have to say a few million with all that property involved. The house is incredible, but it's also been ignored for a long time. It would take someone willing to invest in rehabilitation."

"I want to see it," she said.

"Bring some waders. That creek provides the best way in."

"Your psychopath didn't mention that? He didn't even know there was a gate?"

"My *client* did not, no."

"Hey, you work for a murderer, you better get used to the criticism and name-calling. Anyway, maybe that means the gate is new."

"Probably."

"I wonder who put it up."

"So do I. I'm going to change clothes and drive back down there and check with the auditor, see who has been paying the taxes."

"You're going back today?"

"Uh-huh."

"Lot of driving for one day."

It was, and with any other case I might have delayed the return trip. This was different, somehow. There was something about the place that had gotten under my skin after just one visit, and I wanted to know who was responsible for it, who'd kept it away from a sheriff's sale but still didn't bother to actually take care of the home.

"I'm not busy," I said. "Faster I get this worked out, the faster I can terminate my relationship with Harrison."

Two hours later, wearing fresh pants and shoes, I stood in the recorder's office and stared at a warranty deed confirming that, yes, Alexandra and Joshua Cantrell owned the home. There was no mortgage. They'd paid five hundred thousand for the property alone seventeen years earlier. It was a forty-eight-acre parcel.

So Harrison's information was accurate and up-to-date and the Cantrells still owned the home. Now came the second step, the auditor's office, where I'd find a new address for the couple.

Well, it was supposed to go that way. When I took the parcel number over to the auditor's office and requested the records, though, I learned that the taxes had been paid each year—in full and on time—by one Anthony Child, attorney at law, Hinckley, Ohio. Okay, maybe I was going to need a third step to finish this one off.

———

Child's office was on the second floor of a brick building on the square in Hinckley, which is a town known nationally for Buzzard Day, a bizarre ritual in which people gather each April to welcome a returning flock of turkey vultures. In some places, this return would be cause for alarm, or at least mild revulsion. In Ohio, it's a celebration. Hey, we have long, tedious winters, all right? You take your excitement where you can get it.

Attorney Child was in, and willing to see me. The entire firm seemed to consist of an angry-looking secretary in an outer room and Child alone in the office behind that. The door to the tiny attached bathroom stood open, showing a toilet with the seat up. First class. For a good thirty seconds after I'd been shown into his office he kept his back to me, staring at the TV. Weather report. Can't miss that.

"Hot," he said when he finally clicked the television off and turned to me. "Unusually hot for the first week of May."

"I know it."

"Going to be a rough summer. You can always tell."

Everyone else was rejoicing that winter had finally broken, and this guy was bitching about the summer to come. Cheerful. He sat and stared at me without much interest. Maybe fifty years old, small face with slack jowls and sleepy eyes. His tie was loosened, and his jacket was off.

"I was just explaining to your secretary that I found you through a tax record," I said. "I'm curious about some property, and when I pulled the records I found your office handled the payments."

That was all it took to wake the sleepy eyes up. They narrowed and focused, and he pushed away from the desk and ran both thumbs down the straps of his suspenders.

"What exactly is your line of work, Mr. Perry?"

I took out a business card and passed it across the desk to him. He looked at it long enough to read every word three times and then read them backward. Finally he set the card carefully on the desk and kept one hand on it while he looked back up at me.

"This is about the Cantrell house."

I nodded.

"Who are you working for?"

Here I hesitated, for the obvious reason. Parker Harrison's name hadn't meant anything to me until he'd taken to writing letters, but Child was a good deal older and more likely to remember a murderer from that era than I was.

"Someone who's interested in the property," I said after a beat of silence. "It's a damn expensive home to leave in that condition."

"I take it you've trespassed out there and seen the place? Don't worry, I'm not going to report you. Plenty of people have trespassed there before. It's a damn headache, that house is, and for as little money as I've made off the arrangements, I wish I'd never agreed to it."

He was warming up to me now, waving his hand around while he talked, looking more relaxed.

"You put up the gate," I said.

He nodded.

"At the Cantrells' request?"

A hesitation, as if I'd asked something odd, and then, "No, not exactly. I'd been out to the house a few times and saw that there'd been some vandalism. The sheriff called me to complain, because they'd had to go out there on several occasions and break up groups of drunk kids wandering the grounds. Word got out that the place was empty, and the kids immediately found their way to it. You know how that goes. Then there was a hitchhiker who found it and moved right in, had some insane idea about claiming squatter's rights. Sheriff was irritated, so I went ahead and put up the gate and the fence. It's helped."

"You paid for this?"

"I draw from an account she left. The money was there." He pulled himself back to the desk again, frowning, and said, "Mr. Perry, you clearly don't want to tell me who you're working for and why they want to find her, but I need to tell you this: Any number of people do want to find her, from the police to reporters to people like you, and I can't help. All I ask of you is to make that clear to your client. I don't know how to get in touch with her; I don't know where she is or what she's doing."

"Mr. Child, I don't understand exactly why she'd be so sought after. Who is the woman, anyhow?"

He looked at me as if I'd asked him how to spell my own name. Then his eyes turned reflective and he nodded. "Your client's interested in the property."

"That's right." It wasn't true, really, but I had the sense that was what he wanted to hear as some kind of reassurance.

"So you have no idea . . . shit, you guys really are clueless. Okay. That puts me at peace. It truly does."

"What don't I understand, Mr. Child?"

"Anything," he said. "You don't understand anything. What *do* you know about Alexandra and Joshua Cantrell?"

I shook my head. "Only that their names are on the deed."

"Okay," he said. "Then you absolutely don't understand a damn thing. Now I'm going to tell you two little details, and then I'm going to ask one more time who you're working for, and if you won't answer, I'll tell you to get the hell out of my office."

He braced his elbows on the desk and folded his hands together. "You've done amazingly poor research, Mr. Perry. Here are the two details you need to know: First, Joshua Cantrell is dead. Nobody had heard from him in twelve years, but last winter his bones were found near Pymatuning Reservoir. Buried in the woods. Case still under investigation."

He paused, and I was aware of how quiet it was in his office, so quiet that I could hear the dripping of a faucet in the little bathroom on the other side of the wall, a drop falling into the sink every few seconds. *Plip, plip, plip.*

"Detail number two," he said. "Do you know the lovely Mrs. Cantrell's maiden name?"

"I do not."

"Sanabria," he said. "Alexandra Sanabria."

"Shit," I said. "You're kidding."

He shook his head.

"Maiden name," I said. "Surely she's too old to be the daughter of—"

"Dominic? Yes, too old to be his daughter. Just the right age to be his sister. Sister of Dominic, daughter of Christopher, right there in the trunk of a very infamous family tree. Pride and joy of Crime Town, USA."

It was an old nickname, went back almost fifty years, but people still attached it to Youngstown, a gritty factory town an hour from Cleveland. While the Italian mob's heyday in Cleveland was during the sixties and seventies, Youngstown remained an epicenter for decades longer, featuring constant FBI attention as well as the occasional car bombing or sniper takedown of a major player. During one attempt to pay off the town's mayor, a *priest* was involved as a money handler. Ties run deep in Youngstown, and a lot of them run through the Sanabria family. Christopher was the patriarch, the focus of a major federal investigation when he was killed in the late seventies. Twenty years later, his son, Dominic, appeared in headlines for a few months during the Lenny Strollo and James Traficant trials. Something like seventy convictions were handed down in the fallout of those investigations—Traficant was a U.S. representative at the time, which only added to the circus—but Dominic Sanabria walked away with one of the lightest sentences, two years for minor crimes. It wasn't that he'd been a minor player, but he apparently left less evidence and trusted fewer people. At the time, one of the district attorneys suggested that Sanabria was the most dangerous of the lot, and the media made good use of that quote. People in the Cleveland area remembered the name.

"That house," I said, "is owned by Dominic Sanabria's sister? That's what you're telling me?"

Child's face turned unpleasant as he leaned across the desk, almost pulling out of his chair, and said, "Yes. Now, damn it, I need to know who you're working for."

"That information is confidential, Mr. Child. I'm sorry."

"Then get out. And tell your client to give up his inquiries on that house."

"Where is she?" I said as he got to his feet and walked to the door. "Where's Alexandra?"

I didn't ask because I believed he would provide an answer but simply because I wanted to gauge his reaction for myself, see if I smelled a lie.

He paused with his hand on the doorknob and turned back to me. "Nobody knows. Not me, not her family, and certainly not the police. If they did know, maybe they'd stop calling me all the time."

It felt like the truth.

He twisted the knob and swung the door open for me. "Goodbye, Mr. Perry."

5

Outside, the air was thick with humidity, and a bank of angry dark clouds had gathered in the west. It was a heavy, cloaking warmth, and I opened the second button of my shirt and stood on the sidewalk and stared at the sleepy town square.

Joshua Cantrell is dead . . . bones found last winter . . . buried in the woods. Case still under investigation.

Without leaving the front steps of Child's office, I took out my cell phone and called Amy at the newspaper. For once, she was there. I asked her to do an archives search for Joshua Cantrell.

"The guy who owns the house?"

"Owned. He's dead."

"Lincoln—"

"Run the search, please. I'd like to know when they found the body."

I listened as she clicked keys and people in her office laughed over something. It took a few minutes, and neither of us spoke. Then she found the right article.

"Looks like a hunter found the body on the first weekend of December."

"That's just before Harrison wrote me the first letter. He knew. The son of a bitch knew."

"Lincoln, there's stuff in here . . . hang on. It says that Cantrell is related by marriage to organized crime. To the Sanabria family."

"Yeah," I said. "I was recently informed of that."

"What in the hell is Parker Harrison trying to do?"

"I have no idea, but I guarantee you he knew Cantrell was dead when he sent me out here. He knew, and he didn't tell me."

"You don't think he killed him? That he's playing some sick game now because the body was found?"

"I don't know if he killed him, but, yeah, he's playing some sick game—and I'm going to end it."

I called Harrison from my truck and told him to meet me at the office. I didn't say anything else. The clouds built overhead as I drove back to the city with both hands tight on the wheel and the stereo off, the cab of the truck silent. The rain started when I reached the stoplight across from the office and was falling steadily as I walked into the building, but the air was still warm, reassuring us that this was a spring, not winter, storm. Harrison was already inside, and he met me at the top of the stairs with a smile.

"When you said you'd be in touch, I was expecting a bit more of a wait."

I didn't say a word. Just unlocked the door and walked inside and sat behind the desk and stared at him while he took the chair across from me, waited while his smile faded and his eyes narrowed.

"What's the problem?" he said.

"Did you kill him?"

If I'd been expecting a visceral reaction to that, I was wrong. He lifted his hand and ran his fingertips over the scar on his cheekbone, let his eyes wander away from mine. "No, I didn't kill him. If you're referring to Joshua Cantrell."

"If I'm referring . . . listen, Harrison, you twisted prick, what the hell kind of game is this? Why do I need to play it?"

"Hang on, Lincoln."

"Shut up. I shouldn't have ever let you in the door, and when I made that mistake I *definitely* shouldn't have been stupid enough to buy your story. It was a good one, though, compelling, and you reeled me all the way in with those questions about whether I believed in rehabilitation, whether I believed in the system. A nice, subtle guilt trip. I'm sure there's a better word for it, some psychology term, and you probably know it because you had fifteen years to sit in a cell and read books and come up with games to play. But you shouldn't have involved me, Harrison."

I was leaning toward him, loud and aggressive, and if that made the slightest impact he didn't show it. He waited till I'd wound down, then said, "I told you the truth."

"Like hell you did."

"Lincoln, I worked for the Cantrells as a groundskeeper for one year, and ever since I've wondered what—"

"Oh, stop it already." I waved him off. "All that may be true, and I don't care if it is or if it isn't. What I care about is that you lied to me. You sat there and talked about Joshua Cantrell as if you didn't have the faintest idea that he was dead. Talked about wanting to find him."

"I said nothing about wanting to find him. I said I want to find *her*. In fact, I assured you he was not the reason she had stayed out of touch."

"You already knew he'd been murdered and didn't bother to tell me that. Like it's insignificant information, Harrison, that the guy is dead and the woman is the *sister* of a Youngstown mob figure? How did you get tied up with those guys in the first place? Last I knew, the requirement was to be Sicilian, not Shawnee."

"I was never tied up with them."

"Sure."

"I shared minimal facts," he said. "That I will admit."

My laugh was heavy with disgust. "Shared minimal facts? Shit, that's brilliant. You should've been an attorney, Harrison, instead of a murderer."

That seemed to sting him, and for a moment he looked entirely genuine again. Looked hurt.

"Would you have taken this case," he said, "if you knew all of that before-hand?"

"No."

"See, that was my reasoning. I didn't think you would, but I knew if I could get you to go out to the house, to stand there in that spot under the trees and feel the energy of that place, that things might change. I knew that was possible, because I knew this one was meant for you, that you'd been—"

"*Shut up!*" I hammered my fist onto the desk between us. "I don't want to hear any more of it. I'm not going to take the case. We're done."

I stood up and walked to the door and opened it for him, just as Child had done for me an hour earlier.

"You saw the house?" he said without turning.

"Yeah."

"You didn't feel anything?"

"No, I did not," I said. Was there a tug somewhere along my spine at that? Some twinge that comes from telling a lie? No, couldn't be.

"All right," he said. "I'm sorry you're offended. Sorry you feel betrayed."

"I don't feel betrayed, I feel stupid. I'll give you this heads-up, though: I'm going to track down whatever police agency is investigating Cantrell's death and tell them about your request."

"You think I was involved?" He still had his head down, and now, stand-ing above him, I could see another scar, long and ugly, across the back of his skull and neck.

"I don't know," I said, "but you've killed before, and you seem awfully fascinated with this couple, one of whom happens to be dead. I think the right cops ought to be told about that."

"It's my past that bothers you. That's why you refuse to give me any cred-ibility."

"Yeah, Harrison, that does bother me. Just a touch. Sorry."

"Let me ask you one question," he said, keeping his back to me.

I was silent.

"Can a good man commit a horrible act?" he said.

I stood there at the door, looking at his bowed head, and then I said, "Harrison, get out."

He nodded and got to his feet. "Okay, Mr. Perry. Goodbye."

It was the first time he hadn't called me Lincoln.

I stood at the door while he went through it, and then I crossed to the window and looked down as he walked out of the building and into a hard, driving rain.

6

Amy was in my apartment when I got home, and she was cooking, some sort of Italian dish that had filled the rooms with a thick scent of tomatoes and garlic and made the place feel more welcoming than at any time I could remember.

"Did anyone give you permission to touch my valuable implements?" I said, lifting a cheese grater off the counter. Amy had never cooked a meal in my apartment before.

"You want to be the only one to touch your implements, I can make that happen." She shifted a pan on the stove and adjusted the heat.

"Seriously, to what do I owe this?"

"You sounded a little rough on the phone. Like it hadn't been the best day."

I listened to that, and watched her move around the kitchen, and I was grateful to see her there. She was right; it hadn't been the best day—but those were the sort of days that could stack up on you easily, and it was a new and welcome thing for me to end them with Amy. It beat the hell out of ending it alone, with a bottle of beer and the mindless noise of some TV show.

"Thank you," I said. "Really."

"I wouldn't say that till you taste this."

"What is it?"

"I call it Mafia lasagna. In honor of the Sanabria family."

"Weak humor, Amy. Very weak."

She dried her hands on a towel and turned to face me. "If you're interested, I've got a bunch of printouts discussing Joshua Cantrell—or at least the discovery of his body—over on the table. As for Alexandra, there's not much out there. She's the quiet one of the Sanabria family, I suppose."

I walked over to the table and looked at the stack of papers there. Lots of articles. The discovery of Cantrell's body had made plenty of news.

"I can't believe the name didn't register with me," I said, flipping through the articles.

Amy turned to look at me over her shoulder, a few strands of hair glued to her cheek from the steam rising off the stove. After months of fighting to straighten her naturally curly blond hair, she'd finally given up again, and I was glad to see it. She'd looked too corporate with the straightened hair—an observation that had gotten a pen thrown at me once.

"You've been pretty removed from the news lately." She pulled the oven open and bent to look inside, leaving her voice muffled as she continued to speak. "Can't say the last time I've seen you with the paper."

It was a good point. Ordinarily I would've read about the discovery of Cantrell's body, and probably remembered the name when Harrison said it, but I'd stopped reading the papers and watching TV news shows back in the fall, when I was making all-too-frequent appearances in them. I hadn't gone back to them yet, but now I was thinking maybe I should. It's dangerous to be uninformed, as today had demonstrated.

"That's just good taste," I said. "You know the sort of crap they write in the newspaper these days. It's a wonder they still refer to those people as journalists."

She closed the oven and stood up. "I am close to knives, you know. Large, sharp knives."

"Good reminder." I moved the stack of articles out of the way. They could wait, or maybe I'd never read them at all. There was no need to. I'd taken a silly nibble today, but now I saw the lure and its hooks and knew better than to hang around. The Cantrell case didn't need my attention, and I needed even less the attention of the Sanabria family.

"Food is almost done," Amy said, "and you better realize the only reason I'm feeding you is because I want to hear the story. Not some half-assed version of it, either. The real story, with all the details."

"You'll get it," I said, "but let me pour some wine first."

It was a nice evening that turned into a nice night, and she stayed with me and we slept comfortably and deeply in my bed while another round of storms blew in off the lake and hammered rain into the walls that sheltered us. Amy rose early and slipped out of the house sometime before seven to return to her own apartment before starting the day. We'd been together a while now, but still we both clung to own routines and our own space, and I wondered at times if maybe that wasn't the way it would and should always be, if maybe we were the sort of people who simply didn't cohabit well. At other times, I'd come home and sit alone in the apartment and wonder why in the hell I hadn't proposed.

She'd been gone for almost an hour, and I'd fallen back into a surface layer of sleep, not quite awake but never far from it, either, when the tapping began. A gentle series of taps, five or six at a time, then a pause followed by another sequence. I don't know how many sequences had passed before they finally carved into my brain and I sat up in bed and realized that someone was knocking on my door. Knocking, it seemed, with extraordinary consistency and patience. Never loud, never urgent, but never stopping, either. Tap, tap, tap, tap.

I got out of bed and tugged on a pair of jeans and a T-shirt, made it to the top of the stairs as another calm sequence of knocks began, reached the bottom just as it came to an end. Then I had the door open and was squinting out into the harsh daylight and the face of a small, dark-haired man with a raised fist. There was a ring on his finger that seemed brighter than the sunlight behind him, some hideous collection of gold and diamonds so heavy that I hoped he wore one on the other hand to keep from becoming lopsided. He was getting ready to bring it back down on the door, continue the knocking, but when he saw me he just held the pose for a second and then slowly lowered the hand to his side.

"Good morning, Mr. Perry."

I was barefoot and he was in shoes, but still I had a good four inches on him, and I'm not particularly tall. He was thin across the chest and shoulders, with small hands and weak wrists, and seemed like the kind of guy who would need his wife to open the pickle jar for him. Until you looked him in the eye. There, in that steady and unflinching gaze, was a quality I'd typically seen in much larger men, stronger men. Men who felt invincible.

"Did I wake you?" he said when I didn't respond to the greeting. "I apologize. I'm an early riser, though. Always have been."

He put out the hand with the ring and waited until I shook it, until my palm was firmly held in his, to say, "My name is Dominic Sanabria."

I pulled my hand free and stepped forward, out of my doorway and into the daylight.

"I'm sorry you made the trip," I said. "It was entirely unnecessary, Mr. Sanabria."

"You don't even know the purpose of my trip."

"I know the source of it, though."

"Do you?"

"A lawyer named Child probably gave you a call. Or somebody in the Medina County Recorder's Office, though that seems unlikely. Either way, somebody told you I was inquiring about your sister's home. That information is no longer correct."

"Is it not?"

I shook my head. "I've learned the house is not on the market and will not be on the market, and I've passed that information along to my client. We're done with it now."

He reached up and ran a hand over his mouth, as if drying his lips, and then he spoke without looking at me. "Let's go upstairs and talk—and I'd ask you not to continue lying to me. It's not something I appreciate."

He walked past me and headed up the stairs without another word, and I turned and hesitated and then followed, swinging the door shut and closing out the daylight behind us.

When I got to the top of the stairs he was already in my living room, standing in front of the bookshelf. He slid a Michael Connelly novel out with his index finger and studied the cover.

"I had a brother-in-law who was a big reader," he said. "Not these sort of books, though. Not fiction. He was an anthropologist. Studied people. Studied the, what's the word, indigenous types."

He pushed the book back into place and turned to face me.

"He didn't study me. Did not have the slightest desire to study me, or my people. Wanted very little to do with us. Oh, he was polite, you know, a hell of a nice guy, but he definitely wanted to know as little as possible about me and my associates and what it was that we did. I always liked that about him."

I didn't answer, didn't say a word as he crossed to an armchair and sat carefully on the edge of it. Dominic Sanabria was in my apartment. It was not yet nine in the morning, and Dominic Sanabria was sitting in my living room discussing dead men. I wasn't going to require coffee to get my nervous system energized today.

"My sister is a very special girl," he said, crossing his legs in a manner that would have looked effete from anyone but him. "A woman, of course, but I can't help but think of her as a girl. She's nine years younger than me, you know. By the time she was growing up, there was some awkwardness around my family. Some legal troubles that you might recall, or might not. You're pretty young. Anyhow, my father, who was not without his faults but always loved his children dearly, he thought it would be best to send Alexandra away to school."

I hadn't taken a seat, hadn't moved from the top of the stairs, because I thought it was better to simply stand there and listen. There are guys who bring out the smart-ass in me, the desire to throw some jabs back at them, show them the tough-guy bullshit isn't as intimidating as they'd like it to be. Dominic Sanabria was not one of those guys. All I wanted to do was listen and get him the hell out of my home. Even while that desire occupied my thoughts, though, I hadn't missed the tense shift. He'd referred to Joshua Cantrell in the past, and well he should—Joshua was past tense for this world, no doubt. Alexandra had received present tense. *My sister is a very special girl . . .*

"They found a school out east, somewhere in the Adirondacks, cost a friggin' fortune," he said, "but it was worth it, you know? It was worth it. Because Alexandra, she was always a special kid, but after being out there, being around those sort of teachers and those sort of . . . I dunno, *experiences*, I guess, it made a difference. She was a kind of, you know, a deeper spirit when she came home. A very compassionate person. She was not as close to the family as the rest of us were, but that was good. It was good for her to be around other people. Other influences. Every family has their darling, and she is ours."

He did that thing with his hand again, running it over his mouth, the way you might if your lips were chapped and bothering you.

"When she got married, the guy was, well, a different sort from the type we know. Probably from the type you know. Quiet guy, real studious, shit like that. Nose in a book, right? All the time with that. I liked him. He wasn't real comfortable around me, maybe, but he was good to my sister. They matched up where it counts." He touched his head with two fingers, then his heart. "Where it counts."

Out on the street a truck's gears hissed and someone blew a horn while Dominic Sanabria sat and stared at me.

"I liked Joshua," he said. "Used to call him Josh, and he never bitched about that, but then Alexandra said he didn't like it. Josh*ua*, she said. I liked him. Because I love my sister, and he made her happy."

He sighed and kneaded the back of his neck with his hand and looked at the floor.

"They found his bones a few months ago, and I cannot tell you how unhappy that makes me, because I know how unhappy that makes my sister. I feel that pain in my heart, you know? I feel it for her. There are people out there, somewhere in the world, who know some things that I will need to know."

"I'm not one of them." It was the first time I'd spoken since he entered my apartment.

"Probably not," he said, "but you may be working for one. I believe you probably are. I'd like to speak with that person."

Give him up! my brain screamed. *Give him up!* A quieter voice, the soft whisper of instinct, offered dissent.

"Mr. Sanabria," I said, "I run a business that would not exist without confidentiality. It would disappear if I did not maintain that, and I'd be out on the streets looking for work. I respect you, though, and I respect your interest in this, and here's what I will tell you: My relationship with this client is done. That's a promise, that's a guarantee. I ended it yesterday, and I will not resume it at any time, ever. I don't know anything—*anything*—that can help you. I assume Mr. Child communicated that idea to you. I was utterly clueless when I went into his office, and I remain that way now. Nor do I have any desire to learn more."

"Who hired you?"

I shook my head.

"You've been around," he said. "You understand that people can eventually be convinced to share information."

"I've also seen how stupid and wasteful all that convincing becomes when it doesn't produce any information of value. I've seen the problems that can arise as a result of the effort."

"You were a cop."

"I was."

"Cops tend to feel safe. Off-limits, protected. That sort of thing."

"I've been to a few police funerals. Enough to know better."

"Still you refuse me."

"The name can't help you, Mr. Sanabria. My client is a nobody. *Was* a nobody."

"Maybe you like me," he said. "Maybe you like having me around, want me to drop in again. That must be it, because here you have a chance to send me away for good, and you're refusing that."

"I like you fine. You're terrific, trust me. Even so, I sure as shit don't want you around."

"You sound a little uneasy there."

"I am."

"You sound, maybe, even afraid," he said, and there was a bite in his voice, a taunt.

"I'm afraid of my own stupidity," I answered. "There are people I'd rather not be involved with, at any level, at any time. You are one of those people."

"That could be viewed an insult."

"It should be viewed as a statement of fact. I don't want anything to do with you, and I don't know anything that can help you. Where we go from here, I guess you will decide and I'll deal with."

He nodded his head very slowly. "Yes. Yes, I guess I will decide."

Another pause, and then he got to his feet and walked toward me. Slowed just a touch when he reached me, then turned and went down the steps and opened the door and walked outside. He left the door open. I waited for a few seconds, and then I went down and closed it and turned the lock and sat on the steps. I sat there for a long time, and eventually a car engine started in the parking lot, and then it was gone, and I was alone.

7

For more than a week, it was quiet. At first I checked the locks with extra care, wore my gun when I left the apartment, and held my breath each time I turned the key in the ignition of my truck. Visits from a guy like Dominic Sanabria can make you conscious of such things.

Nothing happened. Sanabria didn't stop by, nor did anyone operating on his behalf. Parker Harrison made no contact. I was quiet, too—despite promising Harrison that I would pass his name along to the Joshua Cantrell death investigators, I didn't make any calls. After Sanabria visited, it somehow seemed better to do nothing. Amy and I discussed the situation frequently for the first few days, but then the topic faded, and soon I was leaving the gun at home and starting the truck without pause. I'd gotten out of the mess early enough, it seemed, and no damage had been done.

"Managed to escape yourself this time," Joe said when I called to say that seven days had passed without disaster following Sanabria's visit. "It's good that you're developing that skill, LP. Without me around, you've actually been forced to learn some common sense."

"Aren't you proud."

"Not particularly. If you'd had even an ordinary amount of that sense, you'd never have agreed to look at the house in the first place."

"Harrison assured me he'd been rehabilitated. What else could I do?"

"I've sat in on parole hearings and listened to true psychotics insist on the same thing."

"You wouldn't release a jaywalker until he'd done five years in solitary, Joe."

The conversation drifted away from Harrison then, on to more important things, like baseball, and eventually Joe asked after the weather.

"Warm," I said. "The sun's shining every day, and it's warm. So why are you still in Florida? I'm pretty sure the rest of your kind has migrated back north."

"My kind?"

"Snowbirds, Joseph. Men who sit around the pool all day talking about their experiences fighting in Korea and working for the Truman campaign. You know, your peers."

"My peers." Joe hated the idea of being one of those flee-for-Florida-in-winter retirees, so naturally I raised the subject during every phone call.

"Perhaps I'm wrong, though," I said. "Perhaps you're not part of that group. Like I said, most of them are already coming back north. So if you need to stay down there this late in the year, you must be even more old and frail."

"That must be it, yes," he said, determined not to rise to the bait this time around.

"When are you coming back?" I asked, serious now. I'd been expecting his return sometime in April, but that month had come and gone and he remained in Florida.

"I don't know yet. We'll see."

"We'll see? If it's pushing eighty degrees up here it has to be, what, a hundred and sixty down there? With ninety percent humidity?"

"Close to that, sure."

"And summer hasn't even hit yet. Only a damn fool would stay in Florida in the summer when he could retreat to a home near the beautiful shores of Lake Erie."

"I'll admit I'm not enjoying the weather as much lately."

"So why not come home? What did you do, meet a woman?"

He didn't answer.

I said, "Joe?"

"Could be the truth, LP. Could be the truth."

I'd made the initial remark as a joke, but his response seemed sincere, and that silenced me. Joe's wife of thirty years, Ruth, had been dead for five now, and in that time he'd not gone on a single date. The few people who'd attempted to make introductions for him had been shut down quickly and emphatically. If Joe was actually seeing someone, it was an awfully big step for him.

"Well, good for you," I said after the pause had gone on too long.

"Oh, shut up with the sincerity. Makes me sick. If I were anybody else, you'd be giving me hell right now, asking which strip club I met her at."

"A stripper? At your age? No way. I just assumed you'd done some volunteering at a home for the blind. Convinced her you were forty years younger and good-looking. Convinced her you were more like me, in other words."

"You're neither good-looking nor forty years younger than me."

"Close enough on both counts, grandpa. Close enough. Can I at least hear the young girl's name?"

"Gena," he said, "and she *is* a few years younger than me, smart-ass."

"You lecherous old dog. How many years? Is she even legal yet? Is this girl—"

"Goodbye, Lincoln."

"Oh, come on, you've got to give me more than—"

"Talk to you soon," he said, and he was laughing as he hung up.

I was laughing, too, and in a good mood as I went downstairs to check the mail, happy for him even if disappointed that this might delay his return. Had a smile on my face until I took the mail out of the box and saw my name written in unpleasantly familiar handwriting on the only envelope inside. *P. T. Harrison*, the return address said, but I didn't need that to identify the sender. I'd seen enough of his damn letters already.

I tore the envelope open as I walked back up the stairs, shook out the contents as I stepped inside the office, dreading whatever twisted manifesto he'd decided to write this time. There was no letter, though. Nothing but a check for five hundred dollars, with *thanks for your time* written in the memo portion.

I threw the envelope in the trash but kept the check in my hand for a minute. It was a simple design, blue on blue, standard font, the sort of check most banks issued cheaply. It told me nothing about Parker Harrison that I didn't already know, except that he had a checkbook. *I have six thousand dollars. I'll spend every dime . . .*

I smoothed the check against the top of the desk and wondered if it would bounce. If not, then Harrison had done all right for himself after serving fifteen years in prison. Managing to stay on the streets for twelve years and save at least a little bit of money might not seem like much, but it was more than most of his fellow offenders managed. Twelve years was a hell of a run for some of them. I had a friend who worked at the Cuyahoga County Jail and referred to the booking area as "the revolving door." Same faces went in and out, year after year, decade after decade. Harrison hadn't done that. From the small amount of research I'd done once he began his letter writing, I'd determined that he'd never been charged with any crime after his release, not even a traffic ticket. I didn't know where he worked or how he lived or what he did with himself, but he hadn't taken another bust. For years, he'd lived quietly and without incident. Then the remains of a former employer turned up in the woods and he'd decided to surface again, surface in my life.

"Go away, Harrison," I said quietly. "Go away." Then I took the check and held it over the trash can, opened my fingers, and watched as it fluttered down. I wouldn't take his money. Didn't want it, didn't need it.

For once, that was true. My former fiancée, Karen Jefferson, had mailed me a check for eighty thousand dollars after my investigation into her husband's death in the fall. She was worth millions now, could certainly afford it, but I'd thrown that check in the trash, too, and the two that followed it. Then she sent another, along with a letter insisting that I take the money. I had. Cashed the check but hadn't spent a dime of it. The money sat in a savings account, earning a pitiful interest rate, but that was enough for me. I didn't want to invest it or spend it, but I appreciated the sense of comfort it provided. The sense of freedom. If I didn't like a client, I didn't have to work for him. If I didn't like a case, I didn't have to take it. If for any reason I didn't feel like working, well, I didn't have to. For a while, anyway. That eighty grand kept me at least a few steps ahead of the thresher.

I spent the rest of the day at my desk writing a case report. A local insurance company had hired me to conduct background investigations on candidates vying for a management job, and by the time I'd summarized the findings on all seven of them it was midafternoon and I was sick of being in the office. I locked up and left, thinking that I'd have an early workout. My energy felt wrong, though, and by the time I got to my building I'd talked myself out of exercise. I got into my truck instead and drove toward Clark Avenue in search of a drink. If you give up on the healthy decision, why not go all out in the opposite direction?

I was headed for the Hideaway, which had reopened in April after being closed for nearly a year from fire damage. I'd found myself down there often in the past few weeks, maybe trying to recapture something that was already gone, maybe just enjoying the place. I didn't want to overthink it. The owner, Scott Draper, had been a good friend once, and maybe could be again. With Joe gone, I'd become more aware of just how many friendships had wandered off or watered down over the years. A lot of that was my fault—I'd retreated from the world for a while after losing Karen and my job. Hell, if Amy hadn't come around back then, when a kid who'd spent a lot of time at my gym was murdered and she was asked to write about it, I'd be pretty damn pathetic by now. Funny how having just one woman around is enough to make you look like a functioning member of society.

A week or even a few days earlier, I might have noticed the car behind me while I was on the highway. When I was riding the peak of my paranoia, I'd done a good job of watching the mirrors. That was past, though, and I didn't pay attention to the cars behind me as I burned up I-71 toward downtown, didn't register any of them until I pulled onto the Fulton Road exit ramp. Even then, it was a cursory thing, just an awareness that I'd been one of two cars leaving the highway.

When I turned off Fulton and onto Clark and the car stayed with me, I finally gave it a few seconds of study, memories of Dominic Sanabria's visit not completely purged yet. It was a Honda Pilot, newer model, red. Not the sort of thing you'd expect a mob enforcer to drive. I put my eyes back on the road and pulled into a parking space on the street a half block from the Hideaway. The Pilot kept going. Nothing to worry about.

By the time I was out of the car, though, I saw that the Pilot's driver had just pulled into a spot across the street, not far away. I stood on the sidewalk and watched as the door opened and a tall guy with blond hair stepped out and walked in my direction.

He came across the street and up the sidewalk without missing a step, even when he realized I was standing there watching him. Walked right up to me, lifted a hand as if he needed to catch my attention, and said, "Lincoln Perry?"

He didn't match the mob-enforcer mold any better than his car. Tall, maybe six three or four, with broad, knobby shoulders under his starched blue shirt. Something about him made me think of a baseball pitcher. He moved well but without any sense of speed or agility, seemed like the sort of guy who'd be good at most sports despite not being particularly athletic. There was a shadow of beard along his jaw, darker than his sandy hair. Light blue eyes.

"Why were you following me?" I said.

"You're Lincoln?"

"You know I am. You were following me."

He held up his hands, palms spread. "Sorry, man. Didn't mean to freak you out. I'd just stopped by the gym and was going down to your office when I saw you get into your truck. I was already in my car, so I just pulled out after you."

"I've never seen you before in my life," I said. "So how did you know that was me, and that it was my truck?"

He smiled. "The lady who was in the gym office looked out at your truck to see if it was still there before she sent me up to your office."

"And your natural inclination was to follow me?"

"Actually, yeah. I'm a PI. You should know how that goes."

"A PI?"

"Name's Ken Merriman. You the sort that likes to see ID?" He reached for his wallet, but I waved him off.

"Don't worry about it, Ken. I'm a little on edge lately. Not your fault."

"No problem—and, hey, give me *some* credit. If I'd been tailing you I could have done a better job than that." He laughed and nodded in the direction of the Hideaway. "You working or grabbing a beer?"

"The latter."

"Well, why don't you let me buy a round, and I'll try to talk you into doing the former."

"That kind of visit, huh?"

"That kind of visit," he said, starting toward the bar.

"Where are you from?" I asked, falling in step beside him. I knew most of the private investigators in the area, by name if not by face, but neither Ken Merriman's name or face was familiar.

"Pittsburgh," he said.

"Keep your voice down, man. People in this neighborhood hear Pittsburgh, they turn violent. It's the home of the Steelers, you know."

"The proud home," he agreed as we reached the front steps.

"I also haven't worked on anything that involved Pittsburgh in a long time," I said, reaching for the door handle. "So whatever brings you up here must have a local tie."

"It did once, at least."

"Did?"

"About twelve years ago."

I was holding the door open for him, but he stopped on the top step, looking at my face.

"Twelve years?" My voice was hollow.

He nodded.

"There's a name I don't want to hear you say," I said.

"Which one? Cantrell or Sanabria?" He winked at me and walked into the bar.

8

Draper wasn't behind the bar, but I didn't care anymore—Ken Merriman had just obliterated my plan for a relaxed evening. I followed him as he walked to the back of the narrow dining room and slid into a booth.

"What do you want to drink?" I said.

"No waitress?"

"Not till five. What do you want?"

"Guinness would be good."

He handed me a ten, and I walked back to the bar and got his Guinness and a Moosehead for myself, then came back and sat down across from him. There'd been a few guys at the bar, but we were the only people in the dining room.

I lifted my beer and nodded at him. "Here's to unwanted visitors from Pittsburgh."

"Come on, don't say that. Here's to fellow PIs, wouldn't that be friendlier?" He grinned and lifted his glass. "To Sam Spade."

"To Sam Spade," I agreed, then touched my bottle off his glass and took a drink. He was a damned likable guy, easygoing and good-humored, but that didn't make the purpose of his visit appealing.

"I wish you'd just made a phone call so I could've told you not to waste your time," I said, "but as long as you made the drive, I'll tell you what I can—*nothing*. Somebody asked me to look into the property, see where the owners had gone. I was dangerously uninformed and had no idea that what was left of one owner was in a coroner's lab somewhere and that the other owner was related to Lenny Strollo's best pal."

Merriman took a drink and shook his head. "Nah, Strollo wasn't that tight with Dominic. Acquainted with him, sure, colleagues you might say, but not that tight."

"What a wonderful reassurance."

He smiled again. "You sound damn edgy about this, Lincoln."

"You would be, too, had Dominic Sanabria paid a visit to your home."

"By all accounts, Sanabria has settled down these days. Living on the straight and narrow. Nary a complaint."

"Be that as it may, there were a few complaints in years past, and some of them involved car bombs."

He acknowledged that with a nod and drank some more of his beer. "Did he threaten you?"

"Not overtly, but he also went out of his way to make sure the notion was in my head. It wasn't a relaxing conversation."

"How do you think he got wind of you so fast?"

"The attorney."

"Anthony Child? That makes sense."

"Of course it does. He called you, too."

He wagged his finger at me. "Wrong. Nice try, but wrong."

"Okay, then who did call you, Ken? Who sent you up from Pittsburgh to ply me with booze and get me to talk?"

"Booze was your idea. I just fell in line."

"We're not going to accomplish much," I said, "if neither one of us is willing to say who we're working for. That's fine with me. There's nothing that I want to accomplish. That doesn't seem to be the case for you."

"If I tell you who tipped me, do I get reciprocity? Will you tell me your client's name?"

I shook my head.

"Damn," he said. "I was afraid of that. But the good news, Lincoln, is that ultimately I'm not too worried about your client. That's not why I'm here."

"No? Then what is it?"

"I want you to work with me. Or, rather, I'd like to work with you. I've done some background research. Seems like you're awfully good. I need help on this one."

"By this one, you mean . . ."

"Finding out who killed Joshua Cantrell."

I shook my head. "No thanks, Ken."

"Sanabria scared you that much, huh?"

"It's not just that, though I'll admit he did a damn good job. There's nothing in it for me. I have no interest in it."

"Really." His Guinness was almost gone. "I'm surprised to hear that. Because what this one has, man, is some intrigue, and most of the detectives I know, well, they go for that sort of thing. The challenge. At least the detectives who are worth a damn."

"Then I must not qualify for that list."

"So if I were to say I could fill you in on Cantrell's history, tell you about the happy couple, what they did up until the time they vanished, you'd say no thanks? Prefer not to hear about it?"

"All I care to hear about is how you learned that I'd inquired about their house."

"You want to know that, I'll tell you," he said, "but you'll have to sit through the rest of it, too. Because if I start, I'm starting at the beginning."

I didn't answer.

He slid out of the booth and got to his feet. "You want a pass on that, I'll walk out the door and drive back home. If you want to hear about it, though, then I think I better buy another round."

Somebody burst into loud laughter at the bar while Ken Merriman stood above me, waiting. Then the laughter faded and it was quiet.

Merriman shifted and spread his hands. "Well?"

"Bring me another Moosehead," I said, "and a bourbon. I think I'll need both."

He'd been hired by Joshua Cantrell's parents, James and Maria, about two months after their son and daughter-in-law left the house near Hinckley for places unknown. It wasn't an especially close-knit family—the Cantrells hadn't been on the best terms with their son in many years, too many social and ideological differences—but it was also unusual for weeks to pass without any word. When they finally called, they learned the phone was disconnected.

"Took them about another month to grow concerned enough to hire me," Ken said. "They drove out and saw the house was empty, then went to the local police, who nosed around enough to determine that Alexandra had made arrangements for the care of the place. That implied a willing departure, not a crime. Nothing illegal about ignoring your parents."

James and Maria Cantrell couldn't believe their son would have made such an abrupt, unannounced departure, and as the weeks went by and still no word came, they grew certain something was terribly wrong.

"When they came to see me that first time, they were petrified," Ken said. "It was difficult to get anything close to a fact out of them."

What he found, once he began looking into the situation, was that there weren't many facts. The only person who'd had any knowledge of the couple's plans to leave was Anthony Child, and he'd been contacted by phone. Child swore that he knew Alexandra's voice and believed without a doubt that she was the one who'd given him his instructions.

"For twelve years the police have refused to look into this because that woman's contact with Child suggested they'd just gotten a wild hair and taken off somewhere," Ken said when he returned from the bar with two more beers and two more bourbons. "Until the body was found, at least. That's shaken things up."

The problem, Ken admitted, was that the couple seemed like the type who *might* get a wild hair and take off. They were an eclectic pair, and most of their interests—holistic practices, faith healing, spiritual retreats—suggested a life outside of the ordinary. Those close to the Cantrells, while surprised by the disappearance, had to admit it seemed to suit them.

Ken worked the case for months and never developed a lead on the missing couple's whereabouts or the reason for their departure. What he did learn was a great deal about their past, including one particularly interesting detail: For years, the couple had maintained a relationship with the state's department of corrections, helping to transition violent offenders through the early stages of parole.

"They met when they were both studying offender rehabilitation in graduate school," Ken told me. "Found some sort of mutual interest there. Academic for Joshua, personal for Alexandra. You can imagine why. Her father had been in and out of jail before being murdered, and her brothers were moving quickly down the same path. Anyhow, once they were married, she and Joshua teamed up to write a few papers, conducted some studies, and got hooked up with an alternative program that snagged a federal grant. At that time, the state was real concerned with engaging the offender's family to help with reentry. The problem that the Cantrells raised was, what about the offender who has no family, or whose family is a cancer to him?"

I sipped my beer and kept my eyes on the table while I listened, not wanting to react in a way that suggested this was anything but new to me. I still hadn't decided whether I'd disclose Harrison's identity, but this twist in the conversation had me wondering if Ken would bring him up of his own accord.

"A police detective called me a few months back, after Cantrell's body was found," he said. "They'd heard I'd investigated in the beginning, and he wanted to know if I'd come across anyone who could work as a homicide suspect. I told him, yeah, I've got twenty-eight names."

The twenty-eight names belonged to the violent offenders Alexandra and Joshua had helped transition back into the world. We had another round of drinks while Ken recited their crimes, which ranged from bank robbery to rape and murder. As of Ken's last count, nineteen of them were still free, and two were dead.

"That means only seven of the offenders who worked with the Cantrells returned to prison," he said. "You know anything about recidivism numbers?"

"Enough to know that's a hell of a lot better than average."

"Yes," he said. "It absolutely is. So whatever they were doing, it seemed to work."

"What were they doing, exactly?"

"At first, they were acting as, well, I guess you'd call it a sort of foster family. They kind of adopted these guys, stayed close to them, counseled them, things like that. By the end, after they bought that land in Hinckley, it changed. They would hire these guys to work for them, kept them on for six months to a year. They paid them well, but the catch was the guys also had to live there."

"In the house?"

"Yes. Imagine that, welcoming convicted killers into your home. Also, while everything out there was modern enough—running water, electricity, all that—they insisted that all the work be done by hand, and without power tools." He grinned at me. "Weird stuff, huh?"

At first I thought they were crazy for requiring that . . . Then I came to understand how important it was. How the sound of an engine would have destroyed what was there.

"Weird," I agreed and finished my beer.

"Alexandra contended that a great contributing factor to recidivism was a loss of touch with the natural world," Ken said. "That prolonged incarceration created this traumatic sense of isolation."

"Okay."

"I talked to a woman with the state parole office who worked with the Cantrells, and she said that Alexandra's vision was for a new sort of prison, one that didn't isolate the inmates from nature. As you can imagine, making *that* sort of change was going to be difficult. So she brought the same ideas over to the reentry side."

"She wanted the parolees to, what, bond with nature?"

"Evidently. She had all these studies. One demonstrated that just a view of nature from a hospital window reduced reliance on pain medication; another showed inmates who participated in a gardening program had improved recidivism rates. Since she couldn't get the support she wanted, she created the program of her desires on a very small scale."

"How were the parolees chosen?" I asked.

"The Cantrells would review their files, their case histories, and then extend the offer. The offenders were under no obligation to accept, but they always did. The pay was good. The Cantrells had one stipulation: They'd only take violent offenders. Preferably murderers."

"That's different from the requirements I've had for roommates over the years."

"Not a request you see in a lot of personal ads, either."

"So how many of these guys did they actually have out there, working for them?"

"Four," he said. "None of those have shown up back in prison—but one is dead."

"How'd he go?"

"Mysterious death," he said. "Not long after leaving the Cantrells' care."

It was quiet for a moment, and then I said, "Seems like it was a hit-or-miss program," and Ken's smile returned.

"Yes. Seems like it was. Apparently they were hoping to use the handful they'd worked with to get a larger program going. Those first four were test subjects, I guess."

"Okay. So you've got twenty-eight violent criminals who worked closely with the couple, and you've got the daughter of a bloody mob legacy. Not hurting for suspects."

"No."

"So where did you get with it?"

He looked down at his glass. Empty again. We'd gone through a few of them by now. I'd lost track. Bourbon with a beer back can do that.

"Absolutely nowhere, Lincoln. I got nothing. I wanted to pursue it, but the parents didn't have much money, and they couldn't pay to keep me running back and forth from Pittsburgh. Originally they hired me because they wanted someone they could meet with face-to-face, someone local, but I blew through their budget and didn't turn up a damn thing, and I couldn't justify taking more of their money. They didn't have much."

"This was twelve years ago?"

"Eleven years ago, by the time they pulled the plug."

"So what the hell are you doing up here now?"

His easygoing humor had faded, and he seemed uncomfortable. "You want another round?"

"I want you to answer the question."

He was quiet.

"Who told you about me?" I said.

"That's what you're worried about? It was your buddy Sanabria."

"*He* hired you?"

"Didn't hire me. I'd crossed paths with him briefly when I got started on this years back, and apparently he hadn't forgotten my name. Called me last week to ask if you were working with me or for Cantrell's parents. I told him no way to the former and no idea to the latter. He seemed dissatisfied with that."

"I've seen that reaction from him, yes."

"So that was how I got your name, and I was curious, right, because this case hadn't left my mind over the years, and it really came back to me when Joshua's body was found. I did a little research on you, saw that you've done some major work—some serious, serious stuff—and I thought, what the hell, why not drive up there and make a pitch."

"I don't understand the pitch."

"I want to work the case, man. With you, ideally. Without you, if you say no."

"You've got no client, Ken. What's the point?"

He braced both forearms on the table and leaned closer. "The point is I've been in this business for fourteen years and never investigated anything that mattered. You know what I've done, year in and year out? Insurance work and infidelity cases. That's it."

"That's how you pay the bills. Isn't that the goal?"

"No! Bullshit it's the goal." He slapped the table and leaned away again. "You're doing this just to pay the bills? Really? That's why you got into the business?"

"I got into the business because I got fired, Ken."

"I know that. You got canned as a police detective, and you set up shop as a private detective. Why?"

"It's all I was qualified for."

He blew out a disgusted breath and looked away from me.

"I get your point," I said. "This has more appeal than an insurance case. If there's one type of detective I've never trusted, though, it's a glory hound."

"That's not what I'm after, damn it. That's not what I mean at all." He sighed and ran both hands through his sandy hair. His face had taken on a flush, and his eyes were beginning to show the booze. "All I'm trying to say is, in fourteen years I've had just *one* case that really mattered, and I didn't accomplish anything on it. Didn't find their son. Now the son has been found, and he's dead, and I'd like to be able to tell them why."

I looked away from him, suddenly wishing I'd let him go for that next round.

"You've had cases like this," he said, voice soft. "I've read about you, Lincoln, I already told you that. You've had cases that mattered. Had cases that . . . that people cared about. People other than you, people other than your clients."

"Ken," I began, but he was still talking.

"My daughter—she's fourteen—she's a fan of the police shows. You know, the TV bullshit, none of it's close to reality, but she enjoys them. There are times . . . times when she asks me about my job, and I find myself . . . not lying maybe, but I'm spinning it, Lincoln. Trying to make it sound like more than it is. More than chasing cheating spouses and taking pictures of accident scenes." He pushed his empty glass away and forced a laugh. "I've had one too many if I'm telling you this."

I didn't say anything.

"You don't have kids," he said.

"No."

He nodded. "You don't have kids, you've never been divorced. You haven't watched some other guy step into your daughter's life. Some other guy who is a damn *doctor*, Lincoln. A surgeon. Saving lives, right? That's what he does. I'm out there taking photos next to a Dumpster, hoping to get a picture of some loser kissing some tramp, hoping to go back to my client and say, yeah, turns out your husband is an asshole—can I have my check now? Meanwhile, my daughter, she's going home to that big house, waiting for her stepfather to drive up in his Porsche with a story about a liver transplant or some shit."

His voice had been rising steadily, closing in on a shout, and he caught it at that point, paused. The bar had filled in as the night grew later, and there were other people in the dining room. I had my back to them, but I could feel the stares. We sat there in silence, though, and once the rest of the room realized

Ken's rant had concluded, they lost interest and went back to their own con-versations and drinks.

"I know it's petty to care," he said. "I know that, but you try not caring about something like that. You give that a shot."

He reached for his empty glass, wrapped his hand around it, and held it.

"Ken," I said. "This case . . . nothing good comes out of working it. You do understand that, don't you?"

He shook his head. "No. No, I do not understand that. What I under-stand is that the man and his wife went missing, Lincoln, vanished and did not appear again until his remains were found. So now he's dead, and she's still missing, and his parents still have no idea what the hell happened. They have no idea what went wrong in their son's life, how his bones ended up in the woods an hour's drive from the million-dollar home he left without a word."

He looked me in the eye. "I want to tell them what happened. I don't give a damn if it's the Sanabria family or the Manson family, or who that guy was married to, I want to be able to go back to those people and tell them, this is what happened to your son."

He lifted the glass, remembered it was empty, and lowered it again. "I'm not good enough to do that on my own."

I shook my head, but he was already shaking his own right back at me.

"Lincoln, I've tried to do it on my own. I didn't succeed."

"There's no reason to think I'd do any better."

"I disagree."

There was a long pause, and then he said, "How about this? How about I bring my case file by your office tomorrow. I run through it with you and talk about approach. Talk about where I'm going from here. You could offer some input, right? Is there a reason in the world why you couldn't at least do that?"

I was sure there was, but it didn't come to mind fast enough to save me.

"All right," I said. "I'll do that much."

He toasted me with the empty glass.

9

That night strips of coal-colored clouds skidded over a bright three-quarter moon, pushed by a spirited wind off the lake. I sat on the roof of my building and marveled at their speed, stared long enough that the lights and sounds of the street below faded and I was held by the rhythm of the clouds, by the vanishing and then resurfacing moon. If I looked long enough, it seemed I wasn't on the roof anymore, could instead be miles out at sea, nothing in sight but that moon and those clouds.

Yeah, I'd had a bit to drink.

I'd called Amy on the drive home, but she hadn't answered, and I'd soon realized that was for the best—I shouldn't have been driving, let alone driving and using a phone. I put the windows down and took Lorain all the way back, a simple and slow drive, stoplight to stoplight until I got home.

I missed her, though. That was different. That was something new. Any night I spent without her, I missed her. Sounds like a bad feeling, but it's not. Having somebody in your life to miss . . . always good. I missed Amy when she was gone, and I'd missed Joe for many months, and all of that meant I wasn't truly alone. There were people who belonged near me, and I felt their absence when it occurred. It was almost a healthy sort of existence. Didn't seem to suit me at all.

It was a warm night, overcast but without rain, and I didn't even turn the lights on in my apartment, just poured a glass of water in the dark kitchen and took it up on the roof. I settled into one of the lounge chairs and watched a sky that seemed determined to entertain.

For a while, bits of the conversation with Ken Merriman played through my head, the most frequent recurrence being the moment he'd confessed it was Dominic Sanabria who'd called him. He'd thrown that out casually enough. *It was your buddy Sanabria.* Too casually? Was it something to wonder about, or just alcohol adding a dose of paranoia to my brain? I meant to ponder that one, but then the wind blew harder and the clouds moved quicker, and eventually the water glass slid from my hand and I was asleep.

I dreamed that I woke. Sounds crazy, maybe, but it happens to me now and then, always when I fall asleep somewhere other than my bed, and often when the mind is encouraged toward odd behavior by alcohol or fatigue. This time I dreamed that when I came out of sleep I was facing the trapdoor that led to the stairs, still in the lounge chair. A figure stood beside the trapdoor, and my dream-mind registered that with surprise but not alarm. I didn't move from the chair, didn't speak, just watched the figure standing there in the dark, and eventually my vision adjusted and I saw that it was Parker Harrison.

He looked at me for a long time, and I knew that I should rise, say something, order him out of my home, but instead I watched silently. The longer I looked at him the more my surprise edged toward fear, a steady crawl, and I held my breath when he reached into the shadowed folds of his clothing with his right hand. The clouds blew past the moon and a shaft of white light fell onto him, and I saw that though his face was normal the flesh on his arm was gone, only thin bones protruding from his sleeve. When his hand came free again, it, too, was nothing but bones, a skeleton hand, and there was a silver coin between his fingers.

He looked across the roof at me, and then he flicked his thumb and spun the coin skyward. The moonlight gave it a bright, hard glint. He caught the coin and flipped it again, and again, and it seemed dangerous now, each flash as wicked as the edge of a sharp blade. My fear built with each toss and burst into pure terror when he caught the coin with an abrupt and theatrical slap of his hand, snatching it out of the air and folding it into his palm and hiding it from the light. When he clasped his hand shut, the bones shattered into a cloud of white powder that turned black as it drifted down to his feet. The coin landed on the roof and spun as the black dust settled around it, and suddenly I was awake and upright, my hands tight on the arms of the chair.

I held that position for a few seconds while the wind fanned over the roof. It was much colder now than when I'd fallen asleep, and below me the avenue was silent. I swung my feet off the chair and stood up, forgetting about the glass resting against my side. It rolled off me and fell away from the chair and shattered on the stone, and I nearly jumped off the roof at the sound.

The sparkle of the broken glass near my feet made me think of the coin from my dream, and like a child who can't trust that the dream world was a false one I turned and looked back at the trapdoor as if expecting to see Harrison there. The door was nothing but a dark square in the surface of the roof, and it was also behind me and not in front of me as it had been in the dream. I took a deep breath and walked toward the door, stepping over the broken glass. That could be dealt with in the morning. Down on the avenue a car finally passed by, rap music thumping out of its speakers, and I was grateful for the noise. I walked to the trapdoor and climbed carefully down the steps and then folded them back into the roof, the door snapping closed with a bang. It was dark inside the building, and my head pounded with a pressurized ache, as if someone had pumped it full of air, searching for leaks in the skull.

"No more bourbon," I said aloud. "No more bourbon."

I groped along the wall for the light switch, flicked it up, and flooded the hallway and stairs with light. Halfway to the apartment door, I paused and turned back, squinting against the brightness, and looked down the steps at the front door. Closed, and with the dead bolt turned. Of course it was. Of course.

I went into the apartment and drank another glass of water, this time with a few ibuprofen tablets, and then went into the bedroom and slept. There were no dreams.

Morning found me at the office with an extralarge cup of coffee and a continued headache, researching Ken Merriman. I spent most of an hour at it, and while everything he'd told me the previous night checked out—he was from Pittsburgh, had worked as a PI for fourteen years, was divorced, and had a fourteen-year-old daughter—there were a few details he'd chosen to omit. Namely, the unpleasant press he'd received from the Cantrell case.

James and Maria Cantrell had given an interview after their son disappeared, imploring the public to help in their quest. As a part of that interview, they let loose on Ken, claiming he'd taken thousands from them and done nothing on the case. James even suggested they would consider a lawsuit against Ken but couldn't afford the legal fees. The reporter had contacted Ken only to be given a "no comment" response. It wasn't necessarily a fair attack—every PI in the business knows the headaches that come from clients who believe they're paying for a specific result, not for work that may produce no result or one contrary to the client's wishes—but it was the sort of publicity that could damage a career, too. I was impressed that Ken had survived it, and I understood a little better why he seemed to be stuck with insurance and infidelity work now. Still, the Sanabria call lingered with me, and that odd personal revelation toward the end of the night. Had it been too much? A melodramatic sales technique?

I knew a PI in the Pittsburgh area through a group called NALI, the National Association of Legal Investigators, a generally high quality group of PIs. His name was Casey Hopper, and he was about Joe's age; he'd been around the business a long time and knew who was worth a shit and who wasn't. I decided it might be worth a call to see if he'd ever heard of Ken.

"Good guy," Casey said as soon as I mentioned the name. "I've worked with him several times."

"You trust him?"

"Much as I trust anyone I don't know particularly well, sure. He's always seemed genuine enough to me, but, you know, there've been some stories about him. Well, one story really."

He then proceeded to relate the Cantrell case to me, and I let him run with it. His take seemed to jibe with every other account—and that included Ken's.

"You thinking about giving him some work?" Casey asked.

"The other way around. He's wanting to partner up on something. I'm not sure about it."

"Well, I can tell you this: He's one hell of a surveillance expert. Good as anybody I've worked with, in that regard. Damn near invisible, and the most patient son of a bitch I've ever seen." He paused, then added, "You know I was a sniper in Vietnam, too."

"Yeah."

"So when I say somebody is patient . . ."

"Yeah."

"Thing with Ken, though, is that's really all the work he gets. He has a steady client base on the surveillance side, insurance and divorce work, shit like that, but as far as a field investigation goes, I don't know that he has much experience at all. I gave him an interview job once when I was out of town, subbed it out to him, and he screwed that up pretty royally. Just didn't know how to take a statement that would be worth a shit in court. So I've avoided giving him anything like that again, and that seems to be the general consensus about him around here. Give him any extra surveillance work you've got; otherwise, find somebody else. He wasn't a cop, wasn't mentored by a good PI, doesn't really have any background on a full-scale investigation, but the son of a bitch can hide in your rearview mirror."

That wasn't exactly encouraging, since the case he wanted a piece of now was going to require the polar opposite of his skill set.

"The Cantrell thing is what he's interested in coming back to," I said. "I bumped into it inadvertently up here, and he looked me up and asked me to help."

"He's back at that? Who the hell is paying him?"

"Nobody. He claims he wants to finish now what he couldn't then. You buy it?"

Casey was quiet for a moment. "Yeah, I probably do. It did some real damage to his career basically *because* he didn't have any other experience to claim as proof that he knew what he was doing. Ordinary people might forget the story, but law firms and agencies who sub out work, the sort of people you need to rely on for quality business, they don't."

I thanked him for the insight and hung up. Then I went back to search for more information and found little else. Beyond that story, there was nothing that stood out, and certainly no indicators that Ken had been telling me anything but the truth. His loyalty to the family seemed odd, considering the charges they'd levied at him, but perhaps his real motivation was in proving them wrong all these years later.

It was ten thirty by the time Ken showed up, and he looked rough. Same clothes as he'd had on the previous day, only now his face had a darker shading of beard and the whites of his eyes wore pink cobwebs. He closed the door behind him with infinite care, as if a loud slam might shatter something in his brain, then looked over at me with a pained smile.

"Maybe I should have told you this last night," he said, "but I'm not a whiskey drinker."

"I like a good Scotch," I said, "but that swill wasn't it. It occurred to me sometime around three in the morning that what the Hideaway considers a well bourbon is probably closer to leaded gasoline."

He groaned and fell onto one of the stadium seats.

"Careful there," I said. "Those seats watched the Cleveland Browns beat the shit out of the Steelers many, many times."

"I'm too hungover to even rise to that argument."

"That bad, eh?"

"Yeah. You bounced back well. Sleep it off peacefully?"

I remembered the slap of Parker Harrison's skeleton hand, the way the bones had burst into powder, how it had looked like fine black dust by the time it settled around the spinning coin.

"Peacefully," I echoed with a nod.

"Wish I could say the same," he said and then held up the scuffed briefcase he'd carried in with him. "Last night you agreed to look this over with me. In fairness, though, I thought I should give you a sober chance to back out of it. You don't owe me anything, and you're certainly not obligated to waste your time on this."

"I can give you a few hours."

He put the briefcase on his lap and folded his arms over it. "Look, Lincoln, I might have gotten a bit more, uh, personal than I should have last night. I mean, shit, you don't even know me, and I was dumping some information on you that probably made the whole thing awkward for you. All of that crap about my wife's new husband—"

"Don't worry about it, Ken."

"No, it wasn't anything you needed to hear, and to be honest, it embarrassed the hell out of me once I got back to the hotel and realized everything I'd said. So, you know, if you could just chalk that up to the booze and forget about it . . ."

"I just said not to worry about it. Okay? It's nothing, man."

He nodded, and an awkward pause settled into the room for a few seconds before he broke it by slapping a hand on the briefcase.

"Well, is this a good time, or you want me to come back in a bit, or—"

"Now's good. Let's see what you've got."

He set the case on the table beside him and opened it, and I raised my eyebrows when I saw all the papers that were inside, hundreds of pages.

"I've got a lot here," he said.

"No kidding."

"I don't want to drown you with shit you're not interested in, so if you've got any idea on where to start . . ."

"I'd be most interested in what you've got from the people who knew them best," I said. "Particularly the people who knew them best at the time they took off. Friends, co-workers, colleagues."

"They didn't work."

I lifted an eyebrow. "Neither of them?"

"Nope. Lived off her money."

"Well, how the hell did she get so much money?"

"The late Christopher Sanabria."

"Surely he wasn't worth that much."

"Was worth a lot, and when he got clipped, the family discovered he'd left the whole pile to Alexandra. It was several million at the time, and she had to wait about eight years until she turned twenty-one and the trust kicked in. By then it was worth a hell of a lot more. Christopher was well invested, it seemed."

"She got every dime?"

"Of his financial holdings, yes. House and possessions split among the sons."

"Nothing to the wife?"

"Wife was dead. Suicide a year before Christopher was murdered. That was the reason Alexandra was sent away. He thought she needed a female influence."

I shook my head. "How many sons did he have?"

"Two. Dominic and Thomas. Thomas was shot and killed by a cop in Youngstown about five years after the father died. Drug bust, but just one cop went in. Odd, right? Said he was checking out a tip he didn't have much faith in. Rumors went around that it was a setup, that the cop was paid for the hit, but nothing ever came of the investigation."

"Alexandra was away at her boarding school for this?"

He nodded. "She left when she was twelve, came back to Ohio after getting out of college."

"To work with the prison system."

"Yes."

I didn't say anything for a minute. I was remembering the way Dominic Sanabria had spoken of his sister. *Every family has their darling. She is ours.*

"Do you know anything about the family relationship after she got back?" I asked. "Was there any bitterness over the money? The mob connections don't even apply to that—father dies and leaves a few million to one kid but not the other, it would start personal problems in most families."

"No sign of that, but I always wondered," Ken said. "By the time she was old enough to take the trust, Dominic was a pretty big deal in Youngstown, had a lot of other things on his mind, and a decent pile of his own cash. He's more than ten years older than her."

I was quiet again, not entirely sold on the idea. Being jilted out of your family money in favor of another sibling was a difficult thing for a man to ignore, particularly a man like Dominic Sanabria. It wasn't easy to imagine the guy going after his own sister, though—that notion of honor among thieves applied more to family than anything else. I wasn't going to figure that out sitting at my desk, though, and I didn't want to have to leave my desk on this. Instead, I waved at Ken's briefcase.

"Well, if their parolees are the only people who saw the Cantrells regularly, what do you have on them?"

"Pretty detailed profiles. There were four of them who worked out there, and three are still alive."

"You ever talk to them?"

"Only two." His head was bowed while he rifled through the briefcase and pulled out a thick manila folder. "Had trouble tracking the other guy down, and then the budget ran out and I was off the case."

He opened the folder and pulled out a stapled sheaf of papers. "The one I never got in touch with, and he was working with them right up until they took off, was a guy named Parker Harrison. So maybe you want to start with—"

"No," I said. "Let's start with the first one, okay? Work forward."

He didn't react other than to nod and slide the Harrison papers back into the folder.

10

The four offenders who'd worked with the Cantrells at their strange home in the woods near Hinckley had all been sentenced for violent crimes. Three had been convicted of murder, another for armed robbery and assault.

The couple's first hire was a Serb named Mark Ruzity, who'd grown up in the Slavic Village on Cleveland's east side. It was a damn hard neighborhood. At one time Ruzity had a bright future. A blues guitarist of some renown, he'd been featured in a few newspaper and magazine articles after landing gigs with national acts. Ken had copies of those stories, glimpses of what could have been. Ruzity's success had always been short-lived, though; his drug problems limited his career. He bottomed out in New Orleans while touring with a band called Three Sheiks to the Wind, attacking an audience member who sat in the front of the club and talked loudly during the performance. Ruzity's luck was poor—not only did he break a good guitar on the gentleman's back, but it turned out his victim was an off-duty cop. That incident landed him in jail for six months, and when he got out he was broke and bandless.

After returning to Cleveland, Ruzity got a job in construction and began playing again, mostly in local bars and for little money. For more than a year he held it together, until he met a leggy redhead named Valerie after a gig one night. She was beautiful, he was stoned, and by morning he was in love. There was just one problem: Valerie was a prostitute.

He didn't remember paying her that night, though he apparently had, and when she informed him the relationship had been strictly professional, he viewed it not as a deal-breaker but as a challenge. The Montagues and the Capulets. After a day of brooding, with a few black beauties and some gin to clear his head, Ruzity determined there was only one way this mess could be sorted out: He murdered her pimp.

The beautiful romantic vision came to a fast and painful end when Valerie herself turned him in. The bad news was that he'd just been caught for murder; the good news was that he'd murdered a pimp with a record. The sentencing judge went easy, and Ruzity spent fifteen years in prison, writing songs and studying the blues. He had no living family and no close friends, and the state's department of rehabilitation placed him in a job with Joshua and Alexandra Cantrell, who had some ideas about offender reentry that seemed worth a try.

Ruzity lived and worked with them for six months before moving back into the city, where he made a living repairing instruments at a pawnshop and teaching guitar lessons.

The second parolee who found his way to Whisper Ridge was Nimir Farah, who'd used a machete in an attempt to murder his own cousin over a suspected affair with Farah's girlfriend. Farah had immigrated to the United States only two years earlier, fleeing a desperate situation in his home country, Sudan. He'd come to Columbus to live with a cousin who'd arrived years earlier on a student visa and was the last living member of Farah's family, or at least the last he'd been able to keep track of as war and famine swept Sudan.

It was thanks only to an exceptional emergency room surgeon that the cousin survived, a point made emphatically clear by the prosecuting attorney in the trial transcript Ken had photocopied. The charge was attempted murder, and the sentence was twenty years in prison. Farah served ten, then managed to avoid a criminal deportation hearing when Alexandra and

Joshua Cantrell stepped in. Ken had tracked down a letter from the couple arguing quite eloquently against deporting Farah to a dangerous country where he no longer had ties. Instead, he was given parole and a job at Whisper Ridge. He worked for the Cantrells for six months, then moved to Cleveland, where he finished the degree in environmental sciences he'd started while in prison. As of Ken's last check, he was employed by a nonprofit that specialized in water sanitation issues—particularly the challenges faced in arid areas much like Farah's homeland.

It seemed to be, once again, a striking success for the Cantrells.

I turned the last page of the Farah file over and found myself staring at a picture of Parker Harrison.

He'd been the third hire, and though I didn't need to refresh myself on his background, I read through Ken's notes anyhow. I wasn't ready to disclose my knowledge of Harrison yet, and skipping over him would be a clear tip of my hand. So I pored over the old information, found nothing new, and then moved to the fourth and final hire, a man named Salvatore Bertoli, who'd been raised in an orphanage after his mother died following their immigration from Italy.

"A lot of different ethnicities passed through," I said. "There a reason?"

"Yeah, that was the idea. Joshua was interested in culture and crime. It was a topic of a lot of the papers he wrote, and how he met Alexandra."

I thought about that and tried to fit Parker Harrison into the mix. His mother had been Shawnee, and he'd told me that Alexandra Cantrell was fascinated by the stories he'd heard and what he knew of the culture.

"I'll tell you something else about their boy Bertoli," Ken said. "He's Italian. As is, you might have heard, that Cosa Nostra thing to which brother Dominic is connected. Allegedly."

"Merriman, you profiling bastard."

He held his hands up. "Just making connections."

"So you think Salvatore was imported by Dominic Sanabria, orphaned, framed for a crime, then paroled and tucked away at the sister's house to steal back the dead father's money?" I considered it and nodded. "Yeah, that works. Let's call it a day."

"I can tell you this, wise-ass—Bertoli had been arrested on two different occasions prior to the one he was finally convicted on. First was a car theft charge, second was assault. In both cases, the guys arrested with him were known associates of Dominic Sanabria."

The smirk dried off my face. "You're sure of that?"

"Positive. Arresting officers confirmed it for me. Said they were insignificant players—I believe he called them grunts—but that guy was an associate of Sanabria's crew. No doubt about it." Ken pointed at the file in my hands. "Interested now? Read on."

I read on. Bertoli's story was far and away the least interesting of the group. He'd beaten and then robbed the drug-pushing manager of a truck stop on I-71, who claimed Bertoli took cash, though when police apprehended him he had no cash but did have some heroin. Truck stops are among the less wise locations for crime. Lonely places along the highway that stay open all night tend to be paranoid about their security. One of the parking lot security cameras caught Bertoli, who was smart enough to wear a mask and use a stolen plate, but not smart enough to use a stolen car. He put the fake plate on his own car—a custom Impala featuring chrome rims with silver diamond cutouts, hardly the sort of thing that stands out. It took police under two hours to locate it and arrest him. Bertoli had a sidekick in the car at the time of the robbery, but it was no high-level mob player. Rather, his passenger was a kid whose name was redacted from the report because he was a juvenile. The arresting officer believed Bertoli had promised to sell the boy the heroin. He was sixteen years old.

The boy wouldn't testify to Bertoli's intent to sell, claiming he was just along for the ride and oblivious to the crime, which weakened the case. Although Bertoli—who was only twenty-three himself—already had three arrests, he didn't have any convictions. He was offered a plea agreement sentence of five years, accepted, and served two and a half.

"Kind of a stiff sentence for somebody who beat up another guy just to take his drugs," I said, "and odd that he didn't want to take it to trial. Makes me wonder if—"

"They tried to get him to roll on somebody and he wouldn't?" Ken said. "That he was scared of that sort of pressure, so he took the deal and did his time with his mouth shut to protect himself? Yeah, that was my idea, too—and where Sanabria figures in, maybe."

"This piece of criminal masterwork that got him busted hardly seems like a major mob play, though. He beats the shit out of some guy and steals a small amount of heroin so he can sell it to an underage kid? Doesn't feel like Dominic Sanabria's work."

"I agree, but Bertoli was associated with those guys, and it makes sense that the prosecutor and the police would have tried to lean on him, doesn't it?"

Yes, it did—but he'd taken his jail sentence instead of talking. Then, with just a few years of time behind him for a relatively mundane crime, he somehow became the next selection of the Cantrell rehabilitation effort. An effort that promptly went awry. Bertoli spent only three weeks on the property before leaving. When I saw Ken's note on the date he left, I looked up from the file.

"Hey," I said, and Ken turned his eyes away from the window as I held up the first sheet on Bertoli. "Is this accurate? The release date?"

"Yes."

I frowned and lowered the sheet. "Harrison was still there. Is that a mistake?"

"No. Harrison was the first one to stay longer than six months. I have no idea why. Maybe they thought he wasn't ready to move on. Maybe he was their favorite felon. I really have no idea. Anyway, he did his six months, stayed on, and then they brought Bertoli in, and the two of them lived there together briefly. Then Bertoli was killed, and the Cantrells took off."

"He was murdered?"

"Officially, no. It's listed as an accidental death. He somehow managed to tumble off the roof of a six-story building. Oops."

He looked at me with a grim smile, and I dropped my eyes and went back to the file and read the details. Bertoli left the Cantrells abruptly, claiming to his parole officer that he was taking a job at a restaurant in Murray Hill, Cleveland's version of Little Italy. He never logged a day of work at the restaurant, though. A few days after he left Whisper Ridge, Salvatore Bertoli fell off the roof of an abandoned warehouse he had no reason to be in, and Joshua and Alexandra Cantrell fell off the face of the earth.

"If there's anything related to the Cantrells that feels wrong, it's Bertoli," Ken said.

He was right. Bertoli felt wrong.

"So let me ask you this," Ken said. "If you've got this case, who of that group interests you the most?"

"On the basis of his connection to her brother and his strange demise, Bertoli," I said. It was as complete a lie as I'd uttered in a while—Harrison interested me most, of course, but Ken's paperwork history pointed in a different direction.

He nodded. "So it would seem, but the detective I talked with, guy named Graham, was interested in only one person out of that group: Parker Harrison."

I was really hoping he'd say Ruzity.

"He tell you why?" I asked, thinking again of Harrison's letters, how they'd started just after Joshua Cantrell's bones were found.

"Nope. Was looking for information, not giving it out. He didn't ask any specific questions about what I'd found on the other guys, though. Just Harrison."

"The current detective? Guy who's working on the Pennsylvania side, where the body was found?"

"That's right. He was entirely focused on Harrison."

I didn't say anything. I'd been holding off on sharing my client's identity with Ken because it felt like the right thing to do, but how honest was it? If I didn't trust the guy enough to tell him that, then what in the hell was I doing offering my help to him? You had to pick a side, sooner or later.

I was quiet for a long time, and Ken was watching me with a touch of confusion, as if he didn't know what I was brooding over.

"Last night you wanted to know my client's name," I said.

Ken nodded.

"Parker Harrison."

He leaned forward, eyes wide. "You're shitting me."

I shook my head. "He'd written me letters for a few months, asking me to look into it, explaining his history to me. I threw them all out. Then he showed up in person and seemed reasonably sane and talked me into it. He didn't mention that Cantrell's body had been found. Once I learned that, I quit."

"Did he know it had been found?"

"Yes. That's what bothered me. It was like he was playing a game."

"You think he could have murdered Cantrell?"

"I have no idea, but now you've got a better idea of why I wanted to stay out of this."

"Did you talk to any cops about him?"

"No."

He said, "Maybe you should. This guy I talked with, Graham."

I didn't answer.

"You say he was writing you letters for a few *months*?" Ken asked.

"Yeah."

"Sounds pretty strange to me, Lincoln."

"He sent the first one the week Cantrell's body was discovered."

Ken leaned back and spread his hands, a what-more-do-you-need gesture.

I looked down at the file, stared at Harrison's photograph for a few seconds, then snapped the folder shut and tossed it on the desk.

"You got Graham's number?"

I called from the office, with Ken listening to my half of the conversation. He didn't hear much. I'd barely begun my explanation when Graham interrupted.

"He was writing you letters? Starting in December?"

"Yes."

"You still have them?"

"No."

"Damn it. That's okay, though. That's okay. You said you're in Cleveland?"

"That's right. Now I only—"

"About a two-hour drive," he said as if I hadn't spoken. "I have a few things to finish up, take maybe an hour, then I can head your way. You give me your address, I can be up there by two, two thirty at the latest."

"I can tell you everything over the phone."

"No, no. I'll come up."

So I gave him the address. When I hung up, Ken said, "Seem interested?"

"Enough to make a two-hour drive without even hearing the whole story," I said, and that made Ken smile. Odd. I didn't feel like smiling at all.

11

Quinn Graham arrived just before two, and it didn't take him long to make me feel like a fool. He was probably in his late thirties, black, with a shaved head and a thin goatee. Not tall but powerful, with heavy arms and a substantial chest.

"So Harrison explained in the first letter that he was a convicted murderer, and you chose not to keep that letter or any that followed it?" he asked about thirty seconds after exchanging greetings.

"That's right."

He didn't shake his head or make a snort of disgust or a wiseass remark. He looked at me thoughtfully.

"Okay. Probably wanted to get it out of your sight. Is that it? Yeah, I don't blame you for that, but I wish you'd held on to them. It's a police thing, though. People with experience tend to be more concerned with potential evidence."

"I know," I said. "I used to be a police detective."

"Oh?" he said and gave me more of that stare, as if he were thinking it was no real surprise that I wasn't still a police detective.

"I remember the letters quite well, though," I said, "and while I do wish

I'd kept them, I'm not sure how much evidentiary value they would have offered."

"We could have analyzed the language, given it to a profiler. Harrison might have even been crazy enough to incorporate some sort of code."

All right, I was an idiot. What else to say? I waited for him.

"Well, they're gone now," he said. "Nothing to do about that."

"Exactly."

"You say you remember them well, so let's hear what you remember."

I took him through the sequence as best as I remembered it, offering approximate dates for the letters, describing each message. Then I told him about Harrison's visit, the simplicity of his request, and the few brief hours I'd invested into working his case.

"Now when you told him off and said you were done," Graham said, scribbling notes onto a leather-bound legal pad on his lap, "was that in person or on the phone?"

"In person." I told him about that final meeting.

"Since then, no communication?"

"He mailed a check."

Graham lifted his head. "I assume you cashed it?"

I shook my head.

"Did you keep *that* at least?"

Another shake.

He frowned and scribbled a few more words onto the pad. "So you have no record of your relationship with Harrison? That's what I'm understanding? No record at all?"

"No, I do not. As I said, I wasn't expecting it would lead to a meeting like this. I just wanted to end it."

"So how *did* it lead to this meeting?" he asked, looking at Ken for the first time. "I've spoken to Kenny here, but how is it that the two of you found each other?"

Ken took it from there. I watched Graham, and when Ken explained that he'd been called by Dominic Sanabria, the pencil stopped moving across the pad, and he lifted his head much slower.

"Dominic Sanabria called you three days ago?"

"That's right. To ask if Lincoln was—"

"I've already heard the reason, Kenny. I'm wishing you might have found that information worthy of my attention. I believe I asked that you pass such things along."

"That was several months ago," Ken said.

"I don't recall putting an expiration date on the request." Graham stared at Ken for a few seconds, then sighed and looked back at his pad. He took his time with it, reading through all of the notes, and then he closed the notebook and set it on the edge of my desk.

"Was supposed to have the day off," he said. "I decided, well, go in this morning, get a few things done, be gone by eleven. Noon at the latest. Now I'm in Ohio. That's the way the damn days off always seem to go. You think you only got a few hours, then you're in Ohio."

"We could've waited," Ken said.

"Oh, no." Graham was shaking his big head. "No, this couldn't have waited. This, boys, this is important."

"Ken told me he had the sense that Harrison was the focus of your investigation," I said, trying to prompt a little information.

He was frowning at his notebook on the desk and spoke again without looking at me. "If you were with the police, then you understand what a nightmare this one is, Linc, my friend."

Apparently Graham liked to dispense nicknames. Too bad there was nobody in the world who called me Linc, and I could tell from Ken's face that he didn't go by Kenny, either.

"It's an awfully cold trail," I said.

"Not the only problem, Linc. Yes, the trail is cold, but it also starts in Pennsylvania, beautiful Crawford County, over which I have jurisdiction." He cocked his head and stared at me. "You know what's in Crawford County? Woods. You know where I'm from? Philadelphia. Now, the woods are nice, sure, but I miss sidewalks. Strange damn thing to miss, but it's true. I miss my sidewalks."

He looked from me to Ken and then back as if he were disappointed that we didn't chime in with our shared love of sidewalks.

"Now I work in Crawford County," he said, "and the wonderful thing about having a body dug up in the woods in Crawford County is that I get to go to work. Bad thing is that in this case, all of the work to be done seems to be in Ohio. That limits me. I've been out here before, spent a few weeks driving back and forth after the body was ID'd, but it's a pain in the ass. An investigation that requires I spend time in Ohio when my superiors would like me to be spending it in the Commonwealth of Pennsylvania, which does in fact pay my salary."

He sighed again. "And, you're right, the trail is cold. Twelve years cold, and the people who left it, well, they're a different sort from you and me. A handful of people who knew them suggested that Joshua might have been suicidal, that he'd been depressed and secretive toward the end. You know what else those people had to say? That if Cantrell actually committed suicide it's possible his wife would have just buried his body, lit a few candles, and marched on. A different sort, yes, they were. Ah, but the family ties? Oh, the family ties, boys, they are *tremendous*. What I've got is a new-age, holistic healer of a sister to a Mafia hit man. How about that? You ever heard anything better?"

He turned his wide eyes to Ken. "Dominic Sanabria called you."

"Yes."

Graham's head swiveled toward me. "And he *visited* you."

"Yes."

"Keeps careful tabs, doesn't he?" Graham's eyes were on his notebook again, and he was frowning, as if he were reading right through the leather cover and didn't like what he read.

"Harrison sent you a check after you told him to get lost," he said. "That's really something. Why give up the money to a guy who said he didn't want it?"

"He was real worked up about giving me a retainer."

"Or maybe his motivations lay elsewhere. Like keeping open that door of communication that he'd been knocking at over several months." He leaned back. "What do you think, Linc? Could we open that door back up?"

"I was pretty happy to extract myself from this situation," I said. "Not as happy to plunge back into it. What's your idea? I'm supposed to play a game with this guy?"

"I love a good game, Linc. That is one hell of an idea. I'm really not sure yet. I'll need a few days to think on it. But I might ask you to play, yes."

I frowned. "Look, Graham, I understand the importance of what you're doing here, but if you expect me to contribute, then I'd like to know more about the situation. You still haven't said why you're so interested in Harrison."

"He lived with the victim at the time of the victim's disappearance."

"That's it?"

He didn't answer.

"Because I don't think that's enough. In fact, from what I've seen, there are plenty of other people worth your time and attention. Like the parolee who had a history of association with Sanabria, went to live with the Cantrells, and died soon after he left."

He nodded enthusiastically. "Oh, Bertoli's part of it, sure."

"Or her brother, shit, that guy—"

"Oh, yes, him, too." Still nodding.

"Seems to me there's more potential in those two areas than with Parker Harrison."

He stopped nodding, made a pained face, and then said, "No, I'm afraid I can't join you there. I was with you right up till the end, though."

"Why? What do you see in Harrison that makes him stand out from the pack?"

"I have my reasons."

"I'm going to need to have them, too, Graham, if you want my cooperation."

He was studying my face, and he kept his eyes hard on mine when he finally spoke again. "Only one of those parolees you mention ever had any direct contact with Dominic Sanabria," he said. "That was Parker Harrison. He made half a dozen phone calls to Sanabria in the same week the Cantrells left their home."

"Looking for information, maybe. Trying to track them down, just like he is now."

"Perhaps. Then there was a twelve-year gap between calls, which ended not long ago, when Harrison made two more calls to Sanabria. That was in December, Linc. Same time Harrison contacted you."

"Following up with him, seeing if he'd heard the news," I said.

"Most interesting thing about the timing of those two calls? Harrison made them a day after the body was discovered."

"So?"

Graham smiled, his teeth brilliantly white against his dark skin. "Took a while to identify the corpse, Linc. Harrison didn't call after the ID. He called after the body was found. A body that, at the time, was an unidentified pile of bones in another state."

I didn't respond to that.

"Let me ask you something," Graham said. "When you talked to Harrison, he say anything about being part Shawnee? Talk about his, uh, culture?"

"Yes."

"Not surprised to hear that," he said. "The folks at Harrison's prison told me he did a lot of reading on the subject. A lot of study."

"That has some significance to you?"

He nodded but didn't speak.

"Well?"

Silence.

"Graham, I'm going to say this again: If you want me to cooperate in whatever game you cook up for Harrison, I'll need to know everything that you do."

"If it leaks," he said, "it jeopardizes an already weak investigation. That cold trail we keep talking about, it's not making this thing easy."

"It's not going to leak," I said. "Not from this room."

He looked at Ken, waited for the nod of agreement.

"We held one detail back from the report on the discovery of Cantrell's body," Graham said. "A detail of potential value."

"What is it?" I said.

"Joshua Cantrell was buried in a grave that was about four feet deep, lined with bark, and laid carefully in an exact east-to-west fashion. Then poles were placed over his body, more bark laid over the poles, and dirt piled on top." He looked at Ken, then back at me. "Those are all elements of a traditional Shawnee burial."

12

Something you learn early as a detective—your work is damn dependent on physical evidence and people who know things relevant to the crime. Have either of those, and you're going to get somewhere. Have neither? Not going far, at least not easily. Quinn Graham had spent six months determining he had none of the former and only suspicions of the latter.

Whatever physical evidence might have existed at Joshua Cantrell's grave at the time he went into it was gone by the time the body was discovered. The evidence techs worked it as thoroughly as they could and came back with nothing. The poles, bark, and arrangement of the grave were physical evidence, yes, but didn't link back to a killer.

"Except in circumstantial fashion," Graham told us, "and you both know that's not worth a shit in court. It's worth something to me, though. That grave and those phone calls to Sanabria, they're worth something to me."

Their worth, it seemed, had been a load of frustration. He'd attempted to talk to Dominic Sanabria and immediately been met by a team of attorneys. Then he'd shifted his focus to Harrison and found the same response.

"Harrison lawyered up?" I said, the surprise clear in my voice.

Graham swiveled his big head to me and nodded. "He's not confirming so much as his own name without his attorney present, Linc. That shouldn't surprise you."

It did. It surprised me because it didn't jibe with the Parker Harrison who'd given up on his letter campaign and come to see me in person, the Harrison who'd gazed at me with a mixture of sorrow and intensity as he implored me to find Alexandra Cantrell. Of course, Harrison hadn't mentioned he knew Joshua Cantrell was dead, either.

"The guy took a sentence for murder," Graham said. "If there's one thing he's not anxious to do these days, it's talk to a homicide detective. Does that imply guilt? Not necessarily, but it doesn't exactly clear his good name, either."

"How much did you push?"

"Interviewed him a few times, and it was an absolute bastard because he had this attorney with him, telling him exactly what to say and when to say it."

"You asked about the phone calls, though? And the burial?"

"Phone calls, yes, burial, no. Like I said, we decided to sit on that. We were hoping for a physical link between him and that grave. Didn't get it, but we're not done yet, either. Sent some of the stuff in for DNA testing months ago, still don't have results. You were on the job, you understand that."

"Cold case, out-of-state case, and a mile-long wait list at the lab."

"Check, check, and check."

"How about the phone calls?" Ken said. "What was his response?"

"Says he called Sanabria after the couple took off, hoping to get in touch with them. Then, after the body was found, says he was merely doing the same thing, checking in again for an update. I pointed out that was a hell of a twist of timing, waiting twelve years to check in and then doing it the same damn week the body was found, but of course he and his attorney refused to go down that road."

"Sanabria confirm that?" I asked.

Graham's face went sour. "Through his attorneys, yes, he did. It's too perfect, man, too rehearsed. They remember these phone calls like they're looking at a transcript."

"Still," I said, "seems to me you've got something to work with there."

"No shit, Linc? Seems that way? Well, hell, buddy, I'm glad to hear you think so. Now let me remind you what my superiors have to say—"

"I get that," I said. "At least I get it from the Pennsylvania side. I'm amazed you haven't stirred somebody with the FBI up about Sanabria."

"That's another part of the problem. I did, but they didn't stir in the way you are thinking and I was hoping. Didn't come into the game looking to help. Instead, they came in warning me that we'd have a nightmare on our hands if we hassled Sanabria. They took their run at him, hard as they could, back in the nineties and didn't get much to show for it. A couple years on a bullshit charge—and they were looking at the guy for, what, five, six murders? Who knows what else? Sense I got from the boys who worked on him back at the time, Linc, was that they didn't want any piece of it. They've kept tabs on him, shit, maybe kept *surveillance* on him, and he hasn't stepped wrong in fifteen years. If he killed his brother-in-law or had him killed, they don't seem to care. There's one guy who felt different, but he's retired now, and what he says doesn't carry water."

We fell silent. Graham got to his feet and walked to the window and stared down at the street.

"If I find Alexandra, it will be put to rest," he said. "That simple. I'm sure of it."

"You've looked for her? Pushed hard?" I said.

"Yes, I've pushed hard," Graham snapped, "and so did your buddy here and a lot of other people before us. Nobody found her. Not me, not anybody else. Right?"

He was looking at Ken, who didn't answer, just stared back at him as if waiting for more. Graham turned away and went back to staring at the street.

"Fact is, I was pretty well distracted from it until today. Got us a couple of dead girls a few months back. Raped, beaten, strangled, and dumped off the highway. Two in two weeks. One was hitchhiking, one a runaway. Two in two weeks, both on my highways . . . yeah, ain't nobody talked about Mr. Cantrell in quite a while."

He turned from the window. "Now you call, and I don't know what the hell to do with what you've got. Don't know yet. All I do know is I'm going to think on it, going to get back in touch, and when I do? I'm expecting cooperation."

He was looking at me, not at Ken. Had himself one hell of a stare. I braved it for a few seconds before I had to nod.

The day after I'd thrown Parker Harrison's check in the trash and promised myself that would be the end of it, I stood in the parking lot below my office and assured a Pennsylvania police detective I'd be willing to cooperate with his investigation if he asked it. I hoped he wouldn't. If he did, I knew my *cooperation* would amount to baiting a psychopath. It would be a game in which Graham would man one side of the board and Harrison the other. Me? The pawn shuffling around in the middle. Yeah, wouldn't break my heart if he decided not to pursue that avenue.

"I've got to head home tonight," Ken said as we watched Graham's Ford Explorer pull onto Rocky River. "How about we grab a bite to eat first?"

It was closing in on four, and we hadn't eaten any lunch.

"We can do that," I said, "and now that you've managed to involve me in the police investigation, I'd say it should be your treat."

We went to Sokolowski's University Inn in Tremont. It was one of my favorite places in the city, a third-generation family-owned restaurant with an exceptional vantage point of downtown. When I was still with the police, Joe and I would stop in and sit at the bar and admire the view. Today, Ken and I walked directly to the back dining room and found a quiet, dark corner.

"Four different varieties of sausage on the menu," he said, dropping his tray onto the table. "This is Cleveland's idea of gourmet?"

"Shut up and taste it."

He bit into the bratwurst and raised his eyebrows. "Okay. Point made."

I'd gotten perch, but the lingering hangover dulled my appetite. Ken, on the other hand, seemed to make a full recovery at the first smell of food.

"Hell of an interesting talk with Graham," he said. "Got more out of him than I'd expected."

"Yeah, it was fantastic. Can't wait till he calls me and asks me to commence the game playing with Harrison."

"I don't know that he will." He cut into his potato pancake, forked about half of it into his mouth. "He gave us some starting points, that's for sure. I'd say it's safe to focus on Harrison."

I sipped some ice water and watched him eat, wondering if he'd stop when he got down to bare plate or just keep right on going until the tray was gone. I've known some people who could chase a hangover away with food, but I'm sure not one of them. Just watching him was making me queasy.

"Safe for *him* to focus on Harrison."

He finished the potato pancake, wiped his mouth with a napkin, and looked at me. "I've already told you. I want this one."

"Then talk to Graham about it."

"I intend to. You heard him bitching about how difficult this is for him when his other active cases are in Pennsylvania, how he's not getting the support he'd like. I think the man would appreciate the help."

"He also would have appreciated a phone call as soon as you heard from Sanabria. So if you're so eager to help him, why'd you wait on that?"

"I already told you, I wanted this one."

"So you've said. Yet you haven't done anything on it."

His face darkened. He looked at the table and slid a thumb along the edge of his knife. "I had some other things going on in my life at that time. Distractions."

"Like?"

"Like losing my daughter," he said and looked up. "My divorce was finalized in January. The ex had a new husband—and my daughter a new stepfather—by March. You do the math on that, Detective."

I nodded, drank some more water, waited.

"So here I am," he said. "Doing something about it, a few months too late—and I've got to thank you for wandering into this by mistake and pissing Sanabria off, because that led to the phone call that got me off my ass. I intend to push it as far as I can, Lincoln. With or without your help and with or without Graham's approval, I intend to do that. Know what I said about being distracted this spring? Well, summer's rolling on in now, buddy, and I'm *looking* for a distraction. This one fits fine."

His easy, amused manner had lost its grip and tumbled free, leaving behind a sheen of bitterness. I could sympathize with some of it—I'd lost a fiancée to another man—but what he was going through as a father was not an experience I knew. Or wanted to know.

"You know why I want that distraction?" he said, his hand returning to the knife. "Because when I have to sit around and think about what's happened in my life in the past year, nine times out of ten I conclude that my wife was right to go, and that my daughter's better off for it." He pressed his thumb into the blade. "That's the truth of it, but as you can imagine, it's not a truth I want to have to spend a hell of a lot of time considering."

"Why do you think it's the truth?"

"Sometimes you make decisions, Lincoln, that seem absolutely righteous at the time. Like there is no other possible option, you know? None. Then the years tick by and you see the way your decisions affected your family, and you wonder if it was a selfish choice."

He didn't offer any more details, and I didn't ask any more questions. There was a piano player in the corner of the room—seemed Sokolowski's always had a piano player—and for a while we just sat and listened to him play "Night Train" and didn't talk. When the song ended, Ken pushed the knife away. There was a hard white line down the middle of his thumb.

"All right," he said. "You've heard me out, and that's more than I had any right to ask, but I'll push it a bit more. I've been up-front with you, at the risk of bruising my ego, and admitted that I've never worked a homicide case. I know my way around an investigation, and I'm good at it, but I don't have the experience or the knowledge on a homicide, and you do. You also have some local credibility, which is going to be important. Those things are why I made the drive. I can move forward on this without you, and I will if I have to, but I'd rather have the help. So I'll ask you just once, with no pressure: Would you be willing to back me up on this?"

The piano player was into something upbeat and jazzy now, the sun was coming in warm through the windows behind him, and it had been many days since Dominic Sanabria stood in my living room. Easy to feel good about things. This one also felt like the sort of job that could get you into trouble, though, and generally you take those only when they're high-paying or personal. I didn't have that kind of excuse this time.

"Graham's assessment didn't exactly encourage me that this is something I want to be involved in, not even in a backup capacity," I said.

"You think he's going to leave you alone now?"

"I can make him. Police can solicit informant help, Ken, but they can't force it."

He shrugged.

It was quiet, and then he smiled, a cajoling, fraternal grin, and said, "Come on, Lincoln. This is what you are."

"Yeah," I said, but I couldn't match the smile. "It is."

"So?"

"Back you up. That was what you said, and it's what I'll hold you to. It's your baby, Ken, but I'll help you in whatever way I can, at least until it seems like that'll get me killed."

He smiled. "Can you ask any more of a man than that?"

13

Joe didn't like it. That was hardly a stunner. He grumbled and grunted and offered dire predictions and then told me I was an ass for not checking Ken's background out before agreeing to help him. When I explained that I had, he just grumbled and grunted some more.

"You had one of Ohio's last major mob figures standing in your apartment after one afternoon of work on the case, LP. That wasn't a clear enough warning sign to you?"

"Warning sign, sure. Stop sign, no."

"I knew there was a reason I always drive when I'm with you."

"Well, why don't you put that damn Taurus in gear and point it north, come back and run the show again."

"In time," he said. "In time."

Amy was a bit more receptive. That, too, wasn't exactly surprising—Amy's curiosity level can generally override her good judgment, a trait that Joe no longer shares. Or never shared. As a kid, he probably did background checks on the neighbors before trick-or-treating at their houses. Still, while Amy was at least lukewarm to the idea, her normal enthusiasm was tempered, and I understood that. It hadn't been so long ago that one of my cases invaded her life in a horrifying way. We rarely spoke of it now, and her typical bravado remained, but I'd also seen the pepper spray she'd added to her purse, and I'd heard the new steel security bar fasten behind me each time I left her apartment. Those were good things, maybe, the sort of precautions that would have pleased me had I not known that I was the reason for them.

"It's a bizarre story, and I can see why you're intrigued, but I also understand what Joe's telling you about the risks," she said as we sat on my roof that night, after Ken Merriman left for Pittsburgh. We had the Indians game on the radio and a bottle of pinot noir within reaching distance. I'd swept up the broken glass from the previous night. Found plenty of dust on the roof, but nothing as black as what had come from Parker Harrison's shattered bones, and no silver coin. Reassuring.

"I understand that, too, Amy, but I only agreed to help the guy. Give him some advice."

"Lincoln Perry, technical adviser?" She rolled her eyes. "Yeah, that'll go well."

"What are you saying?"

"You know, I'm sorry. The more I think about it, the better it sounds. Instead of getting yourself arrested, like normal, you can get *him* arrested."

"It's not a long walk home to your apartment. I'd be happy to throw you down to the sidewalk so you can get a faster start."

"Ha, ha." She stretched out in the chair, put her feet up. "I'm not saying you should pass on this, Lincoln, but you can imagine what's going through my head, too. Sanabria already came to your home once."

The implication was heavy, an unspoken reminder of a day when a man I'd angered had come to her home instead of mine. It was a memory that chased me through my days, that could bring me up short with a grimace of agony seemingly out of nowhere, striking my heart like a sudden and unexpected muscle cramp. The possibilities of what *might* have happened loomed even larger than the pain of what had happened. I'd been in this business for far too long to keep such images at bay; I knew what the world could do, knew the savagery and senselessness of it all too well. It was this that had invaded my mind when Dominic Sanabria came to my apartment, and now she was remembering the same incident and worrying about me. I thought of him again, and of a body laid in a Shawnee grave in Pennsylvania. I thought of those things, and I looked at Amy, and I felt afraid.

"What?" she said. She was watching my face, and a frown had gathered on her own as she studied me.

"I can stay out of it," I said. "I should. It's the right thing for you."

"For *me*?"

I nodded.

"That can't be the issue, Lincoln. It needs to be the right thing for *you*."

"No," I said. "Not anymore. We're together, right? So we make decisions that are the best for both of us. That's the whole point."

She shook her head. "I don't want to let myself be shoved around by fear, Lincoln. It was hard for a while, after what happened. It still is, sometimes, but I'm trying not to let that dictate my life. If you start doing the opposite, you're going to scare me more. Can you understand that? I need support, not protection. There's a difference."

It was quiet for a while, and then I said, "I'm sorry."

"For?"

"For leading the sort of life that makes things like that go through your head."

"Hey, my fault, right? Nobody forced me to date a detective."

"You got a profession you'd prefer? Something safer? Sexier?"

She cocked her head to the side. "Now, that's a good question. What would the ideal profession for a romantic partner be? Hmm . . . do you have one?"

"Reporter, of course."

"Coward. Try again."

"Singer. Jazz or blues, or maybe a country-rock style. Someone with the right voice, you know, kind of smoky and sultry. Bit of an attitude when she's onstage, nice long legs—"

"Pig."

"What?"

"I ask about the ideal *profession* and you start describing the physical features of another woman."

"I was trying to play along."

"Try harder next time. Or smarter, at least." She laced her hands behind her head, smiled. "You know what I'd choose? A carpenter. Strong and capable, right? Handy."

"Hey, I replaced that shelf at your apartment."

She lifted her head and stared at me. "The shelf you broke?"

"Well, be that as it may, I also hung the new one—"

"How many trips to the hardware store did that take you?"

"Just because I didn't have all the materials at first—"

"You tried to put it up without using a level, Lincoln. It wasn't a shelf, it was a ramp."

"I corrected that."

"In a mere five hours. Yeah, stick to detecting, buddy. Even if it gets you into trouble."

I leaned forward and turned the volume on the radio down, a serious concession with two on and two out. "Think about another writer approaching you to guide them through a story, Amy, and then tell me what you'd say. Somebody in your business comes to you for help, you try to do it if you can. At least that's the way I've always operated. He put his ego on the shelf and came asking for help."

"Do you trust him?" she asked.

I hesitated, which is never a good sign when offered in response to a question of trust, but then nodded. "He checks out."

"I didn't ask if he checked out. I asked if you trust him."

"Yes." I nodded again. "So far, I haven't seen anything that warns me not to. The way he showed up after a call from Sanabria, I guess, but since then, in the conversations we've had . . . he seems genuine."

"Same thing you said about Parker Harrison at first."

That stopped me. I gave her a grudging nod.

"Maybe it is, but Ken doesn't share Harrison's history. Besides, I've been in his position, okay? In two regards. Once when Karen left"—Amy made the face one should expect when he mentions his ex—"and once with this sort of case, dealing with a client who came to me hoping I could explain what happened to his family. I remember the way that felt, the sort of burden John Weston handed over to me."

"As I recall, it didn't feel much better when you handed the answers back over to him."

I was quiet, and Amy reached out and laid her hand on my arm.

"I get what you're saying, Lincoln. I do. If you think you can help him and you want to try, then it's a simple choice."

"I really don't know how much of a choice it is. Ken's asked me to get involved. Graham probably will."

I was passing the blame off to every external party, but the truth was it came down to my decision, and I couldn't fully explain the motivation to her. Couldn't explain that when Ken had smiled at me and said, "This is what you are," it had felt less like he was trying to coerce me and more like he was defining me. While his definition was accurate, I didn't know how much I liked it.

This is what you are.

"All of it's irrelevant," I said.

"What do you mean?"

"The idea that I had some sort of choice to make about stepping into this. I was already in it, Amy. From the time Harrison sent that first letter. He picked me, and I've been in it ever since."

"Why?" she said. "Why did he pick you?"

The silence built and hung around us, and eventually I reached out and turned the radio back up. We listened until the final out, but I don't think either of us could have told you the details of the game.

PART TWO

COLD TRAIL BLUES

14

By noon the next day my prediction to Amy was validated. I was involved now—thanks to Ken Merriman's urging and Quinn Graham's approval.

It was Graham who called, but he quickly blamed Ken.

"Your buddy doesn't have the best touch with police," he said. "Calls me up today, says he *wishes to inform me* that he'll be running his own investigation. Wishes to inform me. No bullshit, that's what he said. Not 'Yo, Detective Graham, I was wondering if I might be able to assist.' Not 'Excuse me, Detective Graham, I understand this is a cold case in another state and you might actually, for once in your career, be in favor of a PI's involvement.' No, Linc, instead he *wishes to inform me* that he's going out on his own. Whether I approve or not."

"Hmm," I said.

"Hmm? Hmm? Yeah, hmm is right, Linc. That's about what I had to say, too. Might have added a few more colorful terms, I don't recall. Your buddy, though—"

"Don't know that you can really call him my buddy, Graham. I met him two days ago. You two go back much longer than that. I figure, with that history, maybe he's really *your* buddy."

"Oh, you're not working with him on this? Because he said you were. He said, I believe this is a direct quote—'Perry and I are going to see what we can shake loose.' Shake loose, Linc. You not shaking? He shaking by himself?"

"I said I'd back him up. That's all. You know, give some advice—"

"Oh, some *advice*. Good, good. That's what I want to hear. You're giving advice to a guy who's never been any closer to a murder case than his TV screen."

"You don't want me to help him, then I'll just explain that and stay the hell out."

"Uh, no. Not at this point. Too late for that. Your buddy, he's in the game now. Already *informed* me, as I said. And if he's in the game, Linc? You better be, too. Because at least you been around. At least you know what you're doing. I did a little checking on you. Found out, my man Linc, he's a big shot."

"I wouldn't say that."

"Okay, we won't say that. Here's what we will say: I'm counting on you to keep Kenny from hurting this investigation. If he helps it, great, I'll be the first man down to shake his hand—but I am not going to let him *hurt* it, and I'm counting on you to help."

I rubbed my temples.

"Kenny does bring something to the table," Graham said. "I've got to admit that."

"Yeah?"

"He brings us an excuse to get you back in touch with Harrison. I was worrying on that one while I drove home yesterday. If you blew up on Harrison the way you said, then it'd feel wrong to have you go back, wanting to talk. Don't you think?"

"Sure."

"So we needed an excuse to open that door again. Needed one that felt right. I couldn't decide on it yesterday, but then this morning your buddy calls, and while I'm listening to him go on, I thought, yes, sir, this is the ticket. Kenny is the ticket. It'll be easy to sell as the truth, because it is the damn truth. Kenny looked you up, told you he wanted your client's name, and you agreed to give it to him. You might not want to work for Harrison, but he can. There's money in it, right?"

"Yeah." I could hear loud voices in the background, somebody swearing profusely, everybody else cracking up. Cops. Something about it hit a chord of absence that had been quiet for a long time.

"So you two, you're going to go see Harrison," Graham said. "You're going to talk, and you're going to tape."

"A wire?"

"Yeah. I'll get you set up."

"I've got one. Got a couple."

"Good quality or cheap shit?"

"They're good."

"All right. I'm considering you an informant, not a cop, understand? This isn't your investigation, it's mine. What you hear, I hear."

"Tell it to Ken. I'm just an adviser, remember?" Even I wasn't buying that anymore.

"Yeah, my ass. Anyhow, go easy this first time. Feel Harrison out, check his attitude, see what you think."

"You want me to tape everything?"

"Every word, Linc. Every word. Now, you get a good talk going with him, there's a name I'd like you to drop. Bertoli. Salvatore Bertoli."

"He's of interest?"

"Man died at the same time the Cantrells decided to make their exit. Man also used to run with some boys in Youngstown and Cleveland who were close to Dominic. Man's *plenty* interesting, is what I'm saying."

"Is he tied to Dominic through ten degrees of separation or two?"

"Two would be high, I think. He was definitely in Dominic's circle, though. Definitely."

"Well, that's a hell of an important fact, don't you think? How did he end up with the sister if he's—"

"Just ask Harrison about him. See if he takes you somewhere different than he took me."

"Which was?"

"Nowhere. Now, I don't want you getting too heated with the questioning, Linc. You keep it toned down. We're just feeling our way in the dark here. So you introduce Harrison to Kenny, and if the chance is there, maybe you ask him what he thought of the Italian guy, Salvatore. Whatever, we're treading lightly at the start."

Does it matter how lightly you tread on a land mine? I wondered.

Ken Merriman returned the next afternoon, to a hotel just off I-71 where he'd reserved a room for a full week. It was called a business suite and consisted of a bedroom, living room, and kitchen jammed into the same space as an ordinary hotel room, and when I made a joke about the place he told me I'd be more impressed by it if I'd seen the apartment he'd been living in since the divorce. I didn't make any more jokes after that.

I'd already located Parker Harrison's address and decided the way to approach him was in person and without warning. His sort of style. Besides, I wanted to see where he lived. There aren't many things that give you a sense of people faster than seeing them at home, in their own environment. Maybe he wouldn't let us in, but it was worth the try.

By the time I picked Ken up I was wearing the wire, just a simple seed mike that clipped to the inside of my collar and connected to a digital recorder fastened on my belt. I had a button-down shirt on, untucked over jeans, and it hung low enough that it covered the recorder even when I lifted my arms over my head.

In addition to the recorder, I had my Glock in its holster at my spine, and the feel of those things, the hard press of the gun and the cool, light touch of the wire running along my back, reminded me what I loved about my job. At some point during that preparation, testing the equipment and putting it on, I began to relish my role. After a few weeks of insisting I wanted no part of it, I was ready to go. A man had been killed and buried in the woods, and for twelve years nobody had answered for it. Whether Parker Harrison had killed him or not, he'd wanted to play games with me, writing his letters and telling his half-truths. Well, all right. If he wanted a game, I was ready to give him one.

The adrenaline was still riding with me when I got to Ken's hotel, and as I stood in his cramped room and explained things to him, he began to grin.

"What?" I said.

"You're fired up, aren't you?"

"Just ready to go. That's all."

"I was expecting more of the whining," he said. "You know, gloom and doom, all the reasons we should be playing chess or knitting or whatever instead of working this case."

I thought about what he'd just said and shook my head. Holy shit, I was turning into my partner. I was turning into Joe.

"You want me to take the gun out, fire a few rounds into the ceiling?" I asked. "Maybe bring along a pump shotgun?"

"It doesn't need to be that exciting."

"All right. Then let's get to work."

Harrison lived in an apartment in Old Brooklyn, not far from what had been Deaconess Hospital when I was a kid. My father was an EMT who'd worked out of Deaconess for a while. It was an area that had gone through plenty of cycles in a fairly short time, hit hard by poverty and crime only to come back a few decades later with skyrocketing house values. Harrison's apartment building wasn't attractive—a two-story brick rectangle with all the aesthetic appeal of a shoe box—but it was clean and bordered on either side by nice homes. There were only ten units in the building, and Harrison's was located at the front, on the ground floor. I had no idea what he did for a living or what he drove, so it was anybody's guess whether he'd be home. One way to find out, and that was a knock at the door.

He didn't answer. Nobody did. It was pushing on toward five, but early enough that most people would still be at work. We got back in my truck and went up to Pearl Road, found a restaurant with a bar, and killed an hour and a few Coronas. At six we returned to the apartment building. There were more cars in the lot, including an older Toyota pickup parked directly in front of Harrison's unit.

I pulled in next to it, cut the engine, and resisted the urge to double-check my recorder on the off chance that Harrison was watching. That's one of the challenges of wearing a wire: You're constantly aware of it, but your goal is to make sure nobody else is. I've found the best approach is to try to let it float at the back of your brain. Don't forget you have the thing on—do that and you're bound to screw up—but don't worry about it, either.

When we reached the door, I could hear music inside the apartment, some soft blues that was turned off as soon as I knocked. A brief pause, Harrison probably taking a look through the peephole, and then the door opened inward and he said, "Don't tell me the check bounced."

It sounded like a joke, but his face held all the humor of a brick wall.

"Didn't even cash it," I said. "Mind if we come in?"

He was wearing jeans and no shirt, and his body was more muscular than I would've guessed. Not cut from working out, but strong and free of fat in the way you can be if you eat right. Something told me Harrison probably ate right. He regarded Ken with a curious but not unfriendly gaze, and then he nodded and stepped back, and we followed him into the apartment.

It wasn't spacious—the rooms were narrow, and the ceilings felt low—but it was clean and laid out with a nice touch, furniture carefully situated to keep the small space from seeming cramped. There was a large piece of art on one wall, an elaborate wood carving in a symbol that meant nothing to me.

Harrison watched me look around and said, "It's not my first choice. I don't like living in apartments. I'd rather have some space, but I can't afford that yet, and the neighborhood here is quiet. Besides, I spend all day outside."

"Do you?" I looked away from the wood carving, back at him. "What is it that you do for a living, Harrison?"

"I'm a groundskeeper. For a cemetery."

"Really?"

He nodded. "It suits me."

Ken said, "How unsettling," in a flat voice that was pure Bogart and would have made me smile anywhere and anytime else. Harrison gave him one quick, hard stare, then returned his attention to me.

"Can I ask—" he began, but I interrupted and pointed at Ken.

"He's the one who wants to talk with you. It wasn't my choice."

His eyes went to Ken and lingered there, studying, but when he spoke again it was still to me.

"If he wants to talk to me, why did he go through you?"

"I'll let him explain that." I walked past Harrison and sat on his couch. He watched me but didn't say anything, and after a short pause Ken sat down, too. Harrison stayed on his feet.

"Well?" he said, speaking directly to Ken this time.

Ken launched into his story, explaining the twelve-year-old case, the way it had eaten at him, how he'd promised Joshua Cantrell's parents he'd deliver an answer. I listened and tried to look bored, a little put out, as I was claiming to be. The seed microphone was cool and firm against my collarbone, but so far it hadn't taken in anything worth hearing, just Ken talking and Harrison staying silent.

"So when I found out Lincoln had looked into the house, I asked him about it," Ken was saying. "Wanted to know who his client was, who had an interest in the family."

Harrison looked over at me, no trace of emotion showing yet. "You provided that information."

I nodded.

"That's not confidential?"

"Usually."

He waited for more, but I didn't say anything. Finally he said, "Why wasn't it in my case?"

"You'd already broken my trust, Harrison. I told you that. You sent me out there asking questions like a fool, no idea the man was dead and his sister was related to Dominic Sanabria. You know who showed up at my home the other day? Sanabria. That's your doing, Harrison. You think I owed you confidentiality after that bullshit?"

I'd put some heat into the words, but he didn't change expression or break eye contact. Just listened, gave it a few seconds to make sure I was done, and then turned back to Ken.

"So what do you want from me?"

"A job," Ken said.

"A job?"

"Why not? You wanted Lincoln to work for you, right? Well, he backed out. I won't. I want to see this through, and I need someone to bankroll it,

Mr. Harrison. I'm not going to take any more money from the family, and they don't have any to give me. They're not well off. They still want to know what happened to their son, though, and supposedly so do you."

"What will you do?" Harrison asked. "No offense meant, but if you've had twelve years at this . . ."

I was surprised by the flush that rose into Ken's cheeks. Either he was a hell of an actor or that sort of remark got to him even when it came from the lead suspect.

"It wasn't like I worked at it full-time for twelve years," he said, his voice measured and tight. "When I got started there was no body, no evidence of a crime. They just went away, that's all. Went away and didn't leave a trace. Now there's a trace."

"The buried body," Harrison said. "That's your trace?"

His tone had changed when he said *the buried body*, dropped and chilled. Ken hesitated, as if he'd heard it, too.

"Sure," he said. "That's one hell of a trace, don't you think?"

"The body was found months ago. Has the trace helped you since then?"

It felt cold in the room now, and there was something in Harrison's eyes and the set of his jaw that I didn't like. Ken was sitting forward on the couch, his arms braced on his knees, and I was leaning back, out of his view. Ken shifted his head slightly, as if he wanted to look at me, but then stopped, realizing Harrison would see any exchange between us.

"Well?" Harrison said. "Has the trace helped you?"

"Sure," Ken said.

"In what way?"

Again a pause, Ken unsure of himself now, and Harrison repeated his question.

"In what way?"

"It's given me some suspects."

"Really? Who?"

"Salvatore Bertoli," Ken said.

This was no longer going according to script—Graham had asked that we mention Bertoli, not identify him as a suspect—but Harrison's reaction was worth the gamble. He'd been unusually still, one of those rare people who can stand in front of others without fidgeting or shifting, but now he stepped closer to Ken and took the back of a chair in his hand and gripped it tight.

"Why do you say that?" he asked.

This time Ken did look at me, just one quick glance, and then he said, "You're not my client yet, Mr. Harrison. I'm not going to disclose any of the work I've done. You want to hire me, that would change."

"I'll write you a check tonight," Harrison said, "if you tell me why you said Salvatore's name."

"I've got my reasons."

"I want to hear them."

Ken was in a corner now—he had no reasons for suspecting Bertoli, and no way to avoid answering the question that wouldn't seem false. He was silent for a minute, weighing his options, and I decided to speak for the first time since he'd gotten started, just to divert the conversation if possible.

"You worked with him, Harrison," I said. "So you tell us—what did you think of Salvatore?"

He frowned and shook his head, then pointed at Ken. "I'd like to know why you think he's a suspect."

"He took a tumble off a warehouse roof the same time they disappeared," Ken said. "I've got a feeling those events weren't coincidental."

It was a cop-out, and not enough to satisfy Harrison. He said, "That's all? That's the only reason you called him a suspect?"

"It's the only one I'm prepared to share tonight. Now, if you want to write that check . . ."

"Is he the only suspect?"

"Everyone's a—"

"That's a silly cliché. Is he *your only suspect*?" Harrison was leaning forward now, his weight against the back of the chair, cords of muscle tight in his dark arms.

"He's a favorite," Ken said, still dancing, still evading. It wasn't working well, though. The one thing I was becoming more and more certain about with Harrison was that he could read people, and if Ken kept playing him there was a damn good chance we'd expose too much and learn too little.

Every time Harrison looked at me I felt like he was following the wire with his eyes, tracing its path as if my shirt were transparent.

"He's a favorite," Harrison echoed. "Well, who are the others?"

"Mr. Harrison, do you want me to work for you or not?" Ken said, and I was glad he hadn't answered the question, that he seemed to want to bring this to an end, probably sensing the same dangers I had.

"There are some people who would tell you that I was a suspect," Harrison said.

Ken didn't answer.

"You said you're from Pennsylvania?"

"That's right."

"Have you talked with Detective Graham?"

Again Ken was quiet.

"Of course you have," Harrison said. "That would be a formality. A requirement. Who is his *favorite suspect*?"

"I'm not working with him, or for him."

"Are you not?" Harrison said, and then he turned and looked at me, as if the question applied to us both.

"You told me you didn't kill Cantrell," I said.

"That's right."

"So why are you worried, Harrison?"

His eyes seemed darker now than when we'd walked in. He said, "The evidence can always be twisted, can't it, Lincoln?"

"There something specific on your mind when you say that?"

Harrison looked at me for a long time, and then he let go of the chair and stepped back and turned to Ken. "I'll think about this."

"Well, I'd ask you to think fast," Ken said. "I'll leave a card, and if you could decide by—"

"When I decide, I'll let Lincoln know. You keep your card."

I shook my head. "I'm out, Harrison. If you—"

"No. When I decide, I'll let you know. You brought him to me, Lincoln."

His eyes were hard on me, still searching, distrustful. I felt a tingle at my collarbone, where the microphone rested, and I wanted to cover it with my hands.

Ken got to his feet and offered a hand to Harrison, who shook it after a moment's pause. I stood then, and we moved for the door together. Ken opened it, and I followed him outside, then turned back to face Harrison before closing the door.

"Hey, Harrison. One last question."

He waited.

"Everybody else came and went from the Cantrells' in six months. Everybody else worked alone. Why were you there for a year, and why'd you stick when they hired Bertoli?"

He stood in the doorway, framed by the lighted room behind him.

"Because she asked me to," he said eventually.

"Alexandra?"

A nod.

"Why?"

He stepped out of the apartment, reaching for the door, his hand passing close to my face as he grasped the edge.

"Because she trusted me, and she was afraid."

"Of who? Bertoli? Her brother?"

He pulled away, and my hand fell from the knob as the door swung shut. A second later the lock turned.

15

It was quiet in the truck as I drove away from Parker Harrison's apartment. A disconcerted feeling hung in the air between us, and not just
from Harrison's final statement but from the way Ken had handled the interview. He was older than me by several years, but it didn't feel that way,
because he was so damn green. Anytime I'd done an interview with Joe, I
could afford to worry about my own end of it, assured that Joe, with thirty
years of experience and one hell of an intellect, wasn't going to say anything
that jeopardized us. Ken was a bright guy, certainly, but he didn't have those
thirty years of experience. Didn't have one, even, not in the way that counted.
Working divorce cases and insurance fraud and accident reconstructions
didn't prepare you for a homicide investigation, didn't prepare you for a
back-and-forth with someone like Parker Harrison.

It wasn't just Ken's end of that exchange that left me ill at ease, though.
Harrison had taken a different tone than in either of my previous meetings
with him, somehow both more guarded and aggressive. He'd seemed . . .
cunning. Like he knew not to trust us from the moment we walked through
his door, but he also didn't want to throw us out. Wanted us there, instead,
so he could find some things out for himself. I remembered the way he'd

looked at me when he asked if we were working for Graham, and once again, even in the truck, miles from him, I felt exposed.

"You think anything good was accomplished back there?" Ken said at length.

"We did what Graham asked of us."

"I don't think this was what he had in mind." Ken's voice was low, his face turned away from me, to the window. "I screwed it up, didn't I?"

"Tough to say."

He shook his head. "No, it's not. You were sitting there, you know how it went. He didn't believe a word I was saying."

"Didn't seem to believe much of it," I conceded, "but maybe we were reading too much into it, too. That's how it goes on undercover stuff, you're more sensitive than the target ninety percent of the time."

"Maybe," Ken said, "but that's sure not how I wanted it to play. Doubt it's how Graham wanted it to play, either."

"No."

He was quiet for a while again, then said, "Maybe we could run a few days of surveillance on him. Think that would help?"

"We're not going to do that without Graham signing off on it," I said, "and my guess is he's not going to."

"I might suggest it anyhow."

He was playing back to his strengths, to what he knew—surveillance. The conversation with Harrison had rattled him more than it had me, even, and that was a bad sign. If he wanted to keep moving on an investigation of this magnitude, he was going to need to come up with some confidence fast.

"Lincoln?" Ken said, and I realized I'd tuned him out, fallen away into my own thoughts.

"Sorry," I said. "What was that last bit?"

"Asking if we have to sit around and wait for Harrison to contact us again, or if we can move forward on this in some way. I was thinking if we pursued the Bertoli angle, it'd match up with what we told Harrison."

"Maybe."

"Well, what do you want to do? That's what I'm asking. What's next?"

"I've got to talk to Graham."

He fell silent for the first time as I turned off the interstate at the exit for his hotel. We were waiting at a red light just across from the parking lot when he turned to me and said, "Thank you, Lincoln."

"For?"

"For getting me up here, man. For agreeing to take it on. I needed this. I mean, I *needed* this."

He spoke with intensity, but his eyes were sad. I thought his mind was probably on his daughter again, his daughter and his ex-wife and the new stepfather. What was it he'd said that day at Sokolowski's? *Nine times out of ten I conclude that my wife was right to go, and that my daughter's better off for it.* I wondered which one of the ten he was on right now.

"Maybe tonight wasn't an impressive audition," he said, "but I'm not going to worry about it. I'm here to see it through, and I'll do that."

The light changed, and I pulled across the street and into the parking lot, bringing the truck to a stop outside the door closest to his room.

"I'll talk to Graham, and give you a call in the morning," I said.

"All right." He opened the door, then paused with one foot on the pavement and one still in the cab. "We're going to see this thing to the end, Lincoln. Twelve years I've been waiting for that."

"Maybe we will, or maybe we'll still be talking about it, pissed off and annoyed, ten years from now. That happens sometimes, Ken."

He shook his head. "Not this time. No, I've got a feeling about it."

My apartment was dark and empty when I came inside, and I felt a surge of disappointment that Amy wasn't there. No surprise—we hadn't made plans for the night, and she rarely came by unannounced—but some nights you can't help wishing that someone were waiting for you, had a light on. Of course, the first time that happened I'd probably wince at the sight of the light in the window and think longingly of a quiet, empty, and dark home. What can I say? We private eyes are dualistic creatures. It's one of our human traits.

I wanted to call Amy but figured Graham should come first. Sitting on the couch, I unbuttoned my shirt, removed the wire, and checked the recorder to see if all looked right. It did, but I wouldn't be sure until I hooked it up to the computer, ripped the audio file, and played it back. That would wait until morning. I found Graham's number and called.

"I'm about to get in bed with my wife, Linc. In other words, you best have something worthwhile to say."

I looked at the clock. "It's not even nine, Graham."

"Said I was getting into bed with her. Didn't say anything about sleeping."

"Ah."

"Yeah, ah. Now, what do you have?"

I took him through it as accurately as I could, albeit with a touch of varnish on my description of Ken's contributions. It wasn't a heavy enough coat.

"He told Harrison that Bertoli was a *suspect*?"

"You wanted us to drop the name."

"Drop the name, not call him a suspect! You think that's one and the same?"

"The implication would've been there anyhow."

He grumbled at that but let it go. "So Salvatore's name gave Harrison a little stir, did it?"

"Felt that way."

"Interesting. What do you think of that bit he said to you at the door?"

"That Alexandra asked him to stay because she was afraid? I'm not sure what to think of it."

"I'll ask you this, then—suppose you a woman, and you afraid. A convicted murderer is who you turn to for help?"

"Could be she trusted him."

"Uh-huh, even if I buy that, I still go back to the convicted murderer element. She wants a guy with those credentials around for help, then what do you think she was afraid of?"

"Husband, maybe."

"Guy's a scholar, Linc. Weighed maybe a hundred and forty pounds, spent his day stuck in a book."

"You've been around long enough to know that doesn't mean a thing."

"No, but if she's afraid of him, why not call her brother?"

"So maybe it was the brother she was afraid of."

"That's what I like about your mind, Linc. It works just like mine, only slower."

"That's a big jump, man, suggesting Dominic would go after his own sister."

"Who said anything about going after her? We've got one person confirmed dead, Linc, and it ain't Alexandra."

"You think she was afraid for her husband."

"Makes sense, since he turned up dead," Graham said, but then rushed out, "Look, let's don't get too sidetracked with this. Only reason we're even talking about it is because of what Harrison said, and I don't know how high he'd score in truthfulness. What do you think?"

"About Harrison?"

"Yeah. You were the one sat there and talked with him tonight. Give me your instinct. You feel he's being straight? That he doesn't know a hell of a lot more about this than he's saying?"

I thought about it, remembering his words, his body language, his eyes.

"No," I said. "I don't trust him."

"Exactly. Now, you expect to hear from him? Think he'll take the bait?"

"Here's what I expect—if he takes it, he'll do so knowing damn well that it's bait. He's smart, Graham. He's awfully smart."

"I'm not so sure about that," Graham said.

I was—And that's why, when I got to the office at eight thirty the next morning to discover Harrison had left a message three hours earlier, I didn't view it as any sort of victory.

He'd called at five twenty in the morning and prefaced the message with an apology for the early hour, explaining that he needed to be at work by six.

I know this is your office number, though, so I assume it's not a problem. I gave your offer some consideration, Lincoln, and I've decided to accept. I'll put a new retainer check in the mail today. For one thousand dollars. If that's not enough, let me know. The check will be made out to you. If you'd like to pay Ken Merriman the full sum, that's your decision, but the only way I'll approach this is with you as a go-between. I think that's fair, seeing how you're the one who brought him to me. It wouldn't be right for you to be completely removed from this. I'm not comfortable with that.

He paused there, and I could hear his breathing, fast and shallow, in direct contrast with his patient, careful manner of speaking.

I imagine you might be speaking with Detective Graham at some point. Feel free to give him my regards.

Another pause.

All right, so, I'll mail the check. Now, I don't mean to tell you how to do your business, but I suppose since you're working for me, it's fine if I make a request. Leave Mark Ruzity alone. He shouldn't be of interest to you, and he shouldn't be bothered. I'd like you to keep your distance from Mark.

That was the end of the message. I listened to it a few times before Ken showed up, and as soon as he sat down I played it again and watched his face darken as Harrison talked.

"You get the sense he may know exactly what we're doing?" he said when the message was done.

"I suggested that to Graham last night."

"And?"

"Graham doesn't agree, or doesn't care. I'm not sure which."

"What Harrison said about him . . . that felt like a message, didn't it? Like he was telling us—"

"That he knows we're doing this at Graham's direction? Yeah."

"You talk to Graham since this call?"

"Tried and didn't get him. Left a message."

"Harrison still seems quite taken with you, Lincoln. Supposedly he just hired me, right? But he did that through a call to you and a check made out to you. What do you think of that?"

I shook my head. "No idea. Why'd he come to me in the first place? Why keep writing letters after it was clear I wouldn't respond? Why show up at my office after months of being ignored?"

"You don't like it."

"Would you?"

His grin slipped back into place. "Shit, he's sending you checks. How bad can it be?"

"Yeah, right."

"So what now, we wait on Graham?"

"Uh-huh, that's the drill."

"That last bit of the message is pretty damn strange," Ken said. "Telling us to stay away from Ruzity."

"I was waiting for you to comment on that."

"As far as I knew, the two of them had no relationship. They were with the Cantrells at different times, and I had no idea their paths would have crossed."

"Seems like they did."

"Yeah. With Harrison being our client and all, I suppose we have to respect his wishes and leave Ruzity alone."

"That would be the ethical decision, certainly. We are in his employ."

"So as long as you got that message, we'd be required to keep our distance from Ruzity."

"Exactly."

"Imagine what might have happened if you didn't come into the office right away, though."

I nodded. "Why, there's a chance we might have blundered our way to Mr. Ruzity, oblivious to the wishes of our client. In fact, until that message came through, he *wasn't* our client. He was still considering things."

"An excellent point." He flicked his eyes to the phone, and a smile drifted across his face. "So, let me ask you, Lincoln: When did you play that message?"

"It's tough to recall, Ken. My memory isn't what it used to be. But I can't imagine it was *before* we looked Ruzity up."

"Oh, no," he said. "I can't imagine it was."

16

Finding Mark Ruzity was like looking for a lost dog in a neighborhood overrun by strays—nobody wanted to help, and nobody understood why in the hell you'd want to find him in the first place.

We started at the pawnshop on Storer Avenue where, according to Ken's notes, Ruzity worked repairing guitars. The notes were more than a decade old, though, and the pawnshop was now a vacant building with boarded windows. From there we went to his house on Denison, found nobody home, and started knocking on doors to see if anyone could tell us where to find him. Most of the people on the street seemed to know who he was, but nobody wanted to direct us to him.

"He's one of those guys," said a Puerto Rican woman who kept the chain on the door while she talked to us, "you just keep your distance from him, you know? He's lived here as long as we have, never caused a problem, but he looks like he *could*, right? He don't bother nobody, but I sure as shit wouldn't bother him, either. I don't think you should bother him."

It was the same sentiment Harrison had expressed. For a guy who hadn't taken a fall in fifteen years, Ruzity had one hell of a rep.

Ken finally had the inspiration that got us to him.

"He's a musician, right? Is there anyplace in this neighborhood where a musician would want to go?"

We found one: a used instrument store ten blocks from his house. They knew him, all right.

"Dude can shred a guitar," the kid behind the counter informed us from behind his protective layer of piercings. "I mean just melt the amp, really. But he won't play with anybody else now. Only solo. Calls himself El Caballo Loco."

He paused, waiting for a reaction, and then said, "It means the crazy horse. Badass, right?"

Badass, we agreed. Now where can we find him?

"He's a stone carver, man. Works with a guy named Ben down on Forty-eighth. Does all sorts of cool shit. You should see some of the gravestones."

"Gravestones?"

"Yeah, awesome, right? Like I said, he's pretty badass."

He didn't have an address for the carving shop, but he gave us a close enough description. Ken and I didn't speak until we were back in my truck.

"So he carves the gravestones," Ken said, "and Harrison keeps them clean? That's the idea? A pair of murderers making a living in the cemetery business?"

"Steady work," I said. "They're never going to run out of clients. Hell, they've helped produce some."

The carving shop—Strawn Stoneworks—occupied the bottom floor of a three-story brick building near the old stockyard district. Nobody answered our knock, but there were lights on in the back, and the door was unlocked. We went in.

The front of the room was scattered with samples of carvings laid out on old wooden tables—a fireplace mantel, a small gargoyle, and a handful of headstones. There was a narrow corridor separating this room from the next, and at the opposite end fluorescent lights glowed and a steady tapping sound could be heard. Metal on stone.

I led the way down the hall, and we came out in a workshop that smelled of sweat and dust. There were pieces of stone on the floor and on heavy-duty steel shelves, and tools littered the rest of the space—grinders and hammers and racks of chisels, an air compressor with hoses draped around it. A man was working with his back to us, chipping away at a piece of marble with a hammer and chisel. I was just opening my mouth to speak when he turned and said, "The hell you think you're doing?"

He was of average height, wiry in a hard way, with gray hair and a goatee. He wore an earring, and there were thin lines of sweat snaking down his forehead.

"Hey, sorry, there wasn't anybody out front," I said.

"Strawn left for a while. Said he was getting lunch, but he's probably buying comic books. That's what he does at lunch." He wiped sweat away with the back of his hand. "Anyhow, he's the owner; he's the one you talk to. Not me. And nobody comes back into the workshop."

"We're not looking for Strawn," I said. "We're looking for Mark Ruzity."

He didn't answer.

"Are you—" I began, but then he cut me off.

"Maybe I wasn't clear. Nobody comes into the workshop." He cocked his head and stared us down, first me, then Ken. "Lot of tools back here. People wander in, they could get hurt."

It didn't feel like a public safety announcement.

"Mark," I said, "wouldn't it be easier to answer five minutes of questions?"

"Would be *easiest* to throw your asses out. Nobody—"

"Comes into the workshop. We get it. But if you throw us out now, we'll just have to go back to your place on Denison and wait around. What's the point?"

His eyes flickered and went dark when I said that. Didn't like it that we knew where he lived.

"Okay," he said. "I can tell you what I've told every other cop: I'm clean. Haven't killed anyone in a while. If you're asking about something that went down in the neighborhood, you're asking the wrong man. I'm not involved, and I don't drop dimes."

"It's not about the neighborhood," Ken said. "It's about Alexandra and Joshua Cantrell."

Ruzity seemed to draw in air without taking a breath. Just absorbed it, sucked it right out of the dust-filled room until the walls felt tight around us. He didn't speak, but he looked at Ken in a way that made me wish I were wearing a gun. There were pneumatic hammers on a table beside him, but he was using hand tools, a hammer in his right and a carbide chisel in his left. He turned the chisel in his fingers now. It looked natural in his hand. Familiar.

"I suspect the time has come," he said, "for us to share some names. You already know mine. What are yours?"

We told him. Names and occupation. He kept rotating the chisel. It had a flared point, ridged with small, sharp teeth. Sweat had slipped behind his glasses and found his eyes, and he blinked it away without dropping his stare.

"Private investigators," he said. "Then police didn't send you. So who did? Dunbar?"

I could feel Ken's *who's Dunbar?* question on the way, could also feel the price of it if he let it escape his lips, and rushed out my own response first. "What's your problem with Dunbar?"

Mark Ruzity switched his eyes to me. "My problem? The son of a bitch has spent *twelve years* harassing me and sending cops my way. You ask what my *problem* is?"

I shrugged, and he narrowed his gaze. "Dunbar does his own hassling, though. FBI guys don't hire anybody else to do it for them. So who the hell you working for?"

"If you don't mind," Ken said, "maybe you could answer a question or two and then we will. You know, fair trade."

"Fair trade?" He took a step closer and drew himself up to his full height, and the muscles in his forearms stood out tight around the chisel and the hammer. Then he paused, as if something had interrupted his forthcoming words, and frowned at Ken.

"Merriman," he said. "That's your name?"

"Yes."

"You came around a long time ago," he said. "Back at the start."

"You wouldn't agree to see me," Ken said.

"No. And I won't now. You were working for his parents." His frown deepened. "What in the hell brings you back all these years later?"

"The case remains unsolved, Mark."

"No shit. You been working it for the whole time?"

"No. I'm back because they found his body. It . . . stimulated my interest."

Ruzity pulled his head back, stared down at Ken with his eyes thoughtful and his mouth open, as if Ken had just told him a riddle and Ruzity wanted to be damn sure he got the right answer.

"His body," Ruzity said at length, "doesn't mean shit to me. Okay? Unless you want me to carve his headstone, it doesn't mean shit to me. It shouldn't to you, either."

"No? Like I said, the crime remains—"

"Unsolved," he said. "Yeah, I got it. Maybe it's better that way, too."

"Think you can explain that remark?" I said, and he ignored me, still focused on Ken.

"His parents hired you again when the body turned up? That's what you're telling me?"

"No. I'm not working for them anymore."

"Bullshit. Or, wait—give a shit. As in: I don't. Who sent you here is irrelevant. What's relevant is that you haul your asses out the door and go back to your clients and tell them to stay the hell away from Mark Ruzity."

"Odd response," I said, "coming from someone the Cantrells helped. I'd think you would care about seeing Joshua's death and his wife's disappearance resolved."

His head swiveled to me, and I felt a cold tightness along my spine.

"You think you know something about what the Cantrells did for me?" he said. "You think you know a *damn* thing about that? Let me tell you what they did—showed me that I'm the sort of man who needs his space. Why? To keep from losing a temper that I don't have real good control over. I've controlled it for a while now. Some years, in fact. But it's a daily chore, and it only works when I keep my space, and other people keep theirs."

He lifted the chisel, put the tip to my forehead, and then gave it a gentle tap with the hammer. The tiny teeth bit into my skin. Enough that I felt it, but not enough to draw blood. Ken shifted toward us, but Ruzity appeared unconcerned with him.

"Right now?" he said. "You're in my space, brother."

He'd lowered the hammer but was still holding the chisel against my forehead. Now he leaned close, so close that his goatee brushed my jaw, and spoke into my ear.

"You want to know what Alexandra Cantrell did for me?" he said. "She taught me how to keep myself from putting that chisel through your brain."

He popped the chisel free, and I could feel the imprint of the teeth lingering in my skin.

"The door is where you left it," he said. "Turn your asses around and find it again."

17

Rehabilitated?" Ken said as we walked to my truck. "Really?"
"Clean since the day he stepped out of prison, is what you said."

"It's the truth. But the man seems to have an edge, doesn't he?"

"An edge," I said. "Yeah. That's the word."

"He's the only guy Harrison singled out, the only person he told us not to talk to. I wonder what he—"

"I'll tell you what we need to be wondering about right now: Dunbar. That's the name. You didn't mention him to me before. Have you heard the name?"

"No."

"Ruzity said he was FBI."

"As far as I know, the FBI had nothing to do with the case."

"They shouldn't have," I said, "but evidently they did."

"Think we should track him down?"

"Until I hear otherwise from Graham, yeah. And guess what? Graham still hasn't called."

John Dunbar had retired from the Bureau four years earlier, but fortunately for us he hadn't left the Cleveland area. He was living in Sheffield Lake, a small town west of the city and directly on the shore of Lake Erie. I didn't know the place well, but I'd been there several times, always to a bar called Risko's Tavern. My father had been close with the guy who'd owned the place when I was a kid, and he used to make the drive out there on the weekend to sip a few beers, talk, and watch the water. Every now and then they'd have a clambake or a cookout outside, and he'd take me along. All I remembered of the place from those early visits was that they'd had a piranha tank inside and that my father always seemed to be in a hell of a good mood when he was there. The bar had changed hands since then, but I still stopped in occasionally to sit with a few drinks and some memories.

The waterfront property in the town had gone through a dramatic transformation in recent years, rich people buying up the old cottages that had lined the shore and tearing them down, building ostentatious temples of wealth in their place. When we got out there and I realized from the addresses that Dunbar's property would be on the north side of Lake Road, right on the water, my first thought was one of suspicion—these places were going for several million, so how in the hell did a retired FBI agent afford one? Cop on the take?

Then we found his house and that suspicion faded. It was wedged between two brick behemoths but didn't fit the mold. A simple home, white siding with blue trim, it had just enough room across the front for a door and two square windows on either side. To say the place was tiny didn't do it justice—beside those sprawling homes, it looked like something made by Lionel.

What the house lacked in size, it made up for in location, though. The perfectly trimmed lawn ran all the way down to a stone retaining wall at the lakeshore's edge, and beyond it the tossing, petulant gray water spread as far as you could see. There were some beautiful trees in the front yard, with flowers planted around their bases, but the backyard had been wisely kept free of visual obstructions, letting the lake stand out in all its power. The house was as well cared for as the lawn. When we pulled to a stop behind the carport—there was a Honda Civic parked inside—I could see that all the blue trim was fresh, and the roof looked new.

"Not much house, but I'd take the view," I said.

"No kidding." Ken popped open his door, nodding at the Civic. "We're in luck, too. Looks like somebody's home."

We got out of the car and walked up a concrete path to the front door. There were iron railings beside the two steps up to the door, and those, too, were shiny with a fresh coat of black paint. I pulled open the storm door to knock, but the someone was already at the door, swinging it open.

"Can I help you?"

"Mr. Dunbar?"

"That's right." He was probably late sixties and seemed more like an engineer or a math teacher than a retired cop. Neatly parted gray hair, slight build, three mechanical pencils and one red pen tucked into the pocket of a starched white shirt that he wore with black suit pants but no jacket or tie, so that it looked like a waiter's uniform.

"My name's Lincoln Perry. I'm a PI from Cleveland. Used to be with the department out there."

"Am I the target of your investigation or a potential source for it?" he said dryly, a hint of humor showing in the eyes.

"With any luck, a source."

"Come on in."

We walked inside, and I crossed through the cramped living room to stand at the back window and look out at the lake while Ken introduced himself. Everything in the house spoke of an exceeding level of care, but you could see the age in it, too—old-fashioned doorknobs and hinges, a Formica countertop in the little kitchen beside us.

"Hell of a location," I said when Dunbar finished addressing Ken and they joined me in the living room.

His smile seemed bitter. "You have no idea how often I've heard *that* in the past few years."

"Sorry."

"No, no. It is a great spot, but you've seen what's going up around it. Last fall someone offered me three-quarters of a million for the property. You know what my parents paid for it?"

"Fifty?"

He smiled. "Thirty-eight. We lived in Cleveland, and my father wanted a place on the lake for summer, and back then there was nothing out here."

"You ever consider selling it?" Ken asked. "Money talks, is the rumor."

"Money screams in your ear. No, I haven't and I won't. I'm retired, I live simply, and I cannot imagine being any happier than I am right here."

Retired, and he was wearing a starched shirt and dress pants in his own home. Yes, the more I saw of him, the more he reminded me of Joe.

"Besides, I enjoy my legend in the neighborhood," he said. "Would you believe that the garage next door is more than a thousand square feet bigger than my entire house? The *garage*."

He laughed and turned away from the window, then went and sat on an overstuffed blue armchair and waved at the matching couch across from it.

"All right, if you're not here to buy the house, then what is it? One of you from Cleveland and the other from Pennsylvania, this has to be interesting."

"I'm basically riding shotgun on this one," I said. "It's Ken's case, but I'm helping out with the Ohio end of it. We're trying to find out what happened to a man named Joshua Cantrell. I don't know if that name means anything to you."

Even before I got that last part out, it was clear that the name meant plenty to him. The easygoing look went tense and, maybe, a bit sad.

"Oh, my," John Dunbar said. "That one."

"Yes," I said. "That one."

He was quiet for a moment, looking at the coffee table. "When you say you want to know what happened to him, you mean why was he killed. You mean, of course, what transpired that led to the man's body being buried in the woods."

"Yep," Ken said. "That's the gist."

"Well, you came to the right place," Dunbar said, and when he looked up at us there was no mistaking it this time—his face held sorrow. "I can tell you who I believe murdered him, but I can't prove it. What I can prove, though, is who *got* him killed. There is a difference. Would you like to know who *got* him killed?"

Ken shot me a quick glance, eyebrows raised, and nodded. "We sure would."

John Dunbar lifted his hand and gave us a child's wave, all from the wrist. "Right here," he said. "I got him killed, gentlemen. If you don't mind, I might pour myself a drink before I tell you the story."

18

He went into the kitchen and opened a cupboard and withdrew a bottle of Scotch that was nearly full. We waited while he opened another cupboard and spent a few seconds scanning the inside before selecting a juice glass. When he twisted the cap off the bottle it made a cracking sound, breaking a seal that had evidently enjoyed plenty of hardening time.

"Ken Merriman," Dunbar said in a flat voice. "You're the one the Cantrells hired."

Ken raised his eyebrows. "How do you know that?"

"I was trying to assist with the investigation. The police side. I knew everyone who was involved, at every level. I never spoke with you because, frankly, I wasn't interested in seeing a PI step into the case. Are you still working for them?"

"No."

Dunbar waited, but Ken didn't volunteer a client, so eventually he just nodded and sat down. He took one sip of the whiskey.

"We found you through a man named Mark Ruzity," I said. "He told us you'd been sending police his way for years."

"That's right."

"Why?"

"Because he knows something that could help," Dunbar said, and then he set the whiskey aside and got up and walked into another room, closing the door behind him. He was gone for maybe five minutes before he came back out and dropped a photograph in my lap.

Ken moved so he could look over my shoulder, and we studied the picture. It showed Dominic Sanabria and Mark Ruzity standing together on a sidewalk bordered by a wrought-iron fence. They both looked much younger. Ruzity was saying something to Sanabria, speaking directly into his ear. Whispering, perhaps. He had one hand clasped on the back of Sanabria's neck, and Sanabria was leaning forward and listening with intense eyes.

"They knew one another?" Ken said. "How?"

"I'm not certain," Dunbar said, "but you'll be interested in the date that photograph was taken. It came a matter of days after the Cantrells disappeared."

"Why do you have it?" I asked. "What's your connection to their case?"

"You don't know my personal history with Dominic?" he said, sounding genuinely surprised.

"John, we really don't know much at all," I said. "We're not as far around the curve as you think. More lucky than good, maybe."

"Oh, I doubt that. Still, in the interest of having us all caught up, let me explain. I assumed you read some articles about Dominic, the charges he always managed to slide out from under. I had the bastard once. *Had him.*"

"How so?" Ken said.

Another drink of Scotch, little more than a sip. He hadn't offered us any, which wasn't a problem but confirmed that he wasn't much of a drinker. This glass was for him while he told his story, and it didn't even cross his mind that anybody else would want a drink in the middle of the day.

"There was a motel out on the east side—a big old place with lots of separate units—that Dominic and his team were using. The owner of the place was a sleaze, and he knew they were dirty, but they paid well and tipped better, and so he kept his eyes wide shut to everything they did. Well, I put some energy into turning him, put some pressure on, and he agreed to cooperate with us. The idea was that he'd be a pretty general snitch. I wasn't asking him to do anything out of line, just tip us to comings and goings. I wanted to do some wiretaps out there—the whole reason they were using the place for meetings was to avoid wiretaps—but they were smart enough to get different units every time, and the judge wouldn't sign off on a warrant for the whole damn place. Even if he had, we couldn't have gotten that much equipment. It just wasn't practical.

"So instead I'm using the guy as a source of information on movement, nothing more. About a month after I turned him, I get a call from him. A page, actually—back then we were still using pagers. I call him back, and the guy's frantic. Says Sanabria and another guy had just checked into the motel, and that there were blood splatters on Sanabria's shirt and that he looked all disheveled and out of breath, like he'd just come out of a fight or something. They asked for a unit all the way in the back of the place and then pulled the car up right outside the door, and when they go in Sanabria carries a handgun in with him. This is good news, because he's a convicted felon and not allowed to have a handgun."

This time, Dunbar took more than a sip of the Scotch.

"I haul ass out to the motel. When I get there, the owner tells me somebody else showed up at the room and then drove away, but the car Sanabria and the other guy came in originally is still parked out front. So I go down there, with the owner, and bang on the door, and this guy named Johnny DiPietro answers. Remember that name. He's the guy that checked into the motel with Sanabria. I badge him and tell him I've got the owner there. I stand there in the door, and I say to the owner—this is your property, and I have consent to search. Right? He says yes. All this, DiPietro hears. So then I turn back to him, and I say, okay, you heard that, now are you going to make trouble? He shakes his head and steps aside, and then I say to him, *I repeat it carefully,* I say—do I have your permission to search the room, then? He tells me that I do, he tells me this in front of the hotel owner, who has also given consent, and, you know, it's *his* property anyhow."

Dunbar paused again. There was a flush building in his face.

"I search the room and find a gun and a shirt that's soaking in the shower, has blood on it. DiPietro is panicking now, but Sanabria is gone. He left with the other guy. We arrested him eventually, first for the handgun charge, and then later we got his fingerprints off the gun and a ballistic match to the homicide of a kid named Lamarca, who had just been shot that day. After that, we even got a blood match—Lamarca's blood was on Sanabria's shirt. We had that confirmed by the lab. Ballistic and blood evidence tying Sanabria to a homicide, and if nothing else we've got him on the gun charge."

He paused then, and it was quiet for a moment before Ken said, "So how the hell did he walk?"

I answered for Dunbar.

"DiPietro didn't rent the motel room."

Dunbar raised his eyebrows, then gave a short nod and lifted his glass to me. "Well done, Detective."

"You had ballistic and blood matches that you got through a good-faith search, though," Ken said, incredulous.

"He wasn't a cop," I told Dunbar. "Doesn't know the lovely law of the exclusionary rule."

"Fruit of the poisonous tree," Dunbar said, nodding. "Sanabria, piece of shit that he is, is legally entitled to privacy in a motel room that he rented. If he wants to leave a homicide weapon and a bloody shirt in that room, he's allowed to do that in private. It's his reasonable expectation. Fourth Amendment right."

Ken looked shocked. "You had consent from an occupant and the *property owner.*"

"I know," Dunbar said. "I thought that would be enough. I really did. I knew there was a chance the owner might not be able to grant consent to a rented room without a warrant—honestly, I wasn't sure about that, which I probably shouldn't admit, but then I'm not a lawyer. That's why I used him to bait DiPietro into opening up, though, because I figured DiPietro had to believe it was the owner's right. What I didn't count on was DiPietro being a visitor and not the registered guest. It was Sanabria's room, legally. That means nobody else could give consent."

"So he walked?"

"Yes."

Dunbar put the glass down on the coffee table. "Well, I suppose you don't care about that. I suppose that's not relevant. What you're interested in, I imagine, is how I happened to get Joshua Cantrell killed."

He said this through his teeth, eyes still on the glass. Ken and I were silent.

"So I had Sanabria once and couldn't deliver," Dunbar said. "There's your background. That's all that really need be said. The details, well, the details are mine to worry about, not yours. The point is, we went back after him again. I went back after him. I also went to Joshua Cantrell."

"As an informant?" I said.

"That was the original idea. It didn't go well. Not only did he refuse to talk with us about Sanabria, he insisted he didn't know anything about the man. Said he only knew what his wife told him, and that was old news. His impression was that we knew more of the family he'd married into than he did."

"Did you believe him?"

"Actually, I did. In any event, it was clear he wasn't going to cooperate, so we didn't waste any time on him. I kept tabs on him, though. Made the occasional call. We did that sort of thing with the idea of keeping the pressure up, both on Cantrell and Sanabria. We wanted Sanabria to know that we were always around, always talking to the people who surrounded him, looking for a chink in the armor."

"Was Alexandra a part of this?" Ken asked.

He shook his head. "She wouldn't have anything to do with us. Joshua, though, was almost as scared of us as he was of Sanabria. So while he didn't help, he also didn't refuse to communicate. He was afraid to do that. Now, as I said, we'd check in with him every so often. I caught him alone one day when I came out to their house to show him some photographs. No reason at all that he or Alexandra would be able to ID anyone in the photos, but we wanted to rattle Sanabria's cage a little. He *hated* it when we talked to his family, but we could pretend it was necessary investigation, not harassment. Truth was, we just wanted him sweating.

"So this time, Joshua seemed a little different. He looked at the photographs, told me he didn't recognize any of the people in them, which was of course true, but he was cooperative, too, and as I was leaving he made a remark about wishing he *could* help, and it sounded genuine, and almost angry. We talked for a while, and he told me about the new houseguest they had, a guy who'd done a long stretch for murder. Mark Ruzity."

"Are you saying he wasn't in favor of the hands-on approach his wife brought to the mission?" I said.

"I'm saying he was absolutely opposed to it. The phrase he used was 'she's bringing them into our home.' Apparently against his strongest objections."

"So you made a suggestion," I said. "A pitch. If he was willing to help with Sanabria, why not take advantage of the situation."

His nod seemed embarrassed. "It was almost a joke. On that day, in that conversation, it really was almost a joke. I mean, it was that ludicrous—place an informant in Sanabria's sister's home and use her husband to work him? Crazy, right?"

"But he agreed," Ken said.

"No. He rejected the idea, emphatically, and as time passed, I stopped dropping in on them, refocused in other areas. Then he came back to me. Contacted me by phone and asked if we could meet in person. He seemed very nervous, very agitated. So I drove out to a restaurant in Shaker Heights and met him, and he told me that he'd reconsidered."

"Why the change of heart?" Ken asked.

Dunbar frowned. "The motivation, I'm afraid, was anything but noble. What led him to pick up the phone and call was a complete collapse of his marriage, I believe. His wife wasn't aware of it yet, but that's what it was." He cocked his head at us. "What do you know about Joshua?"

"Quiet, academic sort," Ken said. "Interested in the prison system."

"*Interested*," Dunbar said and nodded. "He was interested in it as a student, not as a participant. Here's what I can tell you about Joshua—he was a nervous man, a scared man. Insecure. I believe that played a role when he met Alexandra. He saw her fascination with those issues of rehabilitation and reentry, and he ran with it. She was a beautiful woman, and a rich one, the sort who had never before given him the time of day. What more motivation did he need?

"Joshua's vision of their married life was that his wife's obsession would pass, or that a few papers, maybe some small donations, would satisfy it. He was wrong. I'm not surprised the final straw came when she began to hire inmates to work for them. As I've said, he was an insecure man. I think those insecurities took his imagination to some wild, dark places."

He looked directly at me with a sudden, sharp gaze. "Understand this—while I sit here and discuss the man's paranoia, I didn't do anything at that time except feed it. I'm not proud of that, but I won't lie about it, either. He felt betrayed by his wife, pushed aside in favor of murderers and thieves, and he wanted to hurt her. That was the sum of it. He wanted to *hurt* her, but he didn't know how. What could he do? Leave her? Then he'd lose everything. Have an affair? He was an awkward, introverted man, hardly capable of becoming a crusading Casanova. Withhold his money? He didn't have any. Alexandra was so much stronger than he was in virtually every way a person can have strength. He saw no way to strike back, no way to retaliate for what he viewed as disregard and betrayal. Until he found my card."

It had started to rain, and the wind was blowing even stronger now. Dunbar turned his head and looked out at the tossing lake.

"He was going to feed you information about his brother-in-law?" Ken said.

"I'm sure he would have been happy to do that," Dunbar said, looking back at us, "provided he knew anything, but he didn't. No, he remembered my earlier proposal, the one I'd made as a throwaway line, about seeing that one of the inmates placed in their care was someone who could snitch."

"Enter Salvatore Bertoli," I said.

"What did he know?" Ken asked. "What was he supposed to know, at least?"

"I told you to remember Johnny DiPietro's name from that story about the hotel. Well, Sanabria and he were both partners and rivals. We heard rumors that Sanabria wanted to clip him even before the motel arrest. After the way DiPietro stood pat and didn't talk he eased up on it temporarily, but before long they were at odds again."

"Over what?"

"Key issues were drugs and associates. Sanabria was very reluctant to be involved with the drug trade at any level. Had heard too many stories about how it brought down his mob buddies all over the country. DiPietro was all about it. DiPietro was also not only willing to network outside the Italians but enthusiastic about it. Sanabria, being old school, didn't support that or trust it. One of the reasons Sanabria was so furious with DiPietro was his tendency to trust people like Bertoli who committed ignorant, poorly thought-out crimes. He also was at odds with him over his desire to move into the east side drug market, which was generally black territory. Eventually the feud boiled over and Sanabria had him whacked. Bertoli was a witness."

"How did you know that?"

"Wiretaps. We got lucky. Almost got lucky, I should say. Caught a conversation between Bertoli and another guy—who's actually in prison now—and Bertoli started in on DiPietro, saying he knew what happened, but his buddy was smart enough to shut him up and get off the phone. Still, it was clear he'd seen it."

"You didn't question him?"

"Of course, but he didn't talk. He was facing prison time on another charge, and we thought we might be able to leverage him then, but . . ." He shrugged. "Sanabria's not the sort of person you want to snitch on. There was a side element, too. When DiPietro was killed, a significant quantity of heroin and coke disappeared. We had credible information that he'd bought into the supply end of things, that he intended to push his influence into the east side drug trade. This was in direct conflict with what Sanabria wanted, and when the hit was made, the drugs seemed to vanish."

"Bertoli's other charge was for beating the shit out of the truck stop guy and stealing his drugs," I said. "You think he went after DiPietro's product?"

"All we're sure of is that the product seemed to disappear from Italian hands. My guess is Sanabria claimed it and got rid of it. Sold it to someone else, outside of his circle, probably. Maybe just destroyed it. He didn't trust drugs."

"Let me be clear on the time line," Ken said. "DiPietro was killed *after* Bertoli was arrested and went to jail, but you somehow think he was a witness? That makes no sense."

"He wasn't in jail yet. He'd been charged, bonded out, and was awaiting trial. Then DiPietro was murdered, Bertoli witnessed it, and we came back at him hard, pushing for him to talk. He panicked and took the plea bargain and did his time. You want to know why? Because he was afraid of Sanabria. He thought going to jail would prove his trustworthiness, prove that he'd kept his mouth shut. He thought, gentlemen, that jail was the safer place to be. As I just said, Sanabria is not the sort of person you want to snitch on."

"You understood that, but you still decided to try again with Cantrell?" I said. "If Bertoli didn't give Sanabria up to avoid prison, why would he do it after he got out?"

"I should have turned him away?" Dunbar snapped. "A potential source of Cantrell's level comes to me and offers to help and I should have turned him away? That's what you think?"

I waited a few seconds, wanting to diffuse the tension, and then spoke as gently as I could. "I'm not second-guessing you. I'm just trying to conceive of the situation—all of them living in that house, working against one another. You turned it into a damned gothic mansion, Dunbar. How surprised could you have been when it imploded?"

"Sanabria had been a target of our investigation for years. *Years.* We'd had him once, and he slipped out, and we were determined to have him again and make it stick."

How'd that work for you? I wanted to ask, but neither Ken nor I spoke, and for a long time all you could hear was the wind.

"I don't feel like that was the end of your story," Ken said eventually. "You told us you got him killed. Who killed him, and why?"

"Sanabria, of course. For the obvious reason. Can I prove that? No. If I could have, that bastard would be in prison where he belongs. So, yes, what you're thinking is right—I screwed up again, and he laughed his way through it again."

"That's not what I was thinking," Ken said.

"Well, it should be. It damn well should be."

"How did it happen?" I said. "Did you have no idea things were going wrong until they disappeared, or . . ."

"I had an idea, but it all went to hell pretty fast. Joshua Cantrell was clumsy in his attempts with Bertoli, displayed his true intentions too early and awkwardly, and Bertoli took off. Moved out of the house. Joshua called to notify me of that, and I thought, well, there's another missed opportunity. That's all that I thought. That we'd taken another swing, hadn't made contact, but no big deal. Then a week later Bertoli was dead. As soon as I found out about that, I went looking for Joshua. He and his wife were gone."

"How are you so sure it was Sanabria, then?" Ken said.

Dunbar frowned. "Did you miss the summary your partner gave? That bit about the gothic mansion? To use his word, it imploded. It surely did. Think about it—we were attempting to get information about Sanabria, we panicked Bertoli, and then he was killed and the Cantrells vanished. Where do you think the blame rests?"

Ken didn't answer. Dunbar stared at him for a moment, and then he said softly, "That's a poor question. The blame, as I've already told you, rests here. Rests with me. But the bloodshed, Mr. Merriman? That's not my doing. That's Dominic Sanabria."

"You must have questioned him," I said. "Tried to connect him to Bertoli's death."

"Of course we did. True to form, he had an alibi seven layers deep. Actually, calling it an alibi wouldn't be fair. He didn't kill Bertoli personally—I'm fairly certain of that—but he had it done. I am even *more* certain of that."

"Then who got the call?" I said, thinking Harrison or Ruzity. "Who carried out the orders?"

"That one, I cannot answer. Only one person alive can. Sanabria himself—and good luck getting him to tell you."

"Two people," I said.

"Pardon?"

"Sanabria could answer it, and so could the person he used. That's who we're looking for."

"I'm not going to be much more help with that," Dunbar said. "You should talk to the detective who got the Cantrell case in Pennsylvania. Graham."

I raised my eyebrows. "You know Graham?"

"Not well. I've had this same conversation with him, that's all." Then, seeing the rise of anger in my face, he said, "Surely you didn't think you were the first people to make these connections?"

"Not anymore," I said. Part of me was embarrassed for being naive enough to believe just that, but more of me was pissed off at Graham. I'd told him I'd help provided I was given the real score, understood the situation as well as he did. The lying prick had promised me that was the case.

"You're sure Sanabria killed Joshua Cantrell, or had him killed," Ken said to Dunbar.

"That's right."

"Well, what about Alexandra?" I said. "Do you really think he murdered his own sister, or do you think she's still alive somewhere?"

"That," John Dunbar said, "is the one question I've been wondering about for the past twelve years."

19

I never knew my mother, but I know plenty of her expressions. She died when I was three, hit by a drunk driver at noon on a Sunday. She'd just left church; he'd just left a tip for the waitress who delivered his fifth Bloody Mary. Ordinarily, we'd have all been in the car together, but my sister and I were sick, sharing some sort of virus, and my father stayed home to watch us. Mom decided to go by herself. Every now and then, generally when my mind's immersed in something, I'll have a sudden sense that I can remember her voice, that I can *hear* the way she spoke. Then my conscious brain shifts over to try to trap it and it's gone. Just that quick. I'll hear her cadence perfectly in some secret lobe of memory, try to focus on it, and scare it off. She's in there somewhere, though. I know that she is.

While the voice eludes me, the expressions do not. My father recalled them often when I was growing up, and in a way that's how she came to exist for me: *Your mother always said . . .*

One favorite phrase, evidently, was head-spinner. As in, *How was your day? Well, it was a head-spinner.* It was how she referred to those days when things came too fast, too unexpected, too complicated.

My day? One hell of a head-spinner.

We'd gone out that morning thinking that Mark Ruzity might be able to give us some insight into the Cantrells. Instead, he'd given us John Dunbar, which at the time had felt like a significant breakthrough. Felt even more like that when Dunbar poured himself a Scotch and settled in to explain how he'd gotten Joshua Cantrell killed. Then he'd delivered the capstone: *Talk to Detective Graham; of course he already knows this.*

A head-spinner.

Had we gained anything? As I sat on the roof watching the sun fade and streetlamps come on and waiting for Amy to arrive, I tried to determine that, and couldn't. A hell of a lot of information had come our way, and that felt like progress. The realization that Graham already had the information, though . . . yeah, that pretty well killed the sense of progress.

A head-spinner. You bet your ass.

I'd dropped Ken at his hotel and left him on his own for the night. Inhospitable, maybe, but I felt a strong need to be away from him and Graham and Dunbar and anyone else who'd ever heard of the Cantrells. We'd meet again in the morning, and then we'd see where it stood. Graham was the one who could tell us that. He hadn't answered when I called him, so I left a message informing him we'd made a major break and he needed to drive up the next morning to discuss it. Since then, he'd called five times and I hadn't answered or called him back. He probably wanted to avoid the trip, and I wanted him to make it. The son of a bitch could explain his lies in person.

Couldn't be mad at him for lying, though. That's what Joe would tell me. I was a civilian, Graham was a cop. Why would he tell me everything he knew? When had I ever done that for a civilian? It was a game, all of it was, and Graham was playing one version with me while I played another with Harrison. I wondered who in the hell kept track of the big board, though.

It was full night when Amy finally arrived, and we sat together as the temperature dropped. No radio tonight, no baseball game. Just talk, lots of it, the two of us tossing questions but no answers.

"You know who I feel sorry for?" Amy said after one long lull. She was curled up tight in her chair, sleeves pulled down over her hands, clearly freezing but not willing to speak of going inside until I did.

"Lincoln Perry, for getting sucked into this nightmare?"

"No, you're doing a good enough job of feeling sorry for Lincoln Perry tonight."

"This is why I gave up being single. Support like that."

"Stop. You know it's true. I've never seen anyone get as melodramatic over anything as you do when you've been lied to."

I smiled. "It's my subtle way of ensuring you always tell me the truth."

"Subtle, sure. Now, can I say who *I* feel sorry for? Alexandra. I mean, step back and think about it. This woman comes from a family that should have its own HBO series, she somehow emerges sane and motivated to help people, and when she tries to do that her husband turns against her, tries to betray her brother, and gets himself killed. All of this just to hurt her."

"Her brother talked about her as if she's alive," I said. "If that's true, how does he know it? And if that's true, how much does she understand?"

Amy tried to nod but lost it in midshiver as the wind picked up. I got to my feet, pulled her up and toward me, and wrapped my arms around her and rubbed her back. She was shaking against me.

"You look like you're ready to go in," I said.

"Only if you are."

I laughed. "Okay, *that's* support."

I turned, ready to move for the stairs, but she stopped me.

"Imagine what that would feel like," she said, her voice muffled against my chest.

"Imagine what?"

"If she is alive, and she does understand. If she knows that her brother killed her husband, and if she knows why it happened."

I didn't answer, just took her hand and guided her toward the steps. The wind was blowing harder now, and I was feeling the cold, too.

Graham rose to the bait. When I finally played his messages the next morning, he cursed me for not returning his calls, then said he'd be up, though not until afternoon. He sounded curious, and I was glad. We didn't have a damn thing that was new to him, but if he wanted to jerk me around, I was happy to return the favor.

Ken came into the office ten minutes after I did, with a cup of coffee in each hand and a stack of papers held between his chin and his chest. He swung the door shut with his foot, set one cup down in front of me, and then lifted his chin, spilling the papers across my desk.

"Thanks."

"No problem."

I took a drink of the coffee and waved at the papers he'd dumped on the desk. "So what's all this?"

"When do you think that first bust with Dunbar and Sanabria went down?" he said. "The one that got screwed up by the informant and the motel room?"

"A while ago. He was talking about using a pager."

"Try twenty years."

"*Twenty?*"

"I was surprised, too. Dunbar talked about it like it had been a few years, right? Not twenty of them."

"I don't suppose it changes anything," I said, gathering the pages into a stack and pulling them toward me. "How'd you find that out?"

"Library. They've got good newspaper archives."

"You went last night?" Now I felt guilty about blowing him off, spending the night with Amy while he was working.

"What else am I going to do? Can only watch so much ESPN."

He'd apparently printed out every article mentioning Sanabria or Dunbar or Bertoli, and it amounted to quite a collection. I flipped through them, skimming most, reading a few completely. Dunbar's account seemed accurate enough.

"Dunbar's been around for a long time," I said, looking at the dates on the articles that referenced him. They started in the late seventies.

"Yeah, he has. Tell you something else that stood out to me from those articles—Bertoli's death was ruled an accident. We already knew that, but reading it again made me think about how firm Dunbar was on the idea that the guy was murdered. He was white on rice with that, you know? Which makes me wonder—if there was an FBI agent involved who knew all the background, and believed Bertoli was murdered, then why rule it an acci-

dent and close the door to an investigation? Why weren't the cops out look-
ing for the Cantrells years ago as witnesses for the Bertoli case? Joshua
Cantrell's parents told me that the police brushed off the idea of a crime.
How could they do that, if what Dunbar told us is true?"

"All good questions," I said. "Bertoli died in Cleveland, didn't he?"

"Yes. Warehouse district, down by the river."

"So it was Cleveland police jurisdiction. Who had the case?"

"His name is in there."

I found the article and read through it, and nodded as soon as I got to the
lead investigator's name—Mike London. I knew he'd take my call.

"How about we get you some answers to those questions while we wait
on Graham's arrival, Kenny boy?"

"Sounds good, Linc. Sounds good."

Mike London always reminded me of a circus bear—enormous and threatening, but a crowd-pleaser at heart. He was one of the better-known wise-
asses in a department full of them, but he was a good detective, too. Didn't have
the sort of mind that Joe or some of the others had, that gift for problem solving, but he compensated with a good eye for detail and a dogged work ethic.
Give Mike thirty leads at the start of the day, and he wasn't going home until
he'd tried all of them, and a few others generated along the way. That effort was
what kept him in favor with the brass despite his sense of humor, which superiors never found quite as hilarious as the rest of the department did.

He was out on the east side when I called, interviewing witnesses to a
drive-by shooting that had missed the intended target and wounded a
sixteen-year-old kid on Euclid Avenue the previous week, and said he'd give
us some time provided I bought him lunch. Mike's appetite had been the
stuff of department lore for years, so that was no small concession.

"Bertoli," he said when I agreed. "That's an old one, Lincoln. Old and cold."

"I know it. Just want to see what you remember about it."

"What I remember is that I did a bunch of interviews out Murray Hill way,
because that's where his family was. Say, you know what Murray Hill makes
me think of?"

"Food?"

"Hell, boy, you always were a good detective. Now, you want to ask me some questions, you can feed me out there at Murray Hill. That little Italian place."

"Murray Hill's nothing *but* little Italian places, Mike."

"The one with all the red, white, and green," he said. Real help narrowing it down. When I finally determined he meant Mama Santa's, we agreed to meet at noon.

Ken and I left early, largely by virtue of having nothing else to do. There'd been no more word from Graham, so I assumed he was still planning to show up that afternoon. If he came by while we were with London, he could wait. I wasn't feeling particularly gracious toward Quinn Graham.

We got to Murray Hill around eleven thirty, which meant we were in for a long wait, because London was never early and rarely on time.

"Here we are," I said as we drove up Mayfield Road and passed by Holy Rosary's brick facade and stained glass windows, the building more than a hundred years old now but still looking solid and clean. "Cleveland's fierce Little Italy. Do you want to go to an art gallery first or a bakery?"

"Yeah, yeah, I get it, not a threatening place anymore—but remember, we're here to talk about a murder. Speaking of murder—"

"I love that segue."

"Thought you would. I forgot to tell you, I checked my office voice mail last night. There was a message from an attorney representing Cantrell's parents."

"Did somebody call them to ask about what you're doing up here?"

"Nope. Wanted to inform me that I may be called for a deposition. They're trying to claim the property."

"That house?"

He nodded. "You've been out there, you know how much it must be worth. The thing's held free and clear in Alexandra and Joshua's names, but they're gone. So his parents want a piece of the estate."

"I don't see how they could get it if there's no proof that Alexandra is dead. The taxes are paid and current, there's no mortgage, no excuse to take it away from her."

"That's what I thought, but their attorney intends to file suit to have her declared dead. They're going to subpoena her attorney to see if he's had any contact with her in the last seven years. Apparently that's some sort of legal standard. They're sure nobody else has been in touch with her for that long."

It sounded crazy, seeking a courtroom ruling over whether or not a life still existed, but I supposed it was reasonable for them to try. Just the night before, Amy and I had wondered if Alexandra was still alive.

"Supposing Child says he hasn't heard from her in the last seven years, then . . ."

"They'll have to publish a notice of her presumed death. Run that for sixty days or something, I'm not sure of the specifics. If she doesn't respond in that time frame, and nobody else comes forward with proof of life, they can get a judge to rule that she's legally deceased. Once that's done, they can put a claim on the property."

I sat with my car keys in my hand and thought about the house, that arched doorway into the earth, the quiet that surrounded it. "They're going to sell it, aren't they?"

"I'm sure that's the idea. They aren't well-off."

It was tough to imagine anyone moving into the place. I tried to picture it—a moving truck parked outside under the trees, a family inside sorting through boxes, kids running around the grounds, ready to transform the empty home into someplace full of life. It didn't seem right.

"That's interesting," I said finally, when I realized Ken was still looking at me and I hadn't said anything for a long time. "I'll be curious to see what happens."

"She'll come back to it," he said.

"What?"

"I think Alexandra will come back to it if she's still alive."

"I don't know why she would."

"Because the place is a grave to her, Lincoln. It's a memorial. You have to see that. She left a home that's worth millions sitting empty and alone for twelve years. She had a damn epitaph carved beside the door. That place means something to her. So let me tell you—if she's alive, I bet she'll come back to see it again."

20

There are plenty of good restaurants on Murray Hill, but Mama Santa's pizzeria is one of the oldest and best known. Ken and I were ahead of the lunch crowd and got a table in the back of the dark, wood-paneled dining room.

"I hope Mike sits next to you," I said as we took our seats.

"He's that big?"

"Three hundred at least."

"That's not tiny."

"I knew a guy who worked a surveillance with him once, said Mike brought this feed bag of beef jerky along, like five pounds of the stuff. Went through that in the first hour, then spent the rest of the night bitching about how hungry he was. Guy said the longer the surveillance went on, the less he liked the way Mike looked at him, started to feel like he was out with the Donner Party."

Ken smiled as he leaned back from the table, stretched out his long legs, and crossed his feet at the ankles. "What's your best surveillance story? Or worst experience, rather. Those usually make the best stories."

"That's easy. I was in an unmarked car by myself not long after I switched

to narcotics and started working with Joe. This is early on, and Joe was something of a legend, so I'm trying to impress, right? Well, it's February, bad
snowstorm had just blown through, left it cold as a bastard, and my lovely
and charming fiancée—yes, I was engaged, and no, it didn't stick—she's feeling bad for me and decides to give me a present. One of these heated pads for
the car seat, you plug it into the cigarette lighter. I was embarrassed by the
damn thing since it didn't exactly feed the tough-guy image I was trying
to cultivate. I threw it in the car, though, because I didn't want to hurt her
feelings.

"So, the night of this surveillance, we sit on the guy's house for hours, and
nothing happens. Started in late afternoon, and now it's two in the morning
and our guy hasn't moved, which means neither have we. It's getting colder
and colder, just crawling into my bones, you know, and I figure, hell, might as
well use her gift for a little while, just long enough to warm up. I plugged it in
for maybe twenty minutes. Half hour at best."

Ken's smile widened as he saw where I was headed.

"Thing warms me up, and now I understand why—it must have been
burning watts like a set of stadium lights. I unplug it about an hour before
our guy moves. He comes out of the house and gets into his car, and I think,
finally, and turn the key."

"Click," Ken said, and laughed.

I nodded. "Click. Absolutely no juice, battery's dead. So I have to get on
the radio with Joe and say, uh, our boy's in motion, but I can't tail him until
I get a jump."

"You tell him what killed the battery?"

"Hell no. You kidding me? I spent the next three weeks bitching about
the shitty unmarked cars they gave us. Joe *still* doesn't know the truth about
that one."

"Nice."

"All right, your turn," I said.

"You'll like this—worst surveillance I ever went on was a fake surveillance."

"A fake surveillance?"

"I have—*had*, rather—a brother-in-law who I simply could not stand. He was older than my wife, had the protective big brother thing going on, but he was also just a dick, you know? Owned a car lot, made piles of money, told bad jokes and laughed at them way too loud. Only his own jokes, though. Never cracked a smile at anything anybody else had to say, but when *he'd* make a joke he always cut up, roared at his own dazzling wit. When we first got married, my patience with him could last about an hour. That's how long I could stand to be in the same room. That time frame diminished over the years."

"I can imagine."

"One Friday night my wife informs me that he's coming by for dinner, and I thought, oh, shit, not on a weekend. Because on the weekends he liked to hit the bottle, and when he did that, he lingered longer and laughed louder. So I thought, just tell one little white lie and give yourself a night off. Tell them you have to work, a rush surveillance job came up, and then go sit in a bar and watch a basketball game."

"Good plan."

"That's what I thought. When I came home that night, I planned to sell the story to my wife by picking up a tripod and acting real annoyed at this last-minute development. Well, the son of a bitch was already there. He'd shown up early. So he started asking a thousand questions about the surveillance, what it is that I do, all of that. I was edging for the door, he was following me with beer in hand, and just as I was about to escape, he turned to my wife and said, 'Hey, you wouldn't mind if I skipped dinner and tagged along with Ken, would you?'"

I started to laugh.

"Yeah," Ken said, nodding. "Of course she agreed to it. So now instead of dealing with this asshole over dinner in my own home, with my wife to distract him, I've got him alone, and in my car."

"Without any surveillance to do."

"Exactly. So I thought, well, what the hell can you do at this point but play it out? I drove us to some apartment complex, just picked one at random, and gave him a story about what we were watching for. We sat there for five hours, him drinking and talking and pointing at every car that came and went—'is that them, is that them?'"

"That's fantastic," I said. "A cautionary tale."

We traded a few more war stories while we waited. Ken asked if I had a surveillance theme song, and I had to laugh.

"A theme song? Are you kidding me? You play the *Mission Impossible* sound track when you're working?"

"Everybody should have a theme song," he said, unbothered, "and, no, mine's not the *Mission Impossible* sound track. Song's called 'Cold Trail Blues.' By a guy named Peter Case. Ever heard it?"

I shook my head.

"Thing speaks to me," he said with a faint grin. "Speaks about the Cantrells, too. All about some guy searching through the gloom, wondering if he'll ever find what he's looking for. Thinking it's too late, and he's too far behind."

"If that's your theme song," I said, "it's no damn wonder that you haven't found Alexandra yet. Encouraging shit."

His smile was hollow. "I'll burn you a copy."

When Mike finally entered, it was twenty past twelve. He wedged in through the door, lumbered across the room, extended his hand, and set to work crushing my fingers. A Mike London handshake was both a greeting and a warning, I always thought.

"How are you, Mike?"

"Hungry. I am hungry, Lincoln, my boy." He turned and cast an interrogator's stare down at Ken. "You're Pennsylvania?"

"Ken Merriman."

"From Pennsylvania," Mike said, as if that dismissed any need for Ken to have a name. A location would suffice. He dropped into the chair beside Ken and heaved his bulk up to the table's edge. I saw Ken trying to slide closer to the wall to make room for him, and I had to hide a grin.

"The way we got to Bertoli," I began, but Mike lifted a hand to silence me.

"I need a menu and a waitress. Then you can tell me all that shit."

We got him a menu and a waitress, and once the food was ordered he drained his glass of water as if it were a shot and said, "All right, get to it."

"Ken was hired by the parents of Joshua Cantrell a while back," I said. "Do you remember that story?"

"Guy went missing with his wife and was found last winter."

"That's him, yeah. We're trying to figure out how he ended up dead and in Pennsylvania, and where the wife went."

"We? How'd you get involved?"

It froze me for a moment, and even Ken gave me an odd look, because it shouldn't have been that difficult a question to answer. Eventually I forced a grin and said, "Just doing what I do, Mike. Just doing what I do."

His eyebrows knit together, as if he thought it was a bullshit answer or at least a strange one, and then he said, "Whatever. None of my business. Let's hear the questions."

"Seems the Cantrells were involved in an offender reentry program, had a bunch of parolees working out at their place, and Bertoli was one of them," I said. It was a cursory version, certainly, but that's all I wanted to give him right now. He didn't need to know about Harrison or Graham or Dunbar. Not yet.

"He was," Mike said, nodding his enormous head. He'd grown a beard since I'd last seen him, which added even more size. "You probably know that their vanishing act was almost simultaneous with Bertoli getting whacked."

"You say getting whacked," Ken said. "That's the perspective we've heard from some others, too, but the cause of death was given as an accident."

"That's right."

"Well, why wasn't there an investigation, if the evidence pointed to homicide?"

"There was an investigation, friend. I ran it. As for the death ruling, you got to look at physical evidence. That's the key. And the *physical* evidence didn't point to a homicide, necessarily. Guy took a fall off a warehouse, clipped his head on a Dumpster, then bounced off the pavement, and turned his face inside out. Nasty way to go, but the cause of death was the fall. That's something I won't dispute. Whether he took that fall willingly . . . I have strong feelings about that, but my strong feelings weren't going to get the cause of death changed. Fall killed him. What triggered the fall, we couldn't say for sure. No physical evidence to suggest that anybody pitched him off the roof. Someone could have, and probably did, but we couldn't prove that."

"There's an FBI agent named John Dunbar," I said, "who knew a hell of a lot about what was going on with Bertoli. Did he approach you?"

Mike smiled. "Oh, you know Dunbar, eh?"

"Uh-huh. You have some problems with him?"

"Not exactly. He was cooperative as hell once Bertoli was dead, but more hindrance than help. He might not have realized it, but other people did."

"What do you mean?"

"Dunbar told you what, exactly? About Bertoli?"

"That he was a potential witness against Dominic Sanabria, and Dunbar was working with Joshua Cantrell to get information out of him."

"He mention that he was retired at the time?"

"What?"

"Yeah, Lincoln. Dunbar was retired from the Bureau when all this shit went down. Everything he told you about his plan with Bertoli and Cantrell is accurate, but it was also unofficial. The Feds had no idea what was going on, because he wasn't working for them anymore. There was no law enforcement involvement, period. Dunbar's idea was that he'd go to them when he had something to show. Didn't pan out, did it?"

My disbelief turned quickly to understanding. The previous day I'd had trouble believing that the FBI could have implemented such a ludicrous plan, placing Bertoli in the home of Sanabria's sister and using Cantrell as an informant. Now I understood—the FBI *hadn't* implemented the plan. It had been Dunbar and Cantrell, working alone.

"That makes sense," I said. "Hell, that's the only way it makes sense. The whole idea was insane. If they never approved it, that means—"

"He was running his own show with Cantrell," Mike said. "Which tells you two things. One, the only official version is the one Dunbar provided, because everybody else who was involved is dead or missing, and, two, the man had a king-sized hard-on for Dominic Sanabria. I mean, he turned Sanabria into a retirement project? Pro bono prosecution? Crazy shit."

Ken said, "So everything Dunbar did with Cantrell was completely—"

"Unsupervised," Mike said. "Yes. When Bertoli took his header off the roof—with or without assistance—and Dunbar came forward with his story, you can imagine how elated his Feeb buddies were. Then the Cantrells bailed, and the whole thing started to smell even worse."

"So they squashed the investigation?" I said. "Are you kidding me? To protect Dunbar?"

"I wouldn't say that they squashed it, really. I mean, I did work the case for a while, and worked it hard. We couldn't get anything convincing to go on. Everybody understood that Sanabria probably had the guy killed, but we couldn't get a lead to work with. Bertoli was a piece of shit anyhow, nobody was crying over his loss, and the last thing the FBI wanted was Dunbar's story going public. Wouldn't have been anything criminal, but it also wouldn't have made them look good. A rogue retiree placing informants without anybody's knowledge, and then the informant gets killed? No, that wouldn't have made them look good."

"Nobody thought it was worth looking for the Cantrells?"

"We looked."

"Not very forcefully," Ken said. "The police told his family that they wouldn't investigate. Told them—"

"Cantrells left of their own volition. That's the way it looked at the time, at least. Packed a bunch of shit into storage and made arrangements for the house. There was no sign that one of them had been killed. Not until the body showed up."

"You said you worked the Bertoli case hard," I said.

"I did. Even if the death ruling wasn't a homicide, we treated it like one as soon as Dunbar came forward. You have to give the guy that much credit, too—at least he showed up and told the truth when Bertoli got killed. A lot of people wouldn't have the balls to do that. He had to know it wasn't going to go over well with his buddies at the Bureau. Took some swallowed pride to come forward, I'm sure."

"You never got anything that showed a connection between his death and Sanabria, though?"

"I got something, but it was weak. It wasn't enough to build a case on." He stopped talking as the waitress passed nearby and eyed her tray hopefully, then sighed with disappointment when she delivered the food to the table beside us.

"What did you get?" I said.

"Lasagna and—"

"Not the food, Mike. I mean on the case. What was the connection?"

"Oh, right. Well, there was a place across from the warehouse where Bertoli died that had parking lot surveillance cameras. It didn't show the scene, but it caught cars coming and going. Problem was, the street was fairly busy. In just one hour around Bertoli's time of death, there were sixty-two cars on the tape. I got all the plate numbers I could, ran registrations."

This was the sort of work ethic that Mike was famous for, a determined pursuit of any angle, no matter how long the odds.

"I got one car, and one car only, that had some possibility," he said. "A tricked-out Oldsmobile Cutlass, all sorts of custom shit on it, spinners and crap like that. The plate ran back to a Darius Neloms. Big D, as he is generally known."

I shook my head. "Doesn't mean anything to me."

"There's a bunch of Neloms in East Cleveland, and the whole family is nothing but pushers and hustlers. Darius runs a body shop over on Eddy and St. Clair."

"Tough neighborhood."

"You ain't kidding. These days, Big D's doing well for himself. Making money putting in hydraulics and fancy rims and stereos, all the toys that the young thugs like, makes 'em feel like they're in a rap video. There was a time, though, when he took a bust for running a chop shop. Taking in stolen cars, repainting them, adding some window tint, maybe changing the headlights or the grille, and sending 'em back out. He didn't take a hard fall because they had trouble proving he knew the cars were stolen. I'm sure that was crap, but the guys bringing him the cars worked for Dominic Sanabria and a guy named Johnny DiPietro."

"Later murdered," I said, "and Dunbar thinks it was by Sanabria, and Bertoli was a witness."

"You got it."

"You think Sanabria hired this Darius guy to kill Bertoli?" Ken asked.

"No way," Mike said. "He would've handled that in-house."

"It was his car at the scene."

"It was registered to him. One of about nine vehicles he had registered to him or his shop. When Bertoli died, Darius was at a party at a nightclub, which I verified by their security tapes."

"So maybe it's a meaningless connection," Ken said.

"Could be, but Darius Neloms was connected to Dominic Sanabria and Johnny DiPietro, had gone to jail for working with them on stolen cars in the past. If somebody in their crew wanted to borrow a car, Darius was a likely source."

"Why in the hell would they borrow a car," I said, "instead of stealing one?"

Mike smiled. "Look at the result. I spent time chasing leads on Darius—and don't kid yourself into thinking the Italians viewed him as some sort of compatriot. A bunch of racist fucks, those guys. They're not above working with a black guy to bring in some dollars, but they damn sure aren't going to worry about redirecting police his way, either."

"You talk to Darius?"

"Uh-huh, and got nothing. 'I own lots of cars, lots of people have access to them cars, no way I could possibly remember who might've been driving that car on that night.'"

"What was your sense of him?"

"That he was lying, of course—but was he lying with a real purpose? Guy like Darius Neloms, he doesn't necessarily need the extra motivation to lie to me. See a badge, lie to the badge."

"So that's where the case died?"

"That's where it died. I ran that up the ladder, you know, showing there was at least a weak link between one of the cars and Sanabria, but of course it wasn't enough. No evidence for a homicide, nobody talking to us, the FBI boys embarrassed by the whole thing because of Dunbar, it's almost surprising I got that far with it."

I saw the waitress headed our way again and figured this time the food would be ours, and that meant Mike wasn't going to be answering any more questions for a while. Best to slide in one more while I had his attention.

"A few minutes ago you made a good point, saying that Dunbar's version is the only official one, since the whole damn circus he put together was so *un*official."

Mike nodded, waiting.

"So I'm wondering—did you believe that version? That one unsupported but also unconfirmed version?"

Mike said, "Look, Dunbar was one of a group of FBI guys that did some righteous work on the mob around here. Put a lot of those boys in prison."

"But?"

"But Dunbar also wore a suit every day, and one of the rules I've developed after twenty years at this game, Lincoln, is never trust a man in a suit."

21

Amazing, the way one fact can change your entire perception of something.

John Dunbar was *retired* at the time he launched his plan with Bertoli and Cantrell? Nobody else approved it, or even knew about it? Yeah, that changed things.

His plan had been terrible, too, a perversion of an old cop game that had never worked well in my experience—planting a snitch in a jail cell. There were plenty of narcs in the prison system, and it was a tactic that had been used for decades, generally off the books, and rarely well. The problem was that the snitches lied, that they had no credibility in court, and that the targets were rarely anywhere near as stupid as required for the tactic to work. Joshua Cantrell had effectively played the role of a jail cell snitch in his own home, welcoming Bertoli in and trying to talk to him about a mob hit. Made it a great deal more difficult to be sneaky about that sort of thing when your wife was the sister of the suspect. They could have concealed that from Bertoli initially—and surely did, otherwise I couldn't imagine he'd have actually agreed to the parole assignment—but eventually it would have had to surface, wouldn't it?

Yes, it was stupid, and Dunbar had known that all along; otherwise he wouldn't have operated without FBI approval, and that made me wonder about both his motivations and his story. I hadn't doubted him at first, not in our initial talk, but at the time I had felt like everything he said was a breakthrough, had been almost overwhelmed by the story he told. Now I looked back on it, playing through the conversation again in my mind, looking for holes, signs of lies.

There were dozens of them. Maybe. Or the whole story could have been entirely truthful. No way to know because every other person who could confirm it was dead or missing, and had been for years.

Except for Parker Harrison.

He was on my mind during our drive back from Murray Hill, and because of that it didn't feel like much of a surprise when I checked the office voice mail and found a message from him.

The request was simple this time, no tips or names or suggestions. Harrison wanted to see me that evening, if possible, and he wanted me to be alone. He didn't leave any other details, just said he'd be home after five and repeated that he wanted it to be only me.

I played the message on speakerphone, so Ken heard it, too.

"Guy doesn't seem to like me, does he?" he said.

"Your client relationship does seem a bit strained."

"Because he knows damn well he's not really a client. The way we tried to play it didn't fool him. Not enough, at least."

"Not at all, would be my guess," I said.

There were no messages from Graham, even though we'd been late getting back from Murray Hill, almost two thirty, and Graham had predicted an arrival time of one. I assumed he would've called if he'd come in early, though; it was too long a drive to give up on us just because nobody was at the office.

I kept staring at the phone, even though the blinking message light was now gone, nobody but Harrison leaving words behind for me. I wished Joe would call, so I could throw all of this at him, let him offer some perspective. It had been a few days since we'd last talked.

"I'll tell you what," Ken said, "the more I think about it, the more I wonder what Harrison did out there. Or what he saw. We're making sense of everything else, slowly but surely. We understand Bertoli's role now, know that they were trying to use him as a witness and it went bad—but Harrison? I can't make sense of him. Not even close."

Nor could I. Or Graham, or Dunbar, or Mike London. A lot of people had considered Harrison, and nobody had made sense of him yet.

While I was staring at the phone and pondering Harrison, there were footsteps on the stairs, and then the door opened without any knock and Quinn Graham entered. He was dressed sharp—black pants with a gold shirt and black-and-gold tie, and when I looked at him I thought of Mike London's warning never to trust a man in a suit and smiled. Most detectives wore suits every day. Only a guy like Mike could distrust the daily wardrobe of his own peers.

"Happy to see me?" Graham said, noting my amused face.

"Sure, Graham. We're elated."

He shook hands with Ken and then took a chair, looked at me, and spread his hands. "Brother, this better be good. I'll tell you something about the drive between my home and here—it ain't pretty. Not gonna be on anyone's scenic route list real soon. I keep making it, though, because of you boys, because of Linc and Kenny. Hope you appreciate that."

"Graham, you'll be thanking us by the time you leave," I said. "We've made some breakthroughs for you, buddy. Big stuff."

"Yeah?" His interest was genuine.

"Yesterday we learned"—I threw in a pause, enjoying the impatience in his eye—"that Salvatore Bertoli was, in fact, placed in the Cantrell home by an FBI agent named John Dunbar."

I said this with heavy drama, straight-faced, as if I really believed he'd be impressed.

"He was believed to be a witness to a killing committed by Dominic Sanabria," I continued after another pause. "Joshua Cantrell was working with Dunbar to extract information from Bertoli. Evidently it did not work well."

Graham stayed silent.

"Pretty big stuff, eh?" I said.

"Right," he said, but the disgust was clear in his voice.

"What's the matter, Graham? You thinking about those hours you wasted on the road?"

"You know all of this is old to me," he said, "yet you made me drive up here."

"I know it's old to *you*, yes. It wasn't old to us, and it's something we wasted a day on, when you could have told us the same things in about fifteen minutes. So you want to worry about the time you spent driving up here, tough shit, man. You let us walk around like a couple of—"

"I didn't want you walking anywhere, Perry. Don't you get that? I don't know how you found Dunbar, but I wish you hadn't. If you'd have called—"

"I did call. Yesterday morning, after we got Dunbar's name and were standing downtown feeling like hot shit. It's embarrassing to admit now, but that's the truth of it. You got a problem with us talking to Dunbar? Well, you could've prevented that easy enough."

He sighed and leaned forward, then ran a hand along the side of his head and gripped the back of his own neck and squeezed as if he were trying to calm himself down.

"I know you were police, Linc," he said, "but you gotta realize, you are *not* police anymore. So when you get all fired up over shit you weren't told, slow down and think about the situation from my point of view, which is: I'm not telling anybody a *damn thing* that I don't have to. Ever. I'm trying to maintain control of my investigation."

It was exactly what I'd expected he'd say, but that didn't mean it pleased me.

"Graham, you asked for our help. Sat right there in that chair and asked for—"

"No, no, no." He looked up, shaking his head. "Didn't ask for anybody's *help*, Linc. What I asked for, and what I expected to receive, was your *cooperation*. Big difference, boy. You had access to Harrison, and that's where I wanted your cooperation. What I did *not* want, at any time, was for you two to go running around the city interviewing people and knocking on doors and potentially damaging my case. I as good as told you that, too."

"When?"

"I said that I was counting on you to keep him from stepping to trouble." Graham jerked his head at Ken, and I saw a flush of anger—or embarrassment—cross Ken's face. "Now I find out I should've been just as worried about you as him."

He sighed again, shook his head again, and then leaned back and loosened his tie. "Here's what I want out of you two, okay? Communication with Harrison. That's it, and that's all. I don't want you to *force* the communication, either. I just want to be aware of it. Tape the talks when he initiates them, and that's great. As far as street work goes, I don't want you on this."

"That's not really your call," Ken said.

Graham looked at him with wide, challenging eyes, his index finger still hooked in the knot of his tie. "It's not? You get in the way of a police investigation, and don't think I can shut you down? Boy, you don't even have a client."

"I do now," Ken said.

"Who?"

"Parker Harrison. He retained me through Lincoln. I believe that scenario was your idea, too."

Graham scowled and released his tie after one last angry jerk.

"Hang on a minute," I said as he was getting ready to start in on Ken again. "We can all fight this one out later. Fact is, Ken's got a client, and you gave it to him, Graham. Regardless, I don't think Ken has any desire to hinder what you've done, or what you're trying to do. If we don't know what that is, though, we're bound to cause you some headaches."

"I told you my reasoning."

"Yes, and I understand it, but what I'd like to hear you say is what you actually think of John Dunbar. I'm assuming you know he was retired at the time all this went down?"

Graham gave one last stare to Ken, not ready to let that battle fade so quickly, but then he returned his attention to me.

"Dunbar's straight," he said. "I know it doesn't feel right, but he's straight."

"How can you say that with any confidence when there's nobody around to support his story?"

"Nobody around to contradict it, either, but the fact is the man could not be more cooperative," he said. "The day after we ID'd the body as Joshua Cantrell, I got a call from Dunbar, wanting to fill me in. He initiated the contact. I had no idea who he was at that point, or what his connection was, and I would've wasted a lot of hours developing that. Instead, he drove out to see me, brought boxes of shit out with him, photos and notes that he'd taken. Left it all with me, for my review. If the man's got anything to hide, he's got a strange manner of hiding it. He was calling me a couple times a week for a while, throwing theories and suggestions until I stopped calling him back because he was underfoot so damn much. Hell, it was him that pointed me to Sanabria's phone records, showed he'd been in touch with Harrison."

"Did you make any attempt to verify his version of events?"

"Of course I did, and the man checks out, Linc. You want to do the same, go ahead. He served thirty years in the FBI, thirty *strong* years, and if you can get anyone to say a bad word about him, it'll be in the way things went with Bertoli."

"Well, I'd imagine. You've got someone murdering an FBI informant that nobody in the FBI knew was an informant, yeah, that's a problem."

"Sure it is. Everyone involved acknowledged that, both at the time and when I got in touch this year. That doesn't make Dunbar corrupt, though."

"What about Mark Ruzity?" I said. "The guy seems to have some anger issues. Put a chisel to my forehead while telling us the case was better off unsolved. Then Dunbar showed us a photo of him with Sanabria just days after the Cantrells vanished. How do you explain that?"

"I can't. You know who took that picture? Dunbar himself. He'd started following Sanabria after he realized Joshua was MIA. Yes, while he was re-tired. Yes, acting unofficially. I get your problem with that, Linc, I do, but I'm telling you the man is truly trying to help. Without him, we'd never know Ruzity and Sanabria had any association."

"So now you know that they do, but you don't know *why*."

"Not yet."

"Bertoli was openly connected to Sanabria's circle before he went into prison," I said. "Now we know that both Ruzity and Harrison had contact with him after they came out. What in the hell was going on in that house, Graham?"

"I'm not sure."

"Yet you want our help, and you expect to get it without telling us a damn thing."

Graham lifted his hands, palms out, and made a patting gesture. Soothing. *Step back, relax, everybody be happy.*

"Look, I understand your irritation, but what we need to make clear is that I can't afford to have you guys in my way. What've you done here, it's no big deal. Talking to Dunbar is nothing, but I can't have you keep after it. Eventually you may talk to the wrong person, maybe before I do, and then we've got a real problem."

"So you're telling us to stop the investigation?" Ken said.

"No, I'm telling you not to harm the *real* investigation. The one that'll get somebody arrested and convicted if it's done right, and will let 'em walk if it's done wrong. I'm here to see that it's done right."

"Which means—"

"Which means you probably ought to go on back home." He said it gently but met Ken's eyes. "That's no disrespect, Kenny. Okay? The truth of it is, man, there ain't nothing for you to do that the police can't do better."

Ken looked at me, eyes hot, as if he were waiting for me to jump into the fray and argue. When I stayed silent, he turned back to Graham.

"What *are* the police doing? A few days ago you were in here telling us how overstretched you are. Sounded to me like you needed the help."

"All right," Graham said, still with the temperate touch in his voice, "then why don't you tell me what you're going to do to help?"

Again Ken looked at me. "Detective work, Graham. That's what we're going to do."

"And that means?"

"Getting out on the street, talking to witnesses, running down leads," Ken said, anger in his voice now. He seemed to think Graham was talking down to him, patronizing, but I didn't read it that way. Graham was trying not to bruise egos, but the reality was he wanted us out of the way because he didn't think we could do anything but harm.

"All of which I've done, and will continue to do," Graham said. "You'll end up right where I am now, Kenny—staring down Sanabria and Harrison."

"So you're saying this one's unsolvable?" Ken said. "Time to put it under wraps, nothing left to do?"

Graham shook his head. "I intend to solve it. I think we will. We should have lab results from the body and the grave in a few months, maybe in a few weeks if we're lucky, and hopefully those will open up some doors. I expect that they will."

"So you want to shut us down," Ken said, "but at the same time you want us to communicate with Harrison. Well, the communication he wants is about our progress on the investigation. Going to be pretty difficult to sit around and chat with him if we're not doing anything."

Graham's jaw worked as he looked at Ken.

"He makes a fair point," I said. "You can't have it both ways, Graham. Either we're involved or we're not. You make the call."

"Okay—you're out."

Ken bristled, but I just nodded. "All right. I guess I better call Harrison, then, tell him tonight's meeting is off."

"You plan a meeting with him?"

"No. He called today and requested one. Seems he's got some things on his mind. Wanted to have a talk."

Graham was looking at me as if considering how satisfying it would be to pop my head right off my neck, but finally he sighed and nodded.

"Go talk to him, then. See what he says, get it on tape, and then call me. Do *not*, under any circumstance, talk to anyone else until you've cleared it with me. Got it?"

"Got it."

"While I'm here, I want a copy of the tape from your last talk, too."

"I burned it onto a CD for you."

"Good. At least I'll get something out of this drive." He stood up and reached for the CD. "You have any idea what Harrison wants?"

"None," I said.

Graham slid the CD into his pocket, then looked at both of us silently.

"Don't worry, Graham," I said. "You'll learn to love us."

"That's what my wife told me when she got a dog—and you know what?"

"What?"

"Time to time, dog still shits on my rug."

22

Ken wanted to ride out to Harrison's house with me, but I didn't like that idea. Harrison had requested a one-on-one meeting, for whatever reason, and I didn't want to irritate him by leaving Ken sitting in my car in the parking lot. So instead I left him sitting at a bar, with Amy for a conversation partner.

"You're not real good with the art of relationships," she observed as I drove her to the Rocky River Brewing Company, a microbrewery that was one of Amy's favorite drinking venues. "It's not exactly standard for a guy to take his girlfriend to a bar and drop her off with orders to entertain another man."

"I'm not telling you to sleep with him. Just buy him some drinks, maybe give him a shoulder rub."

"Yeah, it's a stunner that your fiancée ended up with another guy. A true puzzle."

By the time we got there, Ken was already at the bar, halfway through a beer called the Lakeshore Electric. He stood up when we approached, and I made introductions, wishing like hell that I could just stay with the two of them instead of driving off for yet another strange conversation with Parker Harrison.

"I'll head back this way when I'm done with our boy," I said to Ken. "Until then, watch your ass around Amy. She's a mean drinker."

By the time I got to the door, I could already hear her apologizing for me. It's not an uncommon occurrence.

Then it was back to Old Brooklyn, as the twilight settled in warm and still and with the wet touch of humidity that promised real summer. I kept the windows down and turned James McMurtry up loud on the stereo and thought that it would be a perfect night to sit in the outfield, watching one of those spring games that can't help but be fun because it's too early to feel much concern or disappointment over your team. Maybe if Harrison didn't want too much of my time, we could do that. I knew Amy would be up for it, and what else did Ken have to do?

By the time I reached Harrison's apartment, there was nothing left of the sun but a thin orange line on the horizon, the streetlights were on, and James McMurtry had just finished explaining why he was tired of walking and wanted to ride. I'd put the recorder and wire on before I left my apartment, and now I adjusted my collar and gave one quick look in the mirror to be sure the microphone wasn't visible. It wasn't. I got out and walked up to Harrison's apartment, found the window dark. The door opened at my first knock, though, and Harrison stood in front of me with a dish towel in his hands, his forearms streaked with moisture. Behind him I could see a light on in the kitchen, the living room gloomy with nothing but the fading daylight.

"Lincoln. Come in."

I stepped through the door, and he closed it behind me. Now I wanted a lamp on.

"You mind turning on a—"

"You both need to stop."

"What?"

"You and Ken Merriman. Tell him to keep the money. Or you keep the money. Either way, I think you both need to stop. Send him home."

"Why?"

He didn't answer but also didn't look away.

"Harrison? What the hell is going on?"

He wet his lips. "Lincoln, do you remember what I told you at first? The reason I wanted to find Alexandra?"

"You wanted to be in touch with her."

"No. Well, yes, that was part of it, but what I told you I wanted most was—"

"To know what happened. To know the story."

He nodded. "It's not worth it."

"Not worth *what*?"

He shifted his weight and dropped his eyes for the first time, saw the towel in his hands, and used it to dry his arms.

"Harrison, damn it, tell me what the hell is going on."

"It's not worth the potential for harm," he said.

"Harm to . . ."

"You, Ken Merriman, anyone else. Everyone else. At the end of the day, Lincoln, I think I made a mistake. She left because she wanted to leave, and if she hasn't been back . . . well, I suppose she wants to stay where she is. Right? Unfound and unbothered. If that's what Alexandra wants, then I won't fight for something contrary to it."

"I'm still not following this sudden worry about harm."

"It doesn't matter if you're following it. The last time we talked, you told me you didn't want to work for me, so now I'm giving you good news—I don't want you to work for me, either. Not you, or Merriman, or anybody else."

What had changed his mind? Something we'd done that he knew about? Had he seen us with Graham or Mike London, somehow developed the idea that we were working with police? Or was it entirely different and unrelated to us?

"Harrison—"

"This isn't a discussion. I appreciate your reconsideration, the way you brought an investigator to me, but I'm done."

Now I was more aware of the recorder and the possibilities that were about to be terminated when Harrison threw me out. We'd gotten nothing from him. Not a word that would help the investigation.

"What do you know about the Cantrells?" I said, taking a step toward

him even though there wasn't much space between us. "About what happened to them?"

"What I know isn't enough to matter."

"Bullshit. I saw your eyes when we mentioned Bertoli's name, Harrison.
Why?"

"Lincoln, there's nothing I can say."

"According to the police, that's always been your response. Nothing to
say—but it's a lie, Harrison, and you know it."

"You've talked to the police about me? To Graham?"

I hesitated only briefly. "Of course I did. You're a convicted killer, like it
or not, and you wanted me to look into a murder case. Don't you think that
raised some questions in my head?"

He stood where he was and looked into my eyes as if he were taking in-
ventory, and then he reached out with a quick and sure motion and grasped
the edge of my shirt collar, and tugged it back, tearing the first button loose.
As he did that, he ran his other hand down my spine, checking for a wire. I
tried to counter, shoving his hand away and stepping back, but it was too
late. His eyes had found the thin black wire, standing out stark against my
white skin.

"Whose idea?" he said. "Yours or Graham's?"

"Mine." I took a few steps back, feeling exposed now, vulnerable. He
hadn't moved again, but as I stood there in the dark living room facing him
I found myself wishing I had my gun. I hadn't brought it in because Harrison hadn't seemed the least bit threatening in our previous meetings. Now
his stance and his face made the Glock noticeably absent.

"Leave, Lincoln," he said. "Leave, and let it go. Don't let anybody else
keep you involved. Not Graham, not Merriman, not anybody."

I waited for a moment, staring back at a face that looked to be caught
between fear and anger, and then I went for the door. Harrison didn't move
as I opened it and stepped out.

I stood on the welcome mat in front of his apartment and blew out a
trapped breath and looked down at my shirt, the microphone dangling bare
and obvious. I took it off and untucked my shirt and slid the whole contrap-
tion out and kept it in my hand as I walked to my truck. When I started the

engine, the headlights came on automatically, shining directly into Harrison's windows. The glass reflected an image of my truck back at me, but beyond that I could see the shadows of Harrison's apartment, and his silhouette standing directly in the middle of the room, watching me. He was holding a phone to his ear.

23

I called Graham as I drove away from Harrison's building, got the phone out and dialed without pause because I knew if I stopped to think about it I'd delay calling him. He wasn't going to be pleased with this.

It took about twenty seconds of conversation before he confirmed that idea, breaking into a burst of sustained profanity that might have impressed me had I not been its target. No, he wasn't pleased.

"Graham, there's nothing I would have done differently," I said when he finally paused for a breath.

"*Nothing you would have done—*"

"No. There's not. It was nothing I said that convinced him I was wearing a wire; he was already pretty sure of it. The way he went for my shirt, Graham—he knew I was wearing one. He was sure he'd find it."

"Beautiful, Perry."

"I don't know what to say, Graham. Sorry it went like that, but it was your idea."

"My bad idea," he said. "I'll readily admit that. I let you and your buddy get into this, and I shouldn't have."

I kept the phone pressed to my ear as I hammered the accelerator and pulled onto the interstate, took it up to eighty-five before letting off. It was silent for a while, Graham's breathing heavy with irritation.

"Okay," he said finally. "Okay, it's done. It was a bad idea, and it didn't work, and maybe it did some harm. We can't really tell yet."

"I'm more interested in what changed his mind."

"What changed his mind was the fact that he knew you were trying to con him. What changed his mind was knowing you were taping every conversation."

There was biting accusation in every word, as if he thought I'd gone into Harrison's home with a microphone labeled POLICE PROPERTY in my hand and started asking him questions about Cantrell's death. I gave it a few beats of silence again, not wanting to let this turn into a clash of egos.

"I warned you after our first attempt that I thought he saw through it," I said. "Back then, you didn't want to believe me. That's fine. What I'm telling you tonight is, I don't think that's all there was to it. Something else rattled him."

"That's terrific, Linc. I'll find out what it was. In the meantime, you—"

"He called somebody as soon as I left. You might want to check that."

"How do you know?"

"He was standing with the phone to his ear when I drove away. Kind of curious who he felt deserved such an immediate call."

"Could be somebody called him."

"I didn't hear the phone ring."

"All right, look, I'll see about that, but as I was saying, *in the meantime*, you go find Kenny and you send him home. I want you both off of this, immediately. Like I said before, I take some of the blame. Maybe it was a bad idea from the start, but now it's done. I want you and him as far away from this as possible."

"I'm not sure how easy it'll be to convince Ken."

"It'll be damn easy when I arrest him for interference. You tell him that, and if he has a problem with it, you tell him to call me. He doesn't have a client anymore, and he's not licensed in Ohio. In other words, he's mine, Linc. If I want to shut him down, I can."

Not much was said after that. I disconnected, threw the phone onto the floor of the passenger seat, and drove back to the brewery. It was more crowded than when I'd left; I had to shoulder past people bottlenecked just inside the doors. Amy and Ken were where I'd left them, though, fresh pints on the bar in front of them. They were facing each other, and Ken was grinning at Amy's animated words.

"Hey," she said, turning when she saw Ken's eyes go over her shoulder to me. "I was just explaining my favorite psychological phenomenon to Ken."

"Which one is that?"

"The way the world's most pathologically narcissistic people seem drawn to careers in newspaper management."

Ken started to laugh, but then he stopped, eyes still on me, a frown replacing his smile. "Didn't go well with Harrison?"

I shook my head and leaned on the bar in between them, gesturing at the bartender for a beer. "Didn't go well, no."

"What happened?"

I told them about it while I drank the beer. When I got to the part about Harrison finding the wire, Amy sighed and turned away from me, fear disguised as anger.

"Not your fault," Ken said, shaking his head. "He didn't have to find the wire. He already knew."

"That's exactly what I told Graham."

"Oh, you already talked to him? What'd he have to say?"

I took a long drink of my beer, staring up at the TV. Indians had been up one when I walked in, and now they were down two.

"Well?" Ken said.

"He wasn't happy. Spent a while swearing at me and calling me incompetent before he decided to man up and accept part of the blame, realized it was probably a silly ploy to try in the first place."

"He say what comes next?"

"I assume it'll be back to waiting on the lab work. He seems pretty convinced that's where any break will come from."

"What about us?"

I finished my beer, slid the glass across the bar. "We're done."

"What?"

"He told me in no uncertain terms that we are to stay away from this."

"That's not his decision."

I didn't say anything.

"Is it?" he said. "Lincoln? You want to let that guy back us off?"

"It's not that simple, Ken. He can if he wants to. We don't have a client anymore. If he wants to jump up and down and scream about interference and tampering, he can do that. I don't think he wants to, but I also don't think he's going to let us keep digging on this without a fight."

Amy was quiet, watching us, and I could imagine Ken's expression from the concern in her eyes. This case mattered to him. I knew that by now; he'd made it damn clear. Still, I didn't know what else to tell him.

"So you want to stop?" he said. "This is the end? Go home and forget about it?"

"I'm not saying that."

"Yeah, you're not saying *anything*. What do you think, Lincoln?"

I drummed my fingers on the bar, not looking at either of them for a minute. The bartender pointed at my empty glass and gave me a questioning eye, and I nodded at him. I didn't speak again until the fresh beer was in my hand.

"I think that you care about this one too much to go home and forget about it—but I also want to point out that it's been twelve years since they took off, and six months since his body was found. Plenty of time's already passed, right? So I don't see the harm, really, in letting it breathe for a few more weeks. Let Graham get his lab results. On a case this old, the breaks usually do come from the lab."

"What if they don't?"

"If they don't, we figure out how to move forward, yet after talking to Graham tonight, I think it's a good idea to let it breathe, Ken. At least for a few weeks. We want to assist the police investigation, not slow it down by fighting with them."

He was quiet, clearly unsatisfied. He looked up at Amy as if searching for support, then flicked his eyes down when he didn't find any there.

"So I head home," he said.

"I'm not telling you that. Graham is. Although I think there's probably more smoke than fire to that. Besides, he's angry."

"You just said you wanted to let it breathe."

I shrugged.

"Basically, Graham wants me out of it. Right?"

"It wasn't a one-person decree."

He shook his head. "Maybe not, but I'm the one he doesn't trust in it. What was it he said today? Something about how he'd essentially asked you to babysit me, make sure I didn't cause any trouble. That makes sense, too. I can't fault him for that. You've got the experience on a real investigation. I don't. Hell, I'm the one who already had a shot at this and couldn't come up with a damn thing to show for it, right?"

"Nobody else has, either."

"I guess I can take comfort in being part of a group failure." He sighed and rubbed a hand over his eyes. "So what's your take, then? Should I listen to him and pull off?"

"Let's figure it out tomorrow. Come to the office in the morning and we'll talk."

He nodded, but the energy had gone out of the night, all of us quiet now, flat.

"Hey." I slapped the bar, got both of them to look up. "I think we should tie one on tonight. Go downtown, hit some bars. Got six innings left to play, we could even buy some cheap tickets and watch the end of the game. Drink to crazy graveyard groundskeepers and asshole cops."

"And pompous, untalented editors," Amy said, lifting her glass, trying to fall in line with my forced enthusiasm. "I'm game."

Ken gave an empty smile and shook his head, standing and reaching for his wallet. "I'm out," he said. "Sorry. Not tonight."

"Oh, come on," I said. "What else do you have to do?"

"Call my daughter, for one thing."

"So call her, and then we'll go out. Show you what this beautiful city of Cleveland is all about."

"Not tonight, Lincoln. I think I'll head back to the hotel and go over my case file, make some notes."

"How many times have you been over that file? What's going to be gained from one more look?"

"You never know. Maybe I'll shake something loose yet. Convince Graham he's making a mistake." He tossed some money on the bar, then put out his hand. "We'll talk tomorrow, right?"

"Absolutely," I said, shaking his hand, then watching as Amy stood up to do the same. "Come on down to the office, and we'll get things figured out."

It didn't feel like enough, though.

Last words never do.

24

It took a while for me to determine anything was wrong. I lingered at the bar with Amy long after Ken left, and when we finally departed it was for her apartment and a night that began in the shower and ended in the bedroom. I was aware of her moving around the next morning but managed to tune it out and return to sleep, didn't come fully awake until almost nine.

By the time I returned to my own apartment, showered, shaved, and dressed, it was nearly ten, and when I finally got to the office I expected Ken might be waiting. He wasn't, but a voice mail from him was. His voice was hurried, almost breathless.

Lincoln, I think we've got something. You got us there, we just needed to see it. Last night, I finally saw it. I'm telling you, man, I think you got us there. I'm going to check something out first, though. I don't want to throw this at you and then have you explain what I'm missing, how crazy it is—but stay tuned. Stay tuned.

I called him immediately. Five rings, then voice mail.

"What in the hell are you talking about?" I said. "Get your ass down here and tell me what you've got cooking."

I hung up and sat and stared at the phone, both impatient and irritated. My excitement was up, certainly—or at least curiosity—but I also didn't like being shut out so suddenly. He'd come all the way up here to ask for my help, practically beg for it, and against all better judgment I'd cooperated. Now he felt like he had a break and he'd gone off to field it solo? It was a greedy move, and I'd known some other investigators who pulled it when they had a chance for glory. This case was Ken's baby—he'd been working it for twelve years, not me—but I still wasn't impressed.

Thirty minutes passed. I called him again, got voice mail, didn't leave a message. Waited an hour, called again, left another message, hearing the annoyance in my own voice and not caring. It wasn't just a greedy move, I'd decided, it was a damned foolish one. With his total lack of experience on homicide cases, he could screw this up. Whatever *this* was.

Noon came and went, and I thought about lunch but didn't go for it, not wanting to leave the office phone. I was seething over the fact that he'd called the office line instead of my cell anyhow. He'd wanted to be sure he got a head start on this thing by himself, which was bullshit. I didn't give a damn who got the credit, supposing he *had* made a break—though that seemed like one hell of a long shot to me—but it was my ass that was on the line with Graham.

At two o'clock, Graham called. I recognized his number and hesitated before answering, part of me afraid he was already aware of whatever Ken was attempting and pissed off about it, another part thinking it was my job to warn him. Either way, it wasn't a conversation I wanted to have, but I answered.

"I don't know whether I should give you blame or credit," he said, "but whatever you did to stir Harrison up, he's in action again. That could be good or bad."

"What do you mean, he's in action?"

"I checked the phone call from last night. The one you mentioned."

"Yeah?"

"He called Sanabria."

Neither of us spoke for a minute, just sat there across the miles holding our respective phones and considering the possibilities.

"Okay," I said. "That's one call. Right after I left. Right after he'd told me to hang it up. Were there any others?"

"Uh-huh. One more, made day before yesterday, in the evening."

Just before Harrison had called me to ask for a meeting.

"Sanabria told him to get rid of me," I said.

"Possibly."

"How did he know I was working with Harrison to begin with? You said there hadn't been any other calls between them. Not since the body was discovered."

"They don't always have to use the phone, Linc. In fact, I'm surprised they do it this often."

"I guess."

"Another possibility is your buddy."

"Ken? Are you crazy?"

"Linc, you remember how he found his way to you?"

I was quiet.

"Sanabria," he said. "Right? Dominic Sanabria called him. That's what he told you, that's what he told me. So they've been in communication. Who says it stopped with that call?"

"Do you have any records saying it didn't?"

"No."

"Then I'm not—"

"Remember, there are plenty of other ways they could have had contact. Face-to-face, through an associate, e-mails, other phones. All I'm saying is let's not rule Kenny out of the mix entirely. He around?"

"No."

"Gone home?"

"No. He's in the field."

"In the *field*, you say? Doing what?"

"I have no clue."

"Excuse me?"

I told him about the message and said it was the only thing I'd heard from him all day. He responded, as expected, by reaming me for letting Ken head off into unknown avenues of investigation. My patience wasn't strong enough to take it today.

"I'm not his caretaker, Graham. I don't know the guy any better than you do, and if you want somebody monitoring him, you better get an officer on it. Last night, I told him I was done. That it was time to back off. If he doesn't do that, it's your problem, not mine."

The words sounded childish, petulant, and that only contributed to my growing anger. It had been directed at Ken originally, for cutting me out, now at Graham for blaming me for that, and only built after I hung up the phone. Another hour passed before I finally forced myself to admit that another emotion was bubbling beneath the surface: fear. I was beginning to hear the first drumbeats of dread. Where was Ken?

In the next hour, I called his cell six times and got voice mail every time. I left two messages, then called his hotel and asked to be put through to the room. Again, just rings and a voice mail option.

At twenty till five, I got in my truck and drove to his hotel, went up to room 712 and pounded on the door. No answer. I took the elevator back down to the lobby, stood in the corner, and looked the reception desk over. Two clerks working, one male and one female. I'd talked to a guy on the phone, which meant he'd be more sensitive to Ken's name. Ken had been there a few days, and there was a chance both of the clerks knew him by now, but it was a big hotel, busy, and I thought I'd take a chance. I waited until the guy took a phone call, then approached the woman with a rapid step, feigning great annoyance, and told her I'd locked my keycard in the room.

"Okay, sir, if you could tell me—"

"Room 712, the name is Merriman."

"All right, 712 . . . I've got it. Now, can I see some ID?"

I gave her my best look of condescending patience, as if I were dealing with a child, and said, "Um, I'm locked out, remember?"

She stared at me.

"Wallet's in the room," I said. "I was just running down the hall to get some ice."

No ice bucket in hand, but she didn't seem likely to notice that or care.

"Well, I would have no way of knowing that, would I?" Snippy now, offended. She looked down at the computer screen, then over at her co-worker, who was still talking on the phone.

"I'll just scan you another one. Hang on." She grabbed a blank keycard, ran it through the scanner, hit a few keys, and passed it over. I thanked her and went back to the elevator, rose up to the seventh floor, and walked back to stand in front of the closed door to 712.

I knocked again, just in case. Nothing. Then I slid the key in, waited for the green light to flick on, and pushed the door open.

The so-called living room was in front of me, the bedroom beyond it, with the little kitchen jammed in between. Nothing seemed out of place—no corpse on the bed, no blood splatters on the walls.

Ken's suitcase remained, a pair of pants and a sport coat draped over it. Tossed there casually, the way you would if you knew you were coming back soon. The air-conditioning was humming away even though it wasn't much past seventy outside, turning the room into an icebox. I let the door swing shut, stepped into the cold room, and made a quick circuit through it, looking for anything noteworthy and finding nothing. Housekeeping had already made a pass through—the bed was made and the bathroom cleaned, with fresh towels and soap out. If anything had gone wrong in this room, word would have been out long before I conned my way into a keycard.

I saw a charging cord trailing from the bedside table to a wall outlet, and that made me wonder if he could have left his cell phone behind in the room, explaining why he hadn't answered. I took my phone out and called his number, waiting hopefully as it began to ring, thinking I might hear it in the room. There was nothing, though.

As I stood there amid his things, I began to feel intrusive. I had no right to be there, not just from the hotel's point of view but also from Ken's. He'd been gone a few hours, that was all. Hadn't returned my calls yet. That hardly gave me justification to break into his room and go through his things. Now that I was in here, away from Graham's suspicions and Harrison's questions and the collision those things had with my faith in Ken, the sense of urgency faded a bit. He'd turn up soon, and then I'd have to admit that I'd done this and hope he'd be more amused than angry. It would be an embarrassing moment for me. Right then, though, I was looking forward to that embarrassment. By the time I could feel shame over my actions, he'd be back.

I walked out of the bedroom and back toward the door, then stopped in the living room and looked down at the coffee table. His laptop sat there, closed but with a blinking green light indicating it was still on. There was a blank CD in a clear plastic case on top of the computer. I leaned over and picked it up, read the scrawled *Peter Case, CTB* written with a black marker across the disc. "Cold Trail Blues." The song he'd promised to burn me, his surveillance song.

I put the CD into my pocket. Even the guilt I was feeling about breaking into his room didn't give me pause. I don't know why that was. Maybe it was just that I knew the CD was for me. Maybe it was something darker and more instinctive. Either way, I took it.

I'm glad that I did.

The day faded to evening, and I went back to my apartment and called Amy, asked her to come by. She picked up some Chinese takeout on the way, and while we ate that together I told her about Graham's call and Ken being MIA. She put her fork down and looked at the clock, and her forehead creased with worry lines.

"He's not obligated to call, Amy. He's not our kid, staying out past curfew."

It was forced nonchalance, though, and she knew it.

"You could call someone else, ask if they've heard from him," Amy said.

"Who? His ex-wife?"

That silenced the conversation, but it shouldn't have, because the idea wasn't bad. His ex-wife did hear something before me, when she was called as next of kin and notified that Ken Merriman's body had been found in one of the Metroparks with two small-caliber bullet wounds, one through his heart and one through his forehead.

The ex-wife heard first, and she gave the police my name. Apparently Ken had spoken of me to his daughter. It was eleven thirty when the phone rang. I was sitting on the couch with my arm around Amy, trying without success to focus on the TV, and for a few seconds before I got to the phone I was sure it would be Ken. They were a pleasant few seconds.

I wish I could have them back.

25

Where his life ended, the police weren't sure. They knew only where the body had been found, and at four o'clock in the morning, long after I'd widened their eyes with my list of possible suspects, I stood there alone in the dark.

Ken Merriman's corpse had been discovered on a short but steep hill near the edge of the tree line in Mill Stream Run Reservation, snagged in a thicket of undergrowth that was full and green with late-spring enthusiasm. There was honeysuckle nearby, the sweet cloying scent pushed at me by a breeze that rose and fell like long rollers breaking on an empty beach. The breeze was warmer than the still air, and damp, a messenger sent ahead with promises of rain.

At the top of the hill and beyond the tree line, a small field ran across a parking lot. A walking and bike path snaked away from the lot, a silver thread in the darkness. No cars were in the lot but mine, and no traces of police activity remained. The body had been found at eight that evening, and the Metroparks Rangers who interviewed me said they thought it was found soon after it was dumped. Twenty, thirty minutes earlier and they might've had an eyewitness.

Instead, there'd been only the discovery, made by two brothers from Berea who'd ridden their bikes down past the YMCA camp with a glow-in-the-dark football. The police had the football now, because one end of its neon green body carried a crimson smear. The kids had tossed it into the woods, where it took one good bounce into the thicket and landed directly on Ken's body. Throw got away from him, the older brother, who was fourteen, told the police. Then he started to cry.

Maybe I'd come down here to cry myself. Or maybe to rage and swear. Maybe I thought Ken Merriman would speak to me somehow, that alone in the dark in the place where his blood had drained into the earth and then gone dry under the wind I'd be able to feel his presence, understand something about his end and find direction for the justice this required.

None of that happened. I didn't scream, I didn't weep, I didn't hear any voices of dead men. Instead I smelled the honeysuckle and felt that warm, ebbing breeze and wished that I'd turned Ken away the night he arrived from Pennsylvania.

Where had he gone, what had he done, who had he provoked? Why was his body out here in the brambles instead of mine? We'd worked side by side on this since he'd arrived in Cleveland, right up until those last twenty-four hours when I sat at the office waiting on him to show up and he'd gone out and gotten killed.

What did you do, Ken? What button did you push, what thread did you pull?

There would be no answers here, nothing but wind sounds and sorrow, but I stayed anyhow. When my legs got tired I sat on the top of the hill and stared into the shadows and did not turn when the occasional car passed, disrupting the silence and throwing harsh white light into the trees.

We're going to see this thing to the end, Lincoln. Twelve years I've been waiting for that.

That's what he'd told me at the start, sitting in my truck with one hand on the door handle, ready to go up to the hotel room where he would spend his last night alive, sleeping alone with a too-loud air conditioner blasting away beside him. I'd responded by telling him . . . what had I said? That we might not get there. Something to that effect, some warning that all the effort might yield no result. He'd shaken his head.

Not this time. No, I've got a feeling about it.

My anger rose with the dawn. As the shadows around me changed from shades of dark to patterns of gray and then golden light, I noticed my jaw had begun to ache from the force of my clenched, grinding teeth. I'd had thoughts of Ken earlier in the night, but now he was gone, and Dominic Sanabria and Parker Harrison filled my mind in his stead.

They had done this. I didn't know who had put the bullets through Ken's heart and forehead, didn't know whose hands had carried him from the trunk of a car and released him at the top of this hill, but I knew who'd put it all in motion. I'd seen them personally, looked into their faces and heard their words, and now the intimacy of that filled me with anger that spread like steam. They had left me alive. They had killed Ken Merriman and yet they had left me alive, and in that action their regard for me was clear—they viewed me as impotent. Of course I would accuse them, of course I would come at them with all the resources I could muster. They knew this, and they did not care.

Harrison had told me to step aside before harm was done. That had not been a wild notion, clearly. He'd warned me, and then he'd reached for the phone and called Dominic Sanabria, and a day later Ken—who had not gone home, who had not heeded the warning—was dead.

Harrison had answers.

It was time to get them.

I was close to Old Brooklyn, and that was important, because Harrison left early for work. I didn't know what cemetery employed him, and I didn't want to take the time to find out. The MetroParks Rangers who'd drawn Ken's homicide would surely be looking for Harrison this morning, and I didn't want to follow in on their heels. By then it would probably be too late. The good fortune I had was that they'd been alarmed by all of the information I'd shared. The stories about Sanabria and Harrison and Bertoli had overwhelmed them, and I knew when they finally released me that they'd take a few hours to talk to Graham and others, working to confirm my claims, before they moved in on people with mob ties and murder convictions. I had a window this morning. It was going to be small and closing fast, but I had a window.

By the time I got to Harrison's apartment it was nearly six, and the soft predawn light was giving way to a deep red sunrise, the sort of that age-old sailor's caution. I'd cut it close—almost too close. I was pulling into the parking lot when the door to Harrison's apartment opened and he stepped out. He was wearing jeans and one of those tan work coats favored by farmers, with a thin knit cap pulled over his head. He wouldn't need the jacket and the cap—the day was dawning hot and humid—but he was probably used to chill early morning hours, and he wouldn't yet know of the weather change. He hadn't spent the night sitting in the woods above a body-dump scene.

Harrison didn't look up at my truck as he shut the door and turned to lock it. I pulled in at an angle a few doors down from him, leaving the truck across three parking spaces as I threw it in park and stepped out without bothering to cut the engine. Only then, as he put his key back in his pocket and turned from the door, did he look toward the headlights of my truck. When he saw me his face registered first surprise, then concern, and he said, "What happened?" just as I reached him, grabbed fistfuls of his coat, and pushed him against his own door.

When I left the truck I'd intended to say something immediately, shout in his face, but when I caught him and slammed him against the door I didn't speak at all, wanting instead to just stare into his eyes and see what I saw there. It was only a few seconds of silence as I held him pinned by his shoulders, but what I saw added coal to those fires of anger. His face held secrets. I could no longer tolerate the secrets.

"He's dead, you piece of shit."

"Ken?" he said, and the sound of the name leaving his lips, the way he wanted confirmation of it, was too much for me. I lifted him off the door and then slammed him back into it, maybe three times, maybe four, and when he finally made a move to resist I stepped sideways and sent him spinning off the sidewalk and into the hood of the closest car.

He hit it hard, his ribs catching the bulk of the fall, and when he righted himself and turned back to me I saw a new Parker Harrison. He stood with a wide stance, balanced and ready to move in any direction, and took two steps toward me with his hands raised and no hint of fear or uncertainty in his eyes. He was coming to do harm, coming with violence and confidence, and as I stepped off the sidewalk to meet him I wasn't at all sure that I could win this encounter, knew in a flash of recognition that he had been places and seen things that I had not, and that it was the sort of experience that might well make my advantage in size irrelevant.

That new Harrison lasted only those two steps, though. He brought himself up short as I approached, and there was a moment of hesitation before he moved backward. To a spectator it might have appeared he was giving way to me, but I knew it wasn't that. He didn't fear me at all. Not physically. For a few seconds he'd been sure he could take me and ready to do it. The latter aspect had passed. The former had not.

"What happened?" he said, circling away from me as I continued to pursue him, back on the sidewalk now.

"Somebody killed him, and you know who, you son of a bitch."

"I don't."

"Harrison—"

"I didn't want this," he said. "Lincoln, I did not want this. When I told you to leave it alone, this is what I wanted to avoid."

"What do you know?" I shouted it and was dimly aware of a light going on in the apartment beside Harrison's.

He didn't answer, moving backward in short, shuffling steps.

"This is what you wanted to avoid? How did you know it would happen? *Stop lying and say what you know!*"

We were beside his apartment now, and I punctuated the last shout by pounding my first into his door.

"You called Sanabria," I said. "You told me to quit, and then you called him. Didn't even wait until I was out of the parking lot. Why?"

"How do you know that?"

"Answer the question!"

"You'll have to ask him."

I almost went for him again. Almost gave up the questions and came at him swinging. It was close for a second, but I held back. My hands were trembling at my sides.

"Did Sanabria have you kill him, or did somebody else do it this time?"

"I haven't killed anyone."

"Did fifteen years in prison for shoplifting?"

"That's got nothing to do—"

"It doesn't? You're a *murderer.*"

The muscles in his jaw flexed, his eyes going flat.

"You killed Joshua Cantrell," I said. "Didn't you?"

"No."

"Bullshit. Somebody else gave him a Shawnee burial?"

"I didn't kill—"

"Bullshit!" As I moved toward him, the door to the apartment next door opened and a young woman in a pink robe stepped out and pointed a gun at me.

"Stop it," she said. The voice was weak, but the gun was strong. A compact Kahr 9 mm, and though her voice shook, the gun didn't do much bouncing, just stayed trained on my chest.

"I called the police," she said. "You can wait for them, or you can leave."

Parker Harrison said, "Kelly, go inside. I'm sorry."

She didn't move. Behind her, the door was open, and somewhere in the apartment a child was crying. This woman, who looked maybe twenty-five, was wearing a pink robe and standing barefoot on the sidewalk and was pointing a gun at me while her child cried in their home.

I said, "There's going to be a lot of police here in the next few days, ma'am. They're coming for him, not me."

Neither she nor Harrison responded.

"Do you know he's a murderer?" I said. "Do you know that he killed a man with a knife?"

She said, "Please leave," and now the gun had started to tremble.

I nodded. "I'm going to. I'm sorry. I'm sorry . . . but he . . ." The words left me then, and my strength seemed to go with them, and suddenly standing seemed difficult.

"I'll burn your lies down," I said to Harrison. "All of them. Every lie you've told and every secret you have. Understand that. Tell Sanabria."

I could hear the sirens when I drove out of the parking lot.

26

I went to the office, walked upstairs, and logged on to the computer. For a moment I stared at the phone, thinking of calling Amy. The last time I'd talked to her had been after the police released me and before I'd gone to Mill Stream Run to see the place where Ken's body had been found. She'd been awake then, and I had a feeling she'd be awake now.

I also knew what she'd tell me. She'd tell me to go home, tell me to wait on the police, tell me to do anything but drive out to see Dominic Sanabria. I left the phone untouched while I ran a database search for his address.

A few minutes later, back in my truck with a printed-out map of Sanabria's neighborhood in Shaker Heights beside me, I reached over to the glove compartment, opened it, and took out my gun. It felt good in my hand. Too good. I sat there for a while, caressing the stock with my thumb, and pleasure spread through me and filled my brain and circled around my heart. When I put the gun back, I made sure I locked the glove compartment. Wouldn't want the wrong person getting in there. The sort of person who would use a weapon without need, who'd pull the trigger for reasons of rage and vengeance rather than self-defense. No, I didn't want anybody like that getting ahold of my gun.

It was a slow drive out to Shaker Heights, fighting the build of rush-hour traffic. The house turned out to be in a gated community, which gave me a few seconds of pause, sitting just outside the main drive with my truck idling while I wondered how to get through. I decided it was always a better bet to try the straightforward approach first, so I pulled up to the gate and put my window down and told the kid in the security uniform that I was here to see Dominic Sanabria. I doubted Sanabria had many house calls at eight in the morning, but you never know.

The kid nodded at my request, asked for my name, and then waved me ahead, but he was looking at me strangely as he put the gate up. I kept my eyes in the mirror as I pulled forward and saw that he reached for the phone even before the gate was down. Standard procedure, or was this something he'd worked out with Sanabria, always to call if somebody showed up? Most of the gated communities I'd been through wouldn't let you pass until it had been cleared by the resident. I'd expected him to call before he let me through, not after.

That curiosity stayed with me as I followed the curving road to the right, past dozens of ostentatious homes that all looked generally alike. A few people were out on the sidewalks, walking small dogs that yipped hysterically at my truck. Sprinklers hissed here and there in the perfect lawns, and every car I saw was high-end, lots of Lexus and Mercedes SUVs, one Jaguar sedan. It was a place where most people went off to work each day in law firms or brokerage houses, maybe showing commercial real estate. Sanabria was probably their favorite neighbor. Nothing made better conversation at a cocktail party than saying you had a mob player living in your gated community.

According to my map, Sanabria's house was four right turns—or right curves, really—from the gatehouse, and I made it through all of them before I finally understood why the kid had waved me in and then picked up the phone. The police were waiting.

There was a single cruiser parked on the street across from Sanabria's house, and even before I slowed my truck they hit the lights without turning the siren on. Yeah, they had a description of my vehicle.

I brought my truck to a stop facing the cruiser, and both doors opened and two police in uniform got out. The one behind the wheel was a woman, tall, close to six feet, and her partner was a young guy with a ruddy, freckled face. He hung back while she approached, and when I started to put the window down she shook her head and motioned with her hand.

"Step out, please."

I took a deep breath, put the truck in park, and got out, giving the cruiser another look as I did. Shaker Heights Police Department. All right, they hadn't come here from Harrison's. They'd been sent to wait for me.

"There's no problem," I said as I got out. "I just came here to talk to him."

The cop smiled. She was young, couldn't be thirty yet, but she had cool, no-bullshit eyes.

"I'm sure that's the case," she said, "but we got a call from Cleveland city, said they didn't want you talking to him, Mr. Perry. Said they want to talk to you, and then they'll talk to him."

"I've got every right to knock on the man's door."

She shook her head. "I'm going to have to bring you in to talk to city, Mr. Perry. They have a complaint. Woman says you assaulted her neighbor."

"I didn't assault anyone."

"I'm sure you didn't. Still, like I said, they have the complaint."

"They sent you out here?"

"That's right. They said you threatened Mr. Sanabria."

I started to object again, started to say I'd never threatened anyone, but the energy went out of me then, and I sighed and nodded.

"Call them," I said. "Tell them I'll come in to talk. You don't need to take me."

She frowned. "I was asked—"

"To arrest me, or to keep me from bothering Sanabria? Doesn't look like you're arresting me."

"No."

"Then tell them I'll come in. Tell them I'm cooperative and I'll come in."

She studied me for a moment, then shot her partner a glance and nodded. "Okay. Do me a favor and go wait in your truck. Let me see what they say."

I turned back to my truck, and my eyes passed over it and went up to the house, and I saw for the first time that Dominic Sanabria was standing in front of the door. He hadn't been there when I pulled up, must have come outside when he saw the police lights go on, but now he was standing on his front step wearing workout pants and a fleece jacket, holding a cup of coffee in his hand. I stopped short when I saw him, and when he realized he had my attention he lifted the cup of coffee at me and nodded his head. A neighborly greeting. I was too far away to see if he was smiling, but I imagined he was.

"Mr. Perry?" There was a warning in the female cop's voice, and when I looked at her I saw that she was watching Sanabria, too. "Get in the vehicle, please."

For a moment I didn't move, and then she spoke in a gentler tone. "I know who he is, Mr. Perry. I don't know the details of your situation, but I know who he is. All the same, though, I need you to get in the vehicle."

I nodded without speaking, and I got into the truck, and while I waited on her to come back I did not let myself look at Sanabria. Or at my glove compartment.

27

Things didn't get ugly until Graham got to town. The first few hours I spent with the Cleveland cops who'd responded to Harrison's house and the Metroparks Rangers, getting everyone updated. Nobody arrested me, and it seemed Harrison's version of events had been largely sympathetic. When Graham arrived around noon, I let him have a short briefing and then asked if I could speak to him alone. I wanted it to be just the two of us when I told him about the mistake I'd made, the one I hadn't even considered until I was driving back through the gatehouse of Sanabria's neighborhood.

"You had anything to eat?" he said when the other cops left the room. "Any breakfast, lunch, cup of coffee?"

I shook my head.

"Let's get out of here, then. Go somewhere, grab a sandwich."

He was calm, contained, but he'd never had trouble meeting my eyes before, and today he did. Anger, maybe, but probably some guilt in there, too. Ken was dead, and Graham had been in charge.

We left the station and drove back to my office, Graham following behind me, then walked across the street to Gene's Place. It was close and it was comfortable, and only after we walked through the doors did I remember that it was also where I'd gone for lunch on the day Harrison came to see me and I agreed to take his case. That weird, warm day, when all I'd wanted to do was stand outside and drink in the air, feel the sun and the wind and the knowledge that we'd finally shaken winter.

Graham got a cheeseburger, and I had a cup of soup and picked at a club sandwich while I went through cup after cup of coffee, the fatigue slamming me now. I told him everything I could tell him. He listened and ate his burger and didn't look at me often.

When I was done talking, he leaned back from the table, wiped his mouth with a napkin, and said, "I'm sorry."

"Yeah. Both of us. We're sorry, and he's dead."

His chest filled with air, and he shook his head. "Maybe we didn't do everything perfect, but . . . well, let me correct that, Linc. I *know* we didn't do everything perfect, know that I didn't, but we also didn't kill the guy. We didn't get him killed, either."

The waitress came back and refilled my coffee yet again. "You'll be bouncing off the walls today," she said and laughed. Yeah. Bouncing off the walls.

"No," I said when she was gone, "we didn't get him killed. Sanabria did, I think, and Harrison's involved."

"The phone calls suggest that, at least."

"Speaking of which, why don't you have a damn wiretap on these guys?"

"Don't have the probable cause, and you know that. Maybe I can get it now, but not before."

"Great," I said. "Ken's made a break in the case. That's all the poor bastard wanted to do. Don't think he wanted to die to get it, though."

Graham sighed again. "Linc, how's your head?"

"What, the coffee?"

"No, not the coffee. The way you went at it today, brother . . . I can't have you doing that. You're lucky Harrison's not pressing charges. He may change his mind. Either way, I can't afford to have you—"

"I screwed up with him."

"No shit you screwed up with him, and I'm just saying—"

"No." I shook my head. "You don't understand, Graham. I don't mean in general terms. I mean specifically. In the heat of the moment, when I had him out there in the parking lot, I said something I shouldn't have."

He looked at me like a man who was waiting for a diagnosis and wasn't optimistic.

"I told him you know about the burial," I said. "The Shawnee elements."

Diagnosis delivered, and the result was what I'd expected—a flash of shock, replaced quickly by anger. Deep anger. He stared at me and then turned and looked down at the table and blew his breath out between his teeth.

"You told him we know about the burial. The one thing we've got hope on, waiting on those damn lab results—"

"If you get the lab results, it doesn't matter that he knows. Maybe it doesn't anyhow. How can he prepare to deal with that, Graham? How can that knowledge really help him?"

I was arguing out of a natural sense of self-defense, but I still knew it had been a mistake, and a potentially damaging one. The detail of the grave was the one card Graham had to play on this one, the only thing he'd held back from the media and the only firm link he had to Harrison. It wasn't all that firm—the definition of circumstantial, actually—but it was what he had.

"That's beautiful," he said, shaking his head. "That is just beautiful, Linc."

"Graham, I'm sorry. Like I said, heat of the moment."

"Yeah, heat of a moment you shouldn't have been in. You were *police*, you know better than that." Another head shake. "No, it's on me. It's on me, damn it, I know that, I see that, I got him dead and you knocking suspects around and divulging information and driving out to Sanabria's with intentions I don't even want to guess at . . . yeah, Linc, I made the wrong play when you boys called me. I did. No question."

I didn't say anything to that, didn't want to argue anymore, wanted to try to retain some dignity. Graham and I were feeling a lot of the same things, really. We'd both made some mistakes we'd be thinking about for a long time to come.

"So he knows," Graham said eventually. "He knows what I know now. Level field now, right? Level field."

"It's not level. He knows a hell of a lot more than you do."

He looked up at me then, held my eye for a moment, then nodded. The waitress came back and dropped a check off and Graham reached out and took it and folded it.

"Linc, there's something I need to ask of you."

"You want me out."

"Oh, yeah. Wanted you out yesterday, you know that, but after this morning, the way you went driving around, stirring shit up—that cannot continue."

"Let me head you off here," I said. "I *am* out."

He leaned back and gave me a bemused look, not buying it.

"That's a promise, Graham. The minute you and I finish this talk, I'm done. When I say that, I mean it."

"Why?" he said.

"Why do I want out? Because it's got nothing to do with me."

"Never did, though."

"I know it, and I should have paid more attention to that. Ken showed up and asked, and I went along with him because it is what I do, Graham. This is what I know how to do. He gave me a case and said here is what we know and here is what we need to know, and I couldn't stop myself from joining up. I've done it for too long to stop, evidently. Until today. Because I'll tell you something—I went down to see the spot where his body was found. I stood down there and I thought about my girlfriend's body ending up there instead, or my partner's. They've both come close over the last two years. I stood there and I realized what you just said: that it never did have anything to do with me, and that I can't make a decision to put people in danger for things that aren't personal. Call it a revelation, an epiphany, whatever you'd like. Here's what I'm promising you: I will not put other people at risk for a case anymore. I'm done with it. If I'd sent that poor bastard back to Pennsylvania the day he arrived, he'd be alive, too."

"Can't put all that on yourself, Linc."

"Oh, I'm not. Some of it's on you, and plenty is on him. Then there are the guys who actually, you know, *killed* him. They probably require a bit of blame, too. What I'm saying, though, is that I'm not going to be involved in any attempt to settle up with them. I burned that desire out this morning, and screwed things up for you while doing it. Now I'm just going to apologize and step aside. So save whatever speech you have prepared."

He was watching me with a deep frown, and now he braced his forearms on the table and leaned close, eyes on mine.

"I'll close this case," he said. "Word as bond, Linc, I'll close it."

"I hope so, Graham. You have to try, at least. It's your job—but you know what? It doesn't have to be mine. I'm finally understanding that." I stood up and tossed some money on the table. "I wish you luck, and if you have more questions, you know how to reach me. Otherwise, though, save yourself any worry on my part. I'm gone."

John Dunbar came by my apartment that afternoon. I'd been waiting for Amy, but when I heard a knock instead of a key turning I grimaced, knowing it wouldn't be good. I let him up, and he sat in my living room, loosened his tie, and told me that we had to get to work.

"Look, Perry, I understand how you feel right now. The anger, the sense of futility. You feel that way because you *know* who's responsible and yet he's walking around free. Sanabria's done that too long. We can't let it continue. We can't."

"Did you ever consider," I said, "that you might be responsible for this?"

"What?"

"Everything that happened with the Cantrells. Think about it. Do they ever leave that house if you don't conceive of the brilliant idea of planting Bertoli there? Does anyone ever get killed? Or are they still living in that place and helping people, Dunbar?"

He shook his head. "I'm not going to let you put that at my feet. I didn't invent the trouble they had as a couple, didn't even come to Joshua with the idea. He came to me. I don't regret what we tried to do."

I stayed silent and made a point of looking at my watch. *Anytime you want to leave, Dunbar . . .*

"Your idea," he said, "would be that if we just gave up on justice, fewer people would get hurt? If we just let Sanabria run wild, without persecution or prosecution, the rest of us are fine? That's a pretty selfish idea,

Perry. He killed other people before your friend, and he'll kill other people again."

"How long have you been chasing him?"

He couldn't hold my eyes. "A long time."

"How many years?"

"Twenty. About twenty."

"And you've done nothing but add to his body count."

"I don't have to listen to—"

"If you want him that bad, why didn't you just kill the son of a bitch, Dunbar? You'd have had an easier time doing that and getting away with it than you would have getting anything useful with Bertoli and that half-assed sting attempt."

He got to his feet slowly, his jaw tight. "That's not how it's done. I do it right."

"You haven't yet."

"I will," he snapped. "I will. I'm retired, Perry, and still I'm here, asking for your help. That doesn't mean anything to you? Doesn't tell you anything about me?"

"It means something to me," I said, "but not what you want it to."

He stood there for a moment and stared at me, and I saw contempt in his eyes.

"You could do something about this," he said. "A real detective would."

He left my apartment then. I thought about what he'd said, and thought that a year ago the words would have been coming out of my lips. A year ago, I wouldn't be back in my apartment right now or for many hours yet to come, I'd be chasing every lead, believing that I could do something to set things right. Why didn't I now?

It stacked up on you, after a while. The violence. If you kept your distance, maybe you could avoid that; if every corpse and every crime scene photograph you looked at represented somebody else's friend, somebody's else's brother, somebody else's daughter, maybe you could hold that distance. It wasn't working that way for me anymore, though. I sat in my living room after Dunbar left and I began to see the ghosts, Ken Merriman and Ed Gradduk and Joe before the bullets found him that day by the bridge over

Rocky River. There was Keith Appleton, a sweet kid who'd been one of the first members my gym had and was murdered before his high school graduation, and Alex Jefferson, my onetime nemesis, and Julie and Betsy Weston, mother and child, long gone from this city and still present in my mind every single day.

It stacked up on you.

That afternoon I got out the CD Ken had burned for me and played it for the first time: *Something I need that I just can't find. Is it too late now? Am I too far behind?*

I heard those lyrics, and I thought of Ken, chasing Alexandra twelve years after she'd left, and of Dunbar, pursuing Sanabria two decades after he'd missed a chance to stick him in prison, and I wondered why they no longer felt like colleagues to me, like comrades.

Now there's a whole new crowd out here, and they just don't seem to care. Still I keep searching through this gloom . . .

I wouldn't keep searching through the gloom. Because you couldn't catch them all. Look at Dunbar. A full career behind him, and years after retirement he was still consumed by Sanabria, still hungered for him every day—and if he got him, finally? It wouldn't mean much. There'd be another to take his place. Every detective had his white whale. I wondered how many of them ever lifted their heads long enough to see that the seas were teeming with white whales.

I took the CD out and put it back in its case and put it away, and when Amy came by that night I asked her if she could take a few days off. I wanted to go to Florida, I said. I wanted to see Joe.

"What about the funeral?"

"I don't know anybody he knew, Amy. It'll be a roomful of strangers, maybe strangers who won't want to see me there. He was working with me when he got killed."

"Still, it's a gesture."

"One he's gonna see?"

She didn't answer that, and I said, "Amy, I need to talk things out with Joe. I need you with me."

She nodded. "I'll call my boss."

I went to the Hideaway alone that night. I drank a beer and a bourbon and I toasted to a dead man. Scott Draper, used to dealing with the emotions of the drunk or the emotion-drunk, left me alone until I waved him over and launched into a debate about the prospects of the Cleveland Browns. He saw the forced nature of it, but he asked no questions, and I was glad. I had one last bourbon before calling it a night, muttered a toast to Sam Spade, and then spun the whiskey glass back across the bar. It was done for me now. It was absolutely done for me.

28

We left two days later, took a direct flight from Cleveland to Tampa and then rented a car. Even in the airport parking garage, among the shadows of cold concrete, you could feel the intensity of the Florida summer heat, opening your pores and baking into your bones. I put our bags in the trunk of the convertible Amy had insisted we rent—*if I'm going to sweat, I might as well get tan*—and then tossed the keys to her. I didn't want to drive. Felt more like riding.

We took I-275 south out of Tampa and drove over the Howard Frankland bridge toward St. Petersburg. A few miles past the bridge, I pointed at a sign indicating "gulf beaches," and Amy turned off the interstate. Joe was staying in a place called Indian Rocks, one of the hotel-and-condo communities that lined the beach from Clearwater to St. Pete. The last time I'd been on the gulf side of Florida, I was nineteen and on a spring break trip. We'd been much farther south then, too, so none of this was familiar to me. I could understand why Joe had enjoyed it during the winter, but now, with the unrelenting sun and humidity that you felt deep in your chest, enveloping your lungs, his motivation for staying seemed a little less clear. This Gena must be one hell of a woman.

We hit a stoplight just outside of Indian Rocks and watched an obese man with no shirt and blistered red skin walk in front of the car, shouting obscenities into a cell phone and carrying a bright blue drink in a plastic cup. Amy turned to me, her amusement clear despite the sunglasses that shielded her eyes, and said, "Think Joe's turned into one of those?"

"I'm sure of it."

Joe had told me to call when we got to the little town, so now I took out my cell phone and called, and he provided directions to the condo that had been his home for the past six months. We drove slowly, searching for the place, a different collection of oceanfront granite and glass everywhere you looked. When I finally saw the sign for Joe's building, I laughed. Trust him to find this one.

Squatting beneath two of the more extravagant hotels on the beach was a two-story L-shaped building that looked as if it had been built in the late 1950s and tuned up maybe once since then—perhaps after a hurricane. The old-fashioned sign out front boasted of shuffleboard and a weekly potluck.

"Oh, no," Amy said. "It's worse than I thought."

We pulled into the parking lot and got out and stretched, and then Joe appeared, walking toward us with an easier stride than I'd seen from him in a long time, some of his old athlete's grace coming back.

"Trust LP to wait until it hits ninety-five before he brings you down," he said, going first to Amy, who hugged him hard. He looked good. Some of his weight was back, and the pallor he'd had when he left Cleveland in December was gone, replaced by a tan that made his gray hair seem almost white. He stepped away from Amy and put out his hand, and I liked the strength I felt in his grip, the steady look in his eyes. It was a far cry from the way he'd looked when he left. These months had been good to him.

He let go of my hand but continued to search my eyes. We'd had a few talks since Ken had been killed, but nothing at length. I'm not a big fan of phone conversations.

"Please tell me you don't play shuffleboard," Amy said.

"No. The place is better than it looks, really."

"What's the median age of the occupants?"

"There are some kids. One guy just retired from Visa, can't be more than sixty."

He led us out of the parking lot and around the building, past a sparkling pool with nobody in the water and up the steps to a corner room with a view of the ocean. Now that we were out of the car, the heat was staggering. Even down here on the water the humidity settled on you like lead. There were maybe fifteen steps going up to the second floor, and I felt each one of them the way I'd feel an entire flight of stairs back home. I've never been so happy to hear the grinding of an air conditioner as I was when Joe unlocked the door and let us in.

His room was larger than I would've expected, and bright, with all that sun bouncing in off the water, palm trees rustling just outside. Not a bad place to spend a winter. Also, tucked inside here next to the AC unit, probably not a terrible place to spend the summer. Just don't open that door.

We spent the afternoon in or around his hotel, talking and laughing and generally doing a fine job of pretending this visit was a carefree vacation. He wasn't fooled, though, but he waited, and so did I. We'd get our chance to talk soon enough, but we needed to be alone for it.

In midafternoon I left them in the room and wandered outside and down to the beach and the blistering heat and called the office to check my messages. Nothing new from Graham or Harrison or anyone else. I had an old saved message, though. I couldn't stop myself from playing it again.

Lincoln, I think we've got something. You got us there, we just needed to see it. Last night, I finally saw it. I'm telling you, man, I think you got us there. I'm going to check something out first, though. I don't want to throw this at you and then have you explain what I'm missing, how crazy it is—but stay tuned. Stay tuned.

I played it three times, as if listening to it over and over would reveal something I had missed.

You got us there, we just needed to see it.

I'd gotten us nowhere. In the entire course of our investigation, we had interviewed a grand total of three people beyond Harrison: John Dunbar, Mark Ruzity, Mike London. What had he seen? What could he possibly have seen?

It didn't matter. I told myself that with a silent vigor—it did *not* matter. I was out of it, and needed to stay out.

29

That night we got to meet the much-heralded Gena. Of course, she hadn't been heralded at all—that wasn't Joe's style—which had only made the anticipation greater. If I'd expected someone like Ruth, I was surprised. Gena was about a foot taller, for starters, brunette when Ruth had been blond, blue eyes instead of green, from Idaho instead of Cleveland. She was younger than Joe, too, probably by ten years, and Ruth had been significantly older than him. She was, in almost all ways, the polar opposite of his longtime wife, but that didn't make her any less likable. She was attractive and witty and intelligent, and Joe's eyes lingered on her in a way that made me continuously want to hide a smile.

We left the beach and drove all the way into St. Pete to go to a restaurant Joe liked called Pacific Wave. The food was outstanding, and Amy and Gena ran away with the conversation. Joe hadn't found himself a journalist, but something close. She was an attorney who'd become an advocate for public records and government access, and with those credentials it didn't take long for her to endear herself to Amy. I also began to understand why Joe was still here in the summer but hadn't made any remarks about a permanent relocation. Gena was in Florida only temporarily, as a visiting faculty member at the Poynter Institute, a renowned journalism center in St. Petersburg. She'd come down on a grant, and that grant would be up in September.

"Then it's back to Idaho?" Amy asked.

She nodded, and I saw Joe take his eyes off her for the first time while she was speaking.

"How'd you meet, anyhow?" Amy asked. It was a classic female question, I thought, and one that guys never seemed to ask. They'd met, that was all. Wasn't that enough knowledge? It's no surprise that some of the best detectives I know are women.

"One of my colleagues at Poynter has a time-share up here," Gena said. "I came to a party there, got bored, and went for a walk. Joe was sitting on the beach in his lawn chair. Not so noteworthy, you might think, but this was at ten o'clock at night. It stood out."

Amy looked at Joe, and he shrugged. "There were always a bunch of people out during the day. They got annoying."

"We got to talking a little, and he was explaining why palm trees are so resistant to wind, even in hurricanes," Gena continued, and now it was my turn to look at Joe.

"You learn a lot about palm trees growing up in Cleveland?"

"I did some reading."

"Evidently."

Gena smiled. "After a while I realized I'd been gone too long, and I had to get back, but I also wanted to see him again. He didn't seem to be picking up on that—"

"You can imagine what a great detective he is," I said.

"Well, that's what I finally had to use. By then I knew what he'd done, and he knew why I was here, so I told him I needed to have someone with police experience come speak at one of my seminars. Talk about public access and the back-and-forth with the media, things like that. It ended up being a fine idea, but I'll confess it hadn't been part of the original plan."

"You spoke to students?" I said to Joe. "To *journalism* students?"

He nodded.

"Tell them about the good old days, when there were no recorders in interrogation rooms and every cop's favorite tools were the rubber hose and the prewritten confession?"

"I might have held a few things back."

After dinner, we drove back to Joe's building. He mixed drinks for the three of us and grabbed a bottle of water for himself, and we went out to the patio as the heat faded to tolerable levels and the moon rose over the gulf. It was quiet here, and I thought of Gena's story, of Joe on his lawn chair alone on the dark beach, and I realized that it had probably been a hell of a good choice for him to come here, to be away from the things that he knew and the people that knew him, for at least a little while. We all burn out, time to time. Some people never find that dark beach and that solitary lawn chair, though. I was glad that he had.

At one point, as the conversation between Amy and Gena became more animated and I thought my absence would be less noticed, I got up and walked down to the water and finished my drink standing in the sand. After a while a light, sprinkling rain began, and I realized the voices from the patio had faded. When I went back up, Amy and Gena were gone. Joe was sitting alone, watching me.

"They go inside?" I asked.

He nodded. I took the chair next to him again. It wasn't really raining yet, just putting forth a few suggestions.

"Amy was telling us about your friend," Joe said. "Ken."

"Friend? I'd known him about a week, Joseph."

"That make it easier, telling yourself that?"

I didn't answer.

"I'm surprised you're here," he said. "Right now, I mean. Something like that happens . . . the guy working with you gets killed, I just assumed you'd dig in."

"When your partner gets killed, you're supposed to do something about it, that what you mean? The classic PI line? Well, I don't have it in me anymore. So try not to get killed."

"Understandable. Sometimes it's good to take a few days—"

"No, Joe." I shook my head. "I don't need a few days, and when I say I don't have it in me anymore, I don't mean to go find out what happened to Ken. I should do that, I know. I should be back in Cleveland right now, working on that."

"I didn't say that. I'm just surprised you're not, because it seems to be your way."

"Sometimes your ways change. Or get changed."

He was quiet. The sprinkling rain had stopped, but the wind was blowing harder, and there was no longer any trace of the moon through the clouds.

"Are you coming back?" I said. "It's why I'm here, and you know that. I need to know if you're coming back."

"To Cleveland?"

"No. Well, yes, I care about that, too, but I mean to work. Are you coming back to work with me?"

He said, "I got a call from Tony Mitchell two weeks ago. You remember Tony?"

"Sure. Good cop, good guy. Funny as hell. What this has to do with anything . . ."

"Tony's retired from the department, too. I expected he'd become a Jimmy Buffett roadie, but evidently that didn't work out, because he got himself a job doing corporate security for some big manufacturing firm. Place is constantly hiring new employees, taking in hundreds of applications a month. They've had some problems with bad hires in the past and want to put a preemployment screening program in place. Tony called me, asked if we'd be interested in running it. Would be real steady work."

"Screenings," I said.

"I'd be willing to do something like that," he said. "Make some money, keep busy. The street work . . . I've done it for too long, Lincoln."

"So you're coming back, but you don't intend to do any street work."

"That's about it, yeah."

"Where does Gena figure in?"

"I don't know yet."

I nodded.

"What do you think?" he asked.

"That maybe it's time to fold it," I said and hated the sound of my voice. I'd gone for detached and gotten choked instead.

He didn't answer.

"I don't want to be in this business alone, Joe. I'm not sure I even want to be in it at all anymore, but I don't want to go at it alone. Hell, you're the one who dragged me into it. I was running the gym and—"

"And losing your mind. You were so miserable—"

"That was a different time. I'd gotten fired, I'd lost Karen . . . things were different."

"This job gave you something back. Did it not?"

"Sure," I said. "It gives, and maybe it takes away a little, too. You're proof."

"I'm sorry?"

"Look at yourself. You're happy down here. Are you not?"

"Generally, yeah. It's been good. I'm not sure how—"

"You had to go fifteen hundred miles to separate yourself from it," I said. "From the work. The work was you, and you were the work. I saw it every damn day."

"I could take that comment the wrong way if I wanted to."

"You didn't have anything else, Joe. Nothing."

"I *know* I could take that one the wrong way."

"It was all you were," I said. "Being a detective didn't define you, it devoured you, and you know it. Why else did you have to leave, to go so far and for so long? You did it because if you stayed any closer you knew you'd go right back to the job, and you were scared of that. Scared, or tired."

"You seeing a therapist or just reading their books?"

"Tell me I'm wrong," I said.

He shifted in his chair, shook his head. "I won't argue it. I could, but I won't. Certainly not tonight."

I didn't say anything, and after a while he spoke again, voice low. "I thought the biggest headache would be getting you to let me step aside. Didn't figure you'd be racing me for the door."

"I'm tired of the collateral damage."

"Meaning what?"

It came out in a rush. For a long time, I spoke, and he listened. Never said a word, didn't look at me, just listened. I talked about watching Joe in the hospital when he'd been shot, about John Dunbar's frightening fixation on a case he'd lost, about the way I felt every time I heard that new security bar click into place at Amy's apartment, and the uncomfortable pull my gun had on me while I drove to Dominic Sanabria's house.

"I've seen a lot of people around me get hurt," I said. "You, and Amy, and now Ken Merriman. I'm always untouched, but—"

"You're untouched?"

I nodded.

"Really?" he said. "Because you don't look that way right now, Lincoln. Don't sound it, either."

We let silence ride for a while then. The rain held off, and once I heard a door open and then close again after a brief pause, and I was certain without turning to look that it was Amy, that she'd walked out onto the balcony and seen me down here with Joe and gone back inside.

"So what will you do?" Joe asked.

"I don't know yet. I've still got the gym. Maybe put some of Karen's money into that. Get new equipment, do a remodel, try to expand. Help you out with the employment screening thing, if you need it."

"And stay away from case work."

"Yes. Stay away from case work."

He was quiet again, then said, "I'm sorry it didn't work out better for you, Lincoln. Like you said, I'm the one who brought you into it. At the time, I thought I was doing the right thing. You were a detective. That was as natural and deeply ingrained in you as in anybody else I'd ever seen. I thought it would be good for you, but more than that, I thought you needed it."

That night, when we were alone in our hotel room, I told Amy about my conversation with Joe. I was sitting in a chair by the sliding glass door, she was on the bed and outside the rain fell in sheets. I thought she might make some arguments, raise some of the same points that Joe had, remind me that when we'd met I was trying to make a living off the gym alone and I was a generally unhappy person. She didn't say any of those things, though. When

I was done talking she got to her feet and walked across the room to me and sat on my lap, straddling me, her hands on either side of my face.

"If you can't do it anymore, then there's no decision to be made," she said. "You just need to step back. Don't feel bad about it, just do it."

I nodded.

"One rule," she said.

"Yeah?"

"You can leave the job. You can leave the city if you want to. You can leave damn near anything, but you better not leave me."

I shook my head. "Not going to happen."

"I've invested way too much into this ill-advised Lincoln Perry rehabilitation plan to give up now."

"If anybody ends this, it'll be you."

"Remember that," she said, and then she leaned forward and kissed me before moving to rest her head on my chest. We sat like that for a long time, and then she stood and took my hand and brought me to the bed.

When she was asleep and the rain was gone, sometime around four in the morning, I sat on the balcony with a pad of the hotel stationery and tried to write a letter to Ken's daughter, the one who'd loved TV cop shows. I wanted to apologize for missing the funeral, tell her how much I'd thought of her father, and explain that he'd been a damn fine detective and that his work had mattered, that what he'd been doing on the day he was murdered had an impact on her world. I sat there for more than an hour, wrote a few poor sentences, and then crumpled the pages in my hand and went back inside.

30

Amy and I stayed for a week. We hung out with Joe and sometimes Gena, ate seafood, had drinks of fruit juice and rum, bitched about the heat. All the things you're supposed to do in Florida.

I checked the office voice mail daily. There was no word about Ken. Many days, I played his last message again. I listened to words I already knew by heart, and I tried to imagine what had provoked them. I had no luck. You rarely do with that approach to detective work. The way it gets done is out on the street. I stayed on the beach.

On the day before we left, I ended up sitting on a chair outside Joe's hotel, alone, while he and Amy made a run to the store. Gena was coming by for an afternoon cocktail before dinner, and she showed up before they got back and came down to join me. We made small talk for a bit. I found out that while she had lived in other states and, for one year, in Europe, she always came back to Idaho in the end. Both parents were still alive, and she had two sisters; all of them lived within a fifteen-minute drive.

"So are you going to move to Cleveland or make him move to Idaho?" It was supposed to be a joke, but her pause told me it was a discussion they'd actually had.

"Maybe either, maybe neither, maybe something completely different," she said.

"Egypt?" I was still trying to keep it light, because I was caught off guard by the idea that they were this serious.

"One person moving to join the other is the obvious option," she said, stretching out on the chair beside me and kicking off her sandals, "but there's an element of it that could feel selfish either way, you know? We both have our own lives at home, so to have one person make the sacrifice seems unfair. So we've talked about a compromise. Moving somewhere new to both of us."

"Oh," I said. Can always count on me for insight.

She looked over at me, sunglasses shading her eyes. The wind was fanning her brown hair out. "Would I like Cleveland?"

"Probably not."

"Really?"

"You live in a college town in the mountains, right? Well, the city's a change. Most people head the other way. Leave the city for mountains." I waved out at the water. "Or a beach."

"I lived in New York for seven years. Never minded being in a city. Of course, I was twenty-five then, too."

I didn't say anything.

"Either way, it won't be happening overnight," she said. "Joe's not the sort of person who rushes into things."

That made me laugh. "No, he's not."

She smiled but looked away from me. "He's worried about you."

"Doesn't need to be."

"I couldn't speak to that. I don't know you well enough to say. I do know that he's worried. He's afraid that the way he left was unfair to you. That you're carrying guilt about it when you shouldn't be."

"I got him shot, Gena. Seems to warrant a small dose of guilt. But that's really not the issue, not anymore. He's happy again, and I'm glad of that. Thrilled."

"You're not. Happy, I mean."

"Happy," I said, "seems like a hell of a subjective thing. I'm working on it.

So is Joe. So is everybody. And I can tell you this—you're good for him. I can see that so clearly, and you have no idea how nice it is. He's been alone for a long time."

"Had you, though."

"Yeah, but he never liked my hairstyle as much as yours."

She smiled. "There's one thing I'd like you to know."

"Yeah?"

"When we've talked about moving," she said, "and the things that we'd miss the most, just hate the idea of being away from, I talk about my family. Joe talks about you."

A call from Graham came later that night, and the message he left offered no sense of progress but some news—Joshua Cantrell's family had won a preliminary legal motion to claim the house on Whisper Ridge.

31

Life, or the lack thereof, always seemed to me like something that had to be established medically, not legally, through beating hearts and functioning brains rather than notarized paperwork. That's not always the case. The judge had ruled that the Cantrells were entitled to post legal notice of Alexandra's presumed death, which would run in a variety of newspapers, and there would be a ninety-day period to contest the claim. Either Alexandra herself could appear, proving it wrong while welcoming the approaches of police, or someone else could bring forward proof of life. If those ninety days passed without either occurrence, the Cantrells could begin maneuvering to claim their share of the estate. Graham's understanding was that they'd have to split the estate with Dominic Sanabria.

"He probably killed their son," I said when I called him back the next morning, "and now they're going to have to share the money with him?"

"That's what the law seems to say."

When we got back to Cleveland, I bought a paper in the airport and flipped through it to the public notice section while we stood beside the luggage carousel. There was the first notice of Alexandra Cantrell, buried amid pages of fine-print legalese. It seemed too quiet a way to announce the end of a life.

"You should do an article," I told Amy. "If anything's going to produce Alexandra or proof she's alive, it won't be this notice. It'll take more publicity than that."

She agreed with me, and a day later so did her editor. The story appeared on the following Sunday, front page and above the fold. The TV news picked it up by that evening, and several Associated Press papers around the country ran shortened versions of the "missing, presumed dead" story in the days to come. The story never gathered the national steam I'd hoped for—CNN, talk show features, that sort of thing—but for several weeks, Graham, the newspaper, and the Cantrell legal team were flooded with tips. I called Graham to see if anything was coming of it. Just the tips, he said, most crazy, none credible. If Alexandra was still alive, there was no sign.

I wrapped up what case work I had left when I got back to the city, then put out a memo to our core clients explaining that Joe and I were stepping aside from field investigations. I referred them to other people in town, brushed aside inquiries, and waited for the outcry of disappointment and anger. It never came. Perry and Pritchard Investigations wasn't the community institution I'd believed it to be, evidently.

I listened to Ken's message daily for a while. Then, a month after he'd been killed, the voice mail informed me the message would be deleted from the system. It had been there too long, evidently. You couldn't keep it forever. Eventually the computer decided that the time elapsed required the message to go away even if I didn't want it to. By the next morning, it was gone.

I invested thirty thousand dollars into new equipment for the gym. I paid for a larger phone-book ad and hired a friend of Amy's to create a Web site. I did most of the work on the gym by myself, largely because it kept me busy. When I wasn't working on it, I was working out in it. That summer I took thirty seconds off my time in the mile and added forty pounds to my bench press, got it back up to a max of three hundred and ten pounds, my all-time high and a mark I'd set when I was a rookie. My attention to diet changed, and I started taking amino acids and fish oils and any number of other things that were rumored to have some sort of health benefit. By August, if I wasn't in the best shape of my life, I was damn close to it. My workouts had become feverish, almost obsessive. Do one more rep, Lincoln, run one more mile, take one more pill. You'll be stronger, leaner, faster. You'll have no vulnerability. None.

I'd been spending more and more nights at Amy's apartment, and one evening I felt her eyes on me and turned to see her watching me with a frown from across the room.

"What have I done?"

"Quit your job," she said.

"This is an unemployment lecture?"

"That gym won't be enough for you."

"You don't know that. I could make plenty of money—"

"Not money, Lincoln. It won't be *enough* for you. Don't you get that?"

"You're enough for me," I said.

"Romantically speaking? I sure as shit better be. If I'm not, then you're a cheating bastard. If you mean I'm *enough*, period, all you need . . . that's not true."

"Actually, it is."

"Well, it shouldn't be. You're not enough for me."

I raised my eyebrows. "Gee, thanks. You're a sweetheart tonight."

"I'm serious. I love you, but you don't define my entire existence, either. You wouldn't want to be around me if you did. So to sit there and tell me that I'm *enough* for you, that's a lot of pressure, and when you finally realize it's not the truth, I don't want to be the one who gets hurt."

"I'm not sure I follow your logic there, but I don't intend to hurt you, Amy."

She came over and kissed me, then leaned back and stood with her hands on my shoulders and looked into my eyes.

"You just removed a large piece of yourself, and now you're pretending that it was never there. It's been a hell of a thing to watch, trust me. Impressive at times. You're a master of denial, Lincoln, an absolute master—but I'm scared of where it's going to take you."

She kissed me again then and walked out of the room. I sat and watched her go and thought that I should follow and say more. I didn't know what I would say, though. I really didn't.

At the end of August, Graham called again, this time to tell me that he finally had his lab results on Joshua Cantrell's grave. The backlog had loosened up, and he'd used Ken's murder as a means to bump his request higher in priority.

"We got nothing," he said. "No DNA results. Nothing that connects to Harrison, or anybody else. The only DNA they could find was Cantrell's."

I felt defeat sweep through me, realized just how much hope I'd been holding out.

"What next?" I said.

Graham was quiet.

"You're done?"

"I'm not done, Linc, but it's a cold case, and without new—"

"Ken Merriman was murdered in May, Graham. That's not a cold case."

"That's also not my case. Talk to your boys in Cleveland on that one. I'm sitting here in Pennsylvania with a full caseload and a bunch of supervisors who don't want me spending time in Cleveland. Look, nobody's more disappointed about this than me. I come to a case with one goal—to close it. I haven't done that on this one. I won't deny that, but I also won't bullshit you. My focus has to be out here, where I'm paid to work. I'd love to take Sanabria down, love to take Harrison down, but I can't."

"Somebody will," I said. "In time."

"Right," he said, and then neither of us was comfortable with the other's silence, so we said a hurried goodbye and hung up.

32

The same day Graham gave me the news about the lack of lab results from the grave, he gave it to John Dunbar, who, evidently, had continued his regular calls asking for updates and offering his help. I hadn't heard from Dunbar since I'd asked him to leave my apartment, but at noon on the day after Graham's call he showed up again.

I was on a ladder in the gym, applying paint to a band around the ceiling I'd decided to make a different color than the rest of the wall. It was an aesthetic effect, completely unnecessary, but I'd decided to do it anyhow, because it was good to stay busy. I was finding all sorts of ways to stay busy.

Grace told him where to find me, and he came and stood quietly beneath the ladder and watched me paint until I felt his presence and turned and looked down.

"What are you doing here?" I said.

"Wanted to buy you a beer."

"I don't drink in the middle of the day."

"A cup of coffee, then."

"I'm off caffeine."

"A bottle of water."

He never blinked, just stood with his hands in his pockets and an even stare on his face, watching me. I gave it a moment, and then I sighed and came down off the ladder.

"Let me rinse out the brush."

We walked up the street to an Irish pub that had gone in on the corner. Neither of us spoke. Once inside, I went to a table across from the bar and ordered a beer.

"Thought you didn't drink in the middle of the day," Dunbar said.

I didn't answer.

"So you're not happy to see me," he said. "I get it."

"I just don't know why you came. Why you're not willing to make phone calls instead of personal visits, at least."

"Tougher to blow me off in person," he said. It was a line straight out of Joe's mouth, one of his guiding principles for detective work—you wore out shoe leather before you burned up the phone lines.

"I'll give you that much," I said.

They brought my beer, and he asked for a Jameson and water, and we waited while they poured that and brought it over.

"I talked to Graham," he said after taking an experimental sip.

"As did I."

"Pretty disappointing news."

"It was."

"It'll go back to where it was twelve years ago now," he said. "Go back to nobody looking or even thinking about looking. It'll be unsolved, and forgotten."

I drank some beer.

"Ken Merriman's case is open," he said. "You talked to anybody on that?"

"Not lately."

"I have. I was calling a couple times a week. Guy I've talked to down there got tired of it, though. Asked me to stop. Said he'd let me know if they got an update. So in my professional opinion, that one's moving along about as well as the Cantrell investigation. Which is to say, it's not."

"That could be an unfair assessment."

"You think?"

"The rangers aren't bad at what they do, Dunbar. Give them time."

"Time." He nodded and turned the glass with his fingers. "Twelve years of time, that's what we've had on Cantrell. I don't want to see Ken Merriman's case go another twelve."

"I know it."

"But you're not doing anything to help," he said, "and I don't understand that. Somebody else, sure, they'd feel hopeless and useless and I'd get that. I've read about you though. I've talked to people. Your reputation as a detective is extraordinary, Perry. Good instincts, they tell me, good experience, a real natural—but what people talk about most? It's how damned dogged you've been. How determined. How relentless."

I blew out a breath, looked away.

"I see you've closed your office," he said, "and now it's the middle of the week and you're in the gym, painting. Is that the new you?"

"What if it is?"

"I'd say that's a shame. I'd say that's as much of a shame as anything I've heard in a long time, because the world is full of evil, and there aren't enough people who can do something about it."

He paused. "Dominic Sanabria is a killer. He has gone unpunished for that. He sits around in his fancy house drinking afternoon cocktails and smiling about it. I cannot let that last."

When I didn't answer, a glow of anger came into his face, and he took a deep breath and looked away, as if he couldn't stand the sight of me.

"You remember the kid Sanabria killed, Lamarca?" he said after a while. "I told you about him. It's the case we had him for at the motel if the son of a bitch had only rented his own room."

"I remember."

"The reason he was killed? Sanabria thought the kid was talking to an informant. *Thought* he was. In truth, he wasn't, but that didn't matter to Sanabria. When Joseph Lamarca's body was found, seven of his fingers were broken. Smashed. Bone showing."

It was quiet. He said, "That's what he did to someone he *thought* betrayed him, Perry. Then Joshua Cantrell. Then Ken Merriman. It all goes back to the same place, every single one of those bodies goes back to the damned motel room that he didn't rent. It's about atonement. You bet your ass I'm looking for it, buddy. You better believe it."

I finished my beer, and we sat in silence for a while and watched the TV without really seeing it. Then I ordered another beer and asked if he wanted a second whiskey, and he shook his head. Most of his first was still in the glass.

"I got upset the last time I talked with you," he said eventually, voice soft. "I thought you were being a bastard, to be honest. You said some very cutting things."

"I was having a bad day."

"That doesn't matter. The things you said were cutting, but I know that's because they were true. I screwed that situation up, Perry, I screwed it up *bad*, and a man died. A man was murdered, and I have that blood on my hands. Do you understand that? His blood is on *my* hands."

His eyes were red, and his voice sounded thin.

"I've got to live with that," he said, "and all I can do, the only way I know to cope with it, is by looking for atonement. Because while his blood might be on my hands, I didn't kill him—and if I can see that whoever did kill him is punished? Perry, that's the closest thing I've got to redemption."

I'd lost my taste for the beer now.

"I know Joshua Cantrell doesn't mean anything to you," he said, "but Ken Merriman should. So think of him, and help me. Let's see it through."

"What Ken Merriman means to me," I said, "is that it's time for me to walk away. What you're asking for, I just cannot do. I'm tired of being in the game. Tired of having to spend my days immersed in some filthy, foolish crime, trying to determine what son of a bitch killed a good man and dumped his body in a park where children play. It's not for me anymore. I'm sorry."

"I understand that you're tired," he said, "but I'm trying to tell you that you can't afford to be. Because there are too many people saying they're tired. The whole world is tired now, the whole damn world doesn't have the energy to set anything right. We want to wait on somebody else to do it, and yeah, maybe we believe that it should be done, but we just don't have it in us to *try* anymore. We're a sideline species these days, Perry. We turn the news on and see some tragedy or crisis and shake our heads and say, 'Boy, hope somebody gets to that. It is just outrageous that nobody's addressed that one yet.' Then we put on *American Idol* and go to bed."

"You watch *American Idol*?" I said.

"Don't be an asshole."

It was quiet then, and he waited a while, and eventually I said, "Dunbar, good luck. Really and truly—good luck—but I'm out."

His face fell and he looked away from me. Then he reached into his pocket and pulled out a bill and dropped it on the table. He got to his feet and shook my hand silently, and then he went to the door and stepped out into the wind, shoulders hunched and head down and alone.

33

I couldn't sleep the night after Dunbar's visit. I'd worked out for two hours that afternoon, then gone to the Hideaway and caught up with Scott Draper for a few beers while we watched the Indians game. They were on a losing streak. I knew the feeling.

It was midnight when I got back to my apartment, and I went right to bed, hoping that the lingering effects of the alcohol would take care of the rest, put me to sleep quickly. They didn't. Two hours passed, then three, then four. I stared at the ceiling, wandered out to the couch, went back to bed, turned the TV on, turned it off, tried to read, tried to control my breathing, tried damn near everything I could think of and still couldn't find sleep.

I gave up around five, dressed in workout clothes, and went downstairs, thinking I'd punish my body for refusing sleep by going for yet another run. Break its will before it broke mine. By the time I got outside, though, I knew I didn't have it in me. I stretched out in the parking lot in the dark, breathing in the last cool air of night, another hot and humid day ready to replace it. If not a run, maybe a drive. That seemed better. I could drive to Edgewater Park before the traffic started, watch the sun rise over the lake and the city. I hadn't done that in years. Or maybe go down to the West Side Market, hang around and watch as the vendors arrived and set up their wares before the doors opened. I used to do that when I was a patrol officer, come off a night shift and head down to the market, a place that always felt like a step back in time.

There were plenty of possibilities, and they all sounded good. How I found myself in Old Brooklyn, then, parked across the street from Parker Harrison's apartment building, I really couldn't say.

He left the house just before six, exactly as he had the last time I'd seen him. He walked out of the apartment, turned and locked the door carefully with his key, then tested it once to be sure before he headed to his truck. It was a Chevy S-10, at least fifteen years old, and for a second as he drove out of the lot he was facing directly toward me. Then he made the turn and pulled away and I started the Silverado and followed. I wanted to watch him. That was all. Didn't want another confrontation, didn't want to say a word to him, just wanted to watch him.

He drove to Riverside Cemetery, and I passed the entrance when he turned in, knowing it was too early in the morning not to attract attention by following him in. I gave it fifteen minutes, then circled back around and entered the cemetery, which was one of the city's oldest and largest. It was a beautiful place, really. More than a hundred acres of rolling green valley and flowering trees and marble monuments and the dead. There were plenty of them at Riverside.

I drove through the cemetery until I found Harrison's truck, parked in front of the maintenance building, empty. I'd missed him. I drove back up to the chapel, where I assumed my truck would be less noticeable, parked, and set out on foot. It was a huge place, and it would take a while to find him. I had the time.

I left the road and walked through the grounds, my shoes soon soaked by the dew. After a pass along the south side without any luck, I looped around and headed toward the north, away from the maintenance building. I was not alone in the cemetery. During the walk I saw two people beside graves, paying early-morning respects. I thought that it had been a long time since I'd been to see my mother and father's stones.

I was approaching the northeast bend of the road, ready to head west and walk back toward the entrance, when I heard the buzz of a weed trimmer. A few minutes later I found Harrison trimming the base of a monument, head bowed.

For a moment I just stood there, unsure of what to do. He was at work, and that's all he'd be doing for the rest of the day. No need to watch him tend the grass and weeds in a graveyard. If I really wanted to begin surveillance on him, I could come back in the afternoon, wait for him to get off work, and see where he went. That was what mattered, surely. This did not.

I couldn't leave, though. Now that I'd found him, I wanted to watch just a little bit longer. Just a few minutes. I retreated across the grounds, looking for someplace where I could sit unnoticed and keep an eye on him. Sitting was key. I was suddenly feeling the groggy, mind-numbing weariness of an entirely sleepless night.

About a hundred yards from where Harrison was working, I found an enormous monument with a granite lion resting on top. The lion was lying down with its front paws stretched forward, its head up. The carving job was exquisite. I couldn't imagine how long something like that took. The name on the stone read simply DAYKIN. No first name, no dates. It was probably a family monument, I decided as I looked around the other stones and saw the Daykin name repeatedly. The patriarch making his claim.

I sat in the grass beneath the lion and leaned back until my head rested against the stone. Out across the way, Harrison's weeder buzzed and his shoulders swung back and forth methodically. What a place for a murderer to work.

That thought took me back to Harrison's apartment, to the night Ken and I had made our initial visit and Harrison first told us he worked in a cemetery, told us that it suited him. Ken's response—*how unsettling*.

"How unsettling." I said it aloud and laughed. Man, what a line. How unsettling. I laughed again, softer this time, an under-the-breath chuckle, and then I laid my head back against the stone again and closed my eyes and tried to find a moment of peace. It was there, sitting upright in a graveyard with my head on a piece of granite, that I finally fell asleep.

———

I woke only minutes later, but it felt longer than that, and I came around slowly, like that moment of awakening was at the end of a long, difficult climb. When my eyes opened it took me a second to place myself, and then I realized that Harrison was out of view and I could no longer hear the sound of his machine. I pushed off the stone and looked around and saw him not ten feet away, standing with his arms folded across his chest, watching me.

"Hello, Lincoln," he said. "I'm going to assume this is not a coincidence."

I thought about getting to my feet, but what was the point? Instead, I just leaned forward, rested my arms on my knees, and looked up at him. "Great place to work."

"I like it."

I nodded up at the lion above me. "Hell of a cat, too."

"Do you know who he was?"

"Daykin?" I shook my head.

"A railroad man," Harrison said. "Specifically, a conductor. He was one of the conductors on Lincoln's funeral train. John Daykin. This is one of my favorite monuments in the cemetery."

"You know them all?"

"More than you'd think," he said.

"You keep the graves clean," I said, "and Mark Ruzity carves them. Can you explain that?"

"Alexandra taught us the importance of honoring the dead. Mark took up the carving as his way of doing that. By the time I left Whisper Ridge, he'd met people out here, and got me the job. Not so sinister, really. I hate to disappoint you."

"You know that he's talked to Sanabria?" I said. "There's a photo of it, Harrison. Ruzity and Sanabria together around the time your beloved Alexandra and Joshua disappeared. You were on the phone with Sanabria then, yourself."

He didn't respond. I looked away from him and out across the sea of weathered stones left to mark lives long finished.

"They haven't made an arrest in Ken's murder yet, Harrison."

"If I could tell them who to arrest, I would."

"Yeah?"

"Why are you here? Why would you sit here and watch me work?"

"I need an answer," I said, "to just one question, Harrison. There are so many questions I think you can answer, but I need just this one: Why me? Why did you have to come to me? I ignored your first letter, so you wrote me more. I ignored those, so you came to see me. Why?"

"You've already asked me that."

"I know it. This time I'd like you to tell me the truth."

He sighed and lowered his weed trimmer to the ground, straightened again, and took a rag off his belt and ran it over his face and neck, soaking up the sweat from the morning's rapidly rising heat.

"It was the truth then, and it will be the truth this time, too," he said. "I came to you because of what I'd read. Because of what I hoped you would be."

"What was that?" I said. "Supposing I believed you, which I do not, what was it that you thought I would be, Harrison?"

"Someone who knew how to see the guilty."

"What?"

"Not how to find the guilty, Lincoln. How to see them. How to . . . consider them. The people behind the crime. I'm a murderer. I get that. Well, Joshua Cantrell was murdered, and not by me. I wanted to know who did it—and why."

"That's not what you asked me to do."

"No, and that was my mistake. I held on to the truth when I shouldn't have, but I wanted to get you to the house."

"Why was that so damn special? Why did I have to see the house?"

He spread his hand, waved it around us. "You see all these stones? What are they?"

I sat and stared up at him, searching his face and trying, yet again, to come to a judgment about him. I wanted to believe him.

"What would you call them?" he said. "These stones."

"Graves."

"That's beneath the stone. What are the—"

"Markers, monuments."

He nodded. "Joshua Cantrell has one. You've seen it. That house is his monument. She left it for him, Lincoln. Something to sit in his memory."

It was the same comparison Ken Merriman had made. The sort of comparison that came easily when a house had been outfitted with an epitaph.

"Home to dreams," I said.

"Yes. Dreams she'd shared with her husband. It's important to remember the dead. Alexandra understood that, and so do I. It's why I work here, Lincoln—and before you ask the question, yes, I think of the man I killed. I remember him. Every single day, I think of him, and of what I took from him and those who loved him. It's important to remember."

"You know that she left the house so Joshua would be remembered. You're sure of that."

He nodded.

"Do you know who killed him?"

He shook his head. I watched for the lie and couldn't find it.

"I wanted to know," he said. "That's why I came to you. You wish I never had, and I'm sorry about that. I picked you because I hoped you'd see past my prison sentence, see past my crime. The police can't do that. Neither could you, and that's all right. I took a chance with you. It didn't work out. Sometimes they don't."

"It didn't work out for *you*? Ken's dead, Harrison."

"That wasn't me. I'm sorry about it, more sorry than I can probably make you believe, but it was not me who killed him."

A car passed on the road, circling slowly through the cemetery, and neither Harrison nor I spoke until it was gone.

"Why were you talking to Dominic Sanabria?" I said.

"When?"

"Any of the times. You called him when Cantrell was killed, you called him when the body was found, you called him just before Ken was killed."

He hesitated before saying, "At first I was trying to get information out of him. Trying to get in touch with Alexandra."

"What did you tell him the day before Ken was killed?"

"I told him that you were done with the case. He'd called me earlier to say that his sister and her memory needed to be left alone. That was when I asked you to quit. I was worried for you, and I didn't want to be the one who put you in harm's way. I didn't trust Dominic."

"All of that might be believable, Harrison, but there's one call missing in that explanation. Why did you call him when the body was found? When it was found and *before* it was identified."

He looked uncomfortable, failed to meet my eyes for the first time. "I really can't speak of that."

"You piece of shit." I shook my head in disgust. "You know things that could help, and you won't say them. You don't really want to see anything resolved, don't give a damn about Ken or Cantrell or anybody else. It's all some sort of sick game to you."

"It's not that at—"

"*Then tell the rest of it!*" I got to my feet, shouted it at him.

He stood in silence and watched me. I waited for him to speak, and he did not. After a few minutes of staring at him, I shook my head again.

"I made a promise," he said, his voice very soft, "to someone who mattered more to me than anyone I've ever known. Can you understand that? I gave my *word.*"

"To Alexandra? She's gone, Harrison. Gone, and maybe dead. She's been gone for twelve years. You want to let your promise to her prevent justice?"

No confirmation, no denial, no response.

"Why do you have such loyalty to that woman?" I said, weariness in my voice.

He didn't answer right away. I stood beside the Daykin monument, resting one hand on the lion's side, and I waited. Finally he spoke.

"It's never really quiet in prison," he said. "People think of it as a quiet place, solitary, but it's not. Doors bang, and guards walk around, and the other prisoners talk and shout and laugh and cough. It's loud all the time. Even at night, you hear sounds of other people. You're never really alone."

He paused, and I didn't say anything. Another car drove past.

"You're never alone," he said again, "and it's not an easy place to be. It shouldn't be, right? It's a place where you're sent to be punished, a place that's supposed to painful. You walk around with other murderers, with rapists, drug dealers. Some violent people, some crazy people. You're one of them, and you've got a role to play. You've got to seem more violent and more crazy than them. You got to be the *craziest* man in the place, understand? Because otherwise you will not survive."

He wet his lips, shifted in the grass.

"I'd been in for four years before I decided I couldn't finish. I just gave up, knew there was no way I could make it to the other side. There was a cleaning detail, and I got assigned to that, and I started stealing Drano. They had a big bottle, I knew I'd never get that out, so I emptied toothpaste tubes and filled them with the stuff, brought them back to my cell. You have any idea how hard it is to fill a toothpaste tube with Drano? Takes dedication, I assure you. I waited until I had three of them filled. I did *not* want to have too little to do the job. I thought there would probably be enough in those three tubes to kill me."

"You're still here," I said. "So it wasn't enough?"

"I think it would have been. I didn't take it."

"Why not?"

"It got quiet," he said. "The night I was going to take it, the place got quiet. For one hour. I can tell you that almost exactly. I was waiting, and I was scared, and then it got quiet. I had one silent hour. I couldn't believe it. No-body was talking, or moving, or screaming, and in that hour I remembered, for the first time in a long time, that this was not all that I was. I'd killed somebody, and it was a terrible thing, and I was in this terrible place and I would be for years to come, but that was not all I was. If I committed suicide in there, though, if I died in that place, then it would be different. That would be my identity, all the world would ever know or remember about me, that I was another murderer who died in the place where murderers belong."

He took the rag off his belt again, ran it over his face, soaked up the fresh sweat on his forehead.

"I told that story to Alexandra Sanabria a few weeks before I was re-leased," he said. "She put out her hand and took mine, and she promised me that we would take that one hour and make it my life. That everything I had been and pretended to be aside from it would no longer matter."

He squeezed the rag in his hand, and drops of sweat fell into the grass.

"She kept her promise, Lincoln. So I'll keep mine. I'm sorry, but I'll keep mine."

PART THREE

HONORS AND EPITAPHS

34

The summer went down quietly. The heat broke and the humidity dropped and the kids went back to school. The Indians put together one of their classic late-season runs to ensure you'd spend the winter with that bitter oh-so-close taste in your mouth. The gym attracted a few new members. The PI office stayed closed and locked.

Joe came back to town in the middle of September. He'd been gone for more than nine months without a single trip back, and when he opened up his house and stepped inside and looked around, I couldn't read his feelings.

"So much dust," he said. He'd left Florida at the end of August but headed west instead of north, making the drive to Idaho with Gena. Just keeping her company on a long drive, he'd said. He spent two weeks there, though, and I wondered if it had been a scouting trip of sorts. He'd told me the two of them had not made any future plans but had also not closed any doors. I left it at that.

We reopened the office on the last day of September and devoted a morning to cleaning and reorganizing. We'd share the background check duties and the profits. It wouldn't be enough to support both of us, but that was okay—we each had a supplemental income, mine through the gym and Joe's through his police pension. The screenings provided extra cash as well as something to do.

By mid-October we'd developed a comfortable rhythm, spending a few mornings a week in the office together, processing reports and requesting local court record checks where we needed them. It felt good to have Joe back, good to exchange some of our old jabs and barbs. What we were doing was not detective work, not in any sense that I'd come to know, but it was important, too. We routinely discovered applicants with criminal charges in their histories, from misdemeanors to felonies. These were the kind of people you didn't want in your employ, the sort who could bring real problems inside the walls of your company. In some circumstances, the charges were very old—ten, fifteen, twenty years—but we recorded them just the same. Old charges or not, there was a risk factor associated with the hiring of those people, and our new employer didn't want to take that risk. Couldn't afford to, they told us. Not in this day and age.

It was late October when I heard from Quinn Graham. He called the office and seemed surprised when I answered.

"I thought you'd quit."

"Just case work. We've got some other things on the table."

"I see."

"What's up, Graham? You got something?"

"No," he said, and I could hear embarrassment in his voice. "Not the sort of thing you're looking for, at least."

"Then what is it?"

"Thought you might like to know that Joshua Cantrell's parents won their case yesterday."

"Alexandra's legally declared dead?"

"Yeah, that happened a few weeks back, actually. Yesterday they came to a settlement. The house is going to be claimed by the estate and sold."

"Money split between them and Sanabria?"

"No. Sanabria's attorneys showed up and said he wanted no part of it.

Went through whatever legal process they had to for him to waive his interest. It all goes to the Cantrells now."

At least that bastard wasn't taking the money. It wasn't much, but it helped.

"They going to put the house on the market soon?" I asked.

"Immediately, is my understanding."

We talked a little while longer, and he told me that a few weeks earlier he had made an arrest in the case of the murdered girls that he'd been working that summer. The perp was a thirty-year-old graduate student at Penn State who was working on a thesis about pornography. I was glad Graham got him. I was glad he'd told me about it, too. It was good to know these things.

Two days later a short article ran in the newspaper. It wasn't much, but it explained the legal situation and announced the pending sale of the house. Asking price hadn't been set yet but was rumored to be around four million. The Cantrell family was considering subdividing the land, though, so there would be a delay in the sale while they studied their options.

The morning the article ran, I stopped in the office and asked Joe if he could handle a few days without me.

"Where you going to be?"

"Sitting in the woods with binoculars and a camera."

He looked at me for a long time without speaking.

"I know you'll think it's crazy," I said, "but I want to watch that house."

"The Cantrell house? You want to watch it?"

I nodded. "I want to see who shows."

"What makes you think anyone will except a Realtor?"

"Because that place is sacred to people, Joe. Was, at least. I'd like to know if anyone comes to say goodbye."

"Alexandra?"

"I don't know. There might be a chance. Or maybe Dominic. Or Harrison. Or somebody else entirely."

He frowned. "Even if someone does—and I have trouble believing that anyone will—what the hell will that tell you?"

I didn't answer that. Couldn't. Still, I wanted to see it. I was remembering Ken Merriman's remark that day on Murray Hill. *She had a damn epitaph carved beside the door. That place means something to her. So let me tell you—if she's alive, I bet she'll come back to see it again.*

"If you feel it's worth a shot, then knock yourself out," Joe said. He paused, then said, "Hell, maybe I could take a day or two at it with you. Been a while since I did any surveillance. Old time's sake, why not, right?"

We logged a full week at it. I spent more time there than Joe, rising early each morning and sitting until dusk each night, but he put in plenty of hours. I didn't think it was wise to sit inside the gate, so instead we parked up the road and watched.

In the first two days, there was a decent amount of activity, but it was casual interest, people who drove up to the gate and then pulled back out and went on their way. The newspaper story had sparked some curiosity, that was all.

On the third day, someone drove a black BMW up to the gate, unlocked it, and drove through. I was intrigued by that one until the driver stepped out of the car, and then I recognized him as Anthony Child. Checking on the property one last time, maybe, before it was taken out of his care. He would probably be glad to see the hassle go.

The next afternoon there were more visitors. An old van arrived just after one and parked at the end of the drive. I watched through my long-range camera lens as the doors opened and two men stepped out—Parker Harrison from the passenger side and a rangy, gray-haired guy I'd never seen from the driver's seat. The gray-haired guy was carrying a bouquet of flowers. He kept them in his hand as he and Harrison walked around the gate and began to fight their way up through the woods, just as I had in the spring. I snapped a few pictures before they disappeared into the trees, including one clear shot of the van and the license plate.

Joe had been out with me for the morning but left around noon. I called him at the office now. "Guess who's here. Parker Harrison."

"Really?"

"Uh-huh. Just showed up with another guy I didn't recognize, and they aren't in Harrison's truck. You want to run the plate for me?"

I gave him the license number, and a few minutes later he called back and told me the truck was registered to a Mark Ruzity.

"Mean anything to you?"

"Yeah. He was another of Alexandra's murderers. The first one."

"What do you think they're doing?"

"Paying respects," I said. "He brought flowers, Joe. I'm telling you, the place is a damn memorial at this point."

Ruzity and Harrison came back out twenty minutes later, sans flowers, and got back into the truck and drove away.

So now I had an answer. I'd seen what I told him I wanted to see, and yet I knew nothing more than I had before. Ken's bizarre prediction—*she'll come back to see it*—was as foolish as I should have known it was.

I stayed, though. For the rest of that day, and the three that followed. By the end of the week I was starting to lose my mind from sitting in one spot so long, and Joe was quiet on the topic, which meant he thought it was time to give up. Even Amy asked how much longer I intended to keep watch, and her tone made her feelings clear—it was time to call the surveillance off.

I told them I wanted one more day. Spent twelve hours watching that lonely drive and the gate and didn't see a soul.

"You knew it was a long shot anyhow," Amy said. "Time to let it pass."

I agreed with her, told her the whole thing had gone on too long. Then the next morning I got up and took my camera and my binoculars and drove back and watched nothing. I did it the day after that, too, then came home and told Amy I'd spent the day at the gym. The next morning I rose before dawn and returned.

That was the coldest day of the fall so far, and by seven my coffee was gone and the sun wasn't even up yet and the chill had already filled the cab of the truck and gone to work on my knotted back and shoulder muscles. It was time to quit, I realized. This was lunacy, or close to it.

I was parked just off the road beside a cluster of saplings and brush, squeezed in the back of the extended cab with blackout curtains hung in the windows. I'd now spent about a hundred hours in this position, the most surveillance time I'd logged on a case in years, and I wasn't making a dime from it.

When the headlights crested the hill and slowed near the drive, I didn't even lift my camera. I'd seen too many cars pass to get excited about this one. Then it came to a complete stop, and I sat up and pushed the blackout curtain farther aside and watched as the car—a small red sedan—turned into the gravel track and drove right up to the gate. I finally got my shit together then, reached for the camera and got it up and turned on as the driver's door swung open. My zoom was good, but it wasn't built for low-light conditions, and all I could see in the predawn gloom was that the driver looked like a woman, and she was walking around the gate and through the trees. She was walking toward the house.

35

For a moment, I wasn't sure what to do. I just sat there holding my camera and looking at the dark trees she'd vanished into, wondering if I should wait for her to reemerge and then follow her, or set off now with hopes of catching her at the house. After a brief hesitation, I decided to take action over patience.

I got out of the truck, leaving my camera but wearing my gun, and walked down the road toward the drive. I took my time, knowing that any attempt to follow her quietly through the woods around the creek would be hopeless. It was important to give her a little lead time. When I reached the red sedan, I knelt by the back bumper and took a photograph of the license plate with my cell phone's built-in camera, a device I'd come to appreciate in moments like this. It was an Ohio plate. Surely, then, this couldn't be Alexandra. She couldn't be living so close to home. It would be an aggressive Realtor checking on the house before going to the office, and nothing more. When I walked around to the front of the car I spotted an Avis sticker, though. A rental.

I walked toward the woods bordering the gate. The trees didn't seem nearly so dark when I was in them as they'd looked through the camera, and I found I was able to walk without much difficulty. It was easier now, in late fall, than it had been in spring, when everything was green and growing and the water in the creek rode high on the banks. Once I was around the gate and away from the creek I slowed again, focusing on a quiet approach now. I made my way back to the rutted drive and followed it along, seeing and hearing nothing of the woman ahead.

When the drive curled around its final bend and came out at the base of the hill that hid the house, I stopped and scanned the trees, searching for her. I gave it a careful study, made absolutely certain she wasn't in sight, and then continued forward. I'd taken at least five steps toward the hill when I finally realized she was at the door.

I hadn't seen her at first because the door was beneath that stone arch, covered in shadows, and she was no longer standing. She was kneeling before the door, and as I walked closer, in slow, silent strides, I saw that her head was bowed and her arm extended, her palm resting on the oaken door.

It was her. Other women might make a trip out to this home before the sun rose, but none would drop to their knees and touch its door as if at an altar.

Alexandra had come home.

I stopped walking when I was about thirty feet from her, stood and waited. She held her position for a while, maybe a minute, maybe two. Didn't move at all, didn't make a sound, just knelt there with her head bowed and her hand on the door. When she finally moved it was to rub her hand gently across the wood, and then she got to her feet and turned and saw me.

"It's a beautiful house," I said. "One of a kind. Do you miss it?"

Her eyes left me and flicked to either side, searching for others.

"I'm alone," I said, "and I don't intend to bring you any trouble. I would just like to hear you talk for a while. I'd like you to tell me some things. I need that very much."

She stepped away from the door, out of the stone arch and into the light, toward me. She was not tall, no more than five foot two or three, with a slender build and graceful movements. When she came closer I saw that much remained from the face that had stared at me in photographs—the fine bones and small nose and mouth, the impossibly dark eyes. Her hair was different, chopped short and close to her skull, but for the most part she looked the same.

"I wear a wig most of the time," she said, watching me study her. "I have glasses even though I don't need them. They're clear, no prescription. I wear makeup now when I never used to, lots of eyeliner and foundation and other junk that I just hate to put on my face."

She came to within a few feet of me, then tilted her head, frowned at me, and said, "You're Lincoln."

I hadn't been mentioned in any newspaper article; there was no public record of my involvement with any of the cases surrounding this woman.

"How do you know that?"

She ignored me, turned and looked over her shoulder at the door.

"You were right," she said. "It is a beautiful home, and I do miss it. I miss it terribly, the house and all of the other things I left behind. The life I left behind."

"Alexandra," I said, "how do you know my name?"

"From Ken Merriman."

I stood still and silent and stared at the calm set of her face. Then I said, slowly and carefully, "You don't mean that you spoke to Ken Merriman."

"Of course I do," she said. "I hired him."

36

The sentence left her lips almost carelessly and struck me like lead.

"You hired Ken Merriman?" I said. "You *hired* him?"

She nodded.

"No," I said. "Joshua's parents hired him. That was in the papers. He'd been looking for you for twelve years."

"He looked for me for about nine months," she said, "and then he found me."

"Explain it," I said. It felt hard to get the words out.

"You understand how it began. Joshua's parents hired him. If there is one thing I felt worst about in all of this, it's the uncertainty they had to deal with. That was terrible, I'm sure. They were not kind people, and Joshua's relationship with them had been a painful and difficult one, but that was not enough to justify what I did."

She fell silent for a few seconds before saying, "There's probably no way for people to understand the decisions I made. All I can say is that once I was gone, once it was already under way, I wasn't brave enough to return. There was nothing that could be done to bring Joshua back, not for me or for them."

"Tell me about Ken," I said. The sun was beginning to show pink through the trees. I could hear the birds and the wind but nothing of the road. "How did he find you?"

"The same way you did."

"He watched the house?"

"He asked everyone he talked with about the words by the door, the inscription that's carved there. Everyone told him they'd not seen the carving until we were gone, and he believed that it had been left as an epitaph. He was right, of course."

She lifted her hand and waved at the eastern sky, now beginning to glow red with the rising sun. "Let's walk up top, okay? I loved to sit up there and watch the sunrise. It's just gorgeous."

She moved without waiting for my response, walked around to the side of the hill and started up, following a flagstone path that was now almost completely submerged in weeds. I followed.

When we got to the top of the hill, she moved over to the old well house and leaned against its side, facing the sun. Again I marveled at how completely hidden the house was, nothing but grass and soil evident beneath our feet, only the lip of a stone wall indicating the drop-off on the other side where the windows looked out on the pond. I walked to within a few feet of her and stood silently, arms folded, waiting. She seemed at ease, and for a while she just looked off at the sunrise and did not speak. When she finally broke the silence, she didn't bother to turn around.

"How many days have you been watching?"

"Quite a few."

She nodded. "This was going to be my last visit, you know. It will have to be. The house will have new owners soon. I can't very well come by then."

"If you know everything that's happened, why didn't you announce yourself, prove that you're still alive and keep the home? Why would you let it be sold?"

She didn't answer.

"Did you kill him?" I said.

Now she turned, wounded. "Of course I didn't kill him. Joshua? I loved him so much. So very dearly."

"Then what are you hiding from?"

She stepped away from the well house and dropped down to sit in the grass, cross-legged. It was tall grass, rising well above her waist, but she settled into it comfortably and pushed her sleeves up on her forearms. She was wearing dark jeans and a gray fleece jacket, and there were simple silver bracelets on both wrists. She had to be near fifty now, but she looked like a college student settling down outside of a dormitory. If she weighed more than a hundred and ten pounds I would've been stunned, and her skin was weathered but still smooth, every thin wrinkle looking as if it belonged and added something that you'd miss otherwise.

"Are you going to continue standing?" she said, looking up at me. "It makes me uncomfortable."

So I sat in the grass with her, felt the moisture of day-old rain leave the ground and soak through my jeans, and watched the sun rise behind her as she told me the story.

Alexandra's life was shaped very much by her father's, by the world of crime and violence that had surrounded her childhood. The money he'd left was something she'd viewed as an embarrassment at first and then decided to reinvest into the reentry program. Her vision for Whisper Ridge as a sort of work farm had not received the funding or support it needed. She decided to operate at a smaller level and use success to grow the operation in the future. It was at this point that she began to feel her husband's resistance.

"Joshua was not a direct man in times of conflict," she said. "He wouldn't come out and tell me flatly that he didn't want to open our home to this, but I knew it was the case, and I pushed ahead anyhow. I thought he believed in the ideals, and that time would take care of the rest. It was a selfish thing to do, maybe. I've wondered about that a lot, and I think that it probably was, but at the time I could not imagine . . . I'm sure you know I could not imagine what would come."

What came was an increasingly troubled marriage. Alexandra's version of events meshed well with John Dunbar's. She described Joshua as growing withdrawn and distrustful. Then Parker Harrison was hired, a move that exacerbated the problem at Whisper Ridge.

"My relationship with Parker was very close," she told me. "I'd say that of all of them, of course, but not to the same level. Parker and I, we were similar spirits. I found his story truly tragic."

"I believe the family of his victim would agree," I said.

She stopped speaking and looked at me with a frown that was more sad than disapproving.

"To say one is not to dismiss the other," she said. "Can you understand that?"

"Can I hear the rest of the story?"

"As I said, my relationship with Parker was special. We were so close. I think that fueled the resentment that was already in Joshua."

"You say your relationship with Harrison was special. Was it also sexual?"

"No, no, no. Absolutely not. Although during the first six months Parker was with us, Joshua's personality changed. I now understand this was when he was in contact with the FBI and being pressured to inform on my brother, but I didn't back then."

"It wasn't the FBI," I said. "It was one retired agent with some bad ideas."

"Nevertheless, my husband was withdrawing, and I finally began to understand just how much damage had been done. Then we began to discuss who would replace Parker, and Joshua told me that he wanted to do the interviews and make the offer, which was something I'd always handled in the past. I was confused by that but agreed, because I was so happy to see his enthusiasm returning. Then he decided on Salvatore Bertoli, who was very far from the profile we'd agreed upon at the start."

"You didn't know Bertoli was associated with your brother?"

"No. Salvatore didn't know who I was, either, because my name was Cantrell, and my brother and I were not close. We saw each other, but only rarely, and we did not discuss his . . . associates. All of that is in the past, though. My brother's crimes. He served two years, and when he got out his life changed. He kept no ties. Many who would've posed the greatest problems to him were in prison themselves, and the others accepted his desire to step away. My brother has not been involved with a crime in fifteen years."

"There are police who would dispute that," I said. "I've met some of them."

Her arms unfolded and she leaned forward. "What proof did they show? What evidence? What did they tell you that was current, not historic?"

"Nothing," I said, and then, as the satisfaction crossed her face, "but some of those *historic* events included murder. There are people who feel those things are unresolved."

The satisfaction disappeared, and she dropped her eyes again. "I'm sure that's true. All I can tell you is that he's not been involved in anything criminal in years, that he's led a life that benefits others. He's a businessman now, a generous one. You should see the charities—"

"All due respect," I said, "I'm not here to evaluate your brother's tithing history. I'm glad you don't think he's killed anyone lately. I'd agree that's progress, but it's not what I'm interested in."

I expected that would get a rise, some defensiveness, but instead she just considered me calmly. It was a gaze that made me uncomfortable, as if I fit neatly into a mold she'd been studying her whole life and understood well. When she began to speak again it was without rancor, leaving the subject of her brother behind.

"I was losing trust in my husband and had none in Salvatore. I felt bad things coming into my home, and so I asked Parker to stay. I trusted him. That's the decision that put Joshua over the edge. I didn't see it at the time, of course, but apparently he'd had misgivings and was being bullied along by that FBI agent, Dunbar. When I said I wanted Parker to stay, though, it incensed him, and he decided to go ahead with it. The house became a very ugly place for a while, a distrustful, silent place."

"I've talked to Dunbar," I said, "and he said he conceived the whole thing because he is certain that Bertoli witnessed your brother killing a man named Johnny DiPietro."

"That's not true."

"According to your brother."

"No. According to Salvatore."

"What?"

"He told Parker," she said, "that he understood what Joshua was trying to do and that whoever had put him up to it was absolutely wrong, didn't understand who they should be after, but that it was someone who wouldn't hesitate to kill my husband."

"It seems logical that he'd say that."

"Perhaps, but Parker believed him, and Salvatore moved out."

"At which point Harrison reported all of this to you," I said. "I'm supposed to believe you never chose to confront your husband about it?"

"I did confront him," she said, "and we had a royal battle, a screaming raging fight, and it saved our marriage. It would have saved our marriage."

Her voice faded, tears rose in her eyes, and she dabbed them away gently without shame. She looked hauntingly beautiful in that moment.

"That night was when the silence broke," she said, "and everything that had been held secret was shared. He told me what he'd thought and what he'd done, and I told him how his silence had damaged us, and that night we made love like people *in* love for the first time in years—and we decided we were going to leave."

"For good?"

She shook her head. "No. For a few months, maybe a year. Joshua had been talking about it for a long time, urging for a trip overseas, and at the time I'd refused because I thought it would set us back in what we were doing here. That night, I agreed to it, because I thought that we had to get away to find a shared life again, so we could come back. Otherwise we were going to lose each other. Maybe we would have anyhow, but I like to think differently."

She stopped talking then, and her mouth became a hard line. For a moment I thought she was angry, but then I realized the tears were gaining on her again and she was determined not to be overrun.

"Joshua also thought we had to leave for safety. After what Parker told us, he thought we could be in danger."

"So you planned to leave," I said, "but you never made it. Your husband never made it, at least."

She nodded. "We made calls about arrangements for the house, for the mail, all those things you need to do before going abroad. The last time I saw him, I was heading out to talk to a travel agent and asked if he wanted to come, too. He said he had things to do around the house and I should go alone. I was gone for maybe three hours. When I came back here, I found my husband's body."

She was staring at the well house as if something were crawling out of it.

"He was outside. Just in front of the door. He'd been shot, and there was blood all over the stone, and when I saw his body I was sure that my brother had killed him."

"How did you know?"

"Dominic gave Joshua a present when we got married. It was a ring, this horrible ring with an enormous stone that surely cost a fortune but could not have been less like my husband. He was not a man who wore rings. My brother, at that time, was. He was loud and flashy and wore expensive jewelry and to him the gift meant something. Joshua hated it, though, and the only time he ever wore it was when my brother was around."

She folded her arms across her chest again, even though the wind wasn't blowing and the sun was warm on us through the bare trees, and said, "The ring was lying on his chest. Right there in the blood. It had been dropped in the blood and I understood what it meant. The ring had been a symbol to my brother, a welcome into our family, and Joshua had betrayed that welcome. So my brother killed him, and even as he lied to me about it, he left that ring as a message."

"He was murdered here," I said, "and his body was left at the door."

She nodded.

"Then could you explain how he ended up in the woods in Pennsylvania?"

She looked at me and then away, twisted her torso as if stretching her back, and spoke with her face turned from mine. "I took him there and I buried him."

"I'm glad you lied about that," I said. "Because it tells me how bad a liar you are, Alexandra, and that's going to help me believe the rest of what you've said."

She unfolded the stretch slowly, let her face come back around.

"Parker Harrison buried him," I said. "Now tell me why."

"To help me," she said. "To save me. He'd been gone that afternoon, and when he drove back in, with the truck all loaded up with mulch, he found me sitting there beside Joshua."

"Why didn't you call the police?"

"The police wouldn't bring him back, but they would ask me to stay here and face the investigation and the trial, to prosecute my brother, to deal with the media. All of that would happen if I stayed, and so much more. There were people like Parker, and like Nimir Farah and Mark Ruzity, and I knew the publicity would find them, and I thought that would be a terrible thing. I saw no good coming from it at all, and so much harm."

"What about justice for your husband?" I said. "That meant nothing?"

"Of course it did. My response was one of shock, I'll admit that. The idea of having to bear what would come . . . I decided I couldn't do it. That may seem like cowardice to you, and you may be right. I'll let you make that judgment."

"Mark Ruzity was seen with your brother after you disappeared, after Joshua was killed," I said. "And Parker Harrison called him. Why?"

"I asked Parker to pass along a message to my brother, to tell him that I was leaving, would never speak to him again, and that he should never look for me."

"What about Ruzity?"

She frowned. "Mark is such a good soul, but he struggles with his anger. He really does. He and Parker were close, and I told Parker that he could tell Mark only that I was leaving because of my brother's actions. I didn't trust his reaction to the details. Even so, I suspect Mark might have . . . given a more direct message to Dominic."

"I'm sorry?"

She looked up. "I suspect he threatened to kill him if he pursued me."

I thought of the chisel against my forehead, and then I thought of the photograph Dunbar had taken, the way Ruzity had clasped his hand around Sanabria's neck, pulled him close, and whispered in his ear. There weren't many people who would threaten to kill a mob boss, but Mark Ruzity seemed like he could be one of them easily enough.

"Harrison took the body," I said, "and you took off."

"Yes."

I shook my head, wondering now more than ever why he had decided to darken my door. He knew what had happened. What in the hell had he really wanted?

"Did he know where you went?" I asked. "Did you have any contact with him?"

"No."

So maybe he'd just wanted to find her. Maybe he'd been honest about that much.

"I had no contact with Parker," she said, "until this May. Until the day before Ken was murdered. That day, I called Parker to tell him not to trust you."

"What?"

"I told him that I was safe and well and that I knew he was looking for me but it would be dangerous for him to have any association with police and detectives. He'd buried my husband's body. It was easy to imagine he could be blamed. I said if anything happened, all he needed to do was ask me, and I'd come forward."

The day before Ken was murdered. That was the same day Harrison had told me to quit, but then he'd asked that final question, asked who Ken really was.

"Why didn't you explain Ken to him?" I said.

"Ken was the only person who knew how to find me, and had known for years. Couldn't the police have charged him with something for that? I wanted to keep him out of anything negative."

"Out of anything negative," I echoed. "He's dead. Your decision to leave your husband's murder unanswered is understandable, maybe even acceptable. This isn't."

"I agree."

"Yet you haven't contacted the police, haven't taken any action."

"I didn't know what action to take. I've been gone for twelve years. I have a new life, in a new place. I don't want to destroy that in the way my old life was destroyed."

"But you're the only person who knows anything."

"Here's all I know: that on the morning before he died Ken Merriman left me a message—"

"That's another lie. He didn't leave you a message, Alexandra. All the phone records were checked and rechecked."

"He didn't use his own phone, or mine. He understood my reluctance to give that out, and so years earlier he created an account with a phone message service, some anonymous thing, and he used pay phones and a calling card, just as I did. It was the only way we were in touch. Never in actual conversation, always through an exchange of messages. Now would you like to hear what he said that last day?"

"Yes."

"He said that he believed the two of you were getting close to the truth of my husband's murder, and that it had nothing to do with my brother, and more to do with a car."

37

A car?" I stared at her, and I couldn't speak. A car. What car?
"You don't know what that means?" she said.

"No. I don't know, because he cut me out of it, went off alone on whatever theory he had and got himself killed."

"He cut you out of it because he was waiting for my permission to tell you the truth. To give full disclosure. He thought you could be trusted."

"Would you have given it to him?"

She was quiet for a while before saying, "I don't know. I suppose so. I've told you the truth now."

"Only because I found you." As I said it I realized Ken had told me *how* to find her. That constant insistence that she would return to the house if it were sold, that she'd have to see it one last time. *Let me tell you,* he'd said, the way he started so many sentences, *if she's alive, she'll come back for one more visit before the place is sold.*

"You told him you'd come back here," I said. "When you found out your in-laws were making a claim on the property, you told him you'd come back before it was sold."

"Yes."

He'd led me to her. Brought me here.

"He'd known for years," I said, "and kept the secret. Why?"

"All I told him was what I've told you, only with far less composure. It was my first trip back to the house, and I was already a wreck when he found me. Then that sense of being caught . . . he calmed me down, and he listened to me, and I told him the same story, only without some of the information I have now."

"You told him all of this and then asked him to just go on and pretend he had no idea where you were."

She nodded. "You disapprove, and I'm not surprised. Most people would share your opinion, I'm sure. Ken Merriman was not one of them. He understood when I told him that everything had been taken from me. There were two great loves in my life—my husband and my mission here. They were destroyed. Do you think the state would have continued to work with me? I'd gotten a man killed rather than rehabilitated. My work was destroyed, my husband dead, my brother responsible. I ran from it. I ran, okay? It was wrong, maybe, and weak, certainly, but it is what I did."

I didn't respond.

"I begged Ken Merriman to let me leave, and he did," she said. "He did."

This would have been after the newspaper articles and the public complaints of Joshua Cantrell's parents. After immense damage to Ken's reputation and to his career. He could have played the ultimate trump card by producing Alexandra, silenced every critic and bought himself some amount of fame. It was a hell of a story, a hell of a mystery, and he could have brought it to light. Instead he chose silence, went back to that career of infidelity cases and insurance work, of financial problems and low respect. I thought of the time he'd told me that his wife was right to leave him, what he'd said about making a decision that seemed absolutely right at the time, then seeing the way it affected your family and wondering if it was a selfish choice.

"Do you appreciate the losses he took for you?" I said. "What he gave up?"

"Of course I do. He damaged his own life to protect mine."

"It was the epitaph," I said. "That's what convinced him you'd come back?"

She nodded.

"Who did the carving?"

"Parker. At my request, and after I was gone. I wanted to leave some sense of a memorial, and I wanted the words to speak to my brother. I wanted him to know that I knew he'd killed my husband. Ken Merriman suspected something close, and he thought that if I viewed the house as a memorial, I might return to it. Probably around the last date, April twelfth. So he waited, and he watched. Every day for three weeks."

Three weeks. I wouldn't have lasted that long. I remembered now what Casey Hopper had told me when I called to ask him about Ken—*You know I was a sniper in Vietnam. So when I say somebody is patient . . .*

"You didn't come back on the twelfth?"

She shook her head. "I wanted to, but then I was afraid that might be expected. So I came later."

"He was still waiting."

"Yes. He said everyone told him how important this place was to me, how much hope and excitement I'd held for it, and between that and the epitaph he became convinced I'd come back."

"The house was almost new," I said, "and worth a fortune. You intended to just leave it empty forever?"

"There was nothing left for me here. There was no way I could continue to live here—but sell the house? I could never have done that. Never."

"It's gone now," I said. "I doubt you can reclaim it. It might be too late."

She nodded. "I won't try to stop it. Let them have their money. I owe them that much, surely."

"They did great damage to Ken's career."

"I know, and when he left a message telling me that you'd be inquiring about the house, I said I wanted to hire him to find out who you were working for. I was afraid it was them again, and that Parker would be at risk. I didn't imagine he was the client."

"When you found out, you asked Ken to hang around and keep an eye on things?"

"No. That was on his own. He'd evidently grown doubtful of my brother's guilt."

"You have no contact with your brother?"

"None. As I said, for so many years I believed he killed Joshua. Then Ken left that final message and said he thought I was wrong."

"And that the police needed to pay attention to a car," I said.

She nodded again.

"It needs to be finished," I said. "You have to realize that."

"Will the police be able to finish it?" she said. "After all this time?"

"I'll be able to," I said. "Hell, according to Ken, I already did. Now I just have to figure out *how* I did."

We stayed for another hour, sat there as the sun rose higher and our muscles stiffened, and she told me more of her story but nothing that compared to what I'd already heard. Eventually I asked her where she had been for the past twelve years. She gave more of an answer than I expected.

"I live in a small town not in this country but not so far away, either." She laughed. "How difficult of a riddle is that? Fine, so I live in a small Canadian town. I live under a different name, and I've worn a wig for so long that it feels like part of me. I make a modest living in modest ways and it's all that I need. In my new life, it's more than I need. I've never remarried, and I doubt that I ever will. I have friends whom I treasure, people who mean more to me than I can express, and none of them, not a soul, understands my past. I haven't lied to them, I've just asked for no questions, and they have respected that. Those closest to me have, at least."

I had so many questions myself, but it became clear that she had fewer answers, and after a time the conversation became stagnant and then disappeared altogether. I didn't want to let her go. I also knew we couldn't stay.

"I could hold you here," I said, "and call the police. There are many of them who would like to talk to you."

She didn't answer. Just held my eyes in silence.

"I'm not sure I want to do that," I said. "Maybe I will, soon, but not yet. I'm equally certain it would be a mistake to let you leave."

"Give me your phone number," she said. "I'll call you in a day. I promise I will do that. Whatever you want from me, I'll offer it."

"Including coming forward?"

Again, the silence.

"Ah," I said. "Whatever I want, except that."

"Maybe that. I'm not sure. I've been gone for many years, and I have a new life that would be sacrificed. Surely you know that's not a snap decision."

"No decision that takes twelve years to make is—but I'm not sure it's your decision to make, Alexandra."

We sat and looked at each other for a while, and then I got to my feet. My legs felt foreign. We'd been sitting for a long time.

"I can accept all of this as the truth, and a week from now realize it was a lie and feel a fool for believing you," I said.

"It isn't a lie."

"It may be," I said. "If it is, you can know this—I'll chase you. For as long as it takes me, and as far as it takes me, I'll chase you."

She stood as well, brushed off her jeans, and then stepped forward and offered her hand. I clasped it and held it and looked into her eyes as she said, "I'll say this one more time—it isn't a lie."

She walked away from me then, walked to that short ridge of stone that marked the rear wall of the house and looked down at the pond. She stood there with her hands in the pockets of her jeans and her shoulders hunched, looking down. I gave her a few minutes before I followed.

"I wish you could have seen it," she said when I was beside her.

"I can imagine what it looked like."

"No." She shook her head. "You can't. When Parker was tending the grounds, when everything was at its best, it was beyond what you can imagine. In the spring, when it was all in bloom . . . no, you can't imagine what that looked like."

She took her hands from her pockets and turned away. "It was everything I'd dreamed of. We could have done so much here. We could have done so much."

38

I walked up the drive with her, and neither of us spoke. When she reached her rental car, she turned and faced me.

"I'll call tomorrow," she said, "and we'll figure out how to move forward. You may not believe me, but it is the truth. If I don't call, keep your word. Start the chase."

"That might seem like a joke to you," I said, "but it is not to me. I don't care where you are, Alexandra, I'll find you eventually. Anyone can be found."

"Ken Merriman already taught me that." She took my hand again, squeezed it once, and then turned and opened the driver's door and climbed inside. I waited until she'd started the engine before I left and walked back up the road to my truck. I got inside, started it up, and drove to the highway. I stared at every vehicle that passed and thought, *He said all they needed to do was pay attention to a car.*

There was only one possibility coming to my mind, and Mike London had checked it out. The day Ken and I had lunch with him, he told us about a vehicle he'd seen near Bertoli's murder scene that had belonged to a chop shop affiliated with Dominic Sanabria. What had the owner's name been?

Neloms. Darius Neloms. His alibi checked out solid, though, and the lead dried up. So what could Ken have possibly seen that Mike did not?

Unless it was a different car entirely. If that was the case, then I was as utterly clueless as I had been before talking to Alexandra.

I was halfway back to the city when my cell phone rang, and I saw the call was coming from the office. Joe.

"You're out there again, aren't you," he said when I answered, and then, before I could respond, "LP, you've got to let it go. You've got to stop."

"She came to the house this morning."

For a moment I didn't hear a thing.

"Tell me it is the truth," he said, "and that I don't need to begin searching for the proper institution for you."

I told him what had happened. By the time I was done, I was a mile from the office, and he hadn't spoken for a long time.

"I let her go," I said, "and I know you'll tell me what a terrible mistake that was, but I don't care. I'll find her again if I have to."

"If you believe what she told you, that's not the issue of the day," he said, and something inside me sagged with relief. He agreed with me. Alexandra was no longer the focus.

"I believe it," I said, "because I saw her lie today, and, Joseph, she is not good at it."

"And the car?" he said. "Do you have any idea what that means?"

"Maybe. If I'm wrong, then I've got nothing. We'll have to wait and see."

I hung up with him, and five minutes later I was behind my desk. I told Joe what I remembered from Mike London's investigation, then leaned back with my hands spread.

"That's the best I've got. Darius Neloms was an associate of Sanabria, but he was far from the inner circle. The guy painted stolen cars and sent them back out the door. It's not like he was Sanabria's right-hand man. Even if he was, Ken apparently was questioning whether Sanabria had anything to do with the murder."

"He said the car was important. So maybe he found out who else had access to it."

"Maybe. If it doesn't go back to that chop shop, though, then I have no idea what he was talking about. We talked to Mike the day before Ken was killed, so it would have been fresh in his mind, and if he was giving me credit for getting him to the solution, well, that's the only thing I got him to. Only London mentioned a car."

"Well," Joe said, "I'd say now's the time to call him."

So I called him. Put him on speaker while Joe sat with his chin resting on steepled fingertips and listened. I had not spoken to Mike London since Ken was killed. He'd called after he heard the news, more curious then distressed, and I had never called back.

I'd already decided I didn't want anyone but Joe to know that the new information had come from Alexandra, so I skirted that, told Mike only that Ken had evidently mentioned his belief that a car was the key to the case shortly before he was killed.

"The only car I ever heard mentioned," I said, "was the one you told us about. It belonged to a guy named Darius Neloms, right?"

"Right."

"Who had an alibi that was—"

"Airtight. Yes."

"There's no way you could have been wrong on that."

Silence. Then, "Brother, you want to check up on me, by all means go ahead. Hell, we probably still have the security tapes buried in some evidence locker. But I'm giving you my word that Darius Neloms was nowhere near Bertoli's death scene. A car belonging to him was. I did not find out who was driving the car. I tried, and I did not find out."

His voice was terse and biting, and Joe raised his eyebrows and gave me a little smile. I was stepping into dangerous turf now, with even a suggestion that Mike might have missed something.

"That's good enough for me," I said, trying to soothe, thinking that while I was still going to need to verify, there was no reason to call him out on it now. "I just don't know what the hell to do with this, Mike. If Ken was excited about a car, I think it had to be the one you told us about, but where that took him . . ."

"Like I told you back in the spring, Darius was connected to Sanabria."

"Evidently Ken wasn't sure the murder had anything to do with Sanabria."

"Then I quite simply don't know what to tell you, Lincoln."

I rubbed my forehead and squeezed my eyes shut, trying to think of the right question—hell, of *any* question. What could Ken have seen in that car that neither Mike nor I could?

"You traced the plate, and it ran back to Neloms directly," I said. "Right?"

"Right. Wait, no. It was registered to his shop, which doesn't really make a damn bit of difference. Ultimately still his vehicle. He claimed no idea of who could have driven it, said the keys were inside the shop and maybe somebody took them, then told us the car must have been stolen."

"But it had been returned."

"Uh-huh. I checked out every employee—most of whom were family or friends of his, cousins or nephews or whatever—and didn't get anything, but I don't think whoever was behind the wheel really had much to do with Neloms."

"You think they worked for Sananbria."

"Right. They had a history together."

All of this was recycled, the same damn conversation we'd had six months ago, and all of it pointed back to Sanabria, when Ken's final words pointed in another direction entirely.

"Look, Lincoln, I don't know what else to tell you . . ."

"It's fine, Mike. Don't worry about it. If I think of something else, I'll call."

I thanked him and hung up.

"Mike thinks one of Sanabria's guys drove the car," Joe said.

"Yeah."

We sat in silence and thought.

"This is going to sound crazy," I said, "but what if Bertoli drove himself there?"

He frowned. "His ghost got up off the pavement and drove it back? The car was gone after he died, right? That's why Mike was looking at it as a suspect vehicle."

"Right," I said, "but he had to get there somehow, and whoever killed him would have known that. The guy had just gotten out of prison; it's unlikely he had his own car. So maybe he borrowed one from this Neloms guy.

He drove that car to meet somebody, he got killed, and then someone else—maybe the guy who killed him, maybe not—drove the car back. Having the car gone from the scene is one less thing for the cops to look at, which is what they'd want, and they couldn't have known . . ."

My voice trailed off, and Joe said, "Keep going," but I didn't answer. The notion of Bertoli as the driver had tripped something in my brain, and I got up and went to the file cabinet and pulled out the sheaf of papers Ken had given me on the case. Copies of everything he'd had, or so he'd told me.

It took me a while, but I located the paperwork he'd brought into the office on the morning after our first encounter, the morning after my wild drunken dream about Parker Harrison watching me on the roof. Profiles of all the convicts who'd stayed at Whisper Ridge. I flipped through until I found Bertoli. Read the report once again, the details of his arrest for beating the truck stop manager and stealing his heroin. The police had arrested him within hours. Due to his car.

39

Bertoli used a stolen plate, but it was his own vehicle, an Impala with a custom paint job and chrome rims featuring cutouts in the shape of diamonds.

"Son of a bitch," I said, and then, without bothering to say a word to Joe's questioning glance, I pounded the redial button on the phone and got Mike London back on the line. He sounded weary when he realized it was me.

"One last question," I said. "The car you saw that night, it was an Olds Cutlass, not an Impala, right?"

"Right."

"You said it had custom features on it, though"

"Yeah, all that shit like in a rap video."

"This is a long shot, but do you remember the rims?"

"The *rims*?"

"Yeah."

"Well, they were spinners. You know, the kind that rotate when the engine's on?"

"Right. You remember whether there were diamond etchings in them? Cutouts in the shape of diamonds?"

Silence while he thought, then, "Yeah, maybe. Maybe there were. I'm not sure, but I think that sounds right."

"All right, Mike. Thanks. Thanks a lot."

I hung up with him again, and then I stood and brought the Bertoli report over to Joe's desk and dropped it down, waited while he read it.

"You're thinking that he got his car worked on down there?"

"Yes."

"Makes sense. Of course, we already know Sanabria's guys and Neloms had an association."

"Uh-huh, but read that arrest report again—who was in the vehicle with Bertoli the night he stole the heroin?"

"Unidentified juvenile."

"Right. Name redacted from Ken's report, because what Ken could access was public record, and the passenger was a minor. There's an original police report with that kid's name. I want it."

"I'll call."

Unlike me, he wouldn't use the speakerphone. I heard him say what he wanted and was sure he'd be told to wait for a call back. That's what it would have taken had I called—and if I didn't pick the right person to lean on for the favor, the wait might have extended into the next day. Instead, Joe was on hold for what seemed like all of thirty seconds. He murmured a soft thank-you into the phone, scribbled a name onto his notepad, and then hung up and held the pad a few inches from my face.

Alvin Neloms, black juvenile, sixteen years old.

"A son, probably," I said. "Darius has a son."

"Check on it."

I went back to my computer and ran a database search on Alvin Neloms and pulled up a family history. His father was listed as unknown. His mother had kept her own name, it seemed. According to the family chart the database offered, Darius Neloms was the boy's uncle, not his father. He was from East Cleveland, was now twenty-nine years old, and had been arrested just one time as an adult, for drug possession, charge dismissed. These were all things Ken could have found in a few minutes of research after he made the connection between the cars.

"You know anybody with East Cleveland PD?" I asked.

"Tony Mitchell did some task force stuff with them."

"Ask about this kid, would you? I want to know more before we talk to him."

"We're going to talk to him?"

"Bet your ass, Joseph. We're getting there. Getting *somewhere*."

So Joe got back on the phone and asked for Tony, and they exchanged cursory greetings while I waited impatiently.

"Use the damn speaker, Joe."

He ignored me, then told Tony he was calling to ask if the name Alvin Neloms meant anything to him. He listened for a while with no change of expression, then said, "Could you repeat that, please?" This time he finally hit the speakerphone button.

"I said Cash is the worst they've got," Tony said. "One of them, at least. And down there? When I say he's one of the worst, you know what I'm talking about."

"Cash?" Joe said.

"That's what he goes by, yeah. Comes from an old playground basketball nickname, everybody called him 'Cash Money' when he was a kid because he had a jump shot that just did not miss. In another neighborhood, another school, that kid plays college ball and goes to the league. No question. I've seen him play plenty. We had surveillance details on Cash for years, and even while waiting to bust his ass, I was impressed by his game. He played it like he loved it, you know? Then he'd go off and kill someone. It's sad, is what it is."

"What exactly is his story?" Joe said.

"Drugs and blood. He's top of the food chain out there now. Nobody moves a damn dime bag through East Cleveland that he doesn't know about."

"He's only been arrested one time? Charge dismissed?"

"The boy is *good*, got it? Runs a couple dozen gangbangers and pushers who take his falls for him and isn't a one of them says a word, because if they do, they just dug a grave that fits them nice and tight. Cash runs shit organized, runs it like the damn Mafia."

Joe cocked his head and looked at me. I didn't say anything, didn't respond.

"Unofficial body count credited to Cash Neloms?" Tony said. "Twenty. Maybe twenty-five."

My chest muscles suddenly felt cold and constricted.

"You ever heard of him actually having mob ties?" Joe said.

"Nope. It's all his show, Pritchard. His organization. And that shitty side of town drips with his blood."

"Supposing we wanted to talk to him—" Joe began.

"Talk to *Cash*? On what?"

"Cold case investigation. Twelve years old."

"Twelve years old? *Twelve?* Sweet mother, Pritchard, I'll tell you this one time and make it clear as I can—this ain't a man you *talk* to. Not a PI. I know you were police for a long time, but you're a civilian now, and that's a distinction that means something to Cash. Understand? You walk in that neighborhood asking questions about Cash Neloms, you better be wearing a damn vest and carrying with your finger on the trigger."

"I'm advised," Joe said. "Thanks, Tony."

He disconnected, blew out a breath, and said, "Where are we going, Lincoln? Where in the hell are we going?"

I didn't know. I stood in silence for a minute, trying to think, but there were too many pieces and too many ways they could fit, and I could not see the whole for the sum of its parts, couldn't even get close. Eventually I picked up the phone and held it in my hand, thinking of Quinn Graham. I didn't call, though. I hung up before the dial tone switched over to that rapid off-the-hook beep, and then I lifted the receiver again and called John Dunbar. I used the home number, and he answered.

"Hey," I said, "it's Lincoln Perry. You remember me?"

"You got something?" he said, and it was incredible how much anticipation was in his voice, how much hope.

"Yeah," I said, "I got a question. You have access to phone records from the Cantrell house in the last few months they were there?"

"I've got the actual records. I told you, I kept everything. There's nothing there. I've been over those—"

"Do me a favor," I said, "and go find them. Check and see if there was a call to a guy named Alvin Neloms. Or maybe it was to an auto body shop on the east side. Look for either."

He set the phone down and disappeared. It was maybe five minutes before he came back, and his voice was lower.

"There were three calls to a place called Classic Auto Body, on Eddy Road."

"Were they all during Bertoli's stay?" I said. "The last weeks anyone was in that house?"

"Yes."

"Hang around, Dunbar," I said. "I'm headed your way."

I disconnected then and turned to look at Joe.

"The problem with this job," I said, "is that the guesswork always comes before the facts. I'm pretty sure that system put Ken in his grave."

40

I had to give John Dunbar credit—he didn't balk at the idea. In fact, what I saw in his face when I laid it out for him wasn't denial but shame. He actually seemed to wince when I showed him the police report that mentioned Bertoli's car at the time of his arrest and explained its similarities to a different car that had been near the death scene.

"I knew what kind of car he had," he said. "Of course I knew that, and I knew that's what got him arrested, but I didn't consider that it would have any importance beyond that. I didn't consider it."

He bit off that repeated line, angry, self-reproachful—*I didn't* consider *it.* Joe hadn't said much at all, but he looked at me when Dunbar said that, gave a small nod, showing that he thought it was legitimate.

"I knew it was Alvin Neloms who was in the car with Bertoli the night he was arrested," Dunbar said. "Of course I checked that out, of course I knew it, *of course* I did the same work you just did. Back then he was nothing more than a kid on the corner, someone who watched for police and maybe did a little muling. He was sixteen."

"He's not anymore," Joe said. "According to what we've been told, he's as close to a drug kingpin as the east side has. It's gang country out there; you do well to last six months. Neloms being around this many years later, that tells you something."

Dunbar's eyes flicked side to side but held distance, as if he were watching a film.

"DiPietro was providing some of the east side supply," he said, speaking slowly. "That was the point, see, that's when he and Sanabria had their first falling-out. Sanabria didn't trust drugs, and he certainly didn't trust blacks. His father was of that old school, racist, and I'm sure that stuck with Dominic. He did not want to be involved with the drug trade on the east side. We knew that, knew it from wiretaps and informants and a hell of a lot of work. We knew that Dominic was furious with DiPietro."

He paused and took a breath and then said, "Dominic killed DiPietro," but his voice had gone soft and he wouldn't take his eyes off the police report that detailed Bertoli's car.

As I watched his face, I felt tinged with sorrow. I was looking at an old cop who'd believed something very deeply and was now considering that it might have been wrong.

"You talked with a cop from East Cleveland," he said. "Someone who knows about Neloms."

"Yes," Joe said.

"Can you call him back?" Dunbar said. "Can you ask him a question?"

"What am I supposed to ask?"

"If he has any idea when Alvin made his move into the power structure. If he has any idea where the supply came from. A small fortune of drugs disappeared when DiPietro got whacked. They never turned up with the Italians again."

Joe took his cell phone out and called. He asked for Tony, waited for a few minutes, and then spoke again. He repeated Dunbar's questions, listened as Dunbar and I sat with our eyes on the floor, silent. At length, Joe thanked Tony and hung up. He put the phone back in his pocket and waited for a few seconds before speaking. He did not look at Dunbar when he did.

"The way Tony remembers it, Alvin was a lot like what you say, a corner kid, until he was in his late teens. Then he got his hands on some product. Nobody knew where, or how, but all of a sudden he had product, and then three major players were dropped in a drive-by over on St. Clair, and from that point on Alvin, while still a boy, was also the *man* in East Cleveland. This beginning when he was still in his teens. He was, Tony says, an ambitious young man."

I looked at Dunbar. "DiPietro controlled the drugs you were talking about, right? They were in his possession?"

"You know they were. I already told you that. We looked at every associate, looked at everyone who . . ." his voice faded, and then he said, "Alvin Neloms was a boy. A child."

"Tony also said Alvin and his uncle were tight," Joe said quietly. "Alvin's father is an unknown, disappeared when the mother got pregnant, and Darius looked after the family. Supported the family."

I nodded. "Supported them with a little help from the mob, is what Mike London thought. He said Darius was involved with stolen cars, changing their look and putting them back out on the street."

Dunbar shifted, smoothed his pants with his palms, swallowed as if it were a challenge.

"You never even considered the possibility, did you?" I said.

He looked up. "Neloms? Well, I had no idea—"

"Not Neloms. The possibility that it might have been anybody other than Sanabria, period."

"Of course I did."

"Really?"

His gaze focused again, went defiant. "Perry, that man would've killed anyone who collided with him. You don't understand that about him. I do. He had killed before, and I'd *had* him for it, okay? I told you that story."

"I know," I said. "I'm just wondering which murder you were really chasing him for. The new one you thought he'd committed, or the one he'd already beaten you on."

He held my eyes for a little while and then looked away and ran a hand over his mouth. His hands were dry and white and the blue veins stood out. They matched the strips of stark color under his eyes.

"So what we're thinking," Joe said, "is that Bertoli and Neloms were friends, probably from meeting at the uncle's shop. Neloms is along when

Bertoli beats up the guy at the truck stop, but he doesn't go in, which means that as a kid he's somehow already got people doing the bleeding for him. It also means he was already looking for his own supply at that point, his own drug nest egg. He wanted to run the show, not stand on the corner for somebody else."

"The guy Bertoli beat up didn't have as much product as they thought," I said. "They overestimated his role. Bertoli got busted, but Neloms walked because he was a juvenile."

Joe nodded. "Right. After this, DiPietro is killed, a small fortune of drugs disappears, and suddenly a teenage kid became a deadly force. It was a power play, but one from a player nobody respected or even knew of at the time. This is the scenario?"

"That's the scenario," I said. "Ken Merriman got about ten percent of the way there. He got to the connection between the cars. I bet he didn't get farther than that, but he tried to. He tried to, and he died."

"What would he have done?" Joe said. "Once he connected the cars, what do you think he would have done?"

"Gone and asked about them," I answered, feeling a sick sadness. "He wasn't a street detective. He would have gone right down to that body shop and asked about the car, thinking that was the next step. He might have suspected Cash Neloms was involved by then, but I don't think he had a real sense of how dangerous the guy was. He would have gone down there to ask some questions, and he wouldn't have been very good at it. I saw him in action with interviews, and he was not very good at it."

"Suppose you're right on Bertoli," Dunbar said. "Suppose he was killed by Neloms. That doesn't mean Cantrell was, too. The styles of crime are entirely different. One was killed on scene and the body left without any concern; the other one was buried in another state. Those are two different killings, maybe by two different people."

On the surface he was right, but I understood what he didn't: how Joshua Cantrell's body had been transported, and why. The killings hadn't been different in style at all—both bodies were left where they'd fallen. Same style, same killer. Solve one and you've solved the other.

Thinking about that brought a realization to me. To whoever had killed

Cantrell, the disappearance of his body must have seemed extraordinary. For twelve years, while the rest of the world wondered what had happened to him, one person wondered about the fate of his corpse. Wondered, no doubt, quite intensely.

"I want to talk to Darius," I said. "Not his nephew, not yet. Hit him with the only solid thing we have—that report on Bertoli's car—and see what he'll say."

Dunbar said, "I've got photographs."

"Pardon?"

"I've got photographs of Bertoli, and of his car. I've got photographs of damn near everybody's car, everybody that went near Sanabria."

"How soon can you come up with them?"

He stood up and went into the bedroom. From where I sat I could see through the doorway, and as I watched he opened a closet door. It was a small closet—every space in his house was small—and the clothes that hung in it were pushed far to the side to make room for a clear plastic organizer with drawers. It was the sort a lot of people had in their closets, usually for sweaters and old jeans, things they rarely used or for which they'd run out of shelf space. Dunbar's didn't hold any clothing, though, not a single piece of it. The thing was filled with manila folders, and I could see that each drawer was labeled with a date range.

He'd been retired for nearly fifteen years and had almost no closet space. I looked at that set of plastic drawers and I felt sad for him again.

It didn't take him long. First drawer he opened, first folder he removed. When he came back to the living room he had three photos in his hands; he passed one to Joe and two to me.

"These would have been taken just a few months before Bertoli was arrested, a little before DiPietro was killed. You can see the diamonds carved in the rims. They're tiny, but they're there."

Yes, they were. A half-dozen small diamonds. The car was an Impala, probably midseventies model, painted a metallic black. Bertoli wasn't visible in either of the photographs—the windows were up, and they almost matched the car's paint, clearly an illegal level of tint. Window tint like that pissed off street cops because you couldn't see what was happening in the interior as you approached. The entire car was basically a rolling request to be stopped and searched.

"This is perfect," I said. "Can we borrow these?"

Dunbar nodded, but his eyes seemed faraway again.

I stood up. "Thank you. For the pictures, and the insight."

"I've got some other things I'll go through," he said, not looking up. "I'll do some thinking. I'm not sure you're right . . . but I'll do some thinking."

41

Darius Neloms's shop, Classic Auto Body, was on Eddy Road, which was one of the few streets in the city that I would actively try to avoid while driving. It's an asphalt strip of neglect and anger, a place where as a rookie I'd been called to the scene of a fight and arrived to find a fourteen-year-old boy bleeding to death on the sidewalk from a knife wound to the neck. I'm not one of those PIs who loves to carry a gun, and I usually don't have one in my truck. Eddy Road, though, can make me regret that.

Today I had a gun, and I had Joe in the passenger seat, casting a dour eye over the neighborhood.

"It just gets worse, doesn't it?" he said. "I haven't been down here in a few years, but you can't pick up the paper without seeing something about this neighborhood. It just gets worse, poorer and bloodier."

"And more hopeless," I said, because that's how East Cleveland seemed to me, a legacy of poverty and crime and corruption drowning the people who tried to make a life there.

"Ah, shit, nothing's hopeless," Joe said. "Just ignored."

My mind wasn't on East Cleveland, though. I was thinking of Ken Merriman, of that spot in Mill Stream Run where his body had been dumped, and wondering whether he'd made a drive down Eddy Road on his last day alive. Joe had his face turned away from me, looking out at the neighborhood, and when I glanced at him I had a vision of the bullet holes that hid under his shirt, and then one of the steel security bar that rested across Amy's door.

"Hey," I said, and he turned back to me. "When we talk to Darius, I don't want to give him any names, all right?"

"You mean Cantrell and Bertoli?"

"No, I mean Pritchard and Perry."

He frowned.

"Like I said before, this is a scouting trip, okay? I want to ask the guy about Bertoli's car, drop Cantrell's name, see if we get any sort of response. Feel him out. Then I'll call Graham. It's still his case, you know."

His frown didn't fade. "What's that have to do with names?"

"Nothing."

"Then why—"

"Look, Graham got on my ass about this before, told me to stay out of his way. I don't want to deal with that again."

He looked at me for a long time, then nodded his head at the traffic light ahead.

"You've got a green."

It was closing in on six now, streetlights coming on, but Classic Auto Body was still open. It was an ugly, sprawling place of cinder block, with a stack of tires and a few stripped cars in the parking lot. From the outside it looked like a picture of poverty, but the garage doors were up and two gleaming cars were visible inside, one a new Cadillac and the other a pickup truck that had been painted gold and black and mounted on massive, oversized tires. Two young black men lounged on stools in the garage. A set of speakers stood behind them, playing rap music with a bass line I could feel in my chest.

"Hey," Joe said as we got out of the truck, his voice soft, and when I looked at him he nodded at the black-and-gold pickup truck inside. "Look at the wheels."

There were small diamonds cut out of the chrome rims.

One of the men inside the garage, a thin guy with darker skin and a shaved head, had moved his hand to rest beneath his oversized jacket when we drove in. Now that he saw us, he took it away and exchanged a look with his partner, who got to his feet and stepped over to a closed door. He opened it and said a few words, then shut it and came out to meet us. The guy with the jacket never moved.

"We closed," the one on his feet said, stopping at the edge of the garage. He wore a close-fitting, sleeveless white shirt, ridges of muscle clear beneath it. The music was even louder now, the sound of a ratcheting shotgun incorporated into the beat.

"Doesn't look that way," I said.

"Is, though."

"That's all right. Don't need any work done. Came to see Darius."

He reached up and scratched above his eyebrow, head tilted, studying me. "Darius a busy man."

"I'm sure of it. That's why we don't intend to keep him long. Got a picture to show him, a question to ask, then go on our way."

His eyes flicked over to Joe, whose look and demeanor said *cop* about as subtly as a billboard would.

"I'll give him the picture for you."

Joe shook his head. "We will. Thanks, though."

"Man, Darius ain't available."

"You work with him?"

"That's right."

"Then you know how to get in touch with him. Give the man a call."

While Joe talked, I found myself staring at the man on the stool, that hand resting near his waist. He wasn't looking back at me. He was looking at Joe.

"He ain't gonna answer," the guy in the sleeveless shirt said.

"How do you know that?"

"He busy."

"How about we call him just the same," Joe said.

"No," I said, and they both looked at me with surprise. I shook my head. "If he's not around, he's not around. We'll come back."

He nodded. "You do that, man."

"Thanks."

I turned and walked to the truck. I had the door open and was sitting behind the wheel before Joe even moved. He walked over slowly, got inside, and swung the door shut without a word. The guy from the stool got to his feet and came over to stand with the other man at the edge of the garage. They watched as I drove out of the lot.

"Maybe I misread the situation," Joe said after we were a few blocks away, "but I kind of assumed Darius was inside that office. You know, where the kid poked his head in before he came out to run us off."

"Could be."

"Uh-huh. You want to tell me what we're doing driving away, then?"

"I'm thinking we should pass this off to Graham," I said. "His case, his decisions to make. You saw those diamonds on the rims down here, that's enough, right? Between that and the phone calls, we've got enough. It's time to pass it to him now."

"That's a pretty different stance from the one you had this afternoon."

"Had a few hours to think about it."

"You've done some thinking," he said, "but it's not hours of it that are catching up with you now. It's months."

We didn't say much on the way back to the office. When we got there all he said was "Let me know if Alexandra calls" before he got into his own car and drove away.

I went home, too, called Amy and said I'd come over and I had some news, and then took a shower. Before I got into the water I stood at the sink and stared into the mirror for a long time, waiting for the man looking back to tell me what he wanted to do. What he needed to do. Then the steam spread across the glass and he was gone, no answers left behind.

I did not call Quinn Graham, as I had told Joe I would. I did not call anyone. That night I updated Amy, took her from my conversation with Alexandra Cantrell to my decision at the garage.

"You're really going to back off, pass it to Graham?" she said. "Then why were you there to begin with? Why spend two weeks watching for Alexandra?"

"Just to see if he was right. I had to know. That's all. Now I do."

"If who was right? Ken?"

I nodded.

"You said you were angry with him at first," she said. "Hurt and betrayed, because he lied to you."

"Sure. You think that's abnormal?"

"No. But you don't seem angry now."

"I understand why he did it now."

She nodded. "That makes it easier, doesn't it."

"Of course."

"You know you've been lying to me?"

"What?"

"For three days you've been lying to me. Said you'd given up on the surveillance, stopped going out there—and, unlike you with Ken, I don't understand why."

"I'm sorry," I said. "I didn't think of it as lying, even though it was. I just knew that you and Joe thought I should quit—"

"You told us you already had. Back in the summer, it was *you* who said you were done. Emphatically. Neither of us told you to give up your job, Lincoln, but you did, and then you went back to it in secret. Lying about it. I don't understand."

I didn't know how to make her understand. I couldn't explain to her that she was one of the reasons I'd had to quit, that Ken's murder had been one that hit too close to home. It could be her next time. Or Joe. My decision at the garage today had been made the moment the guy on the stool had reached under his jacket with his eyes on Joe. I understood some things in that moment, understood just how damn close we were to the one thing I could never allow to happen again. I would not bring those I loved into harm's way again. I couldn't.

So if I understood that, then why couldn't I stop altogether? Why had I ever gone back to that damned house in the woods with my camera and my binoculars?

I didn't have an answer for that one. It chilled me, but I didn't. I'd ended up back out there, that was all. The absence of resolution, of truth, had tormented me for too many months. In the end, it won. I was weaker than I'd thought.

"Let me ask you one more thing, and this time, if you care about me at all, tell me the truth," Amy said. She was speaking very carefully, slowly, as if she needed me to feel the weight of the words. "If you don't tell me the truth, we're done, Lincoln. We will have to be done. Because I can't live with you otherwise."

"Ask the question," I said.

"Are you really going to pass this off to Graham, or are you telling one thing to me and Joe and planning another?"

I looked away.

She said, "Lincoln."

"I've got something left to do," I said. "That's the truth. It's something I'm going to do alone. Then I will give this to Graham and, yes, step away. I promise you, that is the truth. I've got one thing left to do."

"What is it?"

"I'm going to get Graham the tape he wanted me to get from Harrison, only this time I'll get it from the right source. I'm going to get him evidence, Amy, get him a case he can prosecute, a case that will end the right way. I don't want to pass this off to him until I know it's ready for that. I can't stand to let it fall apart the way it did with Dunbar and Mike London and Graham and everyone else. Do you understand that? I can't let it fall apart again."

She fell asleep around midnight. I sat beside her in the dark, looking at a pale shaft of light across the carpet that I liked to imagine was the moon but was really from a parking lot light pole. She had not pressed me for more details of what I had planned, and I hadn't offered them. It had been a quiet night. We didn't make love or even talk when we turned out the lights and got into bed, but she fell asleep with her hand wrapped tight around my arm.

After twenty minutes, when her breathing had slowed to the rhythm of true and deep sleep, I got to my feet and found my car keys. She was on her side, face turned into the pillow, and before I left I leaned down and kissed the back of her head, smelled her hair. Then I walked through the dark apartment and opened the door and stepped out into the night. There was no way I could fasten the steel security bar behind me. I regretted that.

I stopped at a convenience store on Rocky River and bought a large black coffee, then drove home, went upstairs, and found the wire I'd used in the early stages with Parker Harrison. I'd never taken it back to the office. We'd had no use for it anymore.

I tested it and then put it on, clipping the microphone lower, near the fourth button instead of the first, remembering the way Harrison had torn at my shirt, how completely exposed it had been then. Once the wire was in place, I got my gun case out of the closet and removed the stainless steel Beretta 9 mm. It had been a while since I'd handled that gun, but I had a shoulder holster for it, and I put that on now and slipped the Beretta inside. I put a jacket on over that, leaving it unzipped, and then I put the Glock into its holster, this one secured on my spine. The East Cleveland Ensemble.

With that preparation complete, I turned off the lights and left the apartment and went to the office. I fired up the computer and then took my PI license out of my wallet and went to the scanner, made a copy of the image and loaded it onto the computer, and made a few changes before printing out a copy. A little trimming work with scissors, a quick pass through the card laminator I'd purchased years ago for just this sort of thing, and then I was done. I tucked the new ID into my wallet in place of the old one, left the office, and drove back to Eddy Road.

42

One version of the neighborhood came to life at dawn, and another went to sleep. It hadn't been a quiet night of surveillance—I'd watched people stumble the sidewalks wrecked out of their minds, seen a fistfight flare and then vanish when a police cruiser drove by, heard the laughter and loud car stereos of those returning from a night at the clubs. That world slid away just before daylight, and then the traffic thickened and stores and businesses opened as the sun rose.

Classic Auto Body was quiet until almost nine, and then someone drove into the parking lot in a sleek black Cadillac CTS and pulled to a stop just outside of the office window, in an area not marked for parking. The driver's door opened and a large black man stepped out with keys in his hand. He unlocked the office door and disappeared inside.

I pushed the blackout curtain aside and climbed into the front seat of the truck and then got out and walked to the shop, tested the door and found it unlocked, and stepped inside.

I'd entered an empty office, but I could hear movement in the garage beyond, someone walking around snapping on light switches. A few seconds passed, and then the door from the garage opened and the Cadillac's driver stepped back into the office and saw me.

"You need help?" he said, not unfriendly, but not thrilled about seeing me there, either.

"Got a couple questions about a car you did."

"Yeah?" He walked around the desk and leaned on its edge, more intrigued now. "Like what you've seen out there, huh?"

"Oh, absolutely. Absolutely."

He was nodding along in agreement, confident in his work. "You got something classic you working on, or is it more of just getting it done up right, something newer but just don't have that *look*, that *style*?"

He appeared even bigger indoors than he had outside. Probably six-four and at least two hundred and sixty or seventy pounds, with a block of a head above a football lineman's shoulders. He looked about forty-five and had a pencil-line beard tracing his massive jaw. Wore baggy jeans and a black jacket open over a T-shirt. There was a chain of white gold or platinum with a glittering medallion in the shape of a diamond around his neck, hanging halfway down his chest.

"I've got some pictures of it," I said, pulling Dunbar's photographs out of my pocket. I nodded at his medallion before I handed them over. "That diamond there, any chance that's, like, your logo?"

"Yeah, man, like a signature, you know? Every artist puts one on their work." He was smiling at me now. "Keeps people from passing off their shit as mine, too. You got these kids, do something on their own, then they want people to think they spent the money, right? Want them to think they got the money *to* spend, so they say, oh, I took it down to Darius. But I got those diamonds I do by hand, man, and there ain't any of them going to try putting *those* on."

"Brand protection," I said. "Trademark."

"Yeah, exactly, a trademark." He put his hand out for the photographs. "What is it you've seen around? Which one of 'em caught your eye?"

I passed them over. "You probably won't remember this. Did it a long time ago."

He took the pictures and studied them one at a time. His face changed to a frown, but it wasn't suspicious, not yet. Just thoughtful.

"Man, you ain't kidding, this is a long time ago. I remember the car, though. This would've been ten years ago at least, got those old dubs on there."

"You did the work, though?"

"Oh, yeah. For sure. That's mine."

"You happen to remember the owner?"

His mouth twisted, and he hesitated, thinking, trying to remember. It took him a few seconds, but when he got it the frown came back, this time with a different quality, and when he spoke his voice wasn't as relaxed as it had been.

"It was an Italian kid, I think. Maybe not. I don't know."

He held the photograph out, and when I didn't take it immediately he gave it a shake to get my attention, as if he were in a hurry to get it out of his hand.

"I don't even know why that piece of shit grabbed your eye," he said.

"You don't like it?"

"You know, I did the work, that's all. People got their own ideas of what looks good, I try to listen. Now what kind of a ride you got? What are we talking about doing?"

"I'm afraid there's been some confusion," I said. "I'm not here to have a car worked on. I'm here about *this* car."

I lifted the photograph and gave it the same little shake he had, but he didn't look, just held my eyes. Now all the good humor was out of his face.

"You a cop?"

"Private."

"It's private whether you a cop?"

"No. I'm a private detective."

"Man, I don't got time for this. That car's so old, I don't remember nothing about it, don't know nothing about that Italian kid, all right?"

"That's fine, Darius. Maybe you could do me a favor, though?"

He waited, suspicious.

"Give your nephew a call, get him down here."

"My family got something to do with you? Man, go on and get out of here. I don't have time—"

"You got nothing to do with Alvin? With Cash, I mean?"

He was giving me flat eyes now, a response to police questioning that he'd spent some years perfecting.

"Maybe you could just give him a message," I said. "Write down my name, tell him that I was down here and that I'd like to speak with him if he gets a chance. That I'd appreciate it if he could give me a call."

"You want to talk to Cash, find him yourself."

"Darius . . ." I spread my hands. "You really want to make this a pain in the ass? All I'm asking is for you to give your nephew my name, tell him I was down here. You do that, and I'm gone."

He scowled and waved his hand at me, impatient. "All right, leave your damn name and get out."

"I'm fresh out of cards," I said. "So you'll have to write it down."

"Man, write it down yourself."

I ignored him, reached in my back pocket and withdrew my wallet, flicked it open to reveal the investigator's license I'd made, and passed it over. He glanced down at it, but it was a cursory look while he picked up a pad of paper and extended it to me.

"Write it here," he said.

I didn't answer, just kept holding the license in front of his face, and this time when his eyes went to it they lingered. He stared at it for several seconds. Too many to be comfortable. Enough to tell me what I needed to know.

"Like I said, you write it down yourself," he said finally, looking away from the license and back at me. His voice was much softer, his eyes much darker.

"Okay," I said, and I closed the wallet and put it back in my pocket and then wrote the name from the license in all capital letters across his pad—KEN MERRIMAN.

He watched me write it and didn't say a word when I dropped the pad on his desk.

"Are you sure," I said, "that you don't want to give your nephew a call right now?"

He looked up at me, and his jaw worked as he studied my eyes.

"It might be a good idea," I said. "Up to you, Darius, but it might be a good idea."

He didn't take his eyes off me as he withdrew his cell phone from the pocket of his oversized jeans.

"You wait," he said, and then he stepped out into the garage and closed the door behind him. I felt my breath go out of my lungs when the door closed, and I looked around the office and through the window out onto the street. Nobody in sight. I would be alone with them when Cash came, just as Ken had likely been. I was more prepared than he had been, though. I had my story ready, had the scenario I needed, and now it was just a matter of playing it through, getting the hell out of here, and handing Graham a case that was ready to close. Simple stuff. Simple. I reached inside my jacket and touched the Beretta once, a gentle tap, and then I dropped my hands back to my sides and waited.

Darius wasn't gone long. Two minutes at most. Then the door opened and he stepped through, face expressionless, eyes flat again.

"You in luck," he said. "Cash is in the area."

"Going to come by?"

He shook his head, and I saw he had his car keys in hand. "You are. I'm going to take you out to see him."

"No need for you to do that," I said.

"Man, I'm helpful like that."

"You want to leave, fine, but I'll wait for him here."

He shook his head again. "You want to see Cash, I take you."

"Maybe you don't understand," I said. "I'm going to wait for him here."

There was real anger showing in him for the first time now, the sort of look that probably didn't meet with opposition very often. He said, "He's not coming here, and you ain't going to stay on my property."

I dropped into one of the plastic chairs that lined the wall across from his desk, crossed one ankle over my knee.

"Try him again, Darius. I think you might be wrong. I think he might be willing to make the trip."

He hesitated. It wasn't me he was worried about, it was his nephew's response. Eventually he turned and went back into the garage, and this time it was almost ten minutes before he returned.

"All right," he said. "He's on his way."

"Terrific," I said.

"Sure is," Darius said. He crossed the office, reached for the blinds, and twisted the rod until they were closed again, and the street was gone and the office was dark. Then he went to the door and locked it and turned the sign to CLOSED.

"Sure is," he said again, and he went behind the desk and sat in his chair, opened a drawer, and withdrew a stainless steel Beretta that looked identical to the one I had under my jacket. He placed the gun on the desk without a word, not pointing at me but close to his hand.

Then we waited.

43

It was about twenty minutes before Cash arrived, and Darius and I did not speak during the wait. If you've ever wondered how long twenty minutes can feel, try spending them in total silence facing a man with a gun.

At some point while we waited, I realized that it was past nine but nobody else had arrived. Then I remembered the extra time that Darius had spent out in the garage before telling me his nephew was on his way. He hadn't turned the CLOSED sign over until after that. Made some extra calls, maybe, told his employees not to come in? I'd chosen to make my return trip out here in the morning for a reason, thinking the place would be more active, but that didn't seem to be the case. Of course, the only employees I'd seen here yesterday weren't exactly the type of guys whose presence would reassure me now. I wondered if much actual work went on down here these days, or if it had become a cover operation for Cash Neloms.

When a car finally pulled in, Darius got to his feet, taking the gun with him, and walked over to unlock the door. He stood beside it and waited, and after a moment the door opened and a slim, athletic-looking black guy stepped inside and shut the door behind him. He looked first at Darius and then turned to me.

"Morning," I said. "Thanks for making the trip."

He was the same height as Darius but about eighty pounds lighter, with a shaved head that glowed under the fluorescent lights in the office. The family resemblance was clear. Same skeptical, watchful eyes and hard-line mouth and strong shoulders. What surprised me most was how damn young he still looked. If I'd seen him on a college campus I wouldn't have even considered that he'd be anything but a student.

"D says you got a question for me?" he said. The words came slow, each one studied on before release.

"That's right." I went through the routine again, took the wallet out and opened it to my Ken Merriman ID and passed it over. With Darius, the idea had worked just as I'd hoped, maybe even better than I'd allowed myself to hope. I'd thought that questioning him and his nephew about Ken might not tell me what I wanted to know. They were used to questioning; they would know how to play the game by now. Pretending to be Ken, though, re-creating his visit as near as I could imagine it had taken place, seemed as if it might produce a different response, put a touch of déjà vu in the air that would be difficult for even veterans like the Neloms to ignore.

Darius had looked at the ID and been momentarily frozen. Cash had the advantage of being forewarned, though, and instead of looking at it he took the wallet right out of my hand, ignored the PI license entirely, and slipped two of my credit cards out. Read the name on them, then held one up for me.

"Looks like you a little confused. Got a couple names, huh?"

I didn't say anything. He waited for a long time, and then he slid the credit cards back into the wallet, closed it, and threw it at me. It hit me in the chest and dropped into my lap. I picked it up and put it back in my pocket, still silent.

Darius was standing by the door, the gun held down against his thigh. He was watching Cash more than me.

"So what you want, man?" Cash said.

I didn't answer.

"You going to speak?"

Again I was quiet. I sat in my chair and did not take my eyes from his, tried to ignore the desire to glance over at Darius and make sure that the gun was still down. I'd see him if he moved. I'd see him.

"Man, say whatever the fuck you got to say." Cash sounded agitated now.

I looked back with what I hoped was a steady, calm stare. He gave it almost a full minute before breaking the silence again.

"All right, then, get out. Come down here and waste my time, waste my uncle's time? Get the fuck out."

His voice was bridling with anger, muscles standing out in his neck. This was what I wanted. To see him frustrated. I wanted to drive him wild with silence. Have him unsteady by the time we got to the real talk.

"I'ma tell you *one* more time—" he began, but this time I spoke.

"I just have a few questions, Alvin."

"Don't call me that."

"My name's Ken Merriman," I said. "I'm a private investigator from Pennsylvania. I was hired by the parents of a man named Joshua Cantrell. He was murdered a few years ago. Twelve years ago, actually. Almost thirteen."

He looked away from me and at Darius, and it took everything I had to keep my hand still, to keep from reaching for the Beretta. Darius hadn't moved. His gun was still pointed down.

"Why you saying you somebody else?" Cash Neloms said. "Come down here and lie to us, you think that's wise? Think that's a good way to stay alive?"

"You're right. I was lying. I didn't come to ask questions. I came to give you some answers, if you wanted them."

"I don't even know who you are. You don't got no answers I need."

"I disagree."

Another look at Darius, and I knew now that this was how it would go. If Cash gave him the right look, that gun was coming up.

"I don't know what you been told, what you think," Cash Neloms said. "I'm *sure* I don't know what kind of fucking fool you are, coming down here, talking crazy shit like this, but, boy, go on and walk out. Right now."

"Don't you even want to know how Cantrell's body ended up in Pennsylvania?" I said.

That stopped him. His mouth closed and his eyes went hard and dull, and for a moment he seemed to have forgotten about Darius in the corner of the room. For a moment he seemed to have forgotten about everything but me.

"I thought you'd like to know that much," I said. "As far as Ken Merriman is concerned, well, I don't need to give you any answers to that one. You already know them. Same story with Salvatore Bertoli. Cantrell . . . I thought you might be curious about that one. Twelve years is a long time to wonder."

"I don't know . . ." It was supposed to be another denial, but he let it die, wiped a hand over his mouth and stared at me and tried to decide what to say. It took maybe ten seconds. "All right. I'm not saying I know what you talking about, but go on and tell it, if that's why you came down here. Go on and tell it."

"You know the name Dominic Sanabria?" I said.

"I might've heard it."

"Yeah, I thought so. He'd like you to do him a favor. Man like that can be a good person to do a favor for, you know?"

"I don't owe him any favors."

"No? He might argue that."

It was quiet again for a while.

"Well," he said, frustration showing again, "what is it, man? You got to say it."

"Dominic's sister has been gone for twelve years. Lot of people looked for her. Police, family, private detectives, reporters. By this time, it seems like if she had anything to say to anybody like that, she'd have said it. Don't you think?"

He didn't answer.

"I'll tell you what she told me," I said. "She has a new life now. Doesn't want to leave it. Doesn't want to come back here, to the questions and the attention."

"Why you telling me that?"

"The favor that Dominic would like you to do," I said, "is pretty simple. I'll put you in touch with her. Get you a meeting. You explain to her that Dominic had nothing to do with her husband's death. That's all."

I expected he might give me disbelief or confusion or anger—anything but acknowledgment—but instead of speaking, he just looked at me for a long time. When he broke that silence, it wasn't with an argument. It was a question, spoken soft and cold.

"Who are you?"

"You saw the name."

"Name don't mean shit to me."

"Here's all you need to know about me—I came here with an offer from Dominic. You've heard it. You going to take it?"

All I wanted now was out. The recorder was running, I had this whole conversation, and I could set up the meeting with Alexandra. There'd be plenty more than Alexandra there, more wires and more cops and a pair of handcuffs ready to fit around Cash Neloms's wrists. I was close now; I just needed to get it done and get the hell out. I just needed to make it through the door.

"Sure," Cash said after a pause. "I'll take it, man."

He was so casual when he said it, his face so utterly relaxed, that if I hadn't been reminding myself to be ready to move if he looked at Darius again I would've died immediately. As it was, I'd been ready for the look, and when he turned to Darius I was already rising, made it out of my chair before Darius lifted the gun.

I reached under my jacket for the Beretta, and I ran straight for Cash and the swinging door to the garage beyond. I was hoping to get behind him or at least close enough to him that Darius wouldn't fire, but that was a hopeless idea; it simply doesn't take that long to lift a gun and pull the trigger.

Darius fired before I cleared my gun, and the bullet hit me on the right side, hit me like the thrust of a metal stake that had been forged to a glowing red heat. The force of it knocked me forward, and his second shot missed high as I fell into Cash Neloms's legs.

I didn't hit him hard, or even intentionally—I was just trying to make it to the door. My weight caught him around the knees, though, and while he didn't go to the floor he did fall backward into the wall, and for a brief moment we were entangled. He came off the wall with his hands reaching for my throat, and by leaning over me like that he blocked any chance of his uncle finishing me off with another shot. By then I had my gun out, and I twisted as his hands clawed at my neck. I saw nothing but the metal desk and Darius Neloms's feet and legs beneath it, but that gave me something to shoot at. I fired once, saw a spray of red burst out of the back of his calf and heard him scream, and then I shoved through Cash Neloms's legs and toward the swinging door that led to the garage. He slammed a punch into the back of my neck and tore at my hand as I went by, and the Beretta came loose and hit the floor. It spun away from me, back toward the desk, but I ignored it and kept scrambling forward. Then I was out of the office and onto the cold concrete floor of the garage. I kicked the swinging door backward as I went, heard it hit something, and then another shot was fired and I felt a second searing pain burn across my thigh.

It was dark in the garage, the doors down and the light off, and I rolled away and hit something that fell all around me, didn't realize until I touched one of them that I'd knocked over a stack of hubcaps. I pulled myself back with my hands, got my torso into an upright position, legs stretched out in front of me, and then I reached behind my back and removed the Glock from its holster. I was slow getting it out, but when Cash Neloms stepped through the door and into the garage, with a gun in his hand, he turned to the left first, reaching for the light switch, thinking that I was now unarmed.

I lifted the Glock and fired twice.

When he dropped, he went backward into the door and it swung open and his head and shoulders fell into the office, nothing of him left visible in the garage but his legs. They moved for a few seconds, heels scraping on the concrete, trying to get upright, and then they went still and it was quiet.

I sat in the pile of hubcaps with the Glock still pointed at the door and waited for Darius. It was hard to hold the gun up now, and the door seemed to be dancing in front of me, waving and undulating and blending with the shadows. I heard motion and fired again before realizing it had been the front door. Darius had just left the office and gone outside. He'd be coming around from a different direction, entering through a different door. I had no idea which way to look. It was his garage. He knew the layout and I did not and it was becoming hard to sit upright and hard to see.

The Glock dropped to my lap, not a mental decision but a physical one, my body giving out, and I twisted onto my side and reached into my pocket for my cell phone. It took two tries to get it out of my pocket. My fingers were slick with warm wet blood.

I got the phone out and open and then I dialed and spoke into it. I could not remember the address where I was, or even the road. All I could tell them was that I'd been shot and Darius was coming back for me. Several times, I said that I did not know what door he would use. That I would not be ready for him when he came.

The phone slid out of my fingers then and bounced off the concrete floor. I could not make myself reach for it even though it was close. There was blood in my mouth now and a terrible high hum in my ears and I could not reach for the phone or lift the gun.

I never heard the sirens.

44

The paramedics found the recorder and gave it to the police. When they listened to that and heard what Joe had to say, it wasn't hard to piece together what had happened. That was good, because I wasn't in any condition to talk.

By the time I got out of surgery, the first media report had leaked, and Alvin "Cash" Neloms was being identified as the alleged killer of Joshua Cantrell. Mike London and John Dunbar were called into the investigation. Quinn Graham drove in from Pennsylvania. The tape was solid, but there was no confession. They needed more. It was Graham who suggested they focus on Ken Merriman, the freshest case and the one that had the best potential for evidence. They found a variety of weapons while searching the properties affiliated with Cash and Darius Neloms, including a handgun and ammunition that were probable matches for Ken's shooting. They would later be proved conclusive matches.

All my concern over Darius Neloms and his unknown path of reentry into the garage turned out to be unnecessary—he'd tried to leave when he saw his nephew fall dead through the door into the office. Dragged his wounded leg along with him and went out and got into his Cadillac and drove away. About two minutes and ten blocks away, he passed out from pain and blood loss and drove up onto the sidewalk and into a telephone pole. They arrested him when he got out of surgery.

By the time the paramedics found me, I was unconscious and in shock. They didn't get me stabilized until I was at MetroHealth's trauma center, the same hospital that had saved Joe. In fact, I had the same surgeon, a Dr. Crandall, who was one of the specialists on gunshot wounds. My surgery was about six hours shorter than Joe's, though. Something he could hold over my head.

Oddly, the chest wound was the lesser of my troubles. Eight inches from being my end—*if it goes in on the left side in the same position, you're dead almost immediately*, Dr. Crandall told me—but the bullet took a ludicrously forgiving trajectory and passed through me, leaving behind a broken rib and some minor soft tissue damage. If it had gone in on the left side, it would have blown right through my heart.

The leg wound, which came when Darius fired at me as I fell through the door and into the garage, was much more serious. The bullet did some arterial damage, and the only reason I didn't bleed out before the EMTs arrived was that I was sitting upright and the wound was on the back of my leg, which offered some level of compression and slowed the bleeding. The crime scene photographs I saw later showed a spray of blood almost six feet from my body that had been released when I leaned onto my side to reach for my phone. If I hadn't rolled back over, pressing the wound against the concrete floor, I would've lost consciousness before I ever got a word out to the 911 operator.

Fall on your ass, save your life. It was a hell of thing to think about.

It turned out there was actually some talk of arresting me, too. I was a civilian, not a cop, and I'd taken a life. We tend to call that murder. The only thing that allowed me to avoid at least preliminary charges was the recording, which supported my story.

I was coherent enough to watch TV on the second day, when I stared through a fog of medication and saw an old booking photo of Cash Neloms fill the screen. He was dead, the anchor explained, but still the focus of several ongoing homicide investigations.

He was dead.

It was over, then. Wasn't it? I thought it was probably over.

No one heard from Alexandra Cantrell in the aftermath of the shootings.

They held me in the hospital for ten days. During that time I refused to see anyone except Amy, Joe, my sister, and the police. My sister, Jennifer, stayed for five days, the longest visit she'd had since she moved from South Bend to Seattle, and the first time she'd met Amy. The two of them seemed to get along well.

Gena came into town, too, and I was happy to hear that. I didn't find out she'd been there until the day she left—Joe told me he'd explained to her that I didn't want a large audience. That rule hadn't applied to her, but it was just like Joe to quietly respect it, no matter what. It was good to know she'd come when he needed her.

I spent a lot of those days asleep. The right kind of drugs will do that to you. I woke once and heard Amy crying in the chair by my bed, but something told me that I should not open my eyes, should not disrupt her. I listened to her cry, and after a while she stopped and reached out and put her hand on my arm, and then I fell asleep again.

Calls came in constantly, most of them from the media. A few other friends tried to call or stop by, and Amy told me that Parker Harrison had come by on three occasions and been turned away. He was holding a card each time, she said, but he would not leave it with the receptionists or with her.

An insider account of the shootings and the crimes that had led to them was released during my hospital stay. It included significant details but was largely unattributed, most of it laid at the feet of "an unnamed source close to the situation." Amy was the source. I'd told her that I wanted to get as much of the detail out as possible, and have it done as early as possible. I also didn't want to give any interviews. That wasn't the sort of balance that pleases the media, but she leaked the story to the right people, people she trusted, and they did the rest.

Darius Neloms was charged with attempted murder. We heard that his attorney would attempt a counterclaim alleging that I had fired first. Amy was worried about that. I told her we'd deal with it when it came. Then Darius and his attorney listened to the tape, and evidently found it more conclusive than they had hoped. By my fourth day in the hospital they were negotiating with prosecutors, suggesting that Darius could produce evidence proving his nephew was indeed the murderer of Cantrell, Bertoli, Ken Merriman, and others. Blood ties meant a great deal to Darius until he was in jail and his nephew was dead, it seemed.

According to Darius, Salvatore Bertoli had sought Cash out to warn him of Joshua Cantrell's attempts to get information about the murder of Johnny DiPietro. Bertoli still believed Cash Neloms to be a friend. In exchange for the warning, Cash killed him and then Cantrell. Housekeeping. His was a different world by the time Bertoli got out of prison; he had an empire to protect, and one did not rule an empire with a soft touch.

While all of this was the focus for me, the police and prosecutors were more interested in what Darius had to say about his nephew's associates. Cash was dead—his network was not. Mike London told me that he was hearing Darius might get a hell of a deal if he rolled on enough people.

I didn't know how to feel about that.

Joe was around often, but he wasn't himself. Anytime he spoke, it tended to be to make a joke, things like suggesting he and I be the stars of a TV commercial for MetroHealth's trauma unit. It was a forced sort of good humor, and while I knew he was worried about my condition, I also sensed something else in the quiet that filled in the spaces between jokes. He was angry.

It wasn't until the day before my release that he was in the hospital room alone with me. Always before Amy had been around, or my sister, or a cop or a nurse. That afternoon, though, Amy had left for a few hours, my sister was on a plane for Seattle, and the cops and nurses had other concerns. Joe sat in the chair under the window. We talked for a few minutes before he lost that false comedic air.

"This is how you like it, right?" He waved at the bed, at the monitors around me.

I smiled. "Sure. My bed at home doesn't have any of this stuff."

He wasn't smiling. "You're okay lying in that bed with me in the chair next to it. That's all right with you."

"What do you mean?"

"Exactly what I said—it's fine with you if you're in the bed and I'm on my feet. Just like you were okay going to see Alvin Neloms alone, nobody aware of what you were doing, because I wasn't there, Amy wasn't there, nobody you care about was there."

"What are you talking about, Joe?"

"You think that if there's nobody around you, then there's nothing for you to fear. If nobody gets hurt but you, then who cares, right? You can deal with that. You can't deal with the other."

"I have dealt with the other."

"Not too well," he said. "Not too well."

I twisted my head on the pillow, turned away from his gaze.

"You sent me home," he said, "and then went back over there alone. Why?"

I didn't answer.

"We could have talked to Darius," he said. "It's what we'd gone over there to do. Then you backed off, said it was a bad idea, that we should pass it to Graham. Told me that, went home and said the same thing to Amy, and then loaded your guns and went back alone, without a word to anyone. I'd like you to explain why you did that."

I reached up and rubbed between my eyes, sucked in a gasp of pain at the movement. It still caught me off guard. I'd spent six days lying here with nothing to think about but the damage the bullets had left behind, and still the pain caught me off guard.

"I guess you're not going to explain why you did it," Joe said. "So I'll go ahead and explain for you. You went down there alone because you're afraid for everybody around you, and not yourself. It's so much easier to isolate yourself, right? Nobody to worry about then. Well, there are a handful of people—poor misguided souls like Amy, like me—who would tell you that's a pretty damn selfish idea."

"You've got a hell of a bedside manner. Should have been a doctor, maybe a chaplain."

"I'm not worried about my bedside manner," he said. "You're fine. Took two bullets. I've taken two of them myself. So if you expect me to sit here and sponge off your forehead, forget it. You'll get better. You're getting better."

I turned back to him. "What do you want me to say, Joe? Apologize for not bringing you along to get shot again?"

"I don't want you to say anything. I want you to *understand* something."

"What's that?"

"What you're doing to yourself, LP."

"I don't know what that means."

"Let me ask you this. Why'd you decide to quit the job back in the summer?"

"I told you—I was tired."

"Tired of what?"

"Everything."

"No. You gave me the phrase, said it right to my face—collateral damage. Ken Merriman got killed, and it was too much. After what had happened to Amy, what had happened to me, it was too much. I understood that. Amy understood that. So we supported you, didn't question it, let you quit. I didn't think it was the right thing for you to do, but I—"

"*You* had already quit, Joe. Don't remember that?"

"I'm also sixty-two years old! I did thirty years as a cop; you did five. Don't see any differences there?"

Neither of us said anything for a few seconds. When he spoke again, his voice was softer.

"I didn't think it was the right thing, but I didn't argue because I don't know that there are many things more deeply wrong than one person telling another how to live. So I let you quit. Now, a few months later, you're in here because you *couldn't* quit."

"Should be a little easier to make it stick now."

Now it was his turn not to answer.

"You remember the way Dunbar looked when we went out there and showed him the Neloms connection?" I said. "You remember how he went into his bedroom and found his files, Joe? In his bedroom? A man who has been retired for years? He was obsessed. And wrong."

"And a different man than you."

"Yeah? I don't know about that. Don't know how different he is from you, either, if you hadn't forced yourself to disappear, forced yourself to quit this work. He's what waits at the end of the tunnel."

"Something you need to understand, Lincoln? There are a lot of tunnels, and you do your own digging."

Neither of us spoke after that. He stayed in the chair until a nurse came in and gave him an excuse to leave.

45

We didn't have another conversation like that. The next time I saw him, there were other people around and he was back to his forced cheerfulness. I'd never seen him so funny, in fact. He seemed like he should have his own late-night show.

I stayed at Amy's apartment after I was released. The stairs were easier to negotiate there, and her place was more open, had better daylight. That sort of thing matters to you when you spend most of the day sitting around.

I was coming back fast. That's what the doctors and the physical therapists told me. Coming back faster than I had any excuse to, in fact, largely because I'd been in outstanding shape at the time I'd taken the bullets. All those obsessive workouts were worth something, then. Good to know.

Amy and I talked about the shooting often, but always in a journalistic fashion—how strong the case against Darius was, what the potential legal ramifications for me might be, things like that. At first I wondered if she was keeping that sort of distance for my sake, and eventually I realized it was for hers. In the silence that grew after one of our conversations, I told her that I was sorry.

"You're sorry?" she said. "For what? Getting shot?"

"For putting you through all of this."

She gave a sad smile. "One of the last things you said to me, the night before you went over there, was that you had to do one last thing, and it had to be done alone."

"I remember."

"Look how well that turned out. In your head, I suppose you were protecting Joe. Probably me, too."

"Oh, no, Joe's shared his psychological insight with you."

"You think he's wrong?" she said. "You have the nerve to look me in the eye right now and tell me that Joe was wrong with what he told you in the hospital?"

I didn't speak.

"Exactly," she said. "You know that he's right—and you know that if a bullet went just a few inches in a different direction, I'd be alone right now, remembering that last night we were together. You think that would be a good memory for me? I couldn't stop thinking about it while you were in the hospital. I decided that it would have made a hell of a fitting epitaph for you. 'He had one last thing to do—alone.' Heaven knows it would be alone."

I didn't say anything.

"I don't think I can explain just how that memory resonated with me while you were in the hospital," she said. "How perfectly and tragically symbolic it seemed. If you had gotten killed out there, and you almost did, that moment would have stayed with me. You know why? Because it felt like you were telling me, '*I have this one last thing to do—alone—and then I can love you without walls.*'"

"Damn it, Amy, you know that I love you."

"I do, but I'm trying to tell you something that you need to understand—you can't protect everyone you love from harm. From the world. Trying to do that will break you, eventually. It will. And you know what? Something bad will still come for the people you love. You can't stop that, and it's not your job to try. It's your job to be there for us when it does."

It was quiet for a moment, and then she said, "Trust me, Lincoln, bad things will happen to the people you love. I'm staring at my boyfriend right now, and let me tell you, he's a pretty pathetic sight. Bullet wound, all bandaged up, can't even get off my couch under his own power."

"I can, too."

"Prove it," she said and walked to the bedroom.

On one of those long days while Amy was at work and I was sitting in her living room alone, I got out a legal pad and a pen, and I sat down to try writing a letter to Ken's daughter again. It came easier this time. I wrote five pages, five pages of apology and sympathy. Then I read through it and thought that it was all wrong, and I threw those away and started over. I left in a few paragraphs of the old stuff, but then I focused on the case. I told her as much as I could. I told her what sort of detective her father had been, how dedicated, how patient. How he had waited day after day to check out a hunch, and in the end the hunch had been right. I couldn't tell her more than that, but I could at least explain that much.

He was a good detective, I wrote, because he stayed at it. Because he craved the truth above all else, above even himself. Certainly above himself.

This time, I mailed the letter.

Late in the week after my release, Joe called to say that Parker Harrison was leaving daily messages at the office. I took down his number and called him back. He asked if he could see me in person, and I gave him the address, and he told me he'd be out in twenty minutes.

It took fifteen. I'd already made my way down to the door and was sitting on the bottom step waiting for him. The steps were difficult. My right leg still screamed if it took the bulk of my weight. I opened the door when he arrived, and I shook his hand, and we went back upstairs. It was slow going. He followed me and didn't say a word.

When we got up to the living room, I fell into my designated corner of the couch, and he sat on the chair across from me. He reached out and handed me an envelope.

"This first," he said. "I tried to bring it to you at the hospital."

I opened the envelope and found a handwritten letter inside. It was a woman's handwriting. Alexandra Cantrell. When I read it, I wanted to laugh. It reminded me so much of the letter I'd written to Ken's daughter—the tone, the words, even some entire phrases. There was a lot of gratitude there, awkwardly expressed. There was also, I discovered when I turned the page over, a phone number and a promise.

If you need or want me to speak to the police, to the media, to anyone, I will do it. This number will reach me, and all you have to do is make the call. I owe you more than I can express, and I feel deeper guilt and agony over the things that have happened to you than you are probably willing to believe. If there is something I can make right, then this is the number to use.

I finished the letter and then folded it again and slipped it back into the envelope. Parker Harrison was watching me.

"I know what she offered," he said, "and it was sincere. If you'd like her to come forward, she will. She wanted to at the start, but I talked her out of it. I told her to wait."

I nodded.

"Will you ask her to come forward?" he said.

"I don't really see the point. It wouldn't give anyone who matters anything new. It would take some things from Alexandra, though. She's already had a lot taken."

That seemed to please him. He looked at the floor for a moment and then leaned forward and said, "Lincoln, the things that happened—"

I held up my hand. "Stop, Harrison. I don't want or need apologies. You could explain some things to me, though."

"Of course."

"Why did you hire me to begin with? Were you worried about being connected to that corpse and wanted to find Alexandra in case you needed a witness?"

He smiled. "Do you know how many times you've asked me the same question? How many times you've asked why I came to you? I told you the truth the first day."

"Not all of it."

"No, not all of it. I apologize for that. My reasons, though . . . those were honest."

"Then why wait twelve years?"

"I'd thought about doing it earlier but always talked myself out of it. Then Joshua's body was found, and I thought it was time. I wanted to speak to her again."

"Ken tried to talk to you during his first investigation. He said you ducked him. Didn't you remember who he was, though?"

He shook his head. "That was twelve years earlier, Lincoln, and I never spoke to him, just ignored the calls and messages. His name meant nothing to me. Then Alexandra made contact, told me that the police were focused on me, and that you were working with them, and she thought I should probably stay away from you."

I recalled the day he'd fired me, how he'd gone straight to the phone when I left. It hadn't been Alexandra that he called.

"You talked to Dominic throughout this. Why?"

"When she left, Alexandra asked me to give him a message."

"To tell him that she wouldn't speak to him again, and he shouldn't look for her," I said. "Yes, that's what she told me. Why did Ruzity go to see him?"

"To threaten to kill him if he looked for her," he said. "I hope you understand that promise didn't come easily for Mark, or lightly. He loved Alexandra, though. The reason I didn't want you to visit him to begin with was that I knew it could go badly, for everyone. He's doing well, though. Ever since he left Alexandra, he has been doing well."

"Why'd you talk to Sanabria after you fired me?"

"To tell him that you'd been working for me but were not any longer, and if any harm came to you I'd hold him responsible."

He'd called, in other words, in an attempt to protect me.

"Quinn Graham said you two didn't have contact for years, but then you did again when the body was found."

He nodded. "I said that I wouldn't go to prison for him. That I'd talk to the police if they came to me, regardless of his sister's decision for silence. He told me then, as he had before, that he hadn't killed Joshua. I found myself, for the first time, starting to believe him. I needed to know the truth, and I needed to talk to Alexandra. So I came to you."

"Because you'd read about me in the papers."

"Because I thought you were the right person for the job," he said. "It's the same thing I told you at the start—it was about how you viewed the guilty. I thought you would be able to look past the things that others would not."

"I didn't, though."

He made a small shrug, as if it didn't matter, and I shook my head.

"No, Harrison. I don't think you understand how badly I failed to be what you hoped I would be. I distrusted you from the start. That never changed."

When I said that, he dropped his eyes and looked at his clasped hands and was quiet for a time.

"I've never asked anyone to forget what I did," he said. "I haven't tried to forget it, either. It demands to be remembered. I carry it with me. I deserve that."

"We all like the idea of rehabilitation," I said. "I just don't know how many of us actually believe in it."

That made him smile, for some reason. "It only takes a few, Lincoln. Alexandra was enough for me."

"Have you talked to her?"

"A few times. As I said, I talked her out of going to the police the day you were shot. I told her to wait."

"I'm glad," I said, and I meant that sincerely. I saw no gain from what would happen if she reappeared. Not for me, or anyone else. Let some mystery linger for the rest of the world. The world probably needed it.

"I have another question for you," I said.

"Yes?"

"What happened to Joshua's ring, the one Dominic left with the body?"

"It's at the bottom of Pymatuning Reservoir." He frowned. "You know, if Alexandra hadn't made the decision she made, her brother might have gone to prison. It was a good way to frame him. It might have worked."

"Yes. It might have."

There was a brief silence, and then he reached in his jacket and withdrew something wrapped in newspaper and passed it to me. It was heavy in my palm.

"What is this?"

"Mark Ruzity wanted you to know he could do other things with a chisel than what he showed you the first time. I think it's his version of a thank-you. Maybe even an apology."

I tore the paper loose and found a beautiful, small piece of granite. Across the front, carved in small but clear letters, it said, *Lincoln Perry, PI.*

"It's for your desk," Harrison said.

"Yeah."

When he got to his feet I started to do the same, but he waved me off.

"Don't make that trip down the stairs for me."

"The trip's good for me, Harrison. It's no fun, but I need it."

I followed him down the stairs, and when we reached the bottom I put out my hand and shook his.

"Thank you," he said. "For what it's worth, Lincoln . . . everything I hoped about you at the start, I still believe now."

He left then, and I turned and took a deep breath and started up the steps again. Back in the living room, I sat down and read the letter from Alexandra one more time, then picked up the nameplate Mark Ruzity had carved and held it in my hands.

Lincoln Perry, PI.

For my desk, Harrison had said. That's what Ruzity had in mind when he carved it, at least. I wondered, though, if it wasn't really the smallest headstone he'd ever done.

46

It was three more weeks before I went to see John Dunbar. By then I was moving better and had some of my weight back. I'd lost almost twenty pounds in the aftermath of the shooting, and it was depressing as hell to consider how weak I'd be when I could finally get back in the gym. I'd been at a strength peak before, and now I'd bottomed out. That's how it goes, though. That's always how it goes.

It was late November when I made the drive, and the lake was hard and cold and whipped into a fury by a strong front out of Canada. Winter on the way, and with it would go Joe. I hadn't been surprised when he told me he was planning on another departure in January, but I was surprised to hear it would be back to Florida, and not Idaho. It seemed Gena was stepping aside from her position and heading south to join him. I remembered what she'd told me about neither of them wanting to be selfish, and how the best thing might be to pick a place that was new to both of them. Florida would be that, and it was also the place where they'd found each other. Maybe they'd stay. Maybe he'd convince her to spend some of the year in Cleveland. It was too early to tell.

Sheffield Lake was quiet; not so many people interested in heading to the lake come November. When I got out of the car and walked to Dunbar's door, the wind was difficult to move through. It seemed to find the bullet wounds somehow, slip through them and carry the chill to the rest of my body.

Dunbar was home, and happy to see me. Ushered me in and took my coat and got me positioned in a chair by the fireplace. It was gas, not wood, but it threw some heat and made the tiny house seem like the perfect place to sit out a howling storm.

"You better let me get you some coffee," he said. "Maybe put in a touch of whiskey, too? Just a warmer. Today's a day for it, if ever there was one."

I said that sounded fine, and then he went out to the kitchen and fixed the coffee, and I sat and watched the storm. When he came back we drank the coffee together, and I listened while he talked about the case, offering updates and theories and connections I might not have heard.

Eventually he burned himself out and set his coffee aside and said, "Well, what brought you out here on a day like this? I'm sure it wasn't for my coffee."

"How sure are you that Alvin Neloms killed Joshua Cantrell?" I said.

He blinked. "Quite sure. How could I not be, at this point? I've heard your tape—he all but confessed. Then Darius provided the details. Why do you . . . I mean, you're sure of it, too. Right? You don't think something else?"

"If I had to guess," I said, "if I had to put every dime I have down on one bet, I'd say he did it, yeah."

"That's what I thought."

"I believe that because of what I saw. Because of how he reacted when I said Cantrell's name. Sometimes, though, I get things wrong. Sometimes I make an assumption based upon what I've seen, and it's wrong."

He was frowning at me, quiet.

"So here's what I have to ask you," I said. "Did you kill Joshua Cantrell, or did you just leave the ring?"

I waited a long time. He did not speak, did not move. Did not look away, either.

"Probably wouldn't have bothered me if I hadn't gotten shot," I said. "Or if it had bothered me, it would have slipped by easier. Since I did get shot, I've had a lot of time to sit around and think. I thought about the way

Neloms had his uncle shoot me, the way he dumped Ken's body, the way he threw Bertoli off a roof. He was not a man who was interested in subtleties. He was interested in making people dead and moving on. Didn't care who got arrested for it, didn't care about framing people."

I leaned forward, feeling a tug in my chest but not the radiating pain that had once been there.

"Alexandra thought her brother killed him, or had him killed. She thought that because of the ring. It's why she left. While I can understand why she thought that, I can't imagine why in the hell Dominic would have left it. As a message? That would have served no purpose. She wasn't a mob rival, she was his sister, and she mattered dearly to him. If he had killed her husband, he wouldn't have left a calling card."

Dunbar's face was still impassive, but his eyes went to the wall above my head.

"It's possible that Joshua Cantrell told Bertoli about that ring," I said, "and that Bertoli told Neloms. Here's the thing, Dunbar: Even if Neloms were to think it wise to frame someone like Sanabria—and he wouldn't—and even if he did know about the ring, he wouldn't have known where to find it. Because Cantrell never wore the thing. I suppose Bertoli could have known, and could have told Neloms, but I don't think so."

It was quiet. Dunbar looked at me for a while, then away.

"Of course I didn't kill him," he said.

"That's your only denial?"

He nodded. "How do you know about the ring?"

"How, indeed."

He sat back in his chair, blew out a shaking breath.

"Tell me what you did," I said.

He turned his hands up. "You know what I did."

"I know you left the ring. I'd like more details."

"Joshua called me and told me that Bertoli was dead and he wanted out. Said they were leaving the country. I told him that he couldn't do that; he had to be a witness for the investigation of Bertoli's murder. He hung up on me. So I went to see him in person, and I found his body."

His mouth worked for a bit without any words coming out, and then he said, "You can't know what I felt then. I can't explain that to you. I knew I was partially responsible, but I also knew who killed him."

"You *thought* you knew," I said. "You were wrong."

That made his jaw clench, but he nodded. "At the time I was *certain*, and I thought, no, I will not let this happen again. I will not let Dominic walk away from this, too."

"You knew where Cantrell kept the ring?"

"It was in a cabinet just inside the door. He kept it there in case Dominic made a surprise visit. So he could put it on at the last minute, you know? The ring was a big deal to Dominic."

He said "Dominic" the way most people say "poison."

"You had a key?"

"Door was unlocked. Open. His feet were still inside the house."

"So you went away, and waited for the discovery."

He nodded, and there was a tremor in his face, near his left eye. "Waited all night, and into the next day. Then I couldn't wait any more, and I went back. He was gone, and the stone was clean. I couldn't believe it. I thought I was losing my mind."

"You didn't call anyone," I said. "With the murder less than two days old, you did not call anyone."

"I had tampered with a homicide scene, and then I had left it."

"There was a murder to be solved. You were the only—"

"*I didn't think it would take twelve years!*" He shouted it at me, and now his hands were trembling, too.

I shook my head in disgust.

"I tried to help," he said. "Anybody would tell you that. I tried to guide things."

"Guide things right to Dominic Sanabria. Right to an innocent man."

"He is *not* an innocent man!"

"He was this time, Dunbar."

"If you had known what I knew—"

"I did," I said. "Me, and every other detective who's looked at it. We fell all over ourselves looking at Sanabria and Harrison and all the rest of them. Shit, there was no shortage of suspects. All of them had been guilty. None of

them were this time. Nobody could ever get it, could ever see the forest because there were too many damn trees. Until Ken Merriman. He got it. Then
he was murdered, and some of that's on your head, Dunbar."

"Everything you just said is true, but it wouldn't necessarily have changed
because they had a corpse. They already had Bertoli's corpse. That didn't
help."

"You're right," I said. "Why would another crime scene possibly have
been a help? Why would Alexandra's testimony possibly have been a help?
You know how long it took me to get to Neloms after I talked to her? One
day. One *day*, you son of a bitch."

He said, "When you *talked* to her?"

"That's right, Dunbar. She's out there—and she's staying out there. You
tell anybody that I've talked to her, and I'll happily distract them with the
rest of this conversation."

"I won't tell anyone," he said. "I just can't believe . . . I never knew . . ."

"She ran away. Because of what *you* did, she ran away. It wasn't the murder. It was the ring and the message that it carried. Remove that, and you
might have had an arrest within a week, might have had twelve fewer years
of Alvin Neloms, might have had Ken Merriman alive."

My voice was rising now, and I wanted to hit him, but instead I reached
out and ran my fingers over my shirt, near the scars.

"I hope it weighs on you," I said. "I hope that burden is terrible, Dunbar.
It should be."

"You *hope* it is? You don't know?"

"I don't know much of anything," I said. "I just do a lot of hoping."

I got to my feet and went to the door, walked back out into the cold
wind.

That night I took Joe and Amy out for dinner at Sokolowski's. I hadn't been
there since that lunch with Ken at the end of the spring. It was edging
toward winter now, and the view of the city's lights was hampered by
rain-streaked windows. It was still beautiful, though. You just had to look
harder.

I told them about my visit to John Dunbar. Joe's initial response was for a call to action—he wanted police, prosecutors, punishment.

"He's an old man now," I said. "A retired and highly regarded FBI agent. You think they'll ever actually let him get to a trial? For a charge of tampering with a crime scene, one that can no longer be proven?"

"It can be testified to."

"By Parker Harrison and Alexandra Cantrell. Those are the people who could testify to it. I ask you this—is it worth it?"

Joe didn't answer. Amy said, "No. I don't think that it is."

"Ken Merriman's daughter might disagree," Joe said. "As Lincoln pointed out, Neloms should have been arrested years before he had a chance to kill Ken."

"Should have been," I said. "Might not have been. Anyway, however corrupt Dunbar's actions, you can be sure he didn't want it to play out like it did. I've seen that man enough to know he won't be able to find peace with this, Joe. Alexandra and Parker Harrison have come closer, and they deserve it more. I suggest we leave them to that."

"What about you?" Joe said. "Have you found peace with it yet?"

"Sure."

He and Amy exchanged a look.

"You remember the conversation we had in the hospital," I said to Joe.

"Yes."

"You were right, of course. I was trying to make this case my life without letting it into my life. Maybe that doesn't make sense, but I don't know how else to phrase it."

"It makes sense," he said. "I've seen plenty of police do it."

"I have, too. They're the ones who eventually end up divorced and drinking and angry. You know that."

He nodded.

"So I see your point, is what I'm trying to say. Still, you have to understand that I've had trouble dealing with what happened when some of these cases found their way into my home, Joe. Found their way to Amy, to you."

"He understands," Amy said. "As do I. Trust me, as do I."

"What are you leading up to?" Joe said. "Are you telling us you want to go back to PI work, or that you're ready to truly quit?"

"I'm telling you I don't have an answer yet. I need some time. There's a part of me that would like to move on. Maybe the largest part of me."

"What would the other part like?" Amy said.

"There are some people who have come to us because they really needed us. I'd like to think we've done some good in those situations."

"You *know* you have," she said.

"Hell," Joe said, "you don't have to look at it like such a crossroads, Lincoln, like it's a right turn or a left and you've got to make the decision now. Hang at the stop sign for a while. Keep it in idle. We still get calls for case work, you know that. Just because you take the calls doesn't mean you have to take the cases. You can listen, and then you can decide."

"That seems right," I said, and it did. For now, that sounded like enough.

I would answer the phone when it rang. I would listen.

DEVELOPMENT
THROUGH
REVOLUTION

Arend Theodoor van Leeuwen

Books by Arend Theodoor van Leeuwen

Development Through Revolution
Prophecy in a Technocratic Era
Christianity in World History

DEVELOPMENT THROUGH REVOLUTION

CHARLES SCRIBNER'S SONS   *New York*

Printed in the United States of America
Library of Congress Catalog Card Number 78-106548

Contents

v

Preface

Although the final manuscript for it was prepared in the silence of a Dutch study, the present book originated and matured during my wanderings abroad on various continents. Looking back over the stages of growth which it has passed through, I remember with gratitude many personal encounters which have contributed to the insights presented in the following pages.

During the first years after the Second World War, Indonesian students in Holland (among them a considerable number of passionate nationalists) gave me the initial essential introduction into the background of the Indonesian Revolution. Since those days I have been unable to overlook the intimate relationship between revolution and war: the big war called world war, as well as the small war called guerrilla. Several years of participation in the life of a Javanese church greatly contributed to my understanding of the drastic spiritual renewal involved in the achievement of national independence. At the same time, my eyes were opened to the immense problems of economic development and postrevolutionary political order that a newly independent country is forced to face.

To these Asian experiences many encounters during the sixties with Christians in Eastern Europe have added a new chapter. I feel particularly indebted to those whose hospitality and friendship I experienced in East Berlin, Czechoslovakia, Hungary, Romania, and the Soviet Union. A number of these contacts were directly or indirectly associated with the Prague Christian Peace Conference. I realize how much the work of its Theological Commission has helped me to discover the promises, dilemmas, and deadlocks of a "theology of revolution" which we tried to develop. The first meeting of this Commission will remain in my memory as a week of abundant hospitality offered by Metropolitan Nikodim and the Leningrad Theological Academy, during which a promising ecumenical confrontation took place between the new theme, Revolution, and the age-old theme, the Incarnation. Last but not least, these contacts with European Socialist countries introduced me to the Christian-Marxist dialogue. Indeed, the final chapter of

this book owes its ambiguous title concerning a post-Christian and a postrevolutionary world largely to this fascinating and sometimes bewildering variety of East European contacts.

The second chapter of this book witnesses to the important contribution of the World Conference on Church and Society, held in 1966 at the headquarters of the World Council of Churches in Geneva. It was for me a privilege, immediately after the impressive encounter during this Conference with the revolutionary mood in present-day Latin America, to be the guest of the Facultad Evangélica de Teologia de Buenos Aires, and its Dean, Professor Miguez Boninos. The days spent there not only meant a first physical contact with that continent, but, through the invitation to deliver the 1966 Carnahan Lectures, laid the cornerstone for this book. The theme of those Lectures, published in Spanish under the title *Desarollo y Revolucion* (Development and Revolution) was seriously tested during the fall of the same year when Princeton Theological Seminary in the United States invited me to deliver a series of lectures. The daily contacts and discussions with many students and with members of the faculty contributed an important enrichment to my understanding of the present-day American scene. I want to express my particular gratitude to President John McCord and to Professors Charles West and Richard Shaull, for their friendship and cooperation.

The invitation of President Gene Bartlett to deliver the four Ayer Lectures during the Eastern Convocation (1968) at Colgate Rochester Divinity School challenged me to a rethinking of the subject, which I titled "Theology Facing Revolution." Only shortly before, I had seen Martin Luther King's dead body, placed on the bier in the Chapel of Spelman College in Atlanta. The months spent in this southern city as a guest lecturer of Candler School of Theology at Emory University stand out in my memory as a dramatic confrontation with the racial crisis in the United States. Participation in a seminar on "Revolution and Christian Responsibility" under the auspices of Professor Theodore Weber not only induced me to deliver a paper on "Christian Mission and Revolutionary Participation," but considerably widened the horizons of my understanding and knowledge. The friendship and hospitality

offered to my wife and me by Dean William Cannon, Professor Mack Stokes, and so many members of the faculty are things we will never forget, and make us regret all the more that circumstances did not permit me to accept the invitation to teach there.

Essential as these preparatory stages have been, the present book is, nevertheless, a rather drastic recasting of preceding lectures, so that the total length is now considerably greater. Wherever it appeared desirable and possible, I have made use of more recent literature. The title of this book represents, in the present stage of my thinking, the most adequate expression of my philosophy on the subject.

Since so many people on various continents have unwittingly contributed to the writing of this book, it does not seem too pretentious to expect some of its readers, by their critical response, to carry forward the theme to a subsequent stage. What more desirable development could there be for a revolutionary theme?

Driebergen, Netherlands   Arend Th. Van Leeuwen
March 1970

CHAPTER ONE

Pitfalls of Universal Change

We are living in a period of turbulent change in almost every aspect of life and in almost every corner of the world. It has rightly been said that President Washington, were he to return for a moment from the grave and cast a glance at the city which bears his name, would probably experience such a shock that he would die of a stroke. Transported to the old city of Babylon at the time of King Hammurabi, he, on the other hand, would feel quite at ease with the tempo of life and the technological level of the city. The only handicap would be the language barrier.

What applies to the pace of the last two centuries is even more valid for the twentieth century, which has witnessed an unprecedented acceleration of technological evolution and social change, and there seems to be no reason to expect an end to this process within the foreseeable future. Our generation is caught up in the midst of a rapid evolution; there is little time left for retrospect and meditation about the good old days, for all our vigilance is required to keep the boat on course and to adapt our groping intelligence to still more rapid changes looming in the near future.

United Nations Development Philosophy

An interesting approach to this process of global change is to be found in the idea of a "development decade," such as was proclaimed at the beginning of the sixties by the United Nations. Since we have now reached the end of this decade and are in the midst of preparations for the Second Development Decade, it is instructive to listen to the evaluation delivered by the Secretary-General of the United Nations when this ten-year program was at the halfway point. In an elaborate analysis looking back and ahead, standing at what he called a "turning point," U Thant developed what could be called a United Nations philosophy on the world-wide socio-economic evolution of our time.[1]

This philosophy can be summarized in a dialectical fashion:

Thesis: (a) The process of development involves all mankind—from the commuter in modern Megalopolis to the herdsmen on the Saharan fringe. *(b)* This process, whereby, at different times and at different speeds, the whole human race is adapting to its use the modern instruments of science and technology, is irreversible. *(c)* The process conceals an increasing interdependence: underneath the vicissitudes of day-to-day politics we begin to discover a substratum of economic and social experience which is more or less common to all the nations of the earth.

Antithesis: The gap in resources between the fully modernized nations and their still-developing neighbors is tending to widen, leaving some two-thirds of humanity below the poverty line, turning the developed societies, whether or not they realize it, into a privileged elite.

Synthesis: The idea of a Development Decade is essentially a focus for action, action to lessen the gap, to speed up the processes of modernization, to release the majority of mankind from crippling poverty, to mitigate tensions and hostilities which must flow from the world's vast inequalities in wealth, to restore solidarity and hope.

This is the general framework of a representative specimen of development philosophy. The thesis states some overt facts, but, on closer analysis, underneath the surface of mere statements, a pertinent philosophy which selects, interprets, and ranges the facts is discernible. Neither the universality, nor the irreversibility, nor the increasing interdependence of the process of development can, in fact, be strictly proved. A gloomy philosophy which would start from a radical unbelief in this perspective of general progress would have at its disposal a number of countertendencies weighty enough to tip the balance toward an expectation of increasing disintegration and regression on a worldwide scale. This type of counterphilosophy could rightly argue that progress, as far as the whole of mankind is involved, is an extremely dubious idea and, besides, that this development is not a "process" in the sense of physical and chemical processes, but is made up of a continuous series of human actions and decisions. These human decisions, although strongly supported by a series of antecedent actions that tend to steer all subsequent actions in the same direction, are not determined like cause and result but are, each of them separately and all of them collectively, conditioned by an underlying conviction. The human heart and the network of civilization are not, however, molded unambiguously by one kind of faith; there are a number of countervailing tendencies crossing the highway of the dominant idea and permanently threatening its supremacy. The idea of progress leads a delicate life and the balance it guarantees is, at most, semistable.

Analogous doubts may arise regarding the supposed universality and the increasing interdependence of the development process. It is obvious that the process tends to penetrate into the most distant corners of the world and that it has an almost irresistible logic and force. Nevertheless, its logic is different from the axiomatic evidence of mathematical logic and its force lacks the absolute character of a physical law. In order for development to take place, the concept of development must be accepted and to some degree acted upon by those who begin to participate; even the "victims" of the development process, who willy-nilly become involved in changes which they have never asked for and which they would

reject if they had the power to do so, begin to breathe the air of the ideas and the ideals which lie at its roots. Universality, far from being a natural fact, is unthinkable without some sort of faith in the meaning, the necessity, or the desirability for the human race to become part of a universal movement. In other words, the idea is based upon an implicit philosophy of history.

To be sure, if we cast a glance at the structure of this underlying philosophy, there is hardly any need to give evidence of its fragility. For the thesis, containing the ideas of irreversibility and universality, is immediately followed by an antithesis that puts the ax to its root. Continual widening of the existing gap between the privileged and the underprivileged reveals not only that the thesis has presented facts but that it is conditioned by a faith. If it is true that two-thirds of humanity exists below the poverty line, then the universal character of the development process becomes dubious, at least. Its irreversibility may still be rightly maintained, but it is reduced to that privileged minority which has been able or lucky enough to catch the train. A reduced irreversibility becomes, however, a different idea, for what was meant in the thesis is the irreversible trend of the development process to become universal. The antithesis deflects, as it were, the direction of the process, and the very irreversibility which in the thesis favors the increasing unity of mankind now turns out to function as a wedge, splitting the human race into two parts.

The next step is the acknowledgment that the antithesis not only follows upon the thesis as its negation, but is its dialectical outcome. For the direct result of the global development process is not growing unity but an increasing disunity of the world. The tree may be good but its first fruits do not give evidence of its health; to the contrary, as compared with the differences which existed in standards of living before the modern development process started, what we are witnessing now is not progress but regression. But if this is the case, why should we hold faith in the truth of the thesis? It is, in any event, a paradoxical truth. No philosophy can afford to leave this paradoxical truth alone, not even a philosophy which proclaims the essential absurdity of history, for that philosophy is forced by its own logic to draw conse-

quences regarding the attitude toward this absurdity. The theoretical philosopher becomes, in the end, a moral teacher. Therefore, it is no reason for amazement if such a rational philosophy like that of the United Nations reveals, in its conclusion, its deep-rooted ethical tendency. The antagonism between thesis and antithesis is reconciled by a conclusive synthesis. Let us look at the various elements of the synthesis successively.

What does it mean to say that the idea of a Development Decade is essentially a focus for action? In the light of the preceding thesis and antithesis, the idea hardly seems fit to serve as a focus for resolute and determined action. This does not pertain only to the program of the sixties but is likely to concern the programs of coming Development Decades as well. If the development process, at least within a foreseeable future (which is the range of knowledge of action), tends to further the disunity rather than the unity of mankind, then any action to lessen the gap has to start on different assumptions from those presented in the thesis. The processes of modernization cannot be reduced to the so-called developing countries, for they bear a global character. It is impossible to speed up those processes in favor of the majority of mankind which has still to be released from crippling poverty and simultaneously to slow them down in the highly developed countries. Modernization cannot be confined to the processes of adaptation to higher stages of development of those parts which are lagging behind. It comprehends a whole complex of technological, social, political, economic, and cultural processes which are on the move, particularly in the most advanced stages of global development. Of course, one can attempt to mitigate tensions and hostilities which must flow from the world's vast inequalities in wealth, but one should not foster the illusion that mitigation of conflicts is the same as restoration of solidarity and hope. It is like a drug which may be temporarily effective but which can never replace a needed operation.

Since it is the very thesis of global unity and irreversibility of the modernization processes which produces the antithesis of the widening gap between the most- and the least-advanced stages, the synthesis of action with a view to lessening the gap cannot follow

from the thesis, let alone from the antithesis. It ignores the paradoxical results emerging from the thesis or, at least, implicitly denies that these negative results should be essential and necessary. It approaches the growing disunity as a temporary phenomenon which can be overcome by resolute action, an action which draws its inspiration from faith in the unity of the human race as the basic truth underlying all phenomena which apparently falsify this faith.

This is the basic pattern of the philosophy of development by which the United Nations is guided. It is worth analyzing the more concrete considerations which fill out this framework, as presented in the following quotations from the Secretary-General's address to which we referred earlier:

"First, it is bluntly acknowledged that many of the basic facts remain as uncompromising as ever: The harsh fact persists that many of the poorest economies have continued to grow most slowly. The growth in developing countries as a whole slowed down; at the same time the growth rate in the economically advanced market economies has accelerated." More important is the statement that the goals of action for which the Development Decade had been initiated were vanishing into a growing distance. One of these goals had been formulated as the need for increasing the transfer of resources to developing countries and the flow of international assistance and capital so that it might reach, as soon as possible, approximately 1 per cent of the combined national incomes of the economically advanced countries. At the midpoint of the Decade, this goal seemed unattainable: ". . . more recently the net flow of international assistance and capital has virtually ceased to increase and progress towards the one per cent goal for resource transfer to developing countries was halted."

We have deliberately chosen an official statement of several years ago, because we are now in a position to evaluate the outcome of these expectations which, indeed, confirms the fear that the Development Decade, as far as the realization of its concrete aims is concerned, has proved a failure. As long as it is not improbable that, at the halfway point of the Second Development Decade, an analogous statement will have to be made, this state-

ment of some years ago represents an instructive specimen of a certain pattern of thought and action.[2]

Thereupon, a realistic sketch of the situation in which two-thirds of mankind is continuously doomed to live is presented. A series of well-known facts passes in review, giving a general impression of human misery and backwardness. Closer analysis, however, raises questions about the homogeneity of the image.

First, the enormous differences in life expectancy, particularly in mortality rates of children, which are five to ten times higher in Latin America than in the countries round the North Atlantic, and in Africa higher still. Enormous disparities in medical services are cited as the cause and, more precisely, the failure to invest adequately in the control of disease and the promotion of health. These glaring differences exist, it is said, in spite of dramatic improvements in the prevention of disease, which over the last decade have added ten to twenty years to life-expectancy figures in the developing countries.

The answer seems to be clear: drastic improvement and extension of medical services. But this conclusion is hardly compatible with the consideration which immediately follows. It is argued that inadequacies in diet and medical care are made more intolerable for about 1,000 million people by the desperate standards of housing which they are forced to endure. The major cities of the developing continents all have their densely crowded shanty towns in which 20 to 30 per cent of the city's inhabitants may be living. "The misery of much of the developing world is a progressive misery. It threatens to grow worse in the second half of the Decade. On present showing the numbers of unemployed and men and women suffering from hunger and malnutrition will be markedly greater in 1970 than today. It is in the poorer countries that the highest growth rate of population is found. In most of Asia and Africa it is over 2 per cent and rapidly approaching the 3 per cent level. In some of the Latin American countries it is higher."

These are the facts. Should we not investigate the causes? Then we will see that the very factor summoned to intensify its activities is one of the main causes of the population explosion. It

is the dramatic improvement in the prevention of disease which, on the one hand, is still not dramatic enough drastically to reduce the mortality rates, and on the other hand, is one of the main causes of the alarming growth rate of population. The misery is intensified by the very factor which should be responsible for reducing it.

Other factors are indicated which have further complicated the problem. Rapid migration to the cities is one of them, often exceeding the rate at which urban employment opportunities have been increasing, with the result that unemployment is rising in many of the developing countries. The city forces the new migrants into the rawest struggle for survival. Yet it is to the cities they come, in a flood far surpassing the general growth of population.

Another factor is the change in people's expectations from life. People clamor for the medical help that then sends the population growth rate leaping still further ahead of available food supplies. Young men stream away from the farms before there is room for them in the cities and while they are still needed on the farms. Parents demand village schools, which youths often leave at the earliest possible moment to seek unskilled jobs in urban centers—the very jobs which a more sophisticated industrialization is beginning to abolish. The conclusion to the Report is worth quoting: "No government of a developing country can escape these dilemmas. But as the Development Decade advances, the impact of all these dynamic forces of explosive change is, on balance, to make their difficulties more complex and their prospects more daunting still."

This is, then, the conclusion of a realistic evaluation of the general situation in which developing countries find themselves. If this were only the conclusion vis-à-vis the antagonistic forces belonging to the realm of the antithesis, there would be no reason for alarm. In this case we could, for encouragement and consolation, turn to the thesis and the synthesis. But this escape is not allowed. The forces which have produced and still continue to produce the bewildering panorama of a developing world are no less intimately connected with the thesis and the synthesis than with the antithesis. The very factors of an increasing unity of mankind and of an

irreversible global modernization and the very endeavor to promote these factors enhance the confusion and create the nearly insoluble dilemmas. Even if it were desirable to do so, it would be simply impossible to divide the world into watertight compartments. Nor is it thinkable that we could reduce modernization processes to those aspects where we expect a favorable influence, while preventing unfavorable results. Modernization is one and indivisible. If this is true, then the idea of development and the program of a Development Decade has lost its suggestion of progress and reveals its paradoxical potentialities and ambiguous consequences. In an open world of total communication where the richer nations daily demonstrate what can be achieved in terrestrial prosperity, the governments of the developing countries are compelled to undertake policies and projects which, in the short run, tend to complicate their already formidable difficulties. Once the magic formula of development has been learned, the forces which have been conjured up begin to lead a life of their own and tend to dominate the sorcerer's apprentice. Let us reject the illusion that the developed countries could play the role of the sorcerer who has only to come home in order to stop the impending flood—for the sorcerer has left forever, and all mankind has to bear the common fate and the common dilemma of the sorcerer's apprentice.

Does this mean that development processes have an innate suicidal tendency? Is this the place for despair? The United Nations philosophy emphatically rejects this suggestion and supports its optimism with a historical example. Even if the distance between the developed and the developing countries sometimes seems unbridgeable, the developed are themselves proof that such chasms can be crossed, such disparities reduced to a more tolerable level. After all, the first decades of technological change within the advanced economies produced conditions which closely resemble the divisions and difficulties of the modern world economy. In the United Kingdom, for example, in the mid-nineteenth century, after some fifty or sixty years of rapid economic growth, society was almost as divided between rich and poor as are the two segments of the modern world—the rich "North" and the still poverty-stricken "South" below the Tropic of Cancer. But a century has

passed and conditions in the developed countries have changed dramatically. Entire communities have made the transition to the standards of middle-class comfort. It has taken time, but the chasm has been bridged. It can be done again.

This argument looks strong and convincing. It is based on the assumption of an essential analogy between two phases of modern history, corresponding to two concentric circles. What happened inside the narrow circle of the Western nations can happen again inside the worldwide circle of global development. Of course, it is acknowledged that the analogy is imperfect, but it can be a source of hope and guidance. In many fundamental ways the processes of economic and social development, precipitated by technological change, resemble each other, in spite of the great variety of cultural and national backgrounds against which they work. The methods by which today's fully modernized societies overcame their internal obstructions are now part of the vital information available to developing societies as they struggle with their own problems. Some of the steps taken in the now-developed societies are relevant to the much wider context of development in general.

There is no reason to belittle the significance of these factors. But there is another side to the coin as well. This is only part of the picture and from the same insight opposite conclusions can be drawn.

All analogy contains a similarity of "logic," or *logos*, between the entities which are compared. A crucial question, therefore, concerns the *logos* which has determined the socio-economic development of the Western nations. Underdeveloped nations have some very critical questions vis-à-vis this logic. Two of these questions are worth mentioning here. If one thing is crystal clear, it is that the logic of capitalism, which has determined the earlier phases of Western development, is neither a rational way to be followed by the developing nations of today and tomorrow, nor an adequate pattern for the development of a world economy. And second, part of this Western development logic was its irresistible inner compulsion to expand its range of influence from the context of the nation to the whole world. This global expansion is also part of

"the steps taken in the now-developed societies" which are "relevant to the much wider context of development in general," but its relevance, far from being a source of hope and guidance, is experienced by the underdeveloped world as a perplexing pressure of colonial imperialism by which it is prevented from enjoying those blessings that a supposed historical analogy would suggest and promise.

Seen from this viewpoint, the analogy argument begins to show a Janus-face.

In the nineteenth century, a stream of discoveries and inventions, coupled with increasing sophistication in their application, pushed back the limits imposed by materials and skills. Certainly, the nuclear and chemical revolutions of our day with their promise of almost limitless power and substitutes are only the last in a sustained series of physical liberations from the old restraints. But why should this be a source of hope for the developing world of today? Is it not evident that the developed countries themselves are the first to profit from this power, which crowns their progress, the mark of modern civilization?

Who would deny that in Western countries technical advances explain the ability of the mass of the workers to capture a much larger share of the economy's production? But is this historical example a stimulus for poor nations of today in their defensive, collective action to increase their earnings in the world market? Or is it a warning that they cannot expect support from Western countries—the very countries whose transition to middle-class comfort came about through processes of economic growth and expansion.

True, Western governments have, through their fiscal, economic, and social policies, lessened the income gap and hastened the growth of productivity in their countries. But is there any evidence that this example is a sufficient stimulus for these governments and peoples to repeat this procedure on a worldwide scale, to be concerned with direct transfers of resources to poor nations to increase their skills and education, their health, social assets and ability to help themselves? Are they aroused to a general effort to extend the concept of sustained and expanding demand from

the domestic economy to the world at large? Or are Western governments and peoples increasingly inclined to realize the weakness and helplessness of this historical concept of sustained and expanding demand vis-à-vis a world economy which ostensibly does not follow the "logic" of the Western example?

The almost invincible optimism of the United Nations philosophy has still other arguments in store. Modern technology is, naturally and inevitably, a chief hope of developing nations for the successful achievement of modernization and for bridging the gap between rich and poor. The poor nations are, in some ways, infinitely better placed than the pioneers of an earlier century. In the first place, they have a hundred years of other nations' experience upon which to draw. A second advantage is the sheer scale of information now available in every field connected with development. A phenomenal increase has occurred over the last fifteen years in the process of humanity educating itself. If the first change in any revolution is to change the way in which people think, the entire world today is mined with explosive change—change in the whole dimension and dissemination of human knowledge, in the power that goes with it, in the expectations to which it gives rise.

This is true: explosive change, a revolution of rising expectations! But what the United Nations philosophy fails to demonstrate is that these explosions are, like the dynamite used to blast out a highway, forces of technological development. Won't some of these explosions destroy the very route that the underdeveloped world is supposed to follow in its search for the promised land? And is it guaranteed that these surging expectations of the poor millions will be fulfilled before they and their children and their grandchildren have died? After all, it is acknowledged by the spokesman of this philosophy that the position of the developing nations, confronted with the vast surge of modern technology, is not all gain. Much of the technology was designed for other societies at other times and does not always fit in with the present needs of emerging states. Worse, it may even involve them in contradictions which more developed societies have avoided. Modern measures of health tend to bring about a very sharp increase in

population before any other factor in the community—food production, educational development, savings, industrial development —has become really dynamic. Another contradiction consists in the effects of a sophisticated technology which dispenses with the only resource that all the developing countries have in overabundant supply—manpower. Third, in the heavy industrial sector which seems to promise the most certain road to growth and independence, capital investments are highest and the returns slowest in coming. Fourth, virtually the entire world expenditure in commercial research takes place in the developed nations. Some substitutes made possible by the chemical revolution are cheaper than natural substances. Technology, used overwhelmingly as a tool of developed societies, can turn into a potent instrument of disruption elsewhere. Last but not least, the underlying pattern of the world market has been brought into being by the developed nations' needs for expansion of their domestic economies and is continually determined by their interests and power. This is reflected in the increasing consciousness of the developing countries of their common grievances against existing arrangements.

Nevertheless, despite these serious contradictions and handicaps, we need not despair. We have to realize how much has already been done, how many international agencies and organizations have been brought into being in recent decades, how rapidly the idea of development as a right of the whole of mankind has grown familiar. Still, what has been done is far from adequate to meet even the absolute minimum necessary to bridge the gap between poor and rich countries, let alone to prevent it from widening.

For instance, in spite of the increase in the flow of long-term capital since the mid-1950's, the target set by the U.N. General Assembly according to which resource transfers to developing countries are to rise to 1 per cent of the national incomes of the developed countries, has not yet been attained. In fact, there has been a leveling off in the flow of funds to developing countries since 1961.

Would not these hard figures be sufficient to destroy any kind of development-optimism? The United Nations philosophy does not

falter, not even at this critical point. We are now, at last, confronted with an apparently invincible argument, the factor of time scale. The richer nations of the West, runs the argument, have tended to approach the whole problem of development with an unrealistic time scale. Bemused by the quick success of the Marshall Plan among a group of essentially already developed nations, they expected that the young economies, supported by aid and mobilized resources, would soon be well on their way to self-sustaining growth. What was insufficiently understood was the fact that even the most favored of the developed nations—the United States—took eighty years to reach industrial maturity. And the most ingenious—Japan—took at least forty for its first revolution and, since the Second World War, fifteen for its second.

Is this a fair argument? What is a realistic time scale? The relevance of such reasoning depends upon the idea of analogy between the development of the now-advanced nations during the last century and the start of underdeveloped countries in our day. But, as we have seen, the logic presupposed in this analogy is the logic of a historic phase, which cannot be imitated within the global context of our present world. Besides, this logic produces contradictory results on a scale and of a kind which turn it into its very opposite. The point at issue is not the time scale which has to be estimated but the question whether a breakthrough is possible across the dividing wall of handicaps that separates the poor from the rich world. Any time scale, condensed or protracted, which lags behind the increase of the countervailing forces, means a failure for the development schedule. The necessary breakthrough may be a qualitative affair, a break with the development logic of the developed countries, instead of a quantitative question of a larger or less portion of time.

It is true that the slow but real progress of development has attracted less public attention than its occasional mishaps. It is true that the developing world, for all its frustrations, is in motion and that this means a considerable advance over the stagnation of the twenties and the thirties. But it is no less true that this motion has to be accelerated to such an extent that the will and the decision to bring it about may be found only in a revolutionary

vision. It is true that the nations have entered an uncharted phase of the world economy. But what should one think of the argument that derives hope from the economic strength displayed in the armaments race? "Although over $120,000 millions are being spent on arms each year, this arms burden has not prevented economic growth in the developed world at an annual rate of 5 to 6 per cent. How much more could be achieved for the benefit of the whole world if even a part of these vast efforts could be redirected from producing the instruments of death to producing the instruments of growth and work and life!" This sounds surprisingly reasonable for its very simplicity. But is it more than an edifying fallacy of the kind which serves to conclude many good, and vain, sermons? For this absurd overarmament is, far from being a casual disease of a healthy society, one of the chief symptoms of the almost ineradicable irrationality which goes hand in hand with the rationale of the development process. The key to the saving vision that will dispel the magic of this rationalized absurdity is not to be found in the wishful thinking of the kind "If all men were wise . . . ." The key may be found only in the collective invention of a radical new rationale.

This optimistic and rationalist philosophy of the United Nations is the expression of a fundamental mentality which pervades a good deal of thinking about the meaning and the perspectives of development. An illustrative example is the list of arguments which the British economist Barbara Ward has enumerated to undergird the idea of a Development Decade, a concept that she called one of the most interesting, most encouraging, most forgotten, and most misunderstood of all the policies being considered these days.[3]

First, in Barbara Ward's list, a Development Decade is a genuine attempt to bring underdeveloped and developed nations together to do something constructive. Second, it attempts to give focus to the joint effort. It begins by establishing the rate of growth that developing nations need to keep ahead of their growth in population and to achieve a small surplus for investment in the whole process of modernization. Such investment in education, in farming, in industrial development is necessary if a community is

going to step over the threshold into the modern economy in which self-sustaining growth becomes possible.

A third advantage of the Decade of Development is its assumption that the problem has to be attacked from many different sides simultaneously. One of the first steps is to look at the pre-investment problem. In nearly every country, however poor, a very large part of its local resources, physical and human, is not yet used. The human element is even more important than the physical one. Possibly as much as 60 per cent of development comes, not from capital but from trained intelligence. Fourth, for the first time aid and trade are being considered together. Fifth, the full process of development planning is beyond the scope of many developing countries, and a transfer of skills is essential if their ambitions are not to end in disillusion as hope far exceeds performance. Sixth, the concept of the Decade of Development provides the first context yet attempted for a genuine effort at joint strategy—for Europe, for Africa, for Latin America, and for Asia and the Far East. A final advantage is the opportunity to focus on the problems of development at least a part of the knowledge that has been acquired in fifteen years of effort. The whole concept of a strategy of development is now better understood than ever before.

These arguments are more than an eloquent and intelligent propaganda for a courageous initiative. They reflect a deep-rooted conviction that under the surface of the global processes of change exists a uniform trend which is called "development," a trend which will reach its ultimate goal of universal welfare and affluence, which is rational and can be understood, which can be steered and mastered.

The Great Revolution

There is, however, another way of characterizing the same under-lying trend, giving expression to the same conviction of universal and rational progress: namely, "revolution." We meet this con-viction in the remarkably similar voices of an American and a

Russian. The American political commentator Walter Lippmann has called this global trend toward a universal society "the Great Revolution." [4] During the long and violent centuries which lie behind us, he argues, only an occasional Utopian thinker dared conceive the construction of an organized international society, embracing all the continents on the globe and all peoples of the human race. Yet, in our time, that Utopian idea has become part of the political calculation of practical statesmen in all governments. The great historical fact is that this century has witnessed the consummation of a phase in human evolution that began in the eighteenth century. In the past two centuries there has been proceeding at an ever-increasing tempo the dissolution of the ancestral order and the disappearance of the old regimes which were built on it; almost every government on earth has been altered radically by revolution. The change from government by tradition to government by consent is perhaps the most unsettling change in the political history of mankind.

However, neither the idea of "human evolution" nor the dramatic series of political overthrows which are called "revolutions" is for Lippmann an adequate expression of the undercurrent of radical change in the human condition. The most fundamental of all the revolutions which destroyed the ancestral order and the old regime is the Great Revolution, which he expects will bring about the peace and stability on which eventually the universal society can flourish. We are still only at the beginning of this new phase in history. It is a product of man's advancing knowledge, his knowledge of how to control the material conditions of his life on earth. This is a unique experience in man's long history. We know in theory and in practice how to produce plenty in place of famine. Fifty years ago this knowledge did not exist. We know, too, how to bring fresh water out of the ocean and how to make the deserts flourish. We know how to control conception and the wild growth of population which threatens to nullify any progress we make in improving the material conditions of life. For the first time in history the conquest of poverty has become a rational object of policy for all states. Many of the superficial revolutions

in human history have come and gone and been forgotten. But a revolution in man's knowledge of the nature of things is irreversible, and on that thesis we can found our faith and future.

The Great Revolution will transcend the Cold War, because it will enable pioneer societies to do what neither capitalism nor Communism has been able to do for them, that is, to move toward a standard of living which is better than any that can be attained by a struggle of classes. The masses of mankind from the poorest to the richest are preoccupied above all else with the problem of living with this Great Revolution which brings the promise and the prospect of the fulfillment of their hopes.

An analogous argument has been presented by Mikhail Millionshchikov, vice-president of the U.S.S.R. Academy of Science, who has taken an active part in the international Pugwash Conferences on Science and World Affairs.[5] He points to the increasing importance of science as a political and social force today. The unity of mankind in our time is evident from the unity and close interdependence of the vital problems facing people wherever they may live. By becoming a direct productive force, science is creating material and spiritual values on an unheard-of, gigantic scale. Science must also see to it that those values are not destroyed. In our era science is called upon to revolutionize not only the economic, social, and political life of society, but also its very way of thinking. By penetrating and dominating all spheres of social activity, scientific reason, as the most highly organized and most disciplined mode of thought, can and must help to find a rational solution for the problems of mankind.

Global Change

Four statements made by persons from different continents, confessing different religions and ideologies, have passed our view. Whatever we may think of the rationalistic optimism pervading them, it cannot be denied that they are deeply concerned with the present phase of mankind's history and, for that reason, help us to define some basic issues on which they agree.

1. Unprecedented change within our century is affecting the human situation on a scale and at a speed never before experienced in history.

2. The character of these changes is defined, on the one hand, by the word "development," but, on the other hand, the need is felt for a second, more radical qualification which assumes this development to be of a revolutionary character. "Development" and "revolution" are, as it were, alternatives of a mutually complementary significance.

3. These turbulent changes, however chaotic and anarchic on the surface, betray a deeper meaning in that they are working toward the unification of mankind. The surprising and often appalling novelty of modern phenomena is closely linked up with the fact that, for the first time in history, the unity of the human race is becoming a plain fact on the level of political, economic, and social decisions.

4. The strategic importance of modern science opens undreamed-of possibilities of exploration and exploitation of material forces to the benefit or the destruction of men; additionally important is the changing function of science as an increasingly integrated and integrating force within the whole social structure.

5. There is an awareness of the comprehensive quality of contemporary development which encompasses all aspects of human life, individual and social, material and spiritual, economic, political and cultural.

A few examples may suffice as illustrations of these points: One example is the rapidly changing and contradictory political scene of the twentieth century. We have, within this century, seen the climax of nationalism and the growth of real international cooperation; the outbreak of the First World War, resulting from national self-idolization, and the eventual choice between a third world war or surrender of national sovereignty; the summit of military power and the end of military solutions as a possible instrument of politics; the emergence of two antagonistic blocs supported by mutually exclusive ideologies and the impossibility for any ideology to solve alone any basic problem for the whole of mankind.

A second example illustrates the universal character of the present-day evolution: the so-called developed countries themselves are actually in a state of rapid development. The most advanced country of the world, the United States of America, is now going through a process of revolutionary transition in many sectors.[6] Its population has recently grown in such measure that the term "population explosion" could rightly apply to this country: the 1948 prediction of the United States Bureau of the Census for the year 2000 was surpassed before 1960. This upsurge in the size of the population is so explosive as to have a major impact upon every important aspect of culture. Dramatic alterations are taking place in the age-composition of the population. The geographic mobility of the population is accelerating, resulting in the growing alienation of the individual. The outstanding demographic trend, the mass-migration of Negroes from the South to the cities in the North, is transplanting the so-called race problem from the South to the large industrial, metropolitan centers of the North, a situation which the North finds itself unprepared to meet.[7] Probably the most dominant aspect of socio-cultural change in recent United States history is the racial revolution. More has happened in the field of race relations during the last two decades than during the entire period from the Civil War to 1950.

These sketchy notes touching on a few of the major factors of rapid social change in the United States today are relevant for various other parts of the world as well. Development processes have a universal character and what concerns a "developing" country is often no less pertinent to "developed" regions.

A third instance of the global character of processes of change in the modern world is the growth of urbanization. In the total perspective of the history of mankind, urbanization is a relatively recent phenomenon. Compared to most other aspects of society, this aspect has developed only in the last few moments of man's existence. But this new development represents a revolutionary change in the whole pattern of social life, which affects every aspect of existence. The general process of urbanization, begun on the foundations of neolithic culture, reached a new phase in Western Europe in recent centuries and achieved in the nineteenth

century a position which entitles us to speak of a true urban revolution. For since then, urbanization means not only the rise of a few scattered towns and cities but the phenomenon of a substantial portion of the population moving into urban centers. And this evolution has gone ahead much faster and reached proportions far greater during the last century and a half than at any previous time in world history. It has been rightly said that the hinterland of today's cities is the entire world. The proportion of people living in cities nowadays is higher than that found in any particular country prior to modern times. The world as a whole is now considerably more urbanized than Britain was in 1800, and the urban population has grown much faster than the growth of the earth's total population since 1800. As yet there is no indication of a slackening of the rate of urbanization throughout the world. If the present rate should continue, more than one-fourth of the earth's people will be living in cities of 100,000 or more in the year 2000, and more than half in the year 2050. Although in the older industrial countries the rate of urbanization is slowing down, the character of the process is changing into a new type of metropolitan expansion which is being felt in less-developed lands. Most of the rapid urbanization now occurring in Africa and Asia, the rate of which has been rising in recent decades, is affected by direct contact with industrial nations. We are in the midst of a worldwide process of urbanization affecting all countries, from the most developed to the most primitive. There is an increasing interdependence between the various phases of urbanization and the different geographical centers.

As a last instance, economic development in modern times illustrates the global setting of present-day changes. Whereas before the First World War economic reasoning was in fact focused upon the wealth and progress of Western countries and functioned predominantly within a national scope, the economic crisis which developed at the end of the twenties and the years of economic malaise which preceded the Second World War awakened the consciousness of international economic interdependence, requiring the concept of a world economy. In Marxist thinking the prophecy of the coming collapse of capitalism in the West developed into

the Leninist theory of imperialism, which is in fact a political concept of world economic developments. In the West during the thirties, principally through the pioneering work of the British economist Keynes, a critical evaluation of fundamental trends of Western economics became possible. Prepared by this prewar development of economic thinking, the decolonization process that started at the end of the Second World War introduced a new approach. The international economic situation was viewed in the perspective of worldwide economic development and the non-Western countries were seen as having a right to participate as full and equal partners.

Terminology

These few indications may suffice to illustrate the rapidity, the extension, and the unprecedented character of the complex of changes which we have been facing in recent decades. There are a number of terms which have become familiar to all of us, serving to characterize in a general way a great variety of phenomena, which have at least this in common, that they confront us with the dynamic situation in which we are forced to live. It is worthwhile to list a number of these terms, which occur in our daily vocabulary and all of which serve to remind us of the dynamic situation in which we are forced to live.

Change, a word that is, so to speak, becoming a cornerstone in the building of social sciences. Sociological studies take increasingly into account the essentially dynamic character of phenomena which traditionally were handled within a much more static setting of social patterns and social structures. This general insight has been intensified by the addition of the adjective "rapid," which has even become a kind of dogmatic assumption in the study-process of the Department for the Study of Church and Society of the World Council of Churches.

Growth, a word serving economic analysis since the Second World War. In a sense economic analysis has, since the beginning of the last century, been preoccupied with this reality, but only

recently has the phenomenon of economic growth grown into a central theme.

Closely connected with this is the word *development*. The overwhelming importance of this concept for the economic and social context of the so-called less-developed world has made it a keyword in modern thinking about processes of change.

With the word *evolution* we are close to the point at which social phenomena touch the wider field of general historical processes covering a wide time span. The history of mankind, viewed as the total evolution of the human species from its earliest phase to the present time, in its turn can be considered the inner circle of a much wider range of biological, geological, and even astronomical evolution.

The aforementioned words have in common an undramatic way of expression, at least at first sight; under deeper analysis they disclose their dramatic potentialities. There is, on the other hand, a different group of words which, in various ways, suggest an unexpected turn of events and a sudden change of direction.

Words like *renaissance* and *reformation,* though particularly referring to certain historical periods of Western civilization, have assumed a certain amount of generalization which makes them applicable to a variety of phenomena in modern civilization throughout the world. Rightly or wrongly, they suggest a new beginning and a fresh inspiration which cannot be explained as resulting from the immediate past.

Other words in popular use to describe the non-Western world of today are *emergent* and *awakening*. It is remarkable that these terms are most often applied to countries whose cultural traditions are much older than the comparatively young history of Western civilization.

A word of wide meaning which, for that reason, is applicable to very different fields of reality, is *crisis*. But whatever its application, the word has a highly dramatic function in that it implies the notion of a radical and unexpected break from tradition and suggests a catastrophic situation that cannot be solved by the familiar means.

Of a hardly less alarming character is the word *explosion*

which has already become part of our daily vocabulary in "population explosion," although it is far from limited to this specific use. It suggests a sudden expansion of piled-up tensions, quite abnormal both for its size and for its range of influence. With the word "crisis," the term shares the connotation of an acute danger that has to be averted by drastic action.

Still more provocative in meaning is the word *revolution*. Its use is particularly notable, both for its unprecedented frequency in the description of political, social, and cultural phenomena in the present-day world and because of its application to such contrasting levels of revolution as the Industrial Revolution, on the one hand, and the variety of political revolutions, on the other hand.

Perhaps the most comprehensive and far-reaching term characterizing the total process of rapid changes is the word *mutation*. Actually the term is derived from the description of biological evolution, and this is precisely its implication when it is applied to the present stage of the history of mankind. It suggests that we are passing through a decisive turn which definitely alters the quality of human culture and society as this has existed until the present time.

Terminology is simultaneously important and unimportant. Words are important for the simple reason that as human beings we need language for orientation and communication. Words may also be significant because they give expression to ideas which allow contradictory interpretations and resist clear definition. If this is the case, analysis of the potential meanings concealed in the womb of one ambiguous term has an importance of its own. For the same reasons, we have to be aware of the relative value of words. They are instruments for distinction and discrimination but they should not be confounded with the realities they try to define. They are signposts and ways of communication but they cannot replace the act of communication itself. To the extent that words acquire a surplus value and virtually grow into motivating forces, their usefulness as tools for definition tends to decrease. Their significance moves to the field of the study of images, ideas, and ideologies.

The words that have been listed above are of the kind which is on the move from analytic distinction to synthetic image. They are related to a dynamic situation which hampers orientation and they tend to grow into dynamizing emotional forces. Two words in this list have acquired in our time a particular significance as indicators of our dynamic era: *development* and *revolution*. There are several reasons why we have chosen these as keywords for our study.

The ambiguity of the words *development* and *revolution* appears from our introductory comments on the United Nations philosophy and on some closely related concepts. It became evident that development processes are pregnant with contradictions and antithetic implications which could better be called "revolutionary." On the other hand, what has been characterized as the Great Revolution is precisely that continuous movement of scientific and technological progress which may appropriately be defined as "development." In other words, the terms cannot be separated into water-tight compartments. They are, in a sense, mutually inclusive. This does not imply, however, that there would not exist a clear distinction between the kind of dynamics to which each word is individually related. "Development" refers to a continuous process during which a reality that was initially "enveloped" becomes gradually "developed" following some innate law of evolution. "Revolution" has, at least in modern speech, acquired the implication of discontinuity, of a break encroaching upon a continuous tradition, of a sudden turn and the introduction of a novelty. If the word is being used with reference to an ongoing process, this makes sense only as an indication of the novelty of the process itself over against preceding processes and as characteristic of its amazing dynamism and its continually surprising capacity to produce unexpected inventions.

A certain ambiguity which makes for some kind of mutual participation of both words and a clear distinction which fixes each term on an opposite course tend, in combination, to produce something like a dialectical relationship between development and revolution. This interplay forces us to beware of an approach which prematurely isolates development from revolution or opposes

revolution to development. We have to follow a stereoscopic method which, while having one word in view, never loses sight of its partner. Or, to use another metaphor, we have to treat the subject like an ellipse with two foci, so that our treatment appears to be following an elliptic circumference: wherever we find ourselves the sum of the relationships to both foci remains constant.

NOTES

1. *The Unesco Courier* (October, 1965), pp. 4f., 8f., 30–34.
2. Cf. "World Economic and Social Development," Report of Section III, Fourth Assembly of the World Council of Churches, Uppsala, 1968: ". . . it would be unrealistic, even irresponsible, to talk about the Second Development Decade . . . without considering why the optimism of the early sixties has given way to recrimination and frustration" (I, par. 10).
3. *World Justice,* Vol. 7, No. 3 (March, 1966).
4. *The Unesco Courier* (October, 1965), pp. 21ff.
5. *The Unesco Courier* (October, 1965), pp. 25f.
6. Report of American Churches to the Division of Inter-Church Aid, Refugee and World Service of the World Council of Churches, made to World Conference on Church and Society; Report prepared by Commission on Social Welfare, National Council of Churches, April 23, 1965.
7. *The American Journal of Sociology,* Vol. 60, No. 5 (March, 1955), pp. 439ff.

CHAPTER TWO

Technical and Social Revolutions

How Many Revolutions?

The word "revolution" has become part of modern language in so many different contexts and with reference to such a bewildering variety of phenomena that its usefulness for scientific analysis may be seriously questioned. The fact remains, however, that it is this very general and fluid term which has become instrumental to scientific description in various disciplines. This can hardly be fortuitous. Apparently the term has an emotional overtone and there are serious reasons for the supposition that it is more than just a nominal collection of unrelated data. There may exist, appearing in variegated colors, a real chameleon whose name is "revolution." Any attempt to lay hands on this mysterious animal has to begin with the first step, namely, to collect a number of applications in modern speech. It seems most appropriate to choose some lists of revolutions which have been assembled with a view to summarizing the dynamics of present history.

The first list is derived from the work of a former President of the United States, the late John F. Kennedy. It is noticeable how frequently Kennedy gave expression to the consciousness of living in a revolutionary world. In his book *Strategy of Peace*[1] he

lists seven peaceful revolutions which "are rocking our nation and our world." They are:

1. The revolution in population.
2. The revolution on the farm.
3. The revolution of technology and energy—the wonders of automation and atomization.
4. The revolution in the standard of living.
5. The revolution in weapons development and its effect on national security. Devastation is literally minutes away.
6. The revolution in the underdeveloped nations of the world.
7. The revolution of nationalism.

Referring to modern Africa, Kennedy states that this continent is "undergoing an agricultural, industrial, technological, urban, social and political revolution. It is passing from a feudal—in some places still prehistoric—stage into the atomic age in a matter of decades. It is recapitulating the history of the last five centuries of European society in 50 years. . . ." This revolutionary stage of the modern world is handled as a challenge which forces "an imaginative and constructive American response to the revolutionary demands of a fast-changing world. . . . It is we, the American people, who should be marching at the head of this world-wide revolution, counseling it, helping it to come to a healthy fruition. . . ."

Over against the challenge of Communism, Kennedy summons the American people to another revolution: "a political, economic, and social revolution far superior to anything the Communists can offer—far more peaceful, far more democratic, and far more locally controlled . . . a revolution of their own making.

"The same revolutionary beliefs for which our forebears fought are still at issue around the globe. . . .

"We dare not forget today that we are the heirs of that first revolution. Let the word go forth from this time and place, to friend and foe alike, that the torch has been passed to a new generation of Americans. . . ."

In "an open letter on foreign policy" [2] which Professor Harrop and Ruth Freeman addressed to Kennedy they present, as a counterpart to the President's enumeration, a list of ten revolutions which are usually considered to be shaping our time:

The *nuclear revolution,* similar to the Industrial Revolution, in which nuclear and solar fuels replace solid and liquid fuels.

The *military revolution,* wherein destructive power has so increased as no longer to permit action to "defend" or "decide" anything.

The *political "power" revolution,* in which "balance of power" or making of decisions through exertion of military or other powers has little chance because nations find it difficult to "confront" each other and a small nation can launch or threaten to launch world devastation without itself having a substantial amount of power.

The *colonial* (i.e., *freedom*) *revolution,* in which "colonialism" is disappearing and nationalism is the pattern.

The *geographic revolution,* in which emphasis has shifted from Europe to Asia, Africa, and South America.

The *nonviolent revolution,* which is demonstrating that political change (India) and social change (southern United States) can be achieved by nonviolence.

The *administrative revolution,* by which national governments have turned to functional or administrative law over court or legislative law and by which demand is being made for international government on the same pattern.

The *human rights revolution,* in which it is recognized that every man in the world has a right to food, work, health, dignity, and freedom, and that fulfillment of these demands is required of government more than are the original "liberties" of free press, religion, and discussion.

The *socialist revolution,* in which all economic systems are being socialized and unrestrained private ownership and management are being replaced everywhere, and in which government is increasingly the capital-former and planner.

The *population-possessions revolutions,* by which the popu-

lation explosion is increasingly highlighting the inequitable distribution of the world's products and facilities.

Another list of revolutions refers particularly to the underdeveloped world. Concerning the development problem, a German demographic scholar, Günther Wollny,[3] enumerates a series of six revolutions which Europe has passed through in modern times:

1. The revolution of the steam engine.
2. The sanitation revolution.
3. The literacy revolution.
4. The agrarian revolution.
5. The revolution of traffic.
6. The monetary revolution.

Wollny's conclusion is that some of these revolutions are accountable for the fatal impasse which the underdeveloped countries are facing today. Only three of the six revolutions, namely those concerning traffic, sanitation, and monetary matters, have been exported to the non-Western world; whereas the other three, namely, the engine, the agrarian, and the literacy revolutions, have been reserved by the colonial system as the white man's privilege.

Another attempt to give a synoptic view of a contemporary complex is the statement on "The Triple Revolution," which was offered in 1964 to President Lyndon B. Johnson by a group of American experts, the Ad Hoc Committee on the Triple Revolution. The statement urged, at this historic juncture for the whole of mankind, a fundamental re-examination of existing values and institutions, and it pointed to three separate and mutually reinforcing revolutions which are taking place:

The Cybernation Revolution. A new era of production has begun. Its principles of organization are as different from those of the industrial era as those of the industrial era were different from the agricultural. The cybernation revolution has been brought about by the combination of the computer and the automated self-regulating machine. This results in a system of almost unlimited

productive capacity which requires progressively less human labor. Cybernation is already reorganizing the economic and social system to meet its own needs.

The Weaponry Revolution. New forms of weaponry have been developed which cannot win wars but which can obliterate civilization. We are recognizing only now that the great weaponry has eliminated war as a method for resolving international conflicts. The ever-present threat of total destruction is tempered by the knowledge of the final futility of war. The need of a "warless world" is generally recognized, though achieving it will be a long and frustrating process.

The Human Rights Revolution. A universal demand for full human rights is now clearly evident. It continues to be demonstrated in the civil rights movement within the United States. But this is only the local manifestation of a worldwide movement toward the establishment of social and political regimes in which every individual will feel valued and none will feel rejected on account of his race.

When we look at these lists of revolutions several things are obvious: First, there is the arbitrary character of the lists. There is no evident reason why precisely the number of seven, ten, six, and three were chosen, for the number of examples could easily be extended or reduced.

Second, there is a variety of phenomena which is gathered into the common denominator of "revolution," but these phenomena play their roles on different levels. The human rights revolution, for instance, is a question of deliberate political and social action, whereas a process like the nuclear revolution or the weaponry revolution is a fruit of new technological inventions which may have their effect on the political and social area but which in themselves have nothing to do with any kind of revolutionary action. The technical revolution has taken place in a different dimension from, say, the education or literacy revolution.

Therefore, the primary function of these lists—and this is our

third remark—is to present a comprehensive qualification of a rather chaotic multitude of contemporary developments, by forcing them into a common frame of reference.

Our final point concerns the strategic term which functions as the denominator under which the whole scale of processes of changes is listed, namely, the word "revolution." One may reasonably question whether all these processes are of such rapidity and dramatic effect that they may rightly be called "revolutionary." Some of these processes have indeed occurred within a very short time span, but others cover a long period, the beginning of which is only to be vaguely defined. The decisive argument consists less in some exact statement of facts than in an emotional response to an overwhelming situation which is shaking the foundations of traditional security.

The fact of this terminological lack of clarity is a characteristic phenomenon in itself and it may point to a fundamental confusion, which is an element of our complex situation. On the other hand, without a minimum of terminological distinctions, there can be no hope of reasonable analysis. Therefore, to begin with, we have to distinguish, on the one hand, processes of change which bear primarily the character of natural processes, no matter how rapid or even turbulent these processes may be. A classical example is the term "industrial revolution." It is interesting that the expression seems to have been coined by a British historian[4] as an analogue to the French Revolution of 1789 for which a parallel event in British history had to be invented. This is obviously a *metabasis eis allo genos,* the application of a term to a completely different area. The invention of the steam engine and the process of industrialization doubtless had an unprecedented impact upon the whole of society and their effect may be much more radical and enduring than all those events which in general are described as revolutionary. Nevertheless, the process itself has nothing in common with social or political upheavals that are the result of violent and deliberate action.

On the other hand, there is in the field of social and political history a definite type of occurrence which is clearly distinct from all other phenomena in that it suddenly brings forth a far-reaching

and violent change in the whole pattern of society, and primarily in the traditional political structure that is being overturned and replaced by a new order. This is the familiar use of the word "revolution" as we have come to know it in our schoolbooks. The classical representative of this concept is the French Revolution of 1789.

However, the interdependence between these two types of "revolution" is so great as to reduce to a minimum of significance the distinction we have tried to make. Sociologists do not hesitate to discuss the Industrial Revolution and the French Revolution in the same context as "two revolutions in joint operation." The attempt, for instance, to characterize the Industrial Revolution as primarily socio-economic and the French Revolution as primarily political and ideological in nature has immediately to be corrected by the addition "that the French Revolution also has all kinds of important social and economic effects, whereas the Industrial Revolution is certainly not devoid of ideological moments, and profoundly affects politics. In accordance with modern views, the French and the Industrial Revolution must not be regarded as single and mere historical events, but as utterly independent processes, set in motion long before their first results are to come to light in the latter part of the 18th century, and gaining momentum, width, and depth ever since." [5] The interplay between these two historical events is, therefore, more than a matter of coincidence; the global expansion of the forces which they have set in motion turns their interdependence into a phenomenon of universal importance. "Just as in our days the so-called developing countries can rightly be considered 'areas in rapid social change,' so there is much sense in stating that in the early part of the 19th century most countries of Western Europe are deeply involved in the all-embracing structural crisis which the French and the Industrial Revolution are bringing about, even if the storm centre of these revolutions is as yet at a distance." [6]

Evidently, we are faced with a complex of rapid developments, taking place interdependently in different aspects and on various levels of culture and society. The socio-economic events cannot be isolated from the ideo-political trends and both aspects are closely related to the changes on the technical and scientific plane.

This complexity is aptly summarized in the title of an important world conference held in 1966 under the auspices of the World Council of Churches in its Geneva headquarters. The theme of the Conference was formulated as "Christians in the Technical and Social Revolutions of Our Time." [7]

Before discussing the specific question of the relationship between these two types, the "technical" and the "social," we should notice the novelty of the revolution theme as such in the history of the World Council of Churches. Of course, the idea of a revolutionary epoch in the midst of which the churches are living has been more or less familiar in ecumenical discussions for several decades, but never before was this theme so central to ecumenical discussion as at this meeting.

Since the set-up of this Conference differed from that of the Assemblies of the World Council of Churches it was in a position to break from the usual dominance of theologians within the existing structure of the Christian churches. The majority of the participants were "laymen: professional men, economists, political leaders, social workers, businessmen, social and physical scientists." And thus the statement of the official report: "the rest were theologians and church leaders." [8] One thing this "rest" could have learned there was that theology and theologians have still to start the adventure of really cooperating and struggling together with this majority of so-called laymen in rethinking the task of the church in the midst of our revolutionary world.

The revolution theme derived a specific significance from the fact that almost half of the participants were from Asia, Africa, and Latin America. The pattern of the discussions and the style of approaching the central theme were largely determined by this

half of the Conference membership. They were able to impart to the theme a sense of urgency, which made the Conference a milestone in ecumenical history.

Technical Revolutions

Hardly less significant than the central function of the revolution theme as such was its treatment. The distinction between technical and social revolutions reveals, on closer analysis, far-reaching implications.

The technical revolution was considered, not for its own sake but because of the impact of the new technology on society. Contributions on this theme came primarily, though not exclusively, from Western scholars. This was to be expected, since the Western world is the main actor on the stage of technological progress. One important consequence of the connection between this half of the theme and Western points of view was a particular interpretation of the "revolutionary" implications of technical innovations in the context of a permanent evolution. There was an explicit tendency in the approach of Dr. Emmanuel G. Mesthene, Executive Director of the Program on Technology and Society, at Harvard University,[9] to belittle the idea of technical "revolutions." After all, he said, the mere prominence today of science and technology is not strikingly new, for the veritable explosion of industrial technology which left a decisive imprint on modern civilization had already occurred two centuries ago and the Newtonian revolution in science had taken place a century before that. It is even not clear that what is new about our age is the rate at which it changes. The curve of growth of the past one hundred years indicates the contrary; it is smooth and will not support claims of explosive change or discontinuous rise. Yet, Dr. Mesthene continued, there is something new in our age. First, we dispose, in absolute terms, of a staggering amount of physical power; second, we are beginning to think and act in conscious realization of that fact. We are therefore in the first age that can aspire to be free of the tyranny of physical nature that has plagued man since

his beginnings. Technology has come of age, not merely as technical capability, but as a social phenomenon. Inventions are now many, frequent, planned, and increasingly taken for granted. The surprising and apparently paradoxical conclusion, therefore, is that technology is becoming less revolutionary. The Industrial Revolution, as we call it, was revolutionary precisely because it ran into attitudes, values, and habits of thought and action that were completely to understand, accept, absorb, and change with it.

Is this an irreversible and necessarily continuing evolution? Mesthene's answer was unhesitatingly affirmative. Technological progress will not be stopped, for three reasons: we do not want to; we cannot; and we should not. The last reason is, of course, the most important one because it reveals a definite faith in the meaning and the blessing of a permanent technological progress. We should not stop because otherwise we would cease to be men. Any admission that the technological race has now been proved incapable of coping with its own creations would be the ultimate in dehumanization, for it would be to surrender the very qualities of intelligence, courage, vision, and aspiration that make us human.

The roots of this faith lie—as was made perfectly obvious by Mesthene—in the Greek concept of the essential intelligibility of the universe, which we are rediscovering in our time. We have the power and will to probe and change physical nature, to control our own biology and that of the animals and plants in our environment, to modify our weather, to alter human personality, to reach the moon today and the rest of the heavens tomorrow. No longer are God, the human soul, and the mysteries of life improper objects of inquiry. We are ready to probe whatever our imagination prompts us to do.

Mesthene's approach to the technical revolution of our time is a fine specimen of a rationalist philosophy as self-expressive of a technological evolution come of age. Whatever may be "revolutionary" in the process of technical change belongs to the past of two or three centuries ago. Technical man has now reached the point where he is capable of understanding and controlling what-

ever impact his technical inventions may make upon nature and civilization.

The French scholar Jaques Ellul, rooted in a different tradition, was far less optimistic in his evaluation of technical progress.[10] But, basically, what we find in his approach is the same assumption that the technological order is a given fact, determined by man's essentially rational capabilities. For this reason he, like Mesthene, strongly criticized the suggestion that we are undergoing a technical "revolution." At most we can speak of "a speed-up in evolution," for the usual concept of revolution is related to the "intrusion of the irrational in history." Needless to say, such a definition of revolution is based on the silent presupposition that history (apart from revolutionary intrusions!) is essentially rational.

On this assumption, Ellul continued, it is a logical step to pose the rational character of technical expansion which enables the technologist to forecast future developments. He can calculate what will be possible, or what will be done, in the year 2000 or in the year 2100, particularly because the expansion of technology is a process of cause-and-effect. The scientist or technologist advances in his scientific technology on the basis of elements that are known to him. On this basis many reports have already been drawn up by scientists forecasting the probable evolution of technology during the next twenty, thirty, or fifty years.

Indeed, on this basis! But Ellul is deeply convinced of the limited range which this rational approach is capable of controlling. There are two dimensions that transcend these limits. First, this method of technological forecasting does not reckon with ultimate objectives, nor with an explicit concept of the most desirable future. Forecasting related to a future aim is always uncertain. Second, it is extremely difficult to forecast the effects of technological development on politics, on society, on man himself, and to a less extent on the economic sphere. Technological development is upsetting everything. It is transforming every traditional situation: everything now depends on technology, in every sphere the evolution is dependent upon technological progress; all other influences are merely secondary.

Both factors in combination reduce the rational character of technological development to a limited sphere. In the political, economic, or social sphere a whole series of value-judgments, aspirations, projects, and patterns are bound to come into play. In these spheres evolution is never the simple effect of technology on a social or political situation; it is "a combination of ideologies and technologies."

The only ideology, however, which Ellul takes into account, is the ideological control of the effects of technological developments as viewed from the standpoint of mature technology. Within a technological society we must have a conscious will in order to hold out and to go on. Every phenomenon that was formerly instinctive has now to some extent become an ethical phenomenon. When man lived in a natural environment he was both similar to, and yet different from, nature. He was adapted to nature, but at the same time he tried to adapt his environment to himself, thanks to his intellectual ability. Today we have to undertake a similar adventure, but in relation to a new human environment. Events and actions must be judged by their foreseeable consequences. The more dangerous and alarming these consequences appear, the more they challenge us, i.e., the more they address a serious, real, crucial call to man to control them. Technology is completely ambivalent, neither to be deplored nor to be construed as in itself meaning progress. It presents a "challenge to man to make progress."

The tendency to a deterministic pessimism, which we meet in several books by Ellul, seems here to be counterbalanced by an ethical appeal to the conscious responsibility of technical man. But, in any case, we don't leave the closed circle of technical evolution.

Very close to the periphery where technical evolution touches the other circle of "social revolution" comes the approach of a British-American social economist, Robert Theobald.[11] Examining the implications of man's growing power in various areas, he takes an important next step. If this power is to be controlled for man's benefit, we have consciously to make "major efforts to alter national and world social structures." The importance of this recog-

nition, in comparison with the philosophies of Mesthene and Ellul, lies in the insight that the technological order does not depend only on the inherent rationality of technology as such, which, if threatened by irrational directions or consequences, has to be restored by the rationality of technical man or by his ethical consciousness. We meet here a new awareness that a technological order is always linked up with a definite social structure which can and should be altered.

Theobald touches upon a number of social structures where a radical change is necessary. The abolition of war is required by technology, but war cannot be abolished until new social means are discovered for settling otherwise insoluble conflicts. Population control is required by the consequences of technology, but population control will not be acceptable until social views change. Permanent economic growth is now possible because of the potential of the new technologies, but many people are not able to compete with the machines which provide the potential for economic growth. And until, in both rich and poor countries, new techniques of income distribution are effected and a person's right to consumption is not made dependent upon his contribution to production, these people will stand no chance in competitive economic growth. Free flows of information are required for the operation of a society in which man has unlimited power to control his environment. New methods of communication are required and are made possible by the new technologies, but man has to make the effort to discover how to communicate objectively and imaginatively, using the new technologies.

This is the voice of a Western expert in the social sciences who clearly recognizes the need for conscious efforts at social change in order to bridge the gap between advanced technologies and retarded social structures. Theobald tries to build a bridge between the technical and the social revolutions of our time, but the initiative for this is still only on the technical side of the gap. Technology is developed into social techniques which now become the saving answer to the needs of a world threatened by anarchy resulting from the disproportion between technical potentialities and social impotence.

Perhaps a reason why none of these three scholars succeeds in placing himself at the starting-point of the social revolutions of our time lies in the limitations common to all three as inhabitants of Western countries. In that case we might expect the decisive step to be taken by a scholar who has spent most of his adult life working with people at the very fringe of civilization. Dr. Margaret Mead is such a person.[12] She has been living and working for many years among the simplest people whom the world knows, the peoples of New Guinea, where among two million people there are 700 languages and where no one knew how to bind more than 500 people together in any sort of community. "From that point of view," Dr. Mead explains, "I can bring a kind of faith and knowledge of how rapidly people can change, because I have seen a single village where I worked 37 years ago skip about 2,000 years since then."

Such an experience has given this outstanding American cultural anthropologist a great respect for the potentialities of modern technology. "Whenever we speak of science and technology and what the new empirical knowledge means for man, we must remember those people to whom it means the first running water so that women did not have to spend three hours a day going to the well, those people for whom it means for the first time light at night." And it is out of this understanding that she urges technically advanced peoples to use the knowledge that exists for the benefit of the whole of mankind. "We now have the responsibility of seeing that only children are born who can be fed and cared for and educated and that we postpone the birth of the others to another generation. We have created this situation in the world and we have knowledge to deal with it and we must use it. If we don't use it then there falls upon us the responsibility that a situation has been created in the world which may bring famine and misery and death to millions of people."

Once more, a Western social scientist looks across the border of the technical evolution and takes account of the dramatic effects upon traditional societies. Once more, this means the extension of Western technology and social science to other parts of the

world and the incorporation of the Third World into the great trend of ongoing technological progress.

This is not to deny that Dr. Mead should have recognized the inner contradiction which is hidden in the application of the concept "revolution" to both the technical and the social realms.

> Revolution has been used here to mean that we face some dramatic changes in the world; the technological, pluralistic, secular revolution means that the changes are so abrupt and involve such discontinuity between parents and children that we can compare them with political revolutions. Revolution is also used here by people whose countries still labour under intolerable conditions that they have found no way to change because they do not have the political apparatus that makes change possible. But the word sends a shudder through the souls of New Yorkers whose notion of revolution is the black-out of electric power and who in New York or London or Berlin realise that in our technologically interdependent society we must if we can find ways to make change that will not endanger the whole elaborate structure.

In other words, the most backward tribes have a right to display their capabilities of extremely rapid adjustment to, and insertion into, the line of technological progress, and the advanced peoples have the obligation to promote this participation by all means. But as soon as this rapid evolution might endanger "the whole elaborate structure" of advanced technology, this social scientist cannot do otherwise than to share the fear and aversion sensed by the affluent society and to hope that the chaos resulting from that social revolution can be prevented. This is a disappointing conclusion to an approach which started so promisingly stretching out hands to those peoples who can only hope to participate in the technical revolutions by passing through social revolutions. It is, once more, an indication of the distance separating the technical from the social revolutions.

The conclusion of Dr. Mead's is confirmed by the analysis of the French economist André Philip.[13] Analyzing the structure of European political life, he starts from the insight that the effects of Europe's new technical revolution far transcend the changes

that occurred at the end of the eighteenth century when the modern industrial age was born. But a political consequence of these radical technical and economic changes, according to Philip's conviction, is the end of the revolutionary spirit. We no longer dream about a future revolution, because we are already living in one, in a continual process of destroying the existing structures and rebuilding them.

Man's role in this ongoing technical revolution is to influence events in such a way as to turn them in the direction he considers favorable. Such action must be technical in character and in no way revolutionary or violent. "In the industrial countries, the technical structure is too elaborate and the different elements overlap too much for any sudden break to be made without upsetting the whole system of production and consequently impoverishing the masses. It is through limited action, which does not jeopardize the structure as a whole, that improvements can be introduced, by methods that are bound to be democratic, attempting creatively to mobilize public opinion as a whole."

Of course, the old revolutionary utopianism and the use of violence that is closely linked with it are still found today in the underdeveloped countries. They are still at the stage at which Europe was living in the fifteenth and sixteenth centuries—the stage during which the national state was being created. In this stage of development violent struggles and revolutionary ideas are inevitable while they attack a past that bars the way to progress. The underdeveloped countries have not yet reached a stage at which they can become involved in our problems, our conflicts, and our organizational difficulties. "It is therefore by respecting their neutrality and by giving them aid with no strings attached that we can best help them to solve some of the problems of their gradual integration into a modern economy."

Gradual integration, that is the saving watchword for underdeveloped areas. Their revolutionary ideas and conflicts are a social and political lag which they have to skip as soon as possible in order to find their place in the unbroken and undisturbed line of technical evolution in which the developed countries take the lead.

Social Revolutions

Such is the viewpoint of those who have profited from several centuries of "technical revolutions" which they, in retrospect, consider as one great and continual process. Is there a bridge from this viewpoint to the other side, the approach of those who are living in the midst of the "social revolutions"?

It is difficult to see how that bridge is to be built, when we listen to the witness of an African leader, 'Bola Ige, a Nigerian expert on questions of agriculture and natural resources.[14] Mr. Ige did not deny the need for technical development, but he did not see here an essential problem for the underdeveloped peoples who, indeed, have the great advantage of having all the culture, all the learning, all the technology, and all the ideologies of the world to choose from.

No, the heart of the matter consists in two other questions. The first, crucial one is the question of politics. Quoting Kwame Nkrumah's famous alteration of a Gospel passage, "Seek ye first the political kingdom and every thing shall be added unto you," Mr. Ige showed how intensively this apparently sacrilegious text fires the imagination of peoples in the nations: "For us, politics is the most important weapon with which to create the new type of man and society, the new and appropriate systems we want, and to build the strength needed to contend with the older powers."

Therefore, closely linked up with the priority of politics is the question of power. Three-quarters of the wealth and 85 per cent of the technology of the world is in the hands of one-third of the world's population. "We do not ask that the wealth and technology which the minority now possesses be necessarily distributed among us. But we demand that we take part in seeing that this enormous wealth and technology is not used to our detriment. It is true that this minority no longer holds visible unfettered political power. But the unseen powers of wealth and technology are more potent, more subtle and more dangerous than naked political power. That is why the struggle against neocolonialism will be more bitter and probably more disastrous than the fight against

imperialism." Mr. Ige compared this demand with the new cry of some young and articulate Negroes in the United States for "Black Power." Charity—called aid—from the rich and the technologically advanced is not the answer; "understanding" is not satisfactory; concession by way of trade is merely an attempt to postpone the evil day. "Nothing short of real participation in the exercise of all-important power will avert the coming revolution. Technology, trade or aid is not our central basis—our own central basis is political power in the world."

Mr. Ige then made a distinction among three attitudes to revolution which one finds among Christians today. The first is a cynical disposition toward revolution. The second attitude is tolerant of revolution, but only as long as it occurs within the structures that we know and does not break any rules or laws. Under these circumstances, persons of this attitude do not mind protest marches, demonstrations, sit-ins, *coups d'état:* after all, the constitution must be upheld. They say "revolutionary" actions are legitimate, and that they are not really violations of the constitution but affirmations of its provisions. They say, "The past can be preserved only as it is being transformed." But this tolerant position presupposes that the constitution is all right. This presupposition was questioned by Mr. Ige. "What if the basic dispute is that the whole constitution, the concept of it, and the whole system should be scrapped? What if the peoples in the new nations say: We do not need the past; we have got to throw it away—including, if necessary, those who held political power in the past"?

Besides this tolerant attitude, which he perceived in some circles of the World Student Christian Federation and among the young leaders of the World Council of Churches, he mentioned a third attitude toward revolution, found among the new technological theoreticians. Revolution, they say, is not necessary, and it is a waste of time because technology and research have built within them the processes which will inevitably bring about change in society and a better outlook for the world.

In the description of this third attitude we easily recognize the point of view which was so clearly formulated by André Philip

and which was more or less implicit in some of the other representatives of the technical evolution. Mr. Ige did not deny the existence of some truth in each of these attitudes. But his point was that they are either unsatisfactory or unconvincing to the peoples of the new nations. "The revolution our people desire is one that will completely knock out all existing suffocating constitutions, systems and the powers that keep them going. They cannot wait for the slow process of data and research. The revolution our people are thinking about is different from those of the past: it is global in its dimensions. And nobody can plan this revolution: its timing will be fixed according to the degree of rottenness of the present dispensation."

Listening to this vehement pleading we may wonder whether there is anything like a bridge between the leaders of the "technical revolutions" and the advocates of the "social revolutions." The Brazilian economist Candido Mendes de Almeida[15] spoke of a fundamental "semantic gap" which exists in the confrontation between the "haves" and the "have-nots." The short-circuit in communication affects not only the relationships between the Third World and the Western nations; it concerns also the relationship between two different approaches which are to be found within Latin America itself. Those groups living on the presupposition that all social dynamisms fit within the classical evolutionary patterns of change try to measure and understand the specific new changes of Latin America in Western categories of historical time. They are the leaders of technical development. Their viewpoint is based on the undeniable truth that transitional change is absolutely dependent on the emergence of a new social order based on planning and on social behavior derived from logical correlations and rational models. But the very truth of this view places tremendous power in the hands of a new priesthood: the economists, the sociologists, the political scientists—all who are concerned with management of the fundamental equations of social changes and the evolution of the policies to assure it. Cognizant of the positions of this power-elite, Dr. Mendes spoke of "the abduction of power by the Technocrat." He warned against the danger of an excess of "technicism" which weakens or even annuls

sensitivity to the historical or meta-economic conditions of the social structure. It leads to the cult of rationality and to the idolatry of the lucid approach, both of which are incompatible with the national procedures that characterize the developing country. The technocrat, seeking the mountain peaks of social progress, may die of suffocation in this rarefied atmosphere in which he has lost contact with the historical and concrete elements required to make viable his stern rational approach toward development.

Lacking this setting, a "conflict between the stiffness of his behaviour and the response from within the community would seem inevitable," Dr. Mendes continued. The reign of the "King Philosophers" is endangered by the rejection of the popular classes. What is really at stake in this drama is "the difficulty of ideological role-playing in the process of transition between total social structures."

Indeed, the relationship and contrast between the viewpoints of the technical and the social revolutions cannot be adequately dealt with except on the plane of ideology. Sketching the ideological scene of his continent, another Latin American observer, Hiber Conteris,[16] tries to fix the limits between which the ideological variants can oscillate. On the extreme right we find plans for development which are approximately parallel to those in the industrialized countries, in the ideology called technocratic. On the extreme left we find a whole series of ideologies which fall into the general category of revolutionary, all deriving their source from Marxism and all sharing the same objective: the socialist state.

What is known as "progressivism"—a term without ideological significance—is represented mainly by the technical organizations that are working to survey the socio-economic level of the regions, notably the Economic Commission for Latin America working under the jurisdiction of the United Nations. This "progressivism" cannot avoid a certain "innocuousness" of "a-sepsis" in its political descriptions. Consequently, leaving political analysis on the second plane, it insists on the importance of the technical bodies and technical posts within the state-system. This attitude

fails, however, to recognize "that the formation of these bodies, without a basic transformation of the power-system and of the political institutions in Latin America, gives no choice for over-coming the irrational factors which have hitherto conditioned progress in Latin America."

The dominant irrational factor indicated by Conteris is the mentality of those groups which identify themselves with the "status quo," i.e., the structure inherited from colonial times. The fact which characterizes those groups that are generally called conservative or reactionary is the absence of ideology, the lack of a coherent scheme of thought and the negation of reflection. The roots and motives for the conservative attitude are irrational: they spring from the desire for power, ambition, the tendency to maintain economic and social differences between men. And the instruments with which these aspirations have traditionally been defended in Latin American society are "violence (legitimized by the use of power), mendacity, the negation of any step which leads to reflection, to awareness of the real situation by the political majorities of Latin America, persecution and the concealment of the rational. It is not unjustified to speak of Latin America's 'mediaevalism,' of a new obscurantism, or of the re-introduction of the inquisition."

It is not being denied by Conteris that in the more flexible and evolved sectors of the higher social classes one does find a certain amount of understanding for the need for social change. This attitude, which may be called the neo-liberalism of Latin America, is, however, also conditioned by irrational motives which spring from the desire to defend positions of privilege. It is limited fundamentally by its aim to preserve the basic structure of the traditional society. Therefore it may be called quasi-ideological, for it presupposes a certain degree of reflection which remains conditioned by irrational factors.

At this point, then, the real cause of the backwardness of Latin American society must be sought. Not its resistance to change, nor its impermeability, is the real danger, but its relative permeability, the limited elasticity of its institutions. It has the effect of "a sedative or an opiate," drugging the capacity of the

masses to react and "delaying the dynamic drive which could produce change at a deeper level and radically transform the socio-economic structures."

The radical transformation, the social revolution which Latin America is desperately in need of, presupposes a clear ideology. In other words, social revolutions have an essentially ideological character, and this ideology is rational, in contrast to the irrational forces which maintain the status quo. Social existence, according to the definition given by Armand Cuvillier, obeys a sort of law of "awareness"; initially, it is simply lived, then it is represented, and lastly it is scientifically known.

Following this definition, Conteris relates ideology to the second stage of this "process of becoming aware." Ideology is "the emergence on the plane of consciousness, under the form of representation, of a situation which until that moment had simply been lived." That representation is, therefore, necessarily affected by a coefficient which is both historical and "situational." This may distort the reality, but it well expresses a reality "from a certain angle, in a particular light."

Opposite Modes of Rationality

If one thing has become obvious from our exposition of different viewpoints, it is the fact that both the "technical revolutions" and the "social revolutions" have a rationale of their own. The "technological" character of the first type may be contrasted with the "ideological" drive behind the second type, but this has nothing to do with their rationality. Both types have, each on its own presuppositions, a rational structure, motivation, and outlook.

In a penetrating analysis of the 1966 World Conference on Church and Society in Geneva, Charles West has characterized this contradistinction as the "confrontation between the technologists and the revolutionaries." [17] It was a confrontation between basically different experiences of reality, where it lies and what its questions are. It was a confrontation between those for whom the

frontier lies in the conquest of nature for the transformation of human life, and those for whom the issue is conflict between man and man, alienation and the achievement of humanity against the all-too-human demons of human power and greed. It was the confrontation "between the traditions of economics and the traditions of politics, and between the apostles of continuity and those of conscious historical break. It was the confrontation of two humanisms, both of which had grown out of the soil of Christendom, taken nurture from rediscovered Greek philosophy, and lost contact with theology as a context for their faith and method and were now trying to reestablish some relation to the Christian faith. It was the meeting of two radically different conceptions of knowledge and relation, of subject and object, and hence of two different methods of thinking and acting."

Dr. West then describes the continuous tragicomedy of misunderstanding taking place between both humanisms. It rests on a different view of the basis and function of thought itself. The technological humanist assumes the rationality of the thinking subject and the objectivity of scientific knowledge. The revolutionary humanist assumes the ideological nature of both. "Thought and forms of understanding are expressions for him of man's relation to his object, of his struggle for self-realization, and of his interests and power in conflict with other men. The roots of this understanding are not in the Enlightenment but in Hegel and Marx; but they do not depend today on the authority of either of these thinkers, or on acceptance of the rest of their systems."

The Theological Problem

Looking at the antithesis between these two humanisms, one may wonder how it is reflected on the theological level. If the gap between the representatives of the "technical revolutions" and the advocates of the "social revolutions" is so broad and deep, is there to be expected from a common theological perspective a "ponti-fical," a bridge-building, contribution? Or are the theological

concepts simply a reflection and continuation of the anthropological differences between the two humanisms, only on another level or, at least, in the language of another discipline?

The ecumenical discussions on the "Christian response to the technical and social revolutions of our time" reflect, indeed, a contrast between two approaches which Dr. West has wittily defined as "theological technocrats" and "theological guerrillas." A theological interpretation and justification of the technical revolutions allows, of course, various accents. Some may prefer to build their concept on the presupposition of the partnership between God's work and man's work in the world. It belongs to man's calling as a rational being, overcoming the resistance of nature, to cooperate with God, who reveals himself as goodness and as eternal possibility. "That is why man's need to know God grows, the more competent he himself grows in the performance of his work" (Mesthene).

Others want to stress the explosive character of the technical revolutions which upsets all traditional Christian concepts and forces the church "to challenge the secular world in a way that it has not done for centuries" (Theobald), requiring a clarity, wisdom and realism which "do not come from nature; they are gifts of the Holy Spirit" (Ellul). Others accentuate the responsibility of modern science and technology to serve the whole of mankind: "the Christian community must demand from the scientist, from the natural scientist and from the social scientist, that they put their knowledge in a form so that it can be used by the ordinary human being" (Margaret Mead). By all means, what has priority for a theological evaluation of technology is the belief that "God still calls man to dominion over the earth, including the imaginative and responsible control of technology." Man's selfishness may turn technology from a blessing into a means of increased exploitation, but this does not modify the "Christian conviction that every man—not just a few—is called by God to take part in the planning and governing of his society." [18] Basically, this theological approach treats man's calling and capacity to overcome the resistance of nature by his scientific and technological potentialities in the same fashion as man's calling and capacity

to avert the dangers of exploitation and enslavement by means of technological power.

On the other side of the cleavage stand the theological revolutionaries who do not believe that this type of enlightened theology is searching and penetrating enough to get to the core of the evil. The Colombian theologian Castillo-Cárdenas[19] sees a basically theological conflict between the two approaches: on the one hand, those who, out of respect for the social and political institutions of the established order, still believe in the possibility of gradual evolutionary change made possible by the rational cooperation of the dominant classes; and on the other hand, those who are convinced of the need and justification of active resistance to the established order, even to the point of subversion, for the sake of the majority. Both positions appear to have some "Christian basis" within the cultural patrimony of classical Christianity. There are those who believe that God's interest is concentrated on the church and on her freedom to fulfill what she considers to be her mission. For them, as long as this freedom is not threatened, there exists a social order that, without being perfect, is at least tolerable. But there are also those pastors and laymen who are convinced that God's interest is concentrated on man's well-being in actual situations, and that the established order in many countries is an affront to God because it is precisely an affront to man. "Active resistance to this 'order,' so as to force the establishment of a new social order rationally planned economically, based on social justice in its internal relations, and on national dignity in its external commitments, should be considered a Christian task."

The heart of the matter for this Latin American theologian lies in the question: Is the renewal of the church possible at all apart from the renewal of Latin American society? He believes that the struggle for a new social order should have precedence, as a Christian task, over the task of renewing the church. This is the convincing lesson which the churches throughout the rest of the Latin American continent have to learn from the Cuban experience: "The Church in Cuba is now passing through a very promising process of renewal which had not been possible before the revolution."

Camilo Torres, the Catholic former priest who was killed in the guerrilla fighting in Colombia in February, 1966, is an inspiring example of the revolutionary theology. His "Message to the Christians," written at the moment of his decision to devote himself fully to the revolutionary cause in Colombia, says: "I have left the privileges and duties of the clergy, but I have not left the priesthood. I believe to have devoted myself to the revolution out of love for my neighbour. I will not say the Mass, but I will realize this love to my neighbour in the temporal, economic and social realms. When my neighbour has nothing against me, when I have realized the revolution, I will then say the Holy Mass again. Thus, I believe to obey Christ's command, 'If you are offering your gift to the altar, and there remember that your neighbour has something against you, leave your gift before the altar and go; first be reconciled to your neighbour, and then come and offer your gift.' "

The question is whether Christians—convinced that the present "order" is an "affront to God and man," and conscious of the multiple forms of violence that the established order exercises against the weak, the deprived, the poor, the disadvantaged people that are the majority—are going to resist this situation effectively, until they attain the goal of a new social order based on justice; or whether, on the contrary, they are simply going to be content with a permanent rebellious attitude that achieves nothing, or with certain isolated reforms equivalent to social anesthesia. Christians who understand the necessity of carrying the struggle to the end see revolution—which can be peaceful if the minorities do not resist violently—as the way in which to attain a social orientation that allows the practice of love for one's neighbor, not only in an occasional and transitory way and for the few, but permanently and for the majority. Revolution not only is permitted, but is obligatory for those Christians who see it as the one effective way of fulfilling love to one's neighbor.

Castillo-Cárdenas comes to the conclusion that the churches are already divided in this respect, even though the two positions wear the same Christian or denominational label. He is wondering "if we Christians in Latin America are not in danger of falling

victims of a conflict between two myths—on the one hand, the myth of peaceful, painless change, that aspires to social transformation without alteration of the system, or great political modifications, or even without touching the centers of power; and on the other hand, the myth of rural guerrilla warfare that has its inspiration and example in Castroism, without distinguishing between the pre-Cuban and the post-Cuban situation in Latin America."

Is there a way out of the dilemma engendered by these opposing myths? Our Colombian guide recognizes the necessity of bridging the gap between the concepts of technical and social revolutions: "Consequently, Christians committed to the struggle for a new social order are beginning to understand the necessity for constant dialogue with technicians and experts in social development, in the search for possible alternatives to the myths we have mentioned."

But on the theological level, he does not go beyond the diagnosis of a "deeper tension between two theologies" which is hidden behind the two approaches that tend to divide the church —"One centered in God, the other centered in man; one, integrist and separatist in relation to society in general, the other solitary and committed to society as a whole; one, attached to dogmas, principles and structures of traditional Christianity, the other committed only to man, in particular situations." He concludes with a quotation from Teilhard de Chardin: "Around us the real struggle doesn't take place between believers and non-believers, but between two kinds of believers, two ideals, two concepts of God. A religion of the earth is being formed against the Religion of Heaven."

On both crucial points the American theologian Richard Shaull has made important contributions which promise a way beyond the deadlock of frustrating divisions.[20] First, he tries to find a new context wherein the contradistinction between technical and social revolutions can be approached in a fruitful way. Whereas André Philip stated that industrialized society means the end of revolution, Shaull opts, rather, for the search for a new strategy of revolution. He doesn't share the trust of so many technologists in the capacity of the established order to renew itself without

strong revolutionary pressures on it. To the contrary, technological advance and the conservation of the established order have, thus far, gone hand in hand. But, as Robert Theobald has pointed out, there is nothing in technology itself which makes this inevitable. In fact, as technology advances, the instruments as well as the atmosphere which it creates could just as easily serve the cause of social transformation and emancipation. Moreover,

> the breakdown of the stable, ontocratic, authoritarian patterns of the past and the dynamic character of modern society create a new potential instability and a very precarious social balance. Sudden pressures applied effectively at the right place at the right time may have a surprisingly wide and deep impact; and small changes can set forces in motion which will produce much greater changes in the future. In this situation, revolutionary strategy is a question of developing those bases from which a system unwilling to initiate major changes when they are most urgently needed, can be constantly bombarded by strong pressures for small changes at many different points. Without such revolutionary forces in our societies today, the prospects for the future are not encouraging. But these efforts could help to keep society open and flexible, renew it in spite of itself, create a new social context for technology, and perhaps lead eventually to the type of social institution that would be sufficiently responsive to human need as to make revolution unnecessary.

In close analogue to the military strategy of guerrilla warfare, Shaull suggests a "strategy for effective political action of a revolutionary type today." This struggle cannot be a matter of isolated, sporadic efforts. It must, rather, include the constant formation throughout society of small nuclei with revolutionary objectives; an intensive effort at the type of education which will open new perspectives on social problems and point the way to new experiments and new solutions.

On the theological level, Shaull opens a perspective which goes beyond the dilemma of a supposed choice between a religion of the earth and a Religion of Heaven. The theological contribution to the revolutionary struggle does not, in the first instance, consist of exposing and challenging the latent idolatry of the ideol-

ogies of total revolution. At this point, other forces in contemporary society are doing a more effective job. Today a strong sense
of the limitations of knowledge about society and of the ambiguities
in a revolutionary struggle can be found among the new revolutionaries in Latin America, the new student left in the United
States, and new groups of philosophers and writers in Marxist
societies. What the new revolutionary needs, if he is to carry on
a long and arduous struggle without absolutes and without utopian
illusions, is the possibility of believing that the future is really open,
the hope that weakness can be victorious over established power,
and that meaning and fulfillment are possible in a life lived in an
intense revolutionary struggle. He needs those resources of transcendence and nonconformity which free him to break the bonds
of the secular, empirical ethos, dream new dreams about the future of man, and cultivate the creative imagination so as to be
capable of thinking about new problems in new ways, and defining
new goals and models of a new society. Therefore, the real question before theology is that of "the vitality of the Judeo-Christian
tradition, in its diverse forms, and its capacity to relate to the human situation today in such a way as to liberate old images, sym-
bols and concepts and create new ones that can perform this task."
Theologians have to "take seriously the fact of the death and resurrection of the Logos as indicating the only road open to us in this
situation."

Responsible Society

It is obvious that these attempts to outline a theological perspective
of social revolution represent a definite step beyond the concept of
the "responsible society" which has been paramount in ecumenical
social thinking for several decades. This concept indicates, in the
words of Heinz-Dietrich Wendland,[21] a decent, human society with
democratic institutions, whose norms are freedom, justice, humanity, and peace. This presupposes that the men and women
living in that society are free persons with a sense of responsibility
toward God and toward their fellow men, who are called to

cooperate freely and responsibly in state and society. An elite of persons and nations must lay the foundation of this "responsible society" of the future, which is already beginning to appear today. This elite, in its turn, must create the bases for democratic states and societies, in places where they do not yet exist (or have only just begun to appear), such as Asia, Africa, and South America.

As has been aptly pointed out by Günther Howe and Heinz Eduard Tödt,[22] the postulate "responsible society" has become less adequate for several reasons. It is often inadequate for Christians in the new nations undergoing revolutionary social and political change. They understand the concept as an alignment with democratic thought and action, especially in the spirit of Anglo-Saxon democracies. Western democratic institutions and ideologies cannot simply be shifted to countries where social, political, and intellectual conditions such as they presuppose are missing. In many cases, such an attempted transfer without modification would appear as tutelage. Further, the limitations of the concept "responsible society" are particularly felt by Christians living under Communist rule. The appeal of Communism for certain countries consists in its dynamic answer to preindustrial circumstances. Lenin's dictum "Communism means Soviet power plus electrification of the whole country," reflects a passion for changing the world by means of science and technology. The ecumenical idea of a responsible society, with its dominant stress on a moral universal law as conceived in the Western Christian tradition, obstructed the view of Communism's dynamic efforts to civilize.

This does not imply that the concept of a responsible society is necessarily static or should allow only a conservative interpretation. The German theologian Wendland has done his best to use it as the basis of a revolutionary, Christian humanism. But the relationship between Christian, revolutionary action and the political-social, revolutionary action of men in history can be established in a responsible way only if "Christians are given an opportunity to understand both in theory and in practice all the chances of transforming society." Wendland raises a warning finger, that "Christians must not be guided by the ideology of the absolute revolution, nor by the Utopia of the perfect society. It

means also that they cannot advocate revolutionising the whole situation by force; they have to take the course of reform." Reform accepts the existing social system, but tries to improve the different institutions in it; these improvements "are based on criticism of society made by different political and social movements within it, and derived partly from the social-ethical thinking of Christians and of the Churches."

However, this Christian "revolutionary" reformism not only is opposed to the ideology of violent social and political revolutions, but is even more definitely distinguished from the technological revolution of our time, which Wendland characterizes as "total revolution," because it tends to overthrow the whole social system. "This upheaval affects every class in society and every sphere of life, including culture, intellectual life and religion. It is this type of revolution which is setting out today to conquer the whole world, supported by the forces of our technological civilisation. This revolution is total, not only in extent, but also in its intensity, because it is based on a new human attitude to the world; and this new human attitude is revolutionary because it has the power completely to transform the world as we know it. It is the creator of a second, artificial world." This means, says Wendland, that man, who is the creator and shaper of the new technological, scientific, rational world makes himself unfree, becomes the slave of his own creation, because the very continuation of his own existence depends on the system which he himself has created with its machinery, apparatus, technology, and scientific and social organizations. Man has released powers of destruction which seem to be completely uncontrollable.

Wendland's treatment of the Christian understanding of revolution is an indication that the concept of the responsible society, even in a revolutionary interpretation, does not touch the heart of either the technical or the social revolutions of our time. The concept is not strong enough or sufficiently realistic to serve as a bridge across the gap separating those who approach the world from either of the two antagonistic types of revolutions, let alone to reconcile the "theological technocrats" and the "theological guerrillas."

Reformation and Revolution

This being the case, what is the particular contribution to be expected from Christians living under Communist rule? Addressing the World Conference on Church and Society, the Russian Orthodox Archpriest Vitaly Borovoy,[23] presented the experience of his church as an enrichment of the total Christian experience and as a challenge to his Western Christian brothers. For the Russian Orthodox Church has for the last half-century been living "in the circumstances of the completely secularized and socialist society which is the fruit of the greatest social revolution in the history of man." As a result of a bitter and open struggle with the Communist government, the church lost millions of believers. But the victorious revolution went its difficult way of consolidation and development without the church. At the same time the overwhelming majority of the masses of believers, who remained true to Christianity and the church, became a constructive element in the building of the new society on the new revolutionary basis, and thus were an example to the clergy and hierarchy who had not welcomed the revolution. Christians, therefore, should

> honourably and actively join in the building of the new life, based on social justice; they should bring a Christian social fervour to the social revolutions of our time and thus avert the de-Christianisation of the contemporary world. This in its turn cannot fail to have an effect on the very nature of the social revolutions. New in its form, but biblical in its content, the theology of development and revolution will have a positive influence on the course of history and on the thinking of the new revolutionary and socialist societies. This theology can and should raise a whole series of questions about the ultimate meaning of the world process, manifesting by word and deed what is good, genuine, eternal and absolute in biblical Christianity as revealed by God. It should help the social revolutions of our time to lead man to his ultimate fulfilment and significance.

The central concept which Borovoy recommends as the cornerstone for this theology of revolution is the concept of

repentance. Repentance is call to renewal, to revolution, to new life. It means a radical break with the former way of life, a radical repudiation of the old sinful ways, and equally a radical acceptance and engagement of one's whole self in the new and perfect life. All this is gladly accepted at the individual level. The strange thing is that "as soon as we start to talk about social renewal, Christians begin to hedge, shunning responsibility and struggle, sometimes openly defending a social sin, simply because an evil which has existed for centuries or even millennia acquires the charm of tradition."

Repentance is the kind of revolution that applies not only to the individual but also to the whole of society, to the nation, to the class, to every social group. The Russian Orthodox Church, says Borovoy, has repented of her Byzantine tradition which contributed, more than any other Christian culture, to the mere sanctification of social evil. It took over without objection the entire social inheritance of the pagan world and gave it a sacral anointing. But "that is radically opposed to the social tradition of early Christianity and the Greek fathers, the messianic preaching of our Saviour and the whole content of the teaching of the Old Testament prophets, which never grows old."

The coincidence of the 450th anniversary of the Reformation and of the 50th anniversary of the Russian October Revolution, two historical turning-points that were commemorated in 1967, gave ample opportunity for Christians to see both events in a common perspective. The Czech theologian Josef L. Hromadka[24] confirmed the fatal consequences of the entanglement of Russian Orthodoxy, before the October Revolution, with the Byzantine order. The bitter sufferings of that church under the Soviet regime prevented the great majority of Christians in the rest of the world from holding an unbiased view of the significance of the Revolution. A Christian layman from the German Democratic Republic, Günther Wirth,[25] referred to a comment of Friedrich Engels which evaluated the Reformation and the Peasant Revolt of the sixteenth century as the first of the "three great bourgeois revolutions" (followed by the English Revolution of the seventeenth and the

French Revolution of the eighteenth centuries), and he recalled the fact that Lenin's remark on the significance of the Reformation refers to this comment of Engels'. "Reformation and Revolution," Wirth concludes, "have a *Tertium comparationis:* the renewal of society which was initiated by the Reformation and—under different historical conditions—has been realized by the October Revolution."

These witnesses of Christians from various Communist countries in Eastern Europe could, in a sense, be evaluated as a link between the viewpoints of the technical and of the social revolutions of our time. For the Russian October Revolution has aimed at a program of "Soviet power plus electrification of the whole country" in which the faith of the technocrats in the irreversible progress of science and technology is merged with the insight into the historical necessity of a total reconstruction of the social order. Where the vision of the October Revolution is related to the original goal of the Reformation, there apparently is dawning, at last, that common perspective for Christians in the midst of the technical and social revolutions of our time for which we have been looking in vain. But this is a deceptive appearance. To a certain extent, what we meet in these Christian evaluations is the East European counterpart of the approach of various "theological technocrats" from Western countries. What is lacking, however, is a concrete and detailed confrontation with the technological order which, after a half-century, has resulted from the October Revolution.

The reason for this default must be sought in the approach of these Christians to the social aspect of that Revolution. Between their viewpoint and the view of the "theological guerrillas" from the Third World lies an enormous gap. Whereas the representatives of the Third World are struggling with a prerevolutionary situation that confronts them with the question of Christian participation in social and political revolution, Christians living under well-established Communist regimes are faced with a postrevolutionary order that does not tolerate any deviation from the planned technological and socio-political evolution going on under its dic-

tatorial supervision. Whereas "repentance" in the Third World implies the decision to make a definite break with the status quo, to Christians in the Communist world who are looking for a positive attitude toward social developments in their country, it means recognition of the decisive turning-point which the Communist revolution meant for the renewal of society and the postrevolutionary situation in which they are living. The establishment of Communism draws the revolutionary sting out of the technical and social revolutions which it has inaugurated and changes them into drastically supervised and well-steered processes of evolution.

Summing up, the several evaluations of technical and social revolutions which we have thus far considered do not succeed in giving that unifying perspective on both types of revolutions for which we were looking. We have, therefore, to seek an answer in another direction. Keeping in mind the problem that the technocrat's concept of revolution, as seen from the viewpoint of social revolutions, is evolutionary rather than revolutionary, the root of the question appears to lie in the concept of scientific and technological evolution. It is for this reason feasible to look in that direction for a deeper understanding of the issues which we are facing.

The Structure of Scientific Revolutions

It is a remarkable phenomenon that historians of modern science are inclined to sketch the development of scientific research and invention during the last four centuries in terms of revolution. This might possibly have no deeper meaning than the use of a glib metaphor, but even in that case the use of such a metaphor in serious historical studies should make us seek the hidden reasons for the choice of exactly this metaphor. But there are very strong indications that this metaphor has a real significance. Indeed, a close parallel between the phenomenon of scientific revolutions and the phenomenon of socio-political revolutions seems to exist.

On first sight the idea of some kind of parallel between the field of science and the field of politics might seem illusory and

even fantastic. To be sure, ever since the days of Aristotle there have been attempts to approach the political realities as an object of scientific analysis. But up to our time this approach has never been able to bridge the gap between the methodology of political science and the methodology of exact science.

There are at least three basic distinctions between the one field and the other. First, whereas exact science is closely related to mathematics, the ways and instruments of political analysis are different. Second, the object of science is nature in contradistinction to the object of political science, which is man in his social relationships. Third, concerning the types of models which are useful in each discipline: science is directed to regular, recurrent and, through experiment, repeatable processes; human society belongs to the historical mode of being which allows the construction of analogies and parallels but which is incompatible with the idea of repetition.

In face of this apparently unbridgeable gap between the sciences and political analysis, any attempt to apply some lessons from a study of the methodology of science to the political field seems from the very outset doomed to frustration. Nevertheless, there is a very special reason for looking in this direction, and it is directly related to the word "revolution."

Let us begin by calling to mind the history of the concept "revolution," which originally belonged to the field of astronomical science. The word clearly indicates a recurring, cyclical movement and is the perfect Latin translation of the Greek word *anakuklosis,* a word which also originated in astronomy. As far back as the pre-Christian era the term was metaphorically applied to the realm of politics by Polybius.[26] It gave expression to the pessimistic Greek outlook, which we also find in Aristotle's *Politics,* of government eternally recurring, "revolving," and with the same irresistible force which makes the stars follow their preordained paths in the skies.[27] In the Middle Ages politics were thought of as depending wholly on the "revolving" wheel of fortune. But by the seventeenth century the new astronomy of Copernicus and Kepler and Galileo had impressed the public deeply enough to make it apply the notion of astronomical revolutions to earthly events. Through this new

usage the laws of nature entered into the world of politics. But it is important to notice that the word "revolution" as used in this sense during the seventeenth and eighteenth centuries rendered to political events a meaning which is the very opposite of the meaning it has received in recent times. "The Glorious Revolution" of 1688 was glorified by the English Whigs as the true "restoration," that is, the return of the legitimate government and constitution which had been upset by Cromwell's "Great Rebellion." "Revolution" was the very opposite and denial of rebellion.

These historical observations may not appear to be an appropriate introduction to the idea of a parallel between the field of science and the field of politics. Indeed, the present use of the word "revolution" seems to deny any analogy between physical and social dynamics. Therefore we have to proceed to the next step of our argument, which focuses, not on the physical object of science but on the *history* of modern science. Writing about the American and the French Revolutions, Hannah Arendt points to the strange fact that the whole notion of novelty and newness as such existed prior to these revolutions of modern times and yet was essentially absent from their beginnings.[28] The men of the revolutions were old-fashioned in terms of their own time, certainly old-fashioned when compared with the men of science and philosophy of the seventeenth century. Galileo stressed "the absolute novelty" of his discoveries and Descartes "insisted that no philosopher before had succeeded in philosophy." But this strange pathos of novelty, so characteristic of the modern age, needed almost two hundred years to leave the relative seclusion of scientific and philosophic thought and to reach the realm of politics. Only gradually, as forced by the facts, the actors of the American and the French Revolutions became aware of the impossibility of restoration and of the need to embark upon an entirely new enterprise. Only gradually did the word "revolution" acquire its new meaning.

This leads us to the third step of our argument. Once this awareness of novelty and discovery of new frontiers, which emerged from the domain of science and philosophy, had penetrated the political atmosphere and had radically altered the significance of the term "revolution," time was ripe for a counter-

movement. From political language, the word gradually moved into scientific and philosophical thought. It is significant that historians of modern science do not hesitate to characterize the whole development of European science between 1500 and 1800 as "the scientific revolution." [29] Herbert Butterfield, in his book *The Origins of Modern Science,* not only makes an explicit and deliberate use of this term[30] but also stresses the overwhelming impact of the scientific revolution upon the whole texture of European civilization.

> Since that revolution overturned the authority in science not only of the Middle Ages but of the ancient world, it outshines everything since the rise of Christianity and reduces the Renaissance and Reformation to the rank of mere episodes, mere internal displacements, within the system of medieval Christianity. Since it changed the character of men's habitual mental operations even in the conduct of the non-material sciences, while transforming the whole diagram of the physical universe and the very texture of human life itself, it looms so large as the real origin both of the modern world and of the modern mentality that our customary periodization of European history has become an anachronism and an encumbrance! [31]

This evaluation by a distinguished historian is noteworthy for two reasons. It reveals the significance of the breakthrough of science in the sixteenth and seventeenth centuries; namely, the basic importance of the new scientific spirit to the political upheavals of the latter part of the eighteenth century. And it assigns to this scientific turn a revolutionary implication which is derived from modern political terminology and which no contemporary man of science, living during that decisive period, would have defined as "revolution." Apparently the cleavage between science and politics is less wide and deep than we first thought. The gap seems to be bridgeable from both sides. On the one hand, the newly awakened interest in the history of science has thrown revealing light on the human actors, the scientists themselves, who, by trial and error and with many gropings in the darkness, probe their way to new discoveries. Thus we see revealed before our eyes the picture of a historical process in which human beings, both

individually and collectively, are being caught up in much the same way as man in his political manifestations. On the other hand, the radical break across walls of traditional concepts, resulting from the surprising discoveries of scientific research, is felt in the very depths of our civilization, wherein also the convulsing forces of political eruptions are being nourished.

Obviously there are serious reasons for approaching the history of modern science with the expectation of learning important lessons that will be applicable to the field of political science. Fortunately, an extremely instructive study comes to our aid, written by Thomas S. Kuhn, professor of the history of science at Princeton University. The book bears the significant title: *The Structure of Scientific Revolutions*.[32] Described as a brilliant, original analysis of the nature, causes, and consequences of revolutions in basic scientific concepts, it has been recommended by Derek J. de Solla Price as "probably the most important contribution to the historiography of science since Butterfield's *Origins of Modern Science*."

Let us turn first to the parallelism, as indicated by Kuhn, between scientific and political revolutions.[33] In the face of the vast and essential differences between political and scientific development, what parallelism can justify the metaphor that finds revolutions in both?

Political revolutions are inaugurated by a growing sense, often restricted to a segment of the political community, that existing institutions have ceased adequately to meet the problems posed by an environment which they have in part created. In much the same way, scientific revolutions are inaugurated by a growing sense, again often restricted to a narrow subdivision of the scientific community, that an existing basic concept has ceased to function adequately in the exploration of an aspect of nature to which that concept itself had previously led the way. Such a basic concept is defined by Kuhn by a technical term which has a pivotal function throughout his study, that is, "paradigm." A paradigm is a universally recognized scientific achievement that for a time provides model problems and solutions to a community of practitioners.[34] Its function in the normal structure of science is comparable to the

function of institutions for the conservation and continuation of normal social and political structures.

A growing sense of malfunction in both political and scientific development can lead to crisis, and this crisis is prerequisite to revolution. That parallelism holds not only for the major paradigm changes, like those attributable to Copernicus and Lavoisier, but also for the far smaller ones associated with the assimilation of a new sort of phenomenon, like oxygen or X-rays. Scientific revolutions seem revolutionary only to those whose paradigms are affected by them. To outsiders they may, like the Balkan revolutions of the early twentieth century, seem normal parts of the developmental process. Astronomers, for example, could accept X-rays as a mere addition to knowledge, for their paradigms were unaffected by the existence of the new radiation. But for those scientists whose research dealt with radiation theory, the emergence of X-rays necessarily violated one paradigm as it created another. Thus these rays could be discovered only when something went wrong with normal research.

This genetic aspect of the parallel between political and scientific development depends upon a second and more profound aspect. Political revolutions aim to change political institutions in ways that those institutions themselves prohibit. Their success therefore necessitates the partial relinquishment of one set of institutions in favor of another, and, in the interim, society is not fully governed by institutions at all. Society is divided into competing parties, differing about the institutional matrix within which political change is to be achieved and evaluated. Because they acknowledge no suprainstitutional framework for the adjudication of revolutionary difference, the parties to a revolutionary conflict must finally resort to the techniques of mass persuasion, often including force. The role of revolutions in the evolution of political institutions depends upon their being partially extrapolitical or extrainstitutional events.

Thomas Kuhn demonstrates that the historical study of change in the so-called paradigm, that is, the traditional scientific concept, reveals very similar characteristics in the evolution of the

sciences. Like the choice between competing political institutions, that between competing paradigms proves to be a choice between incompatible modes of community life. Since at issue is the particular paradigm upon which the evaluative procedures characteristic of normal science depend, each group uses its own paradigm to argue in that paradigm's defense. As in political revolutions, so in paradigm choice—there is no standard higher than the assent of the relevant community.

This is an important statement. As far as political revolutions are concerned, there is nothing surprising in the observation that the shift in political framework which they imply contains many arbitrary elements and has little to do with the struggle between truth and falsehood. But if the same is suggested with reference to the development of science, the implications are highly embarrassing. Nevertheless, this is the very heart of Kuhn's argument. Since this insight may add important depth to our interpretation of the nature of political revolutions, it is worthwhile to look more closely at the development of his analysis.

A scientific revolution would not bear its revolutionary features unless the assimilation of either a new sort of phenomenon or a new scientific theory demanded the rejection of an older paradigm. Why should this be the case? If there are intrinsic reasons for the rejection of an older paradigm, they do not derive from the logical structure of scientific knowledge. In principle, a new phenomenon might emerge without reflecting destructively upon any part of past scientific practice. In the evolution of science new knowledge would replace ignorance rather than knowledge of another and incompatible sort.

Of course, science might have developed in that cumulative manner. But the man who takes historic fact seriously must suspect that science does not develop in this orderly way. Cumulative acquisition of novelty proves to be an almost nonexistent exception to the rule of scientific development and, besides, it is improbable in principle. Unanticipated novelty, the new discovery, can emerge only to the extent that the scientist's anticipations about nature and his instruments prove wrong. There must be a

conflict between the paradigm that discloses anomaly and the one that later renders the anomaly lawlike. There is no other effective way in which discoveries might be generated.

The same argument applies even more clearly to the creation of new theories. There is only one type of phenomenon which might give rise to new theories. That type is the recognized anomalies whose characteristic feature is their stubborn refusal to be assimilated to existing paradigms. Paradigms provide all phenomena except anomalies with a theory-determined place in the scientist's field of vision. But if new theories are called forth to resolve anomalies in the relation of an existing theory to nature, then the successful new theory must somewhere permit predictions that are different from those derived from its predecessor. That difference could not occur if the two were logically compatible. In the process of being assimilated, the second must displace the first.

If existing theory binds the scientist only with respect to existing applications, then there can be no surprises, anomalies, or crises. But these are just the signposts that point the way to extraordinary science. The price of significant scientific advance is a commitment that runs the risk of being wrong. This being the case, then it is small wonder that a new paradigm often necessitates a redefinition of the corresponding science. Some old problems may be relegated to another science or declared entirely "unscientific." Others that were previously nonexistent or trivial may, with a new paradigm, become the very archetype of significant scientific achievement. And, as the problems change, so, often, does the standard that distinguishes a real scientific solution from a mere metaphysical speculation, word game, or mathematical play. The normal-scientific tradition that emerges from a scientific revolution is not only incompatible but often actually incommensurable with that which has gone before.

Changes in the standards governing permissible problems, concepts, and explanations can transform a science. Paradigms provide scientists not only with a map but also with some of the directions essential for map-making. In learning a paradigm the scientist acquires theory, methods, and standards together, usually in an inextricable mixture. Therefore, when paradigms change,

there are usually significant shifts in the criteria determining the legitimacy both of problems and of proposed solutions.

And so the choice between competing paradigms regularly raises questions that cannot be resolved by the criteria of normal science. It is that recourse to external criteria that most obviously makes paradigm debates revolutionary.

Something even more fundamental than standards and values is, however, also at stake. Paradigms are not only constitutive of science. There is even a sense in which they are constitutive of nature as well. Paradigms may also transform the world. Led by a new paradigm, scientists adopt new instruments and look in new places. Even more important, paradigm changes do cause scientists to see the world of their research-engagement differently. Insofar as their only recourse to that world is through what they see and do, we may want to say that after a revolution scientists are responding to a different world.

The history of astronomy provides striking examples of paradigm-induced changes in scientific perception. The Chinese, whose cosmological beliefs did not preclude celestial change, had recorded the appearance of many new stars in the heavens and they had systematically recorded the appearance of sun spots centuries before these were seen by Galileo and his contemporaries. Nevertheless, Western astronomers first saw change in the previously immutable heavens during the half-century after Copernicus' new paradigm was first proposed. After Copernicus, astronomers lived in a different world.[35]

Another striking example is to be found in the work of Galileo. From the properties of the pendulum Galileo derived his only full and sound arguments for the independence of weight and rate as well as for the relationship between vertical height and terminal velocity of motions down inclined planes. All these natural phenomena he saw differently from the way they had been seen before.

It follows from these considerations that the competition between paradigms is not the sort of battle that can be resolved by verification. For verification is like natural selection: it picks out the more viable among the actual alternatives in a particular

historical situation. Whether that choice is the best that could have been made if still other possibilities had been available or if the data had been of another sort is not a question that can usefully be asked. There are no tools to employ in seeking answers to it.[36]

Therefore, the proponents of competing paradigms must fail to make complete contact with each other's viewpoints. Pre- and post-revolutionary normal-scientific traditions are incommensurable. The three reasons for that situation can be recapitulated briefly as follows: In the first place, their proponents will often disagree about the list of problems that any candidate for paradigm must resolve. Second, within the new paradigm, old terms, concepts, and experiments fall into new relationships one with the other. And the third and most fundamental reason lies in their proponents practicing their trades in different worlds.

How, then, are scientists brought to make this transposition from an old to a new paradigm? Part of the answer is that very often they are not.[37] Copernicanism made few converts for almost a century after Copernicus' death. Newton's work was not generally accepted, particularly on the Continent, for more than a half-century after the *Principia* appeared. Darwin, in a particularly perceptive passage at the end of his *Origin of Species,* wrote: "I look with confidence to the future,—to young and rising naturalists." And Max Planck remarked that "a new scientific truth does not triumph by convincing its opponents and making them see the light, but rather because its opponents eventually die, and a new generation grows up that is familiar with it."

In matters like these, neither proof nor error is at issue. The transfer of allegiance from paradigm to paradigm is a conversion experience that cannot be forced. The same assurance which is a source of resistance against a new paradigm is what makes normal, or puzzle-solving, science possible. And it is only through normal science that the professional community of scientists succeeds, first, in exploiting the potential scope and precision of the older paradigm and, then, in isolating the difficulty through the study of which a new paradigm may emerge.

Probably the single most prevalent claim advanced by the proponents of a new paradigm is that they can solve the problems

that have led the old one to a crisis. Copernicus thus claimed that he had solved the long-vexing problem of the length of the calendar year, Newton that he had reconciled terrestrial and celestial mechanics, Lavoisier that he had solved the problem of gas-identity and of weight-relations, and Einstein that he had made electro-dynamics compatible with a revised science of motion. But those claims to have solved the crisis-provoking problems are rarely sufficient by themselves, nor can they always legitimately be made. In fact, Copernicus' theory was not more accurate than Ptolemy's and did not lead directly to any improvement in the calendar. In such a case, persuasive arguments can be drawn from other areas, if the new paradigm permits the prediction of phenomena that had been entirely unsuspected while the old one prevailed. When, sixty years after Copernicus' death, the telescope suddenly displayed mountains on the moon, the phases of Venus, and an immense number of previously unsuspected stars, those observations brought his theory a great many converts, particularly among nonastronomers. When, however, a new candidate for paradigm is first proposed, it has seldom solved more than a few of the problems that confront it, and most of those solutions are still far from perfect. Usually the opponents of a new paradigm can legitimately claim that even in the area of crisis it is little superior to its traditional rival. Until Kepler, the Copernican theory scarcely improved upon the predictions of planetary position made by Ptolemy. And Tycho Brahe's earth-centered astronomical system was a quite successful response to a challenge posed by a new candidate for paradigm. Even in the area of crisis, the balance of argument and counterargument can sometimes be very close indeed. And outside that area the balance will often decisively favor the tradition. Copernicus destroyed a time-honored explanation of terrestrial motion without replacing it; Newton did the same for an older explanation of gravity.[38]

Therefore, the real issue in paradigm debates is not about relative problem-solving ability, but the crucial question is which paradigm should in the future guide research on problems many of which neither competitor can yet claim to resolve completely. A decision between alternate ways of practicing science is called

for, and, under the circumstances, that decision must be based less on past achievement than on future promise. A decision of that kind can be made only by faith. That is one of the reasons why prior crisis proves so important. Scientists who have not experienced it will seldom renounce the hard evidence of problem-solving to follow what may easily prove to be a mere will-o'-the-wisp. But crisis alone is not enough. There must also be a basis for faith in the particular candidate chosen, and sometimes only personal and inarticulate aesthetic considerations can make some scientists feel that the new proposal is on the right track. If a paradigm is ever to triumph it must gain some first supporters, men who will develop it to the point where hard-headed arguments can be produced and multiplied.

Thus have we arrived at the final point of Thomas Kuhn's analysis. If the essential structure of a science's continuing evolution is of this kind, a special problem has simultaneously presented itself: Why should this scientific enterprise move steadily ahead? Why is progress a prerequisite reserved almost exclusively for the activities we call science? [39] Let us recapitulate briefly the main line of Kuhn's historiographic approach. Careful study of the history of science raises strong doubts whether science should develop by the accumulation of individual discoveries. The once-current views of nature were, as a whole, neither less scientific nor more the product of human idiosyncrasy than those current today. If these out-of-date beliefs are to be called myths, then myths can be produced by the same sort of methods and held for the same sort of reasons that now lead to scientific knowledge. If, on the other hand, they are to be called science, then science has included bodies of belief quite incompatible with the ones we hold today. Given these alternatives, the historian must choose the latter.

Out-of-date theories are not in principle unscientific because they have been discarded. That choice, however, makes it difficult to see scientific development as a process of accretion.[40] Observation and experience can and must drastically restrict the range of admissible scientific belief, else there would be no science. But an apparently arbitrary element, compounded of personal and historical accident, is always a formative ingredient of the beliefs

espoused by a given scientific community at a given time. Normal science, the activity in which most scientists inevitably spend almost all their time, is predicated on the assumption that the scientific community knows what the world is like. It is a strenuous and devoted attempt to force nature into the conceptual boxes supplied by professional education and, for that reason, often suppresses fundamental novelties because they are necessarily subversive of its basic commitments. Nevertheless, so long as those commitments retain an element of the arbitrary, the very nature of normal research ensures that novelty shall not be suppressed for very long. Scientific revolutions are the tradition-shattering complements to the tradition-bound activity of normal science.[41] The most obvious examples of scientific revolutions are those famous episodes in scientific development that have often been labeled revolutions before, major turning-points associated with the names of Copernicus, Newton, Lavoisier, and Einstein. But many episodes that were not so obviously revolutionary had no less revolutionary implications. A new theory, however specialized its range of applications, is seldom or never just an increment to what is already known. Its assimilation requires the reconstruction of prior theory and the re-evaluation of prior fact, an intrinsically revolutionary process that is seldom completed by a single man and never overnight.

This extended conception of the nature of scientific revolutions ultimately raises the question: How can scientific development through revolutions be compatible with the apparently unique character of scientific progress? Kuhn's approach to that ultimate question begins with noticing that part of the question is entirely semantic. To a very great extent the word "science" is reserved for fields that do progress in obvious ways. Today, part of our difficulty in seeing the profound differences between science and technology must relate to the fact that progress is an obvious attribute of both fields.[42]

In fact, however, scientific progress is not different in kind from progress in other fields; but the absence, at most times, of competing schools that question each other's aims and standards makes the progress of a normal-scientific community far easier to see. Once the reception of a common paradigm has freed the

scientific community from the need constantly to re-examine its first principles, the members of that community can concentrate exclusively upon the subtlest and most esoteric of the phenomena that concern it. The unparalleled insulation of mature scientific communities from the demands of the laity and of everyday life guarantees for the scientist a position wherein he can take a single set of standards for granted. The effects of this insulation are greatly intensified by the nature of the educational initiation into the professional scientific community. Until the very last stages in the education of a scientist, textbooks are systematically substituted for the creative scientific literature that made them possible.

It is, therefore, only during periods of revolution, when the fundamental tenets of a field are once more at issue, that doubts are repeatedly expressed about the very possibility of continued progress if one or another of the opposed paradigms is adopted. Those who rejected Newtonianism declared that its reliance upon innate forces would return science to the Dark Ages. A similar, though more moderately expressed, feeling seems to underlie the opposition of Einstein, Bohr, and others, to the dominant probabilistic interpretation of quantum mechanics. In short, it is only during periods of normal science that progress seems both obvious and assured. During those periods, however, the scientific community could view the fruits of its work in no other way.[43] Periods of scientific revolution are always followed by periods of normal science during which the harvest of the new discoveries and theories is being reaped. And this is the very reason why progress should be the apparently universal concomitant of scientific revolutions. Revolutions close with a total victory for one of the opposing camps. Will that group ever say that the result of its victory has been something less than progress? That should be rather like admitting that they had been wrong and their opponents right. To them, at least, the outcome of revolution must be progress, and they are in an excellent position to make certain that future members of their community will see past history in the same way.

Do these remarks suggest that the member of a mature scientific community is, like the typical character of Orwell's *1984,* the victim of a history rewritten by the powers that be? Although that suggestion is not altogether inappropriate, no explana-

tion of progress through revolution may stop at this point. The suggestion that in the sciences might makes right fails to recognize the nature of the process and of the authority by which the choice between paradigms is made. If authority alone were the arbiter of paradigm debates, the outcome of those debates might still be revolution, but it would not be *scientific* revolution. The very existence of science depends upon vesting the power to choose between paradigms in the members of a special kind of community. Just how special that community must be if science is to survive and grow may be indicated by the fact that the bulk of scientific knowledge is a product of Europe in the last four centuries. No other place and time has supported the very special communities from which scientific productivity comes. The members of these special communities, as individuals and by virtue of their shared training and experience, must be seen as the sole possessors of the rules of the game of some equivalent basis for unequivocal judgments. To doubt that they shared some such basis for evaluations would inevitably raise the question whether truth in the sciences can be one.[44]

But this raises the final question: What must nature, including man, be like in order that science be possible at all? Why should scientific communities be able to reach a firm consensus unattainable in other fields? Why should consensus endure across one paradigm change after another? And why should paradigm change invariably produce an instrument more perfect in some sense than those known before? The point at stake is this: not only must the scientific community be special. The world of which that community is a part must also possess quite special characteristics. The fundamental problem—What must the world be like in order that man may know it—is as old as science itself, and, within the context of science, it remains unanswered.

Some Conclusions

If Thomas Kuhn's sketch of the structure of scientific revolutions is adequate—and I see no reason to doubt its relevance—then we are facing here an alarming situation. The phenomenon of revolu-

tionary change—which in general confronts us on the socio-political level and, besides, has meaning within the framework of technological developments—now faces us at the very basis of nature itself. In other words, the very ground which we thought to be stable and fixed—whatever may change or be turned upside down on the socio-political and the cultural-technical level—the foundations of natural reality itself appear to suffer from the same type of disease. And this disease is incurable by the methods and instruments of which science itself disposes. The doctor who has almost unlimited knowledge of, and power over, nature is defenseless against the disease which threatens his own security.

Summarized tersely, this means that science has a fundamentally historical character. But even this statement, though of far-reaching consequences, is not radical enough. It still leaves room for the idea of a contradistinction between man and nature, in which the historical character of existence is reserved for man and the realm of nature remains unaffected. As a matter of fact, however, it is nature itself which, in the process of scientific approach, reveals its fundamentally historical character. To prevent misunderstanding, let me point out that I do not refer to the evolution of the universe over billions of years but to the inextricable interdependence between man's scientific analysis of nature and the structure of natural reality itself. This interdependence forbids a simple separation between a knowing subject and a known object. For the heart of the matter is that scientific revolutions, far from originating in man's fragmentary knowledge or lack of insight, are the very outcome of man's effort to penetrate into the more subtle and still unknown secrets of nature. It is nature itself which, again and again, explodes man's scientific concepts. Despite science's continuing struggle to maintain its traditional concepts, it has willy-nilly to surrender to the revolutionary character of natural reality as that reality reveals itself in the process of ongoing investigation.

Enriched by this insight, let us now turn to the socio-political and technological processes of change. The parallel between the structures of scientific and political revolutions, incisively delin-

eated by Thomas Kuhn, may throw a revealing light upon the nature of radical social change.

First, the contradistinction, which we discussed before, between technological and revolutionary humanism may turn out to include two aspects of the same basic structure of reality. The incapability of technological man really to master the material order and to force it within the framework of his technological management is not only revealed by the explosive character of the socio-political order, but is basically akin to the revolutionary structure of scientific research and of nature itself. And, conversely, socio-political revolutions are much more than results of man's collective restlessness; they reflect in a very specific way the essential intractability of reality that scientific knowledge is facing.

Second, the analysis of scientific revolutions explains why socio-political development cannot always follow an unbroken line of gradual change and why revolutions sometimes explode the dominant order in such a violent manner. Revolutions which deserve that name affect the very foundations of the existing order and they cannot be handled according to the categories whereby the traditional order has been accustomed to set its own house in order. Socio-political revolutions, in close analogy to scientific revolutions, replace a traditional concept, or paradigm, by a new concept, or paradigm. Both the tenacious and even fanatical resistance of the adherents of the old order and the no less determined effort of the revolutionaries to win the victory for what they believe to be the only acceptable truth have an unavoidable necessity. There is no impartial judge capable of taking the right decision in the conflict between two parties, for the traditional order is neither more nor less adequate than the new order. Therefore, the conflict is insoluble; it is a conflict between two incompatible concepts of socio-political order. The new order cannot consider itself other than victorious progress, and at the same time it must be rejected by the traditional order, which sees it as the transformation of order into chaos. There is only one argument in favor of the revolutionary concept, and that is the increasing impotence of the ancient order to deal effectively, in traditional terms and by familiar methods, with the challenge of anomalies and crises.

Third, since revolution is not an accidental phenomenon but affects the very foundations of order, every revolution is a double-edged sword. The postrevolutionary order, despite its conviction that it has discovered the panacea for all the incurable evils from which the past order was suffering, is in its turn threatened by the same insecurity and by analogous anomalies and crises, though in a new guise. The truth of revolution consists in its revealing the basic intractability of socio-political order, the essentially historical character of which does not allow any permanent order to be built upon its foundations.

A fourth consequence of the analogy between scientific and socio-political revolutions concerns the interdependence of development and revolution, of gradual and evolutionary change as contrasted with sudden and violent change.

Fifth, the necessity of a sociology of conflict follows cogently from the analogy between the structure of scientific and socio-political revolutions. There is in recent years an increasing acknowledgment of the insufficiency of a dominant type of positivist sociology, which, in fact, is directed by the ultimate norm of the existing, established social order to which the maladjusted individual or group has to become adapted. The insight into the essentially explosive character of socio-political reality of necessity leads to a different approach, of which the emerging sociology of conflict is a specimen.

A sixth conclusion concerns the incapability of scientific as well as of socio-political paradigms to cure the crisis which is permanently threatening their validity. This suggests the necessity of raising the questions on another level where another type of answer is to be looked for. That level is the operational domain of a philosophy of history.

This leads us to our seventh and final point. A philosophy of history will ultimately lead into dilemmas and paradoxes which cannot be dealt with adequately except within the framework of theological categories. In the last analysis, the challenge of revolution conceals a crisis in the theological dimension.

NOTES

1. Kennedy, *Strategy of Peace* (New York, 1960).
2. Harrop and Freeman, *An Open Letter on Foreign Policy* (Boston, 1961), p. 19.
3. Günther Wollny, *Die Zukunft ist anders* (Boppard am Rhein, 1962).
4. Arnold Toynbee, *Lectures on the Industrial Revolution of the Eighteenth Century in England* (London, 1884).
5. P. E. Kraemer, *The Societal State* (Meppel, 1966), pp. 23f.
6. *Ibid.,* p. 27.
7. See *World Conference on Church and Society* (Geneva, 1967), official report of the World Conference on Church and Society held in Geneva, July, 1966, under the auspices of the World Council of Churches.
8. *World Conference on Church and Society,* official report, p. 6.
9. Emmanuel G. Mesthene, "Religious Values in the Age of Technology," address, World Conference on Church and Society.
10. Jaques Ellul, "The Potentialities of the Scientific and Technological Revolutions," address, World Conference on Church and Society.
11. Robert Theobald, "Can Man Benefit from His Technology?" address, World Conference on Church and Society.
12. Margaret Mead, "New Forms of Community in a Pluralistic Society," address, World Conference on Church and Society.
13. André Philip, "The Revolutionary Change in the Structure of European Political Life," in Z. K. Matthews (ed.), *Responsible Government in a Revolutionary Age* (New York and London, 1966), pp. 115ff.
14. 'Bola Ige, "The Political Dynamics of Newly Awakened Peoples," address, World Conference on Church and Society.
15. Candido Mendes de Almeida, "Structural Ambivalence of Latin America," address, World Conference on Church and Society.
16. Hiber Conteris, "Ideological Options and Political Dynamism," address, World Conference on Church and Society.
17. Charles C. West, "Technologists and Revolutionaries," *Background Information for Church and Society,* World Council of Churches (Geneva; May, 1967), No. 38, pp. 2ff.
18. *World Conference on Church and Society,* official report, p. 192.

19. Gonzalo Castillo-Cárdenas, "Christians and the Struggle for a New Social Order in Latin America," address, World Conference on Church and Society.
20. Richard Shaull, "The Revolutionary Challenge to Church and Theology," address, World Conference on Church and Society.
21. Heinz-Dietrich Wendland, "The Church and Revolution," address, World Conference on Church and Society.
22. Günther Howe and Heinz Eduard Tödt, "Peace in the Scientific and Technical Age," *Background Information for Church and Society,* World Council of Churches (Geneva; June, 1966), Nos. 35 and 36.
23. Archpriest Borovoy, "The Challenge and Relevance of Theology to the Social Revolutions of Our Time," address, World Conference on Church and Society.
24. Josef L. Hromadka, "Der Christ inmitten der Weltrevolution," in Gerald Götting (ed.), *Reformation und Revolution* (Berlin, 1967), pp. 61f.
25. Günther Wirth, "Reformation und Revolution," Götting, *op. cit.,* pp. 136f.
26. Cf. Hannah Arendt, *On Revolution* (New York, 1965), p. 35.
27. Eugen Rosenstock-Huessy, *Out of Revolution, Autobiography of Western Man* (New York, 1964), pp. 454f.
28. Hannah Arendt, *op. cit.,* p. 39.
29. A. R. Hall, *The Scientific Revolution, 1500–1800* (London, 1954).
30. Herbert Butterfield, *The Origins of Modern Science* (rev. ed.; New York, 1957), particularly chs. 7, 10, 11.
31. *Ibid.,* pp. 7f.
32. Thomas S. Kuhn, *The Structure of Scientific Revolutions* (Chicago, 1966).
33. *Ibid.,* ch. IX, pp. 91ff.
34. *Ibid.,* ch. X.
35. *Ibid.,* p. 116.
36. *Ibid.,* p. 145.
37. *Ibid.,* p. 149.
38. *Ibid.,* p. 156.
39. *Ibid.,* p. 159.
40. *Ibid.,* p. 3.
41. *Ibid.,* p. 6.
42. *Ibid.,* p. 160.
43. *Ibid.,* p. 162.
44. *Ibid.,* p. 167.

CHAPTER THREE

Development

The American Way

The development of Europe in modern times has been accompanied by a series of revolutions. The United States of America, the most highly developed country in the world, started its route to the top ranks of economic affluence with a revolution. To a certain extent the American Revolution is a part of European history and can be considered as a link in the chain of revolutions which determined Western history in the last three centuries. But, on the other hand, the American Revolution has a peculiar position, and its ambivalent relationship to European revolutions makes it an appropriate starting-point for a discussion of the interdependence of development and revolution.

The ideas and inspiration which gave rise to the American Revolution and the birth of the American nation in 1776 did not appear out of the blue, but were derived from the vision of a whole series of progressive European thinkers like Milton, Locke, Voltaire, Montesquieu, and Rousseau. The War of Independence was the outcome of a struggle which began as no more than the claim to equal rights by an American middle class. Driven by the spirit of their Puritan forefathers in seventeenth-century England, they sought what they believed to be self-evident liberties under the British crown. The philosophy of the Colonies' revolution and of

its new nationhood was formulated by an Englishman, Thomas Paine, who had landed on New World shores only a few months before. His pamphlet *Common Sense* was followed only a few months later by the Declaration of Independence, the content of which reflects the English liberal spirit of Paine's day. On the other hand, the birth of the American nation added something new which had been thus far unknown in European tradition. It was more than just a transplanting of English nationalism to a new continent. The new spirit provided sufficient reason for French forerunners of their own revolution to idealize America as being destined to bring about a new era of humanity, and to contrast it with the decadence and backwardness of Europe. To enlightened Europeans at the end of the eighteenth century, America was a symbol of liberty and natural virtue, a land in whose vast open spaces the natural order could become creative, unhampered by the traditions and superstitions of past ages. This accorded with the sense of universal responsibility that leading Americans had of their own nation, which they believed to be elected to illumine the whole world—Europe in the first instance, followed by Asia and Africa—with truth and liberty.

This exceptional sense of destiny which marked the birth of the American nation was closely related to unique circumstances present in the New World, in contrast with the continent of Europe and Great Britain.

First, as Hans Kohn[1] has pointed out, the American Colonies revolted, not because they were oppressed, but because they were free and their freedom carried the promise of still greater freedom—a freedom unknown in the more settled and static conditions of the old society, but beckoning as a possibility on the new continent. In the wide, open spaces of the yet unexplored continent, common dangers and tasks facilitated the rise of individualism and equality at the same time. Liberty was not a distant ideal, to be realized only after long and painful struggle by suffering generations; it was the long and palpable experience of unlimited opportunities and of a level of prosperity and affluence far beyond anything the Old World had ever been able to provide.

Second, the American Revolution was not, as were revolu-

tions in Europe, a struggle against the fetters of feudalism and absolutism which had held their sway over past centuries, but was the claim of the people of a new continent realizing its autonomy, rooted in and enabled by the simple fact of its geographical distance. The past consisted in primitive Indian history which easily could be blotted out and there was no danger of a relapse, such as France fell victim to within a few years of its revolution.

Third, the social question, which so dramatically prevailed in the French Revolution, was solved in the New World by the manifold opportunities for material happiness and economic equality, which drew the impoverished immigrants from Europe. Jefferson explained the failure of the French Revolution by the fact that it could be accomplished only with the support of the mobs in the cities, debased by ignorance, poverty, and vice, and incapable of rational action. This does not mean that the United States did not face problems of poverty during the nineteenth century, but to a certain extent it was able to brush aside reality until that was forced upon its conscience in recent decades.

A Non-Communist Manifesto

Against this background we must evaluate the faith in economic growth and development which prevails in the United States. Being the most advanced country of the highly developed Western world, it may serve as the most appropriate point of departure for an analysis of the development problem. Probably the best introduction is a study, by one of the leading American economists of our time, which within a few years has become a classic example of Western development-ethos. The author, W. W. Rostow, was at the time of writing his book a professor of economic history at Massachusetts Institute of Technology and more recently has been a leading political and economic adviser in the American government. His study, titled *The Stages of Economic Growth*[2] is significantly subtitled "A Non-Communist Manifesto," and it is a worthy answer to *The Communist Manifesto* of 1848, written by Karl Marx and Friedrich Engels.

Rostow's study sees economic development in five distinctive stages. All societies, in their economic dimensions, are to be identified as lying within one of five levels: the traditional society, the developing conditions necessary for growth, the take-off, the drive to maturity, and the age of high mass-consumption.

The traditional society is one whose structure is developed within limited production functions, based on pre-Newtonian science and technology. This traditional stage had an economic ceiling owing to the absence or nonapplication of the potentialities which flow from modern science and technology. In historical perspective the phrase "traditional society" embraces the dynasties of China, the civilization of the Middle East and the Mediterranean, the world of medieval Europe, and the post-Newtonian societies which, for a time, remained untouched or unmoved by man's new capability for regularly manipulating his environment to his economic advantage.

The second stage of growth embraced societies in the process of transition. The preconditions necessary for eventual take-off were developed in a clearly marked way, in the Western Europe of the late seventeenth and early eighteenth centuries as the insights of modern science began to be translated into new production functions in both agriculture and industry, in a setting given dynamism by the lateral expansion of world markets and the international competition for them. Among the Western European states Britain, favored by geography, natural resources, trading possibilities, and social and political structure, was the first to develop fully the preconditions for take-off.

But the great watershed in the life of modern societies was the third stage in this sequence, the take-off, being the interval when the old blocs and resistances to steady growth are finally overcome. The forces making for economic progress expand and come to dominate the society to such an extent that growth becomes its normal condition. One can allocate the take-off of Britain to approximately the two decades after 1783; France and the United States to the several decades preceding 1860; Germany, to the third quarter of the nineteenth century; Japan, to the fourth quarter of the nineteenth century; Russia and Canada, to the

quarter-century or so preceding 1914; while during the 1950's India and China have, in quite different ways, made their respective take-offs.

After take-off, there follows a long interval of sustained if fluctuating progress, as the now steadily growing economy drives to extend modern technology over the whole front of its economic activity. Some 10 to 20 per cent of the national income is invested, permitting output regularly to outstrip the increase in population. This is the stage in which an economy demonstrates that it has the technological and entrepreneurial skills to produce, not everything, but anything that it chooses to produce.

The fifth stage is the age of high mass-consumption, where, in time, the leading sectors shift toward durable consumer goods and services. For the United States it was in the 1920's, and again in the postwar decade, 1946–1956, that this stage of growth was pressed to, virtually, its logical conclusion. In the 1950's Western Europe and Japan appear to have fully entered this phase, and the Soviet Union is technically ready for it.

This is a rough model of economic history as a sequence of stages. Let us now have a closer look at Rostow's analysis of some of these stages. He has from the outset made a distinction between two different examples of the second stage, in which the preconditions for take-off are developing. The first case, which might be called the general case, fits not merely the evolution of most of Europe but also that of the greater part of Asia, the Middle East, and Africa. In this case, fundamental changes in a well-established traditional society are required, resulting in substantial alterations of the socio-political structure as well as techniques of production. The second case covers the small group of nations, created mainly out of British civilization, which were already far along in the transitional process: the United States, Australia, New Zealand, and Canada. They were founded by social groups who were at the margin of the dynamic transitional process slowly going forward within Britain. Moreover, their physical settings accelerated the transitional process by offering extremely attractive incentives to get on with economic growth. These nations never became deeply enmeshed in the structures, politics, and values of the traditional

society, so the process of their transition to modern growth was mainly economic and technical.

There are, of course, exceptions to the second case; for instance, the southern parts of the United States where a kind of traditional society was created which only in recent decades reached its take-off point. A specific problem is the place of the Latin American states within this categorization. On the whole, they belong in the general case, since they began with a version of a traditional society—often emerging from traditional Latin European and native cultures—but to varying degrees, they also may be regarded as the lucky offspring of an already transitional Europe.

This distinction between the general case—which has to start on the basis of a traditional society—and the specific historical evolution of the United States and the other countries of British origin, confirms the remarks we already made on the situation of the United States within the scope of the dialectical relationship between development and revolution. The preconditions for take-off which determined the economic progress of the United States had already been prepared in the preceding history of the mother-country, Britain, and of Western Europe, and the actual take-off was not burdened with the weight of social and political traditions which were characteristic for the Old World.

The crucial question is, then: By what specific historical preconditions was the first take-off to occur in modern economic history, namely, the breakup of traditional society in Great Britain, determined? The classical answer to this question unfolds from two features of postmedieval Europe: the discovery and rediscovery of regions beyond Western Europe, and the accelerating development of modern scientific knowledge. One of the decisive factors which permitted the first take-off to occur in Britain and not in a neighboring country like France or Holland was the political, social, and religious revolution fought out in Britain by 1688. The roots of modern development are to be found in Europe's revolutionary history.

There is a certain connection between four major revolutions of Western history—the English, the American, the French, and the Russian. In this series, the American Revolution—despite its

close relationship to preceding British history and to the following French Revolution—has a distinctive position. This is acknowledged by Rostow's distinction between the preconditions for economic development which existed in most of Europe, Asia, the Middle East, and Africa, on the one hand, and in the United States (and other countries of British origin), on the other hand. Since his study is labeled a non-Communist manifesto, we may expect the test of his arguments to be found in a comparison between the economic evolution in the United States and in Russia. A special chapter is, indeed, devoted to this subject.

Rostow begins to question the familiar image of Russian economic development as that of a nation surging under a Communist system of state controls into a long-delayed status as an industrial power of the first order, in short, the image of a situation apart which requires forms of analysis different from those applicable in the West. However, despite profound special elements in the story of the evolution of modern Russian society and of its economy, Russian economic development over the past century is remarkably similar to that of the United States, but with a lag of about thirty-five years in the level of industrial output. Moreover, the Russian case, linking the Czarist and Communist experiences, falls, like the case of the United States, well within the broad framework of the stages-of-growth analysis.

There are, of course, some major differences between Russia and the United States. First, whereas Russia had to overcome a traditional society—with well-entrenched institutions of church and state as well as intractable problems of land tenure, an illiterate serfdom, overpopulation of the land, the lack of a free-wheeling commercial middle class, and a culture which initially placed a low premium on modern productive economic activity—the United States was "born free," with vigorous, independent land-owning farmers, and an ample supply of enterprising men of commerce, as well as a social and political system that took easily to industrialization (outside the South).

A second difference consists in the circumstances which conditioned the drive to maturity in both countries: whereas this took place in the United States after the Civil War, in a setting of rela-

tive political freedom (outside the South), and in a society tightly linked to the international economy, at a time of peace, and, generally, with rising standards of consumption per head—in Russia, to the contrary, it occurred in the three decades after 1928, in a virtually closed economy, against a background of war and preparations for war, which did not slow the spread of technology but which did limit the rise of consumption.

But, apart from the military question, the economic difference between the development of both countries is primarily a question of time-lag. As the economist G. Warren Nutter said: "Each son will ultimately catch up to his father in height, and brothers of different age differ less and less in height as they get older." These major differences do not, however, weaken Rostow's statement about the noticeable similarity of United States and Russian economic development over the past century, only with a time-lag of between thirty-five and fifty years.

Some Critical Questions

At this point some basic questions arise with regard to Rostow's model of economic growth. The first question is: Does this kind of model still hold true if the differences between the various cases are considered as more than merely accidental? Rostow's view is determined by the standpoint of a citizen of the northern part of the United States, enjoying all the experiences and blessings of an age of high mass-consumption. And his basic assumption is that the evolution which led to this present stage follows a general model that applies to the economic development followed by any other country from the moment it succeeds in passing through the take-off stage. Is not this assumption, however, dependent upon a *petitio principii*? It makes an important difference whether one looks at a line of evolution from the viewpoint of the realized final stage or from its initial stage. He who has reached the final goal may be inclined to forget or to belittle the enormous handicaps and resistances which have to be overcome by others who have to begin under less favorable circumstances. When, however, this initial

stage is considered as of decisive influence for the course followed by the next stages of the evolution, things will reveal themselves under a different light.

The United States was, indeed, "born free"; in other words, it could start at the point of development which had been reached by Britain and Western Europe in the course of several preceding centuries. But what happened in Western direction—the transplantation of European progressive ideals to the transatlantic world—failed to occur in Eastern direction, so that Russia's situation in the middle of the last century was more backward than the stage of Western Europe's and Britain's society five or six centuries earlier.

Moreover, the differences in circumstances which determined the take-off were of much more than accidental importance. Rostow has himself recognized that, in the course of its take-off, Russia was struck by a major war, "in which the precarious and changing balance between traditional and democratic political elements collapsed in the face of defeat and disorder." The revolutionary situation of 1917 which enabled the Communist Party to seize power never threatened the United States in a comparable stage. The same holds true for the international situation during Russia's drive to maturity, between 1928 and 1958.

Our second question is closely connected with this first question. Rostow rightly criticizes Marxist economic theory on a number of issues and comes to the conclusion that Karl Marx applied his philosophy of history and his economic presuppositions to what he could perceive of one historical case: the case of the British take-off and drive to maturity, the result of which he generalized and projected. It was the British Industrial Revolution and what followed the take-off in Britain that shaped Marx's categories. Moreover, before he died, the failure in his system began to be revealed, namely, the rise in industrial wages in Western Europe and the perfectly apparent fact that the British and Western European working classes were inclined to accept ameliorative improvements and the terms of democratic capitalism. These observations are right, but there are reasons to think that Rostow's theory of economic growth falls a victim to comparable errors, but at the opposite end. He characterizes Communism as "a kind of disease

which can befall a transitional society" and, therefore, the major challenge of our time in Asia, the Middle East, Africa, and Latin America. "For the fate of those of us who now live in a stage of high mass-consumption is going to be substantially determined by the nature of the preconditions process and the take-off in distant nations, processes which our societies experienced well over a century ago, in less searching and difficult forms."

This is a remarkable conclusion which, to be sure, is at variance with the general trend of Rostow's study:

a) Britian's transition period, in which Marx was living, has basic features which are applicable to other countries in a comparable stage;

b) whereas the later development of Britain and Western Europe proved Marx's prophecies wrong, these comparable situations in today's Third World are sometimes even more vulnerable and much more exposed to Marxist infection;

c) the dangers which threaten the Third World are graver than the problems of Western Europe were a century ago; in other words, the model of economic development in this initial stage is not analogous;

d) the stage of high mass-consumption of the most advanced countries is not only determined by the preceding stages which the countries already have passed through, but at the same time and in a no less decisive measure by the trend of initial development which at present takes place in the Third World.

But—and this is our third question—the stage of high mass-consumption is not only co-determined by the stages in which less developed parts of the world find themselves, but is also determined by the inherent logic of accelerated technological evolution. The United States has already entered a new stage which has been characterized as the "cybernation revolution." This includes the development of radically different techniques and the subsequent appearance of novel principles of organization of production, a basic reordering of man's relationship to his environment, and a dramatic increase in total available and potential energy. There is

no question that cybernation would make possible the abolition of poverty at home and abroad. But there are influential voices, like those raised in the American report on "The Triple Revolution" (see p. 30), which question the capacity of the existing industrial system to permit these potentials to become realities. The industrial system, according to their argument, was designed to produce an ever-increasing quantity of goods as efficiently as possible, and it was assumed that the distribution of the power to purchase these goods would occur almost automatically. But they observe in the present trend more and more indications that the capability of machines is rising more rapidly than the capacity of many human beings to keep pace and they fear the permanent establishment of an impoverished and jobless class in the midst of actual and potential abundance. This is not only a fundamental problem for the highly developed countries, but it has its consequences for the perspectives of development on a worldwide scale. David Morse, Director-General of the International Labour Office, examined this issue in the following terms:

> From our present standpoint in time, there is reason to be more optimistic as to the production capabilities of advancing technology than as to employment expansion. Let us look for a moment at the employment needs of the future as measured by changes in the size of the population of working age (during the period 1950–1975). . . .
>
> On a world-wide basis, during this 25-year period, the number of persons of working age will increase by 800 million. From this, it can be estimated with reasonable accuracy that the labor force will be increased by more than 550 million persons—or, in other words, that more than 550 million jobs will be needed. And this figure does not take into account the current backlog of unemployment and underemployment, particularly widespread in underdeveloped countries.
>
> Out of this world total, the increase for the industrially advanced areas of the world would be about 100 million, split in three roughly equal parts among North America, Europe and the Soviet Union. The increase for the underdeveloped areas of the world would be some 450 million, that for Asia alone being estimated at 380 million. For comparison, just this increase in the

labor force in Asia during the 1950–1975 period will be greater than the total labor force of 340 million in the industrially developed world in 1950—North America, Europe and the Soviet Union combined.

That represents a lot of new jobs. And in considering how they might be created, we are confronted with the fact that the technology, whether in agriculture or in industry, which is most capable of yielding the *greatest increases in production* is least capable of expanding employment. This is why automation has become a major public issue in America, because it has been held responsible for the present unacceptable levels of unemployment. I believe automation is only partly responsible; but it is proving to be extremely difficult to adjust policy and particular levels of effective demand to a situation of rapid technological change. Nevertheless, the figures I have cited show that the magnitude of the employment problem will be very substantially greater in the underdeveloped parts of the world.

. . . The world employment problem—and particularly the employment problem in the underdeveloped areas—may grow alarmingly, and prove a source of social and political tension, even as progress is made toward satisfying the production needs of rising populations.[3]

An American economist adds to this the warning that it is time we recognize that the nineteenth-century process of growth, which was achieved by starving the worker and by the voluntary thrift of the manager, has no place in the second half of the twentieth century, when work and saving can be most effectively carried out by the machine. Development theory has failed to keep up with the fact that the world is entering a new era in which the power of the machine (the automatic tool) is being combined with the skill of the machine (the computer) to develop a cybernated system with effectively unlimited productive capacity.

But we need not look to the consequences of technological development for the next decades to discover the inner contradictions hidden within the idea of economic growth as a model to be imitated by each country of the world. If we look at the figure of technological evolution it is obvious that this is passing through an acceleration unprecedented in human history, but an analogous

curve can be drawn in order to represent the population explosion. In the same way that human history can be divided into periods of successive stages of technology, so a historical analysis of the growth of the human species can be made, distinguishing three broad periods:

Period 1, extending from about 600,000 B.C. to 6000 B.C., during which the population grew to about five million and the total number of births did not exceed twelve billion.

Period 2, from 6000 B.C. to A.D. 1650 shows an increase from five million to a half-billion and a total of about 42 billion births.

Period 3, from A.D. 1650 to the present day, shows a sixfold increase, from about a half-billion to over three billion. The total number of births during this period is 23 billion.

It is estimated that at this rate the world population will stand at six billion by the year 2000. In other words, whereas it took more than 600,000 years for the human population to reach the three billion mark, in about another forty years, assuming that the current growth rate remains unchanged, humanity will add another three billion to its number.

Comparison of the acceleration curve of technological evolution on the one hand, and of the population explosion on the other hand, might lead to the conclusion that the human species is passing through a new phase in its evolution which affects all dimensions of human existence and will project the human species into a new way of life and a new mode of existence. It might be rightly assumed the immense problems which arise in the sector of population increase are adequately coped with by the unprecedented increase of potential in the technological sector. This is, broadly speaking, true for the highly developed countries. It is, however, at this point that the fallacy of these figures begins to become manifest. For when we survey the history of mankind it should be realized that only a minority of mankind has reached that most advanced stage of technological evolution which entitles us to speak of a transformation of the human species, but an overwhelming majority still finds itself in a stage which lies between the level

of the Stone Age and the early Middle Ages. When we look at the other figure, which represents the population increase, things are totally different. In this case it is equally fallacious to speak of a worldwide phenomenon, for the overwhelming burden of the increase is to be borne by the underdeveloped world. The rate of population growth tends to be higher in the less developed countries than in the developed countries—about 70 per cent higher on the average. In many less developed countries the rate of population growth exceeds 3 per cent a year. This is a relatively new phenomenon since the First World War, for during the first two decades of the twentieth century, population growth was nearly twice as rapid in the developed parts of the world (North America, Europe including Russia, and Oceania) as in the less developed countries (Japan was an exception). In other words, there is an enormous disproportion in present-day human evolution, and those parts of the world which from the technological point of view have thus far lagged behind are the farthest ahead in the population race.

This is an indication of the contradictions inherent in the phenomenon of development. If mankind were an undivided whole, comparable to the individual in rate of development, there would be no fundamental problems, apart from those of retarded adaptation of one part of the organism to the evolution of other, more advanced, parts. But the problem is much more serious, and described in terms of individual evolution it comes nearer to psychiatric phenomena like schizophrenia, which arise from a fundamental split in the structure of personality.

This leads us to a second consideration. Development always means that one minor part takes a leap ahead and secures an advanced position beyond the rest, which at best does little more than keep its traditional position. The metaphor of a race is, however, only one of the possible descriptions of what really happens when processes of development are taking place.

Another description which may be equally adequate and equally inadequate is in terms of one person standing on the shoulders of two others, who in their turn use the bodies of four fellow men for support. The man who reaches the greatest height

can succeed only by exploiting the muscular energy of a number of other human beings, who not only lend him the necessary support, but by this very service are prevented from harvesting the fruits that have been sown with their help. Our approach to the development problem may vary according to the model of description we have wittingly, or unwittingly, preferred. Let us, for instance, take the lessons of economic and social history since the beginning of the Industrial Revolution.

Looking at it from the point of view of the average British citizen of today the trend of the past 150 years may be considered as a race in which the challenging example of the pioneering middle class has, after two generations, succeeded in evoking the creative response of the labor class which has followed the pioneers on their march to ever-increasing prosperity. But the second metaphor reveals the other side of the coin: the exploitation of at least two generations of industrial proletariat, which was the human cost of this progress, the seed which had to be sacrificed that coming generations might reap a harvest.

A crucial question is: To what extent does the process of development expand its limits? At this point the idea and the reality of modern nationhood play an important role. In spite of the famous statment by Disraeli that nineteenth-century Great Britian was, so to speak, divided into two nations, namely, the bourgeoisie and the proletariat, the social and economic cohesion of the British nation has proved stronger than this conflict. It has in the long run made the blessings of economic progress available to the great majority of the people. But the situation is totally different when it comes to the relationship between nineteenth-century Britain and its colonial empire in British India. The cohesion which, within the boundaries of the British nation, succeeded in overcoming the class conflict was nearly absent in the colonial relationship. And in this case the only chance for the population of India to take-off in the worldwide race for economic progress lay in a national revolution which cut the political bonds of dependence on its colonial master. In other words, a beginning development could not be made without a revolution.

Closely connected with this is a third consideration. The idea

that the process of worldwide development can be compared to a race in which every competitor is free to try and overtake the more advanced competitors is also fallacious, in the respect that it neglects the coexistence of all stages of development in one world. This applies both to the past and to the present. Let us, for instance, take the problem of population explosion in the underdeveloped world. Population increases are closely connected with the application of modern science, and particularly medical and public health breakthroughs, resulting in a rapid decline in the death rate. The one-sided application of modern technology has immensely aggravated the burden of underdevelopment. In other words, the most advanced countries have the advantage not only of having been the first to begin the race of economic progress, but also of dictating their pattern of development to the less developed countries. This advantage implies that to the normal time-lag an abnormal handicap of development pressure is being added. This is another indication of the close connection between development and revolution.

Rostow's stages-of-growth model is a typical specimen of a theory of social evolution which dominated the last quarter of the nineteenth century, following the publication of Darwin's revolutionary idea of biological evolution. But the "stair-step" notion is far from dependent on Darwinist theory; it has gained wide popularity and is alive in the thinking of laymen and in the writings of scholars. As Wilbert Moore[4] has pointed out, in most examples of "stage" theories the discontinuities are caused by changes in man's relation to his environment, that is, in technology. One type of classification concerns primarily the materials used for tools and weapons: the "Old Stone (Paleolithic) Age," the "New Stone (Neolithic) Age," the "Bronze Age," and the "Iron Age." Another method of distinguishing stages concerns itself primarily with the dominant mode of economic production: hunting and food-gathering, pastoral nomadism, settled agriculture, industry. The present and recent past have been characterized by a variety of partially overlapping and partially competing "ages": steam, steel, electricity, automation, nuclear energy, outer space.

Our century has witnessed the downfall of theories of social

evolution, owing in large measure to a paradoxical circumstance, the problem of diversity. Though the diversity of cultures was made central to the evolutionary scheme, the attempt to order differences by resort to "stages" fell under both theoretical and empirical attack. This led to a radical "relativism" in social description. But the *interest* in theories of social evolution has never died and what we are now witnessing is a revival of this interest, which is taking two principal forms. The one attempts to account for diversity by the concept of "multilineal evolution," which means essentially the identification of different sequential patterns for different cultures, or types of cultures.

The other principal emphasis finds the utility of a theory of social evolution at a very general level, without insisting that all structural variations and dynamic processes be subsumed under or be derivable from the general theory. In this approach, culture in general, not particular cultures, is the proper unit for study. This approach serves to emphasize some common elements in the fate of mankind as a distinct biological species, particularly a long-term increase in man's ability to adapt to and control his environment, including the social environment.

Several extremely long-term trends are consistent with this unilinear theory. Moore enumerates four of them:[5]

1. Both survival and expansion of the species *Homo sapiens* bespeak an increasingly effective adaptation, in competition with other species.

2. One of the major factors in man's successful biological survival has been the additive, or accumulative, character of objective knowledge and rational technique.

3. The cumulated "science" has been directed to matters of social organization and control so that the time during which knowledge may survive has been lengthened and the span of social relations has been broadened.

4. The size of human populations and the organized differentiation that size and communication and techniques of control make possible lead to the increasing degree to which virtually all members of the species are part of a single system. Both ideas and

techniques are increasingly drawn from an international or inter-cultural pool to which many systems have contributed and more may do so in the future.

Development Myth

As seen against this broader background of mankind's social evo-lution, the stages-of-growth model reflects the progressive direction of this long-term trend toward a single system that tends to em-brace the whole world. But, at the same time, this mode of think-ing is a rational expression of what has been aptly called the "development myth," the powerful myth behind technological civilization. According to this myth, development actually means acquiring the ways of life of the countries which are most deeply marked by technological civilization. Or to put this even more crudely: economic development aims at making the poor countries like the rich countries.[6]

A dominant expression of this development myth is the widely proclaimed objective of development, i.e., "catching up" with affluent nations. This kind of objective fits perfectly with the stages-of-growth theory and it may be considered as its com-plementary ideology on the part of the developing countries. But, for this very reason, the catching-up notion is no less vulnerable than Rostow's theory as a specimen of the highly developed countries' ideology.

The Indian economist S. L. Parmar[7] has severely criticized the catching-up ideal, since it strongly distorts the real goals for which developing nations need to be striving. Obviously, it is extremely difficult for developing nations to maintain higher rates of growth than the developed countries. Since technology has its own momentum, the rate of technical progress in developed na-tions will be greater. This enhances their productive capacity and enables them to maintain higher growth rates. As regards the narrowing of the income gap, this is made difficult both by the technological lag and the demographic factor. Reduction of the

economic gap can be done only through international cooperation and under international auspices. It is essentially a problem of a more equitable distribution of international resources. No single country, nor a group of developing countries, can do much about it.

The immediate task which Dr. Parmar sees before developing nations is, therefore, different. It is the task to break away from stagnation. They have, in fact, not so much to catch up with others as to maintain a performance better than their previous best. In effect, each nation competes with itself. The quest for development is not so much a quest for "catching up" as for "standing up." The catching-up approach has a number of detrimental consequences. First, it generates frustration and defeatism when, even after sustained efforts, developing nations find that they are still far behind the affluent.

Second, it is lacking in realism. Some estimates about national and per-capita incomes show that even with favorable conditions their relative position vis-à-vis development will not be much better by the year 1980 or even 2000. Such calculations, moreover, estimate a constant level of technology in the developed nations, when the fact is that their level of technology changes at increasingly faster rates in each decade.

Third, using the norms of other nations as criteria for development reflects an element of subservience which can undermine the self-respect and dignity of a people.

Fourth, developing countries have to be low-consumption high-investment economies for a long time. In their eagerness to catch up lies a temptation to imitate the high-consumption pattern of developed economies, with serious consequences to economic efforts.

Fifth, in view of these realities, developing nations need a new concept of development where self-respect is possible even with relative poverty. At the present juncture their sense of economic well-being should come not from having more but from strengthening social and economic structures to produce more. At the same time such strengthening should not be at the cost

of one whole generation in the interest of a future generation, for this does not contribute to the self-respect of either.

Sixth, the quest for development is related to the problems of poor societies. It would be a mistake for developing nations to take over the socio-economic values and structures of affluent nations indiscriminately. Acceptance of a partial concept of catching up may mean accepting the dehumanizing power of things even before liberation from the dehumanizing power of poverty has been achieved. The disappointments of the Development Decade challenge emerging nations to evolve a concept of development more in keeping with their economic, political, and social realities.

After having thus rejected the catching-up notion and having advocated a "development with self-respect" under continuing conditions of relative poverty, Dr. Parmar turns to the only way of narrowing the gap between rich and poor countries: international cooperation. A survey of the four main aspects of international economic cooperation leads him to discouraging conclusions. The transplantation of science and technology in developing nations has, at least in the short run, aggravated some of their problems. Development aid leaves developing nations with the feeling that it represents a form of neo-colonialism. The trend of international trade seems to continue the regressive pattern of colonial trade. The hope that enlightened self-interest would encourage an international policy of development investment has been falsified.

Therefore, the real issue is "to replace structures of stagnation by those conducive to regulated progress. This would mean far-reaching social, economic and political change. Our normal predilection for order needs to be replaced by a passion for justice."

Reviewing these appalling conclusions reached by this leading Indian economist impresses upon one the enormous dilemma facing this approach. Dr. Parmar is an outstanding representative of modern India, of progressive international economic policy-making, and of contemporary ecumenical thinking. For that very reason, his dilemma is a Gordian knot binding together the unanswered questions of influential thinkers concerned with the problems of modern India, the international economy and the ecumenical ethos.

Modern India

The type of middle-class thinking prevailing in leading circles of present-day India reflects the ambivalent position of Indian economic development policy between the threat and challenge of Communist China's example and the promise and frustration of Western economic aid and neo-colonial international patterns of trade and investment. This approach rejects the Communist goal of progress conceived as high growth rate at any cost (material and human) and it wants to measure the sacrifices to be made in keeping with a creative tension between structures and persons. The ideology of this concept of development focuses on the non-economic components of self-respect and determination of a people in its quest for humanization and social justice. It is rooted in the struggle for a new cultural ethos for modern India. In the words of a leading Indian Christian and ecumenical personality, M. M. Thomas, this Indian humanism "means grappling with and reinterpreting the inner being and values of the traditional culture from within the light of their relevance to modernisation." In fact, this development ethos is the continuation of the spirit which enthused the nationalist struggle for political independence as it was guided by Jawaharlal Nehru, "who was never tired of emphasising that the struggle for a new ethos required not cultural imitation but cultural creativity. For him, this meant a journey to discover India in a new way, a search in the Indian tradition for the germs of a humanism on which he could build a new cultural ethos embodying the spirit of modernity." [8]

Obviously, this ethos is not radical enough to produce what Dr. Parmar calls the mutuality between "the technological revolution in developed nations, a revolution of possibilities" and "the social revolution in developing nations, a revolution of aspirations." [9] But he has to acknowledge that from the other side of the gap thus far no solution is to be expected. There is a need for adequate international economic and political structures, but as yet "only limited progress has been made in this direction, and recent trends are discouraging."

International Economy

In fact, the dilemma of international economic policy-making is to a certain extent interwoven with the Indian dilemma. Some aspects of the dilemma have been well described by the outstanding Swedish international economist, Gunnar Myrdal.[10] He agrees that development implies the overcoming of stagnation as people begin to do things in order to improve conditions for themselves. If this is to be accomplished in a democratic way, the people must develop cooperative methods of work. Otherwise, development efforts will be in vain, totalitarian methods will have to be resorted to. "Whether or not the underdeveloped countries outside the Soviet orbit succeed in going the Western way in regard to self-government and voluntary organizations—however different their situation is from that of the Western countries, and however differently their policies must be directed in other and more specific respects—will largely determine not only what sort of economy they will have, but what is to be their national community, and under what type of political system it will operate."

That is one side of the picture, but Myrdal does not forget the other side. He is in full sympathy with Jawaharlal Nehru's conviction that the organs for self-government and cooperation in present-day India should be run by the people themselves and not by the officials. Nehru regularly referred to the experiences in England, Scandinavia, and other Western countries. But Myrdal points out that, in a stagnant society, these institutions do not come into existence except as a result of state policy. The officials have the function of starting them, propagating them, and guiding them. And "it will be a most difficult task to do this in such a way that out of planning and instigation from above comes the surge of a movement from below, strong enough to give them an independent life. This process is a totally different one from the historical process behind the present situation in the Western countries, and the problem of getting the process going by state planning and policies is a totally new one, which the Western countries have never faced."

This is the internal aspect of the Indian dilemma. There is an external, international aspect as well. Gunnar Myrdal shares the common faith in the possibility and the need of a "created harmony" in the direction of a democratic Welfare World. He believes that in spite of the ideological divisions and the wide gaps separating the Western world, the Soviet Union, and the underdeveloped countries in levels and modes of living and working, "we are all existing in the same era of civilization, with a considerable and growing unity of basic ideas and ideals. One such congruity of thoughts and strivings is the dynamic conception implicit in our thinking about the national economy. In all countries we are now striving for 'development.' " [11] He fully understands that, if this urgent need for the development toward the democratic Welfare World is to be realized, very much will depend upon the rapidity and forcefulness of a positive response in the rich countries to a wider sharing of opportunities. But his realism induces him to add emphatically that the main driving force behind such a fortunate development would have to be the exertions of the poor nations themselves. "No upper class has ever stepped down voluntarily to equality with the lower class, and as a simple consequence of a moral conviction given up their privileges and opened entrance to their monopolies. To be induced to do so, the rich and the privileged must sense that demands are raised and forcefully pressed, and that power becomes assembled behind them. At that stage, moral ideals in the upper class are given their chance to play a supporting role." [12]

The question of how to gain and how to exert a sufficient amount of effective power produces an embarrassing dilemma for the international economic model-designing of present-day Western theorists and policy-makers: effective power, internally, in order to push a stagnant economy beyond the critical point where a successful and self-propelling development is being set in motion; effective power, externally, in order to break through the dominant pattern of international economic relationships that is being maintained and reinforced by the overwhelming economic strength of the rich countries. In both respects, a Western-style pattern of economic world order faces its essential limitations.

Regarding the internal aspect, Myrdal frankly admits that developing countries have to follow ways totally different from those which the West followed in past centuries if they wish to reach the West's present stage of development. Vis-à-vis the question of external power, he recognizes that this is the only means whereby developing countries can really force the rich countries radically to change their present self-centered policies.

However, the ethos of this type of international economic theory is too firmly rooted in a technological rationalism to be capable of taking into account the power-issue, which, from its point of view, bears an extremely irrational character. An impressive illustration of this ethos is the study of international economic policy by the outstanding Dutch economist, Jan Tinbergen, and his collaborators, published under the descriptive title *Shaping the World Economy*.[13]

The framework of Tinbergen's rational system of thinking becomes obvious when we look at what he calls "today's challenges." [14] In today's world we are faced with three challenges. The first and greatest is the threat of nuclear war. The second is the misery in developing countries. The third is the challenge of the Communist political economic system." This seems obvious enough, but closer analysis reveals a number of embarrassing questions.

First, who are "we"? Though the author does not attempt to conceal his Western origin and point of view, the force of his approach derives from the very aim to design policy suggestions for tomorrow's world economy and to envisage the economic future of the world as an indivisible whole. As an international economist he tries to reach a supranational and supraideological viewpoint. In fact, the threat of nuclear war is a challenge to the whole world, and the same could be said with regard to the challenge of poverty in developing regions. But the third challenge is clearly only a question for the non-Communist world, and even this not indiscriminately, for many developing countries feel themselves challenged by both the Western and the Communist systems.

Second, the kind of challenge differs very much from case to case. In order to bring the second and the third challenges into line with the first one, it would be fair to speak of the challenge of an

international class struggle between rich and poor countries and of the challenge of the Cold War. Only such emendation would entitle the author to state that "these three challenges are interconnected."

Third, the thesis that "the war threat is directly linked with the contrast between Communist and non-Communist systems" has to be qualified to be a fair diagnosis. The grave danger of proliferation of nuclear weapons does not result from the contrast but from the anomaly of the continuation of sovereign nations in the atomic era. It would be fair to state that Western nations are as unprepared to surrender their national sovereignty as any other nation in the present world. But, this question left aside, the war threat does not result from the contrast between Communist and non-Communist systems but from the contrast between the two big powers, one Communist and one Western, which are so big and so highly developed that they can afford to maintain and develop an atomic-weapons system. The possession of atomic weaponry is a result of, and a display of, technological and economic development.

Fourth, Tinbergen acknowledges that "the Communist challenge, itself a result of the marked inequalities which existed in 19th century European societies, is considerably strengthened by the persistent inequalities in the low-income continents." This is, however, only one part of the truth, for the gravest aspect of the Communist challenge consists in what the author, in another connection, characterizes as the most basic and alarming feature of the underdevelopment problem, i.e., "the fact that in the non-Communist area the gap between the developed and the less developed countries is, generally speaking, increasing in terms of real income per head." [15] It is this fact of the increasing gap which gives the Communist system that basically challenging character, as viewed from the Western approach to international economic policy.

Fifth, for these reasons, Tinbergen's analysis of Communist economy, though adequate in itself, hardly touches the heart of the matter. There is some truth in his thesis of the converging movement of Communist and free economies,[16] but this views the

Soviet system in its stage of maturity and on its way to the stage of high mass-consumption. Hardly less relevant is the question whether Russian development has indeed been more rapid than the development of the Western countries, as the Communist Party claims, and as a number of Western economists deny. For the point at issue is not a comparison of the economic value of the two systems with respect to growth, but the question, What would have happened to Russia if the October Revolution had not occurred, and Russia had been forced to defend its backward position against the Western developed countries without the powerful aid of the Communist political and economic system? The most appropriate Western comment on Communist development, says Tinbergen, may be "that it is only natural that development can be speeded up if a sufficiently large portion of national income is invested and, further, that account must be taken of the sacrifices made in the form of a low level of consumption and the restraint of freedom." [17] However, if this is "only natural," then one may wonder why this solution is not employed by all the poor countries and why Western advisers do not recommend to them this simple and effective solution. Of course, the answer is that many developing countries do not want to make these sacrifices and that Western "doctors" do not want to recommend them. But as yet there is no convincing indication that the Western "doctor" is able to cure the disease without this operation. Tinbergen's belief in "mixed systems" as the optimum between a pure free-enterprise economy and a completely regimented economy[18] may be very well founded, but the crucial question remains: Will this belief produce palpable results in bridging the gap between rich and poor countries and between the Western and Communist worlds?

Sixth, though realizing that "the Communist world cannot be directly influenced by Western countries," and accepting the responsibility "to organize the best conceivable policy for the non-Communist part of the world," the author sees it as a mistake "to confine ourselves to the non-Communist world." He believes that "the ideas set out must be applied to the whole world. They must be used to give strength and perspective to the idea of a

truly *international order,* that is, they must be used to strengthen the United Nations." To those who will point out that the Communist countries may not want to cooperate and may even try to frustrate such activities as may be entrusted to the United Nations and its specialized agencies, his answer is, "first of all, that the aim of increasing world stability and peace is worth some risk; and secondly, that the risks seem to be small in the case of some of the tasks to be given to the United Nations." [19]

Then follow a number of suggestions for alternative possibilities for a world security system under the auspices of the United Nations. They are intended as "examples of a static analysis of security systems which seem to us to make sense even if they are much simpler than the dynamic analysis favored by some other authors." Tinbergen finds some comfort in a remark made by an economist with regard to business-cycle policy but equally applicable here: "We do not need to know the dynamics of the present unstable equilibrium just as an engineer does not need to know the dynamics of a collapsing bridge. What we need to know is the statics of a stable equilibrium, just as the engineer must know the statics of a bridge that will not collapse."

This is an excellent definition of the rationalist ethos behind this Western concept of international economic policy. What is being looked for is "a stable equilibrium, or at least . . . a more stable one." [20] Within the context of this system there can be no room for that revolutionary ethos which desperately needs "to know the dynamics of a collapsing bridge."

What is lacking in this superbly mature diagnostics and therapeutics is the insight that the Western "doctor," while doing his best to cure the ills of a failing world economy, may be himself unwittingly producing the virus which he tries to destroy. The three "challenges" which this policy-making finds itself facing may not emerge as external enemies but, in all probability, are conceived in the womb of the system of which this bridge-building engineering is itself an indissoluble part. The threat of a nuclear war—together with the threat of an international class struggle, the Cold War, and these three closely related challenges—belongs to the warp and woof of the development process; all are part of its

"rationale," of its logic, at least as long as the development process is dominated by this logic—and that is a question of power. The break with this dominating logic and, what is identical with it, the break with its power, is therefore a vehement drive behind those social revolutions which have passed beyond the hope that within the context of the given order any real cure is to be expected.

Ecumenical Ethos

There is no reason for surprise that an analogous ethos such as we have met in the economic reasoning of leading circles in modern India and in the economic policy-making of progressive Western scholars is also recognizable in contemporary ecumenical thinking on issues of world economic development. Needless to say, this ecumenical philosophy also shares its dilemma with the two other areas. Negative reasons for the interconnection among the three areas are to be found in the absence of Communist China on the present-day ecumenical platform and the nonexistence or great weakness of a contribution by the churches living under Communist regimes in the U.S.S.R., Eastern Europe, and Cuba to the shaping of ecumenical thinking on economic questions. Further, such radically critical voices as have been raised by representatives of Latin America (particularly by the Brazilian Catholic economist Candido Mendes de Almeida) are still too new and too rare to exert any perceivable influence on official ecumenical statements. Positive reasons emerge from the long and deeply ingrained Anglo-Saxon tradition of thinking in terms of harmony, equilibrium, balance, integration and cooperation, responsible rationality, and evolutionary change—a tradition which has left its mark, directly and indirectly, on each of the three areas. This tradition forms the backbone of the ecumenical movement to the present day; it is the main source of its greatness and success and, in the world and ecumenical situations which we are going to face in the next decades, the predominance of this tradition will be increasingly challenged. For what in the past has been its strength will become, in the future, its main weakness.

This does not mean that present-day ecumenical thinking on economic development should be unaware of the necessity of radical structural change. In recent official documents there is a definite recognition that "profound changes in the present structure of world economic relations" are needed. "All our fine phrases about 'human solidarity,' 'one world,' etc. sound hollow in the face of increasing international inequalities. If contemporary economic and social policies are failing to arrest this tendency, they must be radically altered." [21] We meet a realistic assessment that "economic and political power is concentrated in a few centres of the developed world," [22] that "our political and social institutions also resist changes" and that, "where fear or rigid unjust structures or the power of vested interests block change, development may be impossible." [23]

It is not denied that revolutionary solutions may be the only way out. "Dare we leave the roads to justice and peace so blocked that men who look to the future have to resort to violence where other ways are possible? It is the work of courageous dynamic love to break through these rigidities. There can be non-violent revolutions. All our efforts must be directed to change without violence. But if injustice is so embedded in the status quo and its supporters refuse to permit change, then as a last resort men's conscience may lead them in full and clear sighted responsibility without hate or rancour to engage in violent revolution. A heavy burden then rests on those who have resisted change." [24] One document acknowledges that "in some countries economic development may demand a profound revolutionary change in the structure of property, income, investment, expenditure, education, and political and administrative organization, as well as in the present patterns of international relations." [25] Another report summons the churches in developing countries to "realize the need for revolutionary change" and recognizes that "the building of political structures suitable to national development involves revolutionary changes in social structures. . . . In countries where the ruling groups are oppressive or indifferent to the aspirations of the people, are often supported by foreign interests, and seek to resist all changes by the use of coercive or violent measures, including the 'law and

order' which may itself be a form of violence, the revolutionary change may take a violent form." Of course, "revolution is not to be identified with violence," and "the churches have a special contribution toward the development of effective non-violent strategies of revolution and social change." But Christians are called "to participate creatively in the building of political institutions to implement the social changes that are desperately needed." [26]

These references to recent ecumenical statements might give the impression of a revolutionary approach to the present world economic situation. However, even a casual reading of the reports is sufficient to falsify this suggestion. Passages like those quoted are rare and the tendency which they seem to support has a very marginal place within the total context. In spite of the existing and increasing tensions which are referred to, the general perspective is that of a great and fascinating call to "world cooperation for development." We live in a new world of exciting prospects. For the first time in history men can see the unity of mankind as a reality. The new technological possibilities turn what were dreams into realities. The adventure of cooperation with all men for the development of the earth for all men is open for all of us. Of course, the worldwide struggle of the less developed peoples to achieve better living conditions is a dramatic feature of our changing world, but this renders even more urgent the task of the prosperous countries to aid the effort; it demands further progress in forms of international collaboration and international organization and requires an "education for world citizenship and development." [27]

Within the context of this great perspective all parts of mankind have to contribute their share. The developing countries must achieve a much more rapid rate of growth, the developed countries must decisively increase the volume and quality of their assistance, the socialist nations of Eastern Europe should be encouraged to expand their efforts to promote development in some countries, the United Nations agencies should be strengthened and utilized more fully, and the United Nations is urged to complete its development strategy for the 1970's with all due speed. [28]

It is obvious that development strategy is basically considered from the viewpoint of a world economic order, which can and should be implemented by the harmonious cooperation of all aspects—social, cultural, religious—of a growing world civilization. The political factor is, of course, not overlooked, but it plays a very subservient role. "The political structures of developed nations must shed all tendencies to exploit economically or to dominate the poorer, and therefore weaker, economies of other nations. More positively, the developed nations must also structure their aid and trade so that these do not become instruments of their own political, ideological and security interests, narrowly conceived; in fact there is need to develop a political climate which can adapt development policies transcending purely ideological and political interests." As an example of the kind of change in attitude which is meant, "the lifting of the economic blockade of Cuba" is mentioned.[29]

The addition of this specific example in the Report of Section III, World Economic and Social Development, of the Fourth Assembly (Uppsala, 1968) of the World Council of Churches deserves in itself a word of appreciation, for it constitutes a concrete application of the generalities which so often fill documents of this type. But what a Report like this terms "maximum" is, in fact, less than a minimum in comparison with the real political issues at stake in a world development strategy. Even the lifting of the economic blockade would not alter anything in the essential power relationships between Cuba and its mighty neighbor. The real question is not whether developed nations are morally obliged to adopt development policies which transcend purely ideological and political interests, but whether developing nations which feel themselves threatened by rich and mighty countries are morally obliged to defend their own development chances with all the means at their disposal and whether they have a right and a duty to structure their policies to the benefit of their own political, ideological, and security interests.

The key role of the state in the process is frankly recognized. It is the function of the state to devise policies "that will encourage the whole citizenry to undertake a creative and disciplined effort

and inculcate in them a sense of responsibility." [30] The government of a developing nation "should be able to enthuse the people to make the sacrifices and to accept the measures necessary for development, by a program of distributive justice." [31] The leaders of developing nations "will have to mobilize and inspire their people and work against the traditions, structures and political forces standing in the way of economic and social progress. To do so will require the use of all avenues of communication and influence." [32] All this is being recognized regarding the internal policies of developing nations. But in an ecumenical philosophy based on the concept of world cooperation for development, the crucial problem is: Are the external policies of developing nations, whose leaders are expected to mobilize and inspire their peoples against the political forces standing in the way of economic and social progress, compatible with this concept of supranational strategy? How is it possible for developing nations to cooperate with the very forces that thwart their development?

It is an essential weakness of the kind of development philosophy presented by ecumenical statements thus far that it deals with the economic issues of world development without the political context of international power relations. The result is a sympathetic Christian idealism, based on lofty moral principles and full of valuable recommendations, which derives its concrete significance from the excellent advices of experts on international economic policy-making. But it is a humanism which hardly touches the hard facts of a revolutionary world and without the backbone of the grim issues of nuclear war threats and guerrilla activities.

Rationality of unbalanced growth. We should not think, however, that the perspective of balance, harmony, and security is the only possible viewpoint for a rational development policy. The very dilemma resulting from the application of this type of perspective to developing societies has challenged social scientists and political economists to draw into the center of their analysis of development processes those elements which do not otherwise receive their due place. Political economist Albert O. Hirschman, who has had intensive experience as an economic consultant in Latin America, conceives development as "a chain of disequili-

bria." [33] This approach places particular importance on pressures, tensions, and disequilibrium. This does not mean that Hirschman disregards the question whether the response to such situations is not at times going to be destructive and whether these tensions could not lead to the adoption of wholly irrational policies.

Nevertheless, Hirschman does not think it desirable to suppress these tensions. His basic argument consists in the consideration that underdeveloped countries already operate under the "grand tension" that stems from the universal desire for economic improvement oddly combined with resistances to change. "Much is to be said for breaking down this grand tension, a highly explosive mixture of hopes and fears, into a series of smaller and more manageable tensions." [34] Development carries with it many strains and stresses, but, and this is even more important, it draws new strength from the tension it creates. Therefore, our aim must be to *keep* rather than to eliminate the disequilibria of which profits and losses are symptoms in a competitive economy. If the economy is to be kept moving ahead, the task of development policy is to maintain tensions, disproportions, and disequilibria. That "nightmare of equilibrium economics, the endless spinning cobweb," is "the kind of mechanism we must assiduously look for as an invaluable help in the development process." Therefore, the sequence that "leads away from 'equilibrium' is precisely an ideal pattern of development from this point of view, for each move in the sequence is induced by a previous disequilibrium and in turn creates a new disequilibrium that requires a further move." [35]

From the viewpoint of the social sciences there are reasons for suspecting the way in which the analysis of the growth processes of advanced industrial countries has yielded an apparatus of ready applicability to the most primitive economies. In principle there is nothing reprehensible in the attempt to make the "economics of development," i.e., of the underdeveloped countries, benefit from the recent vigorous advances of the "economics of growth," i.e., of the economically advanced countries. But there are strong indications that the "economics of growth" is primarily relevant to the conditions under which it was conceived. It grew directly out of the stagnation and economic depression of the late thirties and

fear of what might follow the Second World War. Since the post-war period has been free from the threat of the stagnation for which the growth models were primarily designed, the theory has found its principal field of application in the planning of development for underdeveloped countries. But the model may become a hindrance rather than a help in the understanding of the reality of underdeveloped countries. The economics of development dare not borrow too extensively from the economics of growth; like the underdeveloped countries themselves, it must learn to walk on its own feet, which means that it must work out its own abstractions.[36]

A case in point is the theory of investment, which Hirschman mentions as the most unsatisfactory aspect of the growth models of advanced economies. In these economies investment is constantly living from hand to mouth, it follows hard on the heels of technical progress. From the point of investment incentives, the capitalist system, especially as it existed in the nineteenth century, is hard to beat. The balance between the social costs the entrepreneur caused but escaped and the social benefit he failed to turn into profits was likely to be favorable for many entrepreneurs. This was so particularly with respect to the introduction of new products that competed successfully with close substitutes, and of new technology that resulted in the abandonment of traditional processes. In other words, it was the peculiar lack of internalization implicit in the private-enterprise system—the way in which the institutions of that system concealed certain costs from the entrepreneurs—that was largely responsible for the dynamic economic changes that took place. Hirschman readily admits that "such an explanation of economic progress in the nineteeth century has little in common with Adam Smith's Invisible Hand; it is far more reminiscent of Hegel's *List der Vernunft*"![37]

Economic development brings disruption of traditional ways of living, of producing, and of doing things, in the course of which there have always been many losses; old skills become obsolete, old trades are ruined, city slums mushroom, crime and suicide multiply, etc., etc. And to these social costs many others must be added, from air pollution to unemployment. A major difficulty for the speedy industrialization of today's underdeveloped countries

consists precisely in the fact that they are not prepared to incur those social costs so spectacularly associated with the process during the early nineteenth century in Western Europe. They are forcing their young entrepreneurial class, as well as their taxpayers in general, to internalize a good portion of these costs through advanced social-security, minimum-wage, and collective-bargaining legislation, through subsidized low-cost housing and similar Welfare State measures.

The balanced-growth doctrine is usually invoked to provide a justification for centralized governmental direction and coordination of the development process. However, this has most frequently been urged, not in order to provide more impetus to development through the adding up of all the gains, but to introduce some of the social costs into the economic calculus and thus to temper the ruthlessness and destructiveness of capitalist development. Some sacrifice in the speed of the process of creative destruction is considered worthwhile if it could be made a bit less destructive of material, cultural, and spiritual values. However, centrally planned economies have abundant recourse to the old capitalist trick of shutting out of the economic calculus a variety of social costs that are being incurred in the process of growth. As a result, they may well achieve accelerated growth—not by practicing internalization but by reneging on it.[38]

The Soviet Economy

It is from the viewpoint of a centrally planned economy that the peculiar dynamics of the economics of development are approached by the British economist Alec Nove. Born in Leningrad, Professor Nove's main studies have concerned the development and structure of the Soviet economy. Nove is deeply conscious of the inadequacies of much Western economic analysis of the dynamics of change and he stresses the fact that the problems of underdeveloped countries raise many of the questions with which Soviet economists have been wrestling. Have Western economists, he asks, in fact any sort of agreed approach to the economic problems of development?

Can we really be satisfied with the (usually unconscious) philosophical assumptions underlying welfare economics? In the face of these question marks, he believes that it is as well to approach the errors and omissions of Soviet economists without any undue superiority complex.[39]

If the U.S.S.R. has indeed succeeded in overcoming many serious obstacles to growth, has built up its economic might so rapidly, then perhaps its policies and its economic structure were not, after all, so very irrational. Perhaps the weaknesses and distortions are the obverse side of methods of industrialization which have, or had, a rationality of their own. Unless we appreciate this, we shall be in imminent danger of falling into the error of regarding essential features of the Soviet economic system merely as aberrations, or as the projection into the economic field of the power-seeking megalomania of particular leaders. A particularly useful corrective is to examine those features of the system which arose in response to problems of development as such. This task is facilitated by the growing literature on development, produced by Western economists who have studied how to overcome obstacles.[40] The crucial question is: What constitutes rationality in a developing country, if one takes as given the decision to industrialize and to grow? Any discussion of rationality or waste must be related to some objective or value judgment. There are levels of rationality as well as conflicting kinds of rationality.[41] The Soviet authorities took as axiomatic the political decision that rapid industrialization is the overriding aim of public policy. Of course, it does not follow that they proceeded by the most rational route toward the aim they set themselves. There are at least two senses of the word "rational" which should be carefully distinguished. The first relates to some kind of optimum behavior designed to fulfill the requirements of the existing socio-economic pattern. The second species of rationality takes the aims as determined from outside the economy and then seeks the most efficient way to achieve these results. In some circumstances, what is called "hortatory planning" (targets, strains, campaigns, etc.) may actually be the most rational way to achieve rapid "development" results if certain costs can be disregarded.[42] Development involves

actions which are political and social and have a logic of their own. Insofar as such actions serve the cause of development, they must be held to fulfill economic purposes, yet these same actions *as such* may well inflict economic loss, and if one were merely seeking the *economically* most rational means of achieving given ends, they could well be utterly illogical and pointless. To take a non-Soviet example, the spirit of nationalism might be an essentially unifying factor, a basic motivating force for development, in some countries; this could give rise in certain circumstances to the political necessity of taking measures against foreign firms, measures which, in themselves, actually harm development.[43] Irrationalities at one level may appear logical on another. If the state requires assured service and revenues, it might well see logic in a form of organization which discourages inefficient operation of agriculture. All military organizations stress discipline and obedience, to the detriment of other qualities; the resultant micro-irrationalities and waste are known to everyone who has served in any army. The waste involved is partly the *cost* of the given system.[44]

The Polish Marxist economist Oscar Lange once described the Soviet method of crash-program industrialization as *"sui generis* a war economy."[45] It was a "war economy" because of the element of all-out concentration on politically determined objectives, a situation full of campaigning and of emergency, of acute shortages and arbitrariness, which involved neglect of many economic desiderata. In such circumstances, just as in war economies in Western countries, central decisions about resource allocation became decisive throughout the system. Even the most orthodox economists would probably agree that military operations have a rationality of their own. The creation of capacity to produce guns is no less legitimate an objective than an advertising campaign designed to persuade American housewives that they must throw away their refrigerators or cars in order to buy the very latest model. Anyway, the use of war-economy methods in peacetime to make the means of waging war in wartime is not wholly illogical.[46] The Soviet economy in peacetime was engaged, in effect, in a politico-military operation. Far from being willing to give expression to the socio-economic forces in existence, it was seeking

to alter or to repress these forces. The sheer pace of advance and of change was such that a large part of the demand was itself a consequence of the process of change. The planners were constantly struggling with priority problems, which occupied most of their time and demanded unremitting attention. The existence of a large underemployed peasant population presents economists and politicians alike with problems which are not always to be judged by the criteria of economic rationality that Western economists regard as "normal." In addition, if a deliberate program of modernization is being carried through, there often occurs a long period of extremely uneven development. The industrialization drive itself would not have been launched if criteria of "normal" economic rationality were used. Revolutionary changes were in progress, imposed by a government disinclined to count the cost. There were hardly any periods of normalcy in which the system could settle down. Given the nature of the regime, of the economic tasks with which it was endeavoring to cope, the disturbed history of the period, and also the hostility of the ideology to any talk of economic rationality, the net effect was to perpetuate forms of economic organization designed to achieve rapid results in priority sectors by quantitative direction. Such an approach renders impossible any systematic attempt to achieve rationality in its restricted sense (a fact also encountered in the West during the period of wartime planning).[47]

Of course, the claim that one is pursuing certain aims does not exempt the "pursuers" from criticism at any level of their activities. Some obstacles were tackled with such crude brutality that the damage caused came in itself to constitute an obstacle. Nor is it legitimate to claim that no other way existed for Russia to industrialize. Further, as far as the present stage and the prospects for the near future are concerned, with the transition to a more mature economy, the nature of rationality has, so to speak, changed its meaning. The very considerable slowdown in Soviet economic growth in the most recent years has underlined the fact that the Soviet planners face formidable problems as they search for a way of adapting their system to the requirements of the mid-twentieth century.

Yet, it remains true that what did happen had a certain logic, that it was connected with the problems of rapid development in postrevolutionary Russia, and that many of the problems encountered are common to underdeveloped countries in general. It is the great merit of Nove's picture of the relative efficiency of the Soviet economic system that he takes these things into account. He offers a view of rationality rather wider than that adopted by many Western economists who examine the Soviet scene and development problems in general.[48]

The Great Ascent

The insight that the path of development to be followed by less developed countries must be fundamentally different from the former course of Western countries is common to the type of approach we have been considering. The economist Robert L. Heilbroner sketches the process of economic development as the "Great Ascent" propelling the underdeveloped areas into world history. To most of the backward lands, economic development comes not as the culmination of a long process of social evolution, but as a discontinuous jump from one form of social system to another and radically dissimilar one. Whereas a long period of preparation preceded the commencement of the industrial era in the West, the underdeveloped areas must begin their leap into industrialization without these preconditions. It is only by profound social and political transformation that the Great Ascent will get into motion, and the momentum of the Ascent will itself inaugurate still further social and political change.[49]

These changes are apt to be revolutionary in nature. Characteristically, Heilbroner makes the same kind of distinction between two types of "revolutions" that we discussed in the preceding chapter: "Thus at the heart of the development process lurks a revolutionary potential—revolutionary not in the sense of a gradual redistribution of power and wealth such as accompanied the Industrial Revolution, but in the sense of a drastic, rapid, and painful redistribution such as accompanied the French or Russian

revolutions." It is dangerously wrong to picture economic development as a long, invigorating climb from achievement to achievement. On the contrary, it is better imagined as a gigantic social earthquake, marked not by rising expectations but by a loss of traditional expectations. For the underlying masses, development is apt to be a time of awakening hostilities, of newly felt frustrations, of growing impatience and dissatisfaction. The Great Ascent is likely to be a time of increased disharmony and discontent. The privileged classes in the underdeveloped lands sense the revolutionary potentials which the momentum of economic development could release; thus it becomes associated with political change of a highly charged kind, in which whole social classes can be destroyed and basic institutions remodeled. It is, therefore, hard to see how the elementary preconditions of development can be established short of political revolution. And it seems unlikely, if political revolution does occur, that it will bring to power governments dedicated to the promotion of economic development along nineteenth-century lines.[50]

The price of development is likely to be the exercise of authoritarian power, both political and economic. Mild men will not ride the tigers of development. Neither will mild political or economic systems contain or impel it. The logic of events points to the formation of economic systems and political regimes which will seek to *impose* development on their peoples. But even the most rigorous governments can speed up development only to a degree. The rising level of frustration, unavoidable even under the sternest discipline, will almost surely have to be channeled into directions other than that of economic expectations. Hence a deliberately heightened nationalism, a carefully planned ideological fervor, even military adventures are a likely by-product of development which is more likely to heighten international friction than to constitute a new force for world peace.

Apparently there is a deep-rooted relationship between Communism and economic development. The partial failures of Communist development policies (particularly in the reorganization of agriculture) and its very revolutionary ruthlessness which is the intolerable aspect to many non-Communist peoples must be com-

pared with the greater failure and the even less tolerable situation which exist in the virtual absence of any development in many of the backward lands. What is crucial is that Communism, as an ideology and as a practical political movement, is prepared to undertake the revolutionary reorganization of society—a task from which non-Communist governments shrink. Whether or not the revolutionary regimes of development are finally pushed into the Communist orbit, however, there is no doubt that these regimes will identify themselves as being within the *socialist* orbit. The inner tensions of the development process promise the appearance of "socialism" on a worldwide scale, a fact which presents the capitalist West with a wholly new environment.[51]

This realistic picture of the prospects of the Great Ascent, which Heilbroner aptly characterizes as the "development revolution," confirms our thesis of the inherent revolutionary implications of the development process. Development and revolution are not mutually exclusive, nor is revolution an unlucky exception to the general law of gradual evolution. To the contrary, development is a revolutionary process in its very nature. Development is the great revolutionary agent of modern history.

NOTES

1. Hans Kohn, *The Idea of Nationalism* (New York, 1956), pp. 272ff.
2. W. W. Rostow, *The Stages of Economic Growth* (Cambridge, Mass., 1961).
3. From a speech, September 26, 1963.
4. Wilbert E. Moore, *Social Change* (Englewood Cliffs, N.J., 1965), pp. 35ff.
5. *Ibid.*, pp. 116f.
6. Cf. Michel Bergmann, "Impact of the Development Myth," *The Ecumenical Review,* Vol. XIX, No. 4 (October, 1967), pp. 368ff.
7. S. L. Parmar, "Concern for Man in the Quest for Development," *The Ecumenical Review,* Vol. XIX, No. 4 (October, 1967), pp. 356ff.

8. M. M. Thomas, "Modernisation of Traditional Societies and the Struggle for New Cultural Ethos," *The Ecumenical Review,* Vol. XVIII, No. 4 (October, 1966), p. 435.

9. S. L. Parmar, *op. cit.,* p. 359.

10. Gunnar Myrdal, *Beyond the Welfare State* (New Haven, 1965), pp. 134f.

11. *Ibid.,* p. 40.

12. *Ibid.,* pp. 227f.

13. Jan Tinbergen, *Shaping the World Economy* (New York, 1962).

14. *Ibid.,* pp. 180f.

15. *Ibid.,* p. 8.

16. *Ibid.,* p. 34.

17. *Ibid.,* p. 33.

18. *Ibid.,* p. 181.

19. *Ibid.,* pp. 184f.

20. *Ibid.,* pp. 188f.

21. World Conference on Church and Society, "Economic Development in a World Perspective," Report of Section I, par. 151 and 101.

22. *Ibid.,* par. 109.

23. "World Development: the Challenge to the Churches," Report of the Conference on World Cooperation for Development, submitted to the World Council of Churches and the Pontifical Commission on Justice and Peace (April, 1968), Beirut, Lebanon (Special Report Doc. No. 1, W.C.C. Fourth Assembly, Uppsala, 1968), Ch. 1, par. 14 and 16. Cf. A. McCormack, "World Cooperation for Development—The Beirut Conference," *World Justice,* Vol. X, No. 1 (September, 1968), pp. 5ff. Cf. also Statement of the Beirut Conference on World Cooperation for Development, in *The Ecumenical Review,* Vol. XX, No. 3 (July, 1968), pp. 299ff.

24. Report of the Beirut Conference, Ch. 1, par. 17.

25. Report of Section I, World Conference on Church and Society, par. 47.

26. "World Economic and Social Development," Report of Section III, Fourth Assembly of the World Council of Churches, Uppsala (July, 1968), par. 39 and 15.

27. Report of the Beirut Conference, Ch. 1, par. 4; Ch. 2, par. 1 and 3; Ch. 4, par. 4.

28. *Ibid.,* Ch. 3, par. 2, 34, 41, 48; Ch. 4, par. 18.

29. Report of Section III, Fourth Assembly of the World Council of Churches, par. 17.
30. Report of Section I, World Conference on Church and Society par. 97.
31. Report of Section III, Fourth Assembly of the World Council of Churches, par. 15.
32. Report of the Beirut Conference, Ch. 3, par. 4.
33. Albert O. Hirschman, *The Strategy of Economic Development* (New Haven, 1965).
34. *Ibid.*, p. 209.
35. *Ibid.*, pp. 66f.
36. *Ibid.*, pp. 29ff.
37. *Ibid.*, pp. 33ff., 58f.
38. *Ibid.*, pp. 54ff., 61.
39. Alec Nove, *The Soviet Economy* (rev. ed.; New York, 1965), pp. 302f.
40. *Ibid.*, pp. 304f
41. Alec Nove, "Some Random Thoughts on Irrationality and Waste," *Survey*, a Journal of Soviet and East European Studies (July, 1967), p. 143.
42. Nove, *The Soviet Economy*, p. 155.
43. Gunnar Myrdal, *Economic Theory and Underdeveloped Regions* (London, 1957), p. 73.
44. Alec Nove, "Some Random Thoughts . . . ," *Survey*, pp. 143f.
45. In *Survey, op. cit.*, p. 152.
46. *Ibid.*, p. 153.
47. *The Soviet Economy*, pp. 153ff.
48. *Ibid.*, pp. 310ff.
49. Robert L. Heilbroner, *The Great Ascent:* The Struggle for Economic Development in Our Time (New York, 1963), pp. 8, 124f.
50. *Ibid.*, pp. 17ff., 132ff.
51. *Ibid.*, pp. 20, 135ff.

CHAPTER FOUR

Revolution

Anatomy of Revolution

In *The Anatomy of Revolution*,[1] Crane Brinton has focused his interest upon a definite type of revolution which we meet in modern history. It includes the four great overturns in previously stable political societies in the past: the English Revolution of the 1640's and its sequel in 1688; the American Revolution; the French Revolution and its nineteenth-century sequels; the Russian Revolution of 1917 and its twentieth-century sequels. His focus is on drastic, sudden substitution of one group in charge of the running of a territorial political entity for another group. He does not assume that these four revolutions are typical, nor does he attempt to find a Platonic idea of revolution; he simply takes this series as a starting-point for a work of systematization still in its infancy. He is well aware that there are many other revolutions on record and that anything like a complete sociology of revolutions would have to take into account other kinds of revolutions, notably, three: the revolution initiated by authoritarians, oligarchies, or conservatives, that is, the "Rightist" revolution; the territorial-nationalist revolution; and the abortive revolution. His main scheme has been derived from an analysis of the course of three of the four revolutions he is studying—the English, the French, and the Russian—which have surprisingly similar features. All had a

social or class rather than a territorial or nationalistic basis. All were begun in hope and moderation, reached a crisis in a reign of terror, and ended in something like dictatorship. The American Revolution does not fit perfectly into this conceptual scheme. As a social revolution, it was in a sense an incomplete one, and it does not show the victory of the extremists over the moderates. For this very reason it can serve as a kind of control over against the scheme of the other three revolutions.

A decisive characteristic in the preparation for revolution is what L. P. Edwards in his *Natural History of Revolutions* has described as the "transfer of the allegiance of the intellectuals." Of course, Brinton realizes that the "desertion of the intellectuals" is not a sufficient cause for revolution in itself, for there are many periods in which societies faced a disengagement and bitter criticism of intellectual circles, but it did not lead to an overturn of political and social structures. Certainly, all revolutions have been anticipated by revolutionary ideas and ideals, in other words by a revolutionary ideology.

Another common feature, according to Brinton, is that in the old regime the ruling class seems to be divided, inept, and unsuited to fulfill its functions, whereas among the middle and parts of the lower classes there are more than normally strong sentiments, hostile to the ruling classes. In the first step of a revolution two parties come into clear opposition, and indeed there is violence and by the end of this period the revolutionary party has defeated the old regime, but the miracle is that the hated old regime acquiesced so easily. This honeymoon stage of revolution was most perfectly developed in France, where the revolution came in peacetime, and at the end of a great intellectual movement, called the Enlightenment, which had prepared men's minds for a new and practical miracle. But once the victory has been won, the new government faces a new set of problems and the honeymoon is soon over. It was a French moderate, Vergniaud, who qualified the next stage neatly by the famous phrase: "the revolution, like Saturn, devours its children." Soon after the fall of an old regime, signs become evident that the victors have less homogeneity and party discipline

than appeared to be the case when they were "the opposition." Moreover, they find ranged against them an increasingly strong and intransigent group of radicals and extremists who insist that the moderates are trying to stop the revolution and have betrayed it. Thus, after a period—brief in Russia, longer in France and England—there came a show of force between moderates and extremists, and the latter in their turn took power. Although in the American Revolution the process was not quite the same, the Declaration of Independence was the fruit of the victory of the radicals over the moderates.

In each of these four revolutions, Brinton discovers a tendency for power to shift from Right to Center to Left, from the conservatives of the old regime to the moderates to the radicals or extremists.[2] After each crisis the victors tend to split into a more conservative wing holding power and a more radical one in opposition. Up to a certain point, each succeeding crisis sees the radical opposition triumphant. With the final overthrow of the moderates the revolution may be said to have entered its crisis stage.

In all these societies the successful extremists were few in number and very conscious of their fewness—this is one of the great sources of the extremists' strength, for the masses do not make revolutions. Even twentieth-century revolutions, in spite of their apparent successes in producing a miraculous mass participation, have been achieved by small, disciplined, principled, fanatical bodies. The awareness on the part of the extremists of their few numbers seems to correlate with the intensity of their fanaticism, and with this fanatical devotion one finds a rigid discipline under an effective leadership directed to the realization of the revolutionary ends.

The extremists are not politically inexperienced when they come to power, for they have had long experience with oppression, as well as a briefer but very intensive training in actual government before they attain full power. Their success is due to their admirable adaptation to the special, the unique environment of crisis. This crisis in the "fever" of revolution is commonly called "the

Reign of Terror": the extremists have disposed of all important conflicting groups and have consolidated by installing a centralized system of government.

In his analysis of this crisis period, Brinton makes a sharp distinction between the position of the outsider and that of the insider.[3] For the outsider—the man who makes up the bulk of modern societies, who on the whole accepts what others do in politics, and soon jumps onto the bandwagon—the revolution, especially in this crisis period, is very difficult. It may provide him with a number of spectacles in the form of various celebrations of the new revolutionary cults, but the outsider soon tires of this, as many indications in the French Revolution, for instance, suggest. The revolutionary mania for renaming places and objects also confuses and annoys the outsider. But the heaviest strain is placed upon him by two phases in the Reign of Terror: First, the unmistakable puritanical or ascetic quality, characteristic of all four revolutions at their crisis. And, second, the very strong pressure which the new authorities exert on his privacy. The outsider is not only denied access to what he probably regards as legitimate amusement, but he is not even left to himself. In the crisis period, the revolution hounds the common man in whatever he does: even the conventional backbiting, gossips, dislikes of ordinary social life are intensified beyond endurance.

But what is an almost unbearable pressure to the outsider is the very source of psychological satisfaction for the insider, a satisfaction commonly supplied by what we call religion. In the crisis period the orthodox and successful extremists are crusaders, fanatics, ascetics, men who seek to bring heaven to earth. They are convinced that they are the elect, destined to carry out the will of God, nature, or science. There is, in this respect, uniformity in the English, the French, and the Russian revolutions. Calvinism, Jacobism, Marxism are all rigidly deterministic. "God for the Calvinist, nature and reason for the Jacobin, dialectical or scientific materialism for the Marxist, provide comforting assurance that the believer is on the side that *must* win."[4] The opponents of these revolutions are not just political enemies, not just damned fools; they are sinners, and must be completely wiped out.

If we regard revolutions as a kind of fever, which Brinton does, then the climax of the revolution, the Reign of Terror, can be aptly described as the crisis accompanied by delirium. But this cannot continue for long. After the crisis comes a period of convalescence, perhaps marked by one or two relapses; but finally the fever is over and the patient is himself again, immunized for a while from a similar attack. Following the historical example of the French Revolution, this final phase is characterized as "the Thermidorean reaction." [5] For the end of the crisis in France may be dated from the fall of Robespierre in July, 1794, or in the month Thermidor of the second year of the new French calendar.

There exists a certain kind of uniformity in phenomena in various revolutions. For instance:

The English Revolution was in its Thermidorean period when Cromwell was installed as Protector in 1653 (followed in four years by his appointment as Lord Protector), and with the restoration of the Stuarts in 1660 the great English Revolution may be said to end. In France, the execution of Robespierre was followed some years later by a striking revival of Jacobinism, and when in the last year of the eighteenth century Napoleon Bonaparte had achieved his *coup d'état,* the French convalescence was nearly over. For the Russian Revolution the 1917–1921 period of war may be regarded as its first main crisis, whereas the New Economic Policy of 1921 may be said to have introduced Russia's Thermidor, which still prevails to a degree in the mid-twentieth century. [6]

This sketchy survey of what has been called an "anatomy" of the great revolutions in modern Western history leaves us with some pertinent questions. One concerns the essential function of revolutions in the perspective of history if there is truth in the fever metaphor. Certainly, diseases may be said to have their necessary function within the organic system of the human body, but it cannot be denied that they are diseases, abnormal phenomena, disturbances in the normal equilibrium of physical health. After the disease passes, it should be forgotten. The original equilibrium is restored and the disease has no remaining function. On balance, it belongs to the debit side.

But this kind of approach, which may be adequate to biological phenomena, hardly leads to a real understanding of the deeper meaning of these revolutions. There is a noticeable antithesis between this concept of revolution as a disturbance of normal health and the outspoken conviction of the leaders of the revolutions themselves, who proclaim their goal as the very restoration of health in order to save a deathly sick body. Far from being a kind of dangerous bacilli they consider themselves as the doctors. Not chaos but the bringing of order is their final motive. It is very doubtful, therefore, whether this conceptual scheme of physical health is really adequate, for an anatomy of revolution attempts more than a surface analysis. If we switch from the metaphor of physical health to the dimension of mental health, the evaluation will be much more complicated. It is extremely difficult to measure exactly what type of mental condition is to be considered as normal, for this varies with each person and depends upon the structure of the individual character. Moreover, in the course of personal evolution the norm of mental equilibrium itself may undergo considerable changes. But what is still more important, many creative personalities are far from "balanced," and in individual life the most creative phases are often those which come very near to a state of fever.

There is a series of phenomena which Brinton's surgical knife is able to discover, but it fails to give anything like a satisfactory interpretation. The very fact that modern Western history is marked by a succession of deep incisions should already make us wonder whether these so-called disturbances may, on deeper analysis, prove to be more characteristic than the so-called equilibrium gained after the fever passes. The remarkable phenomenon of the revolutionary mania for renaming—which is, to be sure, the creation of a new language—should be an indication of the radical break which these revolutions pretend to represent. Another indication is the parallel between the self-sacrifice and devotion to religious ideals of the French and the Russian revolutionaries.

The statement that these four revolutions of Western history "show a progressively increasing hostility to organized Christianity"

goes a step further. "There is a secular touch even to the seventeenth-century English revolution, and an overwhelming preponderance of emphasis on the individual conscience over against the corporate church and its traditions; the French and even the American revolution are full in the tide of eighteenth-century secularism; the Russian revolution is proudly materialistic." This progressive hostility to organized Christianity becomes even more interesting when it is deduced from a Christian origin and is considered as a secularization of Christian eschatology. "What separates these revolutionaries from traditional Christianity is most obviously their insistence on having their heaven here, now, on earth, their impatient intent to conquer evil once and for all." [7] The English millenarians expected the second coming year after year. The French Jacobins expected the perfect republic of liberty, equality, and fraternity to restore as it were a new heaven on earth. The Russian Revolution was inspired by the vision of the classless society. Thus it may be asked whether this increasing hostility against Christianity is only a series of fevers or may its remarkable dependence upon Christian eschatology also be interpreted as a desperate attempt to restore the original health of a sick body? And is there some sense in this increase, which is hardly to be understood from the viewpoint of a nearly cyclical concept of revolution?

Another indication of some kind of progress is found in Brinton's remark that these four revolutions exhibit an increasing scale of promises to the "common man," promises which today are made more vigorously in China, in Southeast Asia, and in the Near East. He adds: "It would be folly for us to tell the world that we Americans can fill the promises, especially since we have not filled them at home. Revolution is not a fever that will yield such innocent and deceptive remedies. For a time, at least, we must accept it as being as incurable as cancer." [8]

Pointing in the same direction is his statement that the Russian Revolution is, in a sense, still going on. The fact that, in spite of many signs of a Thermidorean reaction after 1921, the old regime was not restored makes it difficult to dismiss the Russian Revolution as finished. If this is true, then the anatomy of the

Russian Revolution differs from that of the others. But this important concession is a further indication of the failure of this anatomy of revolution to answer the questions it raises. The comparison with cancer goes a step further than the metaphor of fever, for it points to a disease which thus far medical science has not been able to cure.

But why should we approach the enigmatic phenomenon of revolution only from this negative point of view? Since Western history, followed by contemporary world history, is full of revolutions—and history, in spite of increasing risks and dangers, has as yet not succumbed to cancer—there might be hidden in this series of revolutions a creative principle which, far from being pernicious for the human genus, could preserve some elements which are the very source of survival.

The Meaning of Revolution

We need a depth analysis, capable of penetrating into the core of the great revolutionary turning-points that mark modern history and of discovering their hidden meaning. The fundamental weakness of Brinton's anatomy is that it is based on a pattern of thought which is closely akin to the ancient concept of political change. Polybius has given a classical expression of that concept in his description of "the rotation of constitutions," telling how every form of government is doomed to degeneration and failure, not because it is inherently wrong but because it is bound to fall into the hands of the wrong men. There is a cyclic recurrence in human affairs by reason of their always being driven to extremes. Antiquity conceived history as a cycle, in which a course is preordained by the very nature of human affairs and therefore is unchangeable.

Within this concept a real understanding of the meaning of revolution is impossible, for revolutions are the very political events which confront us directly and inevitably with the problem of beginning. This insight is one of the main pillars of Hannah Arendt's study *On Revolution*.[9] The author has made use of the work of

the German historian Karl Griewank, who made a pioneering analysis of the modern concept of revolution.[10] Being herself of German origin and having come to the United States during the Second World War, Miss Arendt has attempted a fascinating confrontation between the political order which has emerged from the American Revolution and the historical fate of the French Revolution and its twentieth-century successors.

The reader will recall that in the course of our discussion of scientific revolutions (see Ch. One), we hinted at what is a keynote in Miss Arendt's study, the notion of novelty. The modern concept of revolution, inextricably bound up with the notion that the course of history suddenly begins anew, was unknown prior to the great revolutions at the end of the eighteenth century. Both the French and the American Revolutions were played out in their initial stages by men who were firmly convinced that they would do no more than restore an old order of things and "revolve" back to former times when things had been as they ought to be.

What made these "restorations" into real revolutions was a new experience, the experience of being free. Only where this pathos of novelty is present and where novelty is connected with the idea of freedom are we entitled to speak of revolution. These two things together—a new experience and man's capacity for novelty revealed by it—are at the root of the enormous pathos which we find in both the American and the French Revolutions, this ever-repeated insistence that nothing comparable in grandeur and significance had ever happened in the whole recorded history of mankind. This means of course that revolutions are more than successful insurrections and that we are not justified in calling every *coup d'état* a revolution or even in detecting one in each civil war. Though words like "rebellion" and "revolt" have had a well-defined meaning since the later Middle Ages, they never indicated liberation as the revolutions came to understand it, and even less did they point to the establishment of a new freedom. For liberation in the revolutionary sense came to mean that the vast majority of mankind, the oppressed and the poor, all those who had always lived in darkness and subjection to whatever powers there were, should rise and become the supreme sovereigns

of the land. This had never happened. The very idea that equality is a birthright was utterly unknown before the modern age.[11]

A third essential element for a true understanding of the spirit of modern revolutions is the role of violence. Of course, violence is no more adequate to describe the phenomenon of revolution than change; only where change occurs in the sense of a new beginning, where violence is used to constitute a new body politic, where the liberation from oppression aims at least at the constitution of freedom can we speak of revolution. This is clearly to be seen in the thinking of Machiavelli, who is rightly considered as the spiritual father of revolution.[12] Machiavelli's insistence on violence was the direct consequence of the twofold perplexity in which he found himself theoretically and which later became the very practical perplexity besetting the men of the revolutions. The perplexity consisted in the task of foundation, the setting of a new beginning, which as such seemed to demand violence and violation. We are vividly reminded of a famous passage in Augustine's great work *De Civitate Dei,* when Miss Arendt refers to "the old legendary crime (Romulus slew Remus, Cain slew Abel) at the beginning of all history." [13] This task of foundation, moreover, was coupled with the task of lawgiving, of devising and imposing upon men a new authority which would supersede the old absolute that derived from a God-given authority. Machiavelli's insistence on the role of violence in politics was due not so much to his so-called realistic insight into human nature as to his futile hope that he could find some quality in certain men to match the qualities we associate with the divine.

The fourth factor in the emergence of the modern concept of revolution is the notion of irresistibility. This connotation of the term in its original astronomical usage, the fact that the revolving motion of the planets follows a preordained path and is removed from all influence of human power, has remained in our own use of the word. It has become common practice to date the new political significance of the word "revolution," which consisted in an exclusive emphasis on irresistibility, from the night of July 14, 1789, in Paris. When Louis XVI heard from the Duc de La Rochefoucauld-Liancourt of the fall of the Bastille, the king, we

are told, exclaimed: "C'est une révolte." But the duke corrected him: "Non, Sire, c'est une révolution." Here the word is used still, and politically for the last time, in the sense of the old metaphor, but the emphasis has shifted from the lawfulness of a rotating, cyclical movement to its irresistibility.[14]

These four notions—novelty, freedom, violence, irresistibility—constitute, so to speak, the cards with which Hannah Arendt plays the game of her historian's philosophy of revolution. She does not conceal her predilection in favor of the original concept of the American Revolution which constituted the body politic of her second fatherland. The historic watershed which separates two fundamentally different concepts lies between the American and the French Revolutions. Whereas the American Revolution was dominated by the political question, it was the social question which decided the course of the French Revolution and its aftermath.

What has posed the most urgent and, politically, the least solvable problem to all other revolutions, i.e., the social question in the form of the terrifying predicament of mass poverty, played hardly any role in the course of the American Revolution. Since the laborers were poor but not miserable, they were not driven by want, and the revolution was not overwhelmed by them. The problem they posed was not social but political, it concerned not the order of society but the form of government. Of course, the absence of the social question from the American scene was, after all, quite deceptive, since abject and degrading misery was present everywhere in the form of slavery and Negro labor. But if Jefferson, and others to a less degree, were aware of the primordial crime upon which the fabric of American society rested, it was because they were convinced of the incompatibility of the institution of slavery with the foundation of freedom, not because they were moved by pity or by a feeling of solidarity with their fellow men. Slavery was no part of the social question, so the social question, whether genuinely absent or only hidden in darkness, was nonexistent for all practical purposes.[15]

To a certain extent this explains the lack of influence of the American Revolution upon the course of modern revolutions. For

it was the question of the priority either of the political or of the social issues about which the founders and the liberators, the men of the American Revolution and the men in France, parted company. The direction of the American Revolution remained committed to the foundation of freedom and the establishment of lasting institutions within the range of civil law. The direction of the French Revolution was deflected almost from its beginning from this foundation through the immensity of the people's misery and of the pity this misery inspired. Robespierre once compared the nation to the ocean; it was indeed the ocean of misery and the oceanlike sentiments it aroused that combined to drown the foundations of freedom. It is as though the American Revolution were achieved in a kind of ivory tower never penetrated by the fearful spectacle of human misery or the haunting voices of abject poverty. "The superior wisdom of the American founders in theory and practice has never carried with it sufficient persuasiveness and plausibility to prevail in the tradition of revolution." [16]

Though Hannah Arendt does not share with Crane Brinton a cyclical philosophy of revolutions, the point of view which both authors have chosen for their survey is the same: the historical event and the political concept of the American Revolution. Both authors express the opinion that the American Revolution represents, in some fundamental respects, an exceptional case as compared with the French and the Russian and, in some degree, even with the English Revolution. It is precisely in this choice of viewpoint that we find some serious limitations in Miss Arendt's analysis.

Basic to her philosophy is what she calls the "alternative between freedom and prosperity." [17] The outcome of the American Revolution, as distinct from its purpose at the start, has always been ambiguous, and the question of whether the end of government was to be prosperity or freedom has never been settled. Even in America where the foundation of a new body politic succeeded and where, therefore, in a sense, the revolution achieved its actual end, the second task of revolution, to assure the survival of the spirit out of which the act of foundation sprang, was frustrated almost from the beginning. The social question interfered

with the course of the American Revolution no less sharply, though far less dramatically, than it did with the course of the French Revolution. For abundance and endless consumption are the ideals of the poor; they are the mirage in the desert of misery. In this sense, affluence and wretchedness are only two sides of the same coin; the bonds of necessity need not be of iron, they can be made of silk. Since America was never overwhelmed by poverty, it was "the fatal passion for sudden riches" rather than necessity that stood in the way of the founders of the republic. Just as the fact that poverty was conquered in America had the deepest repercussions in Europe, so did the fact that misery remained for so much longer the condition of Europe's lower classes have a profound impact upon the course of events in America after the Revolution. The trouble was that the struggle to abolish poverty —one of the greatest achievements of Western history and of the history of mankind—under the impact of a continual mass emigration from Europe, fell more and more under the sway of the poor themselves. Whence came its guidance by the ideals born out of poverty, as distinguished from those principles which had inspired the foundation of freedom. The American dream, as it came to be understood, was the dream of a "promised land" where milk and honey flow. And "the fact that the development of modern technology was so soon able to realize this dream beyond anyone's wildest expectation quite naturally had the effect of confirming for the dreamers that they really had come to live in the best of all possible worlds." [18] In other words, public freedom and public happiness came to be confused with private welfare. The citizen of the revolution was being converted into the private individual of nineteenth-century society.

Within the context of Miss Arendt's philosophy, this fundamental thesis of the complete incompatibility between freedom and prosperity renders the "social question" insoluble, at least insofar as a solution would imply the creation or maintenance of public freedom. Consequently, her thesis is that no revolution has ever solved the social question and liberated men from the predicament of want. All rulership has its original and its most legitimate source in man's wish to emancipate himself from life's necessity, and men

achieved such liberation by means of violence, by forcing others to bear the burden of life for them. This was the core of slavery, but it was not the rise of modern political ideas as such which achieved this emancipation. No, "it is only the rise of technology . . . which has refuted the old and terrible truth that only violence and rule over others could make some men free." [19] The dilemma is obvious. The original concept of civil freedom that inspired the founders of the American Revolution has proved almost impotent for the poor masses of the nineteenth-century immigration. On the other hand, technological development has so far resulted in creating only the mirage of limitless abundance. What remains as the alternative solution of the social question is the concept of the French Revolution, which has turned out to be a complete failure. All revolutions have followed the example of the French Revolution and have used and misused the mighty forces of misery and destitution in their struggle against tyranny or oppression. Although the whole record of past revolutions demonstrates beyond doubt that every attempt to solve the social question with political means leads into terror, and that it is terror which sends revolutions to their doom, "it can hardly be denied that to avoid this fatal mistake is almost impossible when a revolution breaks out under conditions of mass poverty." [20] What this means for our age is that to the original curse of mankind a new curse has been added. Human life has been stricken with poverty since time immemorial, and mankind continues to labor under this curse in all countries outside the Western Hemisphere. But liberation from necessity, because of its urgency, will always take precedence over the building of freedom. The masses of the poor carry with them necessity, to which they have been subject as long as memory reaches, together with the violence that has always been used to overcome necessity. This raging force may well nigh appear irresistible because it lives from, and is nourished by, the necessity of biological life itself.

In spite of its capability of brilliant and illuminating historical analysis, Hannah Arendt's philosophy of revolution leaves us with a dark and gloomy perspective. The reasons behind this deep-rooted pessimism are understandable enough for an author who

has escaped the terror of Hitler's "revolution of nihilism" and has found a safe refuge on the other side of the Atlantic Ocean. Tracing back the origins of the concept of public freedom which is the core of America's political structure, she points to the days of the American Revolution, when "necessity in motion," that "close enormous chain which girds and binds the human race" and can be traced back "to the origins of the world" (Tocqueville), was entirely absent from the range of experiences of American egalitarian society. But this range of experiences belongs definitely to the past, and the enlightened philosophy which inspired and shaped it is too rational and too aristocratic to meet the challenge of the human rights revolution in modern American mass society and the revolution of rising expectations in overpopulated continents.

There is a still deeper reason for the pessimism underlying this type of philosophy. Hannah Arendt has keenly perceived that modern revolutions are confronted with the problem of their ultimate foundation. The problem of an absolute is bound to appear in a revolution, and is inherent in the revolutionary event itself. The English civil war in the seventeenth century, the French Revolution in the eighteenth, and the October Revolution in the twentieth followed the rise of an absolutism which had served as a substitute for the lost religious sanction of secular authority in the person of the king or, rather, in the institution of kingship. The revolutions unmasked this as a pseudo-solution which only served to hide the most elementary predicament of all modern political bodies, their profound instability, the result of some elementary lack of authority. It was precisely the revolutions, their crises and their emergency, which drove the "enlightened" men of the eighteenth century to plead for some religious sanction at the very moment when they were about to emancipate the secular realm fully from the influences of the churches and to separate politics and religion once and for all. The trouble with natural law was precisely that it had no author, that it needed divine sanction to become binding for men.[21] Divine sanction was closely connected with Western mind with what it construed as the quintessence of all laws, the Decalogue of the Hebrew religion.

But it is difficult to agree with the statement that the model itself should not have changed "when in the seventeenth and eighteenth centuries natural law stepped into the place of divinity—into the place, that is, which once had been held by the Hebrew God . . . , a place which then had been occupied by Christ . . . , from whom the Roman popes and Bishops as well as the kings who followed them, had derived their authority, until finally the rebellious Protestants turned to Hebrew laws and covenants and to the figure of Christ himself." [22]

The trouble with the secularization process and its consequence of a lost sanction of religion in the political realm lies precisely in the fact that this model has undergone fundamental changes. In her romantic retrospect to the good old days of the Mayflower Compact and the Declaration of Independence, Miss Arendt has failed to ask whether it might not be the historical calling and service of modern revolutions to reveal the far-reaching and irreversible impact of secularization on the very nature of political structures and concepts.

Autobiography of Western Man

At this very point another German immigrant to the United States, Eugen Rosenstock-Huessy, has tried to shed light on the secular revolutions of modern time. Whereas Crane Brinton and Hannah Arendt take their stand in the event and the philosophy of the American Revolution, Rosenstock-Huessy approaches the history of revolutions from the opposite side. He agrees with Brinton and Arendt that the American Revolution is, to a certain extent, an exception in the series of modern revolutions. Over against the total revolutions on the other side of the Atlantic, the Americans, fighting against Europe for independence and equality, were only interested in a minimum revolution. With a view to introducing Americans to the spirit and history of the total revolutions, Rosenstock-Huessy wrote his voluminous work *Out of Revolution: Autobiography of Western Man*. It is a completely rewritten translation of an earlier work, written in German, titled *Die*

Europäischen Revolutionen und der Charakter der Nationen.[23]

The subtitle of the American edition is an apt expression of Rosenstock-Huessy's vision. He approaches the history of Western revolutions as the "Autobiography of Western Man," i.e., as a history which, far from being a series of disgraceful interruptions between periods of quiet and peace, has the same inner cohesion one would expect to find in the life history of an individual. And, it is an "autobiography" rather than a "biography" because it is based upon introspection and lived experiences rather than on a collection of "objective" facts.[24]

This "autobiography" of the modern revolutionary begins several centuries earlier than is commonly understood and accepted, namely, with the last quarter of the eleventh century A.D. He characterizes the *Dictatus Papae* of 1075 (whereby the Pope, acting as the trustee of all Christendom against imperialism, severed the direct relation between throne and altar) as the "Revolution of the Holy See." It set the precedent for all Europe: the Papal Revolution was the most general and intensive social earthquake Europe had ever seen. The socio-biological phenomenon of total revolution started at the throne of St. Peter.[25] The series of modern "secular" revolutions which have been the consequence of this medieval "clerical" revolution is conceived as beginning with the Reformation, a view which fits into this comprehensive concept of Europe's revolutionary history.

Rosenstock-Huessy traces back the history of modern Europe "from Lenin to Luther." The common quality of the four great forms of government arising between 1517 and 1918 out of the revolutions in Germany, England, France, and Russia consists in their entrusting the regeneration of society to the laymen, to a secular power. All these revolutions stand for a sovereignty of the temporal, they all have one and the same passion: to be free from the visible Catholic Church.[26]

But these four great forms of government which emerged from the four "secular revolutions" also have many other things in common. They are the well-known, ancient forms described by Aristotle: monarchy, aristocracy, democracy, and dictatorship. They follow each other in order, but not within the same country.

Once they have appeared, each in its own country and in its proper order, they coexist. Kings, parliaments, capitalists, and proletariats rule simultaneously. Therefore, the European countries form a unity in spite of their plurality. By acting as independent revolutionary bodies, they have achieved something in common, and each has achieved something for all. The European concert is a common campaign for the best form of government. The ancients knew the rotation of governments. Polybius and Aristotle were considered classics on this topic of the wheel of political fortune. Their pessimistic outlook was justified; the forms of government were mortal and transient. But the Christian era has achieved something very different from the pagans. It has not been content with the rotation of monarchy, aristocracy, democracy, and dictatorship; it has made them coexist. The coexistence of these four political forms in one world means the interpenetration of each one with all the rest. The abuses of one form of government, at the circumference of its sphere of influence, led to reaction. Since Germany's party of religion does not exist in England, the King of England must step down and become the first gentleman of his kingdom. Since the English type of Commonwealth does not exist in France, the aristocrats must step down and become the *élite* in a republic. Since the French variety of capital does not exist in Russia, capital must step down and become one social force among many.[27] Thus, regeneration occurs not at the center, but at the outer fringe. The coexistence of different countries obviates the crude rotation of antiquity. The mutual dependence between cooperating peoples is, by its very nature, opposed to the domination or subjection of one country by another. It is revealed best in times when the motherland of one form is most deeply humiliated in its power abroad.

Each of these forms of government appeared as the result of a tremendous explosion. Protestantism, common law, constitutionalism, Sovietism first tried the way of violent expansion; each belongs to the first chapter of a World Revolution. But they all reached their limits very soon. None of these forms of government was allowed to carry the day completely. Each revolution had to settle down in a particular European area, which was given its

very shape by the fact of its undergoing the immediate influence of one of the World Revolutions. Neither the German, nor the English, nor the French, nor the Russian nation existed in its modern form before the specific revolution which centered within its borders. The successful creation of a new political language by a new class in a new section of the continent is called a revolution; and the territory within which it succeeds and the people whom it transforms are the components of a nation. Nations are the products of revolutions. Each nation depends upon a leading class, which from its inspired stand in the open danger and the open warfare of revolution becomes the governing class in public law and the model of private life. The Bolshevik party in Russia, the religious party in Germany, the parliamentary party in England, the civic party in France are not fractions of an existing nation, but the *raison d'être* of the whole.

The concept of coexistence of all these forms of government in one civilization leads Rosenstock-Huessy to a definite rejection of two theories which, each from an opposite viewpoint, tend to split humanity into meaningless groups: on the one hand, the idealists, the best-government dogmatists, notably orthodox Marxists, who cannot bear the existence of a conflicting form of government, which threatens their most sacred principles; on the other hand, the geographical, nationalistic school, which goes to the opposite extreme and makes government the empirical product of soil, earth, history, climate, and environment. The results of Rosenstock-Huessy's survey go against both: against the destroyer of continuity and the destroyer of our unity in space. Man can neither bear to be cut off from his roots in the past, nor to have all his highest beliefs confined within the bounds of one nation or continent. All these revolutions attempted the same great thing, at different times and with different means, but for exactly the same purpose.

Each revolution, originating at the circumference of a preceding revolution, faced the eternal dilemma of a divine and a bestial nature in man. Each entrusted the solution of this dilemma to a different class, that is, to Nobility, Gentry, Bourgeoisie, Proletariat. In each of these classes, despair over the past and

hope for the future kindled the spark of passionate love for a world reborn. The torchbearers of a new revolution push out the degraded type and commence creation of a new, unknown race.

Another aspect of the rotation of forms of government is a progressive ascent in both space and time. An advance from small territories to large is obvious when we compare the average state of the Reformation with the area covered by Cromwell's first Commonwealth and when it is realized that the area of Russia is forty times as great and contains six times as many people as France had in 1789. And each form has been wrought out on an ascending scale; they follow each other, but by no means repeat each other. Each revolution, standing on the shoulders of the foregoing, dares to go a step further and attack a bigger problem of organization. The rotation is neither mechanical nor meaningless, because the starting-point of the first revolution is preserved in the consciousness of all that follow. If the Marxian revolutionary theory were correct, the revolutions would arise successively in the same territory and in the same nation. Then the "march in echelon" would be impossible. But the whole question of progress depends on the possibility of coexistence of all the rungs of the ladder.

Primitive social groups, because they do not manage to coexist with their enemies, except by devouring them, are bound to rotate in a vicious circle. The meaninglessness of so many South American revolutions is based on the fact that they follow each other in hopeless repetition. But the great European revolutions are sown in a common field of man's experience and hope. They all try to embrace all mankind, one after the other and one beside the other; like separate branches they are all grafted onto the common tree of humanity. The sequence in time and togetherness in space became possible only through a process of branching.

However, the original metaphor which lent its name to the word "revolution" is best suited to express Rosenstock-Huessy's favorite concept of progress. Though the revolutions take their very name from the idea of rotation, of revolving, the wheel of a World Revolution does more than turn in its old orbit. It moves

forward along a new track and creates a new form of recurrent, repetitive life. Evolution is based on revolution; both ideas are reciprocal. "Creation goes on as God's creation has always done. A thunderstorm of destruction clears the air; then follows the low rustle of growth and reconstruction. We may assign the noise to the devil, and the still, small voice to God. But only wishful thinking can exclude either of these sounds." [28] Doubtless, a type of philosophy of history such as underlies this "Autobiography of Western Man" raises a number of philosophical and theological questions; on the other hand, it cannot escape the painful test of detailed historical analysis. After all, our sketchy survey could not give even a glimpse of the rich resources of historical facts which Rosenstock-Huessy has at his disposal, though the way he makes use of them is very difficult to check. But these aspects are not under discussion here. We shall come back, in the sixth chapter of this book, to some questions concerning the consequences of this approach.

At least three important aspects of Rosenstock-Huessy's philosophy contain significant contributions to a deeper understanding of the meaning of the great revolutions of modern time. First, revolutions are not isolated events encroaching upon the normal course of history, but their meaning is illuminated within the context of a great historical drama, a thousand years of evolution of European civilization. Second, instead of neglecting the process of nation-building as a deplorable deviation from the international perspective of world revolution and, on the other hand, avoiding the temptation of a romanticist theory of national existence as an organic whole, Rosenstock-Huessy gives a plausible explanation of the link between Europe's revolutions and the birth of national consciousness. Third, this approach is capable of explaining the inherent tensions between the geographically limited, national self-realization of revolutions and their originally universalist claims. This sheds a revealing light on the present stage of history in which the emerging nations are struggling for a new sense of identity within the context of a coming world civilization. Rosenstock-Huessy is well aware of the fact that

revolution runs the risk of chaos. Revolution feels that an old order has died. When the spirit has left the body of an institution, the revolution breaks out.

In this hour no language exists, or can exist, to lead people on. But in this fatal dilemma between the trite but well-organized language of a dying past and the inspired faith of a group without visible or audible means of self-expression, universal history furnishes the needed generalities for the leaders of the future. The new phase of revolution which is beginning today must put the destructive forces of mankind to use. The present time is bound to attempt an organization of future society by which the dynamite of revolution may be manipulated as consciously as contractors use real dynamite in building tunnels or roads. "The future of revolution and the future of mankind depend on the readiness of the human soul to galvanize political action with a spark of that queer power which regenerates mankind." [29]

The Communist Manifesto

We have deliberately begun this chapter with a discussion of three significant approaches to the history of Western revolutions. No matter how differently Crane Brinton, Hannah Arendt, and Eugen Rosenstock-Huessy may conceive the meaning and the perspective of revolution, their theories have one feature in common: they are primarily concerned with the political structure of revolutions. In a sense, their theories observe revolutionary phenomena from a postrevolutionary point of view; they ask what form of government results from a revolution. This question is not only legitimate, it is even one of the crucial questions which decide the prospect of a revolution, its success or failure, its value and lasting significance.

The political structure is, however, only one aspect of the revolutionary process. In the preceding chapters, we have focused our interest upon the overriding issue of worldwide economic development and upon the ambivalent context of both technical and social revolutions, in which the economic processes are taking place. Chapter Three started with a critical discussion of Rostow's

development model. The limitations and faults of this model have become obvious, notably, its inherent myopy vis-à-vis the revolutionary implications and consequences of development processes. Rostow labeled his theory a "Non-Communist Manifesto." As a matter of fact, whatever the value of this theory may be for economic science as a sample of development philosophy, it is useful and illuminating.

The same reasons are conducive to a discussion of the countermodel which served as reflector for Rostow's philosophy, *The Communist Manifesto* of 1848, written by Karl Marx and Friedrich Engels. This famous document, characterized by the German sociologist Werner Sombart as the most brilliant political pamphlet of the nineteenth century, is, as a matter of fact, still a perfectly adequate model of a philosophy of revolution. Since, until the present date, Marxism has not been seriously threatened by a competitive concept of revolution, this sample may even rightly be presented as the classical model of revolution.

One word of warning may serve as introductory remark. What concerns us here is neither a historical analysis of Marx's thinking, nor a historical sketch of the very complicated and in a sense confusing picture of the variegated, intersecting, interdependent, conflicting and fusing lines of Marxism up to the present day. In the same way as Rostow's study, *The Communist Manifesto* serves as a simplified model of what Kuhn, with reference to scientific concepts, has called a "paradigm."

Let us begin by quoting a passage taken from a later work of Karl Marx in which, eight years after the publication of *The Communist Manifesto*, he wrote down his reflections on the frustrated Revolution of 1848.

> There is one great fact characterizing the nineteenth century which cannot be denied by any party: on the one side, industrial and scientific powers have developed which no former period of history could have fancied; on the other side, there are symptoms of disintegration surpassing even the well-known terrors of the late Roman Empire. In our time everything seems to be pregnant with its contrast. The machine is endowed with the marvelous power to shorten labor and to make it more profitable; and yet

we see how it produces hunger and overwork. The newly emanci-
pated powers of wealth become, through a strange play of
destiny, sources of privation. . . . Mankind becomes master of
nature, but man the slave of man. . . . The result of all our
inventions and progress seems to be that material powers become
invested with spiritual life, while human life deteriorates into a
material force. This antagonism between modern industry and
science, on the one side, modern misery and corruption, on the
other side, this antagonism between the forces of production and
the social conditions of our epoch, is a tangible, overwhelming
and undeniable fact.

Some parties may wish to get rid of the modern capacities
in order to get rid also of the modern conflicts. Or they may
fancy that such evident progress in the realm of production cannot be achieved but by a corresponding regress in the social
political life. But we recognize in this antagonism the clever
spirit (Hegel's "cunning of reason") which keenly proceeds in
working out all these contradictions. We know that the new
form of social production to achieve the good life, needs only
new men.[30]

This is a splendid summary of the contradistinction we noted earlier
between technological and revolutionary humanists (see pp. 35–
42), the first being primarily interested in man's relation to nature,
the second being primarily concerned with the relationship between
man and his fellow man. In Marx's analysis this contrast is rooted
in the essence of the historical process which governs society:
"Mankind becomes master of nature, but man the slave of man."

It is the peculiar character of the historical process that it
must link two contradictory phenomena. The crucial statement
consists in this sentence: "In our time everything seems to be
pregnant with its contrast." Modern socio-economic history seems,
"through a strange play of destiny" to be constrained to bring
forth insoluble contradictions.

Marx, as a pupil of Hegel, claims the ability to decipher the
hieroglyphs of historical necessity. Behind the production of all
these contradictions is the invisible hand of what Hegel called the
List der Vernunft, the cunning of Reason which guides history
through contrast and negation up to the final goal: the birth of

new men who will be able to overcome these contradictions—new men who know how to become masters of nature and at the same time to defend man against enslavement and exploitation by his fellow man. We have deliberately used the term "invisible hand," for this term played a famous role in the enlightened philosophy which served as the motivating force and justification behind the emergence of modern economic science, introduced by Adam Smith in the last quarter of the eighteenth century. One will look in vain for an explicit acknowledgment of this philosophical belief in the economic study of Walt W. Rostow. Likewise, economic treatises written by modern Marxists are silent about Marx's Hegelian idea of a hidden Reason, governing by its cunning ways the socio-political history of human society. Nevertheless there is a common spirit joining antagonists like Marx and Rostow: that is the unquenchable optimism of Enlightenment which believes in the meaning of history as an ongoing progress. And both are convinced that mankind can and will renew itself in such a way as to be able to overcome the dilemmas and to meet the challenges of the present time.

Marx, like Rostow, sees the line of socio-economic history as a line of victorious development. As a matter of fact, *The Communist Manifesto*[31] may be read as one of the most impressive eulogies ever written on the achievements of modern Western bourgeoisie as the glorious product of a long process of development. The word "development" functions as a key word in Marx's description of the rise of the bourgeoisie in recent centuries. But at the same time—and even in perfect parallelism within the same framework—this development is sketched in terms of revolution. Summarizing the short outline of the history of the bourgeois class, it is stated that "the modern bourgeoisie is itself the product of a long course of development, of a series of revolutions in the modes of production and exchange." In other words, development is identical with a series of revolutions which occur on both the socio-economic and the political level.

The word "development" has particular significance in this passage: "Modern industry has established the world market, for which the discovery of America paved the way. This market has

given an immense development to commerce, to navigation, to communication by land. This development has, in turn, reacted on the extension of industry: and in proportion as industry, commerce, navigation, railways extended, in the same proportion the bourgeoisie developed, increased its capital, and pushed into the background every class handed down from the Middle Ages. . . . Each step in the development of the bourgeoisie was accompanied by a corresponding political advance of that class."

This outline of economic and political development, then, is once again summed up in terms of revolution: "The bourgeoisie," thus the basic statement, "historically, has played a most revolutionary part." In other words, the great revolutionary class of modern society is, historically speaking, the bourgeoisie. Its revolutionary significance, which thereupon is described, could be summarized in the following points:

a. The bourgeoisie has revolutionized the feudal order and stripped this order of religious and political illusions which veiled it.

b. The bourgeoisie has been the first to show what man's activity can bring about. During its rule of scarcely one hundred years, it has created more massive and more colossal productive forces than have all preceding generations together.

c. The bourgeoisie cannot exist without constantly revolutionizing the instruments of production, and thereby the relations of production and with them the whole relations of society. Uninterrupted disturbance of all social conditions, everlasting uncertainty and agitation distinguish the bourgeois epoch from all earlier ones. To sum up: "All that is solid melts into air, all that is holy is profaned, and man is at last compelled to face with sober senses his real conditions of life and his relations with his kind."

d. The bourgeoisie has given a cosmopolitan character to production and consumption in every country.

e. The bourgeoisie compels all, even the most barbarian, nations into civilization, i.e., to become bourgeois them-

selves. Just as it has made the country dependent on the towns, so it has made barbarian and semibarbarian countries dependent on the civilized ones, nations of peasants on nations of bourgeois, the East on the West. In one word, it creates a world after its own image.

These last words are essential: the bourgeoisie "creates a world after its own image." The development of the bourgeoisie, identical with a permanent revolution by the restless, unprecedented, radically profane, cosmopolitan activity of a completely new type of man, means a new creation. But this new creation is generating its own destruction—and this is so because of its very nature of being development through revolution. It came into existence as a revolution and it has to die under the blow of a following revolution. History is a series of birth processes. At a certain stage when the fruit which has been generated and fostered within the womb is ripe, the same conditions which up to that moment had promoted its growth become so many fetters. They have to burst asunder and they are burst asunder. In this way feudal society was replaced with bourgeois society: the sorcerer is no longer able to control the powers of the nether world that he has called up by his spells. It has indeed created a world after its own image, but this image is that of the permanent revolutionary. Revolution creates revolution. What appeared to be creation turns out to be an increasingly powerless sorcery.

Development means revolution. The history of industry and commerce is the history of the revolt of modern productive forces against modern conditions of production, against the property relations that are the conditions for the existence of the bourgeoisie and of its rule. The productive forces which, during a certain period of growth, have furthered the development, reach a decisive stage when they become too powerful for these conditions by which they are fettered; and as soon as they overcome these fetters, they bring disorder into the whole of bourgeois society.

Revolt and disorder: they belong to the very essence of the historical process, they are the backbone of development through revolution. They are signs of death and at the same time they are

signs of birth. Death-pangs: the weapons with which the bourgeoisie felled feudalism to the ground are now turned against the bourgeoisie itself. It forged the weapons that bring death to itself. And at the same time birth-pangs: it has also called into existence the men who are to wield those weapons—the modern working class—the proletarians.

This summary of the first chapter of *The Communist Manifesto* may suffice now as an outline of the basic philosophy of history on which Marxist thinking is patterned. It is a philosophy which looks at history as a dialectical series of birth processes and death processes, of development pregnant with revolt, of evolution through revolution. In the background, concealed but perceptible to enlightened eyes, is the "clever spirit," the "cunning of Reason" at work, the higher providence which through crises and contradictions is guiding world history to its final goal: the birth of new man, of a new mankind.

Five years after the publication of *The Communist Manifesto*, Marx, European correspondent for the *New York Tribune,* wrote for that leading radical newspaper of its time an article on "The British Rule in India." [32] The article is a brilliant analysis of the historically decisive role being played by British colonialism in its main Asian colony, a role qualitatively different from all preceding periods. For "the misery inflicted by the British in Hindustan is of an essentially different and infinitely more intensive kind than all Hindustan had to suffer before. All the civil wars, invasions, revolutions, conquests, famines, strangely complex, rapid, and destructive as the successive action of Hindustan may appear, did not go deeper than its surface. England has broken down the entire framework of Indian society, without any symptoms of reconstitution yet appearing. This loss of his old world, with no gain of a new one, imparts a particular kind of melancholy to the present misery of the Hindu, and separates Hindustan, ruled by Britain, from all its ancient traditions, and from the whole of its past history."

England produced "the greatest and, to speak the truth, the only social revolution ever heard of in Asia." In causing this unique social revolution, England was, it is true, actuated only by the vilest

interests, and was stupid in her manner of enforcing them. But, says Marx, that is not the question: "The question is: Can mankind fulfill its destiny without a fundamental revolution in the social state of Asia? If not, whatever may have been the crimes of England, she was the unconscious tool of history in bringing about that revolution."

Here, then, in an analysis which more than a century later has not lost anything of its vigor and has even grown in significance in view of later history, we see once again Marx's philosophy of history transparently clear through the socio-economic surface. Marx wrote this article long before the rise of an Indian nationalist movement. The primary revolutionary force is not the Indians resisting colonialism, but the British intruder uprooting the whole traditional social order of India. And in playing that revolutionary role, she fulfills, as an unconscious tool of history, the destiny of mankind which cannot be realized except through a fundamental revolution in the Asian traditional order.

It has rightly been said that the whole process of history as outlined in *The Communist Manifesto* corresponds to the general scheme of the Jewish-Christian interpretation of history as a providential advance toward a final goal which is meaningful. Historical materialism is essentially, though secretly, a history of fulfillment and salvation in terms of social economy. What seems to be a scientific discovery is, as a matter of fact, from the first to the last sentence inspired by an eschatological faith, which, in its turn, "determines" the whole sweep and range of all particular statements.[33]

In other words, the Marxist model represents a comprehensive philosophy of the interaction between development and revolution, a philosophy which treats the historical logic of development as the very creator of the revolutionary movement. With this model in mind, it is worthwhile to look at the consequences of this interaction in three different settings. Together they determine to a great extent the face of the present world: the setting of established Communist societies in U.S.S.R. and Eastern Europe; the setting of highly developed Western countries; and the setting of the developing nations.

Communist Revolution and Establishment

Leon Trotsky begins his book on the history of the Russian Revolution with an analysis of the peculiarities of Russia's development.[34] He seeks a solution for the great enigma that a backward country was the first to place the proletariat in power, and he finds the solution in the peculiarities of that backward country. A backward country assimilates the material and intellectual conquests of the advanced countries. But this does not mean that it follows them slavishly, reproducing all the stages of their past. The theory of the repetition of historical cycles rests upon an observation of the orbits of old precapitalist cultures. Capitalism means, however, an overcoming of these conditions. It prepares and in a certain sense realizes the universality and permanence of man's development. By this a repetition of the forms of development by different nations is ruled out. Although compelled to follow after the advanced countries, a backward country does not take things in the same order. The privilege of historic backwardness compels the adoption of whatever is ready in advance of any specified date, skipping a whole series of intermediate stages. The development of historically backward nations acquires a planless, complex, combined character. In the Revolution of 1917, the law of combined development emerges in its extreme expression: starting with the overthrow of a decayed medieval structure, the revolution in the course of a few months placed the proletariat and the Communist Party in power.

It is, however, in this very "law of combined development" that the inner contradictions, inherent from the very outset in the Russian Revolution, find their origin. Trotsky conceived this "law" in fact, as an explanation of the socio-economic development a backward country is compelled to pass through, but he also applied this insight to the political form which the Soviet system adopted. Comparing the Russian Revolution with its predecessor, the French Revolution which stepped over the Reformation, he argues that Russia, likewise, stepped over formal democracy. The Russian Revolutionary Party sought an expression for the tasks of the Rev-

olution neither in the Bible (like the English Revolution) nor in that secularized Christianity called "pure" democracy (like the French Revolution) but in the material relations of the social classes. "The Soviet system gave to these relations their simplest, most undisguised and transparent expression. The rule of the toilers has for the first time been realized in the Soviet system, which, whatever its immediate historic vicissitudes, has penetrated as ir- revocably into the consciousness of the masses as did in its day the system of the Reformation or of pure democracy."

But this "realization" of the worker's rule in the Soviet sys- tem is precisely the point where the Russian Revolution has in- creasingly revealed its dilemma. The weakness of Marxist eschatol- ogy consists in its belief that all contradictions which in previous stages of history have of necessity exploded one order of society after another are (at least in principle) overcome in a socialist order by some kind of dialectic miracle. Trotsky's expectation of the world revolution, was, in a sense, an escape from this dilemma, for it pushed the moment of realization into an unlimited future. It was Lenin who acted upon the perception that the very back- wardness of Russian society called for a special form of party or- ganization unknown to the West. As E. H. Carr has pointed out, the attempt to execute a Western political program (which Marx- ism essentially was) within the conditions of the autocratic police state of the Romanovs created a series of contradictions which were the tragic dilemma of the Communist Party and the Bolshevik Rev- olution. On the course set by Lenin, the Party moved inexorably forward within an ever-tightening discipline and an ever-narrowing circle of authority and power. The process had been precisely fore- seen by Trotsky, who predicted a situation in which "the party is replaced by the organization of the party, the organization by the central committee, and finally the central committee by the dicta- tor." The first edition of Stalin's *Foundations of Leninism* con- tained a passage which read too much like an endorsement of Trotsky's "permanent revolution." In the second edition this gave place to a clear and unequivocal statement that socialism could be built in a single country, even in backward peasant Russia. The contradiction in Russia's social development consists in its retarded

character, which had brought it to the point of revolution only when socialism was already knocking at the door and democracy could no longer be realized without socialism; and in its backwardness, which prevented the realization of socialism in free forms.[35]

Of course, Soviet theory has found a solution for any contradictions which may emerge within the setting of the established Soviet system. It makes a distinction between two types of contradictions. The "nonantagonistic contradictions" are not only admitted to exist, but apparently considered to perform a useful signaling and corrective function; they are successfully overcome by the administrative action of the Communist Party and the government. In sharp contrast with it stand the "antagonistic" contradictions which are said to afflict capitalism, and which can be resolved only by revolution. This theory is a fine example of the type of self-justification, whereby an established postrevolutionary system attempts to make itself "revolution-proof" against any upheaval that might emerge from the inherent contradictions lying at the roots of its system. Another indication of the way in which Soviet theory tries to escape the contradictory consequences of rigid orthodoxy is to be found in discussions on the "Asiatic mode of production," the first epoch in the progress of the economic formation of society according to Marx's model of the successive stages of socio-economic development.

Marx and Engels, from 1853 on, had identified Russia as a "semi-Asiatic" society, dominated by an oriental despotism. During the Stalinist era in Soviet-Russia, from 1931 on, an effort was launched to eliminate the concept of Asiatic society because its implications for the character of the Soviet regime were highly embarrassing. The work of advancing the revolution in the so-called backward areas was believed to be enhanced by a return to the unilateral scheme of development under which a universal claim to leadership of social revolution everywhere could be made. From 1962 on, however, there has been a renewal of the discussion of the concept of the Asiatic mode of production. The renewed discussion has made it quite evident that the unchangeable laws of historical materialism have been found unreliable and that the universality of social development, its direction and its sequence, can-

not be accepted as certain and cannot serve as fixed premises for a philosophical system. This example is an indication of the dysfunction of the Marxist model of development, as soon as it receives a dogmatic sanction of the true, infallibly scientific truth. It is, further, a highly interesting symptom of the insoluble dilemma in which Marxism is being caught up by the application to the non-Western world of a model which originally emerged from a typically Western sociology and philosophy of history.[36]

On the other hand, it is interesting to study the problems facing Marxism when it is introduced, not into a less developed country, but into a Western country which has passed through all stages of capitalist economy and industrialization. Yorick Spiegel has made a number of keen observations on the situation of the German Democratic Republic (G.D.R), which he characterizes as the process of "modernizing a modern society." [37] The basic issue of his study consists in the fact that the introduction of socialism in East Germany imposed many problems that were lacking when it was imposed on other countries. Socialism did not have to show its superiority in ruling out still feudal elites, as was the case in Russia, China, and in most of the Eastern countries, but had to demonstrate its superiority over against a liberal economic system, which, however, was no longer the liberal society criticized by Marx. It was now a liberal society which had developed and refined its means of production and of power. The new elite in the G.D.R. had to prove that its ideology was still able to overcome a highly developed capitalistic structure of society. It had to convince the East German that it intended to overcome the "contradictions of capitalism," contradictions that generate aggressive imperial and neo-colonial tendencies. It had to promote the idea that the government had made real efforts to end the exploitation of the workers, to prevent a new rise of Nazism, as in West Germany, and to realize the truly democratic traditions of Germany that created men like Marx and Engels.

A crucial question is the position of the new ideology in its struggle for recognition. To realize its goals, the socialist state must achieve active recognition from the vast majority of its population in a limited number of years. In a highly industrialized society,

passive toleration is not sufficient because qualified work is done only by the worker who is satisfied with his environment. Modern industrial work demands willingness to take responsibility for decision-making. Therefore the indoctrination must generate active personal consent. This is one of the reasons why modern ideologies are so totalitarian. This aspect becomes more important as the process of work becomes more differentiated. It is the same phenomenon that forces the management of a modern capitalistic enterprise to strengthen the interest of their workers in what they are doing. Totalitarianism is clearly distinguished by Spiegel from authoritarianism. In an authoritarian state, the power elite is interested in preserving its value concepts against the majority of the people, as for instance in the aristocratic minorities in the underdeveloped countries. Totalitarianism, on the other hand, aims at the realization of a new order that is based on a new value system and that therefore differs widely from the prevailing social attitudes toward values.

There are three prime reasons why every totalitarian system is forced to use violence. First, the new value system meets a very strong opposition in the old elite which, as circumstances permit, may be supported by related elites in other countries (as, for example, following the French Revolution). Second, the introduction of a new value system would be rather ineffective insofar as it did not include a change in essential social institutions, which is impossible without the use of violence. Third, the change from a revolutionary movement to an established system of power requires new talents. Since the new elite does not have experience in the use of governmental means, severe struggles involving violence cannot be avoided. However, whatever violent means may be necessary, the totalitarian state is based upon the idea of consensus between the party and the population. This can be reached in two ways: by adaptation of the ideology to the traditional value systems and institutions, and—the second way—through the social development's affirmation of the ideology.

The process of adaptation of the ideology characteristically reflects the transition from a revolutionary to a postrevolutionary stage. The Marxist ideology initially was the ideology of a marginal

social group whose protest was formulated as a utopia. Socialization of private property is the key to the realization of the new world, which cannot be reached except by an irrational jump. But at the moment the group becomes a ruling elite, the problems emerging from the transition from a "charismatic" to a "traditional" power structure (Max Weber) become manifest. In Marxist thought this problem is involved in the idea of the opposition of spontaneity and consciousness, or ideology and organization. It is the main theme of the famous discussion between Rosa Luxemburg and Lenin. After the seizure of power the marginal social group is transmuted into a party which has to impose its new value system on the whole of society. The social norms imposed by the S.E.D. (the Communist party of the G.D.R.) are related to the classical Marxist thesis that "the socialist conditions of production . . . set all men in the same relation to the means of production." The concept of the productivity of work is established as a central value. In this way the old proletarian fighter is reoriented toward the *Homo faber*, the technical master of his environment. The productivity of production belongs now to the highest axioms of an ideology primarily oriented toward pragmatic actions, but still connected with a philosophy of history. The ideology has widely developed toward "empty formulas" (as they are called by Ernst Topitsch: *Leerformelin*). This problem is not unlike that of Christian social ethics as it is forced to work with norms like love and justice.

The change in character of the dominating ideology is also related to the seizure of power. From an incentive for fighting, in the years of the utopian struggle, the ideology develops into a means of domination. The character of an empty formula facilitates for the people the evasion of ideological control, just as it becomes more difficult for the Party to retain its control. Besides, after the basic change of their institutions of property, the elite was ready to make some concessions to the traditional ideologies and to use them for a legitimation of the new state and its goals. This process enables the non-Communists to follow the Marxist value system even when they have certain reservations. The same can be said of traditional ideologies, especially nationalism and Christianity.

On its side, the society develops more and more in the direc-

tion of the ideology, following the process of a sort of self-fulfilling prophecy. In underdeveloped countries, the Marxist promises to overcome famine and to end aristocracy's arbitrary actions may be attractive, but in a highly industrialized society this program cannot hope to find any support. However, in such a situation the Marxist ideology sometimes gains, because its program profits from the quasi-natural developmental tendencies of modern society. The development of a modern society needs and creates certain changes in social values that are to an extent immanent in industrial society. The more the Communist Party can realize modern society, the more persuasive is its ideology. To these immanent values and tendencies belong the need for planning, the high prestige of the worker, and the efforts for a better social and legal position for women. The approximation of ideology and social trend is facilitated by the absence of a clear definition of the ultimate goal of a classless society and the fulfillment of all needs. This vagueness not only promotes the assimilation of older democratic traditions but enables the Communist ideology to follow the demands of the industrialized society which have stabilized individualism.

The historical development of Marxism explains in some way the fact that Marxian ideology tries to deny the division between social institutions and private life, which is characteristic of modern man's dual psychological structure. The worker of the nineteenth century could hardly enjoy leisure time, the family was a fighting community. But after the revolutionary struggle is over and the postrevolutionary phase has begun, the immediate needs are gone. The Party is pressed to give more choice in the private sphere. Under these conditions the ideology becomes more and more a means to connect private man with his industrial environment and with the "reality" of the world. Its religious overtone is no longer the redemption of the oppressed, but the liberation of private man from his internal anxieties. With a view to this goal, Marxism emphasizes the personalization of the working situation. As in the liberal political movements in the previous two centuries, this process is dependent upon the depersonalization of the economic power, the transition of the power of the few to the people.

Marxian ideology visualized the conflicts involved in this process by using violence to push society in this direction. But Marxism always depends on the Western world for an example of what personalization means. This contradiction, inherent in Marxism itself, can be solved only when personalization becomes institutionalized in the outer world. It is not the least merit of Spiegel's analysis to have clarified the essential changes which Marxian ideology is bound to undergo when it has entered the stage of an established socialist society, where it has to serve as the mediating sanctification and justification of the factual societal development process which, in general, is characteristic of any industrialized society. His conclusions become even more illuminating if we turn to the contradictions and conflicts inherent in the Western highly developed societies. Then we realize that, on the one hand, Western and socialist-developed countries reveal comparable symptoms of the problems which industrialized societies cannot escape, whereas, on the other hand, looking to each other's conflicts, they find themselves looking in a mirror. If it is true that socialist countries have to wrestle with Western personalization traditions, then it is no less true that Western countries are being faced with the growth of an uneasy consciousness which returns, for its inspiration and enlightenment, to the classics of Marxism.

Conflicts of the Affluent Society

Whereas Marxist ideology has to adapt itself to the development of an established and industrialized socialist order, what we are faced with in Western affluent society is the counterpart. Here, too, the Marxist model which was conceived in the middle of the nineteenth century during the initial stage of industrial capitalism has to come to grips with the realities of an economic system in the stage of high mass consumption and of a technocratic society which is already revealing symptoms of a second industrial revolution. But the problem to be solved is just the opposite of that in socialist countries, where it requires the conversion of a revolutionary in a dominating ideology. Marxism in the West is faced with the fact

that the apocalyptic breakdown of capitalism, despite a series of grave crises, has not occurred, and in the sense originally expected probably never will. Nevertheless, if Marx's critique of the capitalist system was basically right and its inherent contradictions are insoluble without a radical break, then this critique has to be reformulated in new terms on the basis of an analysis of present-day, not nineteenth-century, society.

This process of rethinking is, in fact, a paramount phenomenon in present-day affluent society. Although it is not channeled within a clear-cut movement, group or sect, the term "neo-Marxism" is more or less adequate as an indication of the main trend of thought. As distinguished from the postrevolutionary Marxism of the dominating ideology in the U.S.S.R. and a number of East European countries, this neo-Marxism bears a notably pre-revolutionary character. Clinging to the radical perspective of an impending crisis and overturn of the Western socio-economic, political, and cultural system, it tries to relate this perspective to a factual evaluation of the existing situation.

The influential neo-Marxist philosopher Herbert Marcuse summarizes his critique in the statement that, apparently, Marx's own idea of socialism was not radical enough and not utopian enough.[38] Marx in his time has underrated the level which the productivity of labor under the capitalist system itself could attain and the possibilities suggested by the attainment of this level. His basic concept for the transition to socialism remained that of the development and rationalization of productive forces; their liberation from repressive and destructive controls was to be the first task of socialism. But in spite of all qualitative differences this concept of a "development of the productive forces" establishes a technological continuity between capitalism and socialism. By virtue of this continuity, the transition from capitalism to socialism would at first be a *quantitative* change, greater productivity.

However, this conception corresponds to a stage in the development of the productive forces that is already being surpassed by the advanced industrial societies. The affluent society seems to have mastered one of the unmanageable contradictions leading, according to Marx, to the final crisis of capitalism, for the destructive and

wasteful use of the productive forces proves to be profitable and promotes security. The essential question is therefore this: Has the affluent society indeed succeeded in the containment of radical social change? Or, has it succeeded in containing the revolutionary potential? Marcuse's answer lies in the diagnosis that the affluent society corroborates rather than refutes the internal contradictions which Marx attributed to capitalist development. It is true that these contradictions are suspended and "managed," but they are not solved by either the welfare or the warfare state. Within the system of repressive affluence, a conspicuous radicalization of youth and of the intelligentsia takes place. According to Marcuse, it is a movement which, in spite of all its limitations, tends toward a fundamental transvaluation of values. It is part of the human or social forces which, on a global scale, resist the oppressive power of the affluent society.

Marcuse, in conclusion, attempts a summary identification of these forces within the international and global framework. What happens in Asia or Africa is not external to the system but has become an integral part of the system itself. He sketches the following "syndrome of a revolutionary potential": (1) the national liberation movements in the backward countries; (2) the "new strategy" labor movement in Europe; (3) the underprivileged stratum of the population in the affluent society itself; (4) the intelligentsia, who are the opposition.

Compared with the catalyst potential of the national liberation movements, the radicalization of the intelligentsia seems to be a minor event. But here a broader aspect suggests itself. The historical dialectic here affects dialectical materialism itself. To the degree to which critical consciousness has been absorbed and coordinated by the affluent society, the development not of class consciousness but of consciousness as such, freed from the distortions imposed upon it, appears to be the basic prerequisite for radical change. And as repression is flattened out and extended to the entire underlying population, the "ideological" factors become very material forces of radical transformation.

Marcuse's observations concern several aspects of the present situation and point to different directions. The insight that the his-

torical dialectic affects dialectical materialism itself is confirmed by
the remarkable congeniality and community in critical reassessment
of Marxian philosophy which connects neo-Marxism in socialist
and in Western countries. Two examples of influential thinkers
should suffice. The "heretical" Marxist Polish philosopher Lezlek
Kolakowski published, several years before he was excommu-
nicated from the Communist Party, a number of lectures under the
significant title "Man without Alternatives: On the Possibility and
Impossibility of Being a Marxist." [39] He makes bold to call his own
philosophy a "metaphysics of negation," proposing an attitude of
openness uncolored by hope that it will ever lead to a closed position which is better than all others.[40] History has no preordained
goal which individuals have only to attain. Since the painful experience of Stalinism, under which the authorities had mysteriously
been let into the secret of laws of history that they invoked to justify their deeds, Kolakowski is fiercely allergic to any interpretation
of history in allegedly absolute terms. He will have none of the
Hegelian thesis which Engels introduced into Marxism, that the
necessary is *ipso facto* good as well. Indeed he goes even further
and questions the thesis that history always progresses. "All one
need do in order to believe in the inevitability of progress is believe
at the same time in the progressive nature of all that is inevitable." [41]

Much along the same line, the French Communist philosopher
Roger Garaudy has developed his ideas on a reformation of Marxism which, at the same time, brings it up to date and creates a
"Marxism of the twentieth century." [42] His concept of Marxism
as it was originally meant by Marx himself is a type of philosophy
capable of laying the foundation for man to be an initiator and a
creator in history, the responsible beginner of something new.
Marxism, indeed, has appeared frequently as only a variation of
eighteenth-century French materialism. This precritical conception
of Marxism would be a Marxism that presents itself as if there had
never been a Kant. It claims simply to install itself in things, in a
very simple, uncritical way, and to proceed from there. But Marx,
in his theses against Feuerbach, showed that man reaches out to
things with his projects, his plans, his hypotheses, and his models.

Garaudy radically rejects Stalin's distortion of the notion of dialectics whereby he presented the "dialectic of nature" as a series of laws that, in totality, would govern all reality. In the dogmatic presentation of Marxism, the dialectic is often presented as if history were something already completely written, and as if man were not in history and were not producing history. But the laws of dialectics are always provisional in any stage of the development of science, revisable and to be revised.[43]

This type of neo-Marxist philosophy has already evolved into an influential critique which attracts intellectuals in East and West who feel alienated vis-à-vis a technocratic ideology, whether it is garbed as "socialism" or as liberal capitalism. However, it would bear no relation to Marxism if it did not have direct political consequences. It has played a decisive role in the deep-rooted Czech resistance, inspired as it was by a large group of intellectuals, against Russian imperialism. Of course, the dominating ideology in the U.S.S.R., Poland, and the G.D.R. was quick to label and to denounce this critical Marxism as "revisionism." In Western countries its manifest attractiveness is easily scorned as "opium of the intellectuals." Raymon Aron has analyzed the existentialist Marxist humanism of his compatriot Jean-Paul Sartre as being a subtle version of the Marxian prophetism consisting in the belief that the proletarian revolution will be essentially different from the revolutions of the past, because it alone will permit the humanization of society. This subtle version has not, like the cruder version which counted on the expansion of monopoly and the pauperization of the masses, been refuted by the events of the last century. But it remains abstract, formal, and undefined. However, no matter how abstract, formal, and undefined this neo-Marxist philosophy may appear, the crucial point is that it is directly connected with an international socio-political phenomenon which, in general, represents itself, or is labeled as, the "New Left" and which has grown to a prerevolutionary factor in the widespread and diversified student revolts of recent years. Lezlek Kolakowski's philosophical criticism came into irreconcilable conflict with the dominating regime in Poland when, addressing Warsaw students on the tenth anniversary (1966) of the October uprising, he declared that there

was nothing to celebrate, since hopes had not been fulfilled and political freedom was still cut to the bone. Herbert Marcuse played a role in Germany's student revolt and Jean-Paul Sartre had an influential stake in the French student revolt of May, 1968. Hardly less symptomatic than the international character of these protest movements, which have the character of mass movements, is the confusion they arouse in East and West alike. When Marcuse addressed the Paris students during their May strike, the Russian newspaper *Pravda* suggested that he had been "catapulted from far-away San Diego to Paris in order to sow confusion and to oppose the youth and the students in particular to the fundamental forces of the working class." A pro-Chinese newspaper added sternly: "The students in Eastern Europe are being used by the reactionary ruling cliques to move to the right and unite with U.S. imperialism. . . . Students in Poland can hardly be considered in the vanguard of anything but reaction." [44]

In Western countries the critics were hardly less bewildered. A current question, often merely rhetorical, suggested that the student protests of today only represent a "fascism of the left." Their irrationality appeared to baffle any serious attempt to a reasonable evaluation. "They speak of 'Revolution,' they quote Marx, Mao and Marcuse; and it is not difficult to detect traces of the thought of such various—and, of course, contradictory—*gurus* as Proudhon, Rosa Luxemburg, Artaud, Bloch, Reich, Godard, Ginsberg, Fanon and Stokely Carmichael." [45] Observers were struck by the contradictory character of some of the reasons which had been advanced as causes of student protest in San Francisco, New York, Paris, Rome, Berlin, Warsaw, and Prague. And they concluded that the only common feature of the students' revolt was the rebellious mood, and that its historical originality derived from the fact that it appeared in the highly industrialized countries. "Neither its practice nor its theory are coherent enough to be seen as an attempt to seek rational goals by rational means. . . . In such movements realizable goals are irrelevant, and utopia (i.e., fantasy) is the only satisfactory symbol. This is the emotional background behind the current ideological hotch-potch in which the 'one-dimensional pessimism' of Marcuse is combined with the

'revolutionary optimism' of Mao. It is a mixture in which, ironically, elitist philosophy and dictatorial practice are supposed to serve as a guide to a participatory democracy in a permissive society." Marcuse was, on the other hand, characterized as a "paleo-Hegelian" and, at the same time, compared with Max Stirner, since both thinkers, in fact, come close to a rejection of civilization as such.

Of course, there was frequent reference to the spiritual roots of the student revolts in the traditions of anarchism. The only reason for surprise was the fact that now, for the first time, a radical element has emerged in the industrial countries, claiming Marx as its patron but hankering after the romantic attitudes which are pre-Marxian, and anti-industrial. For radical populism or anarchism is the natural reaction to industrialization in underdeveloped countries. The populist attitude of the intelligentsia has often been explained in terms of the discrepancy between their cultural and national aspirations and the economic backwardness of their countries. Now, history has made a full circle. The scientific-technological revolution of late industrialism has produced its own Luddites, who, unlike the earlier ones, do not smash machines, but want to withdraw from society and (presumably) live on the surplus produced by the computerized economy. "They will then be like the Roman proletariat, which . . . was parasitic on the state. Marxist theoreticians have reached a point where they either have to give up the romantic-utopian ingredients of Marx's early thought, or his later 'productivist' approach to social analysis and history. Paleo-Hegelian neo-Marxists, like Marcuse, and his followers, should logically give up Marx altogether and go back to Arcadia." [46] What is completely lacking in these observations is the crucial question: To what extent are these intellectual protest movements, in their bewildering contradictions, a perfect mirror of the latent and carefully concealed contradictions of an industrial society? What most critics fail to see is the rationality, hidden behind the confusing irrationalities of its ideological claims, of a protest which radically refuses to become absorbed into the perfectly rationalized irrationalities of affluent civilization. It is simply not true that history has made a full circle. The point at stake which, indeed is a reason for surprise, is the novelty of this un-

precedented type of "radical populism," emerging as a symptom of and a reaction against the stage of late industrialism.

It is, therefore, more adequate to evaluate the unknown and unexploited resources which Marxism, as a prospective and comprehensive diagnosis of industrial civilization in its initial phase, has for the ensuing stages of development. It has been rightly stated that within Marxism itself are three divergent conceptions of revolution: (1) a Blanquist conception, the seizure of power by a small group of armed men who, once they are masters of the state, proceed to transform its institutions; (2) an evolutionary conception, according to which the society of the future must gradually mature within the present society until the final redeeming crisis arrives; (3) the permanent-revolution conception, according to which the proletariat party exerts a constant pressure on the bourgeois parties, taking advantage of the reforms grudgingly conceded by the latter to undermine the capitalist order and to prepare at once its own victory and the advent of socialism. Each of these conceptions presupposes the necessity for violence, but the second one would postpone the final outbreak to an indefinite future.[47]

Marx was a great synthesizer and a voracious assimilator of ideas and social facts. Many of his concepts that are most startling to us were commonplaces of the English and Continental radicalism and socialism of his formative years. To a certain extent, Marxism is a much less faithful reproduction of the actual worker's revolutionary feelings than that found in some Chartists (for the British worker) or in Blanqui or Proudhon (for the French). French socialism, whether it is the unreflective philosophy of the *coup d'état* of Blanqui or the free-ranging, universal critique of Proudhon, is a "purer" form of socialism. It represents a more instinctive form of the reaction of the radical part of the working class to industrialization. However, while the theory of Proudhon, of Blanqui, or of Bakunin is as antithetical to Marxism as it is to liberalism, the anti-industrial anarchistic sentiment that underlies their doctrines can often find its effective expression in revolutionary Marxism. The antiauthority premises of anarchism hardly allow it to form an efficient political movement to compete for power. Marxism is the type of socialism that believes in industrialization, but can live as a revo-

lutionary movement of importance only in symbiosis with a widespread anti-industrial feeling. This "in-between" character of Marxism is, in fact, a key to the understanding of the reactions of a radicalized intelligentsia exploding in a series of student revolts in industrialized countries. Adam Ulam describes the evolution of Marxism as "the unfinished revolution." [48] The fact that the modern "Luddites" are no longer smashing machines is a striking indication that late industrialism, particularly where the advent of the second industrial revolution is already perceivable, produces unprecedented reactions of its own.

The future of our society is marked by the unlimited power man has before him in the realm of things. As Bonhoeffer remarked in his *Letters and Papers from Prison,* in former times one overcame nature by the power of soul; now one does it through all kinds of technical means. The immediate reality is no longer nature but organization. The question has now become: What will protect us against the threat of organization? André Dumas commented on these threats born of organization from three points of view corresponding to three characteristics of modern society: quantity, rationality, malleability.

Within a society of abundance the social "left-overs" of the process of growth have a strong chance of developing in the midst of affluence. This underdevelopment seems to be a logical subproduct of growth within societies based on quantity, rationalized and mobile. It is the consequence, the human price that the bad conscience of the unadapted pays to the good conscience of the efficient. However, rationality is made still more questionable by the subjective void it experiences. It looks as if all the goals of men inspired by conviction or feeling, their fears, their hopes, their utopias, religion, nationalism, ideology, all were reduced to their double task as producers and consumers. Of course, it is youth which raises the question. The young are not yet part of the production-consumption cycle and they reject a future reduced to the perpetuation of an aimless machinery. One of the slogans found on the walls of the University of Paris during the student revolt of May, 1968, said: "We reject a world where the certainty not to die of hunger is exchanged for the risk of dying of boredom." An-

other protest slogan started: "The revolution now beginning puts everything in question, not only the capitalist society but the industrial civilization; the society of consumers must die a violent death, the society marked by alienation must disappear from history." Previously, man battled directly with nature, a struggle for life against poverty. Now he is engaged in the indirect trial of struggle with himself, in the battle for culture, for communication, for solidarity in a state of well-being, which intensified isolation. These two threats are linked up with a third threat endangering our future: for some, the impossibility to adapt except through conformity, that is, by denying progressively the creative element of their personality; for others, the impossibility of rejecting without exploding and becoming aggressive. Both groups have no real malleability, only the stiffness of adaptation or refusal. The crisis of the society of consumption lies in this deep feeling of decaying freedom in the mechanism of expanding prosperity.[49]

Black Power

Before turning to the Third World, it is essential to devote some observations to the Negro Revolution in the United States, for the struggle of the American Negroes and their increasing conflict with affluent society reflects, like the student revolts, the inner contradictions of late industrialism and a society of consumption. In a sense, the perplexity of the Negro Revolution results from the complication that a society which technically and economically is already pioneering in the adventure of the second industrial revolution, has allowed its social pattern to foster cruel contrasts, which belong to the initial stage of the first industrial revolution. On the other hand, the Negro Revolution, on account of the simple fact that it is a struggle of black people, cannot be dealt with simply as a phenomenon inside an affluent society: it is part of the worldwide clash between the rich and the poor nations. This double character imparts to the Negro Revolution a global importance which cannot be claimed by a white student revolt or a

white workers' strike, even when these assume the dimension of mass movements.

Insofar as the Negro Revolution is part and parcel of the inner dynamics of present-day American society, it bears an ambivalent stamp which is apparent in the discussion about the truly "revolutionary" character of this emancipation movement. Many Negro intellectuals have reservations about the phrase "the Negro Revolution" even when they use it themselves. As Whitney Young has pointed out, this revolution bears little similarity to the American Revolution or the French Revolution or the Russian Revolution. There is no attempt here to overthrow a government. This is a revolution to gain the rights and respect that should be synonymous with the word "American." It is a revolution not by black people against white people, but by people who are right against those who are wrong. This revolution is unlike others, also, in that, after three hundred years of deprivation, the deprived seek redress for their grievances in an expression of faith in a nation that has done very little to deserve and nurture such faith.[50]

Lewis M. Killian reminds us that the overthrow of a ruling group or the acceptance of a new set of basic, institutional values represents the final act of a long historical process. In many revolutions of the past those revolutionaries who laid the groundwork for the eventual overthrow of a government had no such end in mind. Typically in revolutionary movements the proponents claim that their values are the basic or true values of the society, and it is exactly such ideological competition in the current racial crisis that makes many Negro leaders qualify their use of the word "revolution." They are only seeking to complete the American Revolution begun in 1776, they suggest; it is the white Establishment that has forsaken the basic American values. On the other hand, there are serious reasons for using the word "revolution." Killian sees the question as dependent on the definition one adopts. A revolution may be identified early in its development. Then the definition depends not on the outcome of the movement, but on the means that the movement is forced to use because of the response of the larger society to its demands. A revolution is a

social movement that challenges both the authority of the ruling class and the legitimacy of traditional values. A distinguishing feature of such a movement is that it attempts to create fear, not favorable response, in the public. Under this definition, the Negro protest movement has become a true revolution.[51]

Within the setting of our main theme "development through revolution" it is worth studying the ways and means by which the dominant white elite of present-day American society is trying to meet the challenge of the Negro revolution so that the Negro population may be integrated within the mainstream of American history. An illuminating and outstanding specimen of this type of policy-making is the Riot Commission Report of March, 1968. At the time of its appointment, the Commission was criticized for its moderate character, but the importance of the report, in fact, is that it makes plain that white, moderate, responsible America is where the trouble lies. The key to the report is to be found in the basic charge, in Tom Wicker's introduction,[52] that "white society is deeply implicated in the ghetto. White institutions created it, white institutions maintain it, and white society condones it." Wicker then tries to outline some kind of program that will escape the hopeless illusion of white "moderation" which sets its hopes on impotent efforts toward an integrated society and, at the same time, avoids the blind alley of black "separatism" in an "enriched" ghetto-life. The Commission concluded that the only possible course for a sensible and humane nation was "a policy which combines ghetto enrichment with programs designed to encourage integration of substantial numbers of Negroes into the society outside the ghetto." The core of this recommendation which is, at the same time, its most vulnerable spot, lies in the concept of "integration . . . into the society outside the ghetto." Apparently the Commission did not perceive the contradiction between this concept and the accusation which it acknowledges as substantially true and justified—that white society is deeply implicated in the ghetto which it created, maintains, and condones. However, what does integration into this type of society mean? Or is that society suddenly and by some kind of miracle converted into a new society through its discovery of some of the superhuman

problems of a growing ghetto in the heart of the world's most affluent nation. The Commission itself cannot possibly have fostered this illusion. It describes, with sober and courageous realism, the way to any solution of the problem as "a task that beggars any other planned social evolution known to human history," and it quotes, as the only word of consolation, President John F. Kennedy's maxim that "a journey of a thousand miles must begin with a single step."

Hence, if those are the real dimensions of the issue, then it is surprising to hear the Commission state that the rioters were and are "a time bomb ticking in the heart of the richest nation in the history of the world." Obviously, the report is caught between two incompatible time schedules: that of a journey of a thousand miles and that of a race against the impending threat of a time-bomb explosion. If the latter time schedule is true, then the optimism of Kennedy's maxim cannot be true: there must be a fallacy in the perspective of a journey of a thousand miles. A shortcut must be found and the time bomb dismantled.

Or is the metaphor of the time bomb based on fallacious presuppositions? Do we have to look for the real time bomb at a quite different place from the black ghetto? Is it unthinkable that the core of the problem lies in the structure of the white society itself? There are several indications that the Commission has an uneasy awareness that the heart of the problem should not be looked for in the patient (the black ghetto) but in the doctor (white society). At the same time, it seems to be reluctant to do more than just vaguely hint at this possibility. A first indication of this uneasy awareness lies in the key-function which the report ascribes to the factor of white racism. This seems to be a courageous recognition of the basic disease as consisting in the mentality and pattern of white society. But, strange as it may be, the very idea of white racism being the core-factor of the problem, as far as white society is responsible, works as a fatal escape from the real diagnosis. The factor of racism is made by the Commission into the decisive handicap which prevents the United States from taking the necessary social and political steps. That these steps are unavoidable is clearly stated: "Only a commitment to national

action on an unprecedented scale can shape a future compatible with the historic ideals of American society. The major need is to generate new will—the will *to tax ourselves* to the extent necessary to meet the vital needs of the nation." This would be part of an unprecedented "*planned* social evolution."

But, then, the factor of racism appears and saves the Commission from drawing the necessary conclusions from its own diagnosis. "Until the fact of white racism is far more nearly eliminated than this Commission—or any fair man—could find today, how can that great commitment of money and effort here recommended even be approached, much less made?" This argument appears to invert the sequence of cause and effect. To "tax ourselves" and the "great commitment of money and effort" needed to face the problem are, of course, primarily issues of economic policy which, ultimately, have to emerge from political decisions. White racism is a phenomenon which plays a role on all levels and in all aspects of society and it has, on each of these levels and in each of these regions, to be analyzed and approached within its proper context.

Racism is not only supported and aggravated by social patterns, but it is also heavily dependent upon politico-economic structures. The Commission has half-heartedly admitted this relationship where it fights the fallacy of white middle-class insistence that if immigrants from Europe could rise from the ghetto, so could today's Negroes. The stress is, of course, on the attribute "*today*'s." This is, in itself, already a helpful demythologizing of the race problem, as if it were an eternal or timeless issue simply because it has already existed for several centuries. What we have to cope with is not "the" Negro or "the" white, but Negroes and whites *today*. The Commission, in addition, concretizes this "today" in socio-economic and political terms: "As that cliché is analyzed here, the unskilled labor the black immigrant from the cotton fields can offer is in nothing like the demand that once there was for unskilled labor of the arriving Italian, Irishman or eastern European. Moreover, the power of the urban political machine has declined for many reasons, and today's ghetto resident can exert less organized political pressure than could yesterday's." Indeed,

the demand for unskilled labor has nothing to do with racism but is simply a question of socio-economic development. The United States no longer lives within the era of the first Industrial Revolution; it has already entered the era of the second Industrial Revolution, the era of automation and cybernetics. And the core of the problem lies in the tragic fact that this country has to cope with some of the worst phenomena of the first Industrial Revolution—mass urban poverty—in the era of the second Industrial Revolution.

This question also affects the issue of integration. Somewhat naïvely, the report concludes with surprise: "as for the rioters—those ominous looters and arsonists whose eruption into violence precipitated this massive study—they tended, curiously, to be somewhat more educated than the 'brothers' who remained uninvolved. By and large the rioters were young Negroes, natives of the ghetto (not of the South), hostile to the white society surrounding and repressing them, and equally hostile to the middle-class Negroes who accommodated themselves to that white dominance." And then it concludes, as already quoted: "*They* were and *they* are a time bomb ticking in the heart of the richest nation of the history of the world."

They! That means those very Negroes who were on the margin of that process which the report advocates as part of the solution: integration into the society outside the ghetto! The Commission would have been less naïvely surprised by this discovery had it taken to heart the lesson of the emergence of nationalism and of Communism in the countries of the so-called Third World. Everywhere it was exactly the "somewhat more educated" elements who became the forerunners of political and social protest against the prevailing colonial system. Why? Because "education" is exactly "integration into the society outside the ghetto of nativism and traditionalism." And it is these very marginal elements who begin to feel the paradox of an "education" which aims at "integration" into a society that essentially and unavoidably maintains a system which these "educated" and marginally "integrated" people experience as the very maintenance of social, political, and economic inequality and injustice. In fact the "time bomb" has

already exploded in Asia and Africa and has destroyed, at least politically, the colonial system. The United States is proud never to have participated in the colonialism of the European countries. But now, on a microcosmic scale, it begins to experience the same questions which, on a large scale, have liquidated the colonial system. Can it face, let alone answer, this challenge without a major conversion of its prevailing system, on a scale comparable to the end of colonialism on a worldwide scale?

The Commission claims, in the concluding paragraph of Wicker's introduction to the report, not to have revealed any preference for any political philosophy. But it is noteworthy that it limits this recognition by one condition: "Save for a tacit insistence upon the enormous role the Federal Government, of necessity, must have in raising and spending the sums required." A *tacit* insistence: otherwise this report could not have been written by the "moderate establishment." But nevertheless an *insistence!*

It is a remarkable indication of the dilemma wherein the report is caught up. The core of the question is neither with the rioters of the black ghetto nor in the existence of white racism, but in the overriding question: Which kind of national politico-economic policy will be decided upon to meet the greatest challenge of its traditional system the United States has ever experienced?

The challenge consists in the obvious dilemma that large groups have lost their belief that a mere evolution or further development of present-day society might ever be able to provide a cure for the socio-political ills which have made it sick to the core. On this crucial issue the "New Left" parted company with the "Old Left" from which it sought to differentiate itself between 1960 and 1965. The phrase "participatory democracy," which was the contribution of the New Student Left to political theory, appeared in the Port Huron statement of the founding convention of Students for a Democratic Society in 1962: "In a participatory democracy, the political life would be based on the principle that decision-making of basic social consequence be carried on by public groupings." The advocates of this principle explained that

what they were advocating was a democracy of direct action in which the concerned activists could intervene directly in political process, and affect their outcome without the intervention of an electorate and the machinery of representative democracy. Staughton Lynd, an active civil rights worker and an assistant professor at Yale University, saw participatory democracy as an American version of the Russian Soviet, with admixtures of Gandhi's pro-village ideology, and the back-to-the-people spirit of the Russian student movement of the nineteenth century. In fact, the kinship between "participatory democracy" and "Soviet democracy" which Lynd acknowledges has induced commentators to state that, in essence, it is Lenin's theory of revolutionary action by a small, dictatorial elite translated into the language of the "nonviolent" movement.[53]

No matter how essential the transition from violent to nonviolent action may be, the notion of participatory democracy involved a basic alteration in the concept of civil disobedience. Originally, as conceived by Martin Luther King, Jr., it was an appeal to the conscience of the community; the civil disobedient undertook to violate some unjust or unconstitutional ordinance in order to draw the attention of the electorate and the government to existing wrongs; he still retained a faith in the workings of representative democracy. The New Student Left, on the other hand, began to conceive of civil disobedience as a first step in a confrontation with the power structure. The Student Nonviolent Coordinating Committee (SNCC) came to be characterized as the "new abolitionists." These are young radicals says Howard Zinn; "the word 'revolution' occurs again and again in their speech. Yet they have no party, no ideology, no creed. They have no clear idea of a blueprint for a future society. But they do know clearly that the values of present American society—and this goes beyond racism to class distinction, to commercialism, to profit-seeking, to the setting of religious or national barriers against human contact—are not for them. They are prepared to use revolutionary means against the old order. They believe in civil disobedience. They are reluctant to rely completely on the niceties of negotiation and conciliation, distrustful of those who hold political and economic power. They have a tremendous respect for

the potency of the demonstration, an eagerness to move out of the political maze of normal parliamentary procedure and to confront policy-makers directly with a power beyond orthodox politics—the power of people in the streets and on the picket line."

They are nonviolent in that they suffer beatings with folded arms and will not strike back, but next to the word "nonviolence," what is heard most often is the phrase "direct action." "They believe, without inflicting violence, and while opening themselves to attack, in confronting a community boldly with the sounds and sights of protest. When it is argued that this will inevitably bring trouble, even violence, the answer is likely to be that given by James Bevel: 'Maybe the Devil has got to come out of these people before we will have peace.' " [54]

The battle cry that replaced "Freedom Now" during the critical years of 1965 and 1966 was the enigmatic slogan "Black Power," rooted in the realities of the Negro situation in the mid-sixties. The Negro Revolution had started as a quest for freedom. But the conviction that freedom could be gained only through power and enjoyed only when Negroes have the means in their own hands for guarding that liberty brought power to the forefront as the immediate goal. Stokely Carmichael, who had become chairman of SNCC, used the James Meredith march through Mississippi early in the summer of 1966 as a vehicle for proclaiming "Black Power" as the newest slogan of the revolution. It was a slogan, not an ideology or a program. No fine distinctions were made between kinds of power: political, economic; violent, nonviolent; legal, illegal; loving, hostile. The appeal was simple: let there be power which was new and black. During the ten years preceding the introduction of this slogan there had been a broadening of the values of the revolution. The range of tactics employed by various segments of the Negro Revolution had broadened to include all forms of coercive public protest, even violence, at least as a means of self-defense. Even the most moderate Negro leaders could not afford to condemn rioters in unequivocal terms.

Of essential importance is the connection between the radicalization of the Negro Revolution and the increasing consciousness of solidarity with the opposition in the Third World against

Western (neo-) colonialism and imperialism. The New Student Left had already welcomed the Watts riots of the summer of 1965 as a people's uprising against imperialist America, as part of the same guerrilla warfare which was being carried on from Vietnam to Los Angeles against the United States. The alliance of the radical wing of the Negro protest movement with the anti-Vietnam War movement reflects the intrusion of the Third World theme into the ideology of the Negro Revolution. The struggle of the American Negro was felt to be a part of the broader worldwide struggle of the oppressed, or nonwhite, or colonial peoples.

Carmichael reveals his faith in the Third World when he says: "The colonies of the United States—and this includes the black ghetto within its borders, North and South—must be liberated. For a century this nation has been like an octopus of exploitation, its tentacles stretching from Mississippi and Harlem to South America, the Middle East, Southern Africa, and Vietnam. This pattern must be broken. As its grip loosens here and there around the world, the hopes of Black Americans become more realistic. For racism to die a totally different America must be born." [55]

Stokely Carmichael and Charles Hamilton, significantly enough, introduce their book on Black Power as a political framework and ideology "which represents the last reasonable opportunity for this society to work out its racial problems short of prolonged destructive guerrilla warfare." The book could be read as a passionate comment on Frantz Fanon's *The Wretched of the Earth,* which puts forth clearly the reasons for the relationship of the concept called Black Power to the concept of a new force in the world: "Let us try to create the whole man, whom Europe has been incapable of bringing to triumphant birth. Two centuries ago, a former European colony decided to catch up with Europe. It succeeded so well that the United States of America became a monster, in which the taints, the sickness and the inhumanity of Europe have grown to appalling dimensions. The Third World today faces Europe like a colossal mass whose aim should be to try to resolve the problems to which Europe has not been able to find the answers. It is a question of the Third World starting a new history of man." [56]

The parallelism "white power: the colonial situation" inside the United States and in the world at large is not only the title of the first chapter but also the dominating theme of the book by Carmichael and Hamilton. Integration is being radically rejected because, as a hypothetical solution to the race problem, it demands that the Negro forswear his identity as a Negro. Three myths are exposed as major fallacies. The first one is that in the context of present-day America, the interests of black people are identical with the interests of certain liberal, labor, and other reform groups. The second myth is the fallacious assumption that a viable coalition can be effected between the politically and economically secure and the politically and economically insecure. The third myth assumes that political coalitions are, or can be, sustained on a moral, friendly, sentimental basis, by appeals to conscience.[57] Not too much fantasy is required to translate each of the three myths into terms of the major fallacies concerning the cooperation between the rich and the poor countries.

The book *Black Power* is presented as an essay on "The politics of liberation in America." The word "liberation" could, as well, be replaced by "modernization." The most noteworthy feature of this important witness is that, though the title might suggest a radically revolutionary appeal, what we are offered, in fact, is a penetrating analysis of the paradoxical consequences of rapid development or modernization. The authors agree with the thesis of David Apter, put forward in his *The Politics of Modernization,* that the struggle to modernize has become so compelling a force that we are forced to ask new questions of our own institutions. "Each country, whether modernized or modernizing, stands in both judgment and fear of the results. Our own society is no exception." [58] Whether one is talking about the fantastic changes taking place in Africa, Asia, or the black communities of America, this is the conclusion of the authors: it is necessary to realize that the current turbulent period of history is characterized by the demands of previously oppressed peoples to be free of their oppression. "Those demands will not be quieted by guns or soft talk; those demands have a logic of their own—a logic frequently misunder-

stood by the oppressors. Those demands are part of the on-going process of modernization." [59]

The other side of the coin of Black Power bears the stamp of the term "Black Nationalism." This side provides a no less striking parallelism with phenomena in the Third World. This term, too, is used to express a feeling so far little supported by any detailed plans or serious attempts at organization. The ultra-radical black extremists translate Black Nationalism into the "national liberation struggle" of the Peking-Hanoi-Havana-Algiers varieties. Much is made of the colonial analogy between the American Negro's struggle against white mastery and the struggle of other nonwhites against European white mastery in Asia and Africa. Indeed, as Du Bois suggested nearly seventy years ago and as many others have since, the analogy includes much common experience and many similar emotions.[60]

In the American setting, the political goals of a nationalist struggle to overthrow foreign rule and replace it by national self-rule run into some obvious difficulties. The American black ultras have, however, no interest thus far in any real solutions; the political goals with which they are concerned are the attempt to launch a "guerrilla war" in American cities which will widen the polarization of white and black. The more moderate extremists use the term "Black Nationalism" interchangeably with "Black Power." What they all share, however, is not so much a conversion to a new faith-in-separation as a loss of their old faith-in-the-prospects-of-integration. What they are seeking is a black-imposed and black-controlled separation in which they will be able to improve their own conditions of life.

But, essentially, Black Nationalism is an expression of the long-drawn-out identity crisis of Negroes in America, a reflection of the struggle to find some new resolution of the duality Negro and American. As Harold Isaacs has pointed out, the key word is not "nationalism" but "black." Whatever new revolution in American affairs they may or may not bring about, the new black militants of this generation in America have already sparked a profound revolution in the way Negro Americans see themselves

as black.[61] The elevation of the word "black" to ordinary and aggressive use has a long and complex history and deep psychological roots. The current Black Power movement is the first to succeed in re-establishing the free use of the word "black" in the vocabulary of Negro self-expression. It is a powerful counterassertion and challenge to all the shrinking self-debasement and self-denial of Negroes in the past. Hence the heightened efforts to regain for Negroes a sense of a past in which they can take pride, and the new search for some redefinition of links between Negroes in America and Africans in Africa. The goal of the Negro's struggle in America has been to resolve his duality, to shake the blur into some single or coherent image of himself as a person and as an American.

The Spectrum of Social Time

Black Nationalism in the United States and the nationalism of the emerging countries in the Third World share an essential feature: the struggle for a redefinition of the past and a radical reorientation toward new goals which open perspectives great and inspiring enough to overcome a fatal identity crisis. Therefore, before we enter upon the questions of national revolutions in new states, it is apt to insert some observations on the significance of collective time consciousness for the processes of modernization.

An excellent guide in this field is *The Spectrum of Social Time* by the French philosopher of sociology, Georges Gurvitch.[62] Gurvitch has attempted an analysis of the multiple apperceptions which various types of societies conceive of the time dimension. In the last three chapters Gurvitch attempts an analysis of, successively, the time scales of global societies, of modern societies, and of contemporary societies. Under global societies he includes a variety of social structures from primitive or archaic societies to charismatic theocracies, patriarchal and feudal societies, and the ancient city-states becoming empires. The group of modern societies is divided into nascent capitalistic societies and democratic-liberal societies with developed competitive capitalism. The group

of contemporary societies comprises four types: the managerial society of organized capitalism; the fascist society based on techno-bureaucracy; the planned, centralized, collectivist state; and the planned, decentralized, pluralistic, collectivist society.

One subject of his study is the variety of time scales in these societies: in other words, their concept of social time. Social time is defined as "the convergency and divergency of movements of the total social phenomenon giving birth to time and elapsing in time." But—and this is the other subject of Gurvitch's study—the variety of types of society is seconded by a variety of social classes. Gurvitch defines a social class as constituting a collective whole so vast and rich that it can rival even the time of global society. Each class possesses its own dynamic and its own time scale. This is because each is incompatible with the other classes and resists penetration by the global society to which it belongs. The social time of a rising class, particularly when it begins to take power, is imposed to a large degree on the whole of society. A class, being rebellious toward the hierarchy of functional groupings which characterize the structure of the society in which it is integrated, also rejects the official time scale. A class not in power struggles to get there and moves during this struggle in its own scale of time. If a class disappears, that is because it is a victim of a situation in which its own scale of time is entirely outmoded.

Each class is a world unto itself and aspires to become a unique world. It identifies itself with the existing global society from which the other classes are more or less excluded or at least placed in a subordinate position; or it identifies itself with a future global society in which there is a completely new relationship between the classes, or the class divisions themselves disappear. Or, a class may identify itself with a former global society in which this class played a dominant or at least an important role.

The Marxist analysis is blamed by Gurvitch for a twofold oversimplification. First, Marx has overlooked the complex dialectical game played between the time scale of a social class and the time scale of the global society that is preparing to dominate or is already starting to dominate. He tended to reduce global-society determinism to class determinism, and consequently the

time scale of the global society has been reduced to the time scale of classes. Second, he made the error of contrasting the social classes with only two kinds of particular groupings: the state and political parties. These are generally presented by the Marxist analysis as instruments of the class struggle in modern societies. In this way the macrocosm of groupings within the social classes is partially neglected.

Non-Marxist analysis, however, at present tends to make another error, to the extent of practically denying the existence of social classes and extremely impoverishing the macrocosm of groupings participating in a class. Since the variety of time scales is occasionally concealed in the different social classes, the problem of social time is simply evaded in the non-Marxist approach.

What are the specific features of the different social classes, according to their time scales?

Three social times are found to be most important for the *peasant class:* the enduring time of long duration and slow motion, retarded time turned in on itself, and cyclical time related to the seasons. Erratic time (time of uncertainty, where the present appears to prevail over the past and the future; the time of the technical patterns particularly in the societies of the nineteenth and twentieth centuries), time in advance of itself, and explosive time do not play a role in the time scale produced by the peasant class. Therefore, only crises like religious and civil wars, social and technical revolutions, international wars and epidemics can jolt the peasant-class time. At certain historical junctures, as in the French, Russian, and Chinese Revolutions, the customary time scale of the peasant class is upset by erratic time, and time in advance of itself, and it is only in these extraordinary events that the time scale of the peasant class plays an active role in great social upheavals. But this never lasts long, and, once satisfied, this class turns in on itself and continues to live according to its characteristic scale of time, even if the most modern techniques are put at its disposal, as in the U.S.S.R. and China today.

Quite different is the time scale of the *bourgeois class,* the class which since the beginning of capitalism and up to the twentieth century has been of major importance in our societies and

which has held uncontested power in the industrial societies. This class first played the role of a revolutionary avant-garde, later became moderate, conservative, and finally reactionary. In fully developed organized capitalist societies, e.g., the United States, Great Britain, and West Germany, the managers tend to dominate the industrial and financial factions of the bourgeoisie, and it is that faction which is capable of surviving in collectivist states, even while the disintegration and elimination of the bourgeois class takes place.

The class consciousness of the bourgeois class is characterized by confidence in an unlimited technical and economic progress, confidence in the harmony of the interests of all, in the universal benefits of capitalism and urban culture. Therefore, in direct contrast to the class consciousness of the peasant class, the bourgeois class consciousness lends itself to universal diffusion. Its awareness of time is very well expressed in the saying "Time is money," which relates its own scale of time, considered as universal, to economic profit and production.

The amazing thing to note is that the bourgeois class does not produce the time scale expected in light of its orientation. Because it has always to defend its economic acquisitions and, in order to persist, must partially subordinate the peasant and proletarian classes, its social time scale rather than being time leaping forward is, on the contrary, retarded time masked by advance. The more the bourgeois class feels its very existence menaced by the rising collectivist regimes or by the promotion in its own midst of the managerial group preparing itself to become a class, the more it has tended to favor delayed time turned in on itself, clinging to exhausted or anachronistic political regimes and to organizational methods and technology on the way to being outmoded. The other perspective is the possibility of orientation toward a fascist regime and alliance with technocracy. Only in political revolutions and counter-revolutions where the bourgeoisie, to its own profit, is able to play an avant-garde role, does time in advance of itself come to the surface. This is also the case when, in certain situations, this class becomes a force in colonial, international, and even civil wars. But, even at the height of great turmoil, it remains a prudent

agent, for it has too much to lose in any sort of crisis, in which its very existence is always threatened.

The *proletariat* has been slow to organize and develop class consciousness, which dates back to the beginning of the nineteenth century. Although it was manifested in the various socialist and collectivist ideologies, neither Marxism, which became the dominant expression in a later period, nor any other doctrine has been able to substitute itself for the proletarian consciousness. This consciousness includes among other things the awareness of needs, aspirations of the future, the collective memory of dramatic historical events as political and labor union struggles, etc. It would be erroneous to represent the proletarian class as uniquely revolutionary.

In its scale, time in advance (projecting the future into the present) and explosive time (obliterating the present and the past in the creation of the future) are the generally emphasized times. However, the time in advance of itself is only a time of profoundly uncertain aspirations; whereas explosive time, being the time of the permanent revolution, has seldom an effective duration.

Although the working class remains the greatest revolutionary force in our societies, revolution cannot be permanent. Hence the time ahead of itself moving in the direction of explosive time would last only in a planned economy, directed and controlled by the workers themselves.

It is only during periods of revolution that the proletariat appears to control its time and its scale of time. Its revolutionary consciousness of time is strongly emotional and culminates in utopias and "social myths." Only in controlling the economic planning through democratic self-government is the working class able to reach the point of real mastery of its time. Moreover, the proletarian time scale can be radically changed by other factors. It depends, for instance, on whether the proletariat struggles alone or is allied with other classes; whether it permits a centralized, collectivist state to dominate it temporarily; whether the family or economic strata take an unexpected importance, etc.

The *middle classes* embrace a multiplicity of collectivities—

artisans and small businessmen as well as employees, officials, middlemen and self-employed workers—which do not succeed in finding their place between the working class and the bourgeois class; they have an ambiguous consciousness of their class and can, in the conflict of classes, go in one direction or another, or occupy a position quite apart.

A different case is represented by the *techno-bureaucratic groupings*. The class of managers, which in organized capitalism represents only a fraction of the bourgeois class, has in fascist regimes illustrated its capacity of challenging the very existence of the bourgeois class and of adapting to the social revolutions which create centralized, collectivist structures. However, they have difficulty asserting themselves as a social class, since their different groups do not live in the same social time. The economic planners live in a time ahead of itself, which, in the face of every unforeseen obstacle, is reversed, and becomes a time behind itself. The technical experts live in alternation between advance and delay, precipitated by the rapidity of technical discoveries but with all of its uncertainties. Public-service bureaucrats are often encased in a time of slowed-down, long duration. Therefore, the techno-bureaucrats do not succeed in unifying real time into a scale and are victims of an illusion: they imagine themselves living in a time ahead of itself or even in an explosive time of creation which they think they alone know how to dominate. Consequently, the societies in which they are preparing to seize power risk being carried away by forces moving in times which no class or human power can dominate or arrest.

Moving now from the time scales of social classes to the time scale of *various types of societies,* we are primarily interested in Gurvitch's observations on "modern" and "contemporary" societies. The unforeseen alliance between the territorial state and the newly born town-bourgeoisie provoked the establishment of a new society with its own time scale, resulting in the first phase of capitalism combined with absolute monarchy. This type of society, which gave birth to nascent capitalism and "enlightened" absolutism, was in Western Europe initiated in the second half of the sixteenth century and lived on during the seventeenth and eight-

eenth centuries. In the society of this type, the awareness of time and the conceptualizing of time usually is taken over by the state, on the one hand, and by the bourgeoisie, on the other hand. Both the state and the bourgeoisie are linked with science and technology, which favor the quantification of time.

In industrial technology, international commerce, and scientific knowledge (both technical and philosophical), the bourgeois class and its ideology are essentially in advance. The nobility and the clergy, the agrarian economy and the peasantry are in retardation. The absolute monarchy itself advances by taking important initiatives, but it is retarded in its organization. The monarchic state utilizes enlightened absolutism to maintain a balance between time of advance and time of delay. It does this in order to dominate the erratic time of the masses, which it has itself promoted by favoring industrialization, and the erratic time of social classes competing with the official, already disintegrating, social hierarchy. This mastery of time succeeded in Western societies up to the French Revolution and was maintained to the end of the nineteenth century in Central and Eastern Europe, as for example in Germany, Austria, Hungary, and Czarist Russia.

The *democratic-liberal societies with developed competitive capitalism* were the type of society which, following the British, American, and French Revolutions, dominated Europe and America in the nineteenth century and at the beginning of the twentieth century. In this liberal democratic structure, time pushing forward partially succeeds, having earlier struggled vainly for first place in the structure of the ancient city-states and in enlightened monarchy. The time scale of the proletarian class tends to advance in comparison to that of the global structure of this society, and the time scale of the bourgeois class tends to delay more and more in relation to it—until the moment when this structure either is transformed into that of organized capitalism or else breaks down because of a social revolution or a fascist *coup d'état*.

In many countries where capitalism has achieved prominence or has been introduced into the country from outside, there are tendencies toward the *managerial society of organized capitalism*. This type of society has acquired its greatest prominence in the

United States, and to some degree in Germany before and after Nazism, as well as in France now. The economy is no longer left to free competition; it is planned in the private interest of trusts, cartels, and corporations with the aid of the state which puts its vast bureaucratic machinery at the disposition of the employers. The awareness of time is concentrated in the great bureaucratic machinery, which becomes even more ideological and political and much more dependent on technology than in the liberal democratic regimes.

The knowledge of the time is mechanized here much more easily, as the structure of organized capitalism is not inspired at all by any ideal of the future. These same organized machineries try to dominate the time scale but they achieve only superficial success in this, for they are slaves to the machines they produce. The structure of this society tends once more to be detached from the subjacent total social phenomenon in which time leaping forward and explosive time are more favored than in the superimposed structure's time scale. The structures of organized capitalism are steadily menaced by explosions or attracted by fascists of different kinds.

The structure of the *fascist society* consists of the complete fusion of organized capitalism with the totalitarian state led by the techno-bureaucratic groups arising from the trusts and cartels, banks, high administrative personnel, and specialized career military men. The semicharismatic leader who crowns this edifice is only a straw man, for these groups and the chauvinistic and racial mythology are only a screen behind which is hidden the techno-bureaucratic authoritarianism. The different techno-bureaucratic groupings in power live in mutually contradictory times, whereas the awareness of time attributed to the fascist leader is imaginary and illusory. Because the structure fails to absorb or express the subjacent total social phenomenon, the totalitarian state makes a desperate effort for unification accompanied by economic and military planning which is stalemated in the end. The fascist regimes pretend to be able to master the time scale in which they move, but in reality they are entirely enslaved and carried along by it.

In the *planned, centralized, collectivist state*—the type of society illustrated by Soviet Russia, contemporary China, and most of the so-called people's democracies with the exception of Yugoslavia—the proletarian class, either alone or united with the peasant class, is officially proclaimed "dictator." This dictatorship is exercised by the Communist Party, which itself is in the hands of the organizer technicians. Neither the organs of planning, nor the techno-bureaucracy directing production, nor the state, nor the Party are directly controlled by the proletarians themselves. Only as a catalyst of spontaneous collective creation can the organized superstructure realize effectively its extensive tasks and accomplish its purposes in the interest of all. That would presuppose the predominance of explosive time of creation and of time pushing forward which corresponds to innovating behavior. But for these times to triumph it would be necessary that the interested parties themselves control the organizations. As these conditions till now are not realized in the structure of centralized collectivism, its time scale causes the structure to live in perpetual tension, menaced by fatigue, disillusion, and indifference on the part of the majority of its beneficiaries. Time pushing forward and explosive time are to a large extent sacrificed to the deceptive time of the organized superstructure.

Only a rapid transformation in the sense of the "self-government of the workers" as it is promised now could make this time scale less tense. But the type of the *planned, decentralized, pluralist, collectivist society* has not as yet been completely attempted. Nevertheless, some real, observable tendencies can be seen in certain people's democracies, Yugoslavia, for example; and in certain Western countries when they attempt collectivist economic planning on a democratic base, for instance in the Scandinavian countries and in England at some periods. The structure of this global society would be founded on an attempt to establish a balance between industrial democracy and political democracy. Here the explosive time of creation and time pushing forward appear to have an effective chance to occupy first place. Nevertheless, the creations and the initiatives of different groups might easily be contradictory and conflicting. Time lagging behind would be re-

inforced by the inevitable pre-eminence of law-regulation in this structure, which favors parity and equivalence among a large plurality of groups.

The analysis of Georges Gurvitch, which we have summarized, may be completed by a few observations closely attached to Gurvitch's ideas, which are to be found in a study by Professor Hahn-Been Lee of Seoul, Korea. His study focuses upon the issue of "Developmentalist Time and Leadership in Developing Countries." [63] Among the overwhelming changes which confront the developing countries, owing to the impact of the modern world, there is in general a choice of three attitudes. The positive attitude toward change is forward-looking or "developmentalist." Viewed in a negative way, on the other hand, time becomes a burdensome pressure and leads to an "escapist orientation." A third attitude, torn between the positive and the negative, is present-bound or "exploitationist."

When integration of the past and the future in the present occurs, developmentalist time appears. When it fails to occur, either escapist time or exploitationist time takes hold. Development is a difficult task, precisely because the occurrence of integration of time experience is the exception rather than the rule. Escapist time, though oriented primarily to the past, can also take the form of an escape into the future or a refuge in the present. It can manifest itself in such out-of-time fantasies as "futurism" or "millennialism" and "presentism" as well as archaism. The dominant escapist time is nostalgic for the "good old days." For a nation it usually involves the idea of duplicating a "Golden Age" in the nation's history. The time of refuge in the present is apathetic. A flight into the future has a utopian orientation.

Developmentalist time is essentially an integrated time. It plans ahead and is ready to take risks; its vision of the future is given purpose and precision through the constructive use of the past and its realization is further accelerated through the sacrifices made in the present. This distinction is helpful for analyzing the roles of the various leading groups in developing countries. The traditional elites, i.e., tribal and clan chiefs and members of landed aristocracy, find the new environment of change threatening to

their status, which is based on their past. And they tend to take refuge in an escapist-time orientation. Torn between the system based on their past, and their visible ineptitude at their present tasks, they become increasingly authoritarian in their leadership style.

The exploitationist time is related to a ritualist role pattern. The second-generation elite of postnationalist politicians with a bureaucratic attitude falls into this category. Being highly consumption-oriented and prone to ostentatious public expenditure on all fronts without specific rational priorities, their programs tend to set in motion a vicious circle of high expenditure, inflation, and increased consumption throughout the society.

The innovational and entrepreneurial role pattern, related to developmentalist time, is spread thinly among a relatively small number of politicians and administrators who are most interested in planning for the future and so advocate sacrifices in the present and stress production and investment for long-term gains. Three other groups in addition to the political and administrative elites are also potential sources of "development entrepreneurs." First, the intellectuals. In spite of their utopian predilection, they have an important influence on the course of a nation's modernization. It is particularly the student generation in developing countries, combining idealism and creativity with rebellion, which possesses an explosively utopian time. The second group is the military, which in many developing countries has emerged as a significant candidate for a modernizing role. Nearly all of the new countries have taken the Second World War type of army as their model, thus creating a form of organization peculiar to the most highly industrial civilizations. The unavoidable gap with the traditional value scale of other sections of the society creates tension which in periods of acute social unrest may turn into conflict with civilian society. The time orientation of the military officer corps is, in general, future-oriented but never utopian. Members of the third group, the businessmen, who in developing countries have no time to accumulate experience, in general fall victim to an exploitationist investment. Nevertheless, this group also has the potential to develop an entrepreneurial attitude.

The crucial issue for developing countries is whether they are able to form "innovating enclaves" to intensify the developmentalist potentialities hidden in these forward-looking groups. A second decisive factor is that modernization in the political, the socio-cultural, and the economic spheres is progressing simultaneously. In countries where modernization took place in earlier centuries, social and political developments preceded the industrial revolution, but for the newly developing countries, realism would dictate synchronization of development efforts in all three spheres.

This conclusion of Hahn-Been Lee's analysis confronts the developing countries with the necessity of a syncretist development in various spheres, in other words, with the urge toward a social, political, and industrial revolution taking place at the same time. This necessity would make all the difference between the situation of revolutionaries and developers in developing countries of today and that of their forerunners in comparable stages of Western history in former centuries. The scene is even more confusing and the burden still heavier. The "revolution of rising expectations" in developing countries takes place in a world already witnessing the mature fruits of what was sown by former generations of revolutionaries and developers. In our day there is hardly any room left for utopias. Those who raise the banner for rapid development have to take responsibility for revolution; and, on the other hand, the makers of today's revolutions have to be the planners, managers, and techno-bureaucrats of tomorrow. Once the spell of the unbroken tradition has been broken, there is no return to the good old days, but the way ahead is not a glorious journey toward the eternal sunrise of liberty, equality, and fraternity. The way ahead reveals a very limited number of possible solutions for the development problems. Liberty may be the twin brother of technocratic enslavement, equality another name for bureaucratic collectivism, fraternity the masked appearance of national self-idolization. The years of childhood belong to the past. Our world has come of age.

Revolution of Rising Expectations

"Revolution of rising expectations" is, in fact, a sweeping generalization which has attained a measure of popularity as a general characteristic of the situation in the so-called Third World. ("Third World" is, after all, a no-less-daring generalization and, in that respect, each designation is the other's adequate counterpart.)

Gunnar Myrdal, in his voluminous work *Asian Drama,* while using the phrase "revolution of rising expectations" at the same time puts its generalizing effect to a severely critical test.[64] He recognizes the designation as characteristic of the postcolonial realization of formerly subject peoples that they can shape their own destiny, and this challenges all relationships within society. That the change in attitude has thus far mainly affected the educated class and scarcely touched the lower stratum does not make it less important where that class is dominant. These aspirations, which are bound to rise over time and to spread to an even larger part of the population, have been formulated in the political terms of the modern welfare state of the rich Western countries. They have their roots in the era of the Enlightenment that inspired the American and French Revolutions. Myrdal calls it "one of the ironies of history" that these ideas and ideals were brought to the countries of South Asia mainly by colonialism, "which thereby unwillingly, and unwittingly, destroyed its own foundation." It is worth noticing that Myrdal uses here—probably unwillingly and unwittingly—almost the same expressions that Karl Marx formulated, in the midst of the nineteenth century, to define the paradoxical role of British colonial rule in India. It is even more interesting to see how this "irony of history" has continued its activity in the postcolonial era. As soon as the formerly colonial countries had won their independence, they began to build their constitutional and civic structure on the lines of parliamentary democracy. This resulted from what had been the peculiar, but very real, contact through colonialism of the now newly democratic nations with the colonial powers. However, these democratic concepts had devel-

oped gradually in the rich, progressive nations of the Western world, and began to be realized only during the past generation. A wide gap exists between aspirations and accomplishments within formerly colonial nations which have experimented with ultra-modern political democracy. In other words, the revolution of rising expectations has not only put the ax to the root of the colonial order that had channeled the introduction of explosive ideas and ideals; it goes on undermining the stability of any new order which the new states have attempted to build on the basis of these ideals that they have accepted.

There is truth in Myrdal's criticism that the concept is rather loose and has to be quantified. The idea of the rising expectations as a revolutionary movement among the masses is, in fact, in large part a false rationalization. It reflects the Western observer's and the indigenous intellectual's feeling of how he would react if he had to live in the dire poverty of the masses. The radical tone of most political proclamations in the new states gives expression to the feelings of the members of a privileged class, who are aware of the misery of the broader stratum. Despite the great social distance, they wish to identify themselves with their nation. It is this very struggle to bridge a great social distance that is in the background of a third paradoxical aspect of this "revolution." On a general level, the public debate is filled with pronouncements that a social and economic revolution is needed, particularly under the mounting pressure of a population explosion. But in practice the policies resorted to are piecemeal and gradualist, often to the extreme. The intellectual elite who, on the one hand, are the vehicles for the modernization ideals, on the other hand, largely belong, or have numerous ties, to the privileged groups that have vested interests in the institutional status quo.

This overgradualist approach is supported by other factors. The intellectuals in the new nations are, through their Westernized education and contacts, familiar with the historical development in the Western countries, which on the whole was one of social evolution. The common use of the Western approach in research and planning helps them to overlook the fundamental differences in initial conditions. But also, Western students of developing

nations are biased by their own background in favor of a gradualist approach. They as well as their non-Western colleagues realize that the introduction of sudden changes has often caused disruption. In fact, the developing countries are regarded as unable to master a policy of more rapidly induced change—except by relying on totalitarian and monolithic methods. "Democratic planning" with reliance on persuasion is thus rationalized to defend the avoidance of radical reforms through changing the institutions. So the planners remain in their paradoxical position: on a general and noncommittal level they proclaim the need for radical social and economic change, whereas in planning their policies they tread most warily in order not to disrupt the traditional social order. This contradiction is intellectualized in two opposing views, simultaneously held, on what planning for development really requires in the way of social change. On the one hand, it is asserted that social change must be radical and go very deep. On the other hand, it is stressed that it must proceed with the utmost caution, upsetting the inherited traditional social setting as little as possible.[65]

The Revolution of Nation-Building

The ambiguities implied in the dichotomy between ideals and realities, so characteristic of the self-expression of the revolution of rising expectations in a number of new nations, are essential to the modernization process as such. They result from the fact that this process has been set in motion by the impact of Western countries, whereas the time schedule which the West has followed in the past and is following in the present cannot be imitated by the Third World. "In a sense, the most fundamental difference in initial conditions between the South Asian countries today and the Western countries in any period of their pre-industrial phase is the difference in the pace of history. A telescoping of change has become the only alternative not only to continued stagnation but to regression." [66] This situation is a result of the high levels of economic development now achieved by the developed countries

and the accelerating speed at which they continue to develop. The early development of the Western countries, where economic development originated, was gradual. All the major revolutions of the West, on the religious, intellectual, social, and political levels, occurred long before the Industrial Revolution, and they proceeded slowly. The "coefficient of changeability" (Gerschenkron[67]), starting at a low point in the Middle Ages, rose and then continued to rise at an ever faster rate. Progress in science and technology was a result of and, at the same time, a driving force in this gradual development. In the West, change was indigenous and people became gradually accustomed to the kind of permanent industrial revolution in which they live today. To the underdeveloped countries, however, technological advance is coming as a shock administered by external forces, the dynamics of which are working to the ever-greater disadvantages of their development prospects.

In other words, the succession of "social revolutions" and "technical revolutions" followed in the modernization process of present-day developed Western countries, has, in a sense, been turned upside down in the developing countries of the Third World. This contrast is also clearly visible in the political sector where the development of the modern national state is at stake. In Europe nationalism originated after two great processes of modernization had had time to accrue. The series of transformations, occurring in the Renaissance, the Reformation, and the Enlightenment, paved the way for modern society and culture. The second major fact was the creation of fairly stable states. Both trends preceded the movement of nationalism which, under the stirrings of the French Revolution and the Napoleonic Wars, finally reached fruition in the nineteenth century. Nationalistic ideas gained ground as the economic development toward industrialization gathered momentum. This development is historically associated with the emergence of a new social class, the middle class, which only in the setting of a consolidated national state could unfold its economic, cultural, and social ambitions. However, at the same time of the Industrial Revolution the West European countries were far from being democracies in the modern meaning of the term. Suffrage was generally restricted to

a small, propertied upper class, and it tended to remain that way right up to the twentieth century. The right of workers and poor peasants to the vote had to be fought for through many decades. The ultimate arrival of universal suffrage was a triumph for education, popular agitation, and initiative, in short, of centuries of striving originally started by better-situated groups. In present-day underdeveloped countries, however, the extreme poverty of the common people and the enormous social distance separating them from the very small privileged elite in fact turns what is commonly called the "middle class" into an oligarchic upper class. However, the modernization ideals, which, in Western Europe, had found root in the middle class during an evolution covering a time span of a series of generations, lack national tradition in the Third World and remain more or less rootless. At the same time, as a self-evident implication of the postcolonial attainment of national independence, political rights were granted from above without the masses ever having demanded them.[68]

The prospects of nation-building are, therefore, closely related to the stage of development at which a country has arrived. Generally speaking, the realization of a new concept of nationhood is the universal revolution which mankind has passed through in modern times. The breakup of the old European empires which began after 1918 shattered Central and Eastern Europe into assorted national fragments which have not to this day been brought into any relaxed new pattern of relationships. In the two decades since the Second World War, hundreds of millions of people have become nationals of nations that had for the most part never existed before, certainly not in the forms and with the boundaries they now have. In a world without any more coherent order to share in, colonial peoples who needed to throw off the yokes of foreign power had no choice but national power to put in its place. Nationality has become the paramount link between an individual and the rest of humanity.[69] This being a universal fact, there is at the same time an enormous difference between the political forms which fill the universal model of nationhood. Full democracy with universal suffrage has only been successfully tried out at an advanced stage of economic development. The

experience of the countries in central, eastern, and southern Europe after the First World War suggests that when a democratic form of government is imposed on an economically and politically immature nation it rapidly succumbs to authoritarian pressures. The lessons of recent history in a number of countries of the Third World also point to this relationship.

This issue is clearly illustrated by the different ways pursued in recent decades by the two prominent Asian nations, India and China. Both countries, each of which for centuries has continued a long imperial tradition, have been converted in our century and particularly since the Second World War into nations guided by the modern concept of nationhood and democracy. This is the basic revolution which both have willingly and wittingly accepted, and it is this basic fact which, in a measure, presents both countries with comparable chances, risks, and dilemmas. But the answer which each has decided upon is profoundly different.

Nationalism in India, as it emerged in the last quarter of the nineteenth century, has been the outcome of the impact of European political thought and of the social revolution which India was undergoing as a result of British political and economic dominance. The struggle of the nationalist movement, continued in the Second World War, had borne visible fruits for the national consolidation of this subcontinent. But the national political leaders had, from the very outset, conceived independence as only the initial condition for a much loftier adventure. Gandhi was convinced that independence would be swiftly followed by a social and economic revolution. His view was subscribed to by Nehru and the radical intellectuals he represented. What he wanted was "no change of masters from white to brown, but a real people's rule, by the people and for the people, and an ending of our poverty and misery." [70] This optimism about the country's social and economic prospects was based on the modern Western thought that when the people acquired the power of the ballot they would not permit a minority to monopolize the country's wealth. The notion that in a country like India the right to vote would bring about changes so vast that they could rightly be characterized as a revolution was assumed because of the extreme degree of social

and economic inequality existing there. But the winning of independence failed to implement the expectation that "universal suffrage meant revolution" (Proudhon). It did not touch off the anticipated social and economic revolution.

The ideological reaction to the postponement of the expected economic and social revolution has been complex and contradictory. Generally speaking, forecasts of the future have tended to follow the preindependence view that such a revolution is inevitable. But we also find the contrary idea that democracy dampens efforts to alter conditions in the direction of greater equality. Nehru used to stress the belief that India had chosen the difficult path of democracy even though it meant a slower realization of the goals of planned development than would be possible under Communism. Western observers have expressed their fear that Nehru might be creating urges and expectations which no democratic party will be able to satisfy in the future, thus paving the way for some kind of authoritarianism. "If communism should triumph future historians will be tempted to call Nehru 'the Kerensky of India.' " [71] Myrdal has characterized this embarrassment as emerging from the paramount dilemma of the "Soft State," a label which he considers applicable to all the countries of present-day South Asia. Throughout this whole region, national governments require extraordinarily little of their citizens. The reluctance to enforce policies and to place obligations on people, which derives from the structure of these countries as they have emerged under the impact of colonialism and the fight for independence, is then realized by reference to the concept of "democratic planning," which is often held to be a fundamental difference from the practice in Communist countries. However, what is rarely understood is the fact that this low level of social discipline is also one of the most fundamental differences between the South Asian countries today and Western countries at the beginning of their industrialization.

Preindustrial European societies had widely ramifying and stratified systems of obligations and there is reason to believe that in precolonial times South Asia had somewhat similar systems of obligations. The recent Western development of the welfare state

based on political democracy has meant a radical step toward the more precise definition of these earlier systems of community obligations. South Asia has not experienced a similar evolution from the primitive and static village organization. The colonial period destroyed the old structure of village "integration"; the fight for independence, and the fact of foreign government itself, set in motion attitudes of resistance to authority. The inauguration of the "strong state"—which in principle could be democratic—is handicapped not only by the attitudes and institutions in the villages, but also by inhibitions of the rulers. Nonetheless, rapid development will be exceedingly difficult to engender without an increase in social discipline in all strata and even in the villages. Nationalism would be the necessary force to provide the impulse for radical change—indeed, for all the necessary changes. But the new nationalism in South Asia is something very different from nationalism as it has developed in Europe. "The fundamental reason is that an historical process that in Europe spanned centuries is telescoped within a few decades and that the order of the happenings is deranged." [72]

This conclusion is, in general, applicable to any new nation. The decisive issue is: In what manner will the national evolutions that have occurred in the Third World be able to administer the social, economic, and technical revolutions necessary for the realization of all that they have promised? Therefore, when we now turn our attention from India to China, we can do so within this same framework of a recently attempted nationalist revolution.

It is possible to deal with the Communist revolution as a nationalist movement and it is no less adequate to discuss Leninism and the Russian Revolution as manifestations of nationalism in an underdeveloped country. In an illuminating essay on the politics of development, John Kautsky has defined Leninism as "an adaption of Marxism, a product of the industrialized West, to the conditions of an underdeveloped country." [73]

But he immediately follows this definition with a comment on Lenin's inconsistency. While Lenin—certainly in his practice and to a significant extent also in his theory—carried through that adaption, he was never sufficiently aware of what he was doing to

recognize that the Marxian model of revolution was irrelevant to Russia. He could not see his own revolution as one of intellectuals bent on modernizing an underdeveloped country, that is, as a nationalist movement. For, by Kautsky's definition, nationalism in underdeveloped countries is a modernization movement.

What mattered most to Lenin was the role of the intellectuals in the revolution. The insistence on the leading role of the intellectuals, organized in the Party, and their substitution for Marx's proletariat as the agents of history and the makers of revolution constitutes the core of Leninism. It is also the essence of Lenin's adaptation of Marxism to underdeveloped countries, where the proletariat is nonexistent or small and weak, and the intellectuals are the chief group driving for revolution. Lenin concealed the magnitude of his change from himself and his followers. However, a relatively little known article, written in 1923, titled "Our Revolution" illustrates clearly his view that the revolution itself rather than preceding economic development could create the prerequisites of socialism—industrialization and, with it, an industrial proletariat. It was, hence, a revolution of intellectuals, meant to anticipate the historical development which Marx expected to come only as a result of the growth of industry and a proletariat. The article reveals a tendency to link his revolution to those in underdeveloped countries; it also shows his limited ability to distinguish these sharply from the Western revolutions Marx had used as a model. He sees Russia standing on the borderline between civilized countries and all the oriental, non-European countries. The Russian Revolution was bound to introduce certain novel features in the passage to the countries of the East, and subsequent revolutions in Eastern countries would undoubtedly display even greater peculiarities.[74]

Lenin regarded his own revolution in Russia, not as a nationalist movement in an underdeveloped country, but as a proletarian revolution in an imperialist country. Although the Mexican, Chinese, and Turkish Revolutions were all roughly contemporaneous with the Russian one, nationalism in the underdeveloped countries was as yet hardly recognized. Therefore, it is not surprising that the Russian Revolution should have been widely

viewed as the first successful revolution by an industrial proletariat intent on introducing socialism rather than as one of the first successful revolutions by intellectuals intent on industrializing a backward country independently of Western capital. However, a half century later, and several decades after the movement of decolonization reached its climax, it has become only natural to classify the Russian Revolution as a nationalist revolution in an underdeveloped country. It has even been suggested that future historians may conclude that world Communism, far from exploiting revolutionary tensions in Asia for its own purposes, was but a means by which backward stagnant societies were brought within the orbit of modern civilization. Both in Russia and in China, Communists have failed to achieve what they pretend is their main goal of egalitarianism; but they have achieved national unity and independence, an agrarian revolution liberating the peasants from aggressive landlordism, and capital investment and industrialization.[75]

"Mao Tse-Tung's great accomplishment," wrote Anna Louise Strong in 1946, "has been to change Marxism from a European to an Asiatic form. . . . He has created a Chinese or Asiatic form of Marxism." Mao himself has spoken of the adaptation of Marxism to Chinese conditions. In 1938 he even used the term "Sinification," which he defined as "Marxism applied to the concrete struggle in the concrete conditions prevailing in China." What he called "Sinification" was primarily related to the need for rendering indigenous the form of Marxism. But his contributions to the substance of Leninist theory represent an adaptation of Marxism to Asian conditions rather than a Sinification of Marxism. He elaborated his ideas on the basis of Chinese experience, but the factors underlying these theories—agrarian discontent, impatience with existing conditions, national solidarity in the face of the West—are to a great extent present in many underdeveloped countries. As Stuart Schram has pointed out, in Mao Tse-Tung's revolutionary nationalism two strains are exhibited: the anti-Western political animus, which is common to all nationalists in the underdeveloped countries; and the will to transform society and the Promethean attitude toward nature, which distinguishes revolutionary national-

ism from tradition-oriented nationalism. Whereas Lenin was a European primarily interested in world revolution, Mao is an Asian for whom nationalism is not a necessary evil but an authentic value in itself. While remaining technically an orthodox Leninist, he has succeeded to a considerable extent in incorporating the values and appeals of "populist" nationalism. The radically revolutionary character of this nationalism is, however, derived from another feature, his extreme voluntarism, which attains a kind of apotheosis in the theory of the permanent revolution: "Men are not the slaves of objective reality. Provided only that men's consciousness be in conformity with the objective laws of the development of things, the subjective activity of the popular masses can manifest itself in full measure, overcome all difficulties, create the necessary conditions, and carry forward the revolution. In this sense, the subjective creates the objective." [76]

Lenin's theory that, in periods of revolution, politics takes precedence over economics, was carried a step further by Chinese Communism. China's situation as an underdeveloped country has engendered a mood of impatience, a desire to transform the environment overnight. After some years, during which Mao's government was following a very moderate economic policy, a speed-up was heralded by the announcement, in 1953, of the First Five-Year Plan, in many ways similar to the first Soviet plan. It was, however, commonly believed that China would continue to advance more slowly and prudently than the Soviets had done. Then, in 1955 the political climate and the content of Mao's theories underwent a radical change as the result of his decision to organize the whole of China's peasant population into cooperatives, involving the pooling of the land and the organization of labor into collectives. The acceleration of the Chinese Revolution meant the beginning of what Stuart Schram has called "the Promethean period." Mao's idea of a "war against nature" is a combination of the idea of the rapid transformation of nature with the philosophic conceptions sketched out in his article "On Contradiction." The two basic goals defined in the theory of the permanent revolution —the increasingly rapid transformation of society and of nature —are linked and reinforced by a philosophical theory drawn

essentially from Engels and Lenin. In Mao's writings on contradiction the conception of a universe in ceaseless and perpetual flux is derived from the idea of quantitative change leading into qualitative change. Even after Communism is fully established there will be an endless series of "qualitative changes" labeled "revolutions" emerging from the continual contradictions between the developing productive forces and the relations of production, which in turn will engender contradictions between the members of society. For the moment the antagonistic contradictions of class conflict and the nonantagonistic contradictions of socialist society will continue to exist side by side. But ultimately the development of the productive forces and the efforts of men to adapt to them will replace the class struggle as the matrix of the endless revolutions of the new type to come.[77]

The crucial issue which China has to face is whether the real trend of the "development of the productive forces" is compatible with this concept of the permanent revolution as conceived in Maoist theory. To a certain extent the point at stake is the very counterpart of the decisive issue with which India is confronted. Whereas India's society is threatened with stagnation resulting from the endless postponement of the social and economic revolution that had been anticipated in the struggle for national independence, Chinese society is challenged by technical and objective problems of building socialism which tend to take precedence over the voluntarist ideology of the permanent revolution, which reflects the period of armed revolutionary struggle. As the Marxian myth of the nineteenth-century proletariat has lost a good deal of its relevance for the present-day conditions of Soviet Russian society, it is questionable whether the idea of a "war against nature" will be sufficient for China to solve the problem of the immense and growing role of organization in society and in the economy.

In other words, the question is: Might there not be a functional nexus between "revisionism" and modernization? The more rational economic policies adopted by China's Communist Party in 1961–1962, in the aftermath of the Great Leap Forward, were conducive to the emergence of an incipient "instrumentalism"— the substitution of a largely apolitical production and managerial

ethic for the consumer ethic of the "command economy." The Party's control over the economic life of the country was increasingly challenged by the rise of a "new class" of semi-autonomous managers, administrators, and technocrats, and by the resurgence of vestigial "rural capitalism." Besides, there was a growing apprehension of the party leadership over the trend toward bureaucratization within the party itself. In view of these tendencies, we may raise the question: To what extent is the appearance of certain "heterodox" tendencies in developing Communist societies—tendencies such as instrumentalism and bureaucracy—causally related to the historical transition of these societies from the relatively undifferentiated stage of radical social mobilization and revolution to the more organizationally complex stage of economic rationalization and technological innovation? This notion has, of course, served as a theoretical underpinning for interpretations of the ostensible "erosion of ideology" in the Soviet Union, but it is, in general, applicable to development phenomena in emerging socialist countries.

Richard Baum defines revisionism as "the ideological reflection of the declining relevance of revolutionary norms and values to the solution of qualitatively new, post-revolutionary socioeconomic problems." When viewed in this light, the phenomenon of revisionism becomes readily explainable as a latent function of the modernization process itself. The truth of this maxim is illustrated in the characteristically ambivalent attitudes of Soviet and Chinese Communist leaders toward the modernization process. On the one hand, modernization is positively valued as a social goal, for modernization means economic development and economic development means national power. On the other hand, modernization entails bureaucracy, instrumentalism, and the consequent attenuation and ritual sterilization of ideological principles.[78]

Here is the basis of the contradiction between the values of "red" and those of "expert," which the "Great Proletarian Cultural Revolution" (introduced in late 1965) has been struggling to resolve. The prototypical "red" is the mass-oriented cadre, the combat leader, the highly indoctrinated jack-of-all-trades. His goal

is human solidarity; his vision is of a spiritually integrated society; his outlook is typically utopian and fundamentalist. The prototypical "expert," on the other hand, is the management-oriented technocrat, the professional administrator, the highly skilled specialist; his goal is technical rationality; his vision is of a functionally integrated society; his outlook is typically secular and pragmatic. Several observers tend to link the distinction between these two prototypes with a familiar distinction introduced into an earlier stage of sociology by the German sociologist Tönnies. They suggest a relationship between the "red" vision of a spiritually integrated society with *Gemeinschaft,* and the "expert" vision of a functionally integrated society with *Gesellschaft.*[79]

The different ways being attempted to solve this contradiction are in a measure accountable for the Sino-Soviet ideological competition. The Chinese profound distrust of vertically integrated bureaucracies, highly trained professionals, and narrow economic specialists is closely related to their "populist" approach to social change which calls for the horizontal integration of society on the basis of subjectively mobilized masses under the direct combat-style leadership of "red" cadres. In the Russian case, there is a markedly greater commitment to the goal of professionalism, to the creation of a rational, highly differentiated bureaucratic apparatus, and to a degree of operational autonomy for "expert" hierarchies. Paramount reasons for this divergence are the relatively underdeveloped economic structure of China and the deeply ingrained revolutionary romanticism—the so-called "spirit of Jenan"—of the present Chinese leaders. There is a strange dialectic in this situation. In China, where the Confucian ideal was uncongenial to science, the advancement of science had revolutionary implications. It led to specialization, the cultivation of experts. But these were suspect in Communist China, which, nevertheless (and unlike Confucian China), was absolutely committed to the celebration of science. Marxists traded on the prestige of science, and they knew very well that in everyone's modern world, science had prestige. "When the Chinese communists put scientists down," remarks Joseph Levenson, "they acknowledged that prestige; they did not impugn it; its very universality, its apparent transcendence

of ideology, was a threat to the masters of ideology. Science had to be mastered by the ideologues, or their own occupation would be gone. In a world where science could not be gainsaid, mere experts, practitioners of science, had to be bent to Marxist authority, or Mao, the latest Marxist in line, would have lacked authority himself. Ideology, the correct ideology, must dominate the ostensibly non-ideological expert." [80]

Just as the Confucianist with his nonspecialist ideal had displaced the old aristocracy, and then had taken on an aristocratic aura, so the professional in the modern world, having fragmented that ideal, had the status pride of the aristocrat today. Therefore the Party had to cut him down to size, to vindicate its own version of autocratic rule: "First red, then expert!"

The Cultural Revolution has proved that there are several ways in which a party that monopolizes the instruments of coercion and the channels of social mobility can attempt to control some of the more undesirable consequences of social change. The goal to be attained was the creation of the "new Communist man" who would be both red and expert. However, since ideological fervor tends to decrease in proportion to the acquisition of technical and administrative skills, such a goal would appear, in the long run, highly questionable.

The serious dilemmas which the revolution of nation-building is bound to face in the developing countries of Asia, though differing contexts and under widely varying historical circumstances, are also perceptible in other parts of the Third World. Turning now to the Latin American continent, we choose one characteristic example of nation-building, which has been sketched as "Peace by revolution."

The history of nationalism in Latin America begins at a much earlier date than in the other continents of the Third World. Following the "Age of Discovery," which runs from the late fifteenth to the seventeenth centuries, the "Age of Political Emancipation" began with the nineteenth century, when the Latin American nations one by one won their formal independence. It has been suggested that the third great milestone in the history of Latin America, "the Age of Social Revolution, is now emerging through-

out the Hemisphere, from the Caribbean to Patagonia and from the Atlantic to the Pacific, to remake once more the face and institutions of Latin America. Linked to the great current of modern history, the Latin American social revolution has a close kinship with the revolutionary winds blowing in the Middle East, Africa, and Asia." And in this third period, the Mexican Revolution of 1910 has been characterized as "the first major guidepost in the half-century long, on-and-off march toward the acceptance of social protest as an inevitable Latin-American reality." [81]

The war of independence, fought during the second decade of the nineteenth century, destroyed the governing classes of Mexico, drove the Spaniard from the country, and removed experienced administration from office. But Mexico was not a nation at that time; it was a colony with sharp internal, economic, cultural, and class divisions, in which the army and the church and the large landowner attempted to retain their traditional prerogatives and privileges. The ideas of the French Revolution, although imbibed by a few liberal middle-class people, were not representative of Mexico. During the struggle for independence and after, the new ideas of democracy, liberty, fraternity, and equality were adopted in theory, but they remained foreign to the social and political system and found no application in the new government. The constitution of 1857, adopting the French model, remained inapplicable. The three revolutions which have profoundly altered the structure of Mexican political and social life during the century since 1810 were, first, the independence; second, the *Reforma*; and third, the Revolution of 1910. The first destroyed Mexican dependence upon Spain; the second attempted to destroy the colonial system derived from Spain, and was only partially successful; the third attempted to destroy the plantation system and to free Mexico from foreign tutelage. The first brought the *criollo*, the Mexican whites, into power; the second brought the middle class and the *mestizo* into power; and the third brought the Indian peasant out of oblivion.

Frank Tannenbaum, whose historical sketch we have succinctly followed, also summarizes, from another point of view, the hundred years of conflict as one between two ideals of society.[82]

One group wished to go back to the colonial system. The other group wanted to complete the task undertaken by the war of independence. The church, the army, the large plantation—all would have to be modified or destroyed in order to be brought into conformity with the principles of modern democracy. Both groups had made their peace under the capitalist Diaz regime, which was in power until the end of the first decade of the twentieth century. This compromise was ruptured by the common people, the peasants, the Indians, the city laborers. The Mexican Revolution of 1910 sought to bring a third class into the political arena, and in the process at least temporarily weakened the influence of the feudal and of the capitalist classes.

The leaders of that revolution were children of peasants, Indians. This fact makes for an essential difference from both the French and the Russian Revolutions. There were no important intellectuals on the side of the Revolution. The whole educated class belonged to the dictatorship and its satellites. The gulf between the rich and the poor was so profound that the grievances of the common people found no voice. The great significance of the Revolution of 1910 consisted in the fact that the Indians themselves rose in rebellion and saved themselves from the fate of becoming peons upon the large plantations. During the hundred years since independence, the other institutions implanted by Spain had either been weakened or destroyed, but not so the plantation system. The liberalism of the independence, the radicalism of the struggle against the church, and even the individualism of the Diaz regime, had all served to increase the hold of this feudal institution upon the country. However, neither the Revolution of 1910 nor the revolutionary agrarian program initiated during the following years was able to destroy the plantation system. The agrarian movement proved to be halting, inadequate, and meager. Nevertheless, it was a further step in the process which this Latin American country passed through on its way to nation-building.

A crucial question is, however, whether in the present world this process can be continued gradually and endlessly. Some observers suggest that Latin American nations will have to face the dilemma of the incompatibility between national integrity and

development. "In a world which is being rapidly organized around some powerful poles of development," remarks Professor Jaguaribe, "there is a historical deadline for achieving socio-economic development within a given national configuration. Societies failing to do this will be submitted in the course of time to disruptive pressures. This problem is now faced by Latin America." Professor Jaguaribe assumes that such a deadline is likely to be reached in the next two or three decades. "If this hypothesis is valid, either the Latin American countries . . . will achieve a minimum level of socio-economic development in that lapse of time, or their national configuration will be disarticulated by disruptive processes that will affect the whole of Latin America. In that case, however, the resulting conflict, which would tend to pit the rural central backward sectors against the modern coastal cities, would also reach uncontrollable proportions. Even if the United States interfered in order to prevent such an explosion by helping the forces of the local establishments to contain their own masses, the unsolved contradictions between the huge backward central regions and the tiny strip of the advanced coastal cities would likely be more powerful than any military system of containment."

This analysis leads him to his final conclusion. "Timely and appropriate development, within the framework of the national states in the ambit of a regional Latin American Community, is both a realistic goal and an indispensable necessity. The failure to achieve such goals would probably precipitate Latin America into a continental revolution for which the Chinese Revolution may possibly be an archetype and the Vietnam war, amplified to an incomparably larger dimension, might be a term of reference for understanding the consequence of foreign intervention." This analysis is presented as part of a sketch of the conceptions of the new Latin American intelligentsia. The author is convinced that the kind of problem confronting the new intelligentsia is similar to the one which had confronted Marx: how to understand the world in order to transform the world in accordance with its rational understanding. "The cautious conditional optimism and the alternative sense of tragedy implied in these concepts," concludes Pro-

fessor Jaguaribe, "seem to be the most characteristic features of an outlook that recognizes itself as the last formulation of rational reformism or the first warning of inscrutable revolution." [83]

Reform and *revolution,* indeed, appear to be alternatives. But another view is also possible. Faced with the claims of the Cuban Revolution, on the one hand, and with the demands and promises of the Alliance for Progress, on the other, Latin Americans appear to have these familiar, if stark, alternatives: change through violent revolution or through peaceful reform. However, on the basis of studies of Brazil, Colombia, and Chile, the economist Albert Hirschman argues that this traditional dichotomy does not convey the reality of social and economic change. Actually there are many intermediate stations between effortless and painless reform at one extreme, and total revolution at the other. The Latin American scene appears to be replete with mechanisms which permit the exertion of powerful pressures and the adjudication of conflicts by means equally far removed from traditional concepts of either reform or revolution. "Decentralised, unrequited violence, is frequently found in the role of indispensable midwife to reform." [84]

NOTES

1. Crane Brinton, *The Anatomy of Revolution* (rev. and expanded ed.; New York, 1965).
2. *Ibid.,* p. 123.
3. *Ibid.,* pp. 177ff.
4. *Ibid.,* p. 191.
5. *Ibid.,* p. 205.
6. *Ibid.,* p. 233.
7. *Ibid.,* pp. 196f.
8. *Ibid.,* p. 263.
9. Hannah Arendt, *On Revolution* (New York, Compass Books edition, 1965).
10. *Ibid.,* Ch. I, note 24 (see p. 291), where she refers to Griewank's *Der neuzeitliche Revolutionsbegriff* (1955), which she praises as superseding all other literature on the subject.

11. Arendt, *On Revolution*, p. 33.
12. *Ibid.*, pp. 31ff.
13. *Ibid.*, pp. 40f.
14. *Ibid.*, pp. 16f., 63ff.
15. *Ibid.*, pp. 87ff.
16. *Ibid.*, p. 134.
17. *Ibid.*, p. 137.
18. *Ibid.*, p. 110.
19. *Ibid.*, p. 108.
20. *Ibid.*, pp. 158ff., 190f.
21. *Ibid.*, p. 190.
22. *Ibid.*, p. 190.
23. Rosenstock-Huessy, *Out of Revolution: Autobiography of Western Man* (1st ed., New York, 1938; 2nd ed., New York, 1964). This American edition is based on the author's original German work *Die Europäischen Revolutionen und der Charakter der Nationen* (1st ed., Stuttgart und Köln, 1931; 2nd ed., Stuttgart und Köln, 1951); see author's introduction to 2nd edition, p. xiii.
24. Rosenstock-Huessy, *Out of Revolution*, 2nd edition (1964), pp. 5ff.
25. *Ibid.*, pp. 529ff.
26. *Ibid.*, pp. 453ff.
27. *Ibid.*, pp. 460ff.
28. *Ibid.*, p. 525
29. *Ibid.*, p. 23.
30. "Die Revolution von 1848 und das Proletariat," quoted by Karl Löwith in *Meaning in History* (Chicago, 1949), p. 36.
31. "Manifesto of the Communist Party" in Marx and Engels, *Basic Writings on Politics and Philosophy*, ed. Lewis Feuer (New York, 1959), pp. 1ff.
32. Marx and Engels, *Basic Writings*, pp. 474ff.
33. Karl Löwith, *Meaning in History*, p. 45.
34. Leon Trotsky, *The Russian Revolution* (Garden City, N.Y., 1959), pp. 1–13.
35. E. H. Carr, *Studies in Revolution* (New York, 1964), pp. 131ff., 215.
36. Joseph Schiebel, "Changing the Unchangeable: Historical Materialism and Six Versions of Eternal Laws of Historical Development," *Studies in Soviet Thought*, Vol. VII, No. 4 (Dordrecht, December, 1967), pp. 318ff.

37. Yorick Spiegel, *Modernizing a Modern Society: The Example of the German Democratic Republic* (G.D.R.) (mimeographed paper, Dept. of Sociology of Religion, Harvard University).

38. Herbert Marcuse, "The Obsolescence of Marxism," in *Marx and the Western World,* ed. N. Lobkowicz (Notre Dame, Ind., 1967), pp. 414ff.

39. Lezlek Kolakowski, *Der Mensch ohne Alternative: Von der Möglichkeit und Unmöglichkeit Marxist zu sein* (München, 1964).

40. Lezlek Kolakowski, *Traktat über die Sterblichkeit der Vernunft— Philosophische Essays* (1967). Cf. *Herder Correspondence,* Vol. 4, No. 9, September, 1967, pp. 273ff.

41. Marcuse, *Der Mensch ohne Alternative,* p. 91.

42. Roger Garaudy, *Marxisme du XXe siècle* (Paris, 1966).

43. Cf. *Initiative in History: A Christian-Marxist Exchange,* an Occasional Paper published by the Church Society for College Work (Cambridge, Mass., 1967).

44. Leopold Labedz, "Students and Revolution," *Survey* (July, 1968), p. 11, note 11.

45. John Mander, "An Indispensable Activity," *Survey* (October, 1968), p. 53. Max Beloff, "Universities and Violence," *Survey* (October, 1968), pp. 39, 50.

46. Leopold Labedz, *op. cit.,* pp. 4f., 14 (note 15).

47. Raymon Aron, *The Opium of the Intellectuals* (New York, 1962), p. 47.

48. Adam B. Ulam, *The Unfinished Revolution* (New York, 1964), pp. 107ff., 130. cf. George Woodcock, *Anarchism* (New York, 2nd pr., 1967), pp. 118f.

49. André Dumas, "The Technical Potentialities and the Struggle for New Forms of Community," address, Fourth Assembly of the World Council of Churches, Uppsala, 1968.

50. Whitney Young, Jr., *To Be Equal* (New York, 1964), p. 239.

51. Lewis M. Killian, *The Impossible Revolution? Black Power and the American Dream* (New York, 1968), pp. 4ff.

52. *U.S. Riot Commission Report* (New York, 1968), p. vii.

53. Lewis Feuer, "The Student Left in the U.S.A.," *Survey* (January, 1967), pp. 99ff.

54. Howard Zinn, *SNCC: The New Abolitionists* (2nd ed., Boston, 1965), pp. 13ff.

55. "What We Want," *The New York Review of Books,* September

22, 1966, p. 6. Quoted by Lewis M. Killian, *The Impossible Revolution?* pp. 142f.

56. Stokely Carmichael and Charles V. Hamilton, *Black Power, the Politics of Liberation* (New York, 1967), p. xi. Cf. Frantz Fanon, *The Wretched of the Earth* (New York, 1963), pp. 253f.

57. Carmichael and Hamilton, *op. cit.,* p. 60.

58. *Ibid.,* p. 40. Cf. David Apter, *The Politics of Modernization* (Chicago, 1965), p. 2.

59. Carmichael and Hamilton, *op. cit.,* p. 178.

60. Harold R. Isaacs, "Group Identity and Political Change," *Survey* (October, 1968), pp. 93ff.

61. *Ibid.,* pp. 95f.

62. Georges Gurvitch, *The Spectrum of Social Time* (Dordrecht, Holland). Original French title: *La Multiplicité des temps sociaux.*

63. Hahn-Been Lee, "Developmentalist Time and Leadership in Developing Countries" (paper prepared for presentation to the Comparative Administration Group Research Seminar, University of California, June/July, 1965).

64. Gunnar Myrdal, *Asian Drama,* 3 vols. (New York, 1968), Vol. I, pp. 46f.

65. *Ibid.,* pp. 115ff.

66. *Ibid.,* p. 700.

67. A. Gerschenkron, *Economic Backwardness in Historical Perspective* (Cambridge, Mass., 1962), Ch. 3. Cf. Myrdal, *Asian Drama,* Vol. I, p. 701.

68. Myrdal, *Asian Drama,* Vol. III, pp. 2108f.; Vol. II, pp. 773f.

69. Harold R. Isaacs, "Group Identity and Political Change," *Survey* (October, 1968), p. 79.

70. Jawaharlal Nehru, *The Discovery of India* (4th ed., London, 1956), p. 54.

71. Michael Brecher, *Nehru, a Political Biography* (London, 1959), p. 632. Cf. Myrdal, *Asian Drama,* pp. 794, 781ff.

72. Myrdal, *Asian Drama,* Vol. II, p. 2119; Vol. I, 66; Vol. II, pp. 895ff.

73. John Kautsky, *Political Change in Underdeveloped Countries: Nationalism and Communism* (New York, 1966), pp. 63f.

74. *Ibid.,* p. 65, note 3.

75. *Ibid.,* p. 69, note 2.

76. Stuart R. Schram, *The Political Thought of Mao Tse-Tung* (New York, 1965), pp. 80, 56f., 76ff.

77. *Ibid.*, pp. 48, 54f.
78. Richard D. Baum, "Ideology Redivivus," *Problems of Communism* (May/June, 1967), pp. 2, 7f.
79. *Ibid.*, p. 8. Cf. Franz Schurmann, *Ideology and Organization in Communist China* (Berkeley, 1966), pp. 69f., 99f., 231ff.
80. Joseph R. Levenson, "The Past and Future of Nationalism in China," *Survey* (April, 1968), p. 38.
81. Tad Szulc, *The Winds of Revolution—Latin America Today and Tomorrow* (New York, 1964), pp. 14f.
82. Frank Tannenbaum, *Peace by Revolution* (New York, 1966), pp. 74ff.
83. Jaguaribe, in *Marx and the Western World*, ed. N. Lobkowicz (Notre Dame, Ind., 1967), pp. 251f.
84. Albert O. Hirschman, *Journeys toward Progress: Studies of Economic Policy-making in Latin America* (New York, 1965), pp. 327ff.

CHAPTER FIVE

War

War and Revolution

A realistic treatment of the interaction between development and revolution necessarily involves the phenomenon of war as the third major factor. In fact, there is a certain parallelism between the violence inherent in revolution, ranging from regional rebellion to planned world revolution, and military escalation, beginning with local civil strife and ending in total world war. In sociological studies it has become common to approach the phenomenon of revolution within the setting of "internal war." [1] The term is, however, misleading, for internal wars in our century are hardly to be isolated and they have the tendency to "develop into international events." Internal wars are thus a testing ground in which East and West convey to each other the extent of their aspirations and the depth of their resolve. They are, as it were, a form of communication. Even more, to the extent that they end through negotiations, as in Korea and Laos, they are a form of cooperation—a roundabout way of coordinating mutually exclusive objections in order to preserve a modicum of international stability.[2]

Chalmers Johnson enumerates six types of revolution.[3] The first type, the "Jacquerie" or peasant rebellion is important as a symptom of agrarian unrest, but since it does not aim at a fundamental change in political, social, and economic structure, it can

hardly be defined as a revolution. The "millenarian rebellion" is exceedingly important for the Third World and it bears some essentially revolutionary features. In its expectation of the Millennium, it carries the hope of a complete and radical change in the world, a world shorn of its present deficiencies. More important than the third type, the "anarchistic rebellion" (which is a kind of nostalgic rebellion against changes in the existing political system) is the fourth type, the "Jacobin Communist revolution." The classical example of this fourth type is the French Revolution, and others include the Russian March Revolution of 1917 and the Mexican Revolution of 1910. "Conspiratorial *coup d'état*" is the fifth type, systematically described by Blanqui, among whose disciples in the twentieth century Lenin and some fascist conspirators can be reckoned.

The climax of this typology is to be found in the sixth category, "militarized mass insurrection." Though, in fact, being a better-thought-out and more developed form of the fourth type, the "Jacobin Communist revolution," this final type is dealt with by Johnson separately, and rightly so, for it has a character of its own. Examples of militarized mass insurrection are Ireland (1916–1923) and Algeria (1954–1962), but the classical example is China between 1937 and 1948.

Inasmuch as it tries to qualify the various possibilities of revolutionary violence, this typology is meaningful and useful. But, as is particularly obvious in the character of the sixth type, there are limitations in a theoretical framework that is exclusively concerned with the phenomenon of revolution. Militarized mass insurrection is a form, not only of "internal war," but also of "external war," namely, of the war of liberation. This applies particularly to the case of China, since the 1937 to 1948 period covers the conflict with Japan as well as the Second World War.

For this reason, it is best to discuss the questions of revolutionary violence within the total setting of modern warfare. That there exists a close relationship between revolution and modern warfare is recognized with more or less clarity in recent studies about revolution. Hannah Arendt opens her book *On Revolution* by pointing to this relationship as a specifically modern phenom-

enon, characteristic of fundamental changes in the nature of war. An indication is the introduction of the idea of liberty as a decisive justification of modern war; this concept is absent in the traditional arguments for war. It is being introduced as an emergency-rescue measure, since our technological development has intensified the destructive potentialities of modern armaments beyond any rational purpose. Liberty is a revolutionary purpose and, as a matter of fact, in modern history revolutions have been preceded or accompanied by a war of liberation (as was the case in the American Revolution), or they have resulted in defensive or aggressive wars (as illustrated by the French Revolution). The Russian Revolutions of 1905 and of 1917 were immediate consequences of the troubles resulting from a war situation, and the Second World War may even be interpreted as a civil war on a worldwide scale.

An essential feature, common to revolution and modern warfare, is the unlimited and unconditional resort to violence. The germs of total war were fostered during the First World War, as an unavoidable outcome of the introduction of new types of arms which outdated the traditional distinction between the military and civilians. Toynbee has pointed to the decisive turn in the development of warfare since the outbreak of the French Revolution, a change induced by the energies generated by the recently released forces of Democracy and Industrialism. This bout of violent warfare was not the first in modern Western history, for Western Christendom had been devastated by the so-called Wars of Religion in the sixteenth and seventeenth centuries. Between these two periods of violent warfare was a century in which war was a comparatively mild disease, a "sport of kings," not exacerbated by fanaticism in either the religious or the national vein. This age of relatively civilized warfare came to an end at the close of the eighteenth century, when war became recharged with violence by the impact of Democracy and Industrialism. The first of the modern wars in this sense was the cycle inaugurated by the French Revolution, and in these wars the impact of democracy was all-important. The gospel of fraternity and equality preached by the spokesmen of the French Revolution led to the first of the great modern wars of nationalism. When, in the course of the nineteenth

century, the Industrial Revolution had transformed international commerce from an exchange of luxuries into an exchange of the necessities of life, the democratized nations were irresistibly tempted to fight one another for economic gain.[4]

The influence of the French Revolution on the character and theories of modern warfare is particularly apparent in the lasting importance of German military theoretician Karl von Clausewitz's classical work *On War*. Its influence can still be seen in much of present-day theorizing on military strategy, ranging from American strategic thinking on atomic deterrence to Third World guerrilla-warfare planning.

Clausewitz's famous dictum that "war is nothing but a continuation of political intercourse with an admixture of other means"[5] has to be interpreted against the historical background which the author himself has stressed as essential. The "altered policy which proceeded from the French Revolution not only in France but in the rest of Europe as well" called forth other means and other powers, by which it became possible to conduct war with an otherwise inconceivable degree of energy. "The actual changes in the art of war are a consequence of alterations in policy, and . . . very strong evidence of the intimacy of their connection. Therefore . . . : war is an instrument of policy; it must bear the character of policy, it must measure with policy's measure. The conduct of war, in its major features, is therefore policy itself, which takes up the sword in place of the pen, but does not on that account cease to think according to its own laws."[6]

The complete novelty in the French Revolution of 1793, according to Clausewitz, was that "a force such as no one had previously any conception of appeared. War had again suddenly become an affair of the people, and that of a people numbering thirty millions, everyone of whom regarded himself as a citizen of the State." By this participation of the people in war "a whole nation—instead of a cabinet and an army—entered the scale. Henceforth, the means available—the efforts which might be called forth—no longer had any definite limits, the energy with which the war might be conducted had no counterpoise, and con-

sequently the danger for the adversary had risen to the extreme."
Under Bonaparte, this military power, based on the strength of
the whole nation, marched over Europe with irresistible confidence.
A reaction arose in due time. In Spain, the war became an affair
of the people; in Austria, the government introduced extraordinary
measures; in Russia, in 1812, the example of Spain and Austria
was taken as a model. "Thus the most violent element in war, freed
from all conventional restrictions, broke loose with all its natural
force. The cause was the participation of the people in this great
affair of state, and this participation arose partly from the effects of
the French revolution, partly from the threatening attitude of the
French toward all nations." [7]

Clausewitz's insights are particularly interesting in view of the
position of his fatherland, Prussia, as a backward country facing
the impact of a neighboring country, France, which (in Clausewitz's lifetime) had made a decisive advance in development
through revolution. Born in Prussia in 1780, the son of a minor
tax collector, and dying in 1831, Clausewitz lived in a Europe in
which three powerful currents—philosophical, socio-political, and
military—were undermining existing political and social institutions. Although Prussia had only recently emerged as a first-class
power in Europe, it was already intellectually outmoded. Prussia
was a poor state, governed by an absolute ruler; and the army,
which molded the state to its need, was the principal obstacle to
political or social change of any kind. At the time of the collapse
of the Prussian Army in the war with France in 1806, sympathy
for the French and for Napoleon was still widespread in intellectual
circles, which had at first welcomed the French Revolution, and
among the people. Napoleon initiated reforms in the areas directly
administered by him: feudalism was abolished and the Code
Napoleon was promulgated as the legal code. The Prussian reformers who, under his impact, attempted the regeneration of their
country, recognized that the military reforms needed to raise Prussian military capabilities to the French level would have to be preceded by the political, social, and economic reforms that had
produced the radical increase in French military power. Clausewitz was active in the group that carried out the military reforms.

Recognizing the dependence of military reform upon political reform, they supported the political reformers. The military was thus a leader in producing the reforms absolutely essential to Prussia's regeneration and its emergence from a rigid autocracy to a more flexible, resourceful, and modern state.[8] Thus, there exists a close historical connection between the French Revolution and the War of Revolution as the internal and external aspects of one and the same indivisible, historical movement, and the expansion of the French Revolution by a complex of intellectual, socio-political, and military influences and the chain of reactions it produced inside less advanced countries in the rest of Europe. Since this historical connection is basically significant for the impact of Western Europe upon Eastern and southern Europe and upon the non-European world at large during the nineteenth and early twentieth centuries, the social and political setting within which Clausewitz developed his ideas has, to a certain extent, assumed a universal validity.

With this in mind, we are hardly surprised at the great influence Clausewitz has exerted on the shaping of Communist strategic theory. Communist strategists have devoted particular attention to those elements in his work which pertain to the higher direction of national strategy and the focusing and directing of all elements of national strength. That this interest points to a certain congeniality derives from two aspects of Clausewitz's thought.

The first factor is his contribution to the creation of Prussian patriotism. After the ratification of the Franco-Prussian Treaty in March, 1812, which signaled the climax of Napoleon's rule and the total subjugation of the Prussian army to the interests of the French war with Russia, Clausewitz took service with the Russians against France and Prussia. He was a major figure in the long retreat to Moscow, and later was the principal figure in negotiating the defection of the Prussian corps from the French. This event made possible the reversal of the French-Prussian alliance and marked the climax of Napoleon's disastrous invasion of Russia, thus constituting a major factor leading to his ultimate defeat. Clausewitz's essay *I Believe and Profess,* written in condemnation of the Franco-Prussian Treaty, contains a passionate appeal to

Prussian patriotism. Here we meet a patriotic leader who is arguing that that patriotism has been subject to Napoleon's will.

> I believe and profess that a people never must value anything higher than the dignity and freedom of its existence, that it must defend these with the last drop of its blood; that it has no duty more sacred and can obey no law that is higher; that the shame of a cowardly submission can never be wiped out; that the poison of submission in the bloodstream of a people will be transmitted to its children, and paralyze and undermine the strength of later generations; that honor can be lost only once; that, under most circumstances, a people is unconquerable if it fights a spirited struggle for its liberty; that a bloody and honorable fight assures the rebirth of the people even if freedom were lost; and that such a struggle is the seed of life from which a new tree inevitably will blossom. . . . In my judgment the most important political virtues are: never relax vigilance; expect nothing from the magnanimity of others; never abandon a purpose until it has become impossible, beyond doubt, to attain it; hold the honor of the state as sacred. The time is yours; what its fulfillment will be, depends upon you.[9]

This irrational appeal to the German will eventually enabled the Prussian nation to rise against France and ultimately to defeat Napoleon. This experience, which is a lesson for subjugated and threatened nations of all times and places, was later codified in Clausewitz's work *On War* as the concept of the proper military objective being the destruction of the enemy's forces. This idea was to dominate Prussian military thought throughout the nineteenth century and into the twentieth, and to influence greatly all the world's armies.

The second major factor in Clausewitz's thinking is his recognition of the essential relationship between ends and means. Thus, the first factor, an irrational appeal to the national will, is reinforced by a complementary factor, a rational insight into the limited instruments available. The distinction between these factors is related to the distinction between two kinds of war. The first kind is to be found in his definition of war as "an act of force to compel

our adversary to do our will." [10] In this type of war, each adversary mobilizes all its means and resources in an effort to overthrow the enemy completely and at the same time to avoid being overthrown.

Clausewitz perceived a strong tendency to this type of absolute war in the French Revolution. He believed that the tendency toward pure violence is in almost direct relation to the extent of mass support for war. A greatly aroused public opinion in a democracy increases the tendency for war to become in reality what he conceived war to be in theory: "struggles of life or death, from pure hatred."

In other words, theoretically, the use of force is without limits. "The period just past, in which war reached its absolute strength, contains most of what is universally valid and necessary." But Clausewitz recognized that in actual war this is almost invariably moderated by a number of influences. He considered it "improbable that wars will henceforth have this grand character," and, therefore, pointed out that "a theory which dwells only upon this absolute war would exclude or condemn as errors all cases in which external influences alter the nature of war." [11] In real life, war has a more limited aim: it is part of political relations between national states. It therefore does not make its own laws, but is subject to political guidance. This second type of war, which he considered to be the normal case, is war as the "continuation of politics by other means."

This realistic rationalism is also seen in Clausewitz's firm conviction that defensive warfare is inherently the stronger form. He had seen in the methods of Napoleon the tendency toward "absolute" war, in which a "nation in arms" makes an all-out effort to overthrow an enemy nation by the destruction of the enemy's military force in a decisive battle. After he had left the Prussian service to join the Russian army, Clausewitz influenced the Russian leadership to continue the withdrawal of the Russian army even beyond the ultimate position that had been decided upon for a defensive battle. His account establishes that inability to locate a favorable defensive position, rather than any grand design, was primarily responsible for the long withdrawals which ultimately led to the complete collapse of the French army. Thus, his view

on the strength of the military defensive appears to be directly attributable to his experiences in Russia in 1812.

This viewpoint plays a role within the framework of Clausewitz's definition of strategy and tactics. "Tactics teaches the use of the armed forces in engagements (i.e. single acts, each complete in itself, and strategy, the use of engagements to attain the object of the war)." [12] If he held the strategic defensive, in the final analysis, to be the stronger form of war, this did not imply a mere passive waiting or warding off the enemy's attacks. Rather, strategic defense must be active and vigorous, and have as its ultimate aim the acquisition of strength and creation of opportunity for a decisive attack. "The defensive in war is therefore not a mere shield, but a shield composed of skillfully delivered blows." [13]

With this analysis of some major factors in Clausewitz's views, we may now evaluate the influence of his views on Communist doctrines of conflict. Clausewitz has been carefully studied in the Communist world, and his concept of the nature of war and politics and many of his strategic ideas have been incorporated into Communist doctrine and strategy. Lenin studied Clausewitz's works in late 1914 and early 1915.[14] When Lenin went into hiding after the July, 1917, uprisings, he took with him only two books— Marx's *The Civil War in France* and Clausewitz's *On War*. Lenin saw Clausewitz's work as a practical application of Hegel's dialectical method. The concept he most emphasized was the connection between war and politics, particularly that war is the continuation of politics by other means. To Lenin's dialectical thinking it followed quite naturally that politics is war by other (i.e., nonforcible) means. Thus Clausewitz has been one of the influences in the development of the Communist doctrine of continuous conflict with the non-Communist world. It has been suggested that whereas Marx and Engels "stood Hegel on his head," so Lenin stood Clausewitz on his head. Where Hegel held that ideas determine political and economic conditions, Marx held that economic conditions determine ideas, and hence determine political institutions. Where Clausewitz held that war is a continuation of politics by other means, Lenin and his successors substituted the antithetical idea that politics is a continuation of war by other means. "The

central idea of communist doctrine is thus Clausewitzian, but it is Clausewitz upside down." [15]

Other observers define this dependence by stating that Lenin radically transformed the concept of the revolutionary situation from a tool of social analysis into a clear-cut military analogy. After all, Engels had already discovered in Clausewitz the principle that there is no analytical difference between political and military forms of the class struggle; and to Engels' mind it followed that the methods of military analysis, the study of objectives, capabilities, and conditions, are relevant in the context of any political conflict situation. Quoting Clausewitz, Engels remarked that fighting was to war what cash payment was to trade, for however important it was, it occurred only relatively rarely. "For Communists and their Marxist predecessors," writes Andrew C. Janos, "the political process has referred to the total spectrum of the application of force, of which violence is but one variation." [16]

With these considerations in mind, we are now in a better position to understand the significance of the concept of "militarized mass insurrection," with which Chalmers Johnson ended his typology of revolution. According to Johnson's analysis this type of strategy may be divided into five main components. The spectrum ranges from mobilization of a sustained population and organization of the mobilized population, followed by the building of a large revolutionary army and the perfection of suitable military tactics, to the fifth component, i.e., commitment to a protracted war. These components are the necessary conditions for successful guerrilla warfare, which means the beginning of the end of the revolution. Finally, when victory is certain, the strategy reverts to positional warfare. The battle of Dien Bien Phu is classic in this respect.

The course of Mao Tse-Tung's victory in China is, indeed, a classic example of the strategy of "militarized mass insurrection." Therefore, the significant characteristics of the political and military aspects of Maoism are best seen in the context of the guerrilla warfare which laid the basis for later large-scale Communist success. As Thomas P. Thornton has observed, the Chinese Revolution was of a completely different order from the one that brought the

Bolsheviks to power. Both revolutions had the advantage of operating in wartime choas, and both took place in countries which were ripe for change. However, the Chinese success resulted from a protracted civil war rather than a *coup d'état.* "The difference between their revolutionary experiences was to be of major importance in differentiating the attitudes of the two major Communist states towards revolution. The Russian model established a form of seizing power in which a small party works within an amorphous mass and picks off the fruits of a concurrent revolution. The Chinese, having failed with this method in the 1920's, developed a revolutionary model in which the Communists assert hegemony over a faction of the mass movement at an early stage and then fight their way to power by military means." [17]

This is indeed a crucial point. In a country such as Russia in 1917, where the levers of power could be seized at one stroke, and where the military forces supporting the existing government were in a state of collapse, revolution by armed insurrection was possible. In a country such as China in the late 1920's, where no effective state apparatus existed, and where the armed forces under the command of the partisans of the existing order were, by Chinese standards, exceedingly effective, revolution by insurrection was not possible. However, Mao's "military deviation" was, in fact, more than just an expedient forced upon Mao by circumstances. It was also fully in harmony with the basic bent of his personality. Stuart Schram has pointed out the extraordinary extent to which military metaphors and military habits of thought permeate every aspect of Mao's mentality and his approach to virtually all problems. The idea that war and politics are merely different aspects of the same phenomenon has frequently been formulated by Mao in terms that come from Clausewitz, via Lenin; for instance, in his thesis that "politics is war without bloodshed, and war is politics with bloodshed." [18] But long before Mao had ever heard either of these names, he had undoubtedly read the opening sentences of Sun Tzu's *Art of War*: "The art of war is of vital importance to the state. It is a matter of life and death, a road either to safety or to ruin." [19] Against this background of "Sinification" of Lenin and Clausewitz, we understand the famous opening sentences of Mao's

Report of an Investigation into the Peasant Movement in Hunan of 1927: "In a very short time, several hundred million peasants in China's Central, Southern, and Northern provinces will rise like a tornado or tempest—a force so extraordinarily swift and violent that no power, however great, will be able to suppress it. They will break through all the trammels that now bind them and push forward along the road to liberation. They will send all imperialists, warloads, corrupt officials, local bullies, and evil gentry, to their graves." For, "a revolution is . . . an act of violence whereby one class overthrows the authority of another." [20]

If Maoism may be characterized as a Sinification of Lenin and Clausewitz, then a different type of adaptation of Western ideologies can be found in the views held by Latin American Castroism on the issue of guerrilla warfare, particularly as developed by Ernesto Che Guevara and spelled out in his book *La guerra de guerrillas*. Che Guevara was convinced that the Cuban Revolution contributed three fundamental lessons to the conduct of revolutionary movements in America: (1) Popular forces can win a war against the army; (2) it is not necessary to wait until all conditions for making revolution exist; the insurrection can create them; (3) in underdeveloped Latin America the countryside is the basic area for armed fighting.

At the time of writing, in 1959, Che Guevara was certainly already a Marxist, but definitely not of the orthodox Moscow brand. There is some evidence of Trotskyite and Maoist influence, but Guevara's flat denial of the leading role of the proletariat is directly contrary to Trotskyite doctrine, and even Mao never went as far as Guevara in this direction. Plainly polemicizing against the Latin American Communist parties, Guevara stresses that the third proposition is a fundament of strategy. Those who maintain dogmatically that the struggle of the masses is centered in city movements are entirely forgetting the immense participation of country people in the life of all the underdeveloped parts of Latin America. "In the conditions that prevail, at least in America and in almost all countries with a deficient economic development, it is the countryside which offers ideal conditions for the fight. Therefore the foundation of the social structure that the guer-

rilla fighter will build begins with changes in the ownership of agrarian property. The banner of the fight throughout this period will be agrarian reform." [21]

It would be a serious misunderstanding, however, of the Latin American situation, to link systematic planned violence and guerrilla warfare to a revolutionary ideology of the Castro type. "Violence seems to be institutionalized in the organization, maintenance, and changing of governments in Latin America," writes an observer.[22] His view is supported by many other observations which point to the tendency, inherent in Latin American life, to settle political issues by force. Government by revolution might almost be said to be the rule. A statistical survey counted, since the turn of the present century, an annual average of nearly four successful uprisings per country, and it allows that the number of unsuccessful rebellions during these years may have run into the hundreds.[23] Nevertheless, although violence provides a continuing thread in the fabric of Latin American politics, revolution in the sense of a fundamental transformation of society is rare in Latin America, and even mass participation in violence is only occasionally found. Violence is virtually always present; fundamental change is virtually always absent. Political instability, though chronic and frequently accompanied by limited violence, produces no basic shifts in economic, social, or political policies. The reason is that it does not pose a genuine danger to the control of the conventional economic bases of power. The Latin American *caudillo* operates within a narrowly circumscribed range of power, since he may not tamper with the traditional economic bases of power. In the mathematically formulated definition posed by Merle King, chronic political instability is a function of the contradiction between the realities of a colonial economy and the political requirements of legal sovereignty among the Latin American states.[24]

Structured violence and guerrilla warfare in Latin America are, thus, complex phenomena. A serious study of political violence in rural Colombia has led to the conclusion that the decade since 1948, during which more than 200,000 people were killed in the civil war raging in the rural areas, has to be understood as one of abortive revolution. The inchoate, unconventional civil war in

which mass hysteria and mass homicide became accepted by certain elements of the power structure and by the rural culture on a regional basis, was a violent reaction against the postponement of a structural revolution. "Possibly Colombia," says the sociologist Talcott Parsons, "was responding by a vendetta or guerrilla warfare to the anomie precipitated by the confrontation of old and new, where a decade or two earlier Italy, Germany, and Spain responded to the higher level conflict of the traditionalized and the rationalized by varying expressions of fascism." [25]

Following a distinction made by James Rosenau, the question might be posed this way: Is guerrilla warfare merely a kind of personal war or an authority war; or has it the dimensions of a structural war? Personal wars are fought in order to substitute another person for the existing ruler. In authority wars the governing authority is being replaced (for instance, in decolonization wars). But only a structural war aims at fundamentally changing the socio-political and economic structure (for example, a Communist revolution).[26] History knows many peasant rebellions, but only a structural war has such a close analogy to revolution that it can be considered the continuation of (revolutionary) politics by violent means, as, conversely, the politics of revolution is the continuation of structural war by other means.

War and Development

As there is a close link between war and revolution, another connection, no less intimate, exists between war and development. The literature on either issue can hardly be said to focus attention upon this relationship. In the many studies on development problems, the question is usually neglected. It is to the credit of W. W. Rostow that he paid special attention to it. He sees three particular reasons for this relationship.[27] (1) The theory of the preconditions period—of the supplanting of the traditional society with one form or another of modern society—hinges substantially on the demonstrable effect of the relation between modernization and military power. (2) A creative answer is needed to the challenge of later

Marxist theory which explains modern warfare as a corollary of imperialism viewed as a mature stage of modern capitalism. (3) In this time of precarious nuclear stalemate, we need suggestions as to how the two dominant problems, i.e., the arms race and the organization of a world containing many new nations, can be removed or safely by-passed. He then distinguishes three kinds of wars which have been fought in the past three centuries, since Western Europe began to develop endogenously the preconditions for take-off. Each of these three kinds is related to a distinctive stage in the development process. Of the colonial wars, the wars of independence, from 1776 in America to 1959 in Algeria, are related to the dynamics of the preconditions for the take-off period. Directly from these dynamics a second type of war arose: regional aggression. The wars of the French Revolution became the greatest of all examples of this type, arising from an unresolved transitional process during the preconditions period. Other examples are the American effort to steal Canada during the French wars; Bismarck's expansive military policy against neighboring countries from 1864 to 1871; the Japanese primacy in Korea secured in 1895; and the Russian drive through Manchuria to Vladivostok, leading to the test of strength with resurgent Japan in 1904–1905. The battle cries of nationalist leaders like Nasser on Israel and Sukarno on West Irian and Malaysia represent a contemporary version of this response. These early, limited external adventures appear generally to have given way to a phase of absorption in the adventure of modernizing the economy and society as a whole: post-Civil War America, post-1873 Germany, post-1905 Japan, even post-1920 Russia were for several decades passing through this phase.

The next dangerous age comes with the approach of economic maturity, when one of the available options is the concentration of resources on a more ambitious expansion of external power. There is an inner continuity in the three great military struggles of the twentieth century: the First World War, the Second World War, and the Cold War up to the beginning of the Korean truce negotiations in 1951. To the extent that these struggles have an economic base, that basis lies in the contours of the Eurasian arena of power,

as determined by relative stages-of-growth and by military potential. Within the Eurasian continent, three powers—Germany, Japan, and Russia—were successively tempted to exploit their newly achieved maturity and the vulnerability of the still-transitional societies of Eastern Europe and China, hoping thus to seize control of an emerging industrialized Eurasia.

In the early 1950's the shape of this struggle altered its character and the history of war entered a new phase due, on the one hand, to the full emergence of nuclear weapons, notably the H-bomb, and, on the other hand, to the growing implications of the growth process at many points in the world.

It is obvious that the modern history of economic development and the problems arising from this development cannot be realistically approached without looking at the lessons of modern military history. Let us first consider the development of weapons and the growth of armaments during the last hundred years. Philip Noel-Baker, in an illuminating survey of the modern arms race,[28] points to the decisive impact of the Industrial Revolution on the battlefield, which was revealed in the last quarter of the nineteenth century. For more than five centuries European warfare had been dominated by the use of gunpowder which, although invented by the Chinese, had never been used by them in war. Its introduction onto the European battlefields in the early fourteenth century added a new dimension to warfare. The success of Krupp's steel guns in the Franco-Prussian War and the invention of the machine-gun in the 1880's started a revolution in the armaments of land forces. A period of intense competition followed, and the outbreak of the First World War brought further big improvements in weaponry. After the First World War, the competition to improve the deadly quality of weapons continued without a break: tanks increased in weight, and aircraft increased in speed, range, useful load, and defensive armament. Nevertheless, the Second World War was begun with the weapons of the First War. But before its conclusion, many new weapons had appeared. The scientists, who were given great resources, produced astonishing results: incendiary bombs, the new Tabun gases, the manifold use of radar and electronics, magnetic mines, rockets, and guided

missiles. With the pilotless aircraft, the V1, and the ballistic missile, the V2, Hitler introduced a new kind of war. Finally, in 1945, came the first atomic bombs.

Even more striking than the introduction of these new weapons, Noel-Baker continues, was the unbridled ferocity with which the older "conventional" weapons were employed, first by Hitler and Mussolini, and then by the Western Allies in reply. After the attack of the British Royal Air Forces on Hamburg—which was burned to the ground in reprisal for Hitler's bombing of Coventry, London, and other towns—the destruction of towns and cities by aerial bombardment, and in particular by fire, remained a normal method of warfare on both sides. Some 40,000 British seamen lost their lives from submarine attack (*vs.* 12,000 in the First World War); almost the whole of the German, Italian, and Japanese commercial fleets were sunk by submarines or aircraft.

These methods of warfare were accepted as normal and conventional by all governments. Aerial bombardment and the use of fire marked the operations in Korea and Indochina from the first day to the last, and they were considered normal procedure in the Vietnam war. Even in conventional weapons, says Noel-Baker, there has never been, in a similar length of time, whether in peacetime or in war, anything approaching the present rapidity of progress. This progress, moreover, has greatly increased the speed, "agility," and fire-power of conventional weapons; that is to say, it has increased their offensive power, and thus tipped the balance of advantage still further in favor of the attack as a means of self-defense. Since 1945 all the leading military powers have devoted their main effort to weapons of mass-destruction: strategic and tactical nuclear weapons of many kinds; poison gas, incendiary bombs, and liquids; biological weapons and missiles. The progress made since 1945 with these "modern" weapons dwarfs what has been done with conventional weapons, and the rate of progress continues to increase. Together they have already multiplied the destructive power of the armed forces by a factor of many thousands.

The most important cause of the unbroken expansion of national armaments since 1870 has been the arms race itself. The

construction of the Dreadnought by the British Admiralty in 1907 kindled a frenzied competition with Germany for the construction of Dreadnoughts, and later super-Dreadnoughts. Thus Britain's naval security, on which the Empire and the Commonwealth then depended, was gravely compromised. After the First World War the victorious Allies continued competitive warlike preparations— against each other. The suicidal character of the ever-increasing arms race became obvious after the invention of the atomic bomb. The atomic scientists who, during the Second World War, developed the atomic bomb for the United States believed themselves to be in a life-and-death race against Germany. They also knew the explosive potential of uranium fission. An even more serious choice was President Harry Truman's decision in 1950 to make the H-bomb, after a Russian test of an atomic device had been detected in August, 1949. The alternative to this quantitative lead was the construction of a qualitatively new weapon—as much greater in force than the fission weapons as fission bombs were than conventional bombs. But when Truman made his decision, the Russians had already started the research on an H-bomb which resulted in their 1953 success.

The change in character of the current arms race from previous arms races has been pointed out by the well-known American expert on atomic weaponry, Herman Kahn.[29] Previously, really big wars have tended to occur twenty, thirty, or more years apart, and there has been a tendency for each war to start where the last one left off, or with even more ancient techniques. Now, for the first time in history, we are experiencing a complete technological revolution in the art of war approximately every five years. "As a result, we are now three technological revolutions away from World War II. Any attempts to apply the concepts and rules of common sense derived from that experience run the grave risk of being as outmoded as some American Civil War concepts would have been in World War II. In so far as we are trying to plan for the late sixties and early seventies," said Kahn in 1961, "we are projecting into an environment which is two or three revolutions ahead of where we are today. An examination of the development of military doctrine in the postwar years, in both the official

agencies and the avant-garde, indicates that the possibility of great success in such planning is not high. While doctrine has evolved with meteoric speed as contrasted with the rates before World War II, it has been hopelessly behind events rather than successful in anticipating the future."

The conclusion, therefore, is that the steady acceleration of technological progress makes any reasonable prognosis for the armaments situation in the next decades less and less feasible. We now have to take into account more than just the extrapolation of current technology. We have to consider the possibility of "breakthroughs" and other surprises. Kahn has drawn some extreme conclusions from the present situation. He does not believe that the twentieth century will see a disarmed world, but it may see a world government or the equivalent. An international agency with a near-monopoly for force might come from any of the following possibilities, listed in order of apparent probability rather than desirability:

1. a Soviet- or United States-dominated world, arising most likely out of war;

2. some other results of a war;

3. a Soviet Union–United States combination which is in effect a world government, though it may not be openly called so;

4. some of the NATO nations and China added to the above combination as influential, if not equal, partners;

5. the Haves against the Have-nots, probably without exploitation, perhaps with aid to underdeveloped nations, but with stringent arms control in which authority and responsibility are roughly proportional to military and economic development;

6. a sort of world federal state in which power is proportional to sovereignty and population, as in the United States Congress.

"While many of the above possibilities," he adds, "may strike most people as unpleasant or undesirable, it is quite possible that even a 'bad' world government is preferable to an accelerated and uncontrolled arms race. It is to be hoped this last will not be the only choice available."

In order to think through the ultimate consequences of a

continued arms race and a permanent balance of deterrence, Kahn has drafted the concept of the perfect defense system, for which it would be necessary to construct a so-called Doomsday Machine. Kahn does not believe that the Soviet Union and the United States would build a Doomsday Machine, for the simple reason that they are both status-quo powers. But what about the non-status-quo nations? Many scientists believe that Doomsday Machines will inevitably become much cheaper than the present estimated ten billion dollars, so that the developmental gamble will be much less risky than it is today. In addition, a number of powers which, unlike the United States and the Soviet Union, may not be cautious in outlook, will be getting both richer and more competent technically, yet may retain their non-status-quo outlook. For example, there may be a nation (like the Germany of 1933) which is wealthy enough and technically competent enough to have an advanced military technology, yet desperate or ambitious enough to gamble all. Or some of the underdeveloped nations may become rich in terms of gross national product, but have such a low per-capita income or other social anomaly that they retain attitudes more appropriate to a desperate claimant on the world's resources than a responsible "bourgeois" member of international society.

We have deliberately presented some extreme possibilities, arising from the present paradoxical and suicidal armament situation, because they throw a revealing light on the total complex of the development process both in its advanced stages and in its possible repercussions on less developed stages. With these extreme possibilities in mind, we have now to consider some less hypothetical aspects of the impact of the military factor on the development problem and of the issue of war and peace in relation to the less developed world. The paradox of the military situation after the invention of the atomic bomb might be defined as follows:

In an advanced stage of industrial development, war has actually lost its necessary function; at the same time it is these highly developed countries which present the world with the threat of total annihilation through a third world war. Historically speaking it might be said that war fulfilled a vital function in agrarian societies. The unavoidable corollary of the steady threat

of famine and hunger accompanied the life of agrarian societies. For this type of society there are only three possibilities to relieve the tensions of these permanent, although often latent, threats of famine and hunger; (1) to limit the number of births to the maximum tolerated by the total amount of cultivated area; (2) to strive for expansion by war; (3) to be resigned to an enduring level of undernourishment.

Throughout the history of agrarian societies we see these three possibilities playing a role, and their alternating rhythm had an unavoidable function. After the Industrial Revolution, this function, however, began to lose its meaning. An industrial society is dependent upon a complicated societal system of labor division and upon an extremely vulnerable technical apparatus, so that the risk of destruction which it runs by launching a war does not equal the advantages which may be won by a possible victory. And the development of military technology enhances the annihilating effects of warfare to an extent undreamed of in the history of agrarian societies. But the most important factor is that in a highly developed country the biological drive for war, namely famine and hunger, has been overcome. In an industrial society not only atomic warfare, but war with conventional weapons, has lost its biological urgency and can be maintained only as a cultural and social lag.

Our present world, however, still lives under these preposterous suicidal conditions, the burden of which may seem less crushing with the conclusion of the Atomic Test-Ban Agreement, but which essentially has not lessened in the slightest degree. To the contrary, the arms race has continued. This means that the whole development problem remains in the shadow of the threat of atomic warfare and thus of the consequent arms race. The international economist Gunnar Myrdal some years ago soberly stated that the total amount of international aid to underdeveloped countries is no more than a tiny fraction of what the advanced countries are prepared to pay for their own defense.[30] The United Nations' Experts on economic development calculated that for the underdeveloped countries the capital needed annually from abroad for industry and agriculture alone (excluding complementary social

investments), in order to ensure the very modest increase in per-capital income of 2 per cent a year, would be around ten billion dollars. This would be scarcely 15 per cent of the total expenditure on defense, undertaken after due political process by the citizens of the advanced countries. But even one-tenth of that amount, corresponding to no more than 1 or 2 per cent of real armament costs, would not be forthcoming from the present inadequate basis of human solidarity.

We often hear Western politicians raise the question of a possible disproportion between military and economic aid to developing countries. Even John Foster Dulles acknowledged, in the midst of the Cold War period, that as "an abstract proportion, too much throughout the world is being spent on military and not enough on economic aid." Walt W. Rostow argued forcefully in favor of an aid program designed to assist all countries in achieving a steady, self-sustaining rate of growth irrespective of the short-run political interests of the country. The assumption here is that self-sustaining growth, once attained, will not merely relieve human poverty, but will resolve the Cold War, render military deterrence superfluous, convince the Kremlin that the game for Eurasian power-hegemony is hopeless, and thus, in the long run, accomplish more effectively the defense task that is presently being assigned to military aid and short-term economic aid. This line of thought has met with serious doubts and criticism, however.

The critics have argued that the crucial issue in the Cold War, as far as the developing, non-Communist countries are concerned, is not primarily related to a Sino-Soviet threat to individual freedom and civil liberties, but is directed to the independence of nations from Sino-Soviet control. A major point under discussion was that, unless India, through United States' assistance, can match Red China's economic development, the course of the Free World and its way of life will be damaged beyond repair throughout the underdeveloped parts of the world. The counterargument, launched by the critics who stress the unavoidability of giving priority to military aid, is based on the realistic assumption that, unfortunately, no amount of economic aid will be able to supply India

with the equivalent in capital and working-hours that the Communist regime can extort from its people. It is a fallacy of thought that the time has come to shift from "unconstructive" defense aid (military aid and short-term economic-emergency aid) to "constructive," sound long-term economic-development aid. The latter can at least have a psychological side-effect that will be valuable to the present and exacting defense effort imposed by the Cold War. It is also likely, the argument continues, to have unfavorable effects, such as creating social dislocation, increasing a restless industrial proletariat, or undermining an established cultural and religious order. If external economic aid by the United States helps India over its short-run emergencies, the United States may be doing as much as it can to meet the dangers flowing from a Red Chinese victory in the productivity race.[31]

The debate on this issue has emerged from a fundamental dilemma in which a country on the highest stage of economic and industrial development is being involved as a consequence of its military power and its paradoxical incapacity to make effective use of it. The debate has been continued on the question whether the United States should or should not engage in a radical renewal and expansion of its defense system against atomic attacks, which might mean an investment in the total air defense of fifteen billion dollars.

The former American Secretary of Defense, Robert McNamara, resisted the idea of such a program, not only for military and political reasons, but primarily by demonstrating that security in the future will not depend upon a balance of deterrence, but upon worldwide economic development.[32] In the years between 1958 and 1966, his argument continues, there have been 164 important explosions of violence, fifteen of which resulted in conflicts between governments, the overwhelming majority of them taking place in underdeveloped countries. There exists a direct and constant proportion between the annual number of upheavals —which in eight years has almost doubled—and the economic development of the countries involved. Out of the twenty-seven highly developed countries (with an annual per-capita income of 750 dollars) only one has suffered a major internal upheaval since

1958; out of the thirty-eight least developed countries (with an annual per-capita income of less than 100 dollars) thirty-two suffered outbursts of violence during this period. Eighty-seven per cent of the least developed, 69 per cent of the underdeveloped, and 48 per cent of the half-developed countries have suffered this fate. But out of the 148 revolutions during this eight-year period only fifty-eight were directly related to Communist activity, and of these no less than seven were directed against Communism.

In the 1970's, McNamara pointed out, more than half of the world population will live in the underdeveloped southern part of the earth, but, unless there is a considerable increase in the rate of economic growth, this majority of mankind will have available only one-sixth of the world production of goods and services. By 1975 the number of children in this part of the world under fifteen years of age will equal the total population of the northern, highly developed countries. And still the gap between rich and poor countries grows. In the year 2000 half of the underdeveloped countries will have an annual per-capita income of 170 dollars, while the United States will have reached a level of 4,500 dollars. Safety depends upon development, for, without development, order and stability are impossible and the frustrations engendered by poverty will increase. Order and stability are a shield protecting the development of security. The military problem is only a small facet of the greater problem of security.

This is only one aspect of the development problem, as seen within a broader context. Experience in the postwar decades has proved that the United States economy can very well stand both the burden of modern armament and the consequences of disarmament. In the first year after the Second World War (1945–1946) the United States transferred an absolute amount of manpower and resources from war to civilian employments, more than twice as much as would be involved (in real terms) in total and complete disarmament at present. Although the post-Korean disarmament was less well managed, unemployment dropped again in subsequent years in the face of a continued fall in the real defense burden. Kenneth Boulding[33] has pointed to the fact that the economic burden of a country's military budget in proportion to

the total national income decreases as the country rises to a higher stage of development. In Russia, for instance, though exact information is not available, the proportion of the gross national product going into national security is considerably larger than in the United States—though in an economy that is substantially poorer. National security is correspondingly a much greater economic burden. In the United States the marginal significance of the arms dollar concerns a little more or a little less luxury; in Russia it is much closer to basic comfort, and in India it is close to sheer necessity. In really poor countries like India, Pakistan, and China, arms expenditure literally snatches life from the starving. Economic development is such a tender plant in its early stages that a heavy arms budget may condemn a poor country to stagnation.

Two other questions arise from the close connection between the world's military situation and the problem of world economic development. The first is the relation between atomic, conventional, and guerrilla warfare. It is obvious that these three types of warfare are closely related to the stages of economic development. In a world wherein atomic war would mean universal suicide and conventional warfare, which may inevitably escalate into atomic warfare, is virtually excluded by the big powers as a real factor of foreign policy, the most primitive type of warfare appears to receive an unprecedented opportunity. This question is of major importance for the developing countries; and plays an important role in the Communist theory of just and unjust types of war, and in the conflict within the Communist world between Soviet Russia and China. For a country like China, which is still in the initial stage of development and is struggling with the overwhelming tradition of the agrarian society that prevailed in the past, it is of course normal to approach the problem of war from the point of view that has always been inherent in the agrarian type of society. Moreover, China's specific experiences of the combination of Communist revolution and guerrilla warfare have led her to view this type of warfare as the incomparable instrument for successful revolutions in the underdeveloped world. It has been rightly suggested [34] that, although the Chinese attitude may appear to developed countries—not only the Western nations, but even many

Russian leaders—to be the product of a preindustrial society completely irrelevant in the age of automation, it is in fact shared by large segments of the populations of Asia, Africa, and Latin America. This applies not only to the antiforeign and anti-imperialist drive that accompanies this attitude, but also to the warlike approach which Mao and his colleagues take toward the transformation of nature. Even the failures of China's domestic policies may appear to some in the underdeveloped countries as heroic failures in a common cause.

We have to realize that guerrilla warfare is only one aspect, albeit an important one, of the total amount of possibilities included in unconventional warfare. "Unconventional warfare" embraces a broad spectrum of conflict including such diverse activities as propaganda, economic warfare, sabotage, espionage, subversion, strikes, civil disturbances, terrorism, political warfare, and guerrilla fighting.

It is certainly true that the Communists have practiced unconventional warfare for more than four decades, although they have not called it that. They have used these methods of conflict, either singly or in concert, within the framework of an over-all grand strategy. But it is equally true that unconventional warfare was not originated by Communism. The makers of the French Revolution experimented with many methods of unorthodox warfare, and in the United States, Presidents Thomas Jefferson and James Madison pioneered in such economic-warfare devices as the embargo against Great Britain. Yet, not until the early twentieth century did this mode of conflict come into its own. And it did so for three basic reasons, which have been summed up by James Atkinson as follows:

First, the revolution in the communication of ideas—radio transmission, wireless telegraphy, and photography—provided unconventional warriors with ready-made weapons.

Second, a burgeoning "thinking elite" in modern mass society furnished cadres for, and lent continuity to, revolutionary movements and fifth columns.

Third, modern society has become at once more complex and more vulnerable to attack by unconventional methods. The

West's conspicuous vulnerability to such attack—so much greater than that of the Communists—cannot be laid to a lack of understanding of the capabilities of unconventional warfare. The effectiveness of resistance movements in German-occupied countries during the Second World War demonstrated that the Western countries possess extensive assets and know-how for waging—and waging successfully—this highly specialized version of combat.[35]

However, the reason for this Western vulnerability does not stem, as Atkinson seems to believe, from any supposed peace-loving attitude on the part of Western democracies; it is a simple corollary of the different position within the total scale of the development process. Unconventional warfare is the most adequate type of self-defense and successful attack for those countries which lag behind in economic development and have to resist the pressure of the more advanced countries, which have at their disposal not only economic power, but also instruments of atomic and conventional armaments which they have been able to develop to a superior degree.

The situation is further complicated by a second factor, namely, the coexistence within one world of the three types of warfare—atomic, conventional, and unconventional—and the necessity or supposed necessity for any nation setting high value on its national security and independence to avail itself of all three. We face two paradoxes which are closely intertwined and mutually aggravate each other.

The first paradox is the continued existence of sovereign nations that try to defend their national security by a type of armament, i.e., atomic armament, which by definition implies national suicide at the moment of actual use and which raises problems that can only be solved by the sacrifice of national sovereignty to supranational organizations. The second paradox is the exuberant proliferation of the concepts of nationhood and of national prestige and independence among the less developed world, that part of the world which more than any other is in urgent need of supranational cooperation for economic development. No other segment of the world can less easily bear the burden of military expenditures consequent upon the need to maintain national secu-

rity. The problems might not be insoluble if each paradox could be handled completely separately from the other. But that is not possible in this world. The first paradox is, as it were, being exported to the underdeveloped world, where it immensely aggravates the problems raised by the second paradox. Furthermore, as an indirect result, it makes the problem of atomic disarmament in a world of sovereign nations still less manageable for the big powers.

One need not go so far as to imagine an underdeveloped nation constructing a Doomsday Machine, to illustrate the seriousness of the problem.

Herman Kahn has discussed the possibilities implicit in the production of atomic weapons by China. If one had to explain the rationale of an exchange of several major United States cities for an equal number of Chinese cities, political suicide for the party-in-power in the United States would result. There would also be some signs of instability and distrust in international alliances; but the Chinese government would suffer no more than serious inconveniences. It should, therefore, Kahn continues, be a major objective of arms control to prevent such hypothetical problems from actually occurring, and he sees at this point a clear case of joint Soviet-United States interest.

Kahn himself, however, is very doubtful whether the proliferation of nuclear weapons to an unlimited number of nations can still be prevented. The most advanced nations know, at least in theory, how to make simple nuclear bombs and missiles, and in the absence of explicit or implicit control will be making them in practice. But Kahn goes ahead and assumes a technological breakthrough in the near future, whereby even relatively primitive nations will find it possible to build or to buy a fusion reactor and so acquire a virtually unlimited source of cheap power. He compares the widespread possession of nuclear weapons with situations in physics that may be described as semistable equilibrium, illustrated by balancing a ball on top of a small cup, so that slight movements of the ball can be tolerated, but not big ones. Therefore, his conclusion is that reliable stability can come only through an international agency with effective force.

This very concept of a two-power atomic hegemony of the

United States and the Soviet Union has already been seriously eroded by the attempt of France and China to alter this system of polarization of power through their own nuclear programs. The present situation has, in fact, already crossed the dividing line between the two continental superpowers and the rest. A second qualitative line of division, that between the secondary or medium powers and the small powers, has not yet been reached. If the circle of nuclear powers were to widen to include not merely a few more medium powers but a plethora of small states, this would be as much of a threat to whatever system of nuclear powers may emerge from the nuclear proliferation of the next few years, as it would be to the system of Soviet-American nuclear hegemony. The need to prevent a world of many nuclear powers from developing, or at least to mitigate the consequences of such a development, is likely to be recognized by the major nuclear powers, whether they are two or several.[36]

But what are small states? Couldn't a number of small states join together to form a larger unit—a unit with sufficient nuclear strength to permit them to participate in dictating the conditions of peace to the rest of the world? Are not the underdeveloped countries of today in process of development and is there any guarantee that in the course of this process they will not discover the advantages of the premature possession of nuclear power? Can the second paradox, namely, of the proliferation of nationhood in an era of supranational technology, be adequately approached by those nations who are imprisoned in the vicious circle of the first paradox: the maintenance of national sovereignty by atomic powers whose presumed instruments of security are, in fact, instruments of suicide.

The development problem is one and indivisible; the present-day military problems are one and indivisible. And both problems are indissolubly interconnected.

Strategy and Conscience

In the first part of this chapter we said that Clausewitz's insights into the essential connection between military strategy and politics has, in our century, been seriously studied and practiced by Communist theories on revolution and, more particularly, on the significance of guerrilla warfare. It is not surprising that in recent years the reaction to this fact in Western countries, especially in the United States, has resulted in the development of counterinsurgence theories. In a measure, this means a return to the American experience in guerrilla warfare received in the pre-Revolutionary days when the colonists were engaged in a continuous, unconventional war with the Indians; during the Civil War; and, in general, during a good part of the nineteenth century when American troops were engaged in guerrilla warfare against the Indians.[37]

However important this may be in understanding the type of warfare known to underdeveloped countries, it does not reach the level of Clausewitz's insights, for it means an escape from the essential dilemma on the level of the technology which an atomic power has to face. The real dilemma for highly developed countries is the necessity for, and at the same time the impossibility of constructing, a feasible world order in the atomic era. On this level Clausewitz's principle once more plays a paramount role, and this time his lessons have been very well recognized by Western military and political theoreticians.

Anatol Rapoport, a mathematical biologist at the University of Michigan, has focused some of his studies on the function of modern strategic science, which plays a dominant role in international politics today. He considers modern strategic thinking as a continuation of Clausewitz's famous thesis, but (like the Communist use of the thesis!) in reverse order. To Clausewitz, war was the continuation of politics by other means. Today, international politics has become the continuation of war by other means.[38]

The modern professional strategist stands aloof from the clash of commitments between the peace movement on the left and the defenders of armed might on the right. Modern strategic science

spells out its principles in abstract, often mathematical, terms. Its expertise does not derive necessarily from experience with practical political or military matters but from training in physics, economics, political science, or the abstract principles of strategic thinking. The modern strategist claims objectivity, maturity, and realism. Seen from the strategic perspective, war appears cleansed of its unpleasant features and offers challenging intellectual and organizational problems. There is no question, says Rapoport, that the game of strategy paradigm is the predominant one in the main stream of American thought about international affairs. This is not surprising, since the game of strategy paradigm is attractive to people who associate creative thinking with business acumen and technical know-how. Possibly it explains the fact that the theory of games has aroused intense interest in the United States, unparalleled by any theory of comparable abstruseness.[39] As a matter of fact, in spite of its negligible value as a tool for solving practical problems, games theory brings clearly into focus a conceptual framework in which strategic analogues of conflict situations can be most clearly formulated. In this respect one can speak of a congeniality between strategic and game-theoretical modes of thinking. Game-theoretical analysis is strategic analysis in its most rigorous form. This is because game-theoretical analysis can be applied only when a situation has been stripped of all ambiguity, and the participants have been "purged" of all propensities for error, precipitous decision, etc.

At this point an important conclusion can be drawn. For it appears that even under these idealized conditions it is impossible to prescribe a rational course of action, except perhaps in the simplest cases. The consequent question concerning modern strategic science is, therefore: What can one expect from strategic analysis in real-life situations, where the range of choices is seldom well defined, where estimates of others' utilities are seldom reliable, and where there is no reason to assume that the players are "rational"?

Strategists are, of course, constantly under pressure to formulate situations in such a way as to make strategic analysis relevant. Now, in fact, strategic analysis leads to the most definite con-

clusions in the case of two-person zero-sum games. This is a game played by two persons whose interests are always diametrically opposed. Whatever the outcome of the game, the losses of one player equal the gains of the other. In situations of this kind, strategic analysis leads to a definite conclusion as to what a "rational" player ought to do, assuming that the other player is rational, and that assumption cannot always be made. For example, strategists who devote much of their analysis to the discussion of the techniques of nuclear blackmail have suggested that it might be advantageous for a player deliberately to try to convince the other of his own recklessness. Against a "rational" and believing opponent, this is, of course, a winning strategy, but not against an opponent whose strategist has advised him to do the same thing. The logical conclusion is, therefore, that games theory has nothing to contribute toward a resolution of these ambivalences and paradoxes.

Moreover, strategic analysis presupposes free choice among available strategies. Consequently, in strategic analysis, there is a tendency to ignore the cataclysmic aspect of the conflict. For example, Herman Kahn in his book *On Escalation* describes the forty-four rungs of the so-called "escalation ladder," ranging from an initial "crisis" all the way to the last rung, the "spasm war," in which each side attacks the other with everything it has. Kahn's thesis is that the player of an "escalation game" can move up and down the ladder at will, choosing the level of confrontation so as to maximize his strategic advantage. What is ignored in this picture is the dynamics of escalation itself, which may propel the "players" regardless of their wishes.

For these reasons, Rapoport sees the strategic model of conflict as a typical representative of a deep-rooted faith in man's rationality and free will. He even suggests that the old metaphysical and theological controversy of free will *vs.* determinism meets us here in a new manifestation. The typical representative of determinism is, in this field, the so-called cataclysmic model of conflict. A great example of this determinist type of thinking is to be found in Tolstoy's *War and Peace*. The lesson to be learned from the Napoleonic Wars, according to Tolstoy, is that the power

of potentates is a delusion, for potentates (today we call them decision-makers) are revealed to be the tools, not the makers, of history.[40] Tolstoy said that strategic science was invented by the Germans, whom he described as crackpots. As we saw, Clausewitz drew a very different lesson from the Napoleonic Wars. His strategic concept of war as a political act was diametrically opposed to Tolstoy's fatalism.

For a century, it seemed that Clausewitz's ideals prevailed. No cataclysmic wars erupted in nineteenth-century Europe. Conventional explanations of wars, at least of the European wars in the past few centuries, have been strategic explanations. However, following the First World War, the disillusionment with war, in the Western world, was so general that it appeared for a while as if the characterization of war as a rational political act would be forever rejected. The predominant view was of war as a cataclysmic event.

A specific cataclysmic theory of war was proposed in the years following the First World War. This time the author was not a literary figure but a scientist. Lewis F. Richardson, being a meteorologist, knew that many phenomena which seem totally erratic and unpredictable are nevertheless governed by deterministic laws. In Richardson's models we see an attempt to develop the cataclysmic model of conflict on scientific foundations.[41]

The cataclysmic view emphasizes the uncontrolled, self-propelled features of conflict. Its weakness is that it neglects the purposeful, rational, or quasi-rational features of behavior. The strategic view concentrates on just those features. It is therefore especially congenial to those whose main concern is with the management of conflict. The fact remains, however, that strategic analysis occurs, as a rule, in the context of seeking strategies advantageous to one of the parties to the conflict. Consequently there is constant pressure toward the "zero-sum view."

Neither the cataclysmic nor the strategic view is helpful in the search for creative methods of conflict resolution, mainly because neither poses the problem of analyzing the issues underlying the conflict. Fundamental questions of value are not raised. The

situation can be exemplified by the kind of questions one can legitimately put to a chess player. One can ask him why he made a certain move. It is not legitimate, however, to ask him why he should want to win the game. Once the international conflict is cast into the paradigm of a game, the analogous question loses legitimacy. Yet, it is in a sense a most important question. Why should a nation seek to increase its power or influence? Indeed, why should a nation seek even to "survive" as a nation? The same could be said for the different "ideologies" that are sometimes used as rallying points of the global struggle and in the name of which diplo-military strategies are designed. The "victory" of socialism over imperialism or of democracy over Communism serves the same purpose today as the victory of a nation-state over its "enemies" served yesterday.

A view of conflict which transcends these platitudes must come to grips with the real issues. If neither a strategic nor a cataclysmic model of the present-day anarchy of the international order has anything real to contribute to the growth of a livable, universal political order with its promise of a future for the whole of mankind, then it follows that neither a rationalist free-will philosophy nor an irrationalist determinist philosophy is able to touch the heart of the problem. This implies two things: first, there is the unavoidable self-justification of revolutionary ideologies over against the absence or impotence of any competitive concept of a political world order promising real peace and universal justice; second, just as in the traditional contrast between free-will and determinist metaphysics, so in this new manifestation of the old dilemma the truth is to be found beyond the dilemma.

We are, once more, facing the urgency of an adequate philosophy and theology of history.

NOTES

1. Cf. H. Eckstein (ed.), *Internal War* (New York, 1964).
2. James N. Rosenau, "Internal War as an International Event," in

International Aspects of Civil Strife, ed. James N. Rosenau (Princeton, N.J., 1964), p. 91.

3. Chalmers Johnson, *Revolution and the Social System* (Stanford, 1964).

4. Arnold J. Toynbee, *A Study of History,* abridgement of Vols. I–VI by D. C. Somervell (New York, 1947), pp. 283f.

5. Karl von Clausewitz, *On War,* in *War, Politics, and Power,* being selections from *On War* and *I Believe and Profess,* trans. and ed. with an Introduction by Edward M. Collins (Chicago, 1962), p. 255.

6. *Ibid.,* pp. 267f.

7. *Ibid.,* pp. 227ff.

8. *Ibid.,* Introduction, pp. 3ff.

9. *Ibid.,* pp. 301f.; cf. Introduction, pp. 17f., 48ff.

10. *Ibid.,* p. 63; cf. Introduction, pp. 40ff.

11. *Ibid.,* p. 232.

12. *Ibid.,* p. 141; cf. Introduction, pp. 45f.

13. *Ibid.,* p. 190.

14. Cf. *War, Politics, and Power,* Introduction, pp. 30ff. The account followed there is drawn largely from Stefan T. Possony, *A Century of Conflict* (Chicago, 1953), pp. 20ff.

15. *Ibid.,* Introduction, p. 37.

16. Andrew C. Janos, "The Communist Theory of the State and Revolution," in *Communism and Revolution: The Strategic Uses of Political Violence,* ed. Cyril E. Black (Princeton, N.J., 1964), pp. 33, 36.

17. Thomas P. Thornton, "The Foundations of Communist Revolutionary Doctrine," in Cyril E. Black, ed., *op. cit.,* pp. 65, 69.

18. Quoted in Karl von Clausewitz, *op. cit.,* Introduction, p. 32. Cf. Richard L. Walker, *The Continuing Struggle* (New York, 1958), p. 68.

19. Stuart Schram, "The 'Military Deviation' of Mao Tse-Tung," *Problems of Communism* (January–February, 1964), pp. 52f.

20. Stuart Schram, *The Political Thought of Mao Tse-Tung* (New York, 1963), pp. 179f., 32.

21. Ernst Halperin, "Castroism—Challenge to the Latin American Communists," *Problems of Communism* (September–October, 1963), pp. 11f.

22. William S. Stokes, "Violence as a Power Factor in Latin-American Politics," *Western Political Quarterly,* V (1952), p. 445. Quoted

by Merle King, "Towards a Theory of Power and Political Instability in Latin America," in: *Political Change in Underdeveloped Countries,* ed. John K. Kautsky, p. 127, note 10.

23. Austin F. Macdonald, *Latin American Politics and Government* (2nd ed.; New York, 1954), pp. 11–12; cf. Merle King, *op. cit.,* p. 127, note 10.

24. Stokes, *op. cit.,* p. 461; King, *op. cit.,* pp. 138, 127, note 11; cf. Stokes, *op. cit.,* p. 461.

25. Robert C. Williamson, "Toward a Theory of Political Violence: The Case of Rural Colombia," *The Western Political Quarterly,* University of Utah, Vol. 18, No. 1 (March, 1965), pp. 44, 38.

26. James N. Rosenau, *op. cit.,* p. 90.

27. W. W. Rostow, *The Stages of Economic Growth* (New York, 1960), pp. 106ff.

28. Philip Noel-Baker, *The Arms Race* (London, 1958), pp. 38ff.

29. Herman Kahn, "The Arms Race and Some of Its Hazards," in Donald G. Brennan (ed.), *Arms Control Disarmament and National Security* (New York, 1961).

30. Gunnar Myrdal, *An International Economy* (New York, 1956), p. 123.

31. Arnold Wolfers, "Military or Economic Aid: Questions of Priority," in *American Strategy for the Nuclear Age,* ed. W. F. Hahn and J. C. Neff (New York, 1960), p. 387.

32. Robert McNamara, Speech delivered to the American Society of Newspaper Editors on May 18, 1966, at Montreal, Canada.

33. Kenneth Boulding, "Economic Implications of Arms Control," in *Arms Control, Disarmament and National Security,* p. 161.

34. Stuart Schram, *The Political Thought of Mao Tse-Tung* (New York, 1967), p. 70.

35. James D. Atkinson, "Unconventional Warfare," in *American Strategy for the Nuclear Age,* p. 302.

36. Erasmus, "Polycentrism and Proliferation," *Survey* (January, 1966), pp. 171f.

37. Charles W. Thayer, *Guerrilla* (New York, 1963), pp. 157ff.

38. Cf. Anatol Rapoport, *Strategy and Conscience* (New York, 1964), p. xvii.

39. A. Rapoport, "The Cataclysmic and the Strategic Models," in *Proceedings* of the International Peace Research Association, Inaugural Conference (Assen, 1966), p. 63.

40. *Ibid.,* pp. 78ff.

41. *Ibid.,* p. 89.

CHAPTER SIX

Revolution in a Post-Christian World— Christianity in a Postrevolutionary World

The main theme of this book, succinctly defined in the title *Development Through Revolution,* has been expounded on the basis of two fundamental thoughts. The first idea concerns the interrelationship between the two constituent elements of the main theme, together with its further implications. The second thought is related to the confrontation of this theme with the Christian ethos.

The significance of the first basic thought could be appropriately symbolized by the composition of a triangle, consisting of three mutually connected points: revolution, development, and war.

Revolution, at first sight a linguistic puzzle and a sociological chameleon, reveals on closer analysis a depth-dimension of human existence and natural reality. Ranging from the domain of political and social phenomena to the field of technology and science, in moments of crisis when the traditional system in its totality is passing through a crucial challenge, revolution is surging from the

depth where it lay hidden and breaks out at the surface. At such critical moments, man and world are betraying their apparently uninterrupted, "natural," substantial, continuous character; they are attacked by some mysterious, pernicious disease which threatens the very foundations of health, life, and truth.

But, what to the alarmed observer and to the patient himself frequently appears as a death-blow, may eventually turn out to be the very condition for salvation. Revolution is the dialectical counterpart of evolution and development. The process of development, in the socio-political realm as well as in the realm of science, may follow a continuous and uninterrupted course, as long as a given channel exists. But at the very moment when the adequacy of the traditional channel is being basically questioned and the given system is no longer capable of responding to unprecedented challenges, what seemed to be the safeguard of continuity turns into the enemy of future development, carving out a new channel as it goes along. The established routes are not an unchangeable part of nature; they are historical realities, fixed by man in the course of history and capable of being altered by man in the course of history. The revolutionary character of development is determined by the historical character of human and worldly realities.

Wherever fundamentals of the traditional system are put to the test, a clash of opinions becomes unavoidable. Since the traditional system has lost its relevance for those who have come to question its very foundations, the clash of opinions may eventually assume the dimensions of an irreconcilable collision between truth and truth. In the socio-political realm, a collision of this radical kind cannot but bear a violent character. Social and political revolutions are a form of internal war.

The second idea basic to the development of the main theme of this book concerns the need for a comprehensive confrontation of the Christian ethos with this triangular reality of revolution, development, and war. Throughout the preceding pages we have hinted at the theological implications and perspectives hidden in our main theme; and the second chapter dealt explicitly with a number of Christian approaches to the theme.

The word "ethos" is rather vague and less clearly defined

than "ethics" or "theology." Our predilection for it is associated with our preference for a terminology indicating the essentially historical character of Christianity. Only in the midst of human history and surrounded by all the ambiguities and contradictions inherent in human life and thought can Christian theology and Christian ethics, like the Christian church itself, function as ways to and instruments of the divine Truth. Since our main theme, development through revolution, is directly related to the revolutionary dynamics hidden in the historical background, it would be a grave error if we were to suggest that the Christian response to these realities stems from some metaphysical eternity. The historical character of the Truth sought and proclaimed by Christian believers is not an accidental phenomenon; it derives from the very core of the biblical message.

The title of this final chapter represents an attempt to indicate the radically historical character of the confrontation between the Christian ethos and the threefold challenge emerging from the main theme of this book. A shorter title—for example, "Christianity and Revolution"—would suggest that the subject for analysis concerns the relationship between a metaphysical idea called "Christianity" and an isolated phenomenon called "revolution." But the title we have chosen points to the historical stage of our twentieth century in which the revolutionary era of Christianity belongs to the past and in which the encounter of Christianity and revolution has lost its immediate character. Further, it hints at the fact that the time of a Christian order of civilization and society is gone and that we are living in a post-Christian world. Two additional elements in the chapter title focus on the fact that revolutions, in our present-day world, are immediately related to the realities of a postrevolutionary order, of which history provides so many impressive examples; revolutions occurring in a post-Christian world can no longer bear that unquestionable relationship to Christian theology and ethics and to the existence of the Christian church as in preceding centuries. The historical stage in which we find ourselves has immensely complicated the questions, and only in full recognition of these complications can we hope to find relevant answers. Against the background of these considerations

we will now discuss some paramount issues emerging in the Christian encounter with revolution.

Philosophy of History

We have several times hinted at the fact that any interpretation of the meaning of revolution is rooted in some type of philosophy of history. We have even suggested that any type of philosophy of history has, on closer analysis, theological implications. This is far from being a theoretical statement. To mention one outstanding example: the theories of Karl Marx, even his economic analysis of nineteenth-century capitalism, drew their inspiration and derived their ultimate meaning from his concept of social history as a series of class struggles which will in the future reach its climax in the world revolution and its apotheosis in the classless, universal society. Though this concept was supported by an impressive amount of historical data, and gave impetus to a wealth of concrete economic and sociological research even to the present day, the basic concept was of a philosophical character—a philosophy, however, that was relevant to the actual events of contemporary social and political history.

This relevance of Marxian philosophy stemmed from two factors. First, it was a philosophy of history. The great predecessor and master in whose school such a rebellious pupil as Marx learned the art of creative thinking about human history, Georg Friedrich Wilhelm Hegel, was himself the prototype of the German professor who could only breathe in the lofty spheres of speculative thinking and could hardly stand the emotions of the Revolution of 1830. Nevertheless, historically speaking, Hegel can be rightly characterized as the great philosopher who fundamentally thought about the consequences of the French Revolution. Indeed, it would be hard to find another philosopher who had exerted a comparable influence upon modern social and political movements. Philosophy of history, even when it is born within the pure air of theoretical reflection, has an explosive potential.

The second factor in the relevance of Marxian philosophy

was its conscious bearing upon the historical events which it tried to interpret. The famous thesis of Marx—that the philosophers up to his time had only interpreted the world, but that now the time had come to change the world—did not intend a break with philosophy but, to the contrary, was meant to reveal its ultimate purpose. A philosophy of history, if it is to have any meaning at all, is the expression of man's consciousness of his historical existence; for that reason, it must express his most specifically human way of self-realization, i.e., by making use of his human freedom to encroach upon the necessity of natural processes and radically to change and renew his world and his fate. Another famous dictum of Marx, which sees in philosophy the spiritual weapons of the proletariat as, conversely, the proletariat represents the material weapons of philosophy, is only a different way of giving expression to this essential unity of theory and practice.

There is an important subjective element in any type of philosophy of history, but, unless it degenerates into the production of a series of inferior and arbitrary speculations, this subjective element belongs to the very core of all great philosophy. The theories of Rosenstock-Huessy concerning a thousand years of European history may sometimes seem too speculative, but it can hardly be denied that his thinking represents a courageous and scholarly attempt to come to grips with the unique character of European history. By bringing together in one magnificent survey the great revolutions that have rocked European history, Rosenstock-Huessy has discerned a fine line of continuity stretching from the Papal Revolution of the eleventh century to the Russian Revolution of the twentieth century. This link between such totally unlike poles adds a new dimension to the interpretation of revolution, and its far-reaching implications offer many challenges to Christian thinking on the subject.

Some questions raised are these:

1. What does it mean to say that the second millennium of the history of Christianity has become the scene of this revolutionary history? Does this imply that the first thousand years were, so to speak, a period of incubation and that even the first three

centuries of the early church, when the foundations were being laid for a future which was to outlive the collapsing Roman empire, were only seedbeds in preparation for the coming harvest of the second millennium of Chrisiatn history?

2. If European-Christian history bears this unique revolutionary stamp, is it to be considered as revealing the essence of the Christian message? Is it, in other words, God's purpose not only to plant and maintain his church and to bring many lost sheep to his flock, but also to work in the political, social, and economic structures and even to turn these structures upside down when they thwart his divine purposes which he has decided to fulfill in and through human history? Has this succession of revolutions something to do with the creative action of the Holy Spirit in the social and political domain? Does Jesus' prophecy that "The first will be the last and the last first" apply to more than the Last Judgment? That is, should this revolutionary history be understood as an anticipation of the total revolution which will occur with the coming of the Kingdom of God on earth?

3. If a fundamental relationship exists between the Papal Revolution and the Russian Revolution, as Rosenstock-Huessy has suggested, does this mean that the first can be truly understood only in the light of all its successors, and that this revolution of the twentieth century should be interpreted in the light of its predecessors, back as far as the struggle of the Christian church for independence from the medieval empire? What does this imply for our concept of the church, the medieval church, that of the Reformation, and the modern church? If the great struggles of European church history are indissolubly linked with such secular events as the French and the Russian Revolutions, does this mean that the ultimate consequences of the Christian message are to be revealed, not within the narrow limits of church history, but in the wide and open domain of secular history? And what does this connection imply for these secular events: are they less secular than, on the surface, they appear, and are they to be interpreted as secularized products of the same Spirit which was active in the earlier, more "sacral" periods of European church history?

4. It seems odd that a thinker like Rosenstock-Huessy, who

is far from being a Marxist and whose philosophical system bears a definite non-Marxian and even anti-Marxian character, nevertheless dares to close his survey with the Russian Revolution. His reasons for this strange concept are twofold: a social and a geographical argument. The social argument consists in the idea that the series of European revolutions began at the top of the social pyramid, namely, with the Papal resistance to the monarchic rule of the empire, and moved successively to the bottom, reached in a revolution that was proclaimed in the name of the proletariat. The geographical argument derives from the global dimensions of twentieth-century history which, at the close of the First World War, became manifest in the first "world revolution." Some urgent questions immediately come to mind. Was not the Russian Revolution, in flagrant contradiction to its official claims, the rise to power of a ruthless and well-trained party elite which organized a bureaucratic collectivist dictatorial system? Was not the Russian Revolution, far from being the beginning of the expected world revolution, the emergency substitute for the unrealized hope of a proletarian revolution in the industrialized West? And did not Stalin's victory over Trotsky seal the fate of the world revolution, which was sacrificed to the first priority of building "socialism in one country"? And what about the Chinese Revolution? What about the national revolutions in the Third World? Even if we should recognize that the revolutionary events which have radically changed the scene of Latin America, Africa, and Asia were to a great extent influenced by the spread of European revolutionary history, then this global expansion of what originally played on a very narrow European scene has added an essentially new quality to the history of revolution. Doubtless, Rosenstock-Huessy can be excused for leaving these questions unanswered, for he has consciously limited his survey to the European revolutions. But we are left with these crucial questions.

5. Let us, for a moment, assume that recent and coming revolutions in the Third World are essentially no more than a further harvest of the revolutionary seeds sown by the spread of the French and the Russian Revolutions. Should this imply that Europe has already exhausted the wealth of revolutionary patterns

which the treasure of history holds in store? Would it not be much more adequate to state that the European harvest represents only a fraction of the total harvest which is yet to be reaped in the future, and that the failures and errors of Europe's revolutionary history are still to be corrected and overcome by the new opportunities opening for the Third World? An interpretation of this kind might, on the one hand, do justice to the close link between European and universal history and, on the other hand, fully recognize the essentially new dimension of universal history.

Thus we have some of the questions to be faced when we consider the consequences of this type of philosophy of history. We are beginning to discover the theological nature that lies hidden within a philosophy of history. In his study on the relationship between the secular history of the world and the sacred history of God's saving acts, Karl Löwith[1] outlined the antecedents of the modern philosophy of history, the origins of which he traces back as far as biblical theology. The subtitle of his analysis, therefore, is rightly formulated as "the theological implications of the philosophy of history." Beginning with the modern historian Jakob Burckhardt we are led back through the centuries and brought face to face with a gallery of philosophers of history. Nineteenth century Germany is represented by Marx and his teacher Hegel. France is the scene of the victory of the concept of progress over that of divine providence: we meet Proudhon, Auguste Comte, and such enlightened thinkers as Condorcet and Turgot. The origin of this struggle can be traced back to the eighteenth century, where we meet the French philosopher Voltaire, who was the first to write a genuine philosophy of history which explicitly bore that name. He is preceded by the Italian thinker Vico, who in his *Scienza nuova* (New Science) radically renewed the traditional concept of history and made a definite break with that classical Roman Catholic explanation of God's providence throughout history of which the French thinker Bossuet is the most impressive representative. Then we make a leap of several centuries back to Joachim of Floris, who in the twelfth century designed a magnificent system

in which a trinitarian concept of the three epochs of history resulted in an apocalyptic vision of the coming, in the near future, of the Last Judgment and the Kingdom of God. But at the beginning of this gallery the greatest of all is awaiting us, Augustine, whose work *The City of God,* brought the prophetic vision of the Bible into a powerful system just before the collapse of the Roman empire.

Throughout this dynamic tradition of the philosophy of history which runs from Augustine and his predecessor Orosius to the twentieth century, Löwith discovers a continuous thread of the biblical interpretation of history: despite the most daring modifications it remains the driving inspiration and motivation. The trinitarian concept of the medieval theologian Joachim of Floris appears to have molded the thinking of eighteenth- and nineteenth-century philosophers like Lessing, Fichte, Hegel, and Schelling. Even a radical apostate like Friedrich Nietzsche, who tried to return to the pagan, cyclical concept of the universe, evidently could not detach himself from prophetic and apocalyptic traditions.

Nietzsche's philosophy is an example of the amazing modifications through which the Christian theological tradition has been able to pass in the course of history. This essential inversion of the original Christian expectation into the apocalyptic proclamation of the coming epoch of anti-Christian nihilism is a proof of the power which the Christian pathos has maintained and is still able to exert upon radical opponents of the Christian message. In spite of his superhuman attempt completely to abandon the Christian tradition, Nietzsche did not succeed in reverting to a pre-Christian paganism; his thinking remained dependent upon the Christian belief which he attacked.

The nineteenth-century German philosopher Schlegel said that "the revolutionary desire to realize the Kingdom of God is the principle of modern history." The unlimited political radicalism that has characterized all the great movements of Western history since Charlemagne has its ultimate roots in the radicality of the Christian message. But there exists neither a simple, logical link between the gospel and the philosophies of history that have

emerged in the course of Christian history, nor a causal connection of that kind between certain philosophies of history and political movements which have made use of their concepts.

Certainly, the modern idea of progress developed as a consequence of the proclamation that the coming Kingdom of God will totally renew the old creation and that history is on its way toward that glorious goal. But this does not imply that Jesus or his disciples were themselves, so to speak, responsible for the birth of this modern concept or that we are entitled to interpret the New Testament according to the idea of progress. Likewise, the revolutions which gave birth to modern history—the American, French, and Russian Revolutions—have been definitely inspired by the idea of progress. But it would be too simple to hold the preachers of progress directly responsible for the revolutions, although they helped to pave the way. The great path-breakers of history prepare the way for others, just because they do not walk that way themselves. The French Revolution was being prepared by Rousseau, likewise the Russian Revolution by Marx and the fascist counter-revolution by Nietzsche. But Rousseau would not have recognized his ideas in Robespierre, no more would Marx have done so in Lenin and Stalin, and Nietzsche never would have recognized his ideas in Mussolini and Hitler.

There is a discrepancy between the remote historical results and the meaning of the initial intentions that forbids us to confuse the course of Christian history with any kind of causal determination. In history, "responsibility" has always two sides: the responsibility of those who teach and intend something and the responsibility of those who act and respond. Between intention and response there is no simple equation, but also no independence. Both together produce historical results which are therefore ambiguous and never definite in their potential bearing and meaning.

This consideration should help us evaluate the measure of historical connection which exists between the revolutionary ideas and events that have marked the course of European history and the Christian spirit to which, in their ultimate origin, these ideas and events can be traced.

Revolution in a Post-Christian World

We have already met the names of Hegel, Marx, and Nietzsche, three great philosophers of the nineteenth century, who, so to speak, represent the spiritual trend, following upon the French Revolution in the direction of the Russian Revolution, on the one hand, and of the fascist counter-revolution, on the other hand. A fourth name should be added in order to complete the picture: that of the nineteenth-century Christian thinker Søren Kierke-gaard.[2] These four together can serve as points of orientation for an outline of the Christian ethos vis-à-vis the modern spirit of development and revolution.[3]

Hegel's concept of history as a dialectical process, leading to the final realization of Freedom, can be considered from two points of view: as an attempt to provide a final justification of the Christian faith and as an attempt to provide a final justification of the ideals of the French Revolution. His justification of the Christian faith transformed Christian dogmatics into a philosophy of religion in which Western Christianity is identical with the final stage of the self-liberation of Reason. The conversion of the Germans to Christianity set a process in motion which, through Reformation and Enlightenment, reached its goal in the French Revolution.

Like other philosophers of German idealism, Hegel developed his philosophy largely as a response to the French Revolution.[4] As the philosophers saw it, the French Revolution not only abolished feudal absolutism, replacing it with the economic and political system of the middle class; it also completed what the German Reformation had begun, emancipating the individual as a self-reliant master of his life. Man had passed the long period of immaturity during which he had been victimized by overwhelming natural and social forces, and had become the autonomous subject of his own development. Man now relied on his mind and dared to submit the given reality to the standards of reason. This, according to Hegel, constituted the real significance of the French Revolution in history.

This philosophy of history did not originate with Hegel, for the great theories of the eighteenth century all viewed history as progress. But there was an important difference in Hegel's position. The eighteenth-century philosophers conceived the idea of progress as future-directed. The emerging middle class saw in the concept of progress the interpretation of past history as the pre-history of its own rise to power, which was destined to bring the world to maturity. But since this had not yet materialized, history was still in a state of struggle for the truth to come. Progress implied, not continuation but negation of the given situation. The idea had a revolutionary meaning.

Hegel, too, viewed the struggle for freedom as the only content of history, but he believed this struggle had already ended. He saw his own philosophy as the final realization of the ultimate goals of Christianity. And, in the political realm, his philosophy served to justify Prussian state sovereignty as a necessary element for preserving middle-class society. He saw Napoleon as the historical hero fulfilling the destiny of the French Revolution, the one man able to transform the achievements of 1789 into a state order and to unite individual freedom with the universal reason of a stable social system. Upon the downfall of the Napoleonic system in Germany, Hegel was quite willing to hail the ensuing sovereign monarchy as the genuine heir of the Napoleonic system.[5] In this way, Hegelian idealism justified the given political order, which was interpreted as the highest realization of reason in the process of history.

Hegel's philosophy and the function it fulfilled is highly instructive for the position of nineteenth-century middle-class Christianity. The basic dilemma of Christian ethics vis-à-vis the challenge of revolution is well illustrated by the breakdown of Hegel's system, as represented by the thinking of Kierkegaard, Marx, and Nietzsche. Each in his own way has drawn the unavoidable conclusion that a philosophy which pretends to embody the fulfillment of history means, in fact, the end of history. Since all has been realized, nothing new can be expected. In such a situation, there remains only the choice to accept the status quo or to revolutionize its very foundations.

The Christian thinker Kierkegaard launched a devastating attack upon the bourgeois-Christian order that had found in Hegel its splendid spokesman. The Revolution of 1848, which threatened this order, was to him a symptom of the breakdown of the system, not as an appeal for a social and political revolution but as a sign of the impossibility of ever establishing a Christian order within this world. "The whole of Europe," wrote Kierkegaard, "has with increasing passion and rapidity got entangled in problems which cannot be answered within the setting of the world but only vis-à-vis Eternity." The world could not be saved by the blood of the masses but only by the blood of the Christian martyr. He did not expect any help from soldiers and statesmen, but only from men of spirit who would be able to separate the masses and bring man back to his individual existence. The heart of his message was the renewal of the Christian faith as the responsibility of each individual believer for his eternal salvation over against a collective Christian order which, in fact, could mean only the complete corruption and the death of faith.[6]

Whereas Kierkegaard looked for salvation in a radical renewal of personal faith, a no less passionate attempt to find a way out was being undertaken by the atheist thinker Karl Marx. He, too, discovered that the bourgeois-Christian world had, in Hegel's philosophy, come to an end; but, whereas Kierkegaard took refuge in the radicality of personal faith, Marx proclaimed the coming of a new order which would replace bourgeois capitalism with the classless society and in which an atheist humanism would rise from the grave of Christianity. Where Hegel had tried to prove that the history of progress had been realized, Marx prophesied that history had reached a climax of inner contradictions which doomed it to catastrophe. Where Hegel saw the given order around him as the realization of the already completed French Revolution, Marx looked ahead to the coming revolution that would overturn the present order and establish the utopia that the French Revolution had not been able to realize. Like Hegel, Marx viewed the history of mankind as a great progressive drama which, having begun in the ancient oriental civilizations, was destined, through successive stages of Western history, to reach the ultimate goal of complete

freedom. But there was a fundamental difference between the two concepts. Where Hegel viewed Western Christian history up to his time as the way to the fulfillment of history's destiny, Marx looked upon this period as no more than *prehistory*. In the words of his *Zur Kritik der politischen Ökonomie* of 1859: "In broad outlines we can designate the Asiatic, the ancient, the feudal, and the modern bourgeois methods of production as so many epochs in the progress of the economic formation of society. The bourgeois relations of production are the last antagonistic form of the social process of production. . . . This social formation constitutes, therefore, the closing chapter of the prehistoric stage of human society."

In other words, the whole Christian past and present was relegated, by the verdict of Marx, to prehistory. This had far-reaching consequences for the relationship between Christianity and Marxism. In each of the preceding periods of European Christian history—Greco-Roman, medieval feudal, and modern bourgeois—Christianity had been able to reconcile itself with, to adapt to, or to identify with the given social order. The great significance of Hegel consisted in his attempt to reconcile the Christian religion with the new order emerging from the French Revolution, which had turned the medieval-feudal tradition upside down. Since the French Revolution had been proclaimed by vehemently anticlerical, atheist representatives of the rising bourgeoisie, this kind of postrevolutionary Christian justification was of great importance for a Christian bourgeoisie.

The French Revolution was, however, the final station for Christianity. For the next revolution, preached by Marx, there has not yet risen a new Hegel capable of reconciling Christianity with Marxism, or willing to do so. This might be an indication that the Industrial Revolution, which marked the beginning of a new epoch, is a challenge to the entire Christian past, not only affecting the connection between Christianity and some outdated social order but basically questioning whether or not Christianity has meaning for any social order.

The third great nineteenth-century thinker to draw radical conclusions from the breakdown of Christian bourgeois idealism

was Friedrich Nietzsche. Like Kierkegaard and Marx, he saw the bankruptcy of a Christianity mainly concerned with its traditional position and, like Marx, he was a post-Christian atheist. In radical contrast to Marx, he had no belief whatever in the idea of progress. Therefore, he proclaimed no revolution as a further step on the road of progress; nor did he resort, like Kierkegaard, to the biblical origin of the Christian faith. Where Marx looked ahead to the post-Christian future and Kierkegaard returned to Christ, Nietzsche sought salvation in a return to pre-Christian paganism, which he projected into the future as the coming Revolution of Nihilism.

Hegel, Kierkegaard, Marx, and Nietzsche: four different responses to the challenge of a world that has outlived the Christian tradition. Though they lived in the nineteenth century, the possibilities have not changed fundamentally but have, on the contrary, grown in size and weight. At first sight, Christians might appear to have only the choice between the Hegelian and Kierkegaardian alternatives. Apparently we can choose a Christian middle-class idealism, which defends the given socio-political order of what is generally called the "Free World"; or we can take refuge in the radicality of the Christian faith—a faith that cannot be embodied in, or reconciled with, any kind of worldly order, because it is the unique and unrepeatable decision of each individual person vis-à-vis his Lord and Savior.

Let us, however, have a closer look at these alternatives. Hegel and Kierkegaard were both facing the problem of a Christianity nearly two thousand years of age. Both concluded that only a radically new interpretation could save the Christian religion from the grave. Hegel transformed the Christian faith into philosophical reflection, whereas Kierkegaard looked back to the martyrdom of the early Christians. Each solution, in fact, proved the impossibility of continuing the two-thousand-year tradition of Christianity.

It was this very insight which led Marx, on the one hand, and Nietzsche, on the other, to proclaim a humanist, or an anti-humanist, atheism. Had the gospel been initially proclaimed, not in the Greco-Roman world of the first century A.D. but in Western

Europe of the nineteenth century, we could very well imagine Christianity, instead of socialism and Communism, becoming the ideology of the industrial proletariat. The scene would, then, have yielded a dramatic struggle between a pagan bourgeoisie—aided in part by remnants of the feudal and monarchical past—defending their age-old pagan ideology, and a rising proletariat, inspired by the eschatological expectations of a new heaven and a new earth in which Jesus Christ would bring justice and life to the poor and suppressed. But the nineteenth century was not the first century, and the tradition of nineteen centuries prevented Christianity from fulfilling that role. Nietzsche's prophetic vision of the coming dawn of nihilism was inspired by a vehement resistance to the Christian religion, analogous to the devastating opposition of the Old Testament prophets to the paganism of the Gentiles and of the latent paganism of the Jewish people. His vision of the coming Antichrist was as radically opposed to the Christian tradition as was the New Testament to the Old Testament, and, one might add, no less dependent upon its rejected predecessor.

What is the conclusion from these considerations? It is obvious that the Christian answer to the revolutionary and counter-revolutionary upheavals of the twentieth century cannot consist in a simple choice in favor of Hegel and Kierkegaard as opposed to Marx and Nietzsche. The basic riddle is the "pernicious disease"—as Kierkegaard called it—which has infected the body of Christianity. If the remedy for this disease cannot be found in the message of Marx or in the prophecy of Nietzsche, it is equally clear that Hegel and Kierkegaard have no less failed to provide us with the saving answer. For Hegel wants us to believe in a Christian order that belongs to the past, whereas Kierkegaard simply escapes the question of how to live as a first-generation Christian in a world that has seen some twenty centuries of Christian generations.

But, for the same reason, the Christian conscience cannot simply accept the solutions of Marx and Nietzsche. If Hegel has failed in justifying the results of a long history of steady progress, it is difficult to believe that Marx might succeed in justifying the results of the next stage of this history of progress. And if Kierke-

gaard does not tell us how to live like the early Christians in a post-Christian world, it is hard to follow the naïveté of Marx's belief in a soon to be realized New Paradise and eschatology which nearly twenty centuries of Christianity have not brought near. Likewise, Nietzsche's belief in the rebirth of paganism in a post-Christian world is an illusionary counterpart of the belief of the early Christians in the coming re-creation of Israel in a post-pagan world, and it provides us with overwhelming evidence that post-Christian man can never return to the pre-Christian past.

Nevertheless, if these four possibilities do not appear to offer any solution, at least they may suggest the direction which the Christian ethos should follow. The Christian ethos is, first of all, characterized by hope, as reflected in belief in the coming Kingdom of the Lord. It looks ahead and, for that reason, can never justify past and present orders which, at best, are only preparatory stages of the coming Kingdom, and which, in any event, are affected by the corruptive power of sin and death. Since the Christian ideology that defends the status quo has such influence on the Christian masses, the Christian ethos should be open to a revolutionary criticism which, owing to the pressure of this Christian ideology, must inevitably launch the weapons of hope and expectation against the vested interests of a Christian establishment. On the other hand, the Christian conscience cannot naïvely identify itself with hope based upon a fulfillment of expectations in the near future that have never been fulfilled in the Christian past. Since, however, its hope is directed toward the total renewal that will come as a gift of the Lord—the New Heaven and the New Earth—the Christian conscience can never find the answer to Marx by returning to Hegel. It can only strive for a fundamental renewal of the existing order.

Experience has shown that although Christians are seldom tempted to leap from Hegel to Marx, they will go from Kierkegaard to Nietzsche. Before launching our criticism upon this apparently catastrophic turn of radical faith into radical antifaith, we should try to understand the motivation behind this surprising turn. What Hegel and Marx, for all their mutual antagonism, have in common is an optimistic belief in the progressive meaning of history which

invincibly leads toward the ultimate victory of reason and freedom. Over against this rationalist optimism, we find the Christian thinker Kierkegaard and the anti-Christian thinker Nietzsche joined in an invincible opposition to any such optimism; neither believes in the idea of progress or in the ultimate victory of reason. Both thinkers are extremely antirational, and over against the social ideals of the French Revolution they proclaim a fundamentally individualist message. Kierkegaard believes in the existential truth of personal faith; Nietzsche sets his hope upon the apotheosis of the superman. There is in this antirational philosophy an adamant core which reminds us of the biblical warning that the Christian faith is foolishness and absurdity to those who believe in reason.

Both thinkers emerge as lonely seers of a breakdown of progress, in a century that was full of optimism. It would be unfair to accuse Nietzsche of having prepared the rise of Fascism and National Socialism. It would be more appropriate to see him as a prophet who, decades before the events, revealed the trend of things to come. Both thinkers proclaim the truth that Christianity cannot pretend to fulfill its destiny in the midst of history. The breakdown of this pretension created an abyss from which Marx, on the one hand, and Nietzsche, on the other, raised their voices to proclaim a new faith to a frustrated Christianity. However, the serious temptation of Fascism and National Socialism for millions of Christians in preceding decades remains a vexing problem. In the choice between Marx and Nietzsche there appears to be a definite advantage on the side of Nietzsche. This can be explained only by the complete failure of Hegel's attempt to bridge the gap between the ideals of the French Revolution and the Christian faith. At the very moment that these ideals turn out to be built on illusion, Christians see as their only refuge either an otherworldly, individualistic belief in salvation or a vehemently anti-Christian return to a pagan negation of the meaning of history.

Only a small minority of Christians have the courage to persevere in their belief that history has divine meaning and that it is God's purpose to prepare his coming Kingdom within the tribulations of human history. And so this small minority perceives

in the ideas of the French Revolution a struggle on the road toward the coming Kingdom of God; discovers in the optimism of Hegel and Marx a reflection of the optimism which is a fruit of the gospel of the Risen Lord; does not share Hegel's naïveté that these ideals will be realized within the near future; does not indulge the temptation to fall back upon a fundamental pessimism and anti-rationalism. To the contrary, this small minority derives from the Christian gift of hope the courage and the patience radically to struggle for a renewal of society in the light of that universal justice and grace which will be fulfilled in the New Heaven and the New Earth. Only a small minority has the spirit to pioneer on this road. Or, to put it more appropriately, it is a narrow path which leads across history toward the coming Kingdom.

It is obvious from these considerations that the Christian ethos does not spring full-grown from nowhere, nor can it be construed as a deduction from eternal ethical principles. It takes its place in a specific moment of history and it cannot simply throw off the burden of a series of centuries of Christian history. This has some important implications for our theme.

If the history of the Christian West can be described as a dialectical chain of revolutions, then it must be acknowledged that the nineteenth century made a break in this history. This break is represented, on the one hand, by the French Revolution, the last one still to be incorporated into Christian history and, on the other hand, the Industrial Revolution, which signaled the end of a Christian, predominantly agrarian society and the beginning of a post-Christian civilization. This means that church and Christianity are no longer the forces promoting the revolutionary spirit, nor the setting wherein revolutions find their way. The continuing chain of revolutions moves on, outside of their direct grasp.

This fact, of far-reaching consequences, can be interpreted from two opposite points of view. First, the so-called left wing of a revolution that is predestined to become the initiator of the next revolution can no longer be expected to have a Christian constituency. A reiteration of the English Revolution which emerged from the left wing of the Reformation, or of the American Revolution which originated from the left wing of English Puritanism,

is no longer probable. For church and Christianity this means that, in general, they are lagging behind one or more steps and can at most, later on, try to adapt themselves to the society that has resulted from the revolution.

This applies not only to the Western, traditionally Christian world, but also to the non-Western world. The nineteenth century, which saw the rise of industrialism, was at the same time the age of colonialism; the revolutions of the twentieth century were reactions to both influences. Since colonialism, in the view of non-Western peoples, was linked with the Christian West, and since the Christian churches in the non-Western world are in general only a small and predominantly Western-type minority, the anticolonial liberation movements in the non-Western world were not primarily associated with the Christian church, even though Christians and Christian ideals played an outstanding role in them. In addition, the inner dynamism of the ever-accelerating speed of technological development has replaced the dynamics of the Christian ethos and is pushing the Christian church into the background. Only by displaying the utmost energy can the church hope not to lag too far behind the ongoing development.

To sum up, neither in the West nor in the non-Western world, neither in the industrial and technological nor in the political and social realm are church and Christianity still in a position to start or even to inspire revolutionary events. There are, of course, great differences in the degree of lag. It is obvious, for instance, that the Russian Orthodox Church, which is intimately connected with the Byzantine tradition, is forced to bridge a gap of centuries in order to adapt itself to the industrialized Russia of the second half of the twentieth century. On the other hand, a Christian center like the Center for the Study of Religion and Society in Bangalore, South India, is the spokesman for those advanced circles of the church in present-day India that seek to play an active and pioneering role in modern nation-building. But, immense as the distance may be separating these Indian circles from the Moscow patriarchate, the fact remains that the nationalist movement in India was not born within the Christian church.

Christians should therefore be realistic when they try to de-

termine their stand vis-à-vis the revolutions of our time. They can adapt themselves to a revolution after it has happened; they may eventually go so far as to welcome a revolution when it is on the way; they may, at most, participate in the preparation for it; but they can never claim for it an exclusively Christian responsibility. To the contrary, since church and Christianity are still very tradition-bound, and continue to cling to the preindustrial era of the past, and since theology has, in general, failed radically to come to grips with a postindustrial civilization, the normal situation for church and Christianity is opposition—sometimes vehement, sometimes moderate—to revolutionary developments. The church's preoccupation with "otherworldly" matters often results in an attitude of indifference to events taking place around it in the world. Only after the chaos of revolution has been succeeded by the relative security of "order" does the church gradually temper its resistance to change. Frequently at that point, the church shows a willingness to participate in reaping a harvest for which it had done no sowing.

Christianity in a Postrevolutionary World

This is, however, only one side of the coin; there is another side, too. Revolutions are historical events, they have their inner logic, there are certain patterns of revolutionary processes and, still more important, each revolution is the introduction to a new order. This order may still bear marks of its revolutionary origin and it may try ideologically to eternalize the revolution; this does not alter the sober fact that it is a postrevolutionary order which is first and foremost interested in maintaining itself against any new revolution. It is at this point that the situation of Christianity in modern times may be observed from a second viewpoint. In the period of Christian history when revolutions bore a Christian mark, the postrevolutionary order could not but proclaim itself as the fulfillment of Christian ideals. This applies to Germany after the Reformation, to England since Cromwell and to the United States since the Declaration of Independence. The French Revolution, as a

consequence of its ambiguous character as the last of the Christian and the first of the anti-Christian revolutions, was, in fact, incorporated into nineteenth-century bourgeois Christianity, which, otherwise, did not give up its ideological opposition.

The Russian Revolution of 1917 marked a definite break with the whole history of European revolutions, to the extent that it was impossible for church and Christianity to adapt themselves to the ideology of that revolution. Their resistance continued for decades after bloodshed and martyrdom had been replaced by a postrevolutionary order of an industrialized society on its way toward the stage of economic maturity. On the other hand, the counter-revolutions of Fascism and National Socialism, which proclaimed themselves as the last bulwark of European civilization against the Communist threat, proved to be for millions of Christians an amazingly easy temptation. Obviously, Christianity no longer found itself in a position to identify with a postrevolutionary order. As long as European revolutions had a Christian inspiration and background, this Christian identification with the postrevolutionary order was natural and could be justified, in spite of the dangers inherent in that kind of attitude. But where revolutions arise in opposition to a Christian order—as was the case with the Russian Revolution—the dangers of this attitude become pernicious. The Christian tradition of self-identification with a given order tends to degenerate into the sanctification of a counter-revolutionary order, even to the extent of accepting full-fledged pagan ideologies.

Thus we see that although Christianity has lost its grip on the ongoing history of revolution, it has also lost its traditional naïveté that would sanctify the postrevolutionary order.

At this point our argument must move a step further. If it is true that Christianity can neither make a revolution nor identify itself with a postrevolutionary order—let alone with a counter-revolutionary order—can we then imagine Christianity becoming a dynamic leaven within a postrevolutionary order which itself is in danger of falling into the same trap that had earlier ensnared Christianity? There is a certain irony in the development of socialist countries like Soviet Russia and some Eastern European

countries, in that the governments and the Communist Parties are, so to speak, doomed endlessly to continue and to reiterate the revolutionary ideology that engendered the "First Socialist Country of the World." Now, after a half-century, this ideology is doomed to lose more and more of its flavor as it degenerates into more justification of the established order. We could then imagine Christianity becoming the dynamic force preserving the prophetic and eschatological expectation of a new man and a new world which was at the heart of Karl Marx's message. In such a case, the roles would be changed. Where formerly a renegade of the Christian church like Friedrich Engels supported his Communist faith by appealing to the original spirit of Jesus and his disciples, and where even in the first phase of the Russian Revolution messianic Christian expectations were evident, now we could imagine the prophetic criticism of Christians returning to the original spirit of Karl Marx. This is not a purely theoretical consideration. There is presently developing within philosophical and literary circles in some socialist countries a climate of renewed reflection of, and discussion about, the foundations of Marxist thinking, and this raises new hope for a coming dialogue with a renewed Christianity. When, in a post-Communist order, Communism begins to meet perplexities and frustrations closely akin to those Christianity is facing within a post-Christian order, there may arise a situation in which participation in each other's hopes and disappointments, and sharing of each other's errors and expectations is possible. Such a situation is a challenge for church and Christianity, no longer associates of revolution or establishment, not to retire to the inner security of the soul, but to become a dynamic and renewing force within the structures of society.

If the Christian ethos does not arise from nowhere, neither does it emerge directly from the New Testament nor from the New Heaven and the New Earth.

The ethos of the New Testament was overwhelmingly determined by the expectation of the end of history within the immediate future. We cannot return to that innocent faith and hope. Since the initial period, two things have happened. First, we have the process which has been called *Ent-eschatologisierung,* i.e., the loss of

eschatological tension in the midst of an ongoing history. Second, and the very opposite of this, by the penetration of eschatology into the body of history, there has resulted a kind of latent sickness which may eventually flare up. Over long periods it may seem harmless, but the virus, once it has infiltrated, will never leave. In other words, in the course of Christian history eschatology has brought forth a variety of movements and events, stretching from apocalyptic and messianic movements in the Middle Ages to the rise of the idea of progress in modern times and of Marxism in the nineteenth century.

Of course, as Gurvitch pointed out, certain social time scales are common to all religions and civilizations; but also, as he demonstrates, there emerges in the last two or three centuries of European history an increasing tension from the conflict of time scales between different classes and different levels of development. In the midst of this complex and dynamic reality, church and Christianity are living; their faith and hope are inextricably connected with the Christian expectations of the Kingdom of God, and with the secularized, heretic, pseudo-Christian or anti-Christian expectations of a New World, which have dominated the stage for a long time. Christians cannot behave as if they were proclaiming to a pagan world, as first-generation Christians did, the surprising message that the Kingdom of God is at hand. Christians must discern the time scales within movements and expectations outside the church, and then discover the specific contradictions, tensions, and frustrations inherent in each of them. The Christian message cannot be proclaimed simply in opposition to the expectations that are thriving outside the church, but it has to reveal its relevance in relation to the time scales of other messages and movements.

For instance, faith in continuous progress, which modern techno-bureaucratic society still holds, has, historically, a certain relationship to the Christian message about the ultimate goal of history. This message cannot be proclaimed merely in opposition to secular faith in the saving power of technology, for only in full recognition of the truth presented in the core of that faith can the weaknesses and the sore spots be demonstrated. Marxist expectations of the coming world revolution cannot be answered merely

by the Christian proclamation of the Second Coming of the Lord; this proclamation has to be involved in Marxist thinking as, conversely, Marxist thinking is strongly interwoven with Christian thinking. In the same way, in order to be prophetic criticism, a Christian otherworldly message of personal salvation is the worst kind of answer to fascist pseudo-messianic expectations of the coming superman; for it has first to be revealed for what reasons this return to pre-Christian paganism could become such a Satanic temptation for frustrated and misled Christian masses.

Romans 13

If what Rosenstock-Huessy has pointed out is true, namely, that the series of European revolutions has been constitutive in the creation of European nations, then the Christian question vis-à-vis revolution is closely linked to the questions of the Christian attitude to nationalism and nation-building. The history of the nations in question provides an interesting spectrum of the variety of attitudes which church and Christianity have assumed when facing the national question. In England the spectrum runs from the foundation of the Anglican Church in a struggle for national identity over against the supremacy of Rome, through Cromwell's vision of Britain's election, toward nineteenth-century liberalism, colonialism, and imperialism on the basis of a Christian ideology. Germany's history covers the long road from the myth of the German nation as the heir of the Roman empire, through the struggle of the Reformation for independence from Rome and the nineteenth-century ideology of throne and altar, to the catastrophes of abortive imperialism and the rise of National Socialism. In the case of Russia we would have to describe the breakdown of the mutual involvement between Czarist Russia and the Orthodox Church by the Communist Revolution, and the first signs of a new recognition of the church's contribution to national salvation during the Second World War. All this and much more is possible and has in fact occurred in the course of Christian history. The lesson to be learned from this story is that the nature of national identity is

highly ambiguous. National identity may, in one instance, be the sublime expression of a progressive and universalist struggle for equality, liberty, and fraternity; the same concept may in another case and in a different stage, degenerate into the worst kind of collective self-idolization and tyrannical self-expansion. The frightening fact is that, for both cases and both stages, Christianity can provide, and indeed has provided, the appropriate ideology. What has been said about the impossibility of Christian self-identification either with revolution or with establishment in the modern world, could be, *mutatis mutandis,* reiterated about nationhood and nationalism.

There is a specific aspect of the national question which deserves special attention, that is, the relationship between the traditional Christian doctrine about the state and the traditional Christian attitude toward the problem of war. Put simply, the issue can be defined as follows. Up to the present time the official Christian doctrine favored the maintenance of a just order which, internally, implies the right and duty to defend itself against the threat of revolution and, externally, to defend itself against the threat of competing states. The doctrine suffers from some inner contradictions which in general have been veiled by an appeal to Paul's famous thesis laid down in Romans 13. But obviously, this appeal must fail in more than one respect.

First, with regard to the maintenance of internal order, Paul, though being a son of Israel, abandoned the very right of revolt which, in the eyes of many of his countrymen, was the only safeguard for their national and religious identity against pagan Roman imperialism. It is this very right which, in the traditional Christian doctrine about the state, has served as the cornerstone of Christian resistance to a tyrannical government. It is in this right that the Protestant revolutions, since the time of the Reformation, have found their ultimate justification, but it is impossible to base this right of revolt upon Romans 13.

Second, Paul never envisaged the possibility that two states would launch war against each other and, in mutual competition, would each appeal to the divine right and duty of the state to preserve law and order as described in Romans 13. After all, Paul's

thesis was not related to external warfare but, rather, to the maintenance of internal order. Paul simply identified the Roman empire with the *oikumene,* the total realm of the civilized world which eventually might be forced to self-defense against threats of civilian strife and against upheavals at the barbarian fringe. The possibility of two empires warring against each other was outside his horizon. Obviously, any reference to such an eventuality would have ruined his argument.

Paul's statement in Romans 13 had to be written against an eschatological background: "the night is far gone, the day is at hand" (vs. 12); the Kingdom of God is near at hand. His warning to the Christians never to avenge themselves, but to leave vengeance to the wrath of God, has to be read in that light. This warning is supported by a quotation from Deuteronomy 32:55: "Vengeance is mine, I will repay, says the Lord" (Romans 12:19). Seen in the context of the so-called "Song of Moses," Paul's intention becomes clear. He wants to refer to the eschatological vengeance which will be accomplished by the Lord in order to vindicate his chosen people: then the Lord will "whet" his "glittering sword" and his hand will take "hold on judgment" and he will take vengeance on his adversaries (Deuteronomy 32:9, 36, 41ff.). Viewed in this light, the counterpart of Paul's statement (to be found in Revelation 13) represents the other aspect of the same eschatological theme. In the last book of the New Testament, the state is described as involved in the great apocalyptic struggle wherein its nature is revealed as that of the Beast which, on authority of the Devil, is being given, for a short while, universal power on earth until it will finally be defeated by the Lord God Almighty and the Lamb.

In Augustine's work *De Civitate Dei* this eschatological dimension of the New Testament witness with regard to the state still plays a role. But in later centuries the official Christian doctrine replaced that dimension with a predominant emphasis on the need to maintain enduring law and order in a continuous history. This essential change was closely related to the historical turn following the conversion of Emperor Constantine the Great, and to the inauguration of the period of the *Corpus Christianum. Ent-*

eschatologisierung (loss of the eschatological dimension) and Christianization of the state went hand in hand.

A third historical novelty, far beyond Paul's imagination, was the emergence of two or more rival Christian states, each of which could with equal authority proclaim itself as the right state, governing as God's servant.

These three factors, in combination, have greatly contributed to the inconsistency and self-contradictory character of the official Christian doctrine about state and war. Not only was the appeal to Romans 13 incapable of bridging the gap between the New Testament and the radically different situation which had emerged since the foundation of Christian states, but the doctrine in itself was doomed to becoming increasingly enmeshed in insoluble contradictions.

The evolution of the doctrine in German Protestantism since the Reformation serves as an impressive illustration. Luther appeared at a turning-point in Western Christian history, and his statements reflected the inner tensions and contradictions of that period. He continued, and to a certain extent renewed, the apocalyptic tradition of the biblical message. But, on the other hand, he introduced a trend of thinking which has influenced the further evolution of Lutheran doctrine, even to the present century, in a conservative and eventually reactionary direction. Luther was the last representative of the feudal period; at the same time, he was the precursor of modern nationalism. The onrush of the Turkish Muslims who were threatening Central Europe was viewed by Luther as an apocalyptic foretaste of the impending struggle between the forces of Christ and Antichrist. As a parallel apocalyptic symptom he interpreted the tyranny of the Church of Rome, which tried to suppress the divine Truth, thus displaying the very features of the Antichrist. This parallel accusation was self-contradictory. Over against Islam he appealed to the duty of the emperor, Charles the Fifth, to defend the medieval Holy Roman Empire which, nevertheless, received its deathblow from the Reformation's opposition to the medieval Church of Rome and from the rise of a German nation. In the eyes of Pope and Emperor, Luther not only represented a dangerous heresy; his action

also meant revolution. But when Luther, in his turn, was confronted with the threat of the Peasants' Revolt, which itself was inspired by apocalyptic expectations, he became the stanch defender of the duty of Protestant German kings to maintain, as God's servants, the law and order of the existing state authority. This conservative attitude increasingly dominated the Lutheran doctrine about the state so that in the latter part of the nineteenth century it served as the ideology of the Christian bourgeoisie, in defense against the threat of socialism and Communism. It is not surprising that this Christian conservatism proved defenseless against Adolf Hitler's self-proclamation as the Savior elected to found the Millenarian Empire and to annihilate Communism.

A close parallelism exists between the Christian doctrine of internal self-defense of the state and the doctrine of its external self-defense. During the Crusades the myth of the Holy Roman Empire had underscored the right and duty to go to war against the enemies of Christ, the Muslims. The Reformation meant a definite break with this ideology and introduced a new epoch of religious wars within Christendom itself. As seen from the viewpoint of medieval tradition, Luther destroyed the unity of Western Christendom and, as a fanatic revolutionary, enkindled a civil war which doomed Europe to Christian fratricide. As a matter of fact, the Lutheran doctrine about the just war became an indispensable religious support of warfare between European Christian states. When in the eighteenth century nationalism replaced religion as the ideology in support of warfare, the Christian doctrine of the just war was a useful justification of national self-defense. In Germany, where the medieval myth of the Holy Roman Empire still lingered in the continuation of the German empire until its disintegration at the close of the First World War, there was a specific temptation for this Christian doctrine to back up German imperialism. The Second World War has been characterized as a global war. If this is correct, Germany's role may be interpreted as the culmination of a long history which ranges from the Middle Ages through Reformation and nineteenth-century Christian nationalism to the First World War and its aftermath.

The atomic age has brought full-fledged warfare between

sovereign states to an end. This implies a crisis in the traditional concepts of national sovereignty and of the right to national self-defense by warfare. Since official Christian doctrine has in modern times always justified the violent self-assertion of the national state, it is this doctrine itself which has, in fact, gone to pieces. There is a strange irony in history, in that we are about to return to the kind of universal order which was faced by the New Testament, but with this essential difference, that the limited realm of the Roman *oikumene* now takes on worldwide dimensions.

The Christian ethos is thus entangled in a painful dilemma. If the traditional justification of war as the ultimate means of external self-defense for the sovereign state has lost its validity, then the right and duty of the state to maintain, by violent means, its internal order against the threat of revolution is no less radically questioned. Looking back over history from our vantage point in the atomic age, it is amazing that the same Christian ethos which has willingly blessed the whole course of increasing violence from the Crusades to the atomic explosions over Hiroshima and Nagasaki has reacted so differently in the matter of internal violence. There it has condemned the unhesitatingly less pernicious use of violence and, as a matter of course, has sanctioned the defense of the Christian status quo against overthrow by revolution.

The crisis of the concept of national sovereignty in the atomic age spreads its effects in two directions. First, it stresses the urgency of some kind of world government to maintain peace in the atomic era. Should official Christian doctrine, in the future, develop from a justification of the sovereign state into a well-argued support of the concept of a world authority, then an appeal to Romans 13 would be incomparably more appropriate than the fallacious exegesis which relates the "sword" of the government (vs. 4) to warfare between sovereign states.

The dilemma would, however, be only partly solved; and, for the other part, it would be aggravated. A world government would indeed solve the problem of war, but it would not solve the problem of revolution. To the contrary, a world government, resting upon the collective monopoly of atomic power which has lost any real

significance other than for the preparation of collective atomic suicide, would possess an unprecedented force to maintain its atomic peaceful order against any internal threat. This atomic peace would, in fact, be endangered not only by any actually or potentially independent power in possession of atomic weapons, but even by any minor type of upheaval or political unrest which eventually might escalate into atomic warfare. Obviously, this situation would immensely enhance the tension between the highest stages of technological development, which dispose of a practically unlimited power to maintain the status quo, and the lowest stages of technological development, which have no other means than revolution—more particularly guerrilla warfare—to press for radical change in their own favor. A Christian ethos that would one-sidedly justify the formation of a world order to prevent atomic suicide might, under the guise of an apparently progressive Christian pacifism, contribute to a Christian conservatism which, this time on a worldwide scale, would continue the traditional line. In that case, the Western Christian nations, which in former centuries revolutionized the medieval order and have, along with their technological development, enhanced the potentialities of warfare up to the point of global suicide, would now make a show of their peace-loving intentions. And, while maintaining to their own favor an atomic world peace, they would accuse non-Christian peoples of preparing for revolution. Therefore, the crucial choice facing the Christian ethos in our time is either to be hopelessly corrupted by this notorious kind of hypocrisy or to take the question of revolution as deadly seriously as the question of world peace.

If one thing has become crystal clear, it is the state of crisis in which the traditional Christian ethos finds itself, facing the unprecedented questions of development and revolution in an atomic age. We cannot hope to find solutions by returning to the traditional answers given by the Christian doctrine in preceding periods. A living encounter with traditions will reveal its glaring dilemmas, contradictions, and fallacies, for they can no longer be veiled or overlooked. A fresh encounter with the biblical message becomes imperative.

Biblical Perspectives

A Christian ethos which is coming to grips with the revolutionary dimension of modern history has to face two mutually related but distinct perspectives within the biblical message. The first perspective is apocalyptic, the second prophetic. Each perspective can be aptly defined with reference to a central concept.

A focal point of the apocalyptic perspective is found in the concept of "birthpangs." In Jesus' apocalyptic sermon we read: "And you will hear of wars and rumors of wars; see that you are not alarmed; for this must take place, but the end is not yet. For nation will rise against nation, and kingdom against kingdom, and there will be famines and earthquakes in various places: all this is but the beginning of the sufferings" (Matthew 24:6–8). The last word of this sentence, translated by the Revised Standard Version as "sufferings," means literally: birthpangs, travail. The Greek word *oodin* occurs five times in the New Testament in each instance with reference to the messianic birthpangs, preparing for the coming of the Kingdom of God. In Acts 2:23–24 we read: "this Jesus, delivered up according to the definite plan and foreknowledge of God, you crucified and killed by the hands of lawless men. But God raised him up, having loosed the *pangs* of death, because it was not possible for him to be held by it." Thus, raising Christ from the dead, God has transmitted the pangs of death into pangs of birth. 1 Thessalonians 5:2–3 says: "For you yourselves know well that the day of the Lord will come like a thief in the night. When people say, There is peace and security, then sudden destruction will come upon them as *travail* comes upon a woman with child, and there will be no escape." Revelation 12:1–2, 5 says: "And a great portent appeared in heaven, a woman clothed with the sun, with the moon under her feet, and on her head a crown of twelve stars; she was with child and she cried out in her *pangs of birth*, in anguish for delivery." The woman, threatened by the dragon, brought forth a male child, "one who is to rule all the nations with a rod of iron, but her child was caught up to God and to his throne." In Galatians 4:19, Paul himself speaks of being in

travail with his "little children," the Christians in Galatia, until Christ be formed in them.

All these passages have to be read against the background of Old Testament terminology. In the Psalms and the prophets, expressions like "anguish has taken hold of us, *pain* as of a woman in travail" are established metaphors describing the judgments of the Lord. At the same time, the metaphor refers to the signs of hope and redemption. The Servant of the Lord, as described in Isaiah 42, "will cry out like a woman in travail, he will gasp and pant" as his judgments are passed upon the earth, but only in order to guide the blind in unknown paths and to turn the darkness before them into light (vss. 14–16). And in the last chapter of Isaiah, it is the city of Zion which gives birth before she is in labor and is delivered of sons before her pain has come upon her; and, like a mother, Jerusalem will foster and nourish her children (Isaiah 66: 7–14).

These are the messianic birthpangs which have been fulfilled in the death and resurrection of Jesus Christ. The tribulation (Greek: *thlipsis*) to which his disciples are to be delivered up, being hated by all nations for Christ's name's sake (Matthew 24:9), are the unavoidable ways of participation in Christ's death-and birth-pangs. "When a woman is in travail she has sorrow, because her hour has come; but when she is delivered of the child, she no longer remembers the anguish, for joy that a child is born into the world. So you have sorrow now, but I will see you again and your hearts will rejoice, and no one will take your joy from you" (John 16:21–22). The climax of these sayings is to be found in Paul's vision which sees "the whole creation . . . groaning in travail together until now." World history since the exodus from Paradise has this ultimate meaning: all its anguish and misery will lead to consummation and redemption in the coming Kingdom. The same Lord who banished mankind from Paradise but gave him hope will also set him free from his bondage to earth's futility and will grant him the glorious liberty of the children of God. Jesus Christ, firstborn of the brethren, has, in his death and resurrection, consummated the whole of history, its futility and its hope. The Spirit groans inwardly in those who believe in Christ, as they await,

together with the whole of creation and in conformity to the image of Christ, the redemption of their bodies that they may be adopted as sons. It is with eager longing for the revealing of the sons of God that the creation waits. The night is far gone, the day is at hand (cf. Romans 8:18ff.; 13:12).

It cannot be denied that the apocalyptic vision of history as a protracted process of suffering and travail is an essential part of biblical theology. The necessity of this process is perfectly summarized in Jesus' saying that this "*must* take place" (Greek: *dei*). The metaphor of birthpangs and delivery accentuates the almost biological blindness of the process to which both mother and child are powerlessly and willy-nilly subjected. It is sheer destiny, dark, irrational, chaotic, absurd, ugly, violent, bloody. It could be asked whether or not this process includes anything typically human, for birthpangs are the beginning of all animal life as well. Animals calve, lamb, farrow, whelp, foal, kitten, kid. There is a modern German existentialist philosophy which sees human existence as *geworfen* (dropped) into the world (Heidegger), man in conformity to the beasts who "drop" their young.

Revolutions have this terrible, gloomy aspect in common with the evils of war, with disasters like famines and earthquakes (Matthew 24:7) and with the ugliness of poverty. Any effort to overlook this aspect will always result in a false ideology that, in an attempt to justify the revolution by its ends, tends to belittle the terrible side of its means. But this dark side is only one part of its aspect. The birthpangs of history are more than a subhuman, biological process, for they lead to a high goal: they bring forth sons of God. If a revolution means something more than an outburst of unbearable misery, a rebellion against oppressive tyranny, or an explosion of pent-up hatred, then it must be a cry for righteousness. An apocalyptic approach should open our eyes to the revelation, the *apocalypsis* of the righteousness of God, who listens to the cries of those subjected to misery and tyranny, and who is quick to come to their redemption. In other words, a truly biblical apocalyptic theology of revolution is indissolubly linked up with a *prophetic* approach.

As the word "birthpangs" is central to apocalyptic theology,

likewise the word "conversion" is a focal point of the prophetic perspective. The Greek word for conversion, *metanoia,* is part of the terse summary of the gospel which was proclaimed both by John the Baptist and by Jesus: "The time is fulfilled, and the Kingdom of God is at hand; repent (*metanoite*), and believe in the gospel." Conversion means to turn to the coming Kingdom of God. An illuminating ecumenical study on "Conversion to God and Service to Man" [7] has rightly pointed to the Old Testament roots of the concept of conversion, particularly to be found in one group of words deriving from the Hebrew root *shubh.* This word is used both transitively and intransitively and its main meaning is to "return" or turn back. Theologically the all-important fact is that *shubh* belongs to the covenant context; it means to return to the already given covenant. In consequence *shubh* is seldom applied to people outside Israel. It is the people of God who are called to return, not the heathen! *Shubh* is used primarily in connection with the great occasions in the history of God's covenant with Israel. Its predominant use is in the Deuteronomistic and prophetic material, and each passage in which the word appears concerns a historic moment in the life of Israel. Every time its very existence is threatened, be it by enemy action from outside or by complete alienation from its destiny through apostasy within its own ranks, at stake is not a particular act of degradation but *the* sin in the history of Israel, its repetitive rejection of the Sinai Covenant. *Shubh* is not concerned with acts of individual wrong but with what the Bible calls "sin," Israel's disobedience to God. *Shubh* is therefore closely related to the announcement that Yahweh will come to judge his people. Only after this judgment can a return become reality.

Two elements are essential in this notion of return to God's covenant. They are the call and promise to return to Jerusalem in a geographical sense and the expectation that the Lord will rebuild the walls of Jerusalem and restore the Holy City to a new splendor and glory. "Behold, your God will come with vengeance, with the recompense of God. He will come and save you. . . . And the ransomed of the Lord shall return, and come to Zion with singing" (Isaiah 35:4, 10). "Behold, the days are coming, says the Lord, when the city shall be rebuilt for the Lord from the tower of Hana'el

to the Corner Gate" (Jeremiah 31:38). "The sons of those who oppressed you shall come bending low to you; and those who despised you shall bow down at your feet; they shall call you the City of the Lord, the Zion of the Holy One of Israel. Whereas you have been forsaken and hated, with no one passing through, I will make you majestic for ever, a joy from age to age. . . . Violence shall no more be heard in your land, devastation or destruction within your borders; you shall call your walls Salvation, and your gates Praise. The least one shall become a clan, and the smallest one a mighty nation; I am the Lord; and its time I will hasten it" Isaiah 60:14–15, 18, 22).

But the return of the people of Israel to the Holy City is only the beginning of a much greater and wider movement, the gathering of all nations. The crowning vision is that of all the nations "flowing" to the mountain of the Lord, which shall be established as the highest of the mountains. At that time out of Zion shall go forth the "Torah," and the Lord shall judge between the nations and they shall beat their swords into plowshares and nation shall not lift up sword against nation (Isaiah 2).

This universal peace and righteousness does not come automatically, however. We should not forget that the second chapter of Isaiah, which reveals this grand panorama, is preceded by the first chapter, which proclaims judgment and doom to the existing city and people of Jerusalem: "Hear the word of the Lord, you rulers of Sodom! What to me is the multitude of your sacrifices? says the Lord. . . . Wash yourselves, . . . remove the evil of your doings . . . , learn to do good; seek justice, correct oppression; defend the fatherless, plead for the widow. . . . I will turn my hand against you and will smelt away your dross as with lye and remove all your alloy. And I will restore your judges as at the first, . . . Afterward you shall be called the city of righteousness, . . . Zion shall be redeemed by justice, and those in her who repent, by righteousness. But rebels and sinners shall be destroyed together" (Isaiah 1:10–11, 16–17, 25–28). Who are the "rebels"? Those who refuse to listen to the prophetic call to return and repentance, those who forsake the Lord (Isaiah 1:20, 28).

The Christian ethos facing revolution and rumors and threats

of revolution, through this "small apocalypse," hears the prophetic call to repentance, reformation, renewal, restoration of righteousness, the call to return to the Lord and to rebuild the city of universal peace and justice. The judgment begins with the household of God. Can an age-old "Christian" society, can an established Christendom, can a Christian church deeply integrated with a Christian establishment—can they return to this prophetic vision, can they rejoin their initial revolution?

The answer to the prophetic call to repentance and return has to be given afresh by every new generation and in each period of history. At the same time, it would be unrealistic to disregard the concrete historical setting in which this call is reaching us and in which our response is to be given. Any "theology of revolution" which fails to recognize the full significance of this historical setting, no matter how splendid its biblical analysis and theological argument may appear, will never gain or will quickly lose relevance in the midst of the real revolutionary struggles of our century. The test case of the biblical perspectives, apocalyptic and prophetic, consists in the confrontation of church and Christianity with the concrete process of revolution.

Christianity and the Russian Revolution

An excellent test case for the validity of the Christian response to the revolutionary events of the twentieth century is provided by the history of the Russian Revolution and its aftermath. We begin with two different Christian reactions to the shock of the October Revolution of 1917, representing concrete applications of the biblical apocalyptic and prophetic perspectives to the revolutionary process. The first reaction can serve as a specimen of the prophetic response. In January, 1918, under the fresh impression of the Bolshevik Revolution, the Russian poet Alexander Block wrote his poem "The Twelve." [8] Said to have been written in a single night, this poem has won fame. The Russian writer Ilya Ehrenburg praised it as the greatest phenomenon in Russian literature: "Pushkin was Russia's first love; after him she loved many, but Block she came to

know during fearsome, fatal days, during her great ordeal by fire; when she could not love, she came to know and love him." Another person said that "Block will live as long as dreamers exist—and their tribe is immortal." This magnificent poet succeeded in doing what many an excellent historian, who devoted a lifetime to turning out ponderous tome after ponderous tome, failed to do. "He has epitomized a revolution. And, over and above that, has also epitomized all Revolution, as it always has been, is, and will be."

Block was one of the pioneers of the revolution. Twenty-five years old in 1905, he carried the Red Flag at the head of a procession; in 1917 he was at the front. The heroes of his poem are twelve soldiers of the Red Army, marching across Petrograd one icy winter night, determined to destroy the old world: "In revolution march abreast! Your foe knows neither sleep nor rest! Grip rifle, friend; don't show the white feather: Let Holy Russia have it; fire all together . . . . To bring all bourgeois to ruination, we'll fan a world-wide conflagration—World conflagration, fed by blood. Bless us, O Lord! The old world is a scabby hound—Git! A beating's all you'll get!"

The poem, in a surprising twist, ends as follows: "While the blizzard, laughing snowily, pealed and shrieked and howled and sang. Bang—bang—bang! Bang—bang—bang . . . . Thus they their sovereign march pursue."

> Behind them skulks the hound half-dead;
> Ahead (with flag of sanguine hue)—
> Invisible within the storm,
> Immune from any bullet's harm
> Walking with laden step and gentle
> In snowy, pearl-strewn mantle,
> With small, white roses garlanded—
> Jesus the Christ walks at their head.

The twelve revolutionary soldiers, like twelve disciples, following their Lord Jesus Christ! Small wonder that the poem called forth sharp emotional reactions from both adherents and adversaries of Bolshevism. Among the intelligentsia, and Block himself was one, the poem was considered as an attempt to glorify revolutionary

violence. Members of the church were upset by this blasphemous connection between Christ and an atheist revolution which destroyed sacred tradition. And, last but not least, Communists could not understand the poem except as a satirical comment. Critics on all sides found the connection between Christ and the revolution distasteful.

Alexander Block's enthusiasm for Bolshevism was short-lived. Within two years he was feeling betrayed by the rise of a new bureaucracy which once again strangled the freedom of the spirit. In Block's memorial address in honor of the great Russian poet Pushkin, the central theme was the necessity of freedom, condition for artistic creativity—"not the freedom for propagating liberal ideas, but the creative, mysterious freedom. The poet is dying of lack of breath, life has lost for him its meaning. . . ." In 1921, Block died, a miserable, disillusioned man.

"The Twelve" is a prophetic response to the revolution. The old world of "Holy Russia" is ripe for the final judgment, the new world will arise on its ruins. The prophetic vision, anticipating the coming of the glorious Kingdom of God, does not reckon with a continuous history following upon the foundation of the New Covenant which has replaced the Old Covenant, but it beholds the Day of the Lord near at hand. Block was, indeed, a dreamer; he was not an architect, like Lenin, prepared to use the revolution as the start of "electrification" of the whole country; certainly he was no dictator, like Stalin, ready to transform the revolution into the establishment of "Socialism in a single country." But his dream was real and his poem revealed a transcendent dimension, a hidden meaning in the revolution which neither the success of industrialization and economic development nor the cruelties of Stalinism have been able to annihilate. His dream has, in recent years, come to life once again in the resistance of writers, poets, and artists in their struggle for human, personal, and creative freedom.

Besides the prophetic dimension, the revolution contains an apocalyptic perspective. This apocalyptic dimension has been stressed by the Russian philosopher Nicolas Berdyaev. Born in 1874 of an aristocratic family, Berdyaev turned to Marxism during his student years and was exiled for three years. His philosophy

grew out of the Orthodox tradition, conditioned by nineteenth-century radicalism, and he was the first Christian thinker to take seriously the revolutionary aspect of the Marxist challenge, both in its attack on religious ideologies and in its working view of history. He understood Communism as a religious movement, an essential feature which explained its strength and its demoniacal quality. He found the strength of Communism in its complete design for reconstructing the life of the world, in which theory and practice, thought and will, are one. But the lie of Communism, in his view, is its denial of both God and man in the name of an inhuman collectivity which is its God. "Berdyaev's radical personalist philosophy, his revolt in the name of freedom against all objective authority combined with his complete involvement in history toward its transfiguration," says Charles West, "made him the first to express insights which inform the most effective Christian witness behind the Iron Curtain today." [9] As early as five years after the revolution, Berdyaev went into exile in France, where he lived until his death in 1948.

Berdyaev's study on *The Origin of Russian Communism*[10] views the Russian Revolution against the wider background of the phenomenon of revolution in general, as a special and, in the last analysis, spiritual phenomenon in the destinies of peoples. Rationalist and moralist judgments on revolution are fruitless as are such judgments on war, which is very like revolution. Berdyaev sees revolution as an irrational phenomenon, a sign of the dominance of irrational forces in history. This must be understood in a two-fold sense. It means that the old regime has become entirely irrational and is no longer justifiable in any sense and that the revolution itself comes into being through the unshackling of the irrational elements in the masses. The organizers of a revolution always desire to rationalize the irrational elements in revolution, but all the same they are its instruments. Revolution is destiny and fate.[11] The revolutionaries understand the meaning of revolution less than anybody, for their rationalist ideal has no room for such meaning. Still less are the counter-revolutionaries in a position to understand, for they are fruitlessly and callously facing the past. Objective historians can explain a great deal in the examination of secondary causes, but

the meaning of revolution is not the affair of historical science; it is the business of the philosophy of history.

At this point Berdyaev arrives at his favorite theme. Even the philosophy of history can approach the problem of the meaning of revolution only if it is based upon a religious foundation. As a matter of fact, a philosophy of history is always in a sense a theology of history. For a Christian philosophy of history the fact is revealed that the meaning of revolution is an inward apocalypse of history, i.e., of a judgment upon history within history itself, an exposure of its failure. In our sinful, evil world an uninterrupted progressive development is impossible. In it much evil, much poison is always accumulating. In it the process of dissolution is always going on. Too often it happens that no regenerative forces are to be found in the community, and then judgment upon that community cannot be avoided; then inevitable revolution is ordained in the heavens; then a rupture of time takes place and those forces triumph which, although irrational from a historical point of view, indicate the action of Providence in the darkness.

Berdyaev sees in revolution an ontological meaning.[12] Revolution is like death; and this passing through death is the unavoidable consequence of sin. This is what gives revolution its horror, its grimness, its pattern of death and blood. Revolution is both sin and the evidence of sin, as war is sin and the evidence of sin. War produces still more violence and sheds still more blood than revolution and is, for that reason, often a greater sin than revolution. Therefore it is difficult to understand those Christians who consider that revolution is not permissible because of its violence and bloodshed, and at the same time regard war as wholly permissible and morally justifiable.

It is significant that Berdyaev repeatedly stresses the close parallelism and the historical connection between war and revolution—a close parallelism in respect to the fateful amount of violence and bloodshed; a historical connection insofar as, according to his conviction, the whole fashion assumed by Russian and world Communism was due to the war. This connection is wholly consistent with that part of the Marxist philosophy of history that could be characterized as its apocalyptical trend of thinking. Good is

realized through evil and light through darkness. Marxist philosophy considers a capitalist war as the greatest evil and injustice and at the same time as a necessity for the triumph of socialism. In the capitalist factories the mighty humanity of the future is prepared. It was the war, its methods and its experiences, that regenerated the type of Russian intelligentsia. War methods were transferred to the internal life of the country. "A new type appeared, that of the militarized youth; in contrast with the old members of the intelligentsia he is clean-shaven, alert, with a firm vigorous gait; he looks like a conqueror; he makes no bones about the methods he uses; he is always ready for violence; he is possessed by the will-to-power; he forces his way to the front; he wants to be not only destructive but also constructive and an organizer." [13]

But the heart of the matter is that this Russian Revolution came to birth in misery and from misery, the misery of a disintegrating war; it was not born of a creative abundance of strength. Revolution, as a matter of fact, always presupposes misery, always presupposes an intensifying of the darkness of the past. The disintegration of a war and of armies creates that chaos and anarchy which favor the ripening of the revolutionary harvest.

Revolutions in Christian history, Berdyaev continues, have always been a judgment upon historical Christianity, upon Christians, upon their betrayal of the Christian covenant. For Christians especially, revolution has a meaning, and they, above all, must understand it. It is a challenge to Christians and a reminder that they have not made justice a fact of experience. In revolution judgment is passed upon the evil forces responsible for injustice, but the forces which judge, themselves create evil. To accept history is to accept revolution also as a catastrophic interruption in the destinies of a sinful world.

To deny meaning to revolution brings with it the rejection of history also. But revolution is ugly and violent, as the birth of a child is ugly and violent, as the child who is born is ugly and subject to violence; such is the curse on a sinful world. All history is to a remarkable degree sin, bloodshed, and violence, and it is difficult for the Christian conscience to accept history, for it always passes judgment upon the injustices of history; it does not allow

optimistic views about history. For that reason history must come to an end, must be judged by God, because in history the justice of Christ is not made a fact.

Berdyaev's philosophy of revolution is an outstanding specimen of apocalyptic thinking. Fate and destiny, doom and judgment, the irrationality of darkness and chaos, bloodshed and violence are essential elements of this approach. We are strongly reminded of the "birthpangs" which we recognized as a fundamental concept in biblical apocalyptic language.

Alexander Block's prophetic witness and Nicolas Berdyaev's apocalyptic philosophy are impressive examples of a Christian encounter with the Russian Revolution which goes to the heart of the historical event. They have convincingly applied biblical perspectives to an interpretation of the depth dimension of the revolutionary process. But, at the same time, the disillusionment of the poet and the exile of the philosopher are indications of the difficulties which both the prophetic and the apocalyptic approaches face within the setting of the social and political system built upon the success of the revolution.

The lesson of these historical examples seems to confirm our proposition that Christianity has only an indirect, not an immediate, relationship to the revolutionary process. Archpriest Vitaly Borovoy, whom we quoted in Chapter Two, recognizes that "already well before the revolution, as well as during the revolution itself, large numbers of the revolutionary intelligentsia, workers and youth, left the Church and broke with Christianity. But the victorious revolution went its difficult way of consolidation and development without the Church." He summons Christians to join boldly, honorably, and actively in the building of the new life, based on social justice, to bring a Christian social fervor to the social revolutions of our time and thus to avert the de-Christianization of the contemporary world.[14]

A report of the Theological Commission of the Prague Christian Peace Conference, which attempts a theological understanding of revolution, points out that "the Christian's responsibility does not end with the success of the revolution. He must in good time seek to counteract disillusionment and he must not encourage any

false expectations. He knows that every step forward is only relative." [15] Considerations of this kind enhance the suggestion that Christians, whether their influence is inspiring or moderating, do not find their position in the very heart of the revolutionary process and action, but nearer the periphery. Christianity in a post-Christian and postrevolutionary world cannot have a more immediate relationship to revolution than it has to the biblical—prophetic and apocalyptic—perspective. Its eyes have been opened to the relative significance of any step forward in the course of human history.

Christianity and the Cuban Revolution

Because the Christian church in China is no more than an insignificant minority, the most important test case for the Christian response to revolution since the Russian Revolution is to be found in Cuba. We owe to Leslie Dewart's *Christianity and Revolution* a penetrating and detailed analysis of "the lesson of Cuba." [16] In Cuba, as in many countries of Latin America, the process of liberation from Spanish colonial dominance was accomplished several generations ago. But an established civil order was so far away and the alternation of dictatorial or semidictatorial regimes so much the rule, that Fidel Castro's rise to power was, within that historical setting, hardly a specific problem. Christians could take part in his guerrilla warfare against Batista and, as a matter of fact, in the first stage of his rise to power he was wholeheartedly supported by the bulk of Roman Catholic laymen in Cuba. When shortly after his victory in early 1958, Fidel Castro was asked about the role of the Catholic Church in the revolution's armed struggle, he replied: "The Catholics of Cuba have lent their most decided cooperation to the cause of liberty." Fidel Castro was, at least nominally, Roman Catholic and even until 1960 he wore a medal. What, then, prevented his revolution from becoming a unique case of a Christian revolution in the twentieth century? Fidel Castro owed his life, after his unsuccessful attack of July 26, 1953, on the Moncada Army barracks in Santiago, to a Roman Catholic, Msgr. Pérez Serantes, who intervened in his favor and saved him from

execution. He thus had reason to pay a debt of gratitude to his church. But two decisive elements caused the break between Castro's revolution and the Cuban Roman Catholic Church.

The first element was the increasing confusion of the hierarchy of that church over the fact that Castro, although repeatedly stating his non-Communism, refused to abandon his neutral attitude; they required an unconditional anti-Communism. And that price Fidel Castro was not willing to pay: "Sometimes it has been made to appear in this country that whoever is not sold to the Americans, or is not abjectly and unconditionally for them, is a Communist," said Castro in 1958. "Well," he concluded, "I am not a Communist, but I do not surrender to the Americans either."

The second element was Castro's refusal to sanctify his revolutionary ideology with a public religious confession. It was in the days when Batista was still in power and Castro was leading his guerrilla forces in the Sierra Maestra. Castro refused an unofficial request by Msgr. Pérez Serantes that in one of his statements he mention the name of God, in order to clear up certain misgivings. That was the minimum requirement, but, eventually, the church demanded an identity of purpose between itself and Castro as the condition for helping Castro.

Such was the basic process by which an original benevolence, only faintly marred by a shadow of distrust, produced a crisis of conscience. The attitude toward Batista was diametrically opposite. None, not even his episcopal collaborator from Cienfuegos, approved of him. But some Catholics had this good word to say about him: He fought Communism. In brief, when the question of the church's attitude suddenly arose in the wake of Castro's victory, the hierarchy's past indecisiveness no longer mattered; but their perplexity concerning Castro was something else again. Cuban Communists, on the other hand, were well prepared for the change of regime. They knew exactly what to do: they immediately declared their total and unqualified support of the revolutionary government and of Castro.[17]

Of course, this is not the whole picture. There were notable dissident Catholic voices which lent their support to Castro, among them Angel del Carro, a prominent Catholic intellectual, who sum-

moned his church to adjust to radically new conditions: "Catholics should recognize that Spain's political colonialism gave place to American economic colonialism. The Church must integrally confront the fact that there is a genuine revolution in Cuba . . . the first true revolution. She must play an important role therein or resign herself to losing an appreciable amount of social influence." And in the same year, 1959, Msgr. Diaz supported Castro's Land Reform Law, which, he declared, "is fundamentally in accordance with the mind of the Church regarding the principle of social justice. Its implementation binds the conscience of every Christian who, as such, leaving aside all personal and selfish interests, must contribute to the interests of the common and generously and peacefully." But these were minority views and, as time passed, the minority dwindled.

Leslie Dewart, commenting on this fact of the rapidly increasing counter-revolutionary attitude within the Cuban Roman Catholic Church, draws a parallel with the Roman Church in the sixteenth century in relation to Protestantism. The integration of the Christian and the secular orders made it easy to think that being a Christian was the same as preserving the existing state of affairs. This gave the Catholic Church a tactical inflexibility which ultimately led to the notorious events that "precipitated the greatest tragedy in its history." [18]

The Cuban Revolution has, indeed, raised the question of the relation between the church and the world in the most radical terms. "This event brings to life, with almost brutal evidence, a new form of society, with all its promises and threats—a society that undertakes to revise aims and values, leaves behind all ideological or spiritual homogeneity and takes possession of technical resources for a better mastery of nature and city life, with a population in explosion, restless and, for the most part, secularized." The Argentinian ecumenical expert, Mauricio Lopez, whom we have quoted, commenting on the Cuban challenge to the church, suggests that "what is occurring in Latin America is part of a revolution of worldwide dimensions. It is the elevation of humanity to the technological age." [19]

This comment leads into the heart of the matter and serves

as an apt introduction to a final summary of the perspective and dilemma facing Christianity in the midst of the triangle: revolution, development, and war. No matter whether the strategy of the Cuban Revolution may prove or disprove its relevance to the situation of other Latin American countries, it has produced a shock-effect throughout the Latin American continent and there is no doubt that it is beginning to have the same effect on the ecclesiastical structures. In the words of an Emergency Plan of the Bishops of Brazil, Cuba, a "country no less Catholic than Brazil," is the sad example that the only alternative, if the church does not awaken in time, may be a violent revolution of antireligious and Marxist inspiration.

In the present situation of Latin American society, this alternative leaves its mark everywhere on the shaping of revolutionary thinking and it is in the background of the awakening Christian revolutionary consciousness. Since the Roman Catholic Church has lost its cultural monopoly in Latin America and Protestantism remains on the fringe of the principal social and political concerns, secular or antireligious movements of the political left have forged ahead of all other groups in preaching a new system of social and political values. "Ideologically, Marxism presents itself to the uneasy conscience of the new intellectual generation as the only ideology that explains in a comprehensive manner the present situation, and offers appropriate incentives and instruments to change it." [20] Many Catholics and Protestants who felt increasingly alienated from the people and from national life suddenly discovered themselves in the main current of national life when they participated in the revolutionary struggle. They have been surprised to discover opportunities for encounter with Marxists. "They do not want to accept Marxism but know of no alternative." [21]

Within this ambiguous atmosphere the emergent "theology of revolution" is groping for a new vision and a new inspiration. The attempts to formulate guidelines for a "Christian involvement in revolution" are definitely associated with the political left and its radical tinge. At the same time, to the extent that these attempts are really concerned with a fundamental renewal of church and theological thinking, they have a tendency to "spiritualize" and

"internalize" the political alternatives and directives. "We are now moving along in search of a humanism that can draw on both old and new forces—a humanism that, subjecting both reason and feeling to its discipline, extends the fusion of blood that we already have to a fusion of souls." [22] This theological understanding of revolution, presented as a "theology of Messianism" (Paul Lehmann), focuses on what God is doing in the world to make and keep human life human. "The Christian looks for stability on the other side of change; he is therefore free to be fully involved in the revolution. At the same time, his understanding of what is going on there obliges him to work constantly for reconciliation." [23]

The ambiguity of these theological attempts is evident from two points of view. First, the confrontation with the hard violent core of political revolutionary action is, as much as possible, mitigated. The strategy of guerrilla warfare is recognized as an *ultima ratio* which may be the only alternative left, facing the unbearable pressure of a system of structural violence. But, at the same time, the language of guerrilla strategy is being used, more or less metaphorically, in outlining guidelines for a broad spectrum of social action, undertaken by "small nuclei with revolutionary objectives" (Richard Shaull). In the process of this type of translation, the violent outlook of guerrilla warfare tends to be veiled and, perhaps, transformed into a number of nonviolent choices.

A second ambiguous factor consists in the tendency to understand the revolutionary process and revolutionary action as an instrument whereby God opens opportunities for the proclamation of the gospel. This tendency may eventually manifest itself in a linguistic substitution of "social transformation" for "revolution." In this line of thought, every true struggle to create humane living conditions in which man may express freedom and responsibility is being understood as an attempt to establish a situation in which the call to conversion finds man free to respond. "The transformation of society—in itself a good thing if it involves the changing of injustices into forms of justice—is also a positive fact from the point of view of the preaching of the gospel, since it liberates man for the great decision of his life: his answer to God's call in Christ" (Emilio Castro).[24] In an enthusiastic report by a French priest, the

participation of a great number of Christians in the Parisian student revolts of May, 1968, is welcomed as a great sign of renewal within the church. French Christians were reawakening under the sudden impact of external events upon the churches. The gospel seemed to be more alive in the street than in the church. Thanks to their open participation in the events, Christians acquired the respect and esteem of their nonbelieving comrades in the struggle, since they proved that "God is not a conservative." Many Christians discovered that they themselves were free, responsible, and capable of making history. They experienced the gospel as a power of life that could weigh heavily upon the destiny of mankind. A new relationship to the world was dawning for the churches; no longer the dialogue of two forces or two ideologies, but, rather, a common participation in action.[25]

To the extent that these statements stress the close interconnection between the proclamation of the gospel and given social situations, between renewal of obsolete ecclesiastical structures and renewal of misdirected political structures, they are particularly relevant. Their ambiguity, however, begins where they tend to turn the revolutionary process from a primarily political event into a spiritual experience in which Christians share their own faith and hope. In the French report on the May revolt mentioned above, a distinction is made between two tendencies; a minority of Christians accepted the revolutionary process, its consequences and aims; in other words, they accepted a certain measure of violence and the socialist society. The great mass of "good parishioners," however, desired a return to calm conditions and an evolutionary change of society.

What is defined here explicitly as the goal of a "socialist society" is, obviously, a political aim, based on a political program. No matter how "permanent" the revolutionary process may be, a revolution which deserves the name means a struggle for the restructuring of society according to clear-cut political and economic concepts. In many countries of the Third World some form of "socialism" serves as the ideology of structural change and national development. Revolutions are not being prepared for the sake of revolution or for the promotion of revolutionary experiences, but

for the sake of the sound development of a misdeveloped society. A "socialist society" claims to direct economic development toward the rapid improvement of the lot of the masses and toward the creation of a just society. Economic development in itself is no guarantee that these aims will be implemented; the misdevelopment of many "developing" as well as "developed" countries proves this. But, without economic development, it is certain that the improvement of the lot of the masses will be postponed indefinitely. In other words, the "elevation of humanity to the technological age" is an essential factor in the program for a new society which is to be erected upon the postrevolutionary foundations. During the (pre-) revolutionary stage, that which Indian Christians defined as "Christian participation in nation-building" is identical with the challenge to revolutionary participation. But, in postrevolutionary nation-building, Christianity is confronted with the ideologies of national development and with the realities of a technological age.

The Christian consciousness can no more isolate the question of revolutionary participation from the question of participation in the ongoing technological revolution than it can escape the confrontation with the third factor: warfare. An increasing number of countries of the Third World are being forced to realize that the national revolutions which have liberated them from colonial dominance are only the initial step, and that they need what in Latin America has been aptly called "a second War of Independence," which will lead to the creation of basic conditions for a true and concrete democracy. This is explicitly defined as a war. "If the constitutional means to achieve this aim are blocked for him, the revolution will have to resort to violence and civil war." If the Christian church is really called to join in the struggle "where men dare to oppose unjust laws and crippling social barriers," [26] then eventually Christians will be called to join in civil war. The Cuban Revolution is an excellent example of the fact that in our present-day world guerrilla warfare and civil war cannot be isolated from the highest stages of warfare technology. No sooner had Fidel Castro succeeded in seizing power, and even before economic development planning could envisage the establishment of a national plant for peaceful atomic energy, than Cuba was precipitated into an

international ballistic missile crisis which, for a moment, brought mankind to the edge of atomic war. If the Cuban church, instead of clinging to an anti-Communist attitude, had welcomed Castroism, it would have implicitly assumed full responsibility for the outbreak of the Third World War.

In the second half of the twentieth century, church and Christianity are, willy-nilly, facing the threefold question of development, revolution, and war. The question is one and indivisible, since mankind has become one and indivisible. The Christian response will be neither Christian nor a response, unless it too is one and indivisible.

NOTES

1. Karl Löwith, *Meaning in History* (Chicago, 1949).
2. *Ibid.*, pp. 209ff.
3. Cf. Karl Löwith, *Von Hegel zu Nietzsche* (Stuttgart, 1950).
4. Herbert Marcuse, *Reason and Revolution* (Oxford, 1941), p. 3.
5. *Ibid.*, p. 172.
6. Löwith, *Von Hegel zu Nietzsche*, p. 129.
7. Report, "Conversion to God and Service to Man," in *Workbook for the World Council of Churches Assembly at Uppsala, 1968* (Geneva, 1968), pp. 154ff.
8. B. G. Guerney (ed.), *An Anthology of Russian Literature* (New York, 1960), pp. 15ff.
9. Charles West, *Communism and the Theologians* (New York, 1958), pp. 111ff.
10. Nicolas Berdyaev, *The Origin of Russian Communism* (rev. ed.; Ann Arbor, Mich., 1964), pp. 129ff.
11. Ibid., p. 129.
12. Ibid., p. 131.
13. Ibid., p. 138f.
14. Archpriest Borovoy, "The Challenge and Relevance of Theology to the Social Revolutions of Our Time," address, World Conference on Church and Society, held in Geneva in July, 1966.
15. Report of the Theological Commission of the Christian Peace

Conference, Prague, presented to the Advisory Committee at Sofia in October, 1966. Cf. *Frontier* (Spring, 1967), p. 20.

16. Leslie Dewart, *Christianity and Revolution:* The Lesson of Cuba (New York, 1963).

17. *Ibid.*, pp. 116ff.

18. *Ibid.*, pp. 136, 147, 181.

19. Mauricio Lopez, "The Political Dynamics of Latin-American Society Today," in Z. K. Matthews (ed.), *Responsible Government in a Revolutionary Age* (New York and London, 1966), p. 166.

20. Gonzalos Castillo-Cárdenas, "The Challenge of the Latin American Revolution," in John C. Bennett (ed.), *Christian Social Ethics in a Changing World* (New York, 1966), pp. 202f.

21. Richard Shaull, "The New Revolutionary Mood in Latin America" (a paper presented to the Study Conference, Committee on Cooperation in Latin America, 1962), pp. 7ff.

22. Mauricio Lopez, "The University and Christian Witness in the Latin American Setting," *Federation News* (November, 1962), pp. 23f. Cf. Shaull, "The New Revolutionary Mood," p. 4.

23. Richard Shaull, "Revolutionary Change in Theological Perspective," in John C. Bennett (ed.), *Christian Social Ethics,* pp. 32, 40.

24. Emilio Castro, "Conversion and Social Transformation," in John C. Bennett (ed.), *Christian Social Ethics,* p. 365.

25. Jean Mansir, O.P., *French Christians in a Revolutionary Situation* (Information Documentation on the Conciliar Church, No. 68–48; 11.17.1968).

26. Mauricio Lopez, "The Political Dynamics . . . ," p. 168.

Index

DATE DUE

Demco, Inc. 38-293